The
Many-Colored
Land

The
Golden Torc

The
Many-Colored
Land

The
Golden Torc

Julian May

Nelson Doubleday, Inc.   Garden City, New York

Contents

The
Many-Colored
Land

The
Golden Torc

The Many-Colored Land

VOLUME I IN
THE SAGA OF PLIOCENE EXILE

For Tadeusz Maxim,
the noblest of them all

My heart is sore pained within me:
and the terrors of death are fallen upon me.

Fear and trembling have seized me:
and darkness has overwhelmed me.

And I said: O that I had wings like a dove!
For then I would fly away and be at rest.

Lo, would I flee far away,
and live in the wilderness.

I would wait for him who will save me
from my cowardice and from the storm.

PSALM 55

Contents

PROLOGUE

1

To CONFIRM that it was indeed near death, the great vessel broke through into normal space with lingering slowness. The pain of the usually swift translation was prolonged as well, until the thousand, for all their strength, cursed and wept within their minds and became convinced that they would be trapped. It would be the gray limbo endlessly. That and pain.

But the Ship was doing its best. Sharing the agony of the passengers, it pushed and pried against the tough fabric of the superficies until there were flickers of black against the gray. The Ship and the people felt their anguish dim into a mere harmony of nearly musical vibrations that echoed, damped, and finally snapped off.

They hung in normal space, stars all around them.

The Ship had emerged in the shadow cone of a planet. For long moments, as the stunned travelers watched without knowing what they saw, the halo of pink atmosphere and the pearly wings of the eclipsed sun's corona gave an aureole to the black world. Then the Ship's ominous momentum carried them on; the chromosphere and the orange flames of the sun's limb burst forth, followed by its dazzling yellow substance.

The Ship curved in. The sunlit surface of the planet seemed to roll open beneath them at their approach. It was a blue world with white clouds and snowy mountains and landmasses of ochre and red and gray-green—beyond doubt a world of compatible life. The Ship had succeeded.

Thagdal turned to the small woman at the directive console.

Brede of the Two Faces shook her head. Dreary violet patterns on the motive display made plain that it had been the final effort of the Ship that brought them to this haven. They were fully in the grip of the system's gravity and no longer capable of inertialess locomotion.

Thagdal's mind and voice spoke. "Listen to me, remnant of battle companies. Our faithful craft has all but perished. It subsists only on mechanicals now and they will not serve much longer. We are on an impact trajectory and we must disembark before the hulk enters the lower atmosphere."

Emanations of sorrow, rage, and fear filled the dying Ship. Questions and reproaches threatened to stifle the mind of Thagdal until he touched the golden torc around his neck and forced them all to be silent.

"In the Name of the Goddess, hold! Our venture was a great gamble, with all minds turned against us. Brede is concerned that this place may not be the perfect refuge we had hoped for. Nevertheless, it is fully compatible, in a remote galaxy where none will dare to look for us. We are safe and have not had to use Spear or Sword. Brede and our Ship have done well to bring us here. Praise to their strength!"

The antiphon was raised dutifully. But sticking up out of the symmetry of it was a prickly thought:

Hymns be damned. Can we *survive* here?

Thagdal lashed back. "We will survive if Compassionate Tana wills, and even find the joy that has eluded us so long. But no thanks to you, Pallol! Shadow-sib! Ancient enemy! Trucebreaker! When we are delivered from this immediate peril you will answer to me!"

A certain amount of vulgar enmity swirled up to merge with Pallol's; but it was fogged by the dull-witted tone of mind that comes from the relief of terrible pain. Nobody else really wanted to fight now. Only the irrepressible Pallol was as game as ever.

Brede Shipspouse flowed soothingly over the impending shambles. "This Many-Colored Land will be a good place for us, my King. And *you* need have no fear, Pallol One-Eye. I have already sounded the planet—lightly, of course—and found no mental challenge. The dominant life-form dwells in speechless innocence and can be no threat to us for more than six million planetary orbits. Yet its germ plasm is indeed compatible for the nurturing and the service. With patience and skilled labor we will surely survive. Now let us go forth from here holding to our truce awhile longer. Let no one speak of vengeance, nor of mistrust of my beloved Spouse."

"Well said, Prescient Lady," came the thoughts and spoken words of the others. (Any dissenters were now keeping well submerged.)

Thagdal said, "The small flyers are waiting for us. As we depart, let all minds be raised in salute."

He went stomping from the control deck, golden hair and beard still crackling with squelched fury, white robes brushing over the now dulled metalloid of the decking. Eadone, Dionket, and Mayvar Kingmaker followed after, minds linked in the Song, fingers giving a farewell caress to the fast-cooling walls that had once thrummed with benevolent power. Little by little the others in various parts of the Ship took up the anthem until nearly all of them were in communion.

Flyers spurted away from the moribund vessel. More than forty birdlike machines pierced the atmosphere like glowing darts before decelerating abruptly and spreading their wings. One took the lead and the others formed a stately procession in its wake. They flew toward the world's largest landmass to await the calculated impact, came up from the south and crossed over the most distinctive feature of the planet—a vast, nearly dry sea basin, glittering with salt pans, which cut an irregular gash across the western reaches of the major continent. A snowy range made a barrier north of this Empty Sea. The flyers went beyond the mountains and hovered over the valley of a large eastward-flowing river, waiting.

The Ship entered on a westerly course, leaving a fiery trail as it ablated in the atmosphere. It swept the ground with a horrendous pressure wave that incinerated vegetation and altered the very minerals of the landscape below. Molten globules of green and brown glass showered the eastern highlands as the Ship's integument exploded away. The river waters vaporized from their bed.

Then came the impact—light-burst and heat-burst and sound-burst, as more than two thousand million tons of matter with a velocity of twenty-two kilometers per second inflicted its wound upon the world. The country rock metamorphosed; the substance of the Ship was all but consumed in the holocaust. Nearly a hundred cubic kilometers of planetary crust exploded upward and outward, the finer products rising in a black column to the stratosphere where the high thin winds spread them in a pall of mourning over much of the world.

The resultant crater was nearly thirty kilometers in diameter but not very deep, battered by tornadic storms engendered in the affronted atmosphere above the glowing ulcer in the land. The small flyers circled solemnly above it for many days, oblivious of the muddy hurricane as they waited for the earth-fires to cool. When the rain had done its work, the flyers departed for a long time.

They returned to the grave when their tasks were finally done and rested for a thousand years.

2

THE LITTLE RAMAPITHECUS was stubborn. She was certain that the baby must have gone into the tangle of maquis. His scent was there, distinct in spite of the heavy springtime perfume of heather, thyme, and gorse.

Uttering crooning calls, the ramapithecus forced her way into the ancient burned-over area, moving uphill. A lapwing, vivid yellow and black, gave a *peewit* cry and limped away, trailing one wing. The ramapithecus knew that this charade was intended to distract her from a nearby nest; but thoughts of bird-prey were far from her simple mind. All she wanted was her missing child.

She toiled up the overgrown slope, using a piece of tree branch to beat down the brush that impeded her. She was able to utilize this tool and a few others. Her brow was low, but her face was quite vertical, with a small, humanoid jaw. Her body, a little over a meter in height, was only slightly stooped, and clothed except for the face and palms in short brown fur.

She continued her crooning. It was a message not framed in words, which any young one of the species would recognize: "Here is Mother. Come to her and be safe and comforted."

The maquis thinned out as she reached the crest of the height. Out in the open at last, she looked around and gave a low moan of fear. She stood on the edge of a monstrous basin containing a lake of deepest blue color. The rim curved away to the horizon on either hand, completely barren of vegetation along the narrow lip and down the steep slope to the water.

About twenty meters away from her stood a terrible bird. It was something like a fat heron but as tall as a pine tree and just as long, with wings, head, and tail drooping sadly to the ground. From its belly trailed a knobby appendage with climbing holds. The bird was hard, not made of flesh. It was layered in dust, crusted and scabbed with yellow and gray and orange lichen over what had once been a smooth black skin. Far along the rim of the astrobleme, in both directions, she could see other such birds standing widely spaced, all looking into the dark-mirrored depths.

The ramapithecus prepared to flee. Then she heard a familiar sound.

She gave a sharp hoot. Immediately, a tiny upside-down head popped out of an orifice in the belly of the nearby bird. The child chittered happily. His sounds had the meaning: "Welcome, Mother. This is fun! Look what is here!"

Exhausted, overcome by relief, her hands bloody from breaking through the thorns, the mother howled in fury at her offspring. Hastily, he came down the exit ladder of the flyer and scuttled up to her. She scooped him up and crushed him to her breast; then she put him down and cuffed the sides of his head, left-right, pouring out a torrent of indignant chatter.

Trying to placate her, he held out the thing he had found. It resembled a large ring, but was really two conjoined semicirclets of twisted gold, thick as a finger and rounded, incised with tortuous little markings like the borings of gribbles in sea-logged wood.

The young ramapithecus grinned and snapped open two knobby ends of the ring. The other ends were held by a kind of pivoting hinge that allowed the halves to rotate and open wide. The child placed the ring around his neck, twisted it and snapped the catch shut. The golden torc gleamed against his tawny fur, much too large for him but alive with power nevertheless. Smiling still, he showed his mother what he was now able to do.

She shrieked.

The child leaped in dismay. He tripped over a rock and fell backward. Before he could recover, his mother was upon him, yanking the ring over his head so that the metal bruised his ears. And it hurt! The loss of it hurt worse than any pain he had ever known. He must get it back—

The mother screamed even louder as he tried to grab at the torc. Her voice echoed across the crater lake. She flung the golden thing as far away as she could, into a dense thicket of spiny gorse. The child wailed his broken-hearted protest, but she seized his arm and hauled him toward the path she had made through the maquis.

Well concealed and only slightly dented, the torc gleamed in the dappled shadows.

3

IN THE EARLY YEARS after humanity, with a little help from its friends, had set out to overrun the compatible stars, a professor of dynamic field-physics named Théo Guderian discovered the way into Exile. His researches, like those of so many other unorthodox but promising thinkers of the time, were sustained by a no-strings grant from the Human Polity of the Galactic Milieu.

Guderian lived on the Old World. Because science had so many other things to assimilate in those exciting times (and because Guderian's discovery seemed to have no practical application whatsoever in 2034), the publication of his culminating paper caused only a brief flutter in the dovecote of physical cosmology. But in spite of the prevailing air of indifference, a small number of workers from all six of the coadunate galactic races continued to be curious enough about Guderian's findings to seek him out in his modest home-cum-workshop outside of Lyon. Even as his health failed, the Professor received these visiting colleagues with courtesy and assured them that he would be honored to repeat his experiment for them if they would pardon the crudities of his apparatus, which he had removed to the cellar of his cottage after the Institute disclaimed further interest in it.

It took Madame Guderian some time to become resigned to the exotic pilgrims from other stars. One had, after all, to preserve the social convenances by entertaining the guests. But there were difficulties! She overcame her aversion to the tall, androgynous Gi after much mental exercise, and one could always pretend that the Poltroyans were civilized gnomes. But she could never get used to the awesome Krondaku or the half-visible Lylmik, and one could only deplore the way that some of the less fastidious Simbiari dripped green on the carpet.

What was to be the last group of guests called just three days before Professor Guderian's terminal illness commenced. Madame opened the door to greet two outworld male humans (one alarmingly massive and the other quite ordinary), an urbane little Poltroyan wearing the gorgeous robes of a Full Elucidator, a two-and-a-half-meter Gi (mercifully with clothes on), and—sainte vierge!—no less than *three* Simbiari.

She welcomed them and put out extra ashtrays and wastebaskets.

Professor Guderian conducted the extraterrestrial visitors to the cellar of the large country cottage just as soon as the politenesses had been exchanged. "We will proceed at once to the demonstration, good friends. You will forgive me, but today I am a trifle fatigued."

"Most regrettable," said the solicitous Poltroyan. "Perhaps, my dear Professor, you would benefit from a rejuvenative course?"

"No, no," Guderian said with a smile. "One lifetime is quite enough for me. I feel I am most fortunate to have lived in the era of the Great Intervention, but I must confess that events now seem to be moving faster than my composure can tolerate. I look forward to the ultimate peace."

They passed through a metal-sheathed door into what was apparently a converted wine cellar. An area of stone paving some three meters square had been removed, leaving bare earth. Guderian's apparatus stood in the middle of it.

The old man rummaged for a moment in an antique oak cabinet near the door and came up with a small pile of reading-plaques, which he distributed to the scientists. "A précis of my theoretical considerations and diagrams of the device are contained in these booklets, which my wife has been kind enough to prepare for visitors. You must excuse the simplicity of the format. We have long since exhausted our major funding."

The others murmured sympathetically.

"Please stand here for the demonstration. You will observe that the device has certain affinities to the subspace translator and thus requires very little power input. My own modifications have been designed with a view toward phasing in residual magnetics contained in the local rock strata, together with the deeper contemporary fields being generated beneath the continental platform. These, interacting with the matrices of the translator fields, generate the singularity."

Guderian reached into the pocket of his work smock and took out a large carrot. With a Gallic shrug, he remarked, "Expedient, if somewhat ridiculous."

He placed the carrot on an ordinary wooden stool and carried it to the apparatus. Guderian's device rather resembled an old-fashioned latticework pergola or gazebo draped in vines. However, the frame was made of transparent vitreous material except for peculiar nodular components of dead black, and the "vines" were actually cables of colorful alloys that seemed to grow up from the cellar floor, creep in and out of the lattice in a disconcerting fashion, and abruptly disappear at a point just short of the ceiling.

When the stool and its carrot were in position, Guderian rejoined his guests and activated the device. There was no sound. The gazebo shimmered momentarily; then it seemed as if mirror panels sprang into existence, hiding the interior of the apparatus completely from view.

"You will understand that a certain waiting period is now in order," the old man said. "The carrot is almost always effective, but from time to time there are disappointments."

The seven visitors waited. The wide-shouldered human clutched his book-plaque in both hands but never let his eyes leave the gazebo. The other colonial, a placid type from some institute on Londinium, made a tactful examination of the control panel. The Gi and the Poltroyan read their booklets with equanimity. One of the younger Simbiari inadvertently let an emerald drop fall and made haste to scuff it into the cellar floor.

Numerals on the wall chronometer flickered past. Five minutes. Ten.

"We will see whether our game is afoot," the Professor said, with a wink at the man from Londinium.

The mirrored energy field snapped off. For the merest nanosecond, the startled scientists were aware of a pony-shaped creature standing inside the gazebo. It turned instantly to an articulated skeleton. As the bones fell, they disintegrated into grayish powder.

"Shit!" exclaimed the seven eminent scientists.

"Be calm, colleagues," said Guderian. "Such a dénouement is unfortunately inevitable. But we shall project a slow-motion holo so that our catch may be identified."

He switched on a concealed Tri-D projector and froze the action to reveal a small horselike animal with amiable black eyes, three-toed feet, and a russet coat marked with faint white stripes. Carrot greens stuck out of its mouth. The wooden stool was beside it.

"Hipparion gracile. A cosmopolitan species abundant during Earth's Pliocene Epoch."

Guderian let the projector run. The stool quietly dissolved. The hide and flesh of the little horse shriveled with dreadful slowness, peeling away from the skeleton and exploding into a cloud of dust, while the internal organs simultaneously swelled, shrank, and puffed into nothingness. The bones continued to stand upright, then tumbled in graceful slow arcs. Their first contact with the cellar floor reduced them to their component minerals.

The sensitive Gi let out a sigh and closed its great yellow eyes. The Londoner had turned pale, while the other human, from the rugged and morose world of Shqipni, chewed on his large brown mustache. The incontinent young Simb made haste to utilize a wastebasket.

"I have tried both plant and animal bait in my little trap," Guderian said. "Carrot or rabbit or mouse may make the trip to the Pliocene unharmed, but on the return journey, any living thing that is within the tau-field inevitably assumes the burden of more than six million years of earthly existence."

"And inorganic matter?" inquired the Skipetar.

"Of a certain density, of a certain crystalline structure—many specimens make the round trip in fairly good condition. I have even been successful in circumtranslating two forms of organic matter: amber and coal travel unscathed."

"But this is most intriguing!" said the Prime Contemplator of the Twenty-Sixth College of Simb. "The theory of temporal plication has been in our repository for some seventy thousand of your years, my worthy Guderian, but its demonstration eluded the best minds of the Galactic Milieu . . . until now. The fact that you, a human scientist, have been even partially successful where so many others have failed is surely one more confirmation of the unique abilities of the Children of Earth."

The sour-grape flavor of this speech was not lost on the Poltroyan. His ruby eyes twinkled as he said, "The Amalgam of Poltroy, unlike certain other coadunate races, never doubted that the Intervention was fully justified."

"For you and your Milieu, perhaps," said Guderian in a low voice. His dark eyes, pain-tinged behind rimless eyeglasses, showed a momentary bitterness. "But what of us? We have had to give up so much—our diverse languages, many of our social philosophies and religious dogmata, our so-called nonproductive lifestyles . . . our very human sovereignty, laughable though its loss must seem to the ancient intellects of the Galactic Milieu."

The man from Shqipni exclaimed, "How can you doubt the wisdom of it, Professor? We humans gave up a few cultural fripperies and gained energy sufficiency and unlimited lebensraum and membership in a galactic civilization! Now that we don't have to waste time and lives in mere survival, there'll be no holding humanity back! Our race is just beginning to fulfill its genetic potential—which may be greater than that of any other people!"

The Londoner winced.

The Prime Contemplator said suavely, "Ah, the proverbial human breeding capacity! How it does keep the gene pool roiled. One is reminded of the well-known reproductive superiority of the adolescent organism as compared to that of the mature individual whose plasm, while less prodigally broadcast, may nonetheless burgeon more prudently in the pursuit of genetic optima."

"Did you say mature?" sneered the Skipetar. "Or atrophied?"

"Colleagues! Colleagues!" exclaimed the diplomatic little Poltroyan. "We will weary Professor Guderian."

"No, it's all right," the old man said; but he looked gray and ill.

The Gi hastened to change the subject. "Surely this effect you have demonstrated would be a splendid tool for paleobiology."

"I fear," Guderian replied, "that there is limited galactic interest in the extinct life-forms of Earth's Rhône-Saône Trough."

"Then you haven't been able to—er—tune the device for retrieval in other areas?" asked the Londoner.

"Alas, no, my dear Sanders. Nor have other workers been able to reproduce my experiment in other localities on Earth or on other worlds." Guderian tapped one of the plaque-books. "As I have pointed out, there is a problem in computing the subtleties of the geomagnetic input. This region of southern Europe has one of the more complex geomorphologies of the planet. Here in the Monts des Lyonnais and the Forez we have a foreland of the utmost antiquity cheek by jowl with recent volcanic intrusions. In nearby regions of the Massif Central we see even more clearly the workings of intracrustal metamorphism, the anatexis engendered above one or more ascending asthenospheric diapirs. To the east lie the Alps with their stupendously folded nappes. South of here is the Mediterranean Basin with active subduction zones—which was, incidentally, in an extremely peculiar condition during the Lower Pliocene Epoch."

"So you're in a dead end, eh?" remarked the Skipetar. "Too bad Earth's Pliocene period wasn't all that interesting. Just a few million years marking time between the Miocene and the Ice Age. The shank of the Cenozoic, so to speak."

Guderian produced a small whiskbroom and dustpan and began to tidy up the gazebo. "It was a golden time, just before the dawn of rational humankind. A time of benevolent climate and flourishing plant and animal life. A vintage time, unspoiled and tranquil. An autumn before the terrible winter of the Pleistocene glaciation. Rousseau would have loved the Pliocene Epoch! Uninteresting? There are even today soul-weary people in this Galactic Milieu who would not share your evaluation."

The scientists exchanged glances.

"If only it weren't a one-way trip," said the man from Londinium.

Guderian was calm. "All of my efforts to change the facies of the singularity have been in vain. It is fixed in Pliocene time, in the uplands of this venerable river valley. And so we come to the heart of the matter at last! The great achievement of time-travel stands revealed as a mere scientific curiosity." Once more, the Gallic shrug.

"Future workers will profit from your pioneering effort," declared the Poltroyan. The others hurried to add appropriate felicitations.

"Enough, dear colleagues," Guderian laughed. "You have been most kind to visit an old man. And now we must go up to Madame, who awaits with refreshment. I bequeath to sharper minds the practical application of my peculiar little experiment."

He winked at the outworld humans and tipped the contents of the dustpan into the wastebasket. The ashes of the hipparion floated in little blobby islands on the green alien slime.

PART I

The Leavetaking

1

BURNISHED TRUMPETS sounded a flourish. The ducal party rode gaily out of the Château de Riom, horses prancing and curvetting as they had been trained, giving a show of spirit without imperiling the ladies in their chancy sidesaddles. Sunshine sparkled on the jeweled caparisons of the mounts, but it was the gorgeous riders who earned the crowd's applause.

Greenish-blue reflections from the festive scene on the monitor blackened Mercedes Lamballe's auburn hair and threw livid lights across her thin face. "The tourists draw lots to be in the procession of nobles," she explained to Grenfell. "It's more fun to be common, but try to tell them that. Of course the principals are all pros."

Jean, Duc de Berry, raised his arm to the cheering throng. He wore a long houppelande in his own heraldic blue, powdered with fleurs de lys. The dagged sleeves were turned back to show a rich lining of yellow brocade. The Duc's hosen were pure white, embroidered with golden spangles, and he wore golden spurs. At his side rode the Prince, Charles d'Orléans, his robes particolored in the royal scarlet, black, and white, his heavy golden baldric fringed with tinkling bells. Other nobles in the train, gaudy as a flock of spring warblers, followed after with the ladies.

"Isn't there a hazard?" Grenfell asked. "Horses with untrained riders? I should think you'd stick with robot mounts."

Lamballe said softly, "It has to be real. This *is* France, you know. The horses are specially bred for intelligence and stability."

In honor of the maying, the betrothed Princess Bonne and all her retinue were dressed in malachite-green silk. The noble maidens wore the quaint headdresses of the early fifteenth century, fretted gilt-wire confections threaded with jewels, rising up on their braided coiffures like kitten ears. The crépine of the Princess was even more outlandish, extending out from her temples in long golden horns with a white lawn veil draped over the wires.

"Cue the flower girls," said Gaston, from the other side of the control room.

Mercy Lamballe sat still, gazing at the brilliant picture with rapt intensity. The antennae of her comset made the strange headpiece of the medieval princess out on the château grounds look almost ordinary in comparison.

"Merce," the director repeated with gentle insistence. "The flower girls."

Slowly she reached out a hand, keying the marshaling channel.

Trumpets sounded again and the peasant crowd of tourists oohed. Dozens of dimpled little maids in short gowns of pink and white came running out of the orchard carrying baskets of apple blossoms. They romped along the road in front of the ducal procession strewing flowers, while flageolets and trombones struck up a lively air. Jugglers, acrobats, and a dancing bear joined the mob. The Princess blew kisses to the crowd, and the Duc distributed an occasional piece of largesse.

"Cue the courtiers," said Gaston.

The woman at the control console sat motionless. Bryan Grenfell could see drops of moisture on her brow, dampening the straying tendrils of auburn hair. Her mouth was tight.

"Mercy, what is it?" Grenfell whispered. "What's wrong?"

"Nothing," she said. Her voice was husky and strained. "Courtiers away, Gaston."

Three young men, also dressed in green, came galloping from the woods toward the procession of nobility, bearing armfuls of leafy sprigs. With much giggling, the ladies twined these into head-wreaths and crowned the chevaliers of their choice. The men reciprocated with dainty chaplets for the damsels, and they all resumed their ride toward the meadow where the maypole waited. Meanwhile, directed by Mercy's commands, barefoot girls and grinning youths distributed flowers and greenery to the slightly self-conscious crowd, crying: "Vert! Vert pour le mai!"

Right on cue, the Duc and his party began to sing along with the flutes:

> C'est le mai, c'est le mai,
> C'est le joli mois de mai!

"They're off pitch again," Gaston said in an exasperated voice. "Cue in the filler voices, Merce. And let's have the lark loops and a few yellow butterflies." He keyed for voice on the marshaling channel and exclaimed, "Eh, Minou! Get that clot out from in front of the Duc's horse. And watch the kid in red. Looks like he's twitching bells off the Prince's baldric."

Mercedes Lamballe brought up the auxiliary voices as ordered. The entire crowd joined in the song, having slept on it on the way from Charlemagne's Coronation. Mercy made birdsong fill the blossom-laden orchard and sent out signals that released the butterflies from their secret cages. Unbidden, she conjured up a scented breeze to cool the tourists from Aquitaine and Neustria and Blois and Foix and all the other "French" planets in the Galactic Milieu who had come, together with Francophiles and medievalists from scores of other worlds, to savor the glories of ancient Auvergne.

"They'll be getting warm now, Bry," she remarked to Grenfell. "The breeze will make them happier."

Bryan relaxed at the more normal tone in her voice. "I guess there are limits to the inconveniences they'll endure in the name of immersive cultural pageantry."

"We reproduce the past," Lamballe said, "as we would have *liked* it to be. The realities of medieval France are another trip altogether."

"We have stragglers, Merce." Gaston's hands flashed over the control panel in the preliminary choreography of the maypole suite. "I see two or three exotics in the bunch. Probably those comparative ethnologists from the Krondak world we were alerted about. Better bring over a troubadour to keep 'em happy until they catch up with the main group. These visiting firemen are apt to write snotty evaluations if you let 'em get bored."

"Some of us keep our objectivity," Grenfell said mildly.

The director snorted. "Well, *you're* not out there tramping through horseshit in fancy dress in the hot sun on a world with low subjective oxygen and double subjective gravity! . . . Merce? Dammit, kiddo, are you fuguing off again?"

Bryan rose from his seat and came to her, grave concern on his face. "Gaston—can't you see she's ill?"

"I'm not!" Mercy was sharp. "It's going to pass off in a minute or two. Troubadour away, Gaston."

The monitor zoomed in on a singer who bowed to the little knot of laggards, struck a chord on his lute, and began expertly herding the people toward the maypole area while soothing them with song. The piercing sweetness of his tenor filled the control room. He sang first in French, then in the Standard English of the Human Polity of the Galactic Milieu for those who weren't up to the archaic linguistics.

> Le temps a laissé son manteau
> De vent, de froidure et de pluie,
> Et s'est vestu de broderie
> De soleil luisant—cler et beau.
>
> Now time has put off its dark cloak
> Of gales and of frosts and of rain,
> And garbs itself in woven light,
> Bright sunshine of spring once again.

A genuine lark added its own coda to the minstrel's song. Mercy lowered her head and tears fell onto the console before her. That damn song. And springtime in the Auvergne. And the friggerty larks and retroevolved butterflies and manicured meadows and orchards crammed with gratified folk from faraway planets where the living was tough but the challenge was being met by all but the inevitable misfits who slubbed the beautiful growing tapestry of the Galactic Milieu.

Misfits like Mercy Lamballe.

"Beaucoup regrets, guys," she said with a rueful smile, mopping her face with a tissue. "Wrong phase of the moon, I guess. Or the old Celtic rising. Bry, you just picked the wrong day to visit this crazy place. Sorry."

"All you Celts are bonkers." Gaston excused her with breezy kindness. "There's a Breton engineer over in the Sun King Pageant who told me he can only shoot his wad when he's doing it on a megalith. Come on, babe. Let's keep this show rolling."

On the screens, the maypole dancers twined their ribbons and pivoted in intricate patterns. The Duc de Berry and the other actors of his entourage permitted thrilled tourists to admire the indubitably real gems that adorned their costumes. Flutes piped, cornemuses wailed, hawkers peddled comfits and wine, shepherds let people pet their lambs, and the sun smiled down. All was well in la douce France, A.D. 1410, and so it would be for another six hours, through the tournament and culminating feast.

And then the weary tourists, 700 years removed from the medieval world of the Duc de Berry, would be whisked off in comfortable subway tubes to their next cultural immersion at Versailles. And Bryan Grenfell and Mercy Lamballe would go down to the orchard as evening fell to talk of sailing to Ajaccio together and to see how many of the butterflies had survived.

2

THE ALERT KLAXON hooted through the ready room of Lisboa Power Grid's central staging.

"Well, hell, I was folding anyhow," big Georgina remarked. She hoisted the portable air-conditioning unit of her armor and clomped off to the waiting drill-rigs, helmet under her arm.

Stein Oleson slammed his cards down on the table. His beaker of booze went over and sluiced the meager pile of chips in front of him. "And me with a king-high tizz and the first decent pot all day! Damn lucky granny-banging trisomics!" He lurched to his feet, upsetting the reinforced chair, and stood swaying, two meters and fifteen cents' worth of ugly-handsome berserker. The reddened sclera of his eyeballs contrasted oddly with the bright blue irises. Oleson glared at the other players and bunched up his mailed servo-powered fists.

Hubert gave a deep guffaw. He could laugh, having come out on top. "Tough kitty! Simmer down, Stein. Sopping up all that mouthwash didn't help your game much."

The fourth cardplayer chimed in. "I told you to take it easy on the gargle, Steinie. And now lookit! We gotta go down, and you're half-plotzed again."

Oleson gave the man a look of murderous contempt. He shed the a/c walkaround, climbed into his own drill-rig, and began plugging himself in. "You keep your trap shut, Jango. Even blind drunk I can zap a truer bore than any scat-eatin' li'l Portugee sardine stroker."

"Oh, for God's sake," said Hubert. "Will you two quit?"

"You try teaming with an orry-eyed squarehead!" Jango said. He blew his nose in the Iberian fashion, over the neck-rim of his armor, then locked on his helmet.

Oleson sneered. "And you call *me* slob!"

The electronic voice of Georgina, the team leader, gave them the bad news as they went through the systems check. "We've lost the Cabo da Roca-Azores mainline bore 793 kloms out and the service tunnel, too. Class Three slippage and overthrust, but at least the fistula sealed. It looks like a long trick, children."

Stein Oleson powered up. His 180-ton rig rose thirty cents off the deck, slid out of its bay, and sashayed down the ramp, wagging its empennage like a slightly tipsy iron dinosaur.

"Madre de deus," growled Jango's voice. His machine came after Stein's, obeying the taxi regulation scrupulously. "He's a menace, Georgina. I'll be damned if I drill tandem with him. I'm telling you, I'll file a beef with the union! How'd *you* like to have a drunken numbwit the only thing between your ass and a bleb of red-hot basalt?"

Oleson's bellowed laughter clanged in all their ears. "Go ahead and file with the union, pussywillow! Then get yourself a job to fit your nerve. Like drilling holes in Swiss cheeses with your—"

"Will you cut that crap?" Georgina said wearily. "Hubey, you partner with Jango this shift and I'll go tandem with Stein."

"Now wait a minute, Georgina," Oleson began.

"It's settled, Stein." She cycled the airlock. "You and Big Mama against the world, Blue Eyes. And save your soul for Jesus if you don't sober up before we hit that break. Let's haul, children."

A massive gate, eleven meters high and nearly as thick, swung open to give them entry to the service tunnel that dived under the sea. Georgina had fed the coordinates of the break into the autohelms of their drill-rigs, so all they had to do for a while was relax, wiggle around in their armor, and maybe snuff up a euphoric or two while hurtling along at 500 kph toward a mess under the bottom of the Atlantic Ocean.

Stein Oleson raised the partial pressure of his oxygen and gave himself a jolt of aldetox and stimvim. Then he ordered the armor's meal unit to deliver a liter of raw egg and smoked herring purée, together with his favorite hair of the dog, akvavit.

There was a low muttering in his helmet receiver. "Damn atavistic cacafogo. Ought to mount a set of ox horns on his helmet and wrap his iron ass in a bearskin jockstrap."

Stein smiled in spite of himself. In his favorite fantasies he did imagine himself a Viking. Or, since he had both Norse and Swedish genes, perhaps a Varangian marauder slashing his way southward into ancient Russia. How wonderful it would be to answer insults with an axe or a sword, unfettered by the stupid constraints of civilization! To let the red anger flow as it was meant to, powering his great muscles for battle! To take strong blonde women who would first fight him off, then yield with sweet openness! He was born for a life like that.

But unfortunately for Stein Oleson, human cultural savagery was extinct in the Galactic Age, mourned only by a few ethnologists, and the subtleties of the new mental barbarians were beyond Stein's power to grasp. This exciting and dangerous job of his had been vouchsafed him by a compassionate computer, but his soul-hunger remained unsatisfied. He had never considered emigrating to the stars; on no human colony anywhere in the Galactic Milieu was there a primal Eden. The germ plasm of humanity was too valuable to fritter in neolithic backwaters. Each of the 783 new human worlds was completely civilized, bound by the ethics of the Concilium, and obligated to contribute toward the slowly coalescing Whole. People who hankered after their simpler roots had to be content with visiting the Old World's painstaking restorations of ancient cultural settings, or with the exquisitely orchestrated Immersive Pageants—almost, but not quite, authentic to the last detail—which let a person actively savor selected portions of his heritage.

Stein, who was born on the Old World, had gone to the Fjordland Saga when he was barely out of adolescence, traveling from Chicago Metro to Scandinavia with other vacationing students. He was ejected from the Longboat Invaders Pageant and heavily fined after leaping into the midst of a mock mêlée, chopping a hairy Norseman's arm off, and "rescuing" a kidnapped British maiden from rape. (The wounded actor was philosophical about his three months in the regeneration tank. "Just the hazards of the trade, kid," he had told his remorseful attacker.)

Some years later, after Stein had matured and found a certain release in his work, he had gone to the Saga pageants again. This time they seemed pathetic. Stein saw the happy outworld visitors from Trøndelag and Thule and Finnmark and all the other "Scandinavian" planets as a pack of silly costumed fools, waders in the shallows, nibblers, masturbators, pathetic chasers after lost identity.

"What will you do when you find out who you are, great-grandchildren of test tubes?" he had screamed, fighting drunk at the Valhalla Feast. "Go back where you came from—to the new worlds the monsters gave you!" Then he had climbed up onto the Aesir's table and peed in the mead bowl.

They ejected and fined him again. And this time his credit card was pipped so that he was automatically turned away by every pageant box office . . .

The speeding drill-rigs raced beneath the continental slope, their headlights catching glints of pink, green, and white from the granite walls of the tunnel. Then the machines penetrated the dark basalt of the deep-ocean crust below the Tagus Abyssal Plain. Just three kilometers above their service tunnel were the waters of the sea; ten kilometers below lay the molten mantle.

As they drove two abreast through the lithosphere, the members of the team had the illusion of going down a gigantic ramp with sharp drops at regular intervals. The rigs would fly straight and level, then nose down sharply on a new straight path, only to repeat the maneuver a few moments later. The service tunnel was following the curvature of the Earth in a series of straight-line increments; it had to, because of the power-transmittal bore it served, a parallel tunnel with a diameter just great enough to admit a single drill-rig when there was a need for major repairs. In most parts of the complex undersea power system, service tunnels and bores were connected by adits every ten kloms, allowing the maintenance crews easy access; but if they had to, the drill-rigs could zap right through the rough rock walls of the service tunnel and mole their way to the bore from any angle.

Until the time when the alarm had rung in Lisboa, the mainline bore between continental Europe and the extensive Azores mariculture farms had been lit with the glare of a photon beam. This ultimate answer to Earth's ancient energy-hunger originated at this time of day in the sunshine of the Serra da Estrela Tier 39 Collection Center northwest of Lisboa Metro. With its sister centers at Jiuquan, Akebono Platform, and Cedar Bluffs KA, it gathered and distributed solar energy to be used by consumers adjacent to the 39N parallel all around the globe. A complex of spidery stratotowers, secure against the forces of gravity and high above the weather, gathered light rays from the cloudless skies, arranged them into a coherent beam, and sent this to be distributed safely underground via a web of mainline and local feeder bores. A photon from the Portuguese (or Chinese or Pacific or Kansas) daylight would be directed on its way by means of plasma mirrors operating within the bores, and would reach the fog-bound folk in the farms of the North Atlantic before an eye could blink. The ocean farmers utilized the power for everything from submarine harvesters to electric blankets. Few of the consumers would bother to think where the energy came from.

Like all of Earth's subterranean power bores, Cabo da Roca-Azores was regularly patrolled by small robot crawlers and muckers. These could make minor repairs when the planetary crust shifted in a common Class One incident, not even interrupting the photon beam. Class Two damage was severe enough to cause an automatic shutdown. Perhaps a tremor would shift a segment of the bore slightly out of alignment, or damage one of the vital mirror stations. Crews from the surface would race to the scene of the disruption via the service tunnels, and the repairs were usually made very quickly.

But on this day, the tectonic adjustment had been rated at Class Three. The Despacho Fracture Zone had shrugged, and a web of minor faults in the suboceanic basalt had waggled in sympathy. Hot rock surrounding a three-kilometer section of the paired tunnels suddenly moved north-south, east-west, up-down, crumpling not only the power bore but the much larger service tunnel as well. As the mirror station vaporized in a very small thermonuclear flash, the searing photons of the beam burned undeflected for a microsecond before safety cutoff. The beam punched through the shattered bore wall and continued to burn a straight-arrow path westward through the crust until it broke through the sea floor. There was a steam explosion in the liquefied rock just as the beam died, which effectively sealed the fistula. But a large region that had formerly been fairly stable solid rock was now reduced to a shambles of rubble, cooked oceanic ooze, and slowly cooling pockets of molten lava.

A bypass restored power to the Azores within one second after the break. Until the repairs were made, the islands would take most of their energy from the Tier 38 Collection Center northwest of Lorca in Spain, via Gibraltar-Madeira. Drill crews from both ends of the damaged bore segment would get to clean up the mess, rebuild the mirror, and spin reinforcement sleeves for the tunnels passing through the new zone of instability.

Then there would be light once again.

"Lisbong leader, this is Ponta Del Three-Alfa coming up on Klom Seven-Niner-Seven, c'mon."

"Lisbong Sixteen-Echo gotcha, Ponta Del," said Georgina. "We're at Seven-Eight-Zip and rolling . . . Seven-Eight-Five . . . Seven-Niner-Zip . . . and at the fall, Seven-Niner-Two. You guys gonna take the fistula?"

"Affirm, Lisbong, with one unit on the bore for linkup. Long time no see, Georgina, but we gotta stop meeting like this! Put your best zapper on the mainline rebore, sweetie. She gonna be a sneako rascal, c'mon."

"Have no fear, Ponta Del. See you in a short, Larry lovie. Sixteen-Echo gone."

Stein Oleson gritted his teeth and gripped the twin joy sticks of his rig. He knew he was the best shot Lisboa had. Nobody could zap a truer bore than he could. Lava blisters, magnetic anoms—nothing ever threw him off the true. He got ready to blast.

"Hubert, get on that mainline rebore," Georgina said.

Humiliation and rage twisted Stein's guts. A nauseous blend of bile and herring rose in his throat. He swallowed. He breathed. He waited.

"Jango, you follow Hubey with the sleeve-spinning until you hit the mirror. Then get on that. Steinie, let's you and me open up this service tunnel."

"Right you are, Georgina," Stein said quietly. He thumbed the stud on his right stick. A greenish-white ray blazed out of the rig's nose. Slowly, the two big machines began to cut through the fall of steaming black rock while little robot muckers scuttled about hauling the debris away.

3

THE ENTIRE VOORHEES CLAN had taken to deep space almost immediately after the Great Intervention. It was to be expected of the descendants of New Amsterdam skippers and four generations of

U.S. Navy airmen; a yearning for far horizons was programmed into the Voorhees genes.

Richard Voorhees and his older sibs Farnum and Evelyn were born on Assawompset, one of the longest-settled "American" worlds, where their parents were based with the Fourteenth Fleet. Far and Evvie carried on the family tradition—line officers both, she commanding a diplomatic courier, he the exec on one of the asteroid-sized colonization transports. Both had served with distinction during the brief Metapsychic Rebellion of the 'Eighties, a credit to the family name, to the service, and to humanity at large.

Then there was Richard.

He also went to the stars, but not in government service. The structured military life was repellent to him and he was excessively xenophobic as well. Members of the five exotic races were common visitors at Assawompset Sector Base, and Richard had hated and feared them from the time he was a toddler. Later, in school, he found a rationalization for the dread as he read about the half-century preceding the Intervention on Old Earth, when more and more frequent probings by the eager anthropologists of the Milieu had disturbed and sometimes terrified humanity. The Krondaku had been guilty of particularly tactless experimentation; and crews from certain Simbiari worlds had even descended to mischief-making among the natives when overcome by ennui during long surveillance tours.

The Galactic Concilium had dealt sternly with such transgressions, which were fortunately few. Nevertheless a remnant of the old "alien invasion" psychosis persisted in human folklore even after the Intervention had opened the way to the stars. Mild manifestations of xenophobia were rather common among human colonists; but not many people carried their prejudice as far as Richard Voorhees.

Fanned by feelings of personal inadequacy, the irrational fears of the child matured into full-blown hatred in the grown man. Richard rejected Milieu service and turned instead to a career as a commercial spacer. There he could pick and choose his shipmates and the ports he visited. Farnum and Evelyn tried to be understanding of their brother's problem; but Richard knew all too well that the Fleet officers secretly looked down upon him.

"Our brother the trader," they would say, and laugh. "Well, it's not quite as bad as being a pirate!"

Richard had to pretend to be a good sport about the jibing for more than twenty years, while he worked his way up from spacehand to mate to hired skipper to owner-operator. The day came at last when he could stand at the dock at Bedford Starport and admire the quarter-klom sleekness of CSS Wolverton Mountain, rejoicing that she was his own. The ship had been a VIP speedster, equipped with the most powerful superluminal translator as well as oversized inertialess drivers for slower-than-light travel. Voorhees had the passenger accommodations ripped out and converted her to full-auto express cargo, because that was where the real money was.

He let it be known that there was no journey too long or too dangerous for him to dare, no risk he was not prepared to undertake in the delivery of a rare or desperately needed load anywhere in the galaxy. And the clients came.

In the years that followed, Richard Voorhees made the appalling Hub run eight times before the precarious colonies there were abandoned. He burned out four sets of upsilon energy-field crystals and nearly fused his own nervous system on a record-breaking run to Hercules Cluster. He carried drugs and life-saving equipment and parts to fix vital machinery. He expedited samples of ores and cultures of suspect organisms from outlying human colonies to the vast laboratories of the Old World. He was able to prevent a eugenic catastrophe on Bafut by rushing in replacement sperm. He had given mild gratification to a dying tycoon by speeding one precious bottle of Jack Daniel's from Earth to the faraway Cumberland System. He had toted just about everything but the serum to Nome and the message to Garcia.

Richard Voorhees became rich and a little famous, underwent rejuvenation, acquired a taste for antique aeroplanes, rare Earth vintages, gourmet goodies, and dancing women, grew a big black mustache, and told his distinguished older brother and sister to go screw themselves.

And then, on a certain day in 2110, Richard sowed the seed of his own ruin.

He was alone as usual on the bridge of Wolverton Mountain, deep in the gray negation of subspace, going balls-up for the isolated Orissa system 1870 light-years south of the Galactic Plane. His cargo was a large and intricate temple of Jagannath, including sacred images and rolling stock, intended to replace a religious complex that had been accidentally destroyed on the Hindu-settled planet. Old World artisans, using tools and ancient patterns now unavailable to their colonial kin, had crafted a perfect replica; but they had taken much too long doing it. Voorhees' contract specified that he had to get the temple and its statuary to Orissa within seventeen days, before the local celebration of Rath Yatra, when the god's effigy was scheduled to be transported in solemn procession from the temple to a summer dwelling. If the ship arrvied late and the faithful had to commemorate their holy days without the sacred edifice and images, the shipping fee would be halved. And it was a very large fee.

Voorhees had been confident of meeting the deadline. He programmed the tightest hyperspatial catenary, made sure he had extra dope for the pain of breaking through the superficies on short leash, and settled down to play chess with the guidance computer and trade gossip with the ship's other systems. Wolverton Mountain was completely automated except for her skipper; but Richard had sufficient vestigial social tendencies to program all of the robotics with individual identities and voices, together with input from the scandal sheets of his favorite worlds, jokes, and sycophantic chatter. It helped to pass the time.

"Communications to bridge," said a winsome contralto, interrupting Richard's attack on the computer's queen.

"Voorhees here. What is it, Lily darling?"

"We've intercepted a contemporaneous subspace distress signal," the system said. "A Poltroyan research vessel is dead in the matrix with translator trouble. Navigation is plotting its pseudolocus."

Damn grinning little dwarfs! Probably poking around in their usual busybody way and all the while letting the u-crystals deteriorate without proper maintenance.

"Navigation to bridge."

"Yes, Fred?"

"That vessel in distress is damn near our catenary, Captain. They're lucky. This slice of the hype doesn't get much traffic."

Richard's fist closed around a chess pawn and squeezed. So now he could go nursemaid the little buggers. And kiss half his commission goodbye, like as not. It would probably take several subjective days to make repairs, considering the fumble-fingeredness of the Poltroyans and the fact that Wolverton Mountain carried only three robot excursion engineers. If it was a shipful of humans in distress, there'd be no question of heaving to. But exotics!

"I've acknowledged receipt of the distress signal," Lily said. "The Poltroyan vessel is in a state of life-system deterioration. They've been trapped for some time, Skipper."

Oh, hell. He was only two days out of Orissa. The Poltroons

could certainly hang on for a few days longer. He could catch them on the flip-flop.

"Attention all systems. Carry on original subspace vector. Communications, cease all external transmissions. Lily, I want you to erase from the log that distress signal and all subsequent inter- and intraship communications up to the sound of my mark. Ready? *Mark.*"

Richard Voorhees made his delivery in time and collected the entire fee from the grateful worshipers of Jagannath.

A Lylmik Fleet cruiser rendered assistance to the Poltroyans at about the same time that Voorhees docked on Orissa. The Poltroyans had less than fifteen hours of oxygen remaining in their life-support system when the rescuers arrived.

The Poltroyans turned their recording of Voorhees' initial response to the distress signal over to the Sector Magistratum. When Richard returned to Assawompset, he was placed under arrest on suspicion of violating the Galactic Altruism Statutes, Section 24: "Ethical Obligations of Deep-Space Vessels."

After being convicted of the charge, Richard Voorhees was fined a stupendous sum that wiped out most of his assets. Wolverton Mountain was confiscated and her skipper proscribed from engaging in any aspect of astrogation or interstellar commerce for the rest of his natural lives.

"I think I'll visit the Old World," Richard told his solicitor after the whole thing was over. "They say you can't beat it as a place to blow your brains out."

4

FELICE LANDRY sat erect in the saddle on the back of her three-ton verrul, stun-gun cradled in her right arm. She bowed her head in acknowledgment of the cheers. There were nearly fifty thousand fans in the arena for the big game—a splendid turnout for a small planet such as Acadie.

Landry nudged the verrul into a complicated routine of dressage. The hideous beast, resembling a stilt-legged rhino with a ceratopsian neck frill and wicked glowing eyes, minced in and out of the bodies without stepping on a single one. Of all the players on the green-and-white sawdust grid, Landry was the only one still mounted and conscious.

Other verruls in the sideline pens behind the burladero added their trumpeting to the crowd's applause. With casual skill, Felice had her mount pick up the scarlet ring with its nose horn. Then she sent the animal galloping toward the now undefended Whitewing goal, even though there was no longer any need for speed.

"Lan-*dree!* Lan-*dree!*" screamed the spectators.

It seemed that the young girl and the beast would crash into the cavernous scoop at the end of the field. But just before they were upon it, Landry gave the verrul a sharp crossrein and an unspoken command. The creature wheeled full about, tossing its monstrous head, which was nearly as long as the girl's body. The ring went sailing through the air and entered the scoop dead center. The goal signal lit up and blared in triumph.

"Lan-DREEE!"

She held her gun high and shouted back at the mob. Shock waves of orgasm surged through her. For a long minute she could not see, nor did she hear the single deep peal from the referee's bell that marked the end of the game.

As her senses cleared, she condescended to smile at the leaping, gesticulating throng. Celebrate my victory, people-children-lovers. Call my name. But do not press.

"Lan-*dree!* Lan-*dree!* Lan-*dree!*"

A ref came trotting up with the championship banner hanging at the end of a long lance. She holstered the stun-gun, took the flag, and raised it up. She and the verrul made a slow circuit of the arena, both of them nodding to the deafening plaudits of Greenhammer and Whitewing fans alike.

There had never been such a season. Never such a championship game. Never before the coming of Felice Landry.

The sports-mad people of "Canadian" Acadie took their ring-hockey very seriously. At first, they had resented Landry for daring to play the dangerous game. Then they had devoured her. Short, slightly built but preternaturally strong of mind and body, with an uncanny ability to control the evil-tempered verrul mounts, Felice had vanquished male players of talent and experience to become a sports idol in her first professional season. She played both offense and defense; her lightning-fast stun coups became a legend; she herself had never fallen.

In this, the last match of the championship series, she had scored eight goals—a new record. With all of her teammates downed in the final period, she had singlehandedly fought off Whitewing's last-ditch assault on the Greenhammer goal. Four stubborn giants of the Whitewing team had bitten the dust before she triumphed and went on to score that last go-to-hell goal.

Applaud. Adore. Tell me I am your queen-mistress-victim. Only stay back.

She guided the verrul toward the players' exit, fragile on the back of the monstrous animal. She wore an iridescent green kilt, and green head plumes on the back-tilted helmet. The once buoyant frizz of her platinum hair now straggled in limp ropes against the shiny black leather of her skimpy hoplite-style cuir bouilli armor.

"Lan-*dree!* Lan-*dree!*"

I have poured myself and discharged myself for you, slaves-eaters-violators. Now let me go.

Small medical carts were scuttling through the passageway toward the arena to bring in the stunned. Felice had to keep firm control of the nervous verrul as she moved toward the Greenhammer ramp. Suddenly there were people all around her—assistants, trainers, verrul grooms, second-string benchwarmers, gofers, and hangers-on. They raised a ragged cheer of greeting and congratulation, tinged with overfamiliarity. The heroine among her own.

She gave a tight, regal smile. Someone took the bridle of the verrul and soothed it with a bucket of feed.

"Felice! Felice, baby!" Coach Megowan, hot from the observation booth and still trailing game-plan tapes like a person caught in an old-time ticker tape parade, came pounding down from the upper level of the arena. "You were unbelievable, lovie! Glorious! Pyrotechnic! Kaleidoscopic!"

"Here you go, Coach," she said, leaning down from the saddle and passing him the banner. "Our first pennant. But not our last."

The jostling partisans began to shout. "You tell the world, Felice! Say again, sweetie-baby!" The verrul gave a warning growl.

Landry extended a graceful black-gauntleted arm toward the coach. Megowan yelled for somebody to bring a dismounting platform. Grooms steadied the animal while the girl allowed the coach to hand her down.

Adulation-joy-pain-nausea. The burden. The need.

She slipped off her Grecian helm with its tall green feathers and handed it to a worshipful female trainer. One of her fellow players, a massive reserve guard, was emboldened by the frenzy of victory.

"Give us a big wet smack, Landry!" he giggled, gathering her in before she could sidestep.

An instant later he was spread-eagled against the corridor wall. Felice laughed. A beat later, the others joined in. "Some other time, Benny precious!" Her eyes, brown and very large, met those of the other athlete. He felt as though something had taken him by the throat.

The girl, the coach, and most of the crowd passed on, heading for the dressing rooms where the reporters were waiting. Only the importunate guard was left behind, sliding slowly down the wall to sit, panting quietly, feet stuck out and arms limp at his sides. A medic driving a meat wagon found him there a few minutes later and helped him to his feet.

"Jeez, guy . . . and you weren't even in the game!"

With a sheepish scowl, Benny admitted what had happened.

The medical attendant wagged his head in amazement. "You had a lotta nerve making a pass. Sweet-face that she is, that little broad scares me shitless!"

The guard nodded, brooding. "You know? She *likes* shooting the guys down. I mean, she actually gets her bang from it. Only you can see she'd just as soon the poor sods was dead as snoozing. You grab? She's a freak! A gorgeous, talent-loaded, champion bitch-kitty freak."

The medic made a face. "Why else would a woman play this crazy game? Come on, hero. I'll give you a lift to the infirmary. We've got just the thing for that wonky feeling in your tummy."

The guard climbed onto the cart beside a snoring casualty. "Seventeen years old! Can you imagine what she's gonna be like when she grows up?"

"Jocks like you shouldn't have an imagination. It gets in the way of the game-plan." The medic gunned the cart down the corridor toward the sound of distant laughter and shouting.

Outside in the arena, the cheering had stopped.

5

"TRY AGAIN, Elizabeth."

She concentrated all of her mind's strength on the projective sense, what there was left of it. Hyperventilating and with heart racing, she strained until she seemed to be floating free of the chair.

Project from the plaque in front of you:

SMILE-GREETING. TO YOU KWONG CHUN-MEI THERAPIST FROM
ELIZABETH ORME FARSPEAKER. IF I HAD THE WINGS OF AN ANGEL
OVER THESE PRISON WALLS I WOULD FLY. ENDS.

"Try again, Elizabeth."

She did. Again and again and again. Send that ironic little message that she had chosen herself. (A sense of humor is evidence of personality integration.) Send it. Send it.

The door to the booth opened and Kwong came in at last. "I'm sorry, Elizabeth, but I still don't get a flicker."

"Not even the smile?"

"I'm sorry. Not yet. There are no images at all—only the simple carrier. Look, dear, why don't we wrap it up for today? The vital-signs monitor has you in the yellow. You really need more rest, more time to heal. You're trying too hard."

Elizabeth Orme leaned back and pressed her fingers to her aching temples. "Why do we keep up the pretense, Chun-Mei? We know there is slightly better than zip probability that I'll ever function as a metapsychic again. The tank did a beautiful job of putting me back together after the accident. No scars, no aberrations. I'm a fine, normal, healthy specimen of female humanity. Normal. And that's all, folks."

"Elizabeth—" The therapist's eyes were filled with compassion. "Give yourself a chance. It was almost a complete neocortical regeneration. We don't understand why you didn't regain your metafunctions together with your other mental faculties, but given time and work, you may very well recover."

"No one with my sort of injury ever has."

"No," came the reluctant admission. "But there *is* hope and we must keep trying to get through. You're still one of us, Elizabeth. We want you operant again no matter how long it takes. But you must keep trying."

Keep trying to teach a blind woman to see the three full moons of Denali. Keep trying to teach a deaf woman to appreciate Bach, or a tongueless one to sing Bellini. Oh, yes.

"You're a good friend, Chun-Mei, and God knows you've worked hard with me. But it would be healthier if I just accepted the loss. After all, think of the billions of ordinary people who live happy and fulfilling lives without any metapsychic functions at all. I simply must adapt to a new perspective."

Give up the memory of the mind's angel wings lost. Be happy inside the prison walls of my own skull. Forget the beautiful Unity, the synergy, the exultant bridging from world to world, the never-afraid warmth of companion souls, the joy of leading child-metas to full operancy. Forget the dear identity of dead Lawrence. Oh, yes.

Kwong hesitated. "Why don't you follow Czarneki's advice and take a good long vacation on some warm peaceful world? Tuamotu. Riviera. Tamiami. Even Old Earth! When you return we can begin again with simple pictorials."

"That might be just the thing for me, Chun-Mei." But the slight emphasis wasn't lost on the therapist, whose lips tightened in concern. Kwong did not speak, fearing to cause even deeper pain.

Elizabeth put on her fur-lined cloak and peered through the drapes covering the office window. "Good grief, just look how the storm has picked up! I'd be a fool not to grab at a chance to escape this Denali winter. I hope my poor egg will start. It was the only one in the transport pool this morning and it's very nearly ready for the scrap heap."

Like its driver.

The therapist followed Elizabeth Orme to the door and placed one hand on her shoulder in impulsive empathy. Projecting peace. Projecting hope. "You're not to lose courage. You owe it to yourself and to the entire metacommunity to keep on trying. Your place is with us."

Elizabeth smiled. It was a tranquil face with only a few fine lines about the corners of the eyes, stigmata of deep emotion subsequent to the regeneration that had restored her broken forty-four-year-old body to the perfection of young adulthood. As easily as a crayfish grows new limbs, she had grown new cells to replace smashed arms and rib cage and pelvis, lungs and heart and abdominal organs, shattered bone and gray matter of her skull and forebrain. The regeneration had been virtually perfect, so the doctors had said. Oh, yes.

She gave the therapist's hand a gentle squeeze. "Goodbye, Chun-Mei. Until the next time."

Never, never again.

She went out into the snow, ankle-deep already. The illuminated office windows of the Denali Institute of Metapsychology made squarish golden patterns on the white quadrangle. Frank, the custodian, gave her a wave as he plied a shovel along the walk. The melting system must have broken down again. Good old Denali.

She would not be coming back to the Institute where she had worked for so many years—first as a student, then as counseling farspeaker and redactor, finally as patient. The continuing pain of deprivation was more than her sanity could bear, and Elizabeth was basically a practical woman. It was time for something completely different.

Filled with purpose, clutching the hood of her cloak closely about her head, she headed for the egg park. As was her custom now, she moved her lips as she prayed.

"Blessed Diamond Mask, guide me on my way to Exile."

6

ADMITTING THE HUMAN RACE to the Galactic Milieu in advance of its sociopolitical maturation had been risky.

Even after the first metaphysic human threat to Milieu security had been put down by the venerated Jack and Illusio, there persisted stubborn evidence of humanity's original sin.

People such as Aiken Drum.

Aiken was one of those peculiar personalities who drive behavior

modification specialists to distraction. He was normally chromo-
somed. His brain was undamaged, undiseased, and of superior intelligence quotient. It was crammed with latent metafunctions that
might, in due time, be coaxed into operancy. His childhood nurturing on the newly founded colony of Dalriada was no different from
that of the other thirty thousand nonborns who were engendered
from the sperm and ova of carefully selected Scottish forebears.

But Aiken had been different from the rest of the hatch. He was a
natural crook.

Despite the love of surrogate parents, the devotion of skilled
teachers, and the inevitable corrective courses administered almost
continuously throughout his stormy adolescence, Aiken stubbornly
clung to his destined path of knavery. He stole. He lied. He cheated
when he felt he could get away with it. He took joy in breaking the
rules and was contemptuous of peers with normal psychosocial orientation.

"The subject Aiken Drum," summarized his personality inventory, "displays a fundamental dysfunction in the imaginative sense.
He is essentially flawed in his ability to perceive the social and personal consequences of his own actions and is self-centered to a dele-
terious degree. He has proved resistant to all techniques of moral impression."

But Aiken Drum was charming. And Aiken Drum had a roguish
sense of humor. And Aiken Drum, for all his rascal ways, was a natural leader. He was clever with his hands and ingenious in dreaming up new ways to outrage the established order, so his contem-
poraries tended to view him as a shadow hero. Even Dalriada's
adults, harried by the awesome task of raising an entire generation
of test-tube colonists to populate an empty new world, had to laugh
at some of his enormities.

When Aiken Drum was twelve, his Ecology Corps crew was
charged with the cleanup of a putrefying cetacean carcass that had
washed up on the beach of the planet's fourth-largest settlement.
Saner heads among the children voted for bulldozing the twenty-ton
mess into the sand above high-tide level. But Aiken convinced them
to try a more spectacular means of disposal. So they had blown up
the dead whale with plastic explosive of Aiken's concoction. Fist-
sized gouts of stinking flesh showered the entire town, including a
visiting delegation of Milieu dignitaries.

When Aiken Drum was thirteen, he had worked with a crew of

civil engineers, diverting the course of a small waterfall so that it would help feed the newly completed Old Man of the Mountain Reservoir. Late one night, Aiken and a gang of young confederates stole quantities of cement and conduit and modified the rocks at the rim of the falls. Dawn on Dalriada revealed a passable simulacrum of gigantic male urogenital organs, taking a leak into the reservoir forty meters below.

When Aiken Drum was fourteen, he stowed his small body away on a luxury liner bound for Caledonia. The passengers were victimized by thefts of jewelry, but monitors showed that no human thief had entered their rooms. A search of the cargo deck revealed the young stowaway and the radio-controlled robot "mouse" he had sent foraging, programmed to sniff out precious metals and gemstones that the boy calmly admitted he planned to fence in New Glasgow.

They sent him home, of course, and the behaviorists had still another shot at redirecting Aiken's errant steps toward the narrow road of virtue. But the conditioning never took.

"He breaks your heart," one psychologist admitted to another. "You can't help but like the kid, and he's got a brilliantly inventive mind in that troll bod of his. But what the hell are we going to do with him? The Galactic Milieu just has no niche for Till Eulenspiegel!"

They tried redirecting his narcissism into comedic entertainment, but his fellow troupers nearly lynched him when he queered their acts with practical jokes. They tried to harness his mechanical ability, but he used the engineering school facilities to build outlaw black boxes that gave illegal access to half the computerized credit systems in the Sector. They tried metaphysic deep-redact and deprivation conditioning and multiphase electroshock and narcotherapy and old-time religion.

Aiken Drum's wickedness triumphed over all.

And so, when he reached an unrepentant twenty-first birthday, Aiken Drum was confronted with a multiple-choice question, the answer to which would shape his future:

> *As a confirmed recidivist, counterproductive to the ultimate harmony of the Galactic Milieu, which of these options do you choose?*
>
> *a. Permanent incarceration in Dalriada Correctional Institution*

b. *Psychosurgical implant of a docilization unit*
c. *Euthanasia*

"None of the above," said Aiken Drum. "I choose Exile."

7

Sister Annamaria Roccaro first met Claude when he brought his dying wife to the Oregon Cascade Hospice.

Both of the old people had been salvage exopaleontologists—Claude Majewski specializing in macrofossils and Genevieve Logan in micros. They had been married for more than ninety years and one rejuvenation, and together they had surveyed the extinct life-forms of more than twoscore planets colonized by humanity. But Genevieve had grown weary at last and refused a third lifetime, and Claude had concurred in her decision, as he had throughout most of their time together. They stayed in harness as long as possible, then spent a few declining years in their cottage on the Pacific Coast of Old World North America.

Claude never thought about the inevitable end until it was upon them. He had a vague notion that they would someday drift off quietly together in their sleep. The reality, of course, was less tidy. Claude's Polish peasant body proved in the end to have a much greater staying power than that of his Afroamerican wife. The time came when Genevieve had to go to the Hospice with Claude accompanying her. They were welcomed by Sister Roccaro, a tall and open-faced woman, who took personal charge of the physical and spiritual consolation of the dying scientist and her husband.

Genevieve, riddled with osteoporosis, partly paralyzed and dulled by a series of small strokes, was a long time passing. She may have been aware of her husband's efforts to comfort her, but she gave very little evidence of it. Suffering no pain, she spent her days sedated in a dreamy reverie or in sleep. Sister Roccaro found that more and more of her professional efforts were devoted to dealing with

Claude, who was frustrated and deeply depressed by his wife's slow drift toward life's end.

The old man was still physically sturdy at the age of one hundred and thirty-three, so the nun often took him walking in the mountains. They tramped the misty evergreen forests of the Cascade Range and fished for trout in streams running off the Mount Hood glaciers. They checklisted birds and wildflowers as high summer came on, climbed the flanks of Hood, and spent hot afternoons sitting in the shade on the mountainside without speaking, for Majewski was unable or unwilling to verbalize his grief.

One morning in the early July of 2110, Genevieve Logan began to sink quickly. She and Claude could only touch one another now, since she could no longer see or hear or speak. When the sickroom monitor showed that the old woman's brain had ceased to function, the Sister celebrated the Mass of Departure and gave the last anointing. Claude turned off the machines himself and sat beside the bed, holding Genevieve's skeletal brown hand until the warmth left it.

Sister Roccaro gently pressed the wrinkled coffee-colored lids down over the dead scientist's eyes. "Would you like to stay with her awhile, Claude?"

The old man smiled absently. "She's not here, Amerie. Would you walk with me if no one else needs you for a while? It's still early. I think I'd like to talk."

So they put on boots and went out again to the mountain, the trip via egg taking only a few minutes. Parking at Cloud Cap, they ascended Cooper Spur by an easy trail and came to a halt below Tie-In Rock, on a ridge at the 2800-meter level. They found a comfortable place to sit and took out canteens and lunches. Just below was Hood's Eliot Glacier. To the north, beyond the Columbia River Gorge, were Mount Adams and distant Rainier, both snow-crowned like Hood. The symmetrical cone of Mount St. Helens, to the west downriver, sent up a gray plume of smoke and volcanic steam.

Majewski said, "Pretty up here, isn't it? When Gen and I were kids, St. Helens was cold. They were still logging the forests. Dams blocked the Columbia, so the salmon had to climb upstream on fish ladders. Port Oregon Metro was still called Portland and Fort Vancouver. And there was a little smog, and some overcrowding if you wanted to live where the jobs were. But all in all, life was pretty good out here, even in the bad old days when St. Helens erupted. It was only toward the very end, before the Intervention when the world was running out of energy and the technoeconomy collapsing, that this Pacific Northwest country started to share some of the griefs of the rest of the world."

He pointed eastward, toward the dry canyons and the high-desert scrub of the old lava plateau beyond the Cascades.

"Out there lie the John Day fossil beds. Gen and I did our first collecting there when we were students. Maybe thirty or forty million years ago, that desert was a lush meadowland with forested hills. It had a big population of mammals—rhinos, horses, camels, oreodonts—we call them cookie monsters—and even giant dogs and sabertooth cats. Then one day the volcanoes began to erupt. They spread a deep blanket of ash and debris all over these eastern plains. The plants were buried and the streams and lakes were poisoned. There were pyroclastic flows—kind of a fiery cloud made of gas and ash and bits of lava, racing along faster than a hundred-fifty kloms an hour."

He slowly unwrapped a sandwich, bit, and chewed. The nun said nothing. She took off her bandanna head scarf and used it to wipe the sweat from her wide brow.

"No matter how fast or how far those poor animals ran, they couldn't escape. They were buried in the layers of ash. And then the vulcanism stopped. Rain washed away the poisons and the plants came back. After a while, the animals returned, too, and repopulated the land. But the good life didn't last. The volcanoes erupted again, and there were more showers of ashes. It happened over and over again throughout the next fifteen million years or so. The killing and the repopulating, the shower of death and the return of life. Layer after layer of fossils and ashes were laid down out there. The John Day formation is more than half a klom thick—and there are similar formations above and below it."

As the old man spoke, the nun sat staring at the tableland to the east. A pair of giant condors circled slowly in a thermal. Below them, a tight formation of nine egg-shaped flying craft wafted slowly along the course of an invisible canyon.

"The ash beds were capped with thick lava. Then, after more millions of years, rivers cut down through the rock and into the ash layers below. Gen and I found fossils along the watercourses—not just bones and teeth, but even leaf-prints and whole flowers pressed into the finer layers of ash. The records of a whole series of vanished worlds. Very poignant. At night, she and I would make love under the desert stars and look at the Milky Way in Sagittarius. We'd wonder how the constellations had looked to all those extinct animals. And how much longer poor old mankind could hang on before it was buried in its own ash bed, waiting for paleontologists from Sagittarius to come dig *us* up after another thirty million years."

He chuckled. "Melodrama. One of the hazards of digging fossils in a romantic setting." He ate the rest of his sandwich and drank from the canteen. Then he said, "Genevieve," and was quiet for a long time.

"Were you shocked by the Intervention?" Sister Roccaro asked at last. "Some of the older people I've counseled seemed almost disappointed that humanity was spared its just ecological deserts."

"It was tough on the Schadenfreude crowd," Majewski agreed, grinning. "The ones who viewed humankind as a sort of plague organism spoiling what might otherwise have been a pretty good planet. But paleontologists tend to take a long view of life. Some creatures survive, some become extinct. But no matter how great the ecological disaster, the paradox called life keeps on defying entropy and trying to perfect itself. Hard times just seem to help evolution. The Pleistocene Ice Age and pluvials could have killed off all the plant-eating hominids. But instead, the rough climate and the vegetation changes seem to have encouraged some of our ancestors to become meat eaters. And if you eat meat, you don't have to spend so much time hunting food. You can sit down and learn to think."

"Once upon a time, hunter-killer was better?"

"Hunter doesn't equate with murderer. I don't buy the totally depraved ape-man picture that some ethologists postulate for human ancestry. There was goodness and altruism in our hominid forebears just as there's good in most people today."

"But evil is real," said the nun. "Call it egocentrism or malignant aggression or original sin or whatever. It's there. Eden's gone."

"Isn't biblical Eden an ambivalent symbol? It seems to me that the myth simply shows us that self-awareness and intelligence are perilous. And they can be deadly. But consider the alternative to the Tree of Knowledge. Would anyone want innocence at such a price? Not me, Amerie. We really wouldn't want to give back that bite of apple. Even our aggressive instincts and stubborn pride helped make us rulers of the Earth."

"And one day . . . maybe of the galaxy?"

Claude gave a short laugh. "God knows we used to argue long enough about that notion when the Gi and the Poltroyans cooperated with us on salvage digs. The consensus seems to be that despite our hubris and pushiness, we humans have incredible potential

—which justified the Intervention before we got ourselves too screwed up. On the other hand, the trouble we caused during the metapsychic flap back in the 'Eighties makes you wonder whether we haven't simply transferred our talent for spoiling to a cosmic stage instead of just a planetary one."

They ate some oranges and after a time Claude said, "Whatever happens, I'm glad that I lived to reach the stars, and I'm glad that Gen and I met and worked with other thinking beings of goodwill. It's over now, but it was a wonderful adventure."

"How did Genevieve feel about your travels?"

"She was more strongly tied to Earth, even though she enjoyed the outworld journeyings. She insisted on keeping a home here in the Pacific Northwest, where we had been raised. If we had been able to have children, she might never have agreed to leave. But she was a sickle-cell carrier, and the technique for modifying the genetic codon was developed after Gen had passed optimal child-bearing age. Later on, when we were ready for rejuvenation, our parenting instincts were pretty well atrophied, and there was so much work to do. So we just kept on doing it together. For ninety-four years . . ."

"Claude." Sister Roccaro reached out her hand to him. A light breeze stirred her short curly hair. "Do you realize that you're healed?"

"I knew it would happen. After Gen was dead. It was only her going that was so bad. You see, we'd talked it all out months ago, when she was still in control of her faculties, and did a lot of commiserating and accepting and emotional purging. But she still had to *go*, and I had to watch and wait while the person I loved more than my own life slipped farther and farther away but was never quite gone. Now that she's dead, I'm functional again. I just ask myself what in the world I'm going to do?"

"I had to answer the same question," the nun said carefully.

Majewski gave a start, then studied her face as though he had never seen it before. "Amerie, child. You've spent your life consoling needy people, serving the dying and their mourners. And you still have to ask a question like that?"

"I'm not a child, Claude. I'm a thirty-seven-year-old woman and I've worked at the Hospice for fifteen of those years. The job . . . has not been easy. I'm burnt out. I had decided that you and Genevieve would be my last clients. My superiors have concurred with my decision to leave the order."

Shocked beyond words, the old man stared at her. She continued,

"I found myself becoming isolated, consumed by the emotions of the people I was trying to help. There's been a shriveling of faith, too, Claude." She gave a small shrug. "The kind of thing that people in the religious life are all too likely to suffer. A sensible scientific type like you would probably laugh—"

"I'd never laugh at you, Amerie. And if you really think I'm sensible, maybe I can help you."

She rose up and slapped gritty rock dust off her jeans. "It's time for us to get off this mountain. It'll take at least two hours to walk back down to the egg."

"And on the way," he insisted, "you're going to tell me about your problem and your plans for the future."

Annamaria Roccaro regarded the very old man with amused exasperation. "Doctor Majewski, you're a retired bone digger—not a spiritual counselor."

"You're going to tell me anyhow. In case you don't know it, there's nothing more stubborn in the Galactic Milieu than a Polack who's set his mind to something. And I'm a lot more stubborn than a lot of other Polacks because I've had more time to practice. And besides that," he added slyly, "you would never have mentioned your problem at all if you hadn't wanted to talk it over with me. Come on. Let's get walking."

He set off slowly down the trail and she followed. They tramped along in silence for at least ten minutes before she began to speak.

"When I was a little girl, my religious heroes weren't the Galactic Age saints. I could never identify with Père Teilhard or Saint Jack the Bodiless or Illusio Diamond Mask. I liked the really old-timey mystics: Simeon Stylites, Anthony the Hermit, Dame Julian of Norwich. But today, that kind of solitary commitment to penitence is contrary to the Church's new vision of human energetics. We're supposed to chart our individual journey toward perfection within a unity of human and divine love."

Claude grimaced at her over his shoulder. "You lost me, child."

"Stripped of the jargon, it means that charitable activity is in; solitary mysticism is out. Our Galactic Age is too busy for anchoresses or hermits. That way of life is supposed to be selfish, escapist, masochistic, and counter to the Church's social evolution."

"But you don't think so—is that it, Amerie? You want to go off and fast and contemplate in some lonesome spot and suffer and attain enlightenment."

"Don't you laugh at me, Claude. I tried to get into a monastery

. . . the Cistercians, Poor Clares, Carmelites. And they took one look at my psychosocial profile and told me to get lost. Counseling, they advised! Not even the Zen-Brigittines would give me a chance! But I finally discovered that there *is* one place where an old-fashioned solitary mystic wouldn't be out of place. Have you ever heard of Exile?"

"What paleobiologist hasn't?"

"You may know that there's been a sort of underground railroad to it for a good many years. But you may not know that use of the time-portal was given official Milieu sanction four years ago in response to an increasing demand. All kinds of people have gone into Exile after undergoing a survival regimen. People from every imaginable educational background and profession, from Earth and from the human colonies. All of those time-travelers have one thing in common: They want to go on living, but they can't function any longer in this complex, structured world of galactic civilization."

"And this is what you've chosen?"

"My application was accepted more than a month ago."

They came to a tricky scree slope, the remnant of an old avalanche, and concentrated on traversing it safely. When they reached the other side they rested for a moment. The sun beat down hotly. The retroevolved condors were gone.

"Amerie," the old man said, "it would be very interesting to see fossil bones with flesh on them."

She elevated an eyebrow. "Isn't this notion a trifle impulsive?"

"Maybe I've nothing better to do. Seeing Pliocene animals alive would be an interesting windup to a long career in paleobiology. And the day-to-day survival aspects wouldn't pose any problems for me. If there's one thing you learn out in the field, it's roughing it in comfort. Maybe I could kind of help you get your hermitage set up. That is—if you wouldn't think I was too great a temptation to your vows."

She went into gales of laughter, then stopped and said, "Claude! You're *worried* about me. You think I'll get eaten by a sabertooth tiger or trampled by mastodons."

"Dammit, Amerie! Do you know what you're letting yourself in for? Just because you climb a few tame mountains and catch stocked trout in Oregon you think you can be a female Francis of Assisi in a howling wilderness!" He looked away, scowling. "God knows what kind of human dregs are wandering around there. I don't want to cramp your style, child. I could just keep an eye on things. Bring you food and such. Even those old mystics let the faithful bring 'em offerings, you know. Amerie—don't you understand? I wouldn't want anything to spoil your dream."

Abruptly, she threw her arms around him, then stepped back smiling, and for an instant he saw her not in jeans, plaid shirt, and bandanna, but robed in white homespun with a rope knotted about her waist. "Doctor Majewski, I would be honored to have you as a protector. You may very well be a temptation. But I'll be steadfast and resist your allure, even though I love you very much."

"That's settled, then. We'd better get on down and arrange for Genevieve's requiem without delay. We'll take her ashes with us to France and bury her in the Pliocene. Gen would have liked that."

8

THE WIDOW of Professor Théo Guderian had been astounded when the first time-tripper appeared at the gate of the cottage on the slope of the Monts du Lyonnais.

It happened in the year 2041, early in June. She was working in her rose garden, snipping deadheads from the splendid standards of Mme. A. Meilland and wondering how she would be able to pay the death duties, when a stocky male hiker with a dachshund came striding up the dusty road from Saint-Antoine-des-Vignes. The man knew where he was going. He stopped precisely in front of the gate and waited for her to approach. The little dog sat down one step behind her master's left heel.

"Good evening, Monsieur," she said in Standard English, folding her secateurs and slipping them into the pocket of her black salopette.

"Citizen Angélique Montmagny?"

"I prefer the older form of address. But yes, I am she."

He bowed formally. "Madame Guderian! Permit me to present myself. Richter, Karl Josef. I am by profession a poet and my home has been up to now in Frankfurt. I am here, chère Madame, to discuss with you a business proposal concerning the experimental apparatus of your late husband."

"I regret that I am no longer able to demonstrate the device." Madame pursed her lips. The fine beak of her aquiline nose lifted proudly. Her small black eyes sparkled with unshed tears. "Indeed, I am shortly going to have it dismantled so that the more valuable components can be sold."

"You must not! You must not!" cried Richter, taking hold of the top of the gate.

Madame took a step backward and stared at him in astonishment. He was moon-faced, with pale protuberant eyes and thick reddish brows, now hoisted in dismay. Expensively dressed as for a strenuous walking tour, he wore a large rucksack. To it were lashed a violin case, a lethal-looking dural catapult, and a golfer's umbrella. The stolid dachshund guarded a large parcel of paged books, carefully wrapped in plass and equipped with straps and a carrying handle.

Gaining control of his emotions, Richter said, "Forgive me, Madame. But you must not destroy this so-wonderful achievement of your late husband! It would be a sacrilege."

"Nevertheless, there are the death duties," said Madame. "You spoke of business, Monsieur. But you should know that many journalists have already written about my husband's work—"

"I," said Richter with a faint moue of distaste, "am not a journalist. I am a poet! And I hope you will consider my proposal most seriously." He unzipped a side compartment of the pack and removed a leather cardcase, from which he extracted a small blue rectangle. He held this out to Madame. "Evidence of my bona fides."

The blue card was a sight draft on the Bank of Lyon entitling the bearer to collect an extraordinary amount of money.

Madame Guderian unlatched the gate. "Please enter, M. Richter. One trusts the little dog is well mannered."

Richter picked up his package of books and smiled thinly. "Schatzi is more civilized than most humans."

They sat on a stone bench below a bee-loud arch of Soleil d'Or and Richter explained to the widow why he had come. He had learned of Guderian's time-gate at a publisher's cocktail party in Frankfurt and decided that very evening to sell everything that he owned and hasten to Lyon.

"It is very simple, Madame. I wish to pass through this time-portal and live permanently amid the prehistoric simplicity of the Pliocene Epoch. The peaceable kingdom! Locus amoenus! The Forest of

Arden! The sanctuary of innocence! The halcyon land unwatered by human tears!" He paused and tapped the blue card still in her hand. "And I am willing to pay handsomely for my passage."

A madman! Madame fingered the secateurs deep in her pocket. "The time-gate," she said carefully, "opens in but a single direction. There is no return. And we have no detailed knowledge of what lies on the other side in the Pliocene land. It was never possible to circumtranslate Tri-D cameras or other types of recording equipment."

"The fauna of the epoch is well known, Madame, as is the climate. A prudent person need have nothing to fear. And you, gnädige Frau, must suffer no qualms of conscience in permitting me to use the portal. I am self-sufficient and well able to look after myself in a wilderness. I have selected my equipment with care, and for companionship there is my faithful Schatzi. Don't hesitate, I beg of you! Let me pass through tonight. Now!"

A madman indeed, but perhaps one that Providence had sent!

She remonstrated with him for some time while the sky darkened to indigo and the nightingales began to sing. Richter parried all of her objections. He had no family to miss him. He had told no one of his intentions, so there would be no inquiries made of her. No one had observed him walking on the lonely road from the village. She would be rendering him a blessing, fulfilling for him what had once been an impossible dream of Arcady. He was not committing suicide, he was merely entering a new, more tranquil life. But if she refused him, his Seelenqual would leave him only the grimmest alternative. And there was the money . . .

"C'est entendu," Madame said at last. "Please accompany me."

She led him down into the cellar and threw on the lights. There stood the gazebo with its cables, just as poor Théo had left it. The poet gave a joyous cry and rushed to the apparatus, tears running down his round cheeks.

"At last!"

The dachshund trotted sedately after her master. Madame picked up the parcel of books and placed it inside the lattice.

"Quickly, Madame! Quickly!" Richter clasped his hands in a paroxysm of exaltation.

"Listen to me," she said sharply. "When you have been translated, you must immediately remove yourself from the point of your arrival. Walk three or four meters away and take the dog with you. Is this clear? Otherwise you will be snatched back into the present day as a dead man and crumble to dust."

"I understand! Vite, Madame, vite! Quickly!"

Trembling, she moved to the simple control panel and activated the time-portal. The mirrored force fields sprang up, and the poet's voice was silenced as if by a broken teleview connection. The old woman sank down on her knees and recited the Angelic Salutation three times, then got up and switched off the power.

The mirrors vanished. The gazebo was empty.

Madame Guderian let a great sigh escape her lips. Then she thriftily turned out the cellar lights and mounted the stairs, fingering the small slip of blue plass tucked securely in her pocket.

* * *

After Karl Josef Richter, there were others.

The very first gratuity allowed Madame to pay the inheritance tax and discharge all of her other debts. Some months later, after her mind had been fully opened to the time-gate's profitmaking potential by the coming of other visitors, she let it be known that she was establishing a quiet auberge for walking tourists. She purchased land adjoining her cottage and had a handsome guesthouse built. The rose gardens were expanded and several of her relatives drafted to assist with domestic duties. To the astonishment of skeptical neighbors, the inn prospered.

Not all of the guests who entered chez Guderian were seen to leave. But the point was moot, since Madame invariably required payment in advance.

Some years passed. Madame underwent rejuvenation and displayed an austere chic in her second lifetime. In the valley below the inn, the most ancient urban center in France also underwent graceful transition, as did all of the metropolitan centers of Old Earth in those middle years of the twenty-first century. Every trace of the ugly, ecologically destructive technology was gradually obliterated from the great city at the confluence of the Rhône and Saône. Necessary manufacturing establishments, service and transit systems were relocated in underground infrastructures. As the surplus population of Lyon was siphoned off to the new planets, empty slums and dreary suburbs faded into meadows and forest reserves, dotted here and there with garden villages or efficient habitat complexes. Lyon's historic structures, representing every century for the more than 2000 years of its lifetime, were refurbished and displayed like jewels in appropriate natural settings. Laboratories, offices, hotels, and commercial enterprises were tucked into recycled buildings or disguised to harmonize with the ambiance of nearby monuments. Plaisances and boulevards replaced the hideous concrete autoroutes. Amusement sites, picturesque alleys of small shops, and cultural foundations multiplied as colonials began returning to the Old World from the far-flung stars, seeking their ethnic heritage.

Other types of seekers also came to Lyon. These found their way to the inn in the western foothills, now called l'Auberge du Portail, where Madame Guderian personally made them welcome.

In those early years, when she still regarded the time-portal as a business venture, Madame set up simple criteria for her clientèle. Would-be timefarers had to spend at least two days with her at the auberge while she and her computer checked civil status and psychosocial profile. She would send no one through the gate who was a fugitive from justice, who was seriously deranged, or who had not attained twenty-eight years of age (for the great step demanded full maturity). She would permit no one to carry modern weaponry or coercive devices back to the Pliocene. Only the simplest solar-powered or sealed-pack machines might be taken. Persons obviously unprepared for survival in a primeval wilderness were dismissed and told to return upon acquiring suitable skills.

After thinking deeply on the matter, Madame made a further condition for women candidates. They must renounce their fertility.

"Attendez!" she would snap at the stunned female applicant in her unreconstructed Gallic way. "Consider the inescapable lot of womankind in a primitive world. Her destiny is to bear child after child until her body is worn out, submitting all the while to the whims of her male overlord. It is true that we modern women have complete control of our bodies as well as the ability to defend ourselves from outrage. But what of the daughters who might be born to you in the ancient epoch? You will not possess the technology to transfer your reproductive freedom to them. And with the return of the old biological pattern comes also the return of the old subservient mind-set. When your daughters matured, they would surely be enslaved. Would you consign a loved child to such a fate?"

There was also the matter of paradox.

The notion that time-travelers might disrupt the present world by meddling with the past had seriously troubled Madame Guderian for many weeks after the departure of Karl Josef Richter. She had concluded at last that such a paradox must be impossible, since the past is already manifest in the present, with the continuum sustained in the loving hands of le bon dieu.

On the other hand, one ought not to take chances.

Human beings, even the rejuvenated and highly educated people of the Coadunate Galactic Age, could have little impact on the Pliocene or any subsequent time period if they were restrained from reproducing. Given the social advantage to female travelers, the decision to demand the renouncing of motherhood as a condition of transport was confirmed in Madame's mind.

She would say to the protestors: "One realizes that it is unfair, that it sacrifices a portion of your feminine nature. Do I not understand? I, whose two dear children died before reaching adulthood? But you must accept that this world you seek to enter is not one of life. It is a refuge of misfits, a death surrogate, a rejection of normal human destiny. Ainsi, if you pass into this Exile, the consequences must rest upon you alone. If life's force is still urgent within you, then you should remain here. Only those who are bereaved of all joy in this present world may take refuge in the shadows of the past."

After hearing this somber speech, the women applicants would ponder and at last agree—or else depart from the auberge, never to return. Male time-travelers came to outnumber the female by nearly four to one. Madame was not greatly surprised.

The existence of the time-gate came to the attention of local authorities some three years after the Auberge du Portail commenced operation, when there was an unfortunate incident involving a refused applicant. But Madame's high-powered Lyon solicitors were able to prove that the enterprise violated no local or galactic statute: It was licensed as a public accommodation, a common carrier, a psychosocial counseling service, and a travel agency. From time to time thereafter, certain local government bodies made stabs at suppression or regulation. They always failed because there were no precedents . . . and besides, the time-gate was useful.

"I do a work of mercy," Madame Guderian told one investigatory panel. "It is a work that would have been incomprehensible scarcely one hundred years ago, but now, in this Galactic Age, it is a blessing. One need only study the dossiers of the pathetic ones themselves to see that they are out of place in the swift-paced modern world. There have always been such persons, psychosocial anachronisms, unsuited to the age in which they were born. Until the time-portal, these had no hope of altering their fate."

"Are you so confident, Madame," a commissioner asked, "that this time-portal leads to a better world?"

"It leads to a different and simpler world, at any rate, Citizen

Commissioner," she retorted. "That seems sufficient to my clients."

The auberge kept careful records of those who passed through the Pliocene gate and these would later be fascinating fodder for statisticians. For example, the travelers tended to be highly literate, intelligent, socially unconventional, and aesthetically sophisticated. Above all they were romantic. They were mostly citizens of the Old World rather than of the colonial planets. Many of the timefarers had earned their living in the professions, in science, technology, or other high disciplines. An ethnic assay of the travelers showed significant numbers of Anglo-Saxons, Celts, Germans, Slavs, Latins, Native Americans, Arabs, Turks and other Central Asiatics, and Japanese. There were few African blacks but numbers of Afroamericans. Inuit and Polynesian peoples were attracted by the Pliocene world; Chinese and Indo-Dravidians were not. Fewer agnostics than believers chose to abandon the present; but the devout time-travelers were often fanatics or conservatives disillusioned about modern religious trends, particularly the Milieu dicta that proscribed revolutionary socialism, jihads, or any style of theocracy. Many nonreligious, but few orthodox, Jews were tempted to escape to the past; a disproportionate number of Muslims and Catholics wanted to make the trip.

The psychoprofiles of the travelers showed that a significant percentage of the applicants was highly aggressive. Small-time ex-convicts were common clients, but the more formidable reformed evildoers apparently preferred the contemporary scene. There was a small but persistent trickle of broken-hearted lovers, both homophile and heterosexual. As was to be expected, many of the applicants were narcissistic and addicted to fantasy. These people were apt to appear at the auberge in the guise of Tarzan or Crusoe or Pocahontas or Rima, or else costumed as throwbacks to every conceivable Old World era and culture.

Some, like Richter, outfitted themselves for the journey with Spartan pragmatism. Others wanted to bring along "desert island" treasures such as whole libraries of old-fashioned paged books, musical instruments and recordings, elaborate armories, or wardrobes. The more practical gathered together livestock, seeds, and tools for homesteading in the style of the Swiss Family Robinson. Collectors and naturalists brought their paraphernalia. Writers came equipped with goose quills and flagons of sepia ink—or the latest in voicewriters with reams of durofilm sheets and book-plaque transcribers.

The frivolous cherished delicacies of food and drink and psychoactive chemicals.

Madame did her utmost to accommodate the impedimenta, given the physical restriction of the gazebo's volume, which was roughly six cubic meters. She urged the travelers to consider pooling their resources, and sometimes this was done. (The Gypsies, the Amish, the Russian Old Believers, and the Inuit were particularly shrewd in such matters.) But given the idiosyncratic nature of the timefarers, many preferred to be completely independent of fellow humans, while others ignored practicalities in favor of romantic ideals or precious fetishes.

Madame saw to it that each person had the minimal survival necessities, and extra shipments of medical supplies were regularly sent through the gate. Beyond that, one could only trust in Providence.

For nearly sixty-five years and throughout two rejuvenations, Angélique Guderian personally supervised the psychosocial evaluation of her clients and their eventual dispatch to the Pliocene. As the uneasy cupidity of her early years was finally submerged in compassion for those she served, the fees for passage became highly negotiable and were often waived. The number of prospective travelers increased steadily, and there came to be a long waiting list. By the turn of the twenty-second century, more than ninety thousand fugitives had passed through the time-portal to an unknown fate.

In 2106, Madame Guderian herself entered the Pliocene world called Exile—alone, dressed in her gardening clothes, carrying a simple rucksack and a bundle of cuttings from her favorite roses. Since she had always despised the Standard English of the Milieu as an insult to her French heritage, the note she left said:

"Plus qu'il n'en faut."

The Human Polity of the Galactic Concilium was not willing to accept this "more than enough" judgment however; the time-portal obviously filled a need as a glory hole for inconvenient aberrants. Organized in a humane and somewhat more efficient manner, it was allowed to continue in operation. There was no advertisement of the service, and referrals were kept discreetly professional.

The ethical dilemma of permitting persons to exile themselves to the Pliocene was tabled. Study confirmed that no time-paradox was possible. As for the fate of the travelers, they were all doomed in one way or another anyhow.

9

ALL THE WAY BACK to Earth from Brevon-su-Mirikon, Bryan Grenfell planned the way he would do it. He would call Mercy from Unst Starport just as soon as he got through the decon and remind her that she had agreed to go sailing with him. They could meet at Cannes on Friday evening, which would allow him time to drop off the conference data at the CAS in London and pick up some clothes and the boat from his flat. Fair weather was scheduled for the next three days, so they could cruise easily to Corse or even Sardegna.

In some secluded cove, with moonlight on the Mediterranean and soft music playing, he would nail her.

"This is your Captain speaking. We are five minutes from reentry into normal space above the planet Earth. There will be a momentary discomfort as we pass through the superficies, which may inconvenience sensitive persons. Please do not hesitate to call your flight attendant if you require an anodyne, and remember that your satisfaction is our prime directive. Thank you for traveling United."

Grenfell leaned toward the com. "Glendessarry and Evian." When the drink appeared he tossed it off, closed his eyes, and thought of Mercy. Those sad sea-colored eyes, ringed by the dark lashes. The hair of cedarwood red framing her pale high-boned cheeks. Her body, almost as thin as a child's but tall and elegant in a long gown of leaf-green with trailing darker ribbons. He could hear her voice, lilting and resonant, as they walked in the apple orchard that evening after the medieval pageant.

"There is no such thing as love at first sight, Bryan. There's only sex at first sight. And if my scrawny charms inflame you, then let's lie together, because you're a sweet man and I'm in need of comfort. But don't talk about love."

He had, though. He couldn't help it. Realizing the illogic of the thing, observing himself from afar with a chagrined detachment but still unable to control the situation, he knew he loved her from the first moment they met. Carefully, he had tried to explain without appearing a complete ass. She had only laughed and pulled him down onto the petal-strewn lawn. Their passion had delighted them both but brought him no true release. He was caught by her. He would have to share her life forever or go in misery apart.

Only one day with her! One day before he had to travel to the important meeting on the Poltroyan planet. She had wanted him to stay, suggesting the sailing holiday, but he, duty-bound, had put her off. Imbecile! She might have needed him. How could he have left her alone?

Only one day . . .

Bryan's old friend Gaston Deschamps, encountered fortuitously in a Paris restaurant, had invited him to kill some empty hours observing the Fête d'Auvergne from behind the scenes. Gaston, the pageant director, had called it a droll exercise in applied ethnology. And so it had been—until the introduction.

"Now we will return to those thrilling days d'antan," Gaston had proclaimed after giving him the fifty-pence tour of the village and the château. The director had led the way to a high tower, thrown open the door to the elaborate pageant control room, and she had been sitting there.

"You must meet my fellow wonder-worker, the associate director of the Fête, and the most medieval lady now alive in the Galactic Milieu . . . Mademoiselle Mercedes Lamballe!"

She had looked up from her console and smiled, piercing him to the heart . . .

"This is your Captain speaking. We are now reentering normal space above the planet Earth. The procedure will take only two seconds, so please bear with us during the brief period of mild discomfort."

Zang.

Toothextractionhammeredthumbwhangedfunnybone.

Zung.

"Thank you for your patience, ladies and gentlemen and distinguished passengers of other sexes. We will be landing at Unst Starport in the beautiful Shetland Islands of Earth at exactly 1500 hours Planet Mean Time."

Grenfell mopped his high brow and ordered another drink. This time, he sipped. Unbidden, an ancient song began unreeling in his mind, and he smiled because the song was so like Mercy.

> There is a lady sweet and kind
> Was never face so pleased my mind.
>
> I did but see her passing by,
> And yet I love her till I die.

He would take the tube to Nice and egg on to Cannes. She would be waiting for him at the quay of that peaceful old town, perhaps wearing a green playsuit. Her eyes would have that expression of gentle melancholy and be green or gray, changeable as the sea and as deep. He would stagger up with his dufflebag and a fitted picnic hamper full of food and drink (champagne, Stilton, gooseliver sausage, sweet butter, long loaves, oranges, black cherries), and he would trip over his feet and she would smile at last.

He would take out the boat and make the small boys at the slip stand back. (There were always small boys now that families had rediscovered the quiet Côte d'Azur.) He would attach the thin tube of the tiny inflator and throw the wadded packet of silver-and-black decamole film into the water. Slowly, slowly as the boys gaped, the eight-meter sloop would grow: bulb keels, hull, decks, furniture fixed below, cabin, cockpit, railings, mast. Then he would produce the separate pieces—rudder and tiller, stabilizer, boom with sails still furled, lines, deck seats, lockers, buckets, bedding and all—born miraculously of taut decamole and compressed air. Dockside dispensers would fill the keels and stabilizer with mercury and ballast the rest of the boat and its fittings with distilled water, adding mass to the rigid microstructure of the decamole. He would rent the auxiliary, the lamps, pump, navigear, the gooseneck, CQR anchor, and other hardware, pay off the harbormaster and bribe the small boys not to spit over the quayside into the cockpit.

She would board. He would cast off. With a fresh breeze, it would be up sail for Ajaccio! And somehow, in the next days, he would get her to agree to marry him.

I did but see her passing by . . .

When the starship landed in the beautiful Shetlands it was six degrees Celsius and blowing a dreary northeast gale. Mercedes Lamballe's teleview number responded with a SUBSCRIBER CANCELED SERVICE notice.

In a panic, Grenfell finally got hold of Gaston Deschamps. The pageant director was evasive, then angry, then apologetic. "The fact is, Bry, the damn woman's chucked it. Must have been the day after you went offworld two months ago. Left us flat—and the busiest time of the season, too."

"But where, Gaston? Where's she gone?"

On the view screen, Deschamps let his gaze slide away. "Through that damn time-portal into Exile. I'm sick about it, Bry. She had everything to live for. A bit off her bonk, of course, but none of us suspected she was that far gone. It's a damn shame. She had the best feel for the medieval of anyone I've ever known."

"I see. Thanks for telling me. I'm very sorry."

He broke the connection and sat in the teleview kiosk, a middle-aged anthropologist of some reputation, mild-faced, conservatively dressed, holding a portfolio full of Proceedings of the Fifteenth Galactic Conference on Culture Theory. Two Simbiari who had come in on the same ship with him waited patiently outside for some minutes before tapping on the kiosk door, leaving little green smears on the window.

And yet I love her . . .

Bryan Grenfell held up one apologetic finger to the Simbiari and turned back to the teleview. He touched the # stall.

"Information for what city, please?"

"Lyon," he said.

. . . Till I die.

* * *

Bryan posted the data to the CAS and picked up his own egg in London. Even though he could have done the research just as easily at home, he took off for France that same afternoon. Installing himself in the Galaxie-Lyon, he ordered a supper of grilled langouste, orange soufflée, and Chablis, and immediately began to search the literature.

The library unit in his room displayed a depressingly long list of books, theses, and articles on the Guderian time-portal. He thought about skipping over those cataloged under Physics and Paleobiology and concentrating on the Psychoanalogy and Psychosociology entries; but this seemed unworthy of her, so he poked his card into the slot and resignedly ordered the entire collection. The machine spat out enough thin plaque-books to pave the large hotel room six times over. He sorted them methodically and began to assimilate, projecting some, reading others, sleep-soaking the most tedious. Three days later he fed the books back into the unit. He checked out of the hotel and requested his egg, then went up to the roof to wait for it. The corpus he had just absorbed sloshed about in his mind without form or structure. He knew he was subconsciously rejecting it and its implications, but the realization was no great help.

Broken hearts healed and memories of vanished love faded away, even of this strange love whose like he had never known before. He realized that this had to be true. Measured judgment, consideration of the scary data he had stuffed himself with, common sense uncharged with emotion told him what he must do. Sensibly do.

Oh, Mercy. Oh, my dear. The uttermost part of the galaxy is nearer than you are, my lady passing by. And yet. And yet.

10

ONLY GEORGINA had been sorry to hear that Stein was going. They had got gloriously drunk together on his last day in Lisboa and she'd said, "How'd you like to do it in a volcano?" And he had muttered fondly that she was a crazy fat broad, but she assured him that she knew a guy who would, for suitable consideration, look the other way while they took a research deep-driller out of Messina, where there was this adit that led right into the main chamber of Stromboli.

So what the hell, they egged on over and the guy did let them get away with it. So what if it cost six kilobux? It was seismic down there in the surging lava with colored gas bubbles oozing slowly up the observation window like a bunch of jellyfish in a bowl of incandescent tomato soup.

"Oh, Georgina," he had moaned in the postcoital triste. "Come with me."

She rolled over on the padded floor of the driller cockpit, white flesh turned to scarlet and black by the glare outside, and gave the weeping giant mother-comfort from her melon-sized breasts.

"Steinie. Lovie. I've got three beautiful children and with my genetic quotient I can have three more if I want them. I'm happy as a clam at high tide playing with my kids and torching busted bores and loving up any man who isn't afraid I'll eat him alive. Steinie, what do I need with Exile? This is my kind of world. Exploding in three million directions all at once! Earthlings increasing and multiplying in every nook of the galaxy and the race evolving into something fantastic practically before your eyes. You know that one of my kids is coming out meta? It's happening all over the place now. Human biology is evolving right along with human culture for the first time since the Old Stone Age. I couldn't miss it, lovie. Not friggerty likely."

He broke away and knuckled out tears, disgusted with himself. "You better hope I didn't plant anything in your potato patch then, kid. I don't think my genes'd meet your standards."

She took his face in both hands and kissed him. "I know why you have to go, Blue Eyes. But I've also seen your PS profile. The squiggles in it have nothing to do with heredity, whatever you may think. Given another nurturing situation, you would have turned out fine, laddie."

"Animal. He called me a murdering little animal," Stein whispered.

She rocked him again. "He was hurt terribly when she died, and he couldn't know you understood what he was saying. Try to forgive him, Steinie. Try to forgive yourself."

The deep-driller began to lurch violently as massive eructations of gas rose from Stromboli's guts. They decided to get the hell out of there before the sigma-field heat shields gave way, and burrowed out of the lava chamber via an extinct underwater vent. When they finally emerged on the floor of the Mediterranean west of the island, the driller's hull clanged and pinged with the sounds of rocks falling through the water.

They rose to the surface and came into a night of mad melodrama. Stromboli was in eruption, farting red and yellow fire clouds and glowing chunks of lava that arched like skyrockets before quenching themselves in the sea.

"Holy petard," said Georgina. "Did we do that?"

Stein grinned at her owlishly as the driller rocked on steaming waves. "You wanna try for continental drift?" he asked, reaching for her.

11

RICHARD VOORHEES took the Express Tube from Unst to Paris to Lyon, then rented a Hertz egg for the last part of his journey. His earlier notion of eating and drinking and screwing his way across Europe and then jumping off an Alp had been modified when a fellow passenger on the liner from Assawompset happened to mention the odd Earth phenomenon of Exile.

That, Richard knew instantly, was just the kind of reprieve he needed. A new start on a primitive world full of human beings with no rules. Nothing to bug you but the occasional prehistoric monster. No green Leakie-Freakies, no dwarf Polliwogs, no obscene Gi, no glaring Krondaku making you feel like your nightmares just came true, and *especially* no Lylmik.

He started pulling the strings as soon as he got out of decon and was able to get to a teleview. Most Exile candidates applied months in advance through their local PS counselors and took all the tests before they ever left home. But Voorhees, the old operator, knew that there had to be a way of expediting matters. The magic passkey had come via a big Earthside corporation for which he had done a delicate job less than a year ago. It was to the advantage of both the corporation and the ex-spacer that he exit the here and now as soon as possible; and so with scarcely any arm-twisting at all, the outfit's VP-Operations agreed to use his good offices to convince the people at the auberge to let Richard take abbreviated tests right there at the starport, then proceed directly to Go.

This evening, however, as he glided out of the Rhône Valley toward the Monts du Lyonnais, he still admitted to a few qualms. He landed at Saint-Antoine-des-Vignes just a few kilometers from the inn and decided to have one last meal on free turf. The August sun had dropped behind the Col de la Luère and the resolutely quaint village drowsed in leftover heat. The café was small but it was also dim and cool and not, thank God, too cutesy atmospheric for comfort. As he ambled in, he noted approvingly that the Tri-D was off, the musicbox played only a subdued, jangling tune, and the smells of food were incredibly appealing.

A young couple and two older men, locals by the look of their agrigarb, sat at window tables wolfing large plates of sausage and bowls of salad. On a stool at the bar sat a huge blond man in a glossy suit of midnight nebulin. He was eating a whole chicken prepared with some pinkish sauce and washing it down with beer from a two-liter pewter tankard. After hesitating for a moment, Richard went and took another stool.

The big fellow nodded, grunted, and kept feeding his face. From the kitchen came the proprietor, a jolly pot-bellied man with a heroic aquiline nose. He beamed a welcome to Voorhees, spotting him as an offworlder immediately.

"I have heard," Richard said carefully, "that the food in this part of Earth is never prepared with synthetics."

The host said, "We'd sooner gastrectomize than insult our bellies with algiprote or biocake or any of the rest of that crapdiddle. Ask any gorf in the place."

"Say again, Louie!" cackled one of the oldsters at the window, hoisting a dripping hunk of sausage on his fork.

The proprietor leaned on the counter with hands palm down. "This France of ours has seen a lot of change. Our people are scattered over the galaxy. Our French language is dead. Our country is an industrial beehive underground and a history buff's Disneyland on top. But three things remain unchanged and immortal—our cheeses, our wines, and our cuisine! Now, I can see that you've come a long way." The man's eyelid drooped in a ponderous wink. "Like this other guest here, maybe you still have a ways to go. So if you're looking for a really cosmic meal—well, we're a modest house, but our cooking and our cellar are four-star *if* you can pay for it."

Richard sighed. "I trust you. Do it to me."

"An apéritif, then, which we have chilled and ready! Dom Pérignon 2100. Savor it while I bring you a selection of whimsies to whet your appetite."

"Is that champagne?" the chicken muncher asked. "In that little bitty bottle?"

Richard nodded. "Where I come from, a split of this will set you back three centibux."

"No shit? How far out you be, guy?"

"Assawompset. The old Assawomp-hole of the universe, we call it. But don't *you* try."

Stein chortled around his chicken. "I never fight with a guy till I meet him formal."

The host brought a napkin with two small pastries and a little silver dish full of white steaming lumps. "Brioche de foie gras, croustade de ris de veau à la financière, and quenelles de brochet au beurre d'écrevisses. Eat! Enjoy!" He swept out.

"Financier, huh?" muttered Richard. "There's a good epitaph." He ate the pastries. One was like a cream puff stuffed with delicious spiced liver. The other seemed to be a fluted tart shell filled with bits of meat, mushrooms, and unidentifiable tidbits in Madeira sauce. The dish with white sauce consisted of delicate fish dumplings.

"This is delicious—but what am I eating?" he asked the host, who had emerged to take the credit cards of the local diners.

"The brioche is filled with goose liver pâté. The tart has a slice of truffle, braised veal sweetbread, and a garnish of tiny chicken dumplings, cock's combs, and kidneys in wine sauce. The pike dumplings are served in creamy crayfish butter."

"Good God," said Richard.

"I have an outstanding vintage coming up with the main course. But first, grilled baby lamb filet with little vegetables, and to set it off, a splendid young Fumé from the Château du Nozet."

Richard ate and sipped, sipped and ate. Finally the host returned with a small chicken like that which Stein had lately devoured. "The specialty of the house—Poularde Diva! The most adolescent of young pullets, stuffed with rice, truffles, and foie gras, poached and coated with paprika suprême sauce. To accompany it, a magnificent Château Grillet."

"You're kidding!" Richard exclaimed.

"It never leaves the planet Earth," the host assured him solemnly. "It rarely leaves France. Get this behind your uvula, guy, and your stomach'll think you died and went to heaven." Once again he whirled out.

Stein gaped. "My chicken tasted good," he ventured. "But I ate it with Tuborg."

"To each his own," Richard said. After a long pause for attending to business, he wiped pink sauce off his mustache and said, "You figure somebody on the other side of the gate will know how to brew up some good booze?"

Stein's eyes narrowed. "How you know I'm goin' over?"

"Because you couldn't look less like some colonial gorf visiting the Old Country. You ever thought about where your next bucket of suds is coming from in the Pliocene?"

"Christ!" exclaimed Stein.

"Now me, I'm a wine freak. As much as I could be, dragging my ass all over the Milky Way. I was a spacer. I got busted. I don't wanta talk about it. You can call me Richard. Not Rick. Not Dick. Richard."

"I'm Steinie." The big driller thought for a minute. "The stuff they sent me about this Exile told how they let you sleep-learn any simple technology you think would be useful in the other world. I don't remember if it was on the list, but I bet I could cram brewing easy. And the hard sauce—you can make that outa just about anything. Only tricky bit would be the condensation column, and you could whip that up outa copper-film decamole and hide it in your hollow tooth if they didn't wanta let you in with it on the up. You with your wine, though, you might have a problem. Don't they use special grapes and stuff?"

"Don't they fuggin' ever," said Richard gloomily, squinting through the glass of Grillet. "I suppose the soil would be different back then, too. But you might be able to come up with something halfway decent. Let's see. Grapevine cuttings of course, and definitely yeast cultures, or you'd end up with moose pee for sure. And you'd have to know how to make some kind of bottles. What did they use before glass and plass?"

"Little brown jugs?" Stein suggested.

"Right. Ceramic. And I think you can make bottles outa leather if you heat and mold it in water—Christ! Will you listen to me? The hung spacer carving out a new career as a grape-squash moonshiner."

"Could you get a recipe for akvavit?" Stein was wistful. "It's just neat alcohol with a little caraway seed. I'll buy all you can make." He did a double take. "Buy? I mean barter, or something . . . Shit. You think there'll be *anything* civilized waiting for us?"

"They've had nearly seventy years to work on it."

"I guess it all depends," Stein said hesitantly.

Richard grunted. "I know what you're thinking. It all depends on what the rest of the fruitcakes have been up to all this time. Have they got a little pioneer paradise going, or do they spend their time scratching fleas and carving each other's tripes out?"

The host came up with a dirty old bottle, which he cradled like a precious child. "And here . . . the climax! But it'll cost you. Château d'Yquem '83, the famous Lost Vintage of the Metapsychic Rebellion year."

Richard's face, furrowed with old pain, was suddenly transformed. He studied the tattered label with reverence. "Could it still be alive?"

"As God wills," shrugged mon hôte. "Four point five kilobux the bottle."

Stein's mouth dropped. Richard nodded and the host began to draw the cork.

"Jeez, Richard, can I hit you for a little taste? I'll pay if you want. But I never had anything that cost so much."

"Landlord—three glasses! We will all drink to my toast."

The host sniffed the cork hopefully, gave a beatific smile, then poured three half-glasses of golden-brown liquid that sparkled like topaz in the lantern light.

Richard lifted his glass to the other two.

> A man may kiss his trull goodbye.
> A rose may kiss the butterfly.
> A wine may kiss the crystal glass.
> But you, my friends, may kiss mine ass!

The ex-spacer and the café proprietor closed their eyes and sampled the wine. Stein tossed his down in one gulp, grinned, and said, "Hey! It tastes like flowers! But not much sock to it, is there?"

Richard winced. "Bring my buddy here a crock of eau de vie. You'll like that, Steinie. Sort of akvavit without the seeds . . . You and I, landlord, will continue to bless our tonsils with the Sauternes."

So the evening wore on, and Voorhees and Oleson told each other edited versions of the sad stories of their lives while the proprietor of the café clucked in sympathy and kept refilling his own glass. A second bottle of Yquem was called for and then a third. After a while, Stein bashfully told them what Georgina's *other* farewell presents had been. His new friends demanded that he model them; so he went out into the darkened egg park, got the stuff from the boot, and stalked back into the café resplendent in a wolfskin kilt, a wide leather collar and belt studded with gold and amber, a bronze Viksø helmet, and a big steel-bladed battle-axe.

Richard toasted the Viking with the last of the Château d'Yquem, which he chugalugged from the bottle.

Stein said, "The horns on the helmet were really like ceremonial, Georgina said. Vikings didn't wear 'em in battle. So these are demountable."

Richard giggled. "You look perfek, Steinie ole rascal! Jus' perfek! Bring on th' mashtodons 'n' dinosaurs 'n' whatall. All they hafta do's look at you and they'll piss blue." His face changed. "Why din' I bring a costume? Ever'body goes back in time needs a costume. Why din' I think? Now I'll hafta go through the time-gate in fuggin' civvies. Never did have no class, Voorhees, dumb damn Dutchman. No fuggin' class never."

"Aw, don' be sad, Richard," begged the café man. "You don' wanna spoil yer meal 'n' lovely wine." His beady eyes lit with an expression of drunken craft. "Got it! There's guy in Lyon runs the flickin' opera. Comes up here 'n' eats himself shtooperuss. An' this guy's au ciel du cochon over one kinda wine, 'n' I gotta whole case you c'd use t'bribe 'em if y'could stan' the tab. They got any kinda costume y'd want at the opera. Merde alors, it's not even two hunnerd hours yet! Guy might not even be'n bed! What say?"

Stein whacked his new buddy on the back and Voorhees clutched the edge of the bar. "Come on, Richard! I'll pop for halvsies!"

"I c'd call the guy up ri' now," said the smirking host. "Bet he'd meetcha at the oper'house."

So they did work it out, and in the end Stein piloted the egg with the half-conscious Richard and a case of Château Mouton-Rothschild '95 down to the Cours Lafayette of sleeping Lyon, where a furtive figure guided them into the parking subway and then through a maze of turned-off walkways to the opera's backstage rooms and costumery.

"That one," Richard said at last, pointing.

"So! Der fliegende Holländer!" said the impresario. "Never would have pegged you for that one, guy."

He helped Richard to put on the seventeenth-century garb, which included a rich black doublet with slashed sleeves and a wide lace collar, black breeches, funnel-top boots that folded over, a short cape, and a wide-brimmed hat with a black plume.

"By damn, that's more like it!" Stein whacked Richard on the back. "You make a pretty good pirate. So that's what you're like deep down inside, huh? A reg'lar fuckin' Blackbeard?"

"Black *Mushtash*," said Voorhees. He collapsed, out cold.

Stein paid off the impresario, flew them back to the darkened café to transfer Richard's luggage from the rented egg, and then hopped it for l'Auberge du Portail. By the time they got there, the ex-spacer had revived.

"Let's have another drink," Stein suggested. "Try my oh-dee-vee."

Richard took a swallow of the raw spirit. "Not mush bouquet . . . but con*sider*'ble authority!"

The two costumed roisterers went singing through the rose garden and pounded on the oaken door of the inn with the blunt side of Stein's battle-axe.

The staff responded unperturbed. They were used to having clients arrive in a more or less fuddled condition. Six powerful attendants took charge of the Viking and Black Mustache, and in no time at all they were snoring between lavender-scented sheets.

12

FELICE LANDRY and the psychosocial counselor strolled into the flagged courtyard of the auberge, down an open passage, and into an office that looked out at the fountain and flowers. The room had been copied from the study of a fifteenth-century abbess. The stone fireplace with its bogus coat of arms had a huge bouquet of scarlet gladioli fanned between dog-headed andirons.

"You've come such a long way, Citizen Landry," said the counselor. "It's a pity that your application has encountered such difficulties."

He leaned back in the carved chair, forming a church-and-steeple with his fingers. He had a pointed nose, a perpetual half-smile, and tightly curled black hair with a flashy white blaze in front. His eyes were wary. He had read her profile. Still, she looked docile enough in that gray-blue gown, twisting her poor little fingers in anxiety.

Kindly, he said, "You see, Felice, you're really very young to be contemplating such a serious step. As you may know, the first custodian of the time-portal"—he nodded to an oil portrait of the sainted Madame that hung above the fireplace—"set a minimum age of twenty-eight years for her clients. Now, we may agree today that

Angélique Guderian's restriction was arbitrary, based upon anti-quated Thomistic notions of psychomaturation. But nevertheless, the basic principle does remain quite valid. Fully formed judgment is essential for life-and-death decisions. And you are eighteen. I'm sure you are far more mature than most persons of your age, but nevertheless, it would be prudent to wait a few more years before opting for Exile. There *is* no return, Felice."

I am harmless and afraid and small. I am in your power and I need your help so badly and would be so grateful. "You've studied my profile, Counselor Shonkwiler. I'm rather a mess."

"Yes, yes, but that can be treated, Citizen!" He leaned forward and took her cool hand. "We have so many more facilities here on Earth than were available on your home planet. Acadie is so remote! It's hardly to be expected that the counselors out there would have the latest therapy techniques. But you could go to Vienna or New York or Wuhan, and the top people would certainly be able to smooth out your little SM problem and the male-envious hyperaggression. There would be only the smallest bit of personality derangement. You would be quite as good as new when the course of treatment was finished."

The melting and submissive brown eyes began to brim up. "I'm sure you have only my best interests at heart, Counselor Shonkwiler. But you must try to understand." Pity, aid, empathize, condescend to help the pathetic little one! "I prefer to remain the way I am. That's why I've refused treatment. The thought of other persons manipulating my mind—changing it—fills me with the most dreadful fear. I just couldn't permit it!"

I wouldn't permit it.

The counselor moistened his lips and suddenly realized that he was stroking her hand. He gave a start, dropped it, and said, "Well, your psychosocial problems wouldn't ordinarily preclude transfer into Exile. But besides your youth, there is the second matter. As you are aware, the Concilium does not permit persons having operant metapsychic powers to pass into Exile. They are too valuable to the Milieu. Now, your tests show that you are possessed of *latent* metafunctions with coercive, psychokinetic, and psychocreative potentials of extremely high magnitude. No doubt these were partly responsible for your success as a professional athlete."

She showed a smile of regret, then slowly dropped her head so that the now limp platinum hair curtained her face. "That's all over now. They wouldn't have me any longer."

"Quite so," said Shonkwiler. "But if your psychosocial problems were successfully dealt with, it *might* be possible for the people at the MP Institute to bring up your latent abilities to operant status. Think what that would mean! You would become one of the elite of the Milieu—a person of vast influence—a literal world shaker! What a noble career you might have, spending yourself in service to a grateful galaxy. You might even aspire to a role in the Concilium!"

"Oh, I could never think of doing that. It's frightening to think of all those minds . . . Besides, I could never give up being what I am. There *must* be a way for me to pass through the time-portal, even if I am underage. You must help me find the way, Counselor!"

He hesitated. "The recidivist clause might have been invoked if the unfortunate MacSweeny and Barstow had elected to press charges. There is no age restriction for recidivists."

"I should have thought of that myself!" Her smile of relief was dazzling. "Then it's all so simple!"

She rose and came around to Shonkwiler's side of the desk. Still smiling, she took both his shoulders in her cool little hands, pressed with the thumbs, and snapped his collarbones.

13

CICADAS BUZZED in the branches of the old plane trees that shaded the dining terrace. The scent of mignonette distilled from the gardens in the noontime heat and mingled with the perfume of the roses. Elizabeth Orme toyed with her fruit salad and drank minted iced tea while she marveled over the list that slowly glided over the surface of the plaque-book before her.

"Will you listen to these vocations, Aiken? Architect, Daub-and-Wattle. Architect, Log. Architect, Unmortared Stone. Bamboo Artificer. (I didn't know bamboo grew in Europe during the Pliocene!) Baker. Balloonist. Basketmaker. Beekeeper. Brewer. Candle and Rushlight Maker. Ceramicist. Charcoalburner. Cheesemaker. Dompteur (-euse) . . . What in the world is that, do you suppose?"

Aiken Drum's black eyes flashed. He leapt to his feet, reddish golliwog hair abristle, and cracked an imaginary whip. "Hah, saber-tooth kittycat! Down, sirrah! So you defy the commands of your master? Roll over! Fetch! . . . Not the ringmaster, you fewkin' fool!"

Several of the nearby lunchers gawked. Elizabeth laughed. "Of course. Wild-animal tamers would be very useful in the Pliocene. Some of those large antelopes and things would be valuable if they could be domesticated. Still, I wouldn't want to tackle a mastodon or rhino on the strength of a quickie sleep-course in the art."

"Oh, the people here will do better than that for you, candy-doll. What happens is, you sleep-soak a very basic education in neolithic technology and general survival. Then you'll at least have the wits to dig a latrine that won't swallow you whole, and you'll know what Pliocene fruits aren't going to send you pushing up the daisies. After you sop up the basics, you pick one or more of the japes on that little list to specialize in. They give you a detailed sleeper on it, and lab work, and reference plaques for the tricky bits."

"H'mm," she mused.

"I imagine they try to steer you into a field that isn't already over-crowded. I mean, the folks on the other side of the gate would be apt to get testy if you sent 'em eighty-three lutanists and a taffy puller, when what they really wanted was somebody who knew how to make soap."

"You know, that's not really so funny, Aiken. If there is any kind of organized society on the other side, they'd be entirely dependent on the gate operators to send suitably trained people. Because the women timefarers are sterile, there'd be no young apprentices to re-place workers who died or just wandered away. If your settlement lost its cheesemaker, you'd just have to eat curd and whey until an-other one popped through the gate."

Drum finished his iced tea and began to chew the cubes. "Things can't be too shabby in Exile. People have been going through since 2041. The vocational guidance thing hasn't been perking for any-thing like that long—just the last four years or so—but the older in-mates of the nut-loft must have got *something* going." He thought for a minute. "Figure that most of the ones who went through were macroimmune and maybe even rejuvenated, since that was perfected in the early 'Forties. Barring the expected attrition from accidents, getting eaten by monsters, emigration to the Pliocene Antipodes, or just plain human bloody-mindedness, there ought to be quite a crowd still knocking around. Eighty, ninety thou easy. And like as not with a barter-style economy operating. Most of the time-travelers were damn intelligent."

"And crackers," said Elizabeth Orme, "even as thee and me."

She made an unobtrusive gesture toward an adjoining table, where a great blond man in a Viking outfit drank beer with a saturnine, well-used wayfarer in floppy seaboots and a ruffled black shirt.

Aiken rolled his eyeballs, looking more gnomish than ever. "Do you think that's weird? Wait till you see my rig-out, lovie!"

"Don't tell me. A Highland lad with bagpipe and tartan and a sporran full of exploding joints."

"Pissy patoot, woman. You certainly were telling the truth when you said your mind-reading powers were washed up. Ah-ah-ah! Don't plead with me! It's going to be a big surprise. What I *will* tell you now is my chosen vocation for the Land of No Return. I am going to be a Jack-of-all-trades. Scottish-style Connecticut Yankee in King Arthur's Court! . . . And how about you, my beautiful burned-out brainbender?"

Elizabeth's smile was dreamy. "I don't think I'll take a new persona. I'll just stay me—maybe in red denim—and wear my farspeaker's ring with one of Blessed Illusio's diamonds in remembrance of times past. As for the vocation—" She speeded up the book so that the list of occupations raced past, then turned back to the beginning. Her brow furrowed in concentration. "I'll need more than one trade. Basketmaker, Charcoalburner, Tanner. Put them all together, add one more that begins with B . . . and guess my new profession, Aiken Drum."

"Balls o' brass, woman," he howled, slapped a hand on the table delightedly. The Viking and the pirate stared in mild surprise. "A balloonist! Oh, you lovely lady. You'll soar again in one way or another, won't you, Elizabeth?"

There was a soft chime. A disembodied woman's voice said, "Candidates in Group Green, we would be most pleased if you would join Counselor Mishima in the Petit Salon, where a most interesting orientation program has been arranged for you . . . Candidates in Group Yellow—"

"Green. That's us," said Aiken. The pair of them drifted into the main building of the inn, all whitewashed stone, dark heavy beams, and priceless objects of art. The Petit Salon was a cozy air-conditioned chamber furnished with brocaded armchairs, fantastically carved armoires, and a faded tapestry of a virgin and her unicorn.

This was the first time that the group, which was destined to pass through the time-portal in a body after five days' training, had come together. Elizabeth studied her fellow misfits and tried to guess what exigencies had driven them to choose Exile.

Waiting for them in the otherwise empty room was a lovely pale-haired child in a simple black cheongsam. Her chair was separated from the others by a couple of meters. One of her slender wrists was fastened to the heavy chair arm by a delicate silver chain.

The pirate and the Viking glanced in, looking bashful and truculent because nobody else was yet in costume. They clomped forward and sat down precisely in the center of the row of seats. Another pair that seemed acquainted entered without speaking—a milkmaid-hale woman with curly brown hair, wearing a white coverall, and a stocky man who appeared to be middle-aged, having a snub nose, Slavic cheekbones, and corded hairy forearms that looked able to throttle an ox. A quasi-academic personage in an antique Harris jacket arrived last of all, carrying a briefcase. He looked so self-possessed that Elizabeth found it impossible to imagine what his problem might be.

Counselor Mishima, tall and sleek, came in beaming and nodding. He expressed his delight at their presence and hoped they would enjoy the introduction to Pliocene geography and ecology that he was pleased to present at this time.

"We have among us a distinguished person far more knowledgeable in paleoecology than I," the counselor said, bowing low to the Slavic type. "I would appreciate his interrupting me should my little lecture require correction or embellishment."

Well, that explains *him*, Elizabeth thought. A retired paleontologist bent on touring the fossil zoo. And the dolly on the leash is a recidivist whacko, a few stripes blacker than poor Aiken, no doubt. The boys in fancy dress are your obvious anachronistic losers. But who is the White Lady? And the Thinking Man who wears tweeds in August?

The room light faded and the tapestry rose to reveal a large holograph screen. There was music. (Lord Jesus, thought Elizabeth. Not Stravinsky!) The screen went from black to living Tri-D color in an orbiter's view of Pliocene Earth, six million years—give or take a few —backward in time.

In a long shot, it looked pretty familiar. But then the lens zoomed in.

Mishima said, "The continents, you will observe, are in their approximate modern positions. However, their outlines have an unfamiliar aspect, primarily because shallow epicontinental seas still covered some areas, while others, now lying underwater, were then dry land."

The globe rotated slowly and stopped when Europe was well positioned. The lens zoomed in closer and closer.

"You will all be furnished with a set of durofilm maps—small-scale for the entire Lower Pliocene Earth, one-to-seven-million of Europe, and one-to-one-million of France. Should you plan an excursion to other parts of the world or simply have an interest in them, we will do our utmost to provide you with suitable maps or marine charts."

"How accurate will they be?" asked the pirate.

"Extremely so, we believe." Mishima's response was smooth. "The Pliocene being one of the most recent geological epochs, our computers have been able to map its topography with an accuracy that must approach eighty-two percent. The areas most speculatively derived include fine details of the littoral, minor watercourses, and certain aspects of the Mediterranean Basin."

He began to show them closeup views of different areas, all in vivid relief and supplemented by an outline overlay of the modern landform.

"The British Isles are fused into a single very large mass, Albion, which is probably joined by a narrow isthmus to Normandy. The Low Country area is submerged by the Anversian Sea, as is northwestern Germany. Fennoscandia is an unbroken unit, as yet unsundered by the Baltic. Poland and Russia are strewn with swamps and lakes—some quite large. Another great body of fresh water lies southwest of the Vosges in France, and there are large Alpine lakes . . ."

To the east, the land looked almost completely unfamiliar. A brackish lagoon, the Pannonian Basin, covered Hungary and drained through the Iron Gate and the Dacian Strait to a shallow remnant of the once dominant Tethys Sea, also called Lac Mer. This spread swampy lagoons and salt water far into Central Asia and northward to the iceless Boreal Ocean. In years to come, only the Aral and the Caspian Seas would remain as souvenirs of the vanished Tethys.

"Note also that the Euxinic Basin, which will someday become the Black Sea, is also fresh water. It is fed by the towering ranges of Caucasia, Anatolia, and the Helvetides to the west. A vast swamp occupies the area of the modern Sea of Marmara. Below this is Lake Levant, roughly corresponding to the Aegean Sea of today."

"The Med looks pretty mixed up to me," the Viking observed. "In my line of work I had to know something about the crazy geology of that region. It seems to me you gotta be doing a whole lotta guessing to come up with that layout there."

Mishima acknowledged the point. "There are problems connected with the chronology of the successive Mediterranean inundations. We believe this configuration is most plausible for the early Pliocene. Please observe that the now vanished peninsula of Balearis juts eastward from Spain. There is a single narrow island in place of modern Corse and Sardegna. Italy during that time has only its Apennine spine above sea level, together with an unstable southern area called Tyrrhenis, which once was much larger but now is sinking."

He gave them a closer view of western Europe.

"This is the region that should be of immediate interest to you. The Rhône-Saône Trough contains a great river, draining swamps north of Switzerland and the large Lac de Bresse. The lower Rhône Valley of Pliocene times was probably invaded by the Mediterranean. Many of the volcanoes in the Massif Central were active, and there was also vulcanism in Germany, Spain, central Italy, and in the subsiding Tyrrhenian area. Farther north in France, we see that Brittany is an island separated from the mainland by the narrow Strait of Redon. The Atlantic forms a deep embayment southward into Anjou. Part of Gascony is also inundated by the sea."

"But Bordeaux seems to be all right, thank God," said the pirate.

Mishima chuckled. "Ah! Another connoisseur! You will be delighted to know, Citizen, that a number of other timefarers expressed a wish to settle in the Bordeaux area. They have carried with them certain portable apparatus and cuttings of many different grapes . . . Incidentally, Citizens, such information as we have about these earlier time-travelers is available from our computer at your convenience. And if you wish to have other information—for example, data on religious or ethnic groups, or on the kinds of books, art matériel, or other cultural items known to have been translated— please do not hesitate to request it."

The academic type in the tweed jacket asked, "Will the computer give information on individual persons?"

Aha! thought Elizabeth.

"The usual statistics, similar to those in your own dossiers, are available on those persons who have already passed through. It is also possible to obtain information on the items taken as baggage and the traveler's destination in the Pliocene world, if stated."

"Thank you."

"If there are no further questions—?" Mishima nodded to Felice, who had raised a languid hand.

"Is it true that none of these travelers took any weapons with them?"

"No *modern* weapons were allowed by Madame Guderian, and we have followed her wise dictum. No zappers, no stun-guns, no atomics, no sonic disruptors, no solar-powered blasters, no gases, no gunpowder-based weapons. No psychocoercive drugs or devices. However, many kinds of primitive weaponry from different eras and cultures have been taken into the Pliocene."

Landry nodded. Her face was void of expression. Elizabeth tried, without realizing what she was doing, to throw a redactive probe into her, but of course it was useless. Nevertheless, the ex-meta-psychic was amazed when the young woman turned her head and stared directly at her for a long minute before looking back at the screen.

She couldn't have felt anything, Elizabeth told herself. There was nothing to feel. And even if the carrier went out, there's no way she could have known that it was me. Was there?

Counselor Mishima said, "Let us briefly note some of the names that have been given to the geographical features. Then we will survey the plant and animal life of the so-called Pontian Facies of Lower Pliocene times . . ."

14

Just as soon as the lecture ended, Grenfell hurried to his room and the computer terminal, which was housed in a renaissance credence of wormy fruitwood. He requested the data in permanent durofilm sheets, not really knowing what to expect. What did emerge was pathetically meager—but it unexpectedly included a full-length color portrait, probably taken just prior to her passing through the gate.

Mercy Lamballe was wearing a cowled cloak of deep reddish brown that concealed most of her auburn hair and made dark pits of her eyes. Her face was white and strained. The dress was long, simply cut, of Nile green with a trimming of gold embroidery about the neck, wrists, and hem. Her narrow waist was held in a girdle of some dark color, from which hung a purse and a small scabbard with unidentifiable instruments in it. She wore gold bracelets and a gold necklace, both with purple stones. A large brocaded valise sat beside her. She carried a covered basket and a leather case that looked as though it held a small harp.

She was accompanied by a huge white dog wearing a spiked collar, and four sheep.

He stared at the picture for some time, memorizing it while his eyes stung. Then he read her tersely summarized dossier:

LAMBALLE, MERCEDES SIOBHAN 8-∅49-333-∅32-421F. B: St.-Brieuc 48:31N, ∅2:45W, FrEu, Sol-3 (Earth), 15-5-2∅82, d. Georges Bradford Lamballe 3-946-2∅2-664-117 & Siobhan Maeve O'Connell 3-429-697-551-418. Sb: ∅. M: ∅. D: ∅. C: ∅. Phy: H17∅cm, W46kg, Sfr1, Hrd2, Egn4, DMmole Rscap. Men: IA+146(+3B2), PSA+5+4.2+3.∅-∅.7+6.1, MPQ-.∅79(L) +28+

6 + 133 + 468 + 1. MedHist:NSI, NST, NSS (Supp1). PsyHist: AlienRefr-4 (non-dis), Fug-5 (non-dis), MDep-2 (.25 dis UT) (Supp2). Ed: BA Paris 21Ø2, MA(Anthr) Oxon 21Ø3, PhD(Fr-MedHis) Paris 21Ø4, DLH(CeltFL) Dublin 21Ø5. Emp: ImPag Eire (T4-T1) Ø5-Ø8;(DirAsst3-2) Ø8-Ø9. ImPag France (DirAsst1) Ø9-1Ø. Res: 25a Hab Cygne, Riom 45:54N, Ø3:Ø7E, FrEu, Sol-3. CivSt:*1*A-ØØ1Ø. CrRt: A-Ø1-3. Lic: E3, Tv, Ts, E1Tc2, Dg.

REMARKS: Ent: 1Ø-5-211Ø. VocOpt: Dyer, Sheep Husb, Small-holder, Weaver, Wool Tech. PersInv: (Supp3). Dest: NS. Attmt: NŞ.

TRANS: 15-5-211Ø   REF: J. D. Evans GC2

SUPPLEMENT 3   *Personal Inventory, Lamballe, M. S.*

Clothing: Gown, silk, grn emb-Au. Gown, silk, w emb-r+grn. Gown, polchro, blk emb-Ag-myl. Scarves, silk, 3. Cloak, repelvel, terracotta. Smalls, silk, asst w, 3sts. Hose, silk, w, 3pr. Shoes, low, leather, 2pr. Belt, leather. Purse, leather. Chatelaine, leather + scissors, knife, file, comb, stylus, fork, spoon.

Baggage: Survival Unit A-6*. Smallholder Unit F-1*. Sheep Kit Ov-1*. Fleck, Music, 5Ku, w/AVP (Supp4). Fleck, Library, 1ØKu, w/AVP (Supp5). Decamole appl: spin-wheel, hand-spindle, carder, loom L4H, dye-tub. Valise, leather-brocade. Basket, esparto, cov. Necklace, Au & amethyst. Bracelets, Au & amethyst, 3. Ring, Au & pearl. Mirror, Ag, 1Øcm. Noteplaque, 1Ku. Sewkit S-1* Harp, gilt carved sycamore wood, Celtic, w/case, leather. Harp strings & pegs, asst spare. Fife, open, Ag.

Plants: Strawberry "Hautbois Supérieur 12e," 1ØØ pts. Hemp (Cannabis s. sinsemilla) 15 ctgs. CulHb Unit CH-1* SmGrain Unit SG-1*. Misc seed pkts: Bluebell (Campanula bellardi), Indigo (Indigofera tinctoria), Madder (Rubia tinctorum), Pea "Mangetout."

Animals: Chien des Pyrénées, "Bidarray's Deirdre Stella-Polaris" (1F, pr4M+4F). Sheep, Rambouillet × Débouillet (3F @ pr2F; 1M).

There was more—the supplements with details of her medical and psychiatric history, the library supplements listing her music and books. He skimmed these, then returned to the poignant inventory and the portrait.

Will I find you again, Mercy in your silken gown and golden jewelry, with your harp and your fife and your strawberries and bluebells? Where will you go to tend your pregnant sheep? (Dest: NS.) Will I find you alone, except for loyal Dierdre and her pups, as you've always lived? (Attmt: NS.) Will you welcome me and teach me the songs of old Languedoc or old Ireland, or will your heartswound still be too deep for me to fill? (MDep-2, .25 dis UT.)

What did you find on the other side of the time-portal when you stepped through on your birthday, beginning your twenty-ninth year of life six million years before you were born? And why am I leaving this bravest of all new worlds for a constricting unknown? What's in the dark that I'm so afraid of finding/not finding?

Beguiled my heart, I know not why. And yet I love her till I die.

15

CLAUDE MAJEWSKI opened his eyes, wiped the rheum out of them with a tissue, and removed the earplug that had been teaching him while he slept how to mortise wind beams into the rafters of a log cabin. His left arm was full of pins and needles and his feet were cold. Damn crocky old circulation shot to hell. As he kneaded the blood back into the muscles, he reflected that he would miss the luxury of the auberge's goosedown pillows, liquicelle mattress, and real muslin sheets. He hoped the survival kit they would test today had a decent camp bed.

He padded across the sunny room to the bath. Here the compassion of Madame Guderian was made manifest in black-and-white marble and golden plumbing, in thick towels, perfumed soap and toiletries by Chanel, in sauna and sunlamp and la Masseuse ready to cradle the clients of the inn in soothing elegance after sobering lessons in la vie sauvage.

Some poor timefarers struggling to endure the Pliocene world would remember the last days at the auberge for French cooking, soft beds, and precious works of art. But Majewski knew that his fondest memories would be of the sybaritic john. The warm padded seat that welcomed his spindly shanks! The tissue, like perforated rabbit fur! He harked back to some of the primitive conveniences he and Gen had suffered on boondock planets—portacans with broken heating units; noisome stone and wood tillyhouses full of lurking critters; rough two-holers over flooded trenches; even one ghastly night of storms on Lusatia when he had squatted on a log and *then* discovered that it harbored little mitey monstrosities.

O blessed sanitary plumbing! If no one else invented a Pliocene water closet, Claude intended to give it an earnest shot.

He had a cool perfumed shower, cleaned his teeth (third set, good as new), made a face at himself in the Louis XIV mirror. Not too decrepit. A casual appraisal might judge his age to be late fiftyish. He was vain about his Polish green eyes and striking thatch of waved silver hair, the result of having the male-pattern baldness codons erased from his genetic heritage on the last rejuv. But thank God he'd depilated the rest of his pelt! Characters like that pirate who prized facial hair might have another song to sing in a primitive world—especially a warm and buggy one like Pontian Europe. The old paleobiologist had noted with grim humor that yesterday's lectures and clever animated movies on Pliocene ecology had barely mentioned the insects and other invertebrate denizens. It was more dramatic to show vast herds of hipparions and graceful gazelles being harried by scarcely less graceful cheetahs; or machairodont lions sinking their long canines into bellowing hoe-tuskers.

Claude went back into the bedroom and asked room service to send coffee and croissants. Since this second day was to feature simple survival techniques, he put on the clothing he planned to wear through the gate. Experience had made his choice of kit easy: fishnet underwear, old-fashioned bush shirt and pants made of the best Egyptian long-staple cotton, socks of Orcadian wool with the fat left in, and indestructible boots from Etruria. He had brought along his old backpack even though the auberge stood ready to furnish all equipment. It contained his poncho of breathable grintlaskin and an Orcadian sweater. And in one zip compartment was a beautiful

Zakopane box, all carved and ornamented wood. Gen's box. It hardly weighed a thing.

As he breakfasted, he studied the program for the day's activities. Introduction to Survival Unit A-6*. Shelter and Fire. Minimizing Environmental Hazards (ho ho). Orienteering. Fishing and Trapping.

He sighed, drank the perfect coffee, and munched a flaky bread roll. It was going to be a long day.

16

Sister Annamaria Roccaro had done a fair bit of camping, but the expensive new decamole equipment contained in Unit A-6* was a delight and a revelation to her.

She and the other members of Group Green had first gone to class, where a hearty woman instructor briefed them; then they had paired up and descended to a cavern carved out of the living rock 200 meters below the cellars of the auberge. They were let loose into a sunny meadow with a winding stream and told to become acquainted with their survival gear.

The simulated sun felt hot, even though the reset of their body thermostats was progressing apace. After she and Felice had hiked a short distance, Amerie decided that she would have to forego the sandals that had been her first choice for Pliocene footgear. They were suitably monastic and airy, but they also admitted twigs and small stones. Short buskins or even modern boots would be better for cross-country travel. She also decided that the white doeskin habit was overwarm, even with detachable sleeves. Homespun would be better. She could have a doeskin scapular, cowl, and cloak to keep off the weather.

"Aren't you hot in that outfit, Felice?" she asked her companion. Landry was wearing the green-and-black ring-hockey uniform, which was evidently her choice for the Pliocene.

"It suits me," the girl said. "I'm used to working in it, and my planet was much warmer than Earth. That doeskin looks very high-priestess, Amerie. I like it."

The nun felt strangely flustered. Felice looked so incongruous in her warrior's cuirass and greaves and that Grecian helm with its brave green feathers perched on the back of her head. Stein and Richard had started to tease her when she appeared in the costume that morning; but for some reason, they had broken off almost immediately.

"Shall we camp here?" the nun suggested. A large cork oak grew beside the brook, shading a flat surface that looked like a good place to set up the cabin. The two women shed their packs, and Amerie extracted the fist-sized inflator from hers and studied it. Their instructor had said that the sealed power supply would be good for about twenty years. "Here are two nozzles, one to blow things up and the other to deflate. It says: IMPERATIVE TO SHEATH UNUSED NOZZLE."

"Try my cabin-pak." Felice held out a wad about the size of a sandwich. "I can't believe it'll grow into a four-by-four house."

Sister Roccaro fixed the dangling flat tube of the pak to the inflator, then pressed the activating stud. Compressed air began to spurt into the wad, turning it into a large silvery square. The two women positioned the cabin properly, then watched it grow. The floor thickened to about nine centimeters and became quite rigid as air filled the complex micropore structural web between the layers of film. The walls, somewhat thicker for insulation, grew up, complete with transparent zippable windows and interior screen-curtains. A steeply gabled silvery roof that overhung the doorway inflated last of all.

Felice peered inside the doorless entry. "Look. The floor has sprouted fixed furniture."

There were bunks for two with semidetached pillows, a table, shelves, and at the rear a silvery box with a pipe leading to the roof. Felice read aloud: "BALLAST STOVE WITH SAND OR UNIT WILL COMPRESS UPON COOLING . . . This material must be nearly impossible to destroy!" She reached behind her left greave and produced a glittering little gold-handled dirk. "Can't puncture it, either."

"What a pity they've made it to degrade in twenty years. Still, we should be at one with our environment by then."

Large bucket-shaped hollows in each corner of the cabin had to be ballasted with stones, earth, water, or whatever else was to hand. A very small pocket near the door yielded up a whole handful of pill-sized wads that were to be inflated separately, then weighted with sand or with water. The latter could be injected into the interstitial area by means of a simple collapsible bulb siphon. The pills grew into a cabin door, chairs, cooking gear (with the sand-ballast note), filamentous rugs and blankets, and other miscellany. Less than ten minutes after they had begun to set up camp, the women were relaxing in a fully equipped cabin.

"I can hardly believe it," Sister Roccaro marveled, rapping on the walls. "It feels quite solid. But if there were any wind, the whole cabin would blow away like a bubble unless you weighted it down."

"Even wood is mostly thin air and water," said Felice with a shrug. "This decamole just seems to reproduce the structurally reinforced shell of a thing and let you add mass. Wonder how the stuff compensates for heat and pressure changes? Some kind of valves, I suppose. You'd obviously have to guy this house in a high wind, though, even if you filled most of the wall hollows with water or dirt. But it sure beats a tent. It even has ventilators!"

"Shall we inflate the boat or the minishelter or the bridge sections?"

"They were optional. Now that I've seen how decamole works, I'll take the rest of the equipment on faith." Felice crossed her legs and pulled off her gauntlets slowly. She was seated at the small table. "Faith. That's your game, isn't it?"

The nun sat down. "In a way. Technically, I intend to become an anchoress, a kind of religious hermit. It's a calling that's completely obsolete in the Milieu, but it used to have its fans in the Dark Ages."

"What in the world will you be doing? Just praying up a storm all day long?"

Amerie laughed. "Part of the night, too. I intend to bring back the Latin Divine Office. It's an ancient cycle of daily prayers. Matins starts it off at midnight. Then there's Lauds at dawn. During the daytime there are prayers for the old First, Third, Sixth, and Ninth Hours. Then Vespers or Evensong at sunset, and Compline before going to bed. The Office is a collection of psalms and scripture readings and hymns and special prayers that reflected centuries of religious tradition. I think it's a terrible pity that no one prays it any more in the primitive form."

"And you just keep saying this Office all the time?"

"Good grief, no. The individual hours aren't that long. I'll also celebrate the Mass and do penance and deep meditation with a little

Zen. And when I'm hoeing weeds or doing other chores there's the Rosary. It's almost like a mantra if you do it the old way. Very calming."

Felice stared at her with well-deep eyes. "It sounds very strange. And lonely, too. Doesn't it frighten you, planning to live all alone with nobody but your God?"

"Dear old Claude says he'll maintain me in style, but I'm not too sure I can take him seriously. If he does supply me with some food, I may be able to handcraft some items in my spare time that we can barter."

"Claude!" Landry was contemptuous. "He's been around, that old man. He's not a complete case like those two machos in fancy dress, but I caught him looking at me in a fishy way."

"You can't blame people for looking at you. You're very beautiful. I've heard you were a great sports star on your home world."

The girl's lip curled in a grim little smile. "Acadie. I was the best ring-hockey player of all time. But they were afraid of me. In the end, the other players—the men—refused to come up against me. They made all kinds of trouble. Finally, I was barred from the game when two players claimed I had deliberately tried to do them serious injury."

"Had you?"

Felice lowered her gaze. She was twisting the fingers of her gloves and a flush was rising from her neck into her cheeks. "Maybe. I think I did. They were so hateful." She raised her pointed chin in defiance, the hoplite helmet pushed to the back of her head giving her the look of a miniature Pallas Athene. "They never wanted me as a woman, you know. All they wanted was to hurt me, to spoil me. They were jealous of my strength, and afraid. People have always been afraid of me, even when I was just a child. Can you imagine what that was like?"

"Oh, Felice." Amerie hesitated. "How—how did you ever begin playing that brutal game?"

"I was good with animals. My parents were soil scientists and they were always moving around on field expeditions. Newly opened lands, still full of wildlife. When the local kids in the area would snub me, I'd just get myself some pets for friends. Small creatures at first—then larger and more dangerous kinds. And there were some beauties on Acadie, I can tell you! Finally, when I was fifteen, I tamed a verrul. It's something like a very large Earth rhinoceros. A local animal dealer wanted to buy him for ring-hockey training. I'd never paid much attention to the game before, but I did after I sold the beast. I woke up to the fact that there was a big-money business that might be perfect for my special talents."

"But to break into a professional sport when you were only a young girl—"

"I told my parents I wanted to become an apprentice verrul trainer and groom. They didn't mind. I had always been excess baggage. They just made me finish school and let me go. They said, 'Be happy, baby.'"

She paused and stared at Amerie without expression. "I was a groom only until the team manager saw how I could control the animals. That's the secret of playing the game, you see. The verrul has to make the goals and maneuver to keep you from getting stunned by the short-range weapons the players carry. I played in the preseason as a novelty, to give the Greenhammer box office a hype. The team had been in the cellar for three years running. When they saw that I was more than a publicity gimmick they put me onto the first string in the season opener. I whipped the other clowns on the team into such a froth trying to outdo me that we won the bloody game. And all the rest . . . and the pennant, too."

"Wonderful!"

"It should have been. But I had no friends. I was too different from the rest of the players. Too freakish. And in the second year . . . when they really began to hate me and I knew they would force me out, I—I—"

She pounded both fists on the table and her child's face twisted in anguish. Amerie waited for the tears, but there were none; the briefly revealed hurt was masked almost as soon as it had showed itself. Sitting across the table, Felice relaxed, smiling at the other woman.

"I'm going to be a huntress, you know. On the other side. I could take care of you much better than the old man, Amerie."

The nun rose up, blood pounding in her temples. She turned away from Felice and walked out of the cabin.

"I think we need each other," the girl said.

17

My dear Varya,

We have completed our little games of survival and craftsmanship now, and our bodies are fully acclimated to the tropical world that was Pliocene Earth. There remain only a Last Supper and a good night's sleep before passage through the time-portal at dawn. The apparatus is inside a quaint cottage in the gardens of the auberge, and you can't imagine a more incongruous site for the gate into another world. One looks in vain for the sign above the doorway saying, PER ME SI VA TRA LA PERDUTA GENTE, but the feeling is there all the same.

After five days of working together (more like a holiday camp than basic training, you must understand), the eight of us in Group Green have achieved shaky competence in our chosen fields of primitive technology and a faith in our ability to cope that is probably dangerously inflated. Few of the others seem to appreciate the potential hazard that we might face from our predecessors into Exile. My fellow Greenies are more inclined to worry about being stamped upon by mammoths or bitten by python-sized vipers than to anticipate a hostile human reception committee greedily awaiting the day's grab bag of well-heeled wayfarers.

You and I know that the time-gate arrivals would certainly have been ritualized in some manner by the people on the other side. What the ritual will be is another matter. We can hardly expect to be treated as casual commuters, but whether we shall encounter welcome or exploitation is impossible to fathom. The literature offers certain speculative scenarios that make my flesh crawl. Personnel at the auberge are careful to present a neutral face while at the same time reinforcing our childhood self-defensive training. We will pass through the portal in two groups of four persons, with larger pieces of baggage following. This, I feel, is designed to give us a certain safety in numbers—although the momentary pain and disorientation of ordinary subspace translation will probably affect time-travelers as well, putting us at a tactical disadvantage for the first minute following our arrival in the Pliocene.

Your amused speculations upon my new vocation in the primitive world were much appreciated. However, since the last dinosaurs perished at least 60 million years before the Pliocene Epoch, there will be little call for sweeping up after them! So much for your visions of me as an antediluvian fertilizer tycoon. Prosaically enough, my new job is to be little more than an extension of my erstwhile hobby of sailing. I shall fish for a living and ply the seas on my Quest, and perhaps undertake the odd bit of trade if the occasion presents. The sloop was far too sophisticated a vessel to take to the Pliocene, so I traded her in for a smaller trimaran that can be ballasted with water and sand instead of mercury. If need be, I can whip up a very simple craft from scratch materials as well. We are furnished with toolheads of a gemlike glassy material, vitredur, which stays eversharp and is virtually indestructible for some 200 years, after which it degrades, like decamole. Besides the shipwright's kit, I am equipped with the auberge's survival gear (very impressive) and what they call a Smallholder Unit—tools and decamole appliances for setting up light housekeeping on a subsistence farm, together with a few packets of seeds and a large fleck library with a raft of "how-to" books on every subject from animal husbandry to zymurgy.

The latter, by the way, is the vocation of choice for our Viking. He also confided to me that if there should be a demand for swashbuckling mercenary warriors, he might combine the two trades.

The individual whom I dubbed the Pirate also plans to get involved with alcoholic beverages—wines and brandies, that is. He and the Viking are now the straightest of friends, spending their off-hours tossing down the most expensive spirits that the auberge can supply and speculating on the quality of female consolation that might be available in the By-and-By. (Group Green itself has lean pickings. Besides the Nun, our female members include a sinister Virgin Huntress who seems to have wreaked mayhem or worse on one of the auberge counselors in order to qualify as a recidivist, and an extremely cautious ex-Meta Lady who is, at the moment at least, content to remain just one of the boys.)

Last night we had a fascinating glimpse into the background of the Pirate. His brother and sister turned up unexpectedly to say adieu and turned out to be Fleet line officers of the most impressive stripe. The poor P was very discomfited and the ex-Meta Lady speculates that he must be a cashiered spacer himself. He's a competent sort if you don't mind grouches. I worked with him for a few hours in the Small Boat Handling exercise, which he wanted to cram, and he seemed to have a natural flair for messing about in the water.

Most of the others in Group Green seem to be alone in the world. The Nun received a long conference call from her religious sistren in North America bidding her bon voyage. And earlier today she met with a Franciscan Brother in full conventual fig, no doubt hearing her last confession or whatever. (The friar drove one of those souped-up Gambini eggs with the heat dissipation fins, not the patient gray donkey you might have anticipated from memoirs of Il Poverello.) The Nun was a medic and psychological counselor by profession and plans to retire to a hermitage. I hope the poor woman isn't counting on ministering angels such as the Old Paleontologist overmuch. He's a fine chap with a penchant for carpentry, but I dare say the ex-Meta is right when she pegs him as a death-wisher.

I concur with your analysis of the Little Joker. There must have been some valid square-peg reason for him to be thrown off his home world, but it's a pity that his wild talents couldn't be harnessed for the Milieu. Poor little nonborn. He's endeared himself to the rest of us Greenies—not only for his ghastly sense of humor, but also for his fantastic ability to make something out of nothing. He has assembled a large collection of vitredur toolheads that need only be equipped with shafts or handles to be operational. You get the feeling that after this boy has been in the Pliocene for a week or two, the Industrial Revolution will be raging. He has a whole forge lashup in decamole for his village blacksmith and rustic mechanician acts, and has acquired a plaqueful of geological survey charts to clue him in on metal ores in the unlikely event that none of the other Exiles has gone in heavily for prospecting.

You may be interested in the peculiar social structure of Group Green. The foundress of the auberge was a practical psychologist of no mean ability and realized quite early on that her clients would need support from fellow travelers in order to maximize survival potential beyond the gate. On the other hand, they would tend to be far too eccentric to stand for any of the more obvious schemes of imposed organization. So Madame Guderian fell back on the old "put 'em through hell together and they'll end up buddies" shtick—which you must admit is apt to induce feelings of solidarity in all but the most sociopathic. (And it did, too, with the obvious exception.)

During each day's Group activities we have spent the most strenuous sessions working together, often thrust into outlandish situations where we were forced to cooperate with one another in order to complete a difficult task quickly and well. For example, we bridged a thirty-meter pond full of alligators in one lesson; captured, butchered, and "utilized" an elk in another; and defended ourselves against hostile human stalkers in a third. Ironically, the most accomplished primitive in the Group is the Old Paleontologist, who seems to have knocked about the wilder shores of Galactica for more than a century while gleaning fossil bones.

We are known to each other by first names only, and we may divulge such details of our background as we choose or don't choose. As you may imagine, this leaves a wide margin for parlor psychoanalysis—with the ex-Meta Lady as head gamesmistress. She had me taped as a Questing Lover after the first day, and I'm afraid that she anticipates a melancholy end to my masculine Evangeline-fixe, since she keeps trying to distract me with speculations on rôle playing among the auberge clientèle, the political implications of Exile, and other anthropological amusements.

Do you think I'm doomed, too, Varya? *I* don't, you know.

Late this afternoon I got a call from London, and it was Kaplan and Djibutunji and Hildebrand and Catherwood, bless their bones, telling me goodbye. Aunt Helen sent a note, but she is really nearly gaga now, since declining rejuv.

Your dear letter was in this morning's post. I don't have to tell you how much I appreciate your agreeing to carry on with the liaison committee. It's the one work I really hated to leave unfinished. There is still the ultimate correlation of the pre-Rebellion mazeway material, but I feel that Alicia and Adalberto have that pretty well in hand.

And so I come at last to the farewell, Varya, and I wish I could be eloquent and memorable instead of just my stodgy self. The gaudiness of the act will have to speak for me. Whatever you do, don't mourn. My only hope of happiness lies on the other side of the Exile gate and I must risk going after it. Remember the years we shared as lovers and colleagues and friends and know that I'm glad they happened. Joy and light to you, my Very Dear.

Forever,
BRY

18

WHEN THE LAST SUPPER, with its crazy smörgåsbord of requested dishes, was finally over, the eight members of Group Green took their drinks out onto the terrace, where they instinctively gathered apart from the other guests. Even though it was only half after twenty, the sky over Lyon had turned black as the scheduled weekly storm built up in the north. Pink flashes silhouetted approaching thunderheads.

"Feel the static buildup!" Elizabeth exclaimed. "Even with my metafunctions out, the ionization before a really big storm always gets to me. Every sense sharpens. I begin to feel so clever I can barely contain myself! Capacitor Earth is charging and so am I, and in just a minute or two I'll be able to zap mountains!"

She faced into the strengthening wind, long hair streaming and red denim jumpsuit clinging to her body. The first subsonics of distant thunder curdled the air.

Felice affected a languid tone. "Were you able to move mountains before?"

"Not really. The larger psychokinetic powers are really very rare among metas—almost as rare as genuine creativity. My PK ability was only good for a few parlor tricks. What I specialized in was farspeaking, the glorified telepathy function. It should really be called farsensing because it includes a species of sight as well as hearing. I was also highly operant in redaction, which is the therapeutic and analytical power that most lay persons call mind-alteration. My husband had similar faculties. We worked as a team training the minds of very young children in the first difficult steps toward metapsychic Unity."

"They wanted *me* to go to a redactor," Felice said, her voice thrilling with loathing. "I told them I'd rather die. I don't know how you meta people can stand rummaging around in others' brains. Or always having some other meta able to read your own secret thoughts.

It would be horrible never to be alone. Never to be able to hide. I'd go mad."

Elizabeth said gently, "It wasn't like that at all. As far as metas reading each other . . . there are many different levels to the mind. Modes, we call them. You can farspeak to many people on the declamatory mode, or speak at short range to a group on the conversational mode. Then there's the intimate mode, that only one person can receive from you. And beneath that are many other conscious and unconscious layers that can be screened off by means of mental techniques that all metapsychics learn when they're very young. We have our private thoughts, just as you do. Most of our telepathic communication is nothing more than a kind of voiceless speech and image projection. You can compare it to electronic audiovisuals— without the electromagnetic radiation."

Felice said, "Deep redactors can get into a person's innermost thoughts."

"True. But with them, there is almost always a doctor-patient relationship appertaining. The patient gives conscious permission for the scrutiny. Even then, a dysfunction may be so strongly programmed that the therapist is powerless to get behind it—no matter how much the patient may be willing to cooperate."

"Yeah," said Stein. He tilted his great mug of beer, holding it before his face.

Felice persisted. "I *know* that metas can read secret thoughts. Sometimes the coach of our team would bring in redactors to work on guys in slumps. Metas could always spot the ones who'd lost their nerve. You can't tell me those poor bastards would deliberately let the shrinks find out something that'd get them fired!"

Elizabeth said, "An untrained person, a nonmeta, gives away information in subverbal ways without being aware of it. Think of it as mental mumbling. Haven't you ever stood next to a person who was talking to himself, muttering under his breath? When a person is frightened or angry or trying very hard to work out a problem or even sexually aroused, the thoughts become . . . loud. Even nonmetas can sometimes pick up the vibes—the mind-pictures or subvocal speech or emotional surges. The better the redactor, the better he is at making sense out of the crazy mishmash that human brains broadcast."

Bryan asked, "Is there any way an ordinary person can shut out a mind reader?"

"Of course. It's possible to stymie superficial snooping rather easily. Just keep a firm grip on your mental broadcasting. If you think someone is really digging, think of some neutral image like a big black square. Or do some simple exercise when you're not speaking out loud. Count one-two-three-four, over and over. Or sing some dumb song. That'll block out all but the best redactor."

"I'm glad you can't read *my* mind now, lovie," Aiken Drum put in. "You'd fall into a quagmire of sheer funk. I'm so scared about going through this time-gate that my red corpuscles have gone puce! I tried to back out. I even told the counselors I'd reform if they'd let me stay here! But nobody'd believe me."

"I can't think why," Bryan said.

A reddish bolt of lightning reached from cloud to cloud above the hills; but the sound, when it came, was muffled and unsatisfying, a beat from a dead tympanum.

Aiken asked Elizabeth, "How did the ballooning work out, sweets?"

"I crammed the theory of building one from native materials—tanning fishskins for the envelope and weaving a basket and plaiting cordage from bark fibers. But I did my practicing in one of these." She took a package the size of two large bricks from her shoulder bag. "It blows up five storeys tall, double-walled and semidirigible. Bright red, like my suit. I have a power source to inject hot air. Of course, the power won't last for more than a few flight-weeks, so eventually I'll have to shift to charcoal. Making that's a mess. But it's the only ancient fuel that's suitable—unless I can find some coal."

"No sweat, doll-eyes," Aiken said. "Stick with me and my mineral maps."

Stein laughed contemptuously. "And how you gonna mine the stuff? Draft Snow White and the Seven Dwarfs? The nearest coal's gotta be a hundred kloms north, around Le Creusot or Montceau, and way to hell and gone underground. Even if you reach the stuff without blasting, how you gonna tote it around to where it'll do you some good?"

"So I'll need a week or two to work out the fewkin' details!" Aiken shot back.

"There would be other coal deposits much nearer," Claude Majewski said. "Those modern maps of yours are deceptive, Aiken. They show the strata and deposits as they exist today, in the twenty-second century—not as they were six million years ago. There used to be little limnic coal basins all over the Massif Central and a really large deposit at Saint-Étienne, but they were all worked out late in the twentieth century. Go back to the Pliocene and you'll probably find easy pickings just a few kloms south of here. Find some near a volcano, and you might luck out with natural coke!"

"Better hold off establishing Pliocene Mining, Unlimited, until you eyeball the territory," Richard advised Aiken with a sour grimace. "The local honchos might have their own ideas about us helping ourselves to the natural resources."

"Entirely possible," Bryan agreed.

"We could convince them to let us have a piece of the action," said Felice. She smiled. "In one way or another."

The nun said, "We could also try to avoid conflict by going to an unsettled area."

"I don't think that's Felice's style," Aiken said. "She's looking forward to a little fun and games—aren't you, babe?"

Landry's pale frizzy hair was standing out from her head in a charged cloud. She was wearing the simple cheongsam again. "Whatever I'm looking forward to, I'll find. Right now all I want is another drink. Anybody coming with me?" She strolled back into the auberge, followed by Stein and Richard.

"Somebody should tell those two they're wasting their time," the old man muttered.

"Poor Felice," Amerie said. "What an ironic name for her, when she's so dreadfully unhappy. That aggressive pose is just another form of armor, like the hockey uniform."

"And underneath she's just crying for love?" Elizabeth inquired, her eyes nearly shut and a faint smile on her lips. "Be careful, Sister. That one's standing in the need of prayer, all right. But she's more of a black hole than a black sheep."

"Those eyes eat you alive," Aiken said. "Something damned inhuman is moving around in there."

"Not even normally homophilic," Majewski said. "But I'll certainly grant you the damned."

"That's a cruel and cynical thing to say, Claude!" exclaimed the nun. "You don't know anything of the girl's background, any of the things that have maimed her spirit. You talk as though she were some monster—when all she is, is a pathetic proud child who has never learned how to love." She took a deep breath. "I'm a medic as well as a nun. One of my vows is to help the suffering. I don't know if I can help Felice, but I'm certainly going to try."

A gust of wind lifted Amerie's veil and she clutched it impatiently with one strong hand. "Don't stay up too late, guys. Tomorrow's creeping up on us." She hurried off the terrace and disappeared into the darkened garden.

"Could be it's the nunnie who'll need the prayers," Aiken said, giggling.

"You shut up!" barked Claude. Then he said, "Sorry, son. But you want to watch that smartass mouth of yours. We're going to have enough trouble without your adding to it." He looked at the sky as a prolonged and powerful bolt of lightning descended over the eastern hills. Ground-strokes rose up to meet it and there was a grumble of thunder. "Here comes the storm. I'm going to bed, too. What I want to know is, who the hell ordered the omens for this outfit?"

The old man stomped away, leaving Elizabeth, Aiken, and Bryan staring after him. Three successive thunderbolts gave him a ridiculously theatrical exit; but none of the people still on the terrace was smiling any more.

"I never told you, Aiken," Elizabeth ventured at last, "how much I like your costume. You were right. It's the most spectacular one in the whole auberge."

The little man began snapping his fingers and clacking his heels like a flamenco dancer, turning and posing. Lightning shone on his loose-fitting garment. What seemed to be cloth of gold was actually a costly fabric woven from the byssus threads of Franconian mollusks, famed throughout the galaxy for beauty and toughness. All up and down the arms and legs of the suit were small flapped and fastened pockets; pockets covered the breast area and the shoulders and hips and there was a very large pocket on the back with an opening on the bottom. Aiken's golden boots had pockets. His belt had pockets. Even his golden hat, with the brim tipped up jauntily on the right side, had a band full of tiny pockets. And every pocket, large or small, bulged with some tool or instrument or compressed decamole appliance. Aiken Drum was a walking hardware shop incarnate as a golden idol.

"King Arthur would dub you Sir Boss at first sight," Elizabeth said, explaining to Bryan: "He plans to set himself up as a Pliocene Connecticut Yankee."

"You wouldn't have to bother with Twain's solar eclipse to gain attention," the anthropologist conceded. "The suit alone is enough to overawe the peasantry. But isn't it rather conspicuous if you want to spy out the land?"

"This big pocket on my back has a chameleon poncho."

Bryan laughed. "Merlin won't have a prayer."

Aiken watched the Lyon city lights dim and disappear as the approaching storm curtained the valley with rain. "The Connecticut Yankee had to contend against Merlin in the story, didn't he? Modern technology versus sorcery. Science against the superstition of the Dark Ages. I can't remember too much about the book. Read it when I was about thirteen there on Dalriada and I know I was disappointed with Twain for wasting so much space on half-baked philosophy instead of action. How did it end? You know—I've forgotten! Think I'll go hit the computer for a plaque of the thing for bedtime reading." He gave Bryan and Elizabeth a wink. "But I may decide to aim higher than Sir Boss!"

He slipped off into the auberge.

"And then there were two," Bryan said.

Elizabeth was finishing her Rémy Martin. She reminded him in many ways of Varya—calm, incisively intelligent, but with the shutters always closed. She projected cool comradeship and not the slightest jot of sex.

"You won't be staying with Group Green for long, will you, Bry?" she remarked. "The rest of us have built a dependence in these five days. But not you."

"You don't miss much. Are you sure your metafunctions are really gone?"

"Not gone," she said. "But they might as well be. I've dropped into what we call the latent state because of brain damage. My functions are still there, but inaccessible, walled up in the right half of my brain. Some persons are born latent—with the walls. Others are born operant, as we say, and their mind-powers are available to them, especially if they receive proper training from infancy. It's closely analogous to the acquisition of language by babies. My work back on Denali involved a good deal of that kind of training. Very rarely, we were even able to coax latents into operancy. But my own case is different. I have just a few teaspoonsful of my original cerebrum left. The rest is regenerated. The leavening was enough for a resoul job, and a specialist restored my memories. But for some unknown reason, metapsychic operancy seldom survives a really spectacular brain trauma."

"What happened, if you don't mind my asking?"

"My husband and I were caught in a tornado while we were egging on Denali. It's a sweet little world, with some of the galaxy's worst weather. Lawrence was killed outright. I was broken to bits but ultimately restored. Except for the MP functions."

"And is losing them so unbearable—" he began, then cursed and apologized.

But she was calm, as always. "It's nearly impossible for a nonmeta to understand the loss. Think of going deaf, dumb, blind. Think of being paralyzed and numb all over. Think of losing your sex organs, of becoming hideously disfigured. Put all of the anguish together and it's still not enough, once you've known the other thing and then lost it . . . But you've lost something, too, haven't you, Bry? Maybe you can understand something of the way I feel."

"Lost some*thing*. Perhaps it does make more sense to say it that way. God knows there's no logic to the way I feel about Mercy."

"Where will you look for her? If the others in the Pliocene don't know where she's gone?"

"All I have is an instinct. I'll try Armorica first because of her Breton ancestry. And then Albion—the Britain that will be. I'll need the boat because there's a question whether the Channel was dry land at the precise period we'll be living in. Sea level seems to have fluctuated in an odd way at the beginning of the Pliocene. But I'll find Mercy somehow, no matter where she's gone."

And what will I find in my beautiful balloon, Elizabeth wondered. And what will it matter? Will the Exile world be any less empty than this one?

Perhaps if she and Lawrence had wanted children . . . but that would have compromised the work, and so they had agreed to forego them, finding love fulfillment in each other, mating for life as almost all metapsychics did, knowing that when one had inevitably gone there would still be the Unity, the billionfold mind-embrace of the Galactic Milieu.

Or there would have been . . .

The first large drops of rain made a rataplan on the leaves of the plane trees. Blue-white flashes lit the whole valley and the thunder seemed to shake the mountain roots. Bryan grabbed Elizabeth's hand and pulled her through the porte-fenêtre into the main salon a few seconds before the real downpour began.

19

THE PREDAWN was chilly, with gray clouds scudding southward as though late for an appointment at the Mediterranean. The Rhône Valley brimmed with mist. A small log fire had been lit in the main salon and it was there that the members of Group Green gathered after breakfasting in their rooms. Each person carried the materials for a new life and dressed for the rôle chosen. (Their extra baggage had preceded them to the time-gate staging area: Claude's case of Wybrowa, Bryan's Scotch, Richard's supplies of spices and yeasts and sodium bisulfite, Stein's keg, Elizabeth's liqueur chocolates, and Amerie's large painting of Saint Sebastian.) Richard and Stein whispered together as they stared at the weak flames. Amerie, a half-smile on her lips, fingered the beads of a large wooden rosary that hung from her belt. The others stood apart, waiting.

At precisely five hundred hours, Counselor Mishima came down the broad staircase from the mezzanine and bid them a solemn good-morning.

"Please accompany me."

They picked up their things and followed in single file out of the salon, across the terrace, and into the sodden garden, where the flagstones were still puddled with rain and the blossoms on the rose-standards hung torn and battered from the storm.

The balconies of the main guesthouse overlooked the garden. Up above, dim faces behind glass doors were watching them—just as they themselves had watched other dawn processions of eight time-travelers led by a single counselor. They had seen Gypsies and Cossacks and desert nomads and voortrekkers, Polynesians with feathered capes and warriors with crossbows, swords, and assegais; there had been Bavarian hikers in lederhosen, bearded white-robed prophets, shaven-headed Oriental votaries, sunbonneted American pioneers, cowboys, fetishists costumed in pathetic grotesquery, and sensible-looking people wearing levis or tropical gear. The travelers in the early morning parades had moved through the garden to an old cottage shaded by mulberry trees, its white stucco and half-timbering shrouded in climbing vines. Madame Guderian's lace curtains still hung at the windows and her pink and white geraniums bloomed in earthenware pots beside the large front door. The eight guests and the counselor would enter the cottage and the door would close behind them. After half an hour had elapsed, the counselor alone would emerge.

Bryan Grenfell stood behind Counselor Mishima as he unlocked the Guderian cottage with an old-fashioned brass key. A large ginger cat sat in the dry shelter of the shrubbery, watching the group with a sardonic golden eye. Grenfell nodded to it as he passed inside. You've seen a lot of us go this way, haven't you, Monsieur le Chat? And how many of them by now felt as used and foolish and tired as I do—but still too stubborn to turn back? Here I go, in my pragmatic tropical kit with a haversack full of simple necessities and high-protein food, armed with a steel-tipped walking stick and a small throwing knife hidden beneath the sleeve of my left forearm, and Mercy's dear picture and dossier in my breast pocket. Here I go into the deep cellar . . .

Stein Oleson had to duck his head passing through the door and walk with caution through the hall lest he brush against Madame's tall clock with its wagging brass pendulum, or knock some fragile bibelot from its place on the wall, or catch the curling horns of his Viking helmet on the little crystal chandelier. Stein was finding it more and more difficult to keep silent. Something was expanding inside of him that demanded to cry out, to roar, to vent a great gust of laughter that would make all the rest of the group shrink away from him as from the door of a suddenly opened furnace. He felt his manhood coming alive beneath the wolfskin kilt, his feet itching to leap and trample, his arm muscles tensing to swing the battle-axe or brandish the vitredur-tipped spear he had added to his armory. Soon! Soon! The tangle in his guts would come free, the fire in his blood would power him to heroism, and the joy would be so huge that he would damn near die with the swallowing of it . . .

Richard Voorhees followed Stein carefully down into the cellar. His heavy, folded-over seaboots were awkward on the worn steps. He had a suspicion that he would have to switch to the more comfortable athletic shoes in his backpack once they had passed through the gate and done a first reconnaissance on the other side. Practicalities first, then rôle playing! The secret of success, he told himself, would lie in a swift assessment of the local power structure, covert appeal to the have-nots, and establishment of a suitable base. Once he got the distillery operating (with Stein, and maybe Landry, to keep the locals from muscling in), he'd be on a sound economic footing and ready to jockey for political influence. He smiled in anticipation and carefully adjusted the hipband of the backpack so that it would not wrinkle the skirts of his doublet. Didn't some of those old sea rovers set themselves up as virtual kings in early America? Jean Lafitte, Bloody Morgan, even old Blackbeard himself? And how do you like Richard Voorhees for King of Barataria? He chuckled out loud at the thought, completely forgetting that his costume had not really belonged to an operatic buccaneer, but to a different kind of seafarer altogether . . .

Felice Landry watched Counselor Mishima manipulate the elaborate lock mechanism of the cellar door. It swung ponderously open and they entered the old wine-keep, dank and musty and with a faint overscent of ozone. She stared at the gazebo, that unlikely gate to freedom, and clutched her new arbalest to her black-armored bosom. She was trembling, nauseated, exerting all her willpower to keep from disgracing herself in this ultimate moment. For the first time since early childhood, her eyes, within the T-shaped Grecian helmet opening, were sticky-lashed with tears . . .

"We will translate you in groups of four, as I have already explained," said Counselor Mishima. "Your extra baggage will follow after an interval of five minutes, so be prepared to retrieve it from the tau-field area. And now, if the first people will position themselves—"

Elizabeth Orme watched without emotion as Bryan, Stein, Richard, and Felice crowded closely into the latticed booth and stood motionless. All of them, she thought, have made their plans except me. They have their goals—touching or comical or mad. But I'll be content to drift through the Exile world in my scarlet balloon, looking down on all the people and the animals, listening to wind and the cry of birds, smelling pollen, resin from the forest, smoke from wildfire on the grassland. I'll come to earth only when I feel that the Earth is real again and I am. If we ever can be . . .

Mirrored walls sprang up as Mishima threw the switch. The four people in the gazebo were on their way. Aiken Drum, his golden suit glittering with a hundred reflections from the cellar lights, stepped forward impulsively.

"Damn! So that's all there is to it? Not even enough power drain to dim the lamps!" He studied the vinelike cables that seemed to grow out of the packed soil of the floor and disappear somewhere short of the vaulted ceiling. Mishima warned him to touch nothing, and Aiken gave him a reassuring gesture. But he had to get a close look. The glassy framework was shot through with faintly moving patterns hovering at the edge of visibility. The black bodies of the lattice-nodes each enclosed a tiny point of unwinking light that seemed to be shining at a great distance.

"How long does it take for people to get from here to there?" Aiken asked. "Or should I say from now till then?"

"The translation is in theory instantaneous," replied Mishima. "We maintain the field for some minutes in order to enable a safe exit. And I may say that never once, in the four years that the Human Polity has carried on the work of Madame Guderian, has there been an accident to time-travelers."

Aiken said, "Counselor, I'd like to take one more thing with me into Exile. Can you give me a description and diagram of this device?"

Without a word, Mishima opened the oaken cabinet and took out a small plaque-book. It was obvious that other travelers had made the same request. Aiken kissed the plaque triumphantly and stowed it in a large pocket below the right knee of his shining suit.

Mishima stepped to the control console and switched off the field. The mirror-walls winked out. The gazebo was empty.

"They have passed safely through the portal. Now the rest of you may enter."

Claude Majewski hefted his twenty-kilo pack and was the first inside. Old Man, you're crazy, he said to himself—then smiled because he could hear Gen saying it. On a sudden impulse, he opened the pack compartment that held the carved and inlaid box from the Polish mountains and took it out. Is there really a Pliocene world beyond the gate, Black Girl? Or is it a hoax after all, and do we step out of the glass cage into death? Oh, Gen, go with me. Wherever . . .

Sister Annamaria Roccaro was the last to get into position, smiling in apology as she crowded next to Aiken Drum and felt the hard tools in his pockets pressing through the sleeves and skirts of her habit. Aiken was nearly a head shorter than the sturdy nun, almost as small as Felice but in no way as vulnerable. He'd survive, would Aiken Drum. May the rest of us as well! And now, Mother of God, hear my archaic prayer: Salve Regina, mater misericordiae; vita, dulcedo, et spes nostra, salve. Ad te clamamus, exsules, filii Hevae. Ad te suspiramus, gementes et flentes in hac lacrimarum valle. Eia ergo, advocata nostra, illos tuos misericordes oculos ad nos converte. Et Jesum, benedictum fructum ventris tui, nobis post hoc exilium ostende—

Mishima threw the switch.

There was pain of translation and a momentous snap hurtling them into the gray limbo. They hung without breath or heartbeat, each one screaming alone into silence. And then they felt sudden warmth and opened their eyes to a blinding dazzle of green and blue. Hands were pulling them, voices urging them to step forward out of the shimmering area that had been the gazebo, to step down a little, to come out quickly before the field reversed itself, to enter into Exile.

* * *

THE END OF PART ONE

PART II

The Initiation

1

"COME ALONG, SPORT, come along now. Step down a little. We're the guardians of the time-portal. We're here to help you. Come on. You're feeling zonked-out right now, but that'll pass away right quick. Just relax and come along. You made it safe to Exile. You're safe—you hear me, cob? Come on now. We're all going along to Castle Gateway. You can relax there. We'll have a nice yabber and answer all your questions. Come on."

As the pain receded and his wits phased in again, Bryan was at first aware only of the nagging voice and brilliant light. Such an ordinary twangy voice! Such an extraordinary light! He was conscious of somebody holding him by the right wrist and upper arm, a blurred figure he couldn't quite focus on. Another someone seemed to be vacuuming dust off his clothes with a hand-held machine. Then he was being forced to walk and he looked at his feet and saw them quite clearly, shod in a pair of pigskin boots with crinkled soles, moving first over damp granite, then on thick sod with grass that had been mowed or cropped short. He was stepping on small daisylike flowers. A butterfly with zebra stripes and long swallowtails hung motionless on a dew-spangled weed.

"Wait," he mumbled. "Stop." The insistent tugging left off and he was able to stand still and look about him. The newly risen sun shone over a wide expanse of green tableland going golden in its higher, drier reaches. Tanzania? Nebraska? Dorubezh?

France.

Nearer, there were rounded boulders of crystalline rock. They had been used to mark the sides of a path that led back to a peculiar, indistinct block hanging in the air like a heat mirage. Men dressed alike in white tunics and pants with blue cords about the waist were gathered around Richard and Stein and Felice. Several more guardians stood waiting for the other members of Group Green to arrive. The wavering force field winked out. Bryan insisted upon standing still until it reappeared with four more human figures, which the guardians hastened to lead into open ground.

"All safe, sport. You can come along with me now. The rest'll all be tagging along."

Bryan discovered that the ordinary voice belonged to a skinny, deeply tanned man with grayish-blond hair and a long nose bent to one side. He had a prominent larynx and wore a twisted necklet of dark metal, about as thick and as round as a finger, incised with intricate little markings, and fastened in the front with a knoblike catch. His tunic, apparently of finely spun wool, had a streak of dried food down the front. For some reason, this reassured Bryan. He did not resist when the man began pulling him along the path again.

They were ascending a small hill a couple of hundred meters from the time-portal area. As the anthropologist's mind cleared, he was excited to see a stone fortress of considerable size perched on the eminence, facing east. It did not resemble the fairytale châteaux of France, but rather the simpler castles of his English homeland. Except for the absence of a moat, it was something like Bodiam in Sussex. When they came closer, Bryan saw that there was an outer ringwall of rough masonry about twice the height of a man. Inside this, beyond an encircling space that formed an outer ward, was a four-sided bailey, a hollow square without a central keep, with towers at the corners and a great barbican at the entrance. Above the gate was the effigy of a bearded human face, crafted in yellow metal. When they came close to the outer wall, Bryan heard an eerie howling.

"Right through here, cob," said the guide reassuringly. "Don't pay no mind to the amphicyons."

They went into a passage that led through the outer ward to the portcullis of the barbican. On either side were stout wooden grilles. A dozen huge creatures galloped clumsily up to the bars and began slavering and snarling.

"Interesting watchdogs," Bryan said unsteadily.

The guide kept hustling him along. "Too right! Primitive canids.

Bear-dogs we call 'em. They weigh about three hundred kilos and eat anything that bloody well doesn't eat them first. When we have to secure the fortress, we just lift these grilles and give the beasts access to the whole outer ward."

Inside the large barbican structure was a corridor that branched right and left, leading to peripheral rooms behind the massive curtain-wall. The guide led Bryan up an open stairway to the second level. Here the corridors were whitewashed and there were handsome brass sconces with containers of oil ready to be lighted at nightfall. Deeply bayed windows giving onto the inner court let daylight into the hall.

"We got a small reception room for each of you," the guardian said. "Sit down and rest and have some tucker if you like." He threw open a heavy wooden door and led the way into a chamber that measured about four by four. It was carpeted with a thick wool rug in shades of brown and gray and furnished with surprisingly well crafted chairs and benches of turned wood. Some had corded seats and backs, while others were padded with black woolen cushions. On a low table were ceramic pitchers containing hot and cold liquids, drinking tumblers, a bowl of purple plums and small cherries, and a plateful of seedcakes.

The guide helped Bryan unfasten his backpack. "There's facilities through that curtained door. Some new arrivals feel the need. A chap from the interview committee will come to you in about ten minutes. Meanwhile, just live it cool."

He went out and closed the door.

Bryan walked to an embrasured window in the exterior wall and gazed at the landscape through an ornamental brass grating. He could see amphicyons prowling in the narrow space below. Beyond the outer wall was the pathway and the rock outcropping with its four cornerstones that marked the position of the time-portal. Shading his eyes against the rising sun, he saw the savanna undulating gently toward the Rhône Valley. A small herd of four-footed animals grazed in the far distance. A bird sang an intricate song. Somewhere in the castle, the sound of human laughter echoed briefly.

Bryan Grenfell sighed. So this was the Pliocene!

He began examining his surroundings, his mind automatically filing away the homely details that could tell an anthropologist so much about the culture of a new world. Walls of mortared stone, whitewashed (casein?), with stained oak framing around the doorways and shutters for the glassless window. The convenience had a smaller louvered slit in the wall for ventilation. Its toilet was a simple hole in the masonry reminiscent of the medieval garderobes to be found in English castles. It sported a wooden seat and a nicely carved lid, and had a box of green leaves mounted on the wall beside it. For washup there was a ceramic basin and laver (thrown stoneware, slip-decorated, salt-glazed). The soap was fine-grained, properly aged, and scented with some herb. The hand towel resembled coarse linen.

He strolled back to the reception room. The food laid out on the table added its data to the mass. Bryan ate a cherry, putting the large pit neatly into an empty dish and noting that the flesh was meager but sweet. Probably the original European bird cherry or some close relative. The tiny plums also seemed to be wild. If any time-travelers had brought budwood from improved stonefruits, the resulting trees might have been too susceptible to Pliocene insects and diseases to survive without chemical protection. He wondered about wine grapes and strawberries but seemed to recall that both were rather resistant, and so there was a fair chance that Richard would have his wine and Mercy her strawberries and cream . . .

The cold drink tasted of citrus, and the steaming pitcher turned out to contain hot coffee. Agnostic though he was, Bryan sent up a prayer of thanks for the latter. The seedcakes had a firm texture and a faint aroma of honey. They had been baked properly and decorated with hazelnuts on top. The cookie plate was incised with a simple motif and had a handsome sang de boeuf glaze.

There was a light tapping on the door. The brass latch lifted to admit a mild-looking older man with a neatly trimmed mustache and imperial. He smiled tentatively and sidled in when Bryan gave him a friendly murmur. He wore a blue tunic with a white cord about the waist and had the same necklet of dark metal as the guardians had worn. He seemed ill at ease and perched on the very edge of a bench.

"My name is Tully. I'm a member of the interview committee. If you wouldn't mind—I mean, we can probably help you find your way about and all if you'd tell us just a little about yourself and your plans. Not to pry, you understand! But if we could know just a little of your background and about the trade you've learned, it would help ever so much. I mean, we could tell you which places have need of your—uh—talents if you're interested in settling down. And if you don't want to settle down, perhaps you have questions you'd like to ask *me*. I'm here to help you, do you see?"

He's afraid of me, Bryan realized in amazement. And then he thought of the kind of persons who might come through the gate—persons such as Stein and Felice, for example—who might react to the initial disorientation and culture-shock with violence, and decided that Tully had every reason to be cautious in his initial encounter with new arrivals. He probably rated combat pay. To soothe the man, Bryan leaned back easily in one of the chairs and munched on a seedcake.

"These are very good. Made with oats, are they? And sesame? It's reassuring to be greeted with civilized food. An excellent psychological maneuver on your part."

Tully gave a delighted little laugh. "Oh, do you think so? We've tried hard to make Castle Gateway a welcoming environment, but some of the arrivals are deeply stressed and we sometimes have difficulty calming them."

"I felt a bit wonky at first, but I'm fine now. Don't look so anxious, man! I'm harmless. And I'll answer any reasonable questions."

"Splendid!" The interviewer smiled his relief. He took out a small sheet of writing material (paper? vellum?) from a belt pouch, together with an ordinary twenty-second-century pen. "Your name and former occupation?"

"Bryan Grenfell. I was a cultural anthropologist specializing in the analysis of certain kinds of social conflict. I'm most interested in studying your society here, even though I'm not too sanguine about the possibility of publishing my work."

Tully chuckled in appreciation. "Fascinating, Bryan! You know, there have been *very* few members of your profession to come through the gate. You'll certainly want to go on to the capital and talk to the people there. They'd be most interested in you. You could provide unique insights!"

Bryan looked surprised. "I'm equipped to earn my living as a fisherman or coastal trader. I never thought my academic credentials would be appreciated in the Pliocene."

"But we aren't savages!" Tully protested. "Your scientific talents will very likely prove invaluable to—um—administrative persons, who'll welcome your advice."

"So you do have a structured society."

"Very simple, very simple," the man said hurriedly. "But I'm sure you'll find it worthy of careful study."

"I've already begun on that, you know." Bryan watched Tully's meticulously barbered face. "This building, for instance, has been well designed for security. I'm most interested in knowing what you secure against."

"Oh—there are several kinds of animals that are quite dangerous. The giant hyenas, the machairodus sabercats—"

"But this castle seems more suited to defense against human aggression."

The interviewer fingered his neck-ring. His eyes darted here and there and finally fixed Bryan with a sincere expression. "Well, of course there *are* unstable personalities coming through the portal, and even though we try very hard to assimilate everyone, we have an inevitable problem with the really serious misfits. But you need have no fear, Bryan, because you and the rest of your party are quite safe here with us. Actually, the—um—disturbed element tends to hide away in the mountains and in other remote places. Please don't worry. You'll find that the high-culture persons have complete ascendancy here in Exile. Everyday life is as tranquil as it can be in a —um—*aboriginal* environment."

"How nice for you."

Tully nibbled on the end of his pen. "For our records—that is, it would be helpful if we knew just exactly what kind of equipment you've brought with you."

"To be put into the common store?"

Tully was shocked. "Oh, nothing like that, I assure you. All travelers *must* retain the tools of their trade in order to survive and be useful members of society, mustn't they? If you'd rather not discuss the matter, I won't press. But sometimes people come through with extraordinary books or plants or other things that could be of great benefit to everyone, and if these persons would consent to share, the quality of life for all would be enhanced." He smiled winningly and poised the pen.

"Aside from a trimaran sailing craft and the fishing gear, I have nothing special. A voicewriter with a plaque-converter for the sheets. A rather large library of books and music. A case of Scotch that seems to have gone astray . . ."

"And your traveling companions?"

Bryan said easily, "I think you'd better let them speak for themselves."

"Oh, certainly. I only thought I'd . . . well, yes." Tully put away his writing materials and flashed another bright smile. "Now, then! You must have some questions you would like to ask *me!*"

"Just a few for now. What is your total population?"

"Well, we hardly keep accurate census figures, you understand, but I think a reasonable estimate would be about fifty thousand human souls."

"Strange, I would have guessed more. Do you suffer from disease?"

"Oh, hardly at all. Our ordinary macroimmunization and genetically engineered resistances seem to protect us very well here in the Pliocene, although the very earliest travelers didn't enjoy the full-spectrum coverage of those who have come to Exile within the last thirty years or so. And of course those who were lately rejuvenated can expect a much longer life span than those who were treated with the earlier technology. But most of our—um—attrition has come from accidents." He nodded soberly. "We have physicians, of course. And certain medications are regularly sent through the time-portal. But we cannot regenerate persons suffering really serious trauma. And this world may be said to be civilized, but it is hardly *tame*, if you take my meaning."

"I understand. Just one other question for now." Grenfell reached into his breast pocket and took out the color picture of Mercedes Lamballe. "Can you tell me where I might find this woman? She arrived here in mid-June of this year."

The interviewer took the picture and studied it with widening eyes. He finally said, "I think—you will find she has gone to our capital city in the south. I remember her very well. She made a most vivid impression on all of us. In view of her unusual talents, she was invited to—um—go down and assist with administration."

Bryan frowned. "What unusual talents?"

In some haste, Tully said, "Our society is quite different from that of the Galactic Milieu, Bryan. Our needs are special. All of this will be made clear to you later, when you get a more complete overview from people in the capital. From a professional standpoint, you have some intriguing investigations awaiting you."

Tully rose. "Have a little more refreshment now. Another person would like to interview you in a short while, and then you can rejoin your companions. I'll come for you in about half an hour, shall I?"

Smiling again, he slipped out the door. Bryan waited for a few moments, then got up and tried the latch. It wouldn't budge. He was locked in.

He looked around the room for his iron-shod walking stick. It was nowhere to be found. He rolled up his sleeve to check on the little throwing knife in its scabbard. He was not surprised to find that the leather sheath was empty. Had his introductory "vacuum cleaning" been a frisk with a metal detector?

Well, well, he said to himself. So *this* is the Pliocene!

He sat down again to wait.

2

RICHARD VOORHEES had recognized the psychic disorientation of the time-portal as a variant of that experienced by humans every time that starships passed from the normal universe into the quasi-dimensional gray subspace during superluminal travel. However, the "snap" of temporal translation was prolonged many times longer than that of hyperspace crossover. Richard had also noted peculiar differences in the texture of the gray limbo. There was a dimly perceived rotation about consecutive axes; a compression (was everything, every atom in the universe, subtly smaller 6 million years in the past?); a quality to the gray that was less fluid and more frangible (did one swim through space and smash through time?); a sense of diminishing life-force all about him that would fit in nicely with certain philosophers' notions of the essence of the Milieu.

When Richard dropped through the air a short distance and landed on the granite outcropping of Exile, he was in control of himself almost immediately, as every starship's master had to be after spatial translation. Pushing aside the eager hands of a guardian, he exited from the tau-field under his own power and did a fast eyeball scan while the guide murmured inanities.

Just as Counselor Mishima had promised, the Pliocene Rhône Valley was much more narrow, and the country on this western flank, where the auberge would one day stand on a wooded hillside, was now flatter and less dissected by streams. It was, in fact, a plateau, rising slightly to the south. He spotted the castle. On the skyline behind it, smoking in the early sunlight, were two titanic snowclad volcanoes. The northerly one would be Mont-Dore; the larger cone to the south, the Cantal.

There was grass. There were rabbity critters crouching motionless, pretending to be rocks. Off in a hollow was a grove of trees. Did the little apelike ramapithecines roam those woods?

Guardians were leading Bryan, Stein, and Felice up the path toward the castle. Other men in white helped the second group from the time-gate area. Who was in charge of the place? Some Pliocene baron? Was there an aristocracy here? Would he, Richard, be able to elbow his way into it? His mind tossed up question after question, fizzing with a youthful enthusiasm that astounded and delighted him. He recognized what was happening. It was a belated reprise of the spacer's favorite malady—the New Planetfall Eagers. Anyone who ranged widely throughout the galaxy and endured the boredom of subspace gray was likely (if not too jaded) to work himself into a lather of anticipation over the imminent landing upon a hitherto unvisited world. Would the air smell good? Would the ions vitalize or poop? Would the vegetation and animals delight or disgust the eye? Would the local food ditto the tastebuds? Would the people be successful and sprightly or beaten down by hardship? Would the ladies screw if you asked them to?

He whistled a few notes of the bawdy old ballad through his teeth. Only then did he become aware of the anxious voice and the plucking at his sleeve.

"Come along, sir. Your friends have gone on to Castle Gateway. We've gotta get along, too. You'll want to rest and refresh yourself and like as not ask some questions."

The guardian was a dark-haired man, well built but rather rawboned, with the spurious youthfulness and overwise eyes of a fairly recent rejuvenate. Richard took in the dark metal necklet and the white tunic that was probably a lot more comfortable in this tropical climate than Richard's own black velvet and heavy broadcloth.

"Just let me look around a little, guy," Richard said, but the man kept tugging at him. To avoid argument, Richard began to move along the path leading to the castle.

"That's a nice commanding position you've got there, guy. Is that mound artificial? What do you do for a water supply up here? How far to the nearest town?"

"Easy on, traveler! Just you come along with me. The interview committeeman will be able to answer your questions better than I can."

"Well, at least tell me the prospects for local gash. I mean—back in the present—or the future or whatever the hell you call it here—

we were told that the male-female ratio here was about four to one. I wanta tell you that almost turned me off from coming over! If it wasn't for certain pressing circumstances, I might not have come to Exile at all! So how is it really? You have women up at the castle?"

The man replied austerely, "We're hosting a number of female travelers, and the Lady Epone is temporarily in residence. No women live permanently at Castle Gateway."

"So where do you guys get it? Is there a village or a town for weekend passes or whatever?"

In a matter-of-fact manner the man said, "Many of the castle staff are homophile or autoerotic. The rest are serviced by traveling entertainers from Roniah or Burask. There are no small villages in this area, only widely separated cities and plantations. Those of us who serve at the castle are happy to remain there. We're well rewarded for our work." He fingered his necklet with a small smile, then redoubled his effort to rush the new arrival along.

"Sounds like a real organized setup," said Richard in a dubious tone.

"You've come into a wonderful world. You're going to be very happy here once you've learned a little about our ways . . . Don't mind the bear-dogs. We keep them for security. They can't get at us."

They hurried through the outer ward and into the barbican, where the guardian tried to steer Richard up the stairway. But the ex-spacer pulled away, saying, "Be right back! Gotta take a look at this fascinating place!"

"But you can't—" exclaimed the guardian.

But he did. Clutching his plumed hat, Richard broke into a run that was only slightly slowed by the weight of his backpack. He went clattering over the flagstones into the deep interior of the gatehouse, dodging around corners at random until he emerged into the large inner courtyard of the castle. This early in the morning, the area was deeply shadowed, surrounded on four sides by the two-storey hollow wall with its corner towers and battlements. The court-yard was nearly eighty meters square. At its center was a fountain with trees planted around it in stone boxes. More trees grew at regular intervals around the perimeter. One entire side of the yard was taken up by a large double corral neatly walled in perforated stone. Half of it contained several score large quadruped animals of a type Richard had never seen before. The other half of the corral seemed to be empty.

Hearing the voices of pursuers, Richard dodged into a kind of cloister that ran around the other three sides of the inner ward. He ran for a short distance, then turned into a side corridor. It was a dead end. But on either side were doors leading into apartments within the great hollow wall.

He opened the first righthand door, slipped inside, and closed the door behind him.

The room was black. He stood perfectly still, catching his breath, gratified to hear the sound of running feet grow louder, then fade away. For the moment, he had escaped. He fumbled in one pocket of his backpack for a light. Before he could switch it on, he heard a faint sound. He stood immobile. A line of radiance had sprung into being across the darkened room. Someone was opening another door with infinite slowness and the illumination from the inner chamber swept toward him in a widening beam until he was caught.

Silhouetted in the doorway was a very tall woman. She was dressed in a filmy sleeveless gown that seemed almost invisible. Richard could not see her face but he knew she had to be beautiful.

"Lady Epone," he said, not knowing why.

"You may come in."

He had never heard such a voice. Its musical sweetness held an unmistakable promise that set him on fire. He dropped his pack and came toward her, a figure dressed entirely in black drawn by her bright allure. As she went slowly into the inner chamber, he followed. Dozens of lamps hung from the ceiling, reflecting off draperies of shimmering gold and white gauze that curtained a vast bed.

The woman held out her arms. Her loose gown was of pale blue, unbelted, with long yellow panels floating from the shoulders like misty wings. She wore a golden circlet about her neck and a golden diadem on her blonde hair. The hair hung nearly to her waist and so, if Richard's eyes didn't deceive him, did her incredibly pendulous breasts beneath the gossamer fabric.

She stood nearly half a meter taller than he did. Looking down with unhuman glowing eyes, she said, "Come closer."

He felt the room turn. And the eyes shone more brilliantly and soft skin caressed him until he was drawn into an abyss of joy so intense that it must destroy him. She cried, "Can you? Can you?"

He tried. And he could not.

The sweet breath of light turned into a whirlwind then, screeching and cursing and tearing at him, not at his body but at something cringing apologetically behind his eyes, worthless and deserving to be punished. Torn out, held up to ridicule, flung down and trodden upon, hammered by blasts of hatred, the shapeless thing shrank into a smaller and smaller mass until it was a blot of utter insignificance, finally vanishing in the white blaze of pain.

* * *

Richard woke.

A man in a blue tunic knelt at his feet, fumbling with his ankles. Richard was clamped into a heavy chair, seated in a small room with walls of unadorned gray limestone blocks. The Lady Epone was standing in front of him, her eyes flat and jade-colored, her mouth curved in a smile of contempt.

"He's ready, Lady."

"Thank you, Jean-Paul. The headpiece, if you please."

The man brought a simple silver coronet with five points and placed it on Richard's head. Epone turned to a construction on a table beside the chair, which Richard had mistaken for some kind of elaborate jeweled metallic sculpture. The apparatus glowed faintly in its crystalline parts, the multicolored lights waxing and waning in what was evidently some malfunction. Epone gave the largest prism, a pinkish thing the size of a fist, an impatient flick with thumb and forefinger.

"Ah, bah! Will nothing function in this cursed place? There! Now we will begin."

She folded her arms and inclined her gaze on Richard. "What is your given name?"

"Go to hell," he muttered.

A tremendous throb of agony seemed to lift the top of his skull.

"Please speak only to answer my questions. Obey my orders at once. Do you understand?"

Sagging against the chair clamps, he whispered, "Yes."

"What is your given name?"

"Richard."

"Close your eyes, Richard. Without speaking, I wish you to send out the word *help*."

Sweet Jesus, that was an easy one! Help!

A man's voice said, "Minus six farspeak."

"Open your eyes, Richard," commanded Epone. "Now I want you to listen carefully. Here is a dagger." She drew a silver blade from somewhere within her draperies and held it toward him on both open hands. The palms had only a few faint lines in their milky softness. "Force me to plunge the dagger into my heart, Richard. Revenge yourself on me. Destroy me by my own hand. Kill me, Richard."

He tried! He willed the death of the monstrous bitch. He tried.

"Minus two point five coerce," said the minion standing behind the chair.

Epone said, "Concentrate on what I am saying to you, Richard. Your life and your future here in Exile depend upon what you do in this room." She cast the dagger down onto the table, less than a meter away from his pinioned right arm. "Make the knife rise up, Richard. Send it at me! Drive it into my eyes! Do it, Richard!"

There was a terrible eagerness in her tone this time, and he tried desperately to oblige her. He knew now what was happening. They were testing him for latent metafunctions—this one psychokinesis. But he could have told them—

"Minus seven PK."

She leaned close to him, fragrant, lovely. "Burn me, Richard. Bring up flames from your mind and let them blacken and cook and turn to ash this body that you will never know because you are not a man but a poor worm without sex or sensibility. Burn me!"

But he was the one who burned. Tears coursed down his cheeks and caught in his mustache. He tried to spit at her but his mouth was clotted and his tongue swollen. He twisted his head because his eyes would not close to shut out the blue and primrose coolness of her cruelty.

"Plus two point five create."

"Interesting, but not good enough, of course. Rest for a moment now, Richard. Think of your companions upstairs. One by one they will come to this room as so many others have come, and I will get to know them as I know you. And some will serve the Tanu in this way and others in that, but all *will* serve, save a few blessed ones who will find that the gate into Exile is the door into paradise after all . . . You have one last chance. Come into my mind. Feel me. Probe me, take me to bits and reassemble me in a more compliant image." She bent closer and closer toward him until the flawless skin of her face was only a few handsbreadth from his own. No pores, no creases on that face. Only pinpoint pupils in the nephrite eyes. But beauty! Vile and tantalizing beauty of incredible age.

Richard strained against the clamps of the chair. His mind screamed.

I hate you and violate you and diminish you and cover you with excrement! And I call you *dead!* I call you *rotted!* I call you writhing in pain everlasting, stretched on the rack of the superficies until the exhalation of the universe dies and space falls in upon itself . . .

"Minus one redact."

Richard fell forward. The coronet dropped from his head to strike the stone flags with a bell tone of finality.

"You've failed again, Richard," Epone said in a bored voice. "Inventory his possessions, Jean-Paul. Then put him in with the others for the northern caravan to Finiah."

3

Elizabeth Orme was so dazed by the shock of the translation that she scarcely felt the guiding hands that urged her up the pathway toward the castle. Someone relieved her of her pack and she was glad. The soothing mumble of the guide's voice carried her back to another time of pain and fear long ago. She had felt herself awakening in a cushioning womb of warm solution where she had been regenerating for nine months in a web of tubes and wires and monitoring devices. Her eyes blinded, her skin deprived of tactile sensation by the long immersion in amniotic fluid, she could nevertheless hear a gentle human voice that calmed her fear, told her she was whole again and shortly to be freed.

"Lawrence?" she whimpered. "Are you all right?"

"Come along now, missy. Just come along. You're safe now and you're among friends. We're all going up to Castle Gateway and you'll be able to relax there. Just keep on walking like a good girl."

Strange howls of maddened animals. Open the eyes in horror and shut them again. *Where is this place?*

"Castle Gateway, in the world you call Exile. Take it easy, missy. The amphicyons can't get us. Just up these stairs now and we'll have you lying down for a nice rest. Here we go."

Opening doors and a small room with—what? Hands were pressing her to sit down, to lie down. Someone lifted her feet and arranged a pillow under her head.

Don't go away! Don't leave me here alone!

"I'll be back in just a few minutes with the healer, missy. We won't let anything happen to *you*, bank on that! You're a very special lady. Relax now while I get somebody to help you. Washroom behind that curtain."

When the door closed she lay motionless until a surge of nausea rose in her gorge. Struggling up, she lurched into the washroom and vomited into the basin. An excruciating pain lanced her brain and she nearly collapsed. Leaning against the whitened stone wall, she gasped for breath. The nausea receded and so, more slowly, did the agony in her head. She became aware of someone else entering the room, two persons speaking, arms supporting her, the rim of a thick cup pressed to her lips.

I don't want anything.

"Drink this, Elizabeth. It will help you."

Open. Swallow. There. Good. Now sit again.

A voice, deep and honey-rich. "Thank you, Kosta. I'll take care of her now. You may leave us."

"Yes, Lord." Sound of door closing.

Elizabeth clutched the arms of her chair, waiting for the pain to come back. When it didn't, she let herself relax and slowly opened her eyes. She was sitting at a low table that held a few dishes of food and drink. Across from her, standing beside a high window, was an extraordinary man. He was robed in white and scarlet and wore a heavy belt of linked squares of gold set with red and milk-white gemstones. Around his neck was a golden torc, thick twisted strands with an ornamented catch in front. His fingers, holding a stoneware cup with the medicine, were oddly long, with prominent joints. She wondered vaguely how he had managed to slip on the many rings that gleamed in the morning sunlight. The man had blond shoulder-length hair cut in a fringe above his eyes, which were very pale blue, seemingly without pupils, and sunken deep into bony orbits. His face was beautiful despite the fine webwork of lines at the corners of his smiling mouth.

He was nearly two and a half meters tall.

Oh, God. Who are you? What is this place? I thought I was going back in time to Pliocene Earth. But this is not . . . this can't be . . .

"Oh, but it is." His voice, with a musical lilt, was kind. "My name is Creyn. You are indeed in the time-epoch known as Pliocene and on the planet Earth—which some call Exile and others the

Many-Colored Land. You've been disoriented by your passage through the time-portal—perhaps more seriously than the rest of your companions. But that's understandable. I've given you a mild strengthening draft that will restore you. In a few minutes, if you please, we'll talk. Your friends are being interviewed now by people of our staff who welcome all new arrivals. They're resting in rooms like this one, having a bit of food and drink and asking questions that we're doing our best to answer. The guardians of the gate alerted me to your distress. They were also able to perceive that you are a most unusual traveler, which is why I am interviewing you myself . . ."

Elizabeth had closed her eyes again as the man droned easily on. Peace and relief permeated her mind. *So there really is a Land of Exile! And I've really managed to come into it safely. Now I can forget what I've lost. I can build a new life.*

She opened her eyes wide. The tall man's smile had become ironic.

"Your life will certainly be new," he agreed. "But what is lost?"

You . . . can hear me.

Yes.

She leaped to her feet, drew breath, cried out in a shattering scream. *Vocalization of ecstasy. Life found restored renewed. Gratitude.*

Softly! she told herself. Draw back from the pinnacle. Gently. After that first mad interior leap, go cautiously. Reach out at the simplest possible mode, at wide wide focus, for you are weak with rebirth.

I/we rejoice with you Elizabeth.

Creyn. You permit shallowquestion?

Shrug.

Elizabeth slipped clumsily beneath the surface of his smile, where a neat reticulation of data waited passively for her study. But the deeper layers were shielded by warning hardness. She snatched up the proffered information and got out quickly. Her throat had gone dry and her heart pounded with the shock of the assimilation. *Gently! Gently. Two mental blows within a few minutes on her raw tenderness. Suspend heal allow selfredaction. He cannot read deeply or far. But coerce yes. Redact yes moststrongly. Other abilities? No data.*

She spoke out loud at last in a calm voice. "Creyn, you are not a human being and you are not a true operant metapsychic. These two things contradict my experience, so that I am confused. In the world I come from, only persons with operant metapsychic powers are able to communicate in purely mental speech. And only six races in all our galaxy possess the genes for metability. You belong to none of them. May I probe deeper to learn more about you?"

"I regret that I cannot permit it at this time. Later there will be suitable opportunities for us to . . . get to know one another."

"Are there many of your people here?"

"A sufficient number."

In the split second that he replied she hurled a redactive deep-probe with all her strength right between his pale-blue eyes. It bounced and shattered. She had to cry out with the violence of the rebound, and the man named Creyn laughed.

Elizabeth. That was most impolite. And it won't work.

Shame. "It was an impulse, a social error I apologize for. In our world, no metapsychic would dream of probing without invitation unless placed in a threat situation. I don't know what came over me."

"You've been discomposed by the portal."

Wonderful dreadful pitiless one-way portal! "It's more than that," she said, sinking back into the chair. She did a swift tour of her mental defenses. Up and fairly secure, rawness crusting over, familiar patterns reasserting.

"Back on the other side," she said, "I suffered a serious brain injury. My metafunctions were obliterated in the regeneration process. It was thought that the loss was permanent. Otherwise"—she gave it mental underlining—"I never would have been allowed to cross into Exile. Nor would I have wanted to come."

We are most fortunate. Welcome from allTanu.

"You've had no other operant metas come through?"

"A group of nearly one hundred arrived abruptly some twenty-seven years ago. I'm sorry to say they were unable to adapt to our local conditions." *Cautioncaution. Wallup.*

Elizabeth nodded. "They would have been fugitive rebels. It was a sad time for our Galactic Milieu . . . Are all of them dead, then? Am I the only operant in Exile?"

Perhaps not for long.

She braced herself on the table, rose and walked closer to him. His amiable expression changed. "It is not our custom to enter lightly into another's private space. I request you in courtesy to withdraw."

Polite regret. "I simply wanted to look at your golden collar. Would you take it off so that I can examine it? It seems to be a remarkable piece of craftsmanship."

Horrors! "I'm sorry, Elizabeth. The golden torc bears a weight of religious symbolism among us. We wear it as long as we live."

"I think I understand." She began to smile.

PROBE.

Elizabeth laughed aloud. Now *you* must apologize Creyn!

Chagrin unease. Regrets Elizabeth. You will take some getting used to.

She turned away. "What will become of me?"

"You'll go to our capital city, rich Muriah on the White Silver Plain. It lies in the south of this Many-Colored Land. We'll have a wonderful welcome for you there among the Tanu, Elizabeth."

She spun around and met his eyes. "Those that you rule. Will they welcome me, too?"

Caution. "They will love you as they love us. Try to suspend judgment on us until you have all of the data. I know that there are aspects of your situation that trouble you now. But have patience. You are in no danger."

"What happens to my friends? The people who came through the time-portal with me?"

"Some of them will be coming to the capital. Others have already indicated that they prefer to go elsewhere. We'll find good places for all of them. They'll be happy."

Happy ruled? Unfree?

"We do rule, Elizabeth, but kindly. You'll see. Don't judge until you see what we've done with this world. It was nothing, and we've transformed it—just this little corner—into something marvelous."

It was too much . . . her head began to throb again and vertigo came. She dropped back into the soft cushions of the bench. "Where—where did you come from? I know every sentient race in our Milieu six million years into the future—coadunate and non. There is no people resembling you—except for humans. And I'm certain you're not of our genus. Your mental pattern is different."

Differences similarities parallels starwhirlpools in countless numbers to the uttermost limit.

"I see. No one in my future time has managed intergalactic travel.

We have not yet been able to supersede the pain barrier of the necessary translation. It rises geometrically with the increase in distance."

Mitigant.

"How interesting. If it were only possible to transmit information about that back through the portal."

"We can discuss this later, Elizabeth. In the capital. There are other possibilities even more intriguing that will be made clear to you in Muriah." Distraction. He fingered his gold necklet and at once there was a tapping on the door. A nervous little man in blue stepped into the room and saluted Creyn by placing his fingers to his forehead. The Tanu gave a regal gesture of acknowledgment.

"Elizabeth, this is Tully, one of our trusted interviewers. He's been talking to your companions, discussing their plans for the future and answering their questions."

"Have all of them recovered from the passage?" she asked. "I'd like to see them. Talk to them."

"In good time, Lady," said Tully. "All of your friends are safe and in good hands. You mustn't worry. Some of them will be going south with you, while others have chosen to travel to another city in the north. They feel their talents will be appreciated more up there. You'll be interested to know that caravans will be leaving here this very evening, going in both directions."

"I see." But did she? Her thoughts were muddled again. She threw a tentative query at Creyn, which he parried neatly.

Trust in me Elizabeth. All will be well.

She turned back to the little interviewer. "I want to be sure of saying goodbye to those of my friends who are going north."

"Certainly, Lady. It will be arranged." The little man put a hand to his necklet and Elizabeth looked at it closely. It seemed identical to the one worn by Creyn except for the dark color of the metal.

Creyn. I want to put thisone to the question.

Disdain. He is under ourprotection. Would you distress him in prematureattempts to satisfy curiosity? Questioning would distress him verymuch. Perhaps permanent harm. He has little data. But do asyouwish with him.

"Thank you for telling me about my friends, Tully," she said in a gentle tone.

The man in blue looked relieved. "Then I'll just run along to the next interview, shall I? I imagine Lord Creyn has already answered all of your questions about—um—*general* matters."

"Not quite all." She reached for pitcher and glass and poured some of the cold drink. "But I expect he will, in time."

4

No SOONER had the blue-clad interrogator left the room than Aiken Drum was testing the wooden door, discovering that it was locked, and doing something about it.

He used the tough glassy needle of a leatherworking fid to probe the slot where the brass latchbar came through until he was able to lift a concealed pawl that was preventing the notched bar from moving. Opening the door carefully, he saw the device on the other side that activated the locking mechanism. A tiny stone from the floor served to jam it.

He pulled the door shut and went creeping down the hallway, passing other closed rooms where he assumed his comrades from Group Green were incarcerated. He wouldn't let them out yet; not until he looked things over to see how he might take advantage of this strange situation. There was something powerful as well as peculiar at work here in the Pliocene, and it was obvious that it would take more than the simple-minded schemes of Stein and Richard to con the local yokels.

. . . Look out!

He darted into one of the deep window bays that overlooked the castle's inner courtyard. Whipping out his chameleon poncho, he hunkered down in the shadows and tried to blend inconspicuously into the stone floor.

Four sturdy guardians, led by a man in blue, went dashing down the corridor in the direction from which Aiken had come. They never looked in his direction and in a moment the reason became apparent.

There was a roar of rage in the distance and a muffled crash.

Heavy blows began to ring against the inner side of one of the reception room doors. Aiken peered from his alcove in time to see the group of castle lackeys cringe away from the first door at the head of the stairway. Even from his viewpoint more than ten meters away, Aiken could see the slabs of thick oak tremble from the force of rhythmic smashes.

The guardian in blue paused outside the door and fingered his torc in an agony of apprehension. The four other men gaped as their leader screeched, "You let him keep the iron axe? You stupid *turds!*"

"But, Master Tully, we put enough soporific in his beer to stun a mastodon!"

"But not enough to even slow down this Viking maniac, that's obvious!" Tully hissed. The door vibrated with a particularly mighty blow and the point of Stein's axe blade showed momentarily through broken wood before it was pulled back. "He'll be out of there in minutes! Salim, run for Lord Creyn. We'll need a *very* large gray torc. Alert Castellan Pitkin and the security squad, too. Kelolo, bring more guardians with a net. And tell Fritz to close the portcullis in case he gets away down the stairway. Hurry! If we can net this bastard as he breaks through we might just *salvage* this crock of shit!"

The two guardians raced off in opposite directions. Aiken shrank back into the shadows. Good old Steinie. Somehow he'd seen through the façade of phony goodwill and decided to take direct action. Drugged beer! Good God—suppose the coffee had been doped, too? He hadn't taken more than half a cup, though. And he'd tried to play the game their way when Tully interviewed him. He felt certain he had put himself over as a potentially useful but harmless little clown-handyman. Maybe they only drugged the big, dangerous-looking types.

"Hurry, hurry, hurry *up*, you fools!" Tully wailed. "He's breaking out!"

This time Aiken didn't dare look. But he heard a triumphant bellow and a squawk of splintering wood.

"I'll teach you to lock me in!" Stein's voice called out. "Wait till I get my hands on that little white-bellied prick who juiced my beer! *Yah! Yah! Yah!*"

A very tall figure dressed in scarlet and white went striding past Aiken's refuge, trailed by a jangling squad of warriors, all human, wearing domed kettle-helmets and heavy coats of yellowish scale-armor.

"Lord Creyn!" came Tully's voice. "I've sent for the net and more men . . . Oh, thank Tana! They're here!"

Lying flat on the floor under the poncho, Aiken wormed over the stones until he had a good view down the corridor. Stein, yelling with each blow of the axe, had enlarged the hole in the door until it was nearly large enough to permit his escape. The people from the castle had regained their discipline with the coming of Creyn and stood waiting.

Six armored men had a strong net deployed on the floor. Two more soldiers poised on either side of the disintegrating door with clubs as thick as a man's arm and studded with rounded metal knobs. The unarmed guardians fell back in a protective line before the towering form of Creyn.

"Hee-*yah!*" cried Stein, kicking the last obstructing pieces of oak from the opening. His horned Viking helmet popped out for an eye-blink and then withdrew for the charge.

He emerged with a leap that carried him nearly to the opposite side of the broad corridor, beyond reach of the net and into the midst of the guardians gathered about their awesome master. Men in white flung themselves at the berserker with despairing screams. Stein hewed at them, both hands swinging the battle-axe in short vicious arcs that sheared through flesh and bone and sent pathetic severed things bouncing from walls and along the floor, fountaining crimson as they rolled. The armored soldiers clubbed at him without effect and tried to seize his arms while he kept chopping at the barrier of living and dead men separating him from Creyn. In some way, Stein knew very well who his principal enemy was.

"I'll get you!" the Viking roared.

Creyn's robes showed scarcely any white now. He stood impassively against the wall, fingering the golden ring about his throat. One soldier finally snatched the horned helmet from Stein's head while another swung a club, catching the giant at the back of the neck with a force that would have crushed the bones of a less heroic vertebral column. For three long seconds, the Viking stood like a grotesque statue, his axe raised within easy striking distance of Creyn's head. Then Stein's fingers loosened. The weapon went tumbling down behind his back. His knees bent slowly and his head fell onto his breast as the net was belatedly flung over him.

One of the warriors drew a short bronze sword and rushed forward, eyes glittering. Before he could strike, he halted as though paralyzed. Another soldier pried the blade from his hand.

"No one is to harm this one," the Tanu overlord said. He moved through the shambles until he could look down upon Stein's unconscious body. Kneeling on the gory flags, Creyn held out his hand for the short sword and used it to cut the meshes covering Stein's head. Then he took a gray metal torc from a large pouch at his belt and fitted it about the fallen rock driller's neck.

"He is harmless now. You may remove the net. Take him to a fresh reception room and clean him up so that I may treat his wounds. He'll be most welcome in the capital."

Rising, Creyn beckoned for a pair of soldiers to accompany him. All three of them made bloody footprints as they walked toward Aiken's hiding place, slowed, and stopped.

"Come out," Creyn said.

"Oh, well!" Aiken gave him a grin as he scrambled to his feet. He flourished his hat in a mock salute and bowed from the waist. Before he realized what was happening, Creyn bent down and snapped something around his neck.

Oh, Christ, Aiken thought. Not me, too!

You are a completely different breed of cat, Aiken Drum, and bound for more sophisticated amusements than your muscular friend.

Aiken craned his head to look into the wintry eyes far above him. The Tanu's hair that had been so sleek and shining was clotted now with the blood of men who had died defending him—died unwillingly, from the sound of their hopeless screams, freed from the symbol and source of their bondage only at the moment that Stein's blade severed their heads from their bodies.

"I suppose you can do what you like with us, once you've put on these fewkin' dog collars," Aiken said bitterly, touching the thing about his own throat. It was warm. For one fraction of a second he felt a flash of pleasure born in his loins go racing along his nerves like lightning through wires before it exited his body through tingling fingers and toes.

What the *hell!*

Did you like that? It's only a sample of what we can give you. But our greatest gift will be the fulfillment of your own potential, freeing you even as you serve us.

The way these poor sods served? Headless trunks piled limbs awash in blood?

Amusement. Your own torc is silver and not gray. As befits a latent metapsychic made operant. You're going to enjoy the Pliocene very much, my lad.

"Well, I'll be damned!" Aiken exclaimed aloud. Delight. *Delight.* *DELIGHT!* "How many of the functions am I strong in?"

Find out for yourself.

A built-in master control mechanism in the collar for you guys I presume.

What do you think?

Aiken gave a crooked grin. "Better than gray, less than gold. Tell you what. I'll take it!" He folded his poncho carefully and stowed it back into his lumbar pouch. "What next, Chief?"

"We'll let you wait in a fresh reception room for now. One with a more effective lock. In a few hours, you'll be leaving for our capital city, Muriah. Don't be apprehensive. Life here in Exile can be very pleasant."

As long as I know who's boss?

Affirm.

The guards hustled Aiken Drum through a door. He called over his shoulder, "Have one of your flunkies bring me a good stiff drink, will you, Chief? All this fighting raises a terrible thirst in a man."

Creyn had to laugh. "It will be done." Then the guards slammed the door and barred it.

5

AMERIE HAD HEARD the sounds of fighting in the corridor outside and pressed her ear to the boards of the locked door to confirm her suspicions. It had to be Stein or Felice. Could one of them have been driven insane by the shock of the translation? Or was there a good reason for the violent outburst?

She tore open her backpack and rummaged in the Smallholder Unit for the small plass envelope holding the cord-saw. Dragging one of the benches over to the window, she tucked her skirts into her rope belt and jumped up.

Cut halfway through the upper bars of the brass grille on the inside! Cut all of the way through the bottom bars, then lever the whole thing outward with the top of another bench after I smash it apart! I could unbraid the rug and make a rope out of the wool—but wait! The decamole bridge sections would work—two for a ladder and the third to cross over the area with those damn bear-dogs—

"Oh, Sister. What are you *doing?*"

She whirled around, hampered by both index fingers being engaged in the rings of the cord-saw. Tully and a burly guardian stood at the open door. The little interviewer's tunic was covered with dark stains.

"Please come down, Sister. What a dreadfully reckless thing to think of! And all so unnecessary. Believe me, you are in no danger."

Amerie locked eyes with him, then stepped down, resigned. The big guardian held out his hand for the saw and she gave it to him without a word. He tucked it into one of the pockets of her pack and said, "I'll carry this for you, Sister."

Tully said, "We are having to expedite our usual interview program because of a most regrettable accident. So if you will accompany Shubash and me—"

"I heard sounds of fighting," she said. "Who was hurt? Was it Felice?" She strode to the open door and looked out into the corridor. "Merciful God!"

Guardians had removed the dead and injured, and cleanup crews were sluicing the walls and floor with big buckets of water; but traces of mayhem were still sickeningly apparent.

"What have you done?" Amerie cried.

"The blood is that of our own people." Tully was somber. "It was shed by your companion, Stein. He, by the way, is unhurt except for bruises. But five of our men are dead and seven others seriously injured."

"Oh, Lord. How did it happen?"

"I'm sorry to say that Stein went berserk. It must have been a delayed reaction to the temporal translation. Passage through the time-portal sometimes triggers deeply buried psychic explosives. We try to protect both the travelers and ourselves by confining new arrivals to these reception rooms for a while during the recovery period —which is why *your* door was locked."

"I'm sorry about your people," she told him with sincere regret. "Steinie is—strange—but a dear man when you get to know him. What will happen to him now?"

Tully fingered his gray collar. "We who guard the gateway have our duty and at times it is a heavy one. Your friend has received treatment that should preclude another attack. He won't be punished any more than a sick man is punished for his illness . . . Now, Sister, we must hurry you along to the next phase of our interview. The Lady Epone requires your assistance."

They passed through the dreadful hallway and down the stairs to a small office on the other side of the barbican. Felice Landry was waiting alone, seated in an ordinary cushioned chair beside a table that held a metal sculpture all studded with jewels. The two men conducted Amerie inside and withdrew, closing the door.

"Felice! Stein has—"

"I know," the athlete interrupted in a whisper. She put one gloved finger to her lips, then sat silent, holding her emerald-plumed leather helmet demurely in her lap. With her hair standing out from her head and her enormous brown eyes wide, she looked like a pretty child waiting to be forced onstage for some sinister theatrical performance.

The door opened and Epone glided in. Amerie stared at the immensely tall figure in astonishment.

"Another sentient race?" the nun blurted out. "Here?"

Epone inclined her majestic head. "I will explain it to you shortly, Sister. Everything will be clarified in good time. For now, I require your assistance in gaining the confidence of your young companion for a simple test of mental abilities." She picked up a silver coronet from the table and approached Felice with it.

"No! No! I told you, I won't let you!" the girl shrieked. "And if you try to force me, it won't register. I know all about these rotten mind tricks!"

Epone appealed to Amerie. "Her fears are irrational. All of the newly arrived timefarers consent to the test for latent metabilities. If we discover that you possess them, we have the technology to bring them up to operancy so that you and all of the community may enjoy their benefits."

"You want to *probe* me," Felice spat out.

"Certainly not. The test is a simple calibration."

Amerie suggested, "Perhaps if you tested me first. I'm quite sure that my own MP latencies are minimal. But it would probably reassure Felice if she could see just what happens in the test."

"An excellent idea," Epone said, smiling.

Amerie took Felice's hand and raised her from the chair. She could feel the trembling fingers even through the leather glove, but the emotion hidden in those unfathomable eyes was something much different from fear. The nun spoke soothingly. "Stand there, Felice. You can watch while I go through this, and then if the idea still distresses you, I'm sure this lady will respect your personal convictions." She turned to Epone. "Won't you?"

"I assure you, I mean you no harm," the Tanu woman replied. "And as Felice has said, the test will not give proper results unless the subject cooperates. Please be seated, Sister."

Amerie unfastened the pin that held her black veil, then slipped off the soft white wimple that had covered her hair. Epone set the silver coronet on the nun's brown curls.

"First we will test the farsensing function. If you would, Sister, without speaking, attempt to tell me *greetings*."

Amerie squeezed her eyes shut. One point of the coronet acquired a faint violet spark.

"Minus seven. Very weak. Now for the coercive faculty. Sister, exert all of your willpower upon me. Force me to close my eyes."

Amerie glowered in concentration. Another point of the coronet grew a somewhat more intense bluish spark.

"Minus three. Stronger, but still far below the potentially useful range. Now let us test psychokinesis. Try very hard, Sister. Levitate yourself in your chair just one centimeter above the floor."

The resultant rosy-gold spark was hardly visible and the chair stayed firmly on the flagstones.

"Ah, a pity. Minus eight. Relax now, Sister. In testing the creative function, we will ask you to spin an illusion for us. Close your eyes and visualize a common object—perhaps your shoe!—suspended in midair before you. *Will* this object to appear before us. Try hard!"

A greenish spark like a miniature star. And—was it really there?—the faintest phantasm of a hiking boot.

"Do you see, Felice?" the Tanu exclaimed. "Plus three point five!"

Amerie's eyes popped open and the illusion vanished. "Do you mean I actually did it?"

"The coronet artificially enhances your natural creativity, converting it from latent to operant. Unfortunately, your psychic potential in the faculty is so low as to be virtually useless, even with maximum gain."

"It figures," said the nun. "Veni creator spiritus. Don't call me, I'll call you."

"There is one more test, for the MP function that is to us most important of all." Epone manipulated the crystalline device, which had begun to flicker. When the glow in the jewels had steadied, she said, "Look into my eyes, Sister. Look beneath them, into my mind if you are able to. Can you perceive what is hidden there? Can you analyze it? Collate its scattered bits back to coherency? Heal its wounds and scars and voids of pain? Try. Try!"

Oh, poor one. You want to let me, don't you? But . . . strong, too strong. Looking out at me beating on transparent walls so strong and now darkening darkening. Black.

A red spark had flared for a brief moment, a microscopic nova. It dimmed to near invisibility. Epone sighed.

"Minus seven ultimate redact. I would have given much—but enough." She removed the coronet and turned to Felice with a kindly expression. "Will you permit me to test you now, child?"

Felice whispered, "I can't. Please don't make me do it."

"We can wait until later, in Finiah," Epone said. "Very likely you are a normal human woman, as your friend is. But even for you, without metafaculties, we can offer a world of happiness and fulfillment. All women enjoy a privileged position in the Many-Colored Land because so few pass through the time-portal. You will be cherished."

Amerie paused in the act of restoring her headdress and said, "You should know from a study of our customs that some of our priests are consecrated virgins. I'm one. And Felice is not heterosexually oriented."

Epone said, "That is a pity. But given time, you will adjust to the new status and be happy."

Felice stepped forward and spoke very quietly. "Do you mean to tell us that women are sexually subservient to men here in Exile?"

Epone's lips curved upward. "What is subservience and what is fulfillment? It is feminine nature to be the vessel yearning to be filled, to be the nurturer and sustainer, to spend the self in giving care to the beloved other. When that destiny is denied, there can only be a void, weeping and rage . . . as I and so many other women of my race know only too well. We of the Tanu came here long ago from a galaxy at the farthest limits of Earth's visibility, exiles driven forth because we refused to modify our lifestyle according to principles abhorrent to us. In many ways, this planet has been an ideal refuge. But its atmosphere fails to screen out certain particles that are detrimental to our reproductive capacity. Tanu women produce healthy children rarely and with great difficulty. Nevertheless we are vowed to racial survival. We prayed through the hopeless centuries and at length Mother Tana answered us."

A dawning realization came to Amerie. Felice showed no emotion. The nun said, "All of the human women going through the time-gate have been sterilized."

"By reversible salpingotomy," said the serene exotic.

Amerie sprang to her feet. "Even if you undo it, the genetics—"

"—are compatible. Our Ship, who brought us here (blessed be its memory), chose this galaxy and this world for the perfect compatibility of the germ plasm. It was expected that aeons would have to ensue before we achieved full reproductive potential, even using the native life-form you call ramapithecine as a nurturer of the zygote. But we live so very long! And we have such power! So we endured until the miracle occurred and the time-portal opened and began sending you to us. Sister, you and Felice are young and healthy. You will cooperate, as others of your sex have done, because the rewards are great and the punishments insupportable."

"Fuck you!" said the nun.

Epone walked to the door. "The interview is at an end. You will both prepare for the caravan journey to Finiah. It is a beautiful city on the Proto-Rhine, near the site of your future Freiburg. Humans of goodwill live happily there, served by our good little ramas so that they are relieved of all drudgery. You will learn contentment, believe me." She went out and softly closed the door.

Amerie turned to Felice. "The bastards! The rotten bastards!"

"Don't worry, Amerie," said the athlete. "She didn't test me. *That's* the important thing. I kept smearing pathetic whinings over my thoughts all of the time that she was near me, so if she could read me at all, she probably believes I'm nothing but a poor little leather gal."

"What are you going to do? Try to escape?"

Felice's dark eyes glowed and she laughed out loud. "More. I'm going to take 'em. The whole goddamned lot."

6

THERE WERE benches under the trees of the walled compound, but Claude Majewski chose to sit on the pavement in the shade of the animal-pen partition where he could watch the living-fossil beasts and brood. He turned the carved Zakopane box over and over in his big hands.

A fine end to your frivolity, Old Man. Sold down the river in your one hundred and thirty-third year! And all because of a crazy whimsical gesture. Oh, you Polacks always were romantic fools!

Is that why you loved me, Black Girl?

The really humiliating aspect was that it had taken Claude so long to figure the thing out. Didn't he welcome the first friendly contact, the attractive sitting room with the food (and the john), all nicely calculated to soothe the frightened old poop after the stress of translation? Wasn't Tully genial and harmless, drawing him out and flattering him and dishing the codswallop about the great life of peace and happiness they would all enjoy in Exile? (All right, Tully *had* overdone it just a little.) And the first sight of Epone had all but stupefied him, the unexpected presence of an exotic on Pliocene Earth numbing his natural prudence while she measured him, found him wanting, and dismissed him.

Even when the armed guards led him politely across the courtyard he had been docile as a lamb . . . until the last minute when they took away his pack, opened the gate, and pushed him into the people pen.

"Easy does it, traveler," one guard had said. "You'll get your pack back later if you behave yourself. Make trouble, and we have the means to subdue you. Try to escape and you join the bear-dogs for dinner."

Claude had stood there with his mouth open until a sane-looking fellow prisoner in Alpine climbing kit came over and led him into the shade. After an hour or so, Claude's pack was returned by a guard. Any equipment that might have aided in escape had been removed. He was told that the vitredur woodworking tools would be returned to him when he was "safe" in Finiah.

After the first shock had passed off, Claude explored the people pen. It was actually a large and well-shaded yard with ornamental walls of pierced stonework more than three meters high, patrolled by guards. An indoor extension led to a fairly comfortable dormitory and a washroom. The compound held eight women and thirty-three men. Claude recognized most of them from having watched their early morning march through the auberge gardens to the Guderian cottage. They represented approximately one week's bag of time-farers, with the missing ones presumed to have been sorted out by Epone's test and shunted to some alternate destiny.

Claude soon discovered that the only one of his comrades from Group Green in the pen was Richard. He lay in an ominous sleep on one of the dormitory bunks. He would not awaken when the old man shook him by the shoulder.

"We've a few others like him," said the Alpine climber. His face was long, weathered, and finely wrinkled with the indeterminate middle-aged look of decaying rejuvenation. He had humorous gray eyes and ash-colored hair beneath his Tyrolean hat. "Some people just seem to drop out of it, poor devils. Still, they're better off than the lizzie who hanged herself day before yesterday. You lot today are the last of the week's consignment. Tonight we'll move out. Just be glad you haven't had to stick it out here for six days like some of us."

"Did any try to escape?" Claude asked.

"A few before I came. A Cossack named Prischchepa from my group. Three Polynesians yesterday. The bear-dogs even ate their feathered cloaks. Pity. Do you like recorder music? I feel like a bit of Purcell. Name's Basil Wimborne, by the way."

He sat down on a vacant bunk, took out a wooden flute, and began to play a plaintive melody. The old man recalled that Bryan had often whistled snatches of it. Claude listened for a few minutes, then wandered back outside.

Other time-travelers were reacting to their imprisonment according to their individual psychology. An aging artist bent over a sketch pad. Side by side under a tree sat a young couple dressed as Yankee pioneers, caressing one another in oblivious passion. Five Gypsy men argued conspiratorially and practiced close-combat lunges with invisible knives. A perspiring middle-aged male in a rabbit-trimmed toga and kidskin domino kept demanding that the guards give him back his discipline. Two Japanese ronin, sans swords but otherwise attired in handsome fourteenth-century armor, were playing goban with a decamole board. A lovely woman veiled in rainbow chiffon resolved her tensions in dance; the guards outside had to keep discouraging her from climbing up the walls and leaping into space like a billowy butterfly, crying, "Paris—adieu!" In a shady spot sat an Australoid black man in a crisp white shirt, riding breeches, and elastic-sided boots; the four tiny speakers of his music library were arranged about him, endlessly alternating "Der Erlkönig" with an antique cut of Will Bradley's "Celery Stalks at Midnight." A fellow dressed in jester's motley juggled three silver balls with persistent lack of skill before an audience of an elderly woman and her Shih-Tzu puppy, which never tired of chasing the balls. Perhaps the most pathetic of the prisoners was a tall robust man with a ginger beard and hollow eyes, beautifully accoutered in imitation chainmail and a medieval knight's silken surtout emblazoned with a golden lion. He strode about the compound in a frenzy of agitation, peering through the holes in the wall and crying, "Aslan! Aslan! Where are you now that we need you? Save us from la belle dame sans merci!"

Claude decided that he was up a very shitty creek indeed. For some perverse reason he felt almost pleased with himself.

He picked up a fallen leafy twig and poked it through one of the ornamental apertures into the adjacent animal corral.

"Here, boy. Here, boy."

One of the creatures on the other side of the wall pricked its tufted, horselike ears and ambled over for a taste. Claude watched it in delight as it first nipped off the leaves with tiny cropping teeth, then champed the woody parts with its strong molars. When the tidbit was swallowed, the animal gave him a look that plainly reproached his lack of generosity, so he got it more leaves.

It was a chalicothere, a member of one of the most peculiar and fascinating families of Cenozoic mammals. Its body was massive and deep-chested, nearly three meters long and with a horselike neck and head that testified to its perissodactyl affinities. Its front legs were somewhat longer than the hind ones and at least twice as stout as those of a draft horse. Instead of terminating in hoofs, the feet bore three toes ending in huge semiretractile claws. The inner ones on the front feet were nearly the size of a human hand, with the others only half as large. The chalicothere's body was clothed in a short hairy coat of bluish gray, dotted with white spots about the withers, flanks, and hindquarters. Its tail was rudimentary, but the creature did boast a fine mane of long black hair, a black streak down the spine, and flashy black featherings at the fetlocks. The intelligent eyes were set a bit farther forward on the skull than those of a horse and were fringed with heavy black lashes that the beast batted fetchingly. It wore a leather bridle and was thoroughly domesticated. The corral held at least sixty of the animals, most of them dapple-gray, with occasional white or sorrel individuals.

The Pliocene sun ascended over the barbican and finally shone directly into the courtyard, driving all but the most hardy prisoners into the relative coolness of the stone dormitory. A surprisingly decent noon meal of bayleaf-seasoned stew, fruit, and wine punch was served. Claude again tried vainly to awaken Richard and finally stowed the pirate's food under his bunk. After lunch most of the prisoners retired for a siesta, but Claude went back outside to pace his digestion into submission and speculate on his fate.

About two hours later, stablehands dressed in gray began toting in large baskets of gnarled tubers and fat roots resembling mangelwurzels. They dumped these into troughs for the animals. While the chalicotheres were feeding, the men mucked out the pen with big twig brooms and wooden shovels, dumped the manure into wheeled carts, and trundled it off toward the corridor leading to the castle's postern gate. Two of the hands stayed behind with a portable pump apparatus, which they immersed in the central fountain. While one man pumped a stirrup, the other unreeled a stiff canvas hose with which he washed the floor of the corral, the excess water draining off into gutters. When the pavement was clean, he turned the spray onto the feeding animals. They uttered whickers and squeals of delight.

The old paleontologist nodded with satisfaction. Water lovers. Root eaters. So chalicotheres *were* denizens of the damp semitropical forest or muddy river bottomlands. And they did use their claws to dig for roots. A minor mystery of paleobiology was solved—for him, at least. But were the prisoners actually going to have to ride such archaic steeds? The beasts wouldn't be as fast as horses, but they looked as though they had a lot of endurance. And their gait—! Claude winced. If one of those creatures cantered with him aboard, his old knees and hip joints were going to shatter like antique Christmas-tree ornaments.

A sound in the shadowed cloister caught his attention. Soldiers were leading two new prisoners to the back door of the compound, which opened into the dormitory. Claude saw a waving green plume and a glimpse of black and white. Felice and Amerie!

He hurried inside and was standing there as the two women were led into the prison. One guard put down their packs, which he had carried, and said in a friendly fashion, "Won't be long to wait now. Better get something to eat from the leftovers on the table over there."

The knight errant came running over to them with a tragic expression. "Is Aslan on his way? Have you seen him, good Sister? Perhaps this warrior-maid is of his entourage! Aslan must come or we be doomed!"

"Oh, piss off," muttered Felice.

Claude took the knight by one mailed elbow and led him to a bunk near the other door. "Stay here and watch for Aslan." The man nodded solemnly and sat down. Somewhere in the dimness, another prisoner was weeping. The Alpinist was playing "Greensleeves" on his recorder.

When Claude returned to his friends, he found Felice rooting in her pack and cursing. "All missing! The arbalest, my skinning knives, the ropes—just about every damn thing I might have used to get us out of here!"

"You might as well forget it," Claude told her. "If you resort to violence, they'll collar you. That fellow playing the flute told me about a prisoner who went bonkers and attacked a mess attendant. Soldiers clubbed him down and put one of those gray metal neckrings on him. When he stopped screaming and recovered his senses, he was as mild as milk. Couldn't get the collar off, either."

Felice swore more eloquently. "Are they planning to collar us all, then?"

Claude glanced around, but nobody was paying the slightest attention to them. "Evidently not. As nearly as I can judge, the gray collars are a crude type of psychoregulator, probably linked to the golden ones worn by the Lady Epone and other exotics. Not all of the castle personnel wear collars. Soldiers and guardians do, and straw bosses like the worthy Tully. But the stablehands don't have collars, and neither do the mess attendants."

"Not in sensitive enough positions?" suggested the nun.

"Or maybe the hardware is in short supply," Claude said.

Felice frowned. "That could be. It would need a sophisticated technology to manufacture things like that. And so far, this outfit looks damn Mickey Mouse. Did you see how that mind calibrator kept fritzing out? And no running water in those reception rooms."

"They didn't bother to take any of my pharmaceuticals," said Amerie. "The collars must protect the guards from any drugging we might be tempted to try. Handy gadgets. No slave overseer should be without some."

"They may not need to collar people to keep them down," Claude said, grim. He gestured at the dormitory's listless inmates. "Just look at this crew! A few lively ones tried to escape and they were fed to the bear-dogs. I think that most folks falling into a nightmare like this are so traumatized that they just float for a while and hope things won't get worse. The guards are cheerful and spin yarns about the good life waiting for us. The food's not bad. Wouldn't *you* just take it easy and see what develops, instead of fighting it?"

"No," said Felice.

Amerie added, "The women's expectations aren't quite so rosy, Claude." She told him tersely of their interview with Epone, and of the origins and reproductive predicament of the exotic race. "So while *you* may be able to live peacefully building log cabins, Claude, Felice and I are going to be turned into broodmares."

"Damn them!" whispered the old man. "*Damn* them!" He stared at his big hands, still strong, but blotched with liver spots and corded with blue veins. "I wouldn't be worth a fart in a teacup in any real dustup. What we really need is Stein."

"They took him," Amerie said, and explained how Tully told her that the Viking had been "treated" to prevent further trouble. They all knew what that had to mean.

"Are any of the others here?" Felice asked.

"Just Richard," said the old man. "But he's been asleep ever since I was put in here this morning. I couldn't wake him, either. Maybe you ought to take a look at him, Amerie."

The nun took her pack and followed Claude to Richard's bunk. It was surrounded by empty beds for a reason that was easily apparent. The sleeping man had soiled himself. His arms were folded tightly over his breast and his knees were drawn up nearly to his chin.

Amerie lifted one eyelid, then took his pulse. "Jesus, he's close to catatonic. What could they have done to him?"

She searched in her pack and came up with a minidoser, which she pressed to Richard's temple. As the bulblet collapsed and the powerful drug entered the unconscious man's bloodstream, he gave a faint moan.

"There's a chance this might bring him around if he's not too far gone," the nun said. "Meanwhile, will you guys help me clean him up?"

"Right," said Felice, starting to shuck her armor. "His pack's here. He ought to have other clothes."

"I'll get water," Claude said. He headed for the washroom, where there was a stone tank supplied by a conduit from the fountain. He filled a wooden bucket and brought soap and quantities of rough towels. As he sloshed back between the bunks, one of the Gypsies eyed him.

"You help your friend, old man. But maybe he's better off the way he is. Useless to them!"

A woman with a hairless head clutched at him. She wore wrinkled yellow robes and her Oriental face was ravaged by scars, an unusual sight. Perhaps they were part of her religious devotion. "We wanted to be free," she croaked. "But these monsters from another galaxy will enslave us. And the worst of it is, they look *human*."

Claude pulled away from her. Trying to ignore other cries and whispers, he made his way to Richard's bed.

"I gave him another shot," Amerie said grimly. "It'll bring him around or kill him. Damn—if only we could give him a sugar drip."

The knight gave a shout. "They're starting to saddle the faerie steeds! We'll soon be on our way to Narnia!"

"See what's going on, Claude," Felice ordered.

He pushed through others who were hurrying outside and managed to get close to the perforated wall nearest the central court. Stablehands were leading pairs of chalicotheres from the corral to ranks of hitching rails across the yard. More servitors brought out piles of tack and started placing pads on the animals' backs. To one side, eight of the beasts were segregated for special treatment, their bronze-studded harness and other equipment marking them as soldiers' mounts.

An amused voice at Claude's shoulder said, "Don't seem to think we'll need much guarding on the trip, do they?" It was Basil, the Alpine hiker, watching the proceedings with interest. "Ah! There's the explanation. Catch the clever modification of the stirrups?"

Bronze chains dangled from them. They were padded with narrow leather sleeves and would probably hang loosely enough about the ankle to be only minimally uncomfortable when fastened.

The saddling took some time and the sun westered behind the castle. It was obvious that they were scheduled for a night march in order to avoid the daytime heat on the savanna. A squad of four troopers led by an officer wearing a short blue cloak came marching to the compound gate and unbarred it. The soldiers were attired in light bronze kettle-helmets and piece-armor, worn over tan shirts and shorts. They were armed with intricately pulleyed compound bows, bronze short swords, and vitredur lances. As the soldiers entered the pen, the prisoners fell back. The officer addressed the crowd in a matter-of-fact voice.

"All you travelers! It's nearly time to move out of here. I'm your caravan leader, Captal Waldemar. We're gonna get to know each other pretty good in the next week or so. I know you've had a hard time, some of you, staying in this hot compound while you waited for the contingent to be complete. But things will be better soon. We're on our way north to the city of Finiah, where you'll be making your home. It's a good place. A lot cooler than here. The journey is about four hundred kilometers and it will take us about six days. We'll go by night for two days here in the hot country, then switch to day travel when we hit the Hercynian Forest.

"Now, you travelers, listen! Don't give me any trouble and you'll get good food at stations along the way. Fuck up and you'll be short-rationed. Make me really unhappy and you won't eat at all. Any of you travelers who think you'd like to escape, just think about the fossil zoo waiting bright-eyed and bushy-tailed for stragglers on foot. We got sabertooth cats like superlions and hyenas the size of grizzly bears. We got wild boars bigger'n oxen that take a human leg off with one bite. We got rhinos and mastodons that'll stomp you to death if they even catch sight of you. And the deinotheriums, the hoe-tusker elephants, they like to use people for cute tug-o'-war games and then dance on the pieces! They only stand four or five meters at the shoulder, by the way. You escape the big buggers and you can get nailed by the small fry. The creeks are full of pythons and crocs. The woods have poisonous spiders with bodies like peaches and fangs like gaboon vipers. You get away from the animals and the Firvulag will track you down and play devil-tunes on your mind until you go mad or die from the horrors.

"It's bad out there, travelers! It's not the pretty Eden world they told you about in A.D. 2110. But nobody has to worry if they stick with the caravan. You're gonna ride those critters that you been looking at in the pen next door. They're chalicotheres, kind of a distant relative of the horse, and we call 'em chalikos. They're smart and they like people, and with those claws they have, nothing messes with 'em much. Be nice to your chaliko. He's transportation and a bodyguard in one package . . .

"Now, in case any of you travelers feel like riding off into the tall timber—forget it. These torcs, these necklets that us soldiers wear, they let us keep complete control of the chalikos. You leave the driving to us. And we'll also have trained amphicyons ranging along the flanks of the caravan. Those bear-dogs know that any rider who tries to light out is fair meat. So live cool and we'll all have a good ride.

"Right! Now I want you to get your stuff together. You can either transfer your things from packs into saddlebags or just lash your rig behind the cantle of the saddle. I understand two of you have pet animals with you. We'll have pannier baskets that they can ride in. The guy that brought the pregnant goat . . . your animal will have to stay here until the weekly trade and supply caravan brings it on. Most of your proscribed tools and weapons and the bulky stuff taken from you when you first arrived will be carried on our pack animals. You may get most of the things back eventually, if you behave.

"Everything clear? Right! I want all of you lined up here, two by two and ready to ride, in half an hour. When you hear a big bell ring, you know you got just five minutes to line up or it's your ass. That's *all!*"

He turned on his heel and marched out with his detail following. They didn't even bother to bar the gate.

Murmuring, the prisoners began shuffling back inside to gather their belongings. Claude reflected that night travel was another demoralizing factor calculated to stifle notions of escape, as were the inflated descriptions of Pliocene fauna. Spiders as big as peaches forsooth! Next it would be the Giant Rat of Sumatra! On the other hand, the amphicyons were a real enough menace. He wondered how fast they could run on those primitive digitigrade feet. And what in the world were the horrendous Firvulag?

Across the yard another party under guard was emerging from the gatehouse. Hostlers cut out six animals from the main remuda and led them to a mounting platform. Claude saw one slim figure in gold lamé being helped aboard a saddled chaliko, and there was another standing by in a scarlet jumpsuit and a third—

"Aiken!" the old man shouted. "Elizabeth! It's me! Claude!"

The figure in red began to remonstrate with another blue-caped captal of the guard. The arguing got louder and louder and finally Elizabeth stamped her foot and the man shrugged. She broke from the group and ran across the courtyard, the officer following at leisure. She pulled open the people-pen gate and threw herself into the white-haired paleontologist's arms.

"Kiss me," she whispered breathlessly. "You're supposed to be my lover."

He folded her to his breast while the soldier eyed him with interested speculation. Elizabeth said, "They're sending us to the capital, Muriah. My metafunctions are returning, Claude! I'm going to do my best to get away. If I do, I'll try to help you all, somehow."

"That's enough now, Lady," said the soldier. "I don't care what Lord Creyn told you. You've got to get ready to ride."

"Goodbye, Claude." She gave him a real kiss, full on the lips, before she was hurried back across the courtyard and helped onto her mount. One of the soldiers fastened the slender chains about her ankles.

Claude raised one hand. "Goodbye, Elizabeth."

From a covered area beyond the main animal pen came a majestic figure riding a snow-white chaliko with scarlet and silver trappings. The captal saluted. Then he and two soldiers swung into their saddles. A command rang out.

"All ready! Portcullis up!"

The file of ten riders went slowly into the arched passage of the barbican. There was a distant excited howling from the bear-dogs. The last prisoner in line turned to wave at Claude before he disappeared into the shadowed opening.

And goodbye to you, Bryan, thought the old man. I hope you find your Mercy. One way or another.

He went back into the dormitory to help with Richard, feeling old and weary and not at all pleased with himself any more.

7

THE PARTY OF TEN formed up to ride two by two as soon as they had quit Castle Gateway. Creyn and his captal led and the two soldiers followed behind the small group of prisoners. The sun was just down and they traveled eastward into the dusk, down the gradual slope of the plateau toward the twilit Rhône-Saône Valley.

Elizabeth sat easily in her saddle, eyes closed and hands clasped on the pommel while the reins lay free. It was fortunate that the chaliko did not require guidance from its rider; because Elizabeth was fully occupied in listening.

Listen . . . but be unaware of the sounds made by the mounts plodding over soft earth. Do not hear the crickets, the frogs tuning up in the misty swales scattered in the hollows of the tableland. Be deaf to the birds' evensong, the distant yelping of hyaenids emerging for the night's hunt, the murmuring voices of companion riders. Listen not with the ears but with the newly recovered metapsychic farsensing faculty.

Reach out afar, afar. Search for other minds like your own, other speakers, other please-God *truepeople*. (Shame on you for that, arrogant sickee, but be forgiven just this once.)

Listen, listen! The reborn ultrasense is not yet fully operant, and yet there are things to be heard. Here in the party: the guarded exotic consciousness of Creyn in converse with his captal, dark-minded Zdenko, the two concealed behind a torc-generated screen easily breached; but forebear, since they would be aware of the penetration. Pass over Aiken and the other silver-torc prisoners, the man Raimo and the woman Sukey, their infantile mental babblings as grating as the efforts of fledgling violinists importuning the ears of a cranky virtuoso. Ignore the gray-torced guards and poor unconscious Stein, and Bryan with his brain still unfettered except by chains of his own forging. Leave them all and journey afar.

Listen back at the castle where another exotic voice is—yes—singing. Lesser notes of silver and gray respond in dim echoing of the golden tone. Listen ahead, closer to the great river, to a complex alien mutter: exultation, impatience, anticipated dark joy, cruelty. (Drop *that* horrid thing until later.) Listen farther east, north, northwest, and south. Perceive other concentrations, golden amorphous clots betokening the presence of still more of the artificially enhanced exotic minds, their thoughts too numerous and unfocused for your convalescent mind to sort, their harmonies and occasional peaks of power so strange, yet so achingly familiar in their resemblance to the metapsychic networks of the dear lost Milieu.

Listen to the anomalies! Soft gibberings and puerile thrusts. Other unhuman minds—unaugmented by torcs, perhaps genuinely operant? What? Who? Where? Data inconclusive, but there are many. Listen to faint traceries of dread-patterns and pain-patterns and resignation-loss-patterns coming from God knew where or what. Shrink back. Press past them and beyond, listening. Listening.

That! A fleeting contact from the north that winks out in a spasm of apprehension as soon as you touch it. Tanu? Enhanced human farspeaker? Call out, but receive no response. Project friendship and need, but hear no answer . . . Perhaps you imagined it after all.

Listen afar, afar. Sound the entire Exile world. Are any of you here, sisters and brothers of the mind? Do any farsense in the uniquely human mode that the exotics cannot know? Answer Elizabeth Orme farspeaker redactor searcher hoper prayer! Answer . . .

Planet aureole. Emanations of lower life-forms. Mental whispers from normal humanity. The jabber of the Tanu and their torced minions. An ambiguous murmur from the other side of the world, evanescent as a remembered dream. Is it real or reverberate? Imagination or reality? Track it, lose it. Hover despairingly and know that it never was. The Earth is mute.

Go out beyond the world-halo and perceive the diapason roar of the hidden sun and the thinner arpeggios of stars near and distant, tingling with their own planets and life. No metapsychic humanity? Then call to the ancient-in-your-day Lylmik race, frail artisans of mental prodigies . . . but they do not yet exist. Call to the Krondaku, brothers-mental despite their fearsome bodies . . . but they, too, are a race still in embryo, as are the Gi, the Poltroyans, and the rude Simbiari. The living universe is uncoadunate, mind still chained to matter. The Milieu is in its childhood and Blessed Diamond Mask unborn. There is no one to answer.

Elizabeth withdrew.

Her eyes beheld her own hands, the diamond ring symbolic of her profession faintly luminous, mocking. Banal mental images lapped and splattered her. The wide-open subvocalization of the soldier Billy, brooding over the aging but available charms of a female tavern keeper at a place called Roniah. The other guard, Seung Kyu, preoccupied with a wager he plans to make upon some contest, the outcome of which might now be modified by the participation of Stein. The captal broadcasting pain waves from a boil in his armpit that is aggravated by the bronze breastplate of his light armor. Stein seemingly asleep, calmed by his gray torc. Aiken and the woman named Sukey weaving a crude but effective screen over some mental shenanigans. Creyn now deep in verbal conversation with the anthropologist, discussing the evolution of Tanu society since the opening of the time-portal.

Elizabeth wove a shield behind which she could mourn, impervious as the diamond of her future patron saint. And when it was finished she let the bitter sorrow and rage blaze up. She wept for the irony of having fled from loneliness and bereavement, only to encounter it transformed and fresh. Cocooned, wrapped in the fire of loss, she drifted. Her face was as tranquil as that of a statue in the bright light of the Pliocene stars, her mind as inaccessible as they.

* * *

". . . the Ship had no way of knowing that this sun was shortly to enter into a prolonged period of instability, triggered by a nearby supernova. Within a hundred years of our arrival, only one conceptus in thirty survived until term. Of those that were born, only about half were normal. We live long, by human standards, but we faced extinction unless the disaster could somehow be ameliorated."

"You couldn't simply pack up and leave?"

"Our Ship was a living organism. It died heroically when it brought us to Earth, making an intergalactic leap unprecedented in the history of our race . . . No, we could not leave. We had to find another solution. The Ship and its Spouse had chosen Earth for us because of a basic compatibility between our plasm and that of the highest native life-form, the ramapithecines. This enabled us to dominate them with our torc technology—"

"To enslave them, you mean?"

"Why use such a pejorative term, Bryan? Did your people speak of enslaving chimpanzees or whales? The ramas are scarcely more sentient. Or would you have had us live in a Stone Age culture? We came here voluntarily in order to follow an ancient lifestyle no longer permissible on the worlds of our galaxy. But we hardly desired to subsist on roots and berries or live in caves."

"Perish the thought. So you made the ramas your servants and went your merry way until the sun went spotty. And then your genetic engineers found a new use for the ramas, I presume."

"Don't equate our technology with your own, Bryan. At this late stage of our racial life we are very poor engineers—genetic, or otherwise. All we were able to do was utilize the rama females as planting beds for our fertilized ova. It increased our reproductive rate only slightly and was a lame expedient at best. You can see how the arrival of human time-travelers—genetically compatible and virtually immune to the effects of the radiation—would seem providential to us."

"Oh, very. Still, you have to admit that the advantages are mostly one-sided."

"Are you so certain of that? Recall what kind of misfit human beings make the decision to come to Exile. We Tanu have a great deal to offer them. Better things than they ever dreamed possible, if they possess latent metafunctions. And we really ask so little in return."

* * *

Something came jabbing Elizabeth.

Stop that.

Jabjabjab.

Go away.

Jab. Jabjab. Come out help I've screwed it.

Stop small pecking childmind Aiken.

JAB!

Vexing insect swat you Aiken! Bother someone else.

JabscratchPOUND. Dammit Elizabeth she's going to bollix up STEIN.

Slowly, Elizabeth turned in her saddle and stared at the rider next to her. Aiken's mind nattered on as she brought into focus a woman-form in dark flowing robes. Sukey. A tense face with plump cheeks and a button nose. Indigo eyes set too closely together for beauty, glazed with panic.

Elizabeth went into her without invitation and grasped the situation in an instant, leaving Aiken and the late-arriving Creyn to watch from outside in helpless impotence. Sukey was in the grip of

Stein's enraged mind, her sanity almost overwhelmed by the mental power of the wounded man. It was plain what had happened. Sukey was a potentially strong latent redactor and her new silver torc had made the metafunction operant. Egged on by Aiken, she had tested her ability by snooping into Stein, intrigued by the apparent helplessness of the sleeping giant. The young woman had slipped in beneath the low-level neural bath generated by the gray torc, which Creyn had set up to soothe the berserker and block out residual pain from his healing injuries. Under this lid, Sukey had seen the pitiful state of Stein's subconscious mind—the old psychic ulcerations, the newly torn rents in his self-esteem, all gurging about in a maelstrom of suppressed violence.

The tempter had whispered to Sukey, and her innate compassion had responded. She had begun a hopelessly incompetent redact operation on Stein, confident that she could help him; but the brute resident in the pain-filled Viking soul had reared up and attacked her for her meddling. Now both Sukey and Stein were caught in a fearsome conflict of psychoenergies. If the antagonism were not promptly resolved, the outcome could be total personality disjunction for Stein and imbecility for the woman.

Elizabeth sent one blazing thought to Creyn. She dove in and folded the great wings of her own redactability about the frenzied pair. The young womanmind was flung unceremoniously out, to be fielded by Creyn, who let Sukey down easily and then watched with a respect tinged by some other emotion as the mischief was undone.

Elizabeth wove restraints, stopped the psychic whirlpool, calmed the heaving pit of fury. She plucked away the jerry-built mind-alteration structure confected by Sukey, with its naive and impudent drainage channels that were too puny for true catharsis. She bore Stein's damaged ego up with loving force while melting the edges of the wounds and pressing the torn parts back so that healing could begin. Even the older psychic abscesses swelled and burst and vented some of their poison through her. Humiliation and rejection diminished. The father-monster shrank toward pathetic humanity and the mother-lover lost some of her vesture of fantasy. Stein-Awakened looked into Elizabeth's mirror of healing and cried out. He rested.

Elizabeth emerged.

The party of riders had come to a halt, crowding closely around Elizabeth and her mount. She shivered in the sultry evening air. Creyn took his own soft scarlet-and-white cloak and draped it about her shoulders.

"It was magnificent, Elizabeth. None of us—not even Lord Dionket, our greatest—could have done better. They are both safe."

"It still isn't complete," she forced herself to say. "I can't finalize him. His will is very strong and he resists. This took—all I have now."

Creyn touched the circle of gold about his neck. "I can deepen the neural envelope generated by his gray torc. Tonight, when we reach Roniah, we will be able to do more for him. He will recover in a few days."

Stein, who had not once moved during the metapsychic imbroglio, uttered a vast sigh. The two soldiers dismounted and came to adjust his saddle cantle so that it became a high supporting backrest.

"There's no danger of his falling now," Creyn said. "We'll make him more comfortable later. Now we had better ride on."

Bryan demanded, "Will somebody tell me what the hell is going on?" Lacking a torc, he had missed a great deal of the byplay, which had been telepathic.

A stocky man with tow-colored hair and a vaguely Oriental cast to his features pointed a finger at Aiken Drum. "Ask that one. He started it."

Aiken grinned and twiddled his silver torc. Several white moths appeared suddenly out of the darkness and began orbiting Sukey's head in a crazy halo. "Just a little do-goodery gone baddery!"

"Stop that," Creyn commanded. The moths flew away. The tall Tanu addressed Aiken in a tone of veiled menace. "Sukey was the agent, but it is obvious that *you* were the instigator. You amused yourself by placing your friend and this inexperienced woman in mortal danger."

Aiken's golliwog face was unrepentant. "Ah. She seemed strong enough. Nobody forced her to mess with him."

Sukey spoke up. Her voice had a ring of stubborn self-righteousness. "I was only trying to help. He was in desperate need! None of the rest of you seemed to care!"

Creyn said with asperity, "This was not the time or the place to undertake a difficult redaction. Stein would have been treated in good time."

"Let me get this straight," said Bryan. "She tried to alter his mind?"

"She tried to heal him," Elizabeth said. "I suppose Aiken urged her to try out her new metabilities, just as he's been testing his own. But she couldn't handle it."

"Stop talking about me as though I were a child!" Sukey exclaimed. "So I bit off more than I could chew. But I meant well!"

There was a harsh laugh from the towhead, whose silver torc was nearly concealed by a plaid flannel shirt. He wore heavy twill trousers and woodsman's boots with lug soles. "You meant well! Some day that'll be humanity's epitaph! Even that damned Madame Guderian meant well when she let people pass into this hell-world."

Creyn said, "It will be hell for you only if you make it so, Raimo. Now we must ride on. Elizabeth—if you feel able, would you help Sukey to understand something of her new power? At least advise her of the limitations she must accept for now."

"I suppose I had better."

Aiken rode close to scowling Sukey and patted her shoulder in a brotherly fashion. "There now, sweets. The past mistress of mind-bendery will give you a flash course, and then you can work on *me!* I guarantee not to gobble you alive. We'll have lots of fun while you straighten out the kinks in my poor little evil soul!"

Elizabeth's mind reached out and gave Aiken a tweak that made him squawk out loud. "Enough of you, my lad. Go practice working your will on bats or hedgehogs or something."

"I'll give you bats," Aiken promised darkly. He urged his mount forward along the wide track, and the cavalcade began to move once more.

Elizabeth opened to Sukey, gentling the woman's fear and discomfiture.

I would like to help you. Little mindsister. Be at ease. Yes?

(Bloody-minded stubborn chagrin breaking down slowly.) Oh why not. I did make a terriblehash of it.

All over now. Relax. Let me know you . . .

Sue-Gwen Davies, aged twenty-seven, born and raised on the last of the Old World orbital colonies. A former juvenile officer full of sturdy empathy and maternal concern for her wretched young clients. The adolescents of the satellite had mounted an insurrection, rebelling against the unnatural life chosen for them by technocratic idealist grandparents, and the Milieu had belatedly ruled that the colony must be disbanded. Sukey Davies had rejoiced even as her job became redundant. She had no loyalty to the satellite, no philosophical commitment to the experiment that had become obsolete at the very moment that the Great Intervention commenced. All of Sukey's working hours had been spent trying to cope with children

who stubbornly resisted the conditioning necessary for life in an orbiting beehive.

When the satellite colony was terminated, Sukey came down to
Earth—that world seen below for so many aching years. Paradise and
peace existed down there. She was sure of it! Earth was Eden. But
the real promised land was not to be found on Earth's manicured,
busy continents.

It was inside the planet.

Elizabeth came up short. Sukey's mind was moderately intelligent,
strong-willed, kindly, latent in high redactability and moderate farsense. But Sukey Davies was also firmly convinced that the planet
Earth was hollow! Old-fashioned microfiche books smuggled onto
the satellite by bored eccentrics and cultists had introduced her to
the ideas of Bender and Giannini and Palmer and Bernard and
Souza. Sukey had been enthralled by the notion of a hollow Earth
lit by a small central sun, a land of tranquillity and invincible
goodness, peopled by dwarfish gentlefolk possessing all wisdom and
delight. Had not the ancients told tales of subterranean Asar,
Avalon, the Elysian Fields, Ratmansu, and Ultima Thule? Even
Buddhist Agharta was supposed to be connected by tunnels to the
lamaseries of Tibet. These dreams seemed not at all outré to Sukey,
the inhabitant of the inside surface of a twenty-kilometer-long spinning cylinder in space. It was logical that Earth be hollow, too.

So Sukey came down to the Old World, where people smiled as
she explained what she was looking for. Quite a few helped relieve
her of her severance pay as she pursued her quest. There were not,
she discovered from expensive personal inspection, mirage-shielded
polar apertures leading to the planetary interior, as claimed by some
of the old writers; nor was she able to gain entrance to the under-
world via the purported caves in Xizang. Finally she had gone to
Brazil, where one author said there was a tunnel to Agharta located
in the remote Serra do Roncador. An old Murcego Indian, sensing
an additional gratuity, told her that the tunnel had indeed once
existed; but unfortunately it had been closed by an earthquake
"many thousands" of years in the past.

Sukey had pondered this pronouncement for three tearful weeks
before concluding that she would surely be able to find the way into
the hollow Earth by traveling back into time. She had dressed herself in robes reflecting her Welsh heritage and come eagerly to the
Pliocene, where—

Creyn says *his* people founded the paradise!

Oh Sukey.

Yesyes! And I powerfulhealer can belong! Creyn's promise!

Calm. You can become metapractitioner of stature. But not instantly. Much much to learn dear. Trustlistenfollow *then* act.

Want/need to. Poor Stein! Other poorones I can help. Feeling them all around us do you feel too? . . .

Elizabeth withdrew from the fidgeting immaturity of Sukey's mind and cast about. There *was* something. Something completely alien to her experience that had only glimmered on the fringes of her perception earlier in the evening. What was it? The enigma would not resolve itself into a mental image she could identify. Not yet. And so Elizabeth put the problem aside and returned to the task of instructing Sukey. The job was a difficult one that would keep her busy for quite some time, for which thanks be to God.

8

BOUND FOR the River Rhône, the party rode for three more hours into the deepening night and coolness, coming down from the plateau via a steep trail with precarious switchbacks into a forest so thick that the bright light of the stars was blocked out. The two soldiers ignited tall flambeaux; one man rode in the van and the other at the rear. They continued their eastward progress while eerie shadows seemed to follow them among the massive gnarled trees.

"Spooky, isn't it?" Aiken inquired of Raimo, who was now riding beside him. "Can't you just imagine these big old cork oaks and chestnuts reaching out to grab you?"

"You talk like an idiot," the other man growled. "I worked in deep forests for twenty years in the B.C. Megapod Reserve. Ain't nothing spooky about trees."

Aiken was unabashed. "So that's why the lumberjack outfit. But if you know trees, you must know that botanists credit them with a primitive self-awareness. Don't you think that the older the plant, the more attuned to the Milieu it must be? Just look at these trees along here. Don't tell me they had hardwoods eight-ten meters across on the Earth we knew! Why, these babies must be thousands of years older than any tree on Old Earth. Just reach out to 'em! Use that silver torc of yours for something besides an Adam's apple warmer. Ancient trees . . . evil trees! Can't you feel the bad vibes in this forest? They could resent our coming here. They might sense that in a few million years, humans like us'll destroy 'em! Maybe the trees hate us!"

"I think," said Raimo with slow malevolence, "that you're trying to make a fool outa me like you did with Sukey. Don't!"

Aiken felt himself hoisted up from his saddle. His chained ankles caught him like a victim on a rack. Higher and higher he rose, until he was suspended dangerously close to the branches overhanging the trail.

"Hey! It was only a joke and that *hurts!*"

Raimo began to chuckle and increased the tension still more.

Squeeze. Pummel the glacial mind-grip of the Finno-Canadian and make him let go, let go, let go!

With a crash that made the startled chaliko squeal, Aiken plummeted back into his saddle. Creyn turned around and said, "You have a penchant for cruelty that will have to be curbed, Raimo Hakkinen."

"I wonder if all your kind would think so?" inquired the former woodsman in an insolent tone. "Anyhow, you can make this little shit stop bugging me. Tree-spooks!"

Aiken protested, "A lot of old-time cultures believed that trees had special powers. Didn't they, Bryan?"

The anthropologist was amused. "Oh, yes. Tree cults were almost universal in the ancient world of the future. The Druids had an entire alphabet for divination based on trees and shrubs. It was apparently a relic of a more widespread tree-centered religion that derived from utmost antiquity. Scandinavians revered a mighty ash-tree named Yggdrasil. Greeks dedicated the ash to the sea-god Poseidon. Birches were sacred among the Romans. The rowan was a Celtic and Greek symbol of power over death. The hawthorn was associated with sex orgies and the month of May—and so was the apple. Oak trees were cult objects all over preliterate Europe. For some reason, oaks are especially vulnerable to lightning, so the ancients connected the tree with the thunder-god. Greeks, Romans, Gaulish Celts, the British, Teutons, Lithuanians, Slavs—they all held the oak to be sacred. The folklore of almost all European countries featured supernatural beings that dwelt in special trees or haunted the deep woods. The Macedonians had dryads and the Styrians had vilyas and the Germans had seligen Fräulein and the French had their dames vertes. All woodland sprites. Scandinavian people believed in them, too, but I've forgotten the name they gave them—"

"Skogsnufvar," said Raimo unexpectedly. "My grandfather told me. He was from the Åland Islands, where the people spoke Swedish. Full of dumb fairytales."

"Nothing like ethnic pride!" chortled Aiken. And that brought on another row, as the forester lashed out again with his enhanced PK function and Aiken fought back with his coercive power, trying to make Raimo ram his own forefinger down his throat.

At last Creyn cried, "Omnipotent Tana, enough!" Both men groaned, clutched at their silver torcs, and subsided like a pair of whipped schoolboys, silent but unrepentant.

Raimo pulled a large silver flask from his pack and began nursing from it. Aiken curled his lip. The forester said, "Hudson's Bay Company Demerara, one-fifty-one proof. Grownups only. Eat your heart out."

Elizabeth's cool voice requested, "Tell us about the Skogsnufvar, Bryan. Such an awful name. Were they beautiful?"

"Oh, yes. Long flowing hair, seductive bodies—and tails! They were your standard archetypal anima-female menace, luring men into the deep woods in order to sleep with them. And ever after, the poor chaps were completely in the power of the elf-women. A man who tried to leave would sicken and die, or else go mad. Victims of the Skogsnufvar were written about well into the twentieth century in Sweden."

Sukey said, "Welsh folklore had such creatures, too. But they lived in lakes, not forests. They were called the Gwragedd Annwn and they came up to dance on the water in the misty moonlight and lured travelers into their underwater palaces."

"It's a common folkloric theme," Bryan said. "The symbolism is easily grasped. Still—one has to feel a bit sorry for the poor male elves. They seem to have missed out on a lot of good dirty fun."

Most of the humans laughed, including the guards.

"Are there any parallel legends among your people, Creyn?" the anthropologist asked. "Or didn't your culture produce tales of enchantment?"

"There was no need," the Tanu replied in a repressive tone.

An odd notion occurred to Elizabeth. She attempted to slide a microprobe through Creyn's screen without triggering his awareness.

Ah Elizabeth don't. These petty aggressions games idle scrabblings for superiority.

(Innocent incredulity scorncolored taunt.)

Nonsense. I am oldtired civilized of goodwill to you and yours even ultimately crushable. But others mykind not. Beware Elizabeth. Reject not Tanu lightly. Remember puffin.

Puffin?

Childpoem your folk from humaneducator among us long deceased. Lonelybird only one of kind ate fishes bewailed solitude. Friendship proffered by fishes if bird refrained devouring. Deal accepted mealhabits changed. Fishes only game in town for puffin.

As you Tanu are for me?

Affirm Elizapuffinbeth.

She burst out laughing and Bryan and the other humans looked at her in blank astonishment.

"Somebody," Aiken remarked, "has been whispering behind our minds. Are you going to let us in on the joke, lovie?"

"The joke's on me, Aiken." Elizabeth turned to Creyn. "We'll have a truce. For now."

The exotic man inclined his head. "Then permit me to change the subject. We are approaching the bottomlands of the river, where we'll have our night's rest in the city of Roniah. Tomorrow we shall resume our journey in a more agreeable fashion—by boat. We should arrive in the capital city of Muriah in less than five days, if the winds are right."

"Sailboats on a turbulent river like the Rhône?" Bryan said, aghast. "Or—is it calmer here in the Pliocene?"

"You'll have to judge that for yourself, of course. However, our boats are quite different from those you may have been accustomed to. We Tanu are not fond of water travel. But with the coming of humanity, safe and efficient boats were designed and river commerce became extensive. We now use boats not only for passenger travel but also to ship vital commodities from the north—especially from Finiah and from Goriah in the area you call Brittany—to the southern regions where the climate is more to our taste."

"I've brought a sailboat with me," the anthropologist said. "Will I be permitted to use it? I'd like to visit your Finiah and Goriah."

"As you'll see, upstream travel is generally not feasible. We rely on caravans for that, using either chalikos or larger beasts of burden called hellads—a species of short-necked giraffe. In the course of your researches you will doubtless make visits to several of our population centers."

"Without a torc on him?" Raimo interjected. "You'd trust him?"

Creyn laughed. "We have something he wants."

Bryan flinched; but he knew better than to rise to the bait. He only said, "These vital commodities you ship. I suppose they include mostly foodstuffs?"

"To some extent. But this Many-Colored Land is literally overflowing with meat and drink for the taking."

"Minerals then. Gold and silver. Copper and tin. Iron."

"Not iron. It is unnecessary in our rather simple technoeconomy. The Tanu worlds have traditionally relied on varieties of unbreakable glass in those applications where humanity utilized iron. It is interesting that in recent years you, too, have come to appreciate this versatile material."

"Vitredur, yes. Still, your fighting men seem to prefer the traditional bronze in their armor and weapons."

Creyn laughed quietly. "In the earliest days of the time-portal it was considered wise to restrict human warriors in that way. Now, when the restriction has become obsolete, humans continue to cling to the metal. We permit a bronze technology to flourish among your people where it does not conflict with our own needs. We Tanu are a tolerant race. We were self-sufficient before humans began to arrive and we are by no means dependent upon humanity for slave labor—"

Elizabeth's thought loomed large: OTHER THAN REPRODUCTIVE ENSLAVEMENT.

"—since the tedious and difficult work such as mining and agriculture and comfort maintenance is undertaken by ramas in all but the most isolated settlements."

"These ramas," Aiken broke in. "How come there weren't any back at the castle to do the dirty work?"

"They have a certain psychic fragility and require a tranquil environment if they are to function with minimal supervision. At Castle Gateway there is inevitable stress—"

Raimo gave a derisive grunt.

Bryan asked, "How are the creatures controlled?"

"They wear a much simplified modification of the gray torc. But you must not press me to explain these matters now. Please wait until later, in Muriah."

They rode into an area where the trees were not so thickly clustered, among giant crags at the base of a sparsely forested ridge. Up where the crest met the starry sky was a glow of colored light.

"Is that the town up there?" Sukey inquired.

"Can't be," Raimo said contemptuously. "Look at the thing move!"

They reined in their chalikos and watched the glow resolve into a thin skein of luminescence that twisted in and out of the distant silhouettes of the trees at considerable speed. The light was a blend of many hues, basically golden but with knots that flared blue, green, red, and even purple in a panoply of sparkling commotion, wild and urgent.

"Ah!" Creyn said. "The Hunt. If they come this way you'll see a fine sight."

"It looks like a giant rainbow glowworm racing up there," Sukey breathed. "How lovely!"

"The Tanu at play?" Bryan asked.

Sukey uttered a disappointed cry. "Oh—they've gone over the ridge. What a shame! Tell us what the Hunt is, Lord Creyn."

The exotic man's face was grave in the starlight. "One of the great traditions of our people. You'll see it again, many times. I'll let you discover for yourselves what it is."

"And if we're good," Aiken put in impudently, "do we get to join in?"

"Possibly," Creyn replied. "It is not to every human's taste—nor even to every Tanu's. But you . . . yes, I think perhaps the Hunt would appeal to your particular sporting instinct, Aiken Drum."

And for an instant, the healer's emotional tone was plain for Elizabeth to read: disgust, mingled with an age-old sense of despair.

9

RICHARD saw flames.

They were moving toward him or he was moving toward them and they were vivid orange and resin-smoky, rising tall into a wavering queue in the nearly windless dark.

He saw that it was a pile of burning brush the size of a small hut, crackling and hissing but throwing no sparks, seeming to draw abreast of him, pass him by and recede, disappearing at last behind a grove of black trees that had crept up unseen in the night but now stood backlighted by the bonfire's glow.

It hurt his neck to look back. He let his head loll forward. There was something bulky just in front of him that had long hair and moved rhythmically. It was very strange! He himself was rocking, firmly supported in some kind of seat that held him upright. His legs were thrust forward at an angle, the calves resting on unseen supports, feet braced against wide treads. His arms, clad in the familiar sleeves of a master spacer's coverall, rested in his lap.

A funny kind of starship, he mused, with a hairy control console. And the environmental must be on the fritz because the temperature was nearly thirty and there was dust in the air and a peculiar smell.

Trees? And a bonfire? He looked around and saw stars—not the proper colored stars you see in deep space, but little twinkling specks. Far away, in the black below the starry bowl, was another small exclamation point of fire.

"Richard? Are you awake? Would you like some water?"

Well! Would you look at who was flying the righthand seat of this crate? None other than the old bone hunter! Would have thought he was too creako to qualify. But then you don't need much finesse to fly on the ground . . .

"Richard, if I pass you the canteen, can you hold on to it?"

Smells of animals, pungent vegetation, leather. Sounds of creaking harness, brisk clumping feet, huffing exhalations, something yip-ping in the distance, and the voice of the persistent old man beside him.

"Don't want water," said Richard.

"Amerie said you'd need it when you woke up. You're dehydrated. Come on, son."

He took a closer look at Claude there in the darkness. The old man's figure was illuminated by starlight; he was astride a huge horselike creature that was loping easily along. Damnedest thing! *He* was riding one, too! There were the reins draped over the pommel of a saddle right in front of him below the hairy control console —neck—of the critter. And it was trotting straight and level without any guidance at all.

Richard tried to pull his feet up and discovered that his ankles were fastened somehow to the stirrups. And he wasn't wearing his seaboots, and someone had exchanged his opera costume for the spacer's coverall with the four stripes on the sleeves that he had stuffed into the bottom of his pack, and he had an imperial grand champion hangover.

"Claude," he groaned. "You got any booze?"

"You can't have any, boy. Not until the drug Amerie shot into you wears off. Here. Take the water."

Richard had to lean far out to grasp the canteen and the starry sky lurched. If his ankles had not been fastened, he would have fallen from the saddle.

"Jesus, I been chewed up and spit out, Claude. Where the hell are we? And what's this thing I'm riding?"

"We're about four hours out from the castle, riding due north and parallel to the Saône River. As near as I can judge, you're riding a nice large specimen of Chalicotherium goldfussi, which the locals call a chaliko, not a calico. The beasts travel a pretty fair clip here on the plateau, maybe fifteen or sixteen kloms an hour. But we lost time fording creeks around a little swamp, so I guess we might be thirty kloms above Lyon. If there was a Lyon."

Richard cursed. "Bound where, for God's sake?"

"Some Pliocene metropolis called Finiah. From what they told us, it's on the Proto-Rhine about in the position of Freiburg. We get there in six days."

Richard drank some of the water and discovered he was very thirsty. He could remember nothing beyond the welcoming smile on Epone's face as he followed her into the dazzling inner chamber of the castle. He tried to marshal his wits, but all he could rake up were tattered dreams in which his brother and sister seemed to urge him to get up or he'd be late for school. And the penalty for that would be cruising the gray limbo forever and ever, searching for a lost planet where Epone would be waiting.

After a while, he asked, "What happened to me?"

"We aren't sure," Claude temporized. "You know, don't you, that there were exotics in the castle?"

"I remember a tall woman," Richard muttered. "I think she did something to me."

"Whatever it was, you were out for hours. Amerie got you semiconscious so that you'd be able to move out with the rest of us in the caravan. We thought you'd prefer that to being left behind alone."

"Christ, yes." Richard took slow swallows of water, leaned back, and watched the sky for a long time. There were a hell of a lot of stars, and pearly streaks of luminescent cloud toward the zenith. As the caravan began descending a long downhill slope, he could see that he and the old man were near the tail end of a long double file of riders. Now that his eyes worked properly again, he discerned other dark shapes coursing along both sides of the column with awkward humping strides.

"What the devil are those things out there?"

"Amphicyons riding herd on us. We have a guard of five soldiers, too, but they hardly ever bother to check up. There are two bringing up the rear and three in front with the Exalted Lady."

"The *who?*"

"Epone herself. She comes from Finiah. These exotics—they're called Tanu, by the way—seem to have widely scattered settlements, each with a central urban area and satellite supporting plantations. My guess is that humans function as slaves or serfs, with some exceptional types enjoying special privileges. Evidently the Tanu cities take turns collecting a week's worth of time-travelers at Castle Gateway, minus the specials who get siphoned off to the capital and the unlucky ones who are killed trying to escape."

"We *aren't* special, I take it."

"Just part of the grunt-pack. Amerie and Felice are in the caravan, too. But the four other Greenies were sifted out and sent south to the big time. Group Green seems to have been unusual in having so many taken. There were only two other people sent to the capital from the rest of the week's contingent."

As they rode along, the old man told Richard as much as he could about the day's events and the presumed fate of Aiken, Elizabeth,

Bryan, and Stein. He also summarized Waldemar's little speech and reluctantly told of the future in store for the women of the party.

The ex-spacer ventured a few questions, then fell silent. Too bad about the nun going to an exotic harem. She'd been decent to him. On the other hand, that stuck-up Ice Queen of an Elizabeth needed a good stoking. And Felice, that sly little bitch—! Richard had offered her a harmless little suggestion back at the auberge and she'd sent him up like a holiday firework. Damn teasing little snatch! He hoped the exotics had peckers like baseball bats. It would serve her right. Might even make a real woman out of her.

The caravan moved steadily down the incline, heading a little east of north now and coming closer to the river. The beacon fire was their landmark. Claude had told him that similar fires were spaced about two kloms apart all the way from the castle. A scouting party must be riding in advance of the caravan along the track, torching the waiting piles of brush if all was well.

"I think I see a building down there," Claude said. "Maybe it's the place where we stop for a break."

Richard sure as hell hoped so. He had drunk too much water.

From the head of the column came the silvery notes of a horn sounding a three-toned call. This was echoed distantly. After a few minutes had passed, a dozen or so tiny pinpricks of fire emerged from the vicinity of the downslope bonfire and approached the caravan in a sinuous line: riders carrying torches, coming to escort them.

By the time that the groups converged, Claude and Richard could see that the last beacon fire burned outside of a walled enclosure resembling an ancient American plains fort. It stood on a bluff above a tree-crowded watercourse that must drain into the Saône. The caravan halted momentarily, and Lady Epone and Waldemar went forward to greet the escort party. In the torchlight, Richard unconcernedly admired the stately Tanu woman, who was riding a white chalicothere of exceptional size and wearing a dark-blue hooded cloak that floated behind her.

After a moment's conference, two of the soldiers from the fort rode off to one side and in some manner called in the pack of amphicyons. The bear-dogs were led away on a side path while the rest of the escort fell in beside the caravan for the last part of the journey. A gate in the palisade opened and they rode inside, two by two. Then, in what was to become a familiar procedure, the prisoners had their mounts tethered to posts in front of double troughs of feed and water. At the left of each chaliko was a dismounting block. After the soldiers unlocked their chains, the muscle-sore travelers descended and gathered in an untidy group while Waldemar addressed them once again.

"All you travelers! We'll rest here for one hour, then go on until early morning, another eight hours." Everybody groaned. "Latrines in the small building behind you, get your food and drink in the bigger building next door. Anybody sick or gotta complaint, see me. Be ready to remount when you hear the horn. Nobody comes into the area beyond the hitching rail. That's *all*."

Epone, who was still on chalikoback, guided her beast delicately through the throng until she loomed over Richard.

"I'm glad to see you're recovering."

He gave her a quizzical look. "I'm just dandy. And it's nice to know you're a lady who cares about the health of her livestock."

She threw her head back and laughed, cascades of sound like the deep strumming of a harp. Her partially hidden hair gleamed in the torchlight. "It really *is* too bad about you," she said. "You've certainly got more spirit than that silly medievalist."

She turned her animal away, rode to the opposite side of the compound, and was helped out of the saddle by obsequious men in white tunics.

"What was that all about?" inquired Amerie, who had come up with Felice.

Richard glowered. "How the fuck should I know?" He went tottering off toward the latrine.

Felice watched him go. "Are all your patients this grateful?"

The nun laughed. "He's coming along just fine. You know they're on the mend when they bite your head off."

"He's nothing but a stupid weakling."

"I think you're wrong about that," Amerie said. But Felice only snorted and went off to the mess hall. Later, when the two women and Claude were eating cheese and cold meat and maize bread, Richard came and apologized.

"Think nothing of it," the nun said. "Sit down with us. We've got something to talk over with you."

Richard's eyes narrowed. "Yeah?"

Claude said softly, "Felice has a plan for escape. But there are problems."

"No shit?" the pirate guffawed.

The little ring-hockey player took Richard's hand and squeezed. His eyes bulged and he pressed his lips together. "Less noise," Felice said. "The problem isn't in the escape itself, but in the aftermath. They've taken our maps and compasses. Claude has a general knowledge of this part of Europe from his paleontology studies more than a hundred years ago, but that won't help us if we can't orient ourselves while we're on the run. Can you help us? Did you study the large-scale map of Pliocene France when we were back at the auberge?"

She dropped his hand and Richard stared at the whitened flesh, then threw her a glance of pure venom. "Hell, no. I figured there'd be plenty of time for that once we arrived. I brought a self-compensating compass, a computer sextant, all the charts I'd need. But I suppose all the stuff was confiscated. The only route I looked at was the one west to the Atlantic—to Bordeaux."

Felice grunted in disgust. Claude persisted in a peaceable tone, "We know you must be experienced in navigation, son. There's got to be some way we can orient ourselves. Can you locate the Pliocene polestar for us? That would be a big help."

"So would a frigate of the Fleet Air Arm," Richard grumbled. "Or Robin Hood and his merry men."

Felice reached out for him again and he dodged back hastily. "Can you do it, Richard?" she asked. "Or are those stripes on your sleeves for good conduct?"

"This isn't my home planet, dykey-doll! And the noctilucent clouds don't make the job any easier."

"A lot of vulcanism," Claude said. "Dust in the upper atmosphere. But the moon has set and there aren't any ordinary clouds. Do you think you'd be able to get a fix as the glowing patches come and go?"

"I might," Richard muttered. "But why the hell I should bother beats me . . . What I want to know is, what happened to my pirate outfit? Who put this coverall on me?"

"It was there," Felice said sweetly, "and you needed it. Badly. So we obliged. Anything to help out a friend."

Claude hurried to say, "You got all messed up in some fight you were in back at the castle. I just cleaned you up a bit and washed your other clothes. They're hanging on the back of your saddle. Should be dry by now."

Richard looked suspiciously at the smirking Felice, then thanked the old man. But a fight? Had he been in a fight? And who had been laughing at him with lofty contempt? A woman with drowning-pool eyes. But not Felice . . .

Amerie said, "Please try for the polestar if you feel well enough to manage it. We only have one more night of travel on this high north road. Then we'll be angling off every which way and traveling in the daytime. Richard, it's important."

"Okay, okay," he grouched. "I don't suppose any of you Earthworms knows the latitude of Lyon."

"About forty-five north, I think," said Claude. "Around the same as my boyhood home in Oregon, anyhow, from the way I remember the sky over the auberge. Too bad we don't have Stein. He'd know."

"A rough guess is good enough," Richard said.

The nun lifted her head. The sound of a horn came from outside in the fort's yard. "Well, here we go again, Group. Good luck, Richard."

"Megathanks, Sister. If we follow any escape plan *this* kid dreams up, we're gonna need it."

* * *

They rode on through the night, traveling from beacon to beacon along the plateau trail with the river valley at their right and the scattered small volcanoes of the Limagne giving an occasional ruby pulse in the southwest. Constellations totally unfamiliar to the Earth natives of the twenty-second century crowded the sky of Exile. Many of those stars were the same ones that would be visible in the planet's future; but their differing galactic orbits had twisted the familiar star patterns all out of recognition. There were stars in the Pliocene sky that were destined to die before the time of the Galactic Milieu; others that Milieu people would know were at this time still dark in their dustcloud wombs.

Richard viewed the Pliocene heavens with nonchalance. He'd seen an awful lot of different skies. Given plenty of time and a fixed base for observation, finding the local Polaris would be a snap, even with eyeball instrumentation alone. It was only the fact that they were moving on animal-back, and the need for a quick fix, that made the thing a bit tricky.

Now. *If* the old fossil-flicker was right about the rough latitude, and *if* they were on a near-northerly course on this trail as Claude thought they'd have to be, given the lay of the land, *then* the polestar should be about halfway between the horizon and the zenith somewhere in . . . there.

He had picked up a couple of stiff twigs from the litter back at the fort and now bound them together into a cross-sight with a hair from his mount's mane. Each stalk was twice as long as his hand. He hoped the field wouldn't be too limited.

Adjusting his position in the saddle to minimize the effect of the chaliko's rocking gait, he memorized the constellations that had to be roughly circumpolar. Then he held the cross-sight at arm's length and aligned the vertical axis with the straight track ahead (analog: two upright chaliko ears) and centered it on a likely star he had tentatively selected. He carefully noted the positions of five other bright stars within the quadrants of his sight and then relaxed. Three hours from now, when planetary rotation had made those six stars seem to change position slightly, he'd take another sighting. His near-photographic memory would do an angular comparison within the field of the cross-sight, and with luck he would be able to discern the imaginary hub in the sky about which all those stars were turning. The hub would be the pole. It might or might not have a star on it or near it that could be dubbed Pliocene Polaris.

He would center the cross-sight anew on this point in the sky and try to verify the pole's position before dawn with a two-hour shot. Failing that, he would check it tomorrow night with a good long time interval for maximum rotation.

Richard set his wrist chronometer's alarm for 0330, glad that he hadn't followed the impulse to throw the thing away back in Madame Guderian's rose garden on that rainy morning when he had abandoned his universe . . .

Less than twenty hours ago.

10

EVEN THOUGH he had been partially briefed by Creyn on what to expect, Bryan found the reality of the riverside city of Roniah nearly overwhelming. The party of riders came suddenly upon the place after wending their way through a dark canyon where the guards' torches barely illuminated a narrow trail cut in buff sandstone. The caravan emerged onto a knoll overlooking the confluence of the Saône and the Rhône and saw the town below on the west bank, just south of the snout of forested crags where the two great rivers joined.

Roniah was built on a rise adjacent to the water. Twisting around the hill's base was an earthen rampart crowned by a thick fortified wall. All along the top of this, glittering like lavish strings of orange beads, were closely spaced little fires. High, square watchtowers jutted out from the wall every hundred meters or so, and these, too, were outlined in pricks of fire all along their crenellated battlements, around the windows, and even up and down the corners and angles of the walls. A massive city gate had almost every detail of its architecture picked out in small lamps. Leading to the gate was a colonnaded avenue half a kilometer long, every column of which was capped with a huge flaming torch. The midway was flanked with spangled geometrical patterns that might have been lamp-bordered lawns or flowerbeds planted in parterre designs.

From the caravan's vantage point above the town, Bryan could see that Roniah was uncrowded, its mostly small houses laid out along wide curving streets. Since it was well past midnight, most of the dwellings showed no window lights; but along the edges of the roofs were little dots of fire; and the parapets that fronted the houses were also illuminated by thousands of the evenly spaced lamps. Closer to the riverside were a number of larger structures bearing slender towers of varying heights. The walls and major features of these buildings were outlined in light as elaborately as the city gate was— but instead of oil-lamp orange, the façades glowed with blue, bright green, aquamarine, and amber. Many of the towers had their windows ablaze.

"It's like fairyland," breathed Sukey. "All those little sparkling lights!"

"Each inhabitant is obligated to contribute to urban illumination by maintaining the lamps of his own house," Creyn said. "The common fuel is olive oil, which is extremely plentiful. The taller Tanu dwellings are lit by more sophisticated lamps energized by accumulations of surplus metapsychic emanations."

They rode down, following the track until it merged with a road paved in granite setts that widened to nearly eighty meters as it approached the avenue of fire-topped columns. Between the great pillars stood neat frameworks of bamboo arranged in aisles, separated by dark shrubbery and clusters of palm trees. Creyn explained that booths for a market were set up in this exterior garden every month, featuring the goods of local artisans as well as luxury products of all kinds brought in by caravans. Once a year there was also a Great Fair, which attracted people from all over western Europe.

"You have no daily market for foods, then?" Bryan asked.

"Meat is the great diet staple," Creyn replied. "Professional hunters, all human, bring in large quantities of game to the plantations in the more northerly reaches of both the Saône and Rhône. It is sent downstream daily to the town provisioners on barges, together with grain, fruit, and other produce from the farms, such as olive oil and wine. Most of the food processing is done at the plantations by rama workers. In years gone by, our own people supervised the plantations. Now almost all of them are overseen by humans."

"And you see no potential hazard in such an arrangement?" Bryan asked.

Creyn smiled, the flickering lights striking sparks from his deep-set eyes. "No hazard at all. The humans engaged in critical occupations all wear the torc. But try to understand that coercion is seldom necessary. For all but the most deeply disturbed of your people, the world of Exile is a happy one."

"Even for the women?" Elizabeth inquired.

The unperturbed Tanu said, "Even the lowliest nonmeta women of the commonalty are completely free from drudgery. They may engage in the occupations of their choice or live in indolence. They may even pleasure themselves as they will with human lovers. The only restriction is that their children must be by us. The more fortunate humans possessing genetic codons for metafunction enjoy a privileged position. They are welcomed into our society as probationary equals. In the fullness of time, those who have proved their loyalty to the Tanu may exchange their silver torcs for gold."

"Both men and women?" Aiken asked, his lips twitching.

"Both men and women. I'm sure you can appreciate our reproductive strategy. We not only strengthen our line against the effects of the local radiation but also incorporate your genes for latent and operant metability. Ultimately, we may hope to evolve fully operant metapsychics"—he nodded at Elizabeth—"even as you will have done six million years from now. We will then be freed from the limitation of the golden torcs."

Elizabeth said, "Quite a grand design. How do you reconcile it with the reality of this planet's future . . . with no Tanu?"

Creyn smiled. "The Goddess wreaks as she wills. Six million years is a long time. I think we Tanu will be grateful to settle for a small portion of it to call our own."

They approached closer to the great gate, which was twelve or thirteen meters wide and almost twice as high, fashioned of titanic balks of timber heavily reinforced with bronze plates.

"Not much action outside here at night, is there?" Aiken commented.

"There are wild animals and other dangers," Creyn said. "The night is not a time for humans to be abroad unless they are going about the business of the Tanu."

"Interesting," Bryan said. "These city walls and the rampart must be effective against almost any kind of night prowlers. They're certainly overelaborate as a protection from animal menaces. Or even aggression from outlaw humans—and I understand there are some here and there."

"Oh, yes," Creyn admitted, with a dismissing wave of his hand. "Little more than a minor nuisance."

"Then what purpose do the fortifications really serve?"

"There are always," Creyn said, "the Firvulag."

They came to a halt immediately in front of the gate. Above its arch was the same golden mask emblem that had adorned the entrance to Castle Gateway. Captal Zdenek, accompanied by one torch-bearing soldier, rode to a shadowed niche and detached a stout chain that dangled from the soffit of the overhanging archway. The chain had a ball of metal-caged stone on the end that measured a good half-meter in diameter. Zdenek rode out a short distance holding the ball and then turned, took aim, and let it swing back toward the gate in a pendulum arc. It struck a blackened bronze lens set into the timbered valve and there was a deep-throated *boom,* as from a huge Old World church bell. Even as the soldier caught the returning ball and put it back into its niche, the ponderous gate began to swing open.

Creyn rode forward alone, rising above the saddle to his full height so that his scarlet and white robes streamed back in the breeze rushing from the widening aperture. He cried out three words in an exotic tongue, simultaneously transmitting a complex mental image that the torc-wearing humans and Elizabeth were unable to decipher.

Two squads of human soldiers with crested helmets stood at attention on either side of the open entrance. The engraved plates and scales of their ceremonial bronze armor gleamed like gold in the light of countless flaming lamps. Beyond the gate, lining the otherwise deserted street for almost an entire block on both sides, were the ramas. Each small ape wore a metal collar and a blue and gold tabard. Each held a wand of some glassy material tipped with a blue or an amber light.

Creyn and his retinue passed between the ranks of ramapithecines, and the little animals turned and pattered alongside the chalikos, escorting the riders through the streets of the sleeping town. At one plaza, where the waters of a large fountain splashed onto floating lanterns, Captal Zdenek saluted Creyn and rode off toward a dim barracks with the soldiers Billy and Seung Kyu, their night's work at an end. The timefarers gaped at the houses, dark except for the myriad twinkling oil lamps along every roof gutter, garden wall, and balustrade. Exile architecture in the human quarter was a mélange of mortared stonework, half-timbering, and quasi-biblical mudplaster, with thick walls for coolness, tiled roofs, vine-hung loggias deep in shadow, and small patios planted with palms, laurels, and aromatic cinnamon trees.

"Munchkin Tudor," Bryan decided. Humanity had retained its sense of humor in spite of the six-million-year banishment.

They saw no people at all; but here and there other child-sized ramas, wearing tabards of differing colors, went about mysterious errands, pushing little covered carts. Once, in an oddly reassuring incident, an unmistakable Siamese cat streaked across the main avenue and disappeared into the open window of a house.

The chaliko riders neared a complex of larger buildings close to the river. These were constructed of a material resembling white marble and set off from the rest of the town by an ornamental wall breached at intervals by wide stairways. The parapet at the top was decorated with planter-urns spilling flowers. In place of the homely town lamps of ceramic or metal fretwork, torchères like great silver candlesticks lit the precincts of the Tanu. The dwellings were hung with chains of faceted glass lanterns, their blue and green and amber making an eerie contrast to the friendly warmth of the oil lamps on the streets of the outer town. There were a few familiar touches: waterlilies in tiled pools, climbing yellow roses supported on delicate trellises of marble filigree, a nightingale, wakened by the sound of their passage, that uttered a few sleepy notes.

They passed into a courtyard hemmed by ornate frosty buildings. Here a large door was suddenly flung open and golden radiance streamed forth, catching them by surprise. As the ramas stood solemnly by, human servitors came rushing out to take the bridles of the chalikos, unlock the ankle chains of the prisoners, and help them to dismount.

Then came the Tanu—twenty or thirty of them, laughing and calling out greetings to Creyn in the exotic tongue and chattering in animated exuberance over the time-travelers in musical Standard English. The Tanu wore thin flowing gowns and robes of vivid tropical colors, together with fantastic jewelry—wide yoke-collars all gemmed and enameled, with brocaded and jeweled ribbons dangling front and rear. The women had wired headdresses all hung with gemstones. Here and there among the lofty exotics were a few smaller human figures, just as gaudily dressed, but wearing silver torcs instead of the Tanu gold. Bryan studied these privileged humans with interest. They seemed to be socially integrated with the taller ruling race and just as anxious to make the acquaintance of the overawed prisoners.

Among the arrivals, only Aiken was completely at ease. With his pocketed suit flashing like liquid metal, he fairly hopped about the courtyard, making mocking obeisance to the laughing Tanu ladies, most of whom were nearly a third taller than he was. Bryan stood apart from the others and watched. The Tanu nobles were solicitous of the comfort of the prisoners, joking over the incongruity of the situation, somehow managing to make the newly met exiles feel wanted and welcome. Bryan had no doubt that mental speech was flying about as fervidly as the vocal sort. He wondered what kind of psychic stimulant might be operating at the lower levels of consciousness to make even sullen Raimo and the aloof Elizabeth slowly unbend and join in the conviviality.

"We don't want you to feel left out, Bryan."

The anthropologist turned and saw a slender exotic male garbed in a simple blue robe smiling at him. He had a handsome but sunken-eyed visage, lined about the mouth as Creyn's was. Bryan wondered whether this might be a sign of extreme age among these inhumanly youthful-looking people. The man's hair was of the palest ivory and he wore a narrow coronet of a material resembling blue glass.

"Permit me to welcome you. I am your host, Bormol, like yourself a student of culture. How eagerly we have awaited the arrival of another trained analyst! The last anthropologist who came to us arrived nearly thirty years ago and he was unfortunately in frail health. And we need your insights so urgently! We have so much to learn about the interaction of our two races if this Exile society is to flourish to our mutual advantage. The science of your Galactic Milieu can teach us the things we must know in order to survive. Come—we have good food and drink waiting for you and your friends inside. Share with us some of your first impressions of our Many-Colored Land. Give us your initial reactions!"

Bryan managed a rueful laugh. "You flatter me, Lord Bormol. And overwhelm me. I'm damned if I can make head or tail of your world as yet. After all, I've only just arrived. And excuse me, but I'm so tired out after this bloody shocking day that I'm ready to drop in my tracks."

"Forgive me. I'd completely forgotten you're without a torc. The mental refreshment that our people have been lavishing over your companions hasn't affected you. If you wish, we can—"

"No, thank you!"

Creyn came up and smiled ironically at the anthropologist's sudden alarm. "Bryan would prefer to do his work without the consolations of the torc . . . in fact, he has made this a condition of cooperation."

"You don't have to coerce me," Bryan said testily.

"Don't misunderstand!" Bormol appeared pained. He gestured at the gaudy throng, now leading the other prisoners inside with every evidence of good fellowship. "Are your friends being coerced? The torc isn't a symbol of bondage but of union."

Bryan felt a surge of anger and dreadful weariness erupt in him. His voice remained calm. "I know you mean well. But there are many of us humans—one might say most of us in my world of the future, most of the *normal* members of humanity—who would rather die than submit to your torc. In spite of all its consolations. Now you must excuse me. I'm sorry to disappoint you, but I'm not up to any learned discussions right now. I'd like to go to bed."

Bormol bowed his head. One of the human servants came running up with Bryan's pack. "We will meet again in the capital. I hope you will have modified your harsh opinion of us by then, Bryan . . . This is Joe-Don, who will take you to a retiring room at once. Rest well."

Bormol and Creyn glided away. Almost everyone else had already left the courtyard. "Right this way, sir," Joe-Don said, his breezy aplomb equal to that of a bellman in one of the Old World's posher hostelries. "We've got a nice room ready for you. But too bad you'll miss the party."

They went off into corridors decorated in blue and gold and

white. Bryan caught a glimpse of the unconscious Stein being borne away on a litter by four more human attendants.

"If there's a doctor in the house, Joe-Don, that man could use looking after. The poor chap got clobbered both physically and mentally."

"Don't worry, sir. Lady Damone—Bormol's missus—is an even better medic than Creyn. We get a lot of whacked-out specimens passing through here, the time-portal being the shock that it is. But most of the casualties get fixed up pretty good. This Tanu bunch don't have anything like the tank regeneration equipment we grew up with, but they slop on through pretty good regardless. They're mighty tough themselves and they can heal most injuries and diseases with the help of the torcs. Lady Damone'll give your pal a good veinfeed and see to his scattered marbles. Another day, he'll be as good as new. Quite a pile of muscle, isn't he? They must have him tapped for the Grand Combat."

"And what," Bryan asked quietly, "might that be?"

Joe-Don blinked, then grinned. "Kind of sports event they have a couple of months from now, around the end of October. Traditional with these folks. They're great ones for traditions . . . Well, here's your room, sir."

He threw open the door to an airy chamber that had white draperies billowing in front of a large window. A vertical string of sapphire lanterns hung beside a cool-looking bed. More-conventional oil lamps cast a pool of yellow radiance on a table where a simple supper had been laid out.

Joe-Don said, "If you need anything, just pull this ring beside the bed and we'll come running. I don't suppose you'll require any consoling companionship? No? Well, sweet dreams anyhow."

He whisked out and closed the door firmly behind him. Bryan didn't bother to test the lock. He gave a great sigh and began unbuttoning his shirt. Somehow, although he had not been aware of moving upward, he had come to the topmost floor of the Tanu mansion. The view from his window overlooked much of the town and gave him a distant glimpse of the city gate. Roniah lay silent and glittering, an earthbound constellation, reminding him of a Christmas display he had seen long ago on one of the more extravagant Hispanic-heritage worlds.

He wondered in a perfunctory fashion what kind of exotic cheer his companions were presently enjoying down at the Tanu party. No doubt he'd hear all about it tomorrow. Yawning, he folded the shirt . . . and felt the small bulk of the durofilm sheets tucked into the breast pocket. He took them out and there was her picture, glowing dimly with its own light.

Oh, Mercy.

Have they taken you and made you one of themselves, as they are trying to do with my friends? Thin sad woman with yearning sea-deep eyes and a smile that keeps me bound despite all reason! I have never heard you play your harp and sing; but my mind's ear creates you:

> There is a lady sweet and kind
> Was never face so pleased my mind.
> I did but see her passing by,
> And yet I love her till I die.
>
> Her gestures, motions, and her smile,
> Her wit, her voice my heart beguiled,
> Beguiled my heart, I know not why.
> And yet I love her till I die.

A deep brazen note sounded, snatching him from his fatigue-drugged reverie. It was the great gong at the city gate. The portal swung open in response, seeming to admit the rising sun.

"Christ!" whispered Bryan. He watched transfixed as the Hunt came a-homing.

A rainbow poured down the main avenue of the town, taking the same route that their own party had followed not long before. Flaring and twisting, the creature of light resolved itself into a procession of splendidly mounted Tanu leaping about with the antic joy of a Novo Janeiro Mardi Gras parade. Both chalikos and riders glowed with an internal effulgence that continually shifted up and down the entire spectrum. The Hunt came closer and closer and eventually passed almost under Bryan's window. He saw that the participants, men and women alike, were arrayed in bizarre armor, apparently of gem-studded glass, adorned with spikes and knobs and other decorative excrescences that gave them the look of humanoid crustaceans fashioned out of diamonds. The chalikos were partially armored with the same material and wore shining gems on their foreheads. Both mounts and riders trailed brightly colored streamers of gossamer fabric that emitted sparks from the tapered ends.

The Hunt made a triumphant noise. The men struck their bejeweled shields with glowing glass swords to produce a musical clangor; some of the women sounded weirdly twisted glass horns with animal-head bells, and others chanted at the top of their powerful voices. Near the end of the parade were six riders glowing a uniform neon-red, evidently the heroes of this particular chase. They held tall lances, upon which were mounted the night's trophies.

Severed heads.

Four of the heads had belonged to monsters—a fanged and wattled horror gleaming black and wet, a reptile with ears like batwings and a fringe of tentacles at its cheeks that still twitched, a thing having branched golden antlers and the face of a bird of prey, a nightmare simian with pure white fur and still-blinking eyes the size of apples.

The other two heads were smaller. Bryan saw them quite clearly as the procession passed by. They had belonged to an ordinary little man and woman of late middle age.

11

IT WAS THE UNEXPECTED re-creation of old pain that finally gave Amerie her insight.

The swollen ankles chained immobile to the high stirrups, the stretched muscles on the insides of her thighs, the horde of imps twanging the spiral ganglia in the small of her back, the cramps in calves and knees—she remembered them. It had been just like this twenty-six years ago.

Her father had told the family that descending into the Grand Canyon of the Colorado on a mule would be a wonderful adventure, a trip through a cut-open layercake of planetary history that they would all look back on and savor after they'd gone out to far Multnomah. And it had started out fine. On the trail down, Amerie the child delighted in fingering the strata of colored rock that became older and older, until at the bottom she had picked up a two-billion-year-old fragment of black glittering Vishnu schist and studied it with suitable awe.

But then had come the journey back up to the Canyon's rim. And pain. That endless trip, with aching legs that finally went into spasms as she subconsciously tried to help the mule on its upward climb. Her parents were experienced trailriders and knew how to sit the slope. Her little brothers with their wire-and-plass toughness were happy to let their mounts do the work. But she, the conscientious one, had known the dreadful job that the mule was doing and had unwittingly demanded to share it. Toward the end she was crippled and weeping, and the others had sympathized with poor little Annamaria, but of course it was better to keep on riding and get to the top so that it would be over, rather than stop on the trail and delay the whole party. And Dad had urged her to be his big brave girl, and Mom had smiled pityingly, and the two little brothers had looked superior. Back on the South Rim, Dad had taken her into his arms and carried her to their room and put her to bed. She had slept for eighteen hours, and the brothers teased her for missing out on the egg ride to the Painted Desert, and she had felt guilty. That had started it all.

Mom and Dad and the boys, all gone now. But the big girl still tried to carry her load no matter how much it hurt. So there. Now you begin to understand why you have come here and all the rest of it. This pain and the remembered old ones trigger the realization. And now, just as scab-rip and toothpull and boneset can help true healing begin, now you can recover! But God, what a fool you have been. And now here you are *here* and the insight has come too late.

Amerie rode her chaliko in the Pliocene sunrise. Felice was asleep on the mount to her left, having told the nun that riding these animals was a pleasure after the half-tamed verruls of Acadie. All around the train of slumped riders, the birds of the plateau were clamoring in the dawn chorus. Should she sing her own song of praise in spite of everything? The sleep-learned Latin phrases presented themselves. Wednesday in Summer. She had forgotten Matins at midnight, so better do that before the Lauds that properly belong to dawn.

She chanted softly as the eastern sky turned from purplish gray to yellow with cirrus wisps like torn vermilion chiffon.

> Cor meum conturbatum est in me:
>   et formido mortis cecidit super me.
> Timor et tremor venerunt super me:
>   et contexerunt me tenebrae.
> Et dixit: Quis dabit mihi pennas sicut columbae,
>   et volabo, et requiescam!

Her head sank upon her breast and tears fell onto the white homespun of her habit. From the next rider ahead of her came a quiet laugh.

"Interesting that you pray in a dead language. Still, I daresay we could all do with a bit of Psalm Fifty-Five."

She looked up. It was a man in a Tyrolean hat, turned partway around in his saddle and smiling at her.

He declaimed: "'My heart is sore pained within me! And the terrors of death are fallen upon me. Fear and trembling have seized me, and darkness has overwhelmed me. And I said: O that I had wings like a dove! For then I would fly away and be at rest.' . . . What's next?"

She said miserably, "'Ecce elongavi fugiens: et mansi in solitudine.'"

"Oh, yes. 'Lo, I would flee far away and live in the wilderness.'" He waved a hand at the emergent landscape. "And here it is! Magnificent. Just look at those mountains in the east. They're the Jura. Amazing the difference six million years makes in them, you know. Some of those ridges must be at three thousand meters—perhaps twice as high as the Jura of our time."

Amerie wiped her eyes on her scapular. "You knew them?"

"Oh, yes. I was very keen. Tramped and climbed all over the Earth, but liked the Alps best. I'd planned to climb them again in their juvenile aspect. My reason for coming to Exile, you see. In my last rejuv, I had my lung capacity upped twenty percent. Had the heart and large muscles fortified as well. I'd brought all kinds of special climbing gear along. D'you know—parts of the Pliocene Alps might be higher than the Himalaya we knew? Our Alps were greatly eroded by the Ice Age that'll be along in a few million years. The really high country would be farther south, around Monte Rosa on the old Swiss-Italian border, or southwest into Provence where the Dent Blanche nappe overrides Rosa's. There could be folds down there pushed above nine thousand meters. There could be a mountain higher than Everest! I hoped to spend the rest of my life climbing these Pliocene mountains. Even the Alpine Everest, if I managed to find a few kindred souls to accompany me."

"Perhaps you still will." The nun tried to force a smile.

"Not friggerty likely," he replied cheerily. "These exotics and their flunkies will put me to work hewing wood or drawing water when they find out that my only talents are classical donning and falling off alps. If I'm lucky and have any spare time after slavery,

I'll tootle tunes for drinks in the local equivalent of the village pub."

He apologized for interrupting her prayers and turned forward again. In a few moments, Amerie heard the soft sounds of his flute mingling with the birdsong.

She resumed her own quiet chanting.

The caravan was on a downhill slope once more, still traveling northward parallel to the Saône. The great river was invisible, but its course was marked by a wide belt of mist-hung forest far down in the valley. The countryside beyond the woodland on the opposite bank was much flatter, a prairie dotted with trees that gradually blended into a marshy plain with many small meres and sloughs that sparkled as the sun climbed. Tributary streams twisted through the eastern swamp; but the west bank of the Saône that they traveled was several hundred meters higher, cut only by widely separated creeks and gullies, which the patient chalikos plodded across while scarcely breaking stride.

Now that it was fully light, Amerie could see the other people in the train—the soldiers and Epone riding three or four ranks ahead, the pairs of prisoners strung out behind at neatly maintained intervals. Richard and Claude were near the baggage animals and the rear guard. The outriding amphicyons galumphed stoically on either side, sometimes closing in, so that she saw their evil yellow eyes or smelled the carrion reek of their bodies. The chalikos had their own distinctive smell, odd and sulfurous, like a flatus of turnips. It must be from the roots they eat, she thought wearily. All that food that made them so big and strong and *wide*.

She groaned and tried to ease her tormented muscles. Nothing helped, not even prayer. Fac me tecum pie flere, Crucifixo condolere, donec ego vexero. Oh, shit, Lord. This isn't going to work.

"Look, Amerie! Antelopes!"

Felice was awake, pointing to the savanna on their left where a golden rise of land seemed strangely overgrown with dark stalks that waved in all directions. Then Amerie realized that the stalks were horns and the entire hillside was thick with reddish-tawny bodies. Thousands upon thousands of gazelles were grazing the dried grass. They were undisturbed by the passing caravan and raised mild black-and-white faces, seeming to nod their lyre-shaped horns at the amphicyons, which ignored them.

"Aren't they beautiful?" cried Felice. "And over there! Those little horses!"

Hipparions were even more numerous than the gazelles, roaming the uplands in huge loose herds that sometimes seemed to cover an entire square kilometer. As the party of travelers came into lower elevations where the vegetation was more lush, they saw other grazers—goatlike tragocerines with mahogany coats, larger harnessed antelopes that had thin white stripes on their fawn sides, and once in a scrubby little grove of acacias, massive gray-brown elands bearing stout spiraling horns—the bulls, with their drooping dewlaps, standing over two meters tall at the shoulder.

"All that meat on the hoof," Felice marveled. "And only a few big cats and hyenas and bear-dogs for natural enemies. A hunter would never starve in this world."

"Starving," the nun said dourly, "hardly seems to be the problem." She hoisted her skirt and began to massage her thighs by pounding them with the sides of her hands.

"Poor Amerie. Of course I know what the problem is. I've been working on it. Watch this."

As the nun stared, puzzled, Felice's chalicothere drifted casually toward her own until the sides of the two animals touched lightly. Then Felice's mount moved away, maintaining its steady pace as it trotted a good arm's length to the left of its proper position in line. After just half a minute of this aberrant movement, the beast slipped back into its normal caravan slot. It moved sedately for a few moments, then broke stride so that it decreased the distance between it and the animal ahead by a meter and a half. The chaliko continued tailgating while Amerie began to comprehend what was happening. It fell back into its usual place just as a suspicious bear-dog let out a howl.

"Mamma mia," murmured the nun. "Can the soldiers tell you're doing it?"

"Nobody's fighting my override of their control. There probably is no feedback at all, just the preset command for the entire train that keeps them moving at speed in the selected intervals. You remember when those blue partridges spooked the chalikos early last evening? The guards came back to see that we were all properly lined up again. They wouldn't have had to do that if they had feedback from our mounts."

"True. But—"

"Hang onto your wimple. Now it's your turn."

Amerie's pain and spiritual malaise were swept away in a sudden wash of hope—for her own chalicothere was now duplicating the earlier motions of Felice's animal. When the eerie solo dance had been completed, both of the creatures performed identical maneuvers in concert.

"Te deum laudamus," Amerie whispered. "You just might pull it off, child. But can you reach *them?*" She nodded in the direction of the nearest amphicyon.

"It's going to be hard. Harder than anything I ever did back in the arena on Acadie. But I'm older now." At least four months older. And it isn't a stupid game anymore with me hoping that they'd learn to care instead of only being afraid. But here she is now trusting and even the others would if only they knew. They would trust and admire. But how to test? Must not give the thing away. So hard. Which way would be best?

The bear-dog running twenty meters off Felice's left flank came slowly closer, lolling tongue dripping saliva. The brute was nearly exhausted after its long trek. Its wits were slowed and its willpower diminished. The pricking within its mind that urged it onward and kept it alert was being callused round with fatigue and hunger. The call to duty was now weak in comparison to the promise of high meat in the trough and a bed of dry grass in a shady place.

The amphicyon ranged closer and closer to Felice's chaliko. It whimpered and snorted when it realized that it had lost control of itself, shaking its ugly head as though trying to dislodge pesty insects. The heavy jaws clashed, scattering slobber; but still it came closer, pacing together with the chaliko in the dust cloud that swirled about the mount's clawed feet. The amphicyon glared in helpless rage at the small human sitting high above it—the human that was forcing, bending, compelling. It growled its fury, curling its lip above discolored teeth almost the size of Felice's fingers.

She let it go.

The effort had dimmed her vision, and her head ached abominably from the resistance of the stubborn carnivore mind. But—!

"You did that, didn't you," Amerie said.

Felice nodded. "Damn hard, though. The things aren't on light autopilot like the chalikos. It was fighting me every minute. Bear-dogs must work by training-conditioning. That's harder to crack because it's well bedded in the subconscious mind. But I think I've got it figured. Best to go after them when they're worn out, at the end of the day's travel. If I can hang onto two, or even more . . ."

Amerie gave a helpless gesture. It was incomprehensible to the nun, this direct impact of mind upon mind, this operation of a power beyond her own mental capability. What would it be like to be a metapsychic—even an imperfect one such as Felice? To manipulate other living things? To move and reform inanimate matter? What would it be like to *really* create—not merely the ghost of a hiking boot, as she had done with the aid of Epone's device, but a substantial illusion, or even matter and energy themselves? What would it be like to link in Unity with other minds? To probe brains? To enjoy angelic powers?

A bright planet shone in the east near the rising sun. Venus . . . no, call it by its other, more ancient name: Lucifer, bright angel of morning. Amerie felt a tiny frisson of fear.

Lead her not into temptation, but forgive us as we warm ourselves at Felice's fire, even as she burns . . .

The caravan marched down into the lowland, off the plateau into another river valley that opened westward through the Monts du Charolais. The scattered dwarf palmettos, pines, and locust trees of the heights gave way to maples and poplars, walnuts and oaks, and finally to a deep humid forest with sourgum, bald cypress, thickets of bamboo, and huge old tulip trees more than four meters in diameter. Lush shrubbery abounded, making the landscape seem the very exemplar of a primeval jungle. Amerie kept expecting dinosaurs or winged reptiles to appear, knowing at the same time that the notion was idiotic. The Pliocene fauna, when you came down to it, was very similar to that of the replenished Earth six million years in the future.

The riders caught glimpses of small deer with bifurcated horns, a porcupine, and a gigantic sow followed by cunning striped piglets. A troop of medium-sized monkeys swung through the upper storey of the woods, following the caravan and shrieking but never coming close enough to be seen clearly. In some places shrubs and small trees had been uprooted and stripped of green. Piles of droppings smelling of elephant identified this as the work of mastodons. A feline roar of uncanny power caused the bear-dogs to howl back defiantly. Was it machairodus, one of the leonine sabertooth cats that were the commonest large predators of the Pliocene?

After the prisonlike environment of the castle and the numbing transition of the night journey, the time-travelers now became aware of a new feeling that overcame even their fatigue and soreness and the memory of broken hopes. This forest, pierced by the slanting rays of morning sunlight, was unmistakably another world, another Earth. Here in vivid reality was the unspoiled wilderness they had all dreamed of. Blot out the soldiers and the chains and the exotic slave mistress—and this Pliocene woodland could still be apprehended as paradise.

Dew-strung giant spider webs, incredible masses of flowers, fruits and berries shining like baroque jewels in settings of many-hued green . . . cliffs with thin waterfalls dropping into pools in front of mossy grottoes . . . throngs of fearless animals . . . the beauty was real! In spite of themselves, the prisoners discovered that they were scanning the jungle for more marvels as eagerly as any pack of thrill-seeking tourists. Amerie's pain faded before visions of scarlet-and-black butterflies and gaudy treefrogs chiming like elfin bells. Even in August the birds sang their mating songs, for in a world without true winter they had not yet begun to migrate and could raise more than one brood a year. An improbable squirrel with tufted ears and patches of greenish-and-orange fur scolded from a low tree limb. Another tree was draped with a motionless python, its body as thick as a beer barrel and as gorgeously colored as a Kermanshah rug. There went a tiny hornless antelope with legs like twigs and a body no larger than a rabbit's! There flew a bird with a raucous crow voice, feathered in a splendor of violet and pink and darkest blue! By a stream stood a huge otter, poised on hind limbs and seeming to smile amiably at the prisoners riding by. Farther down the creekbed were wild chalicotheres somewhat smaller and darker than their domesticated cousins, ripping up bulrushes for breakfast and managing to look dignified in spite of their mouthfuls of dripping greenery. In the short grass beside the trail grew crowds of mushrooms—coral, red with white spots, sky-blue with magenta gills and stems. Creeping amongst them was a many-legged millipede the size of a salami, looking as though it were freshly enameled in oxblood-red with cream racing stripes . . .

The horn sounded its three notes.

Amerie sighed. The echoing reply set off the wild things farther along the trail, so that the caravan met its escort in a tangled voluntary of bird and animal voices. The forest thinned and they came into a parklike area beside a slow-flowing river, some western tributary of the Saône. The trail led over a lawn beneath venerable cypresses and through the gate of a large palisaded fort almost identical to the one they had stopped at during the night.

"All you travelers!" Captal Waldemar bellowed, when the last of the caravan had entered the gate and the wooden doors were swung shut. "This is our sleeping stop. We'll rest here until sunset. I know you're feeling pretty used up. But take my advice and soak in the big hot-tub in your bathhouse before you fall into the sack. And eat, even if you think you're too tired to be hungry! Take your packs with you when you dismount. Anybody sick or gotta complaint, see me. Be ready to remount this evening after supper when you hear the horn. You feel like trying to escape, remember that the amphicyons are outside and so are the sabertooth cats and a really trick orange salamander the size of a collie dog with venom like a king cobra. Have a nice rest. That's *all*."

A white-clad hostler helped Amerie from her saddle when she was unable to get down on her own.

"You want to give yourself a good soak, Sister," the man said solicitously. "It's the best thing in the world for trail soreness. We heat the water with a solar setup on the roof, so there's plenty."

"Thank you," she murmured. "I'll do that."

"You could do something for us here at the fort, too, Sister. If you're not too tired and stiff, that is." He was a short, coffee-colored man with graying kinky hair and the preoccupied air of a minor civil servant.

Amerie felt that she could fall asleep standing up if only there were something to lean against. But she heard herself saying, "Of course I'll do anything I can." Her racked leg muscles spasmed in protest.

"We don't often get a priest here. Just a circuit-rider every three or four months—old Brother Anatoly out of Finiah or Sister Ruth from Goriah, way over to the west. We have maybe fifteen Catholics among the men here. We'd really appreciate it if—"

"Yes. Certainly. I suppose you'd prefer the votive Mass of St. John the Beloved Disciple."

"First your nice bath and supper." He picked up her pack, draped her arm over his shoulders, and helped her away.

As soon as Felice had dismounted, she rushed over to Richard and said, "Well? Did you get it?"

"Dead easy. And there's a second-magnitude sparkler sitting right on top of it." He looked down at her from the high back of his chaliko. "Since you're in such good shape, gimme a hand down off this brute."

"Easiest thing in the world," she said. Stepping onto the dismounting block, she put her little hands under his armpits and swung him off in one motion.

"Sweet Jesus!" exclaimed the pirate.

"I could use a little of that, too, Felice," came Claude's dry voice. The ring-hockey player went to the next chaliko and plucked the old man out of the saddle as though he were a child.

"What kinda gravity you have on Acadie, anyhow?" Richard growled.

She bestowed a condescending smile. "Point eight-eight Earth normal. Nice try, Captain Blood, but no joy."

"You mustn't try anything rash here, Felice." Claude was anxious. "I should think they'd be very alert in a place like this."

"Don't worry. I've—"

Richard hissed, "She's coming—watch it! Her nibs!"

The white chaliko bearing Epone paced majestically through the clutter of weary prisoners and their baggage.

"No dust or sweat on that one," remarked Felice bitterly, slapping at the filthy green skirts of her hockey uniform. "Looks like she's ready for the fuckin' beaux-arts ball. Must be ionized fabric in the cloak."

A few of the travelers were still astride their mounts—among them the sturdy ginger-bearded man with the lion emblazoned on his knightly surtout. He had both elbows resting on the pommel of his saddle. His hands covered his face.

"Dougal!" Epone's voice was at once wheedling and commanding.

The knight leapt in his seat and stared at her wildly. "No! Not again. Please."

But she only signaled for hostlers to take the bridle of the knight's chaliko.

"O thou belle dame sans merci," he groaned. "Aslan. Aslan."

Epone rode away across the fort compound toward a small structure with pots of flowers hanging from its veranda roof. The hostlers led tall Dougal after her.

Claude watched them go and said, "Well, now you know, Richard. It's a good thing you're out of it. She looks like mighty rough trade."

The ex-spacer swallowed the bile that had risen in his throat at memory's slow return. "Who . . . who the hell is Aslan?" he managed to ask.

"A kind of Christ figure in an old fairy tale," the old man replied. "A magical lion who saved children from supernatural enemies in a Never-Never Land called Narnia."

Felice laughed. "I don't think his franchise extends to the Pliocene. Would either of you gentlemen care to join me in a hot tub?"

She marched off to the bathhouse, dusty feathers awave, leaving the others to limp slowly after.

12

OH, WHAT A NIGHT it had been!

Aiken Drum lay sprawled on snowy sheets and let his silver torc give him a replay of the high. Fizzy exotic booze. Delicious exotic food. Fun and games and music and dance and romping and stomping and flying and galloping those exotic broads with their crazy boobs down to there. Sweet houghmagandy! Hadn't he shown them that he was big enough! And hadn't he found his heart's home at last . . . Here in Exile, among these people who loved to laugh and venture as he did, he would thrive and grow and *shine*.

"Gonna be Sir Boss!" he giggled. "Gonna roj this whole fewkin' world until it yells quits! Gonna fly!"

Oh, yes. That, too.

Slowly, his naked body rose from the bed. He spread his arms wide and soared toward the ceiling where the morning sunlight shining through the drapes made ripple-bars of greeny gold. The bedroom was an aquarium and he was a swimmer in the air. Zoom! Bank! Roll! Dive! Let go and fall bouncing back to the bed shouting with delight, for it was a rare gift even among the talented Tanu, and the ladies, especially, had greeted his discovery of it with great excitement.

Wonderful silver torc!

He scrambled off the bed and went to the window. Roniah down below was awake and going about its business—human figures strolling or bustling, stately Tanu mounted on gaily caparisoned chalikos, and everywhere the little ramas at work—sweeping, gardening, fetching and carrying. Kaleidoscopic!

. . . Hey, Aik. Where you be, buddy?

The mental hail came to him hesitantly and garbled at first, then with increasing confidence. Raimo, of course. The surly woodsman had undergone a remarkable change of attitude as Aiken's new meta-functions became increasingly manifest at the party. Raimo left off his shit-kicking and got friendly. And why not? He could sense a winner, that one!

You there, Ray? You talking at me, Woodchopper?

Who the hell else? Hey, Aik—if this is a dream, don't wake me up.

No dream. It's realio-trulio and we are in for one helluva good time. Hey! What say we bust out and do a little sightseeing in the town?

They got me locked in, Aik.

You forgot what we learned at the party? Hang on a nanosec while I put my clothes on and I'll be right there.

Aiken threw on his golden costume, checked to be sure that no Tanu was watching, then launched himself out of his bedroom window. Hovering above the mansion like a great gleaming insect, he sent his seekersense homing in on Raimo's querulous thought pattern, then dived at the open window of his buddy and popped into the room crowing, "Tah-*dah!*"

"Damn, you really do know how, don't you?" Raimo said with some envy. "Seems I'm only good for pickin' up furniture." By way of demonstration, he caused the bed to dance and sent tables and chairs flying about the room.

"Everybody's different, Chopper. You got your talents, I got mine. You could have diddled the mechanism of the lock to escape, you know."

"Shit. Never thought of it."

Aiken grinned. "You'll be thinking of a lot of things from now on, Ray—and so will I. Last night was some kinda eyeopener, no?"

The former woodsman laughed out loud and the two of them wallowed in a mutual replay, chortling over the discomfiture of the scandalized Sukey and Elizabeth, who had retired abruptly when the members of the Hunt joined the festivities. Poor straity-ladies! No sense of humor and probably fridgies to boot. It had been good riddance when they left, and party had gone on until dawn, featuring entertainments increasingly delightful that the two men could savor to the full, strengthened by their silver torcs. Good old metaboodly psychokinoodly!

Aiken gestured out of the window. "Come on. Let's see how the human half lives. I'm curious about the way the normals operate in this Exile setup. Don't sweat the flying bit, Ray. I can hold up the both of us."

"They'll spot us."

"I've got another metafunction. The illusion thing. Check this!"

There was a soundless snap and the small golden man disappeared. A tiger swallowtail butterfly flapped up and landed square on Raimo's nose. "Keep those paws down or I go hornet," said Aiken's voice. The butterfly vanished, and there was the practical joker again, standing in front of Raimo with one finger resting on the forester's nose.

"Hell's bells, Aik! You are *loaded!*"

"Say again, Chopper. Gimme your hand. Come on—don't be a poop. We're off!"

Two yellow butterflies flew away from the Tanu dwelling and over the town of Roniah. They swooped above the workshops of potters and rooftile makers and weavers and carpenters and metalsmiths and boatwrights and armorers and glassblowers and sculptors. They intruded upon lapidaries and painters and basketmakers and rehearsing musicians; sipped nectar from the jasmine that bloomed beside swimming pools where pregnant women lounged and laughed; flew into an open-air schoolroom where a dozen blond, lissom children pointed their fingers in amazement and a startled Tanu teacher sent a dangerous query arrowing back toward Bormol's mansion.

"To the docks!" Aiken ordered, and they flew toward the riverside. Broad flights of steps led down to a busy landing stage. Rama stevedores unloaded barges while human dockhands and boatmen, many of them naked to the waist in the morning heat, went about their jobs or loafed in shady places waiting for some other man to finish his.

The two butterflies landed atop a fat mooring bollard and turned back into Aiken and Raimo. One dockworker gave a shout. Seagulls rose up from the pavement and pilings, squawking an alarm. Aiken strolled off the bollard, leaving Raimo sitting there and blinking, and struck a pose in thin air. A burly bargee gave a shout of laughter and exclaimed, "Well—if it ain't Peter Pan hisself! But you better send that there Tinkerbell back for a refit!"

The dockside loafers roared. Up on the bollard, Raimo extended both of his arms to the side. His slanty-eyed Finnish face wore a crooked grin and a look of odd concentration. Immediately a dozen gulls fluttered down and aligned themselves from his wrists to his shoulders.

"Hey, Aik! Shootin' gallery! Zap before crap or you lose!"

The hovering little man in gold took aim with his forefinger. "Pam!" he said. "Pam-pam-pammidy-*pam!*"

Small flashes ran along Raimo's plaid-flanneled arms. He was engulfed in a cloud of smoke and fragmentary white feathers. The audience whistled and applauded while Raimo sneezed. "Attaway, li'l biddy buddy!"

"And for my encore," Aiken cried, making a pass with both hands at the bollard itself, "I give you—*shazoom!*"

There was a sharp explosion. The heavy timbers of Raimo's perch disintegrated, leaving him suspended above the water wearing a look of pained surprise.

"Was that nice?" the ex-forester expostulated. He floated over to the chuckling Aiken, grasped him by the epaulets of his golden suit, and suggested, "Maybe we should cool off with a swim!"

The two airborne figures began to wrestle, bouncing low over the muddy yellow waters of the Rhône among the moored lighters and wherries and barges like wind-tossed carnival balloons. The men on the docks cackled and stamped, and terrified ramas dropped their burdens and covered their eyes.

Enough!

Creyn's mental command whipped out, hauling the two back to the quayside and depositing them onto the pavement with a painful jolt. Four attendants from Bormol's mansion stepped forward to take firm hold of the still snickering miscreants. With the fun clearly at an end, the dockworkers and boatmen began drifting back to their jobs.

"I am programming mental restraints upon your major metapsychic functions until you have received proper training at the capital," Creyn said. "We'll have no more of this childish behavior."

Aiken waved at Elizabeth, Bryan, and Sukey, who were being escorted down the quay stairs together with Stein on his litter.

Raimo said, "Aw, Chief. How else we gonna learn what we can do?"

Aiken added, "Lord Bormol told us last night to get right into it. And did we ever!" He winked at Sukey, who glared at him.

Creyn said, "From now on, you'll do your learning in a controlled environment. Lord Bormol doesn't need you repaying his hospitality by destroying his wharf."

The little man in gold shrugged. "Don't know my own strength yet is all. You want me to try putting that thing back together again?"

Creyn's eyes, opaque blue in the sunlight, narrowed. "So you think you could? How very interesting. But I think we'll wait, Aiken Drum. It will be far safer for all of us if you stay on the leash for the time being."

Elizabeth's thought came stealing gently along . . .

So many wild talents you do have Aiken. What else is hidden in there? Let me look.

She sent a probe boring into him. It caromed off a hastily erected but effective barrier.

"Cut it out, Elizabeth!" Aiken cried aloud. "Quit or I'll fewkin' well zap you!"

She regarded him sadly. "Would you, really?"

"Well—" He hesitated, then gave her a lopsided smile. "Maybe not, sweetie-face. But I can't have you messing about with me, you know. Not even in fun. I'm not Stein . . . or Sukey, either."

Creyn said, "Our boat is waiting for us at the end of the landing stage. We must be on our way." But as they all went down the dock, the Tanu man reached out to Elizabeth on a narrow-focus mode that spoke to her mind alone:

Did you see how he did that?

Primitive/effective. Even versus me unprepared. Concerned?

Appalled actually.

How effective torcrestraint?

Adequate now while he still unuse fullpotential. Later silver never suffice will seize gold. Educators face dilemma that one. May require termination. Not my decision Tanabethanked.

Capable vastmischief even when latent. Rare old humantype uncommon in Milieu: clownmeddler.

Type not unknown among Tanu alas. Predict kid smashhit Muriah. Query Muriah survive impact.

Ironical justdeserts to you slavemasters. Humanity preyperilous. Ah Elizabeth.

Deny? Laugh. Manipucraftylators! Desocialization/resocialization exiles shrewdly essayed. Example: castle environment anxiety-provoke. Follows party warmthfriendshippowersexgoodies. Reinforce lesson severed heads. Crude goodguy/badguy punish/reward terror/relief mindforming. Aiken + Raimo + (Sukey?) yours. Both Hunts victorious.

How else integrate minimal delay? Some types e.g., Aiken super-hazard.

More like you than you?

Perceptive Elizabeth. Angelic aloof overflyer despising pathetic exilemisfits.

!

"Ah, Elizabeth. We get to know one another better and better."

* * *

The skipper who welcomed them to the unusual boat that would take them downriver wore khaki pants and a sweat-stained T-shirt. His belly overflowed his waistband. A crinkly peppered-salt mustache and fringe-beard bracketed the jovial smile on his mahogany face. He flicked Creyn a casual salute, one finger tapping the bill of a decrepit U.S. Navy cap of twentieth-century vintage.

"Welcome aboard, milord and ladies and gents! Skipper Highjohn at your service. Take any pew you like, but the best view is up forward. Bring that stretcher over here and lash it to the tie-downs."

The human travelers came onto the strange craft and settled somewhat apprehensively into the seats, which were pneumatically cushioned and form-fitting, with elaborate harnesses that the skipper helped them to fasten.

"Is the river very rough, Captain?" Sukey inquired. She had positioned herself near Stein and kept darting uneasy glances at the sleeping giant while the attendants secured him with strong webbing.

"Don't you be concerned. I've done this Rhône-Med run for sixteen years and never lost a boat." Highjohn flipped a lid on the chair arm and revealed a hidden container. "Little barfbucket if you need it."

Aiken piped up, "You may not have lost a boat—but how about a passenger?"

"You look like you got a strong ticker, boy. If things get too wild for you, Lord Creyn will program a calmative into your torc. Everybody set now? We'll be stopping for lunch at Feligompo Plantation around noon for any of you who have appetites. Tonight we'll be at Darask, which is below the site of the future Avignon. You know—the place with the bridge. See you later."

With a friendly wave, he went forward. The attendants from the mansion who had carried on Stein and their baggage now trooped ashore. Dockhands began scurrying about the vessel, preparing it for castoff. The passengers watched with mingled interest and unease.

The riverboat was similar in design to most of the others at the quayside, measuring about fourteen meters from its high, knife-sharp bow to its gluteally rounded stern. It was a distant cousin to the inflatable rafts and foldboats used by sportsmen and explorers on the whiter waters of the Galactic Milieu. The hull—stenciled on both sides with the name of the boat, Mojo—was a tough air-filled membrane with fat exterior corrugations and pillowlike fenders jutting out at regular intervals along the waterline. It looked as if it could be deflated and disassembled for shipment upstream via caravan. Tightly covered hatch openings fore and aft gave access to cargo holds, while the passenger accommodation was in an open area amidships that was arched over with a series of half-hoops. The dockworkers quickly covered this frame with panels of deeply tinted transparent film resembling decamole. When the last section of the bubbletop was sealed, an air blower began to operate inside the boat, providing ventilation for the occupants and rendering the waterproof canopy rigid.

Sukey turned to Elizabeth, who sat in the seat beside her. "I didn't like the way the Captain talked. What are we getting into?"

"An interesting ride, at any rate, if the signs and portents add up. Bryan—do you know anything at all about the River Rhône?"

"It was all cut up with dams and locks and bypass channels in our time," the anthropologist replied. "The gradient is probably a lot steeper here in the Pliocene, so there are bound to be rapids. When we approach the Avignon region about a hundred-fifty kloms south of here, we'll be in an area that very likely has a deep gorge. In the twenty-second century it was stoppered by the Donzère-Mondragon Barrage, one of the largest dam projects in Europe. What we'll find down there now . . . well, it can't be too bad or they wouldn't try to navigate it, would they?"

Aiken uttered a shaky laugh. "Good question. Well, ready or not, guys, we're off to the races."

A rather stout telescoping mast was rising up behind the passenger compartment. When it reached its full height of four meters, the top section opened to disgorge a boom with a roller sail, looking for all the world like an old-fashioned portable movie screen. The sail unfurled and gave a few tentative swiveling motions. Dockhands cast off the boat's mooring warps, and vibration in the deck betokened the operation of a small auxiliary engine. The Mojo began threading in and out of the other shore traffic on its way to the mainstream, leading Bryan to deduce that it must utilize more than one rudder for maximum maneuverability.

They angled sharply away from the shore. As the current took them, the walled city of Roniah fell away astern with amazing swiftness. It was not too easy to estimate their speed, since they were a good two hundred meters from either shore; but Bryan guessed that the sediment-laden flood was racing along at a minimum of twenty knots. What would happen when this great volume of water was compressed between high rock walls farther downstream challenged the imagination of the anthropologist. His speculations were of a decidedly queasy sort.

Raimo, in the seat next to him, had found his own brand of solace. He took a pull from his replenished silver flask and offered it to Bryan rather half-heartedly. "Tanu popskull. Hardly Hudson's Bay standard, but not too bad."

"Maybe later," Bryan said, smiling. Raimo grunted and took another swallow. The euphoria of his morning adventure had faded away, leaving the ex-forester brooding and ill at ease. Bryan tried to draw Raimo out with questions about the previous night's revelry but received only the curtest replies.

"You hadda be there," Raimo said, and lapsed into silence.

For nearly an hour they moved easily through a wide bluff-sided channel—the forested foothills of the Alps on their left hand and arid tablelands rising above the near-jungle of the humid bottoms on the right. Occasionally, Creyn pointed out the location of a plantation; but the trees were so thick that it was impossible to see any details of the settlements ashore. They glimpsed smaller boats plying the shallows and once they overhauled a long covered barge riding deep in the water, baremasted and having only a small bubble over the midships steersman's cockpit. The bargee greeted them with a toot from his airhorn, to which Skipper Highjohn responded with a syncopated blast of his own.

The river made a wide curve and the channel passed between a tall headland and a group of craggy islets. Small mechanical sounds announced the furling of their sail, the boom's folding, and the withdrawal of the telescoping mast back into its housing. Far from losing speed, the boat moved along faster rounding the point. It seemed to Bryan that they must be making thirty knots or more. Simultaneously he became aware of a deep vibration transmitted by the water through the sealed hull of the boat, the inflated headrest of his seat, and the very bones of his skull. The vibration increased to an audible roar as the boat came charging around a sharp bend. The walls of a canyon rose on both sides.

Sukey screamed and Raimo yelped an obscenity.

Ahead of them the narrowing Rhône slanted downhill at a one-in-five gradient, the river lashed to a foaming frenzy by the rocks of its tilted bed. The boat seemed to dive into the rapids and a great avalanche of ochre water crashed over the canopy and temporarily engulfed them. Then Mojo broke free and came to the surface, planing along among monstrous standing waves and granite boulders, rolling so steeply that yellow water climbed halfway up the watertight bubble first on one side, then on the other. The noise was almost insupportable. Raimo's mouth was wide open but his yells went unheard amidst the uproar of the cascading Rhône.

A dark mass loomed ahead. The boat heeled nearly sixty degrees to starboard as they went whipping around a tall rock pinnacle into a crooked slot between files of huge boulders. The air was so filled with flying spume that it seemed impossible that their skipper could see where he was going. Nevertheless the boat continued to zig and zag among the rocks with only an occasional bump against the pneumatic fenders.

A respite came in the form of a deep cut where the river flowed free. But the voice of Highjohn called, "One last time, folks!" and Bryan realized that they were rocketing through the defile toward a veritable fence of sharp crags, fanglike chunks of broken granite against which the yellow river waters crashed in overlapping curtains of spray. There seemed to be no way through. The stunned time-travelers gripped the arms of their seats and braced for the inevitable impact.

Mojo raced toward the tallest of the rocks, pitching violently. It crashed into the foam—but instead of hitting solid rock or sinking, it rose higher and higher on some unseen surge. There was a thrumming blow against the port side as they bounced off a rock face, completely drowned in the opaque pother. The boat seemed to roll a full 360 degrees and then wallow free to sail through the air. It landed with a bone-jarring impact, water closing again over the top of the canopy. Almost immediately it popped to the surface, floating in complete tranquillity across a broad pool that spread between low walls. Behind them was the cut they had just traversed, spewing a horsetail cataract, like the outflow of a titanic drain, into the basin thirty meters below.

"You can unfasten your safety belts now, folks," the skipper said. "That'll be all the cheap thrills for this morning. After lunch, it *really* gets rough."

He came back into the passenger compartment to check the canopy for possible leakage. "Didn't take in a drop!"

"Congratulations," whispered Bryan. With one trembling hand he fumbled with the buckles of the harness.

"Give you a hand?" suggested Highjohn, bending over to help.

Released, Bryan rose weakly to his feet. He saw that all of the others, including Creyn and Elizabeth, were motionless in their seats, eyes closed, apparently asleep.

Fists on hips, the riverman surveyed the passengers with a slow shake of his head. "Every goddam time. These sensitive Tanu types just can't take Cameron's Sluice, being afraid of water as they mostly are. So they zonk out. And if the torc-wearing humans show any distress, the Tanu just program a zonk for them, too. Kinda disappointing—you know? Every artist likes to have an audience."

"I take your point," Bryan said.

"I don't often get a rarey like you, no torc and all and man enough to come through it without a case of the yammering fantods. This lady without the torc"—he pointed to Elizabeth—"must have just fainted away."

"Not likely," Bryan said. "She's an operant metapsychic. I dare say she just did her own calming mental exercise and napped through the excitement, just as Creyn did."

"But not you, eh, sport? I suppose you've been on rough water before."

Bryan shrugged. "Hobby sailor. North Sea, Channel, Med. The usual thing."

Highjohn clapped him on the shoulder. His eyes twinkled and he gave Bryan a comradely smile. "Tell you what. You come on forward with me and I'll show you a thing or three about driving this tub before we reach Feligompo. If you enjoy it—who knows? There's lots worse jobs you could settle into in this Exile."

"I'd enjoy riding with you in the wheelhouse," Bryan said, "but I won't be able to take you up on your offer of an apprenticeship." He grinned ruefully. "I believe the Tanu have other plans for me."

13

CLAUDE AWOKE. A cool breeze blew through hanging strings of wooden beads that screened all four sides of the prisoners' dormitory and kept insects from flying in. Two guards paced around and around outside the shelter, bronze helmets turning as they scanned the inmates, compound bows strung and ready, resting lightly on their shoulders where they could be drawn in an instant.

The old man tested his limbs—and by God, they worked. His field adaptation system was still Go after all the years. He sat up on his pallet and looked around. Almost all of the other prisoners were still lying as though drugged. But Felice was up, and Basil the Alpine climber, and the two Japanese ronin. Faint yapping sounds came from a closed basket next to a sleeping woman. There were snores and a few moans from the other sleepers.

Claude quietly watched Felice. She was talking in low tones with the three other men. Once one of the ronin tried to protest something she was saying. She cut him short with a fierce gesture and the Oriental warrior subsided.

It was very late in the afternoon and quite hot. The space within the walled fort was deep in green shade. A smell of cooking wafted from one of the buildings, making Claude's mouth water. Another meat stew, and something like fruit pies baking. Whatever its other flaws, the Exile society certainly ate well.

Having finished her discussion, Felice crept across the crowded floor to Claude's resting place. She looked keyed up and her brown eyes were wide. She wore the sleeveless kilt-dress that was the undergarment to her hoplite armor, but had put off the rest of the uniform with the exception of the black shin guards. The bare areas of her skin were lightly sheened with perspiration.

"Wake Richard up," she whispered peremptorily.

Claude shook the shoulder of the sleeping ex-spacer. Muttering obscenities, Richard hoisted himself onto his elbows.

"We'll probably have to do it tonight," Felice said. "One of the fort people told Amerie that by tomorrow we'll be into very heavy country where this plan of mine wouldn't have much chance of working. I need open space to see what I'm doing. What I'll do is pick a time before dawn tomorrow when it's still fairly dark and the bear-dogs are running on the dregs of their second wind."

"Now wait a minute," Richard protested. "Don't you think we'd better discuss this plan of yours first?"

She ignored him. "Those others—Yosh, Tat, Basil—they'll try to help us. I asked the Gypsies, but they're half crazy and won't take orders from a woman anyway. So this is what we do. After the midnight break, Richard changes places with Amerie and rides beside me."

"Come on, Felice! The guards'll spot the switch."

"You change clothes with her in the latrine."

"Not on your—" Richard blazed. But Felice caught him by the lapels and dragged him over the floor on his stomach until they were nose to nose.

"You shut up and listen, Captain Asshole. None of the rest of you have a hope in hell of getting out of this. Amerie pumped one of the guards after she said Mass for them this morning. These exotics have metafunctions that can zap out your brain and turn you into a lunatic or a fuckin' zombie. They can't even be *killed* with ordinary weapons! They've got some system for controlling their slave-cities that's almost perfect. Once we arrive at Finiah and they test me out and find I'm latent, they'll collar me or kill me and the rest of you'll be lucky to spend your lives shoveling shit in the chaliko barns. This is our *chance*, Richard! And you're going to do as I say!"

"Let him go, Felice," said Claude urgently. "The guards."

When she dropped him, Richard whispered, "Damn you, Felice! I didn't say I wouldn't help. But you can't treat me like a friggerty baby!"

"What else would you call a grown man who craps up his bed?" she inquired. "Who changed your dydees when you drove starships, Captain?"

Richard went white. Claude was furious. "Stop it! Both of you! . . . Richard, you were sick. A man can't help himself when he's sick. For God's sake, forget the matter. We were glad to help you. But you've got to pull yourself together now and join with the rest of us in this plan to escape. You can't let your personal feelings toward Felice wreck what may be our only chance to get out of this nightmare."

Richard glared at the little ring-hockey player, then gave her a twisted grin. "You may be the only one of us who's a match for 'em at that, sweetie-babe. Sure. I'll go along with whatever you say."

"That's fine," she told him. She reached behind the black leather of her left greave and extracted what looked like a slender golden cross. "Now the first good news is that we aren't completely weaponless . . ."

* * *

They rode away in the evening with a crescent moon shining through the cypresses. After fording the shallow tributary, the trail climbed to the Burgundian plateau and once more resumed its northerly course. Fire-beacons lit the way through deepening twilight. After a time they were able to look down on a vast heaving region of mist marking extensive swamplands where the Pliocene Saône was born from the prehistoric Lac de Bresse. The lake waters stretched northward and eastward into the distance like a sheet of black glass, drowning the entire plain below the Côte d'Or. Richard entertained the old paleontologist with descriptions of the legendary wines that would be produced in this district six million years into the future.

Later, when the stars were bright, Richard took one last sighting of Pliocene Polaris. It was the brightest star in a constellation that the two men dubbed the Big Turkey.

"That's a good job you've done," Claude said.

"The whole business may turn out to be academic if we end up dead or brain-burned . . . You think this scheme of Felice's might really work?"

"Think about this, son. Felice would be able to escape by herself fairly easily. But she's worked out this plan to give the rest of us a chance, too. You may hate the little lady's entrails, but she just might bring this thing off. I'm going to do my damnedest for her, even though I'm just an old poop one step this side of fossilization. But you're still a young man, Richard. You look like you could handle yourself in a fight. We're counting on you."

"I'm scared outa my motherin' mind," the pirate told him. "That little bitty gold knife of hers! It's nothing but a toy. How the hell am I going to do it?"

The old man said, "Try Amerie's prescription. Pray a lot."

* * *

In the forward part of the caravan, Basil the Alpinist was saluting the sinking crescent moon by playing "Au claire de la lune" on his recorder. The little butterfly dancer from Paris, who rode beside him, sang along. And amazingly enough, Epone herself joined in in a soprano voice of melting richness. The exotic woman continued to sing as Basil played several more songs; but when he began "Londonderry Air," one of the soldiers galloped back on his chaliko and said, "The Exalted Lady forbids the commonalty to sing that song."

The climber shrugged and put his flute away.

The butterfly dancer said, "The monster sings that song with her own words. I heard her, back at Castle Gateway on the first night that we were imprisoned. Isn't it odd that a monster should be musical? It's like a fairytale—and Epone is like a beautiful wicked witch."

"The witch may sing a different song before dawn," Felice said; but only the nun heard her.

The trail came closer and closer to the western shore of the great lake. The caravan would have to skirt it before heading east into the Belfort Gap between the Vosges highland and the Jura, which led to the valley of the Proto-Rhine. The lake waters were utterly calm, reflecting the brighter stars like an inky mirror. As the curve of the trail took them around a promontory, they saw a distant beacon reflected as well, a streak of orange stabbing toward them across a broad bay.

"Look—not one fire but *two*." Felice's voice held a note of anxiety. "Now what the devil do you suppose that means?"

One of the soldiers from the rear of the caravan galloped past them to confer with Captal Waldemar, then returned to his position. The chalikos slowed to a walk and finally halted altogether. Epone and Waldemar rode off the trail to the top of a small rise where they could survey the lake.

Felice gently pounded one fist into the palm of her other hand and whispered, "Shit shit shit."

"There's something out there on the water," said Amerie.

A light mist filmed the reaches of the bay. One part of it seemed to thicken and grow bright as they watched, then break into four separate, dimly shining masses, fuzzy and amorphous. As the will-o'-the-wisps approached, they grew larger and glowed in color—one faintly blue, another pale gold, and two deep red. They bounced up and down as they followed a devious path over the water to a place not far offshore from the halted caravan.

"Les lutins," said the butterfly dancer, her voice rough with fear.

The central portion of each mass now revealed a form suspended within the glow, rounded bodies with dangling appendages that flexed. They were at least twice as tall as a human being.

"Why, they look just like giant spiders!" whispered Amerie.

"Les lutins araignées," the dancer repeated. "My old Grandmère told me the ancient tales. They are the shape-shifters."

"It's an illusion," Felice decided. "Watch Epone."

The Tanu woman had risen in her stirrups so that she stood high above the back of her motionless white chaliko. The hood of her cloak dropped so that her hair was luminous in the multihued light radiating from the things out on the lake. She placed both hands at her neck and cried out a single word in the exotic language.

The flame-spiders elevated their abdomens at her. Filaments of purple light rocketed toward Epone and over the heads of the prisoners. The people exclaimed in wonderment, hardly conscious of fear. The episode was so bizarre that it seemed like a light-show performance.

The bright webbing never reached the ground. As it shimmered above them, it began shattering into a myriad of glittering fragments like dying fireworks. The outer edges of the individual spiders' haloes started to disintegrate in the same corruscating fashion, enveloping the phantoms in a cloud of swirling sparks. The glowing spiders became krakens with writhing tentacles, then monstrous disembodied human heads with Medusa hair and fiery eyes, and finally featureless balls that dwindled, dimmed, and winked out.

Only stars and the beacon fires gleamed on the lake.

Epone and the captal rode back to the trail and resumed their places at the head of the procession. The chalikos snorted and whiffled and set out again at their usual trot. One of the soldiers said something to a prisoner at the head of the column, and the word passed slowly back.

"Firvulag. Those were Firvulag."

"It was an illusion," Felice insisted. "But something sure as hell caused it. Something that doesn't like the Tanu any more than we do. That's very interesting."

"Does this mean you'll have to change your plan?" Amerie asked.

"Not bloody likely. It may even help. If the guards are on the lookout for ghoulies and ghosties and long-leggety beasties, they'll pay less attention to *us*."

The cavalcade came around the bay to the place of the double beacon, where the prisoners entered another fort for the midnight rest. Felice dismounted quickly and came to assist all three of her friends, and several other riders as well. And later, when it was time to climb back into the saddle, she was there again to help the tired people fit their feet into the stirrups just before the soldiers came around to lock on the bronze ankle chains with their enveloping leather sleeves.

"Sister Amerie isn't feeling well," the little athlete told the guard who locked her onto her own beast. "Those strange creatures out on the lake gave her a bad turn."

"Don't you worry about the Firvulag, Sister," the man told the veiled, drooping rider. "There's no way they can get you as long as the Exalted Lady is with us. She's tops as a coercer. You just ride easy."

"Bless you," came a whisper.

When the soldier moved away to tend to Basil and the dancer, Felice said, "You just try to go to sleep, Sister. That's the best thing for nerves." In a lower tone she added, "And keep your cunnilingin' trap shut like I told you!"

The poor sick nun invited Felice to take an unlikely anatomical excursion.

*   *   *

They went on, following the shore but still trending northward. After an hour had passed, Claude said, "I'm free. How about you, Amerie?"

The rider beside him was incongruously garbed in a starship captain's coverall and a wide-brimmed black hat with dark plumes. "My chains are broken. What an incredible child Felice is! But I can understand why she was ostracized by the other ring-hockey players. It's too freakish, all that strength in such a doll-like body."

"Her *physical* strength is something the others could live with," Claude said, leaving it at that.

Presently, Amerie asked, "How many people did she set free?"

"The two Japanese riding behind her. Basil, the fellow in the Tyrolean hat. And that poor medievalist knight, Dougal, just ahead of Basil. Dougal doesn't know that his chains have been weakened enough to be broken. Felice didn't think he was stable enough to let in on the scheme. But when the thing starts we might get him to break loose and help. Lord knows he's big and strong-looking, and maybe he hates Epone enough to snap out of his funk when he sees others in action."

"I hope Richard will be all right."

"Don't worry. I think he's ready to do his part—if only to show Felice that she's not the only one with balls."

The nun laughed. "What a collection we are! Exiles and losers all. We got just what we deserved—running away from our responsibilities. Look at me. A lot of people needed my ministry. But I had to brood and maunder about my own precious spirituality instead of getting on with my job . . . You know, Claude, most of last night was hell for me. There's something about riding that hits me in the worst way. And while I was hurting, I found I was shrinking myself. I think I finally understand the reasons why I got into this mess. Not just coming to Exile—the whole thing."

The old man said nothing.

"I think you figured it out, too, Claude. Quite a while ago."

"Well, yes," he admitted. "When we talked about your childhood that day on the mountain. But you had to find it out for yourself."

She said softly, "The firstborn daughter with the Little Mama thing in the warm Italianate family. The hard-working professional parents depending on her to help raise the cute little brothers. She loving to do it, power-tripping on the responsibility. Then the family gets ready to emigrate to a new world. Exciting! But the daughter screws up by straining some muscles and then breaking her leg in a fall."

. . . But just one short week in the tank, dear, and you can come out to us on the next ship. Hurry and get well, Annamaria. We're going to need your help more than ever on Multnomah, big girl!

And you hurried. But by the time you were well they were all dead—killed in a translational malfunction of their starship. So what could you do but atone? Try through all the years to show them you were sorry that you had not died along with them. Dedicate yourself to easing the passing of others as you were not able to ease theirs . . .

"But fighting it at the same time, Claude. I realize that now. I wasn't really a morbid person and I was glad to be alive and not dead. But that old guilt never let me go, even though it was so well sublimated in my vocation that I didn't realize how it was undermining me. I went along for years doing work that was very hard and refusing to take holidays or sabbaticals the way the others did. There was always a case that needed my special help and I was always strong enough to give it. But in the end it all became a sham. The demons weren't exorcized any more. The emotional fatigue of the job and the buried guilt all mingled and became unbearable."

The old man's voice was compassionate. "So when the contemplative orders justifiably turned you down, you scratched around and found what looked like an even better form of atonement . . . Can't you see that you haven't loved *yourself* enough, Amerie? This hermitage-in-Exile idea was the ultimate chair in a corner facing the wall."

Her head was averted from him so that the broad-brimmed hat hid her face. She said, "So the Exile anchoress turns out to be just as much of a fraud as the ministering nun in the hospice for the dying."

"That last bit isn't true!" Claude snapped. "Gen didn't think so and neither did I. And neither did the hundreds of other suffering people you helped. For God's sake, Amerie, try to keep a perspective! Every human being has deep motives as well as superficial ones. But the motivation doesn't invalidate the objective good we do."

"You want me to get on with my life and quit picking scabs. But, Claude—I can't go back now, even though I know the choice was wrong. I have nothing left."

"If you've got any faith remaining at all, why not believe that you're here for a reason?"

She gave him a crooked smile. "It's an interesting idea. Suppose I spend the rest of the night meditating on it."

"Good girl. I have a feeling you won't have much time for meditation later on, if Felice's plan works out . . . I tell you what. You meditate and I'll snooze, and we'll both do ourselves good. Wake me as soon as Basil starts playing the signal. It'll be just before dawn."

"When it's darkest," sighed the nun. "Go to sleep, Claude. Pleasant dreams."

* * *

There were no more double beacons, which seemed to have been the scouting party's warning of Firvulag in the vicinity. The caravan had come down from the plateau now and traversed open wooded slopes cut by little brooks that foamed whitely over boulders, calling for tricky footwork by the chalikos as they picked their way along in the starshine. The country became rougher and there was a tang of conifer resin in the air. As the night wore on, a breeze sprang up, ruffling the lake and making the beacon fires near the shore lean and twist. It was very quiet. Aside from the noise of the moving caravan, only owl hoots were to be heard. There were no lights of villages or farms, no sign of habitation at all. So much the better if they did manage to escape . . .

They came to a deep gorge lit on both sides by bonfires, where a lonely guardpost secured a suspension bridge over a cascading stream. Three torch-bearing men in bronze armor stood at attention as Epone and Captal Waldemar crossed the swaying structure. Then the soldiers led small groups of prisoners over, bracketed by amphicyons.

When they resumed their march, Richard told Felice, "It's after four. We been losing time fording the creeks."

"We'll have to wait until we get far enough away from that damn guardpost. I hadn't planned on that. There are more than three soldiers manning it, count on that. Epone will be able to send them a telepathic call for help and we've got to be sure they'll get to us too late. I want to wait another half hour at least."

"Don't cut it too fine, sweets. What if there's another post? And what about the scouts ahead who light the beacons?"

"Oh, shut up! I'm juggling factors until I'm dizzy trying to optimize this thing. Just be sure *you're* ready . . . Did you lash it firmly to your lower arm?"

"Just like you said."

Felice called out, "Basil."

"Righto."

"Would you play some lullaby tunes for a while?"

The notes of the woodwind rose softly, soothing the riders after the brief anxiety caused by the bridge-crossing. The double file of chalikos and their flanking bear-dogs now moved among titanic black conifer trunks. The trail was soft with millennia of needle duff, muffling their passage and sending even the most uncomfortable riders into a doze. The track rose gradually until it was more than a hundred meters above the Lac de Bresse, with occasional sheer drops to the water on the caravan's right. Too soon, it seemed to Felice, the eastern sky began to lighten.

She sighed and pulled down her hoplite helmet, then leaned forward in the saddle. "Basil. Now."

The Alpine climber played "All Through the Night."

When he finished it and began again, four amphicyons went

charging soundlessly to the head of the procession and hamstrung Epone's chaliko with simultaneous slashes of their teeth. The exotic woman's mount uttered a heart-stopping shriek as it went down in a welter of dark bodies. The bear-dogs, with barking roars, leaped upon Epone herself. Soldiers and the front ranks of prisoners gave shouts of horror, but the Tanu slave-mistress did not cry out.

Richard thumped his free feet against his mount's neck and held tightly to the reins as the creature took off. He galloped into the midst of the quartet of soldiers trying to come to the assistance of Epone. Waldemar was shouting, "Use your lances, not the bows! Lift them off her, you stupid bastards!"

Richard's chaliko reared and crashed down upon the captal, knocking him from the saddle. A figure in white robes and a black veil leapt down as if to help the fallen officer. In the moment that Waldemar took to gasp astonishment at seeing a mustache on a nun's face, Richard slipped Felice's little dirk from its golden scabbard and pressed the steel blade home twice below the two corners of Waldemar's jaw, just above the gray metal necklet. His carotid arteries severed, the captal clutched at the false nun with a bubbling cry, gave a peculiar smile, and died.

Two riderless chalikos were thrashing together in the semidarkness, inflicting ghastly wounds upon one another with their huge claws. Replacing the dirk in its sheath on his forearm, Richard seized the dead officer's bronze sword and backed off, cursing. There were confused shouts and a long scream of pain from the tangle of amphicyons and armed men. The two soldiers of the rear guard came pounding up to assist their comrades. One of the men charged with lance couched, spitting a small bear-dog that dashed in from the side and hoisting it high into the air. Then another hulking form came darting among the mounted guards, snapping at the heels of the enraged, screeching chalikos.

Felice sat her beast, motionless, as though she were merely a spectator to the carnage. One of the ronin, heels drumming the shoulders of his mount, rushed into the free-for-all and hauled back on his reins. The chaliko reared and brought its scimitar claws down onto the rump of a soldier's animal. The Japanese warrior, shouting an ancient battle cry, forced his own mount to ramp again and again with terrible driving blows that crushed the soldier and his chaliko into the tangled mass already on the ground. The second ronin came up on foot and grasped a lance from its scabbard on the fallen man's saddle.

"A bear-dog! Behind you, Tat!" Richard yelled.

The warrior whirled around and braced the spear on the ground as the amphicyon leaped. Transfixed through the neck, the animal body continued forward on momentum and crushed the ronin named Tat beneath its great bulk. Richard ran forward and stabbed the struggling monster in its near eye, then tried to haul it off the warrior. But someone shouted, "Here comes another one!" And Richard looked up to see a black shape with gleaming eyes not four meters away.

Felice gazed impassively at the fight, her face almost hidden within the T-shaped helmet opening.

The charging amphicyon swerved away from Richard and ran over the edge of the steep embankment, squalling in midair and striking the water with a tremendous splash. Basil and the knight Dougal rode their mounts impotently around the edge of the bedlam of noise, hesitating before the flailing bloody claws and struggling shapes. Ripping off the impeding veil and wimple, Richard picked up another lance and tossed it to Basil. Instead of stabbing with it, the climber hoisted the thing like a javelin, threw, and hit one of the soldiers high on the armor of his upper back. The point of the weapon skidded up beneath the man's kettle-helmet, penetrating the base of his skull. He fell like a bag of sand.

Felice watched.

No more bear-dogs came from the shadowy perimeter. All that were left alive were busy worrying something lying next to the body of a dead white chaliko. A single soldier stood upright among them, hacking slowly at the snarling amphicyons like some freshly painted red automaton.

"You must kill him," Felice said.

They could not find any more lances. Richard ran to the mounted knight, handed up his bronze sword, and pointed. "Take him, Dougal!"

As if in a trance, the elegant medievalist grasped the weapon and waited for a suitable moment before riding into the mass of dead and dying animals and men. He decapitated the futile chopping figure with a single blow.

There were two bear-dogs left alive as the last soldier fell. Richard found another sword and prepared to stand his ground if they came after him; but the creatures seemed seized with a kind of fit. They backed away from their prey reluctantly, giving vent to agonized howls, then turned and went leaping to their doom over the edge of the lakeside cliff.

The sky was becoming rose-colored. There were gagging sounds and hysterical sobs as the stunned prisoners, who had been herded into a compact group by Claude and Amerie during the embroilment, now came slowly forward to look. Noises from dying chalikos were cut short as the surviving ronin went about with a dispatching sword. The first morning notes of song sparrows, simple and solemn as Gregorian chant, echoed among the lofty sequoia trunks.

Felice rose up in her saddle, arms wide, fingers grasping, head in its plumed helmet thrown back as she writhed, cried out, then slumped back inertly against the high cantle.

The Japanese bent over the gory carcass of the white chaliko. He grunted and beckoned to Richard. Numbed now, feeling only curiosity, the former starship captain went stumbling into the fleshly wreckage, hindered by his incongruous nun's garb. On the ground amidst the bodies was a hideously gnawed limbless trunk swathed in bloody rags. The face was torn to the bone all along one side, but the other was still beautiful and untouched.

An eyelid opened. A jade-green orb reached out at Richard. Epone's mind took hold of him and began to drag him down.

He screamed. His bronze sword hewed and stabbed at the thing down there but its inexorable grip held firm. The dawnlight began to fade and he was being taken to a place from which he would not return.

"Iron!" the high-pitched voice of the knight called out. "Iron! Only thus may the faerie perish!"

The useless sword fell and Richard fumbled at his wrist. As he continued to sink he clutched at the instrument of redemption and sent its steely potency deep—between the heaving white-scarlet ribs without breasts to the raging heart, stilling it and quenching the body's resident spirit which took flight, releasing as it was released.

Basil and the ronin hauled Richard out of there by the arms. He was wide-eyed and still screaming but holding tight to the gold-handled knife. The three of them paid no attention to the demented Dougal, who leaped from his saddle and began stomping something beneath his mailed feet.

Felice shouted a warning.

Ignoring her, the knight picked a blood-smeared golden hoop from the mess and scaled it far out over the lake, where it sank without a trace.

14

THE RIVERSIDE PALACE at Darask was in an uproar when the southbound travelers broke their journey there on the second evening. The mistress of the establishment had been brought to childbed with twins and her labor was proving dangerously prolonged. Creyn went off to volunteer his medical services, leaving the prisoners in the care of a silver-torced major-domo, a black Irishman who forthrightly introduced himself as Hughie B. Kennedy VII and led them under guard to a large chamber high in one tower of the palace.

"You'll have to rough it tonight, friends," Kennedy said. "Boys and girls together here where we can keep you secure easily. We can't spare the guards tonight for single quarters, not with our poor Lady Estella-Sirone hovering on the brink and the buggerin' Firvulag gathering round, knowing what's in the wind. You'll be cool up here at any rate, and above the mosquitoes. There's a good supper out on the balcony table."

The escorting palace guards carried in Stein's litter and rolled the Viking onto one of the netting-draped bedsteads. Sukey protested. "But he needs care! He hasn't eaten or drunk all day or—anything."

"Don't fret yourself over him," Kennedy said. "When they're put under with the torc"—and he fingered his own—"they're like in suspended animation. Your friend's just a hibernatin' animal, metabolism all slowed down. He'll keep until tomorrow. By then, please Jesus, all'll be well with our Lady, and we can spare some time for him." The major-domo gave Sukey a shrewd look. "Likely you'll keep a good eye on your friend."

The prisoners were allowed to take a change of clothing but nothing else from their packs, which were then removed by the guards. Kennedy apologized once more for the meagerness of their welcome and prepared to lock them in. Elizabeth came to him and said in a low voice, "I must speak privately to Creyn. It's important."

The major-domo frowned. "Ma'am, I realize that you're a privileged person, but my orders were to install all of you together here."

"Kennedy, I'm an operant metapsychic and a trained redactor. I can't get through to Creyn, but I can farsense your lady and her unborn babies and I know that right this moment they're in serious trouble. I can't help them from here, but if you take me down to the birthing room . . . there! Creyn's calling for me!"

Kennedy had heard the telepathic summons, too. "Come along, then." Taking her by one arm, he drew her into the tower corridor and slammed the door shut.

Raimo said sourly, "That was nice going. We get stuck here, but Little Red Riding Britches gets to see the fireworks."

"I never would have pegged you as an obstetrics freak," Aiken jeered.

"Didn't you hear that guy?" Raimo's pale eyes glistened and he licked his lips. "He said the Firvulag were gonna lay siege to the place! I wanna see that. Maybe get in on the fighting."

Sukey's face was twisted with scorn. "You just can't wait to join the Hunt, can you? Can't wait to get some monster's head on a pike. But you weren't so brave when we were shooting those rapids today!"

Leaving them to their bickering, Bryan and a strangely subdued Aiken Drum went out to the balcony. The promised supper had enough food for a dozen people; but all of it was cold and bore evidences of hasty preparation. Aiken picked up the leg of a roast fowl and took an uninterested bite, meanwhile inspecting the security arrangements of the balcony. It was completely enclosed in a cage of ornamental brass grillwork.

"I won't be flying out of here very quickly, will I? I suppose I could saw through the bars with one of the little vitredur gizmos I have in my pockets. But it hardly seems worthwhile trying to escape. They've got me so curious about the Tanu good life that running away seems stupid."

"I believe that's the attitude you're supposed to form," Bryan said. "You were allowed to taste just enough of your new powers to want a whole lot more. Now they've taken your metafunctions away until you submit to their training regimen down in the capital and they make you into a good little copy of themselves."

"So you think that'll happen, do you?" Aiken's golliwog grin was as wide as ever, but his black button eyes held an ugly glitter. "You don't know a fewkin' thing about me and the way my mind works.

As for the metabilities, you're only a *normal*. You've never tasted the powers and you never will, so don't give me any of your high-ass professor's predictions about the way I'm going to behave!"

"They've got you collared and liking it," Bryan said mildly.

Aiken touched the silver neck-ring with a dismissive flick. "This thing! It's only put a clamp on my metafunctions. The clamp is effective now because I haven't figured how to turn it off. But I'm working on it. You think they've got me under control? What Creyn did at the very beginning was program this inhibitory thing on us. There's this little nagger in the skull that hints at horrible things happening to us if we try to escape or do anything to threaten the peace and good order of our wonderful Tanu friends. You know how much that inhibition is worth, influencing *me*? It isn't worth shit. Little Sukey and dumbo Ray in there are safe—but not Aiken Drum."

"The torcs . . . have you discovered how the different kinds work?"

"Not the details, but enough. One of the Tanu women at the Roniah party spilled a lot when I put it to her nicely. The old torcs are the basic article, the mental amplifiers that turn latents into operants. They're stuffed with barium chips all latticed with microscopic amounts of rare earths and bits of other junk that these jokers brought with them from their home galaxy. They handcraft the torcs and have a machine to grow and print the chips. They hardly understand how the machine functions, and most of 'em know even less about the theory behind the torcs themselves, the whole metapsychic thing. The technology of it is handled down in the capital city by some outfit called the Coercer Guild."

"Do the golden torcs have differing powers of—uh—magnification?"

"They're all exactly the same. And all they magnify is what the individual's got. If a guy's got one weakie ability latent, he becomes an operant weakie. If he's loaded with all five metafunctions in wholesale lots, he becomes operant as the Wizard of Oz. Most of the Tanu are fairly strong in just one metafunction and they tend to club up with others of the same type. The folks who have several strong powers are the real aristocrats. Just what you'd expect. It's the same sort of setup that you get in the Milieu—only on a pipsqueak scale, with everyone pretty much out for what he can get. Near as I can tell so far, there are no masterclass metas here and nothing like the Milieu's psychounion."

Bryan slowly nodded. "I'd already sensed a lack of hierarchy among these people. I wouldn't be surprised to find them still at the clan level of socialization. Fascinating—and almost unprecedented, given the high-culture trappings."

"They're barbarians," Aiken stated flatly. "That's one of the things I like about 'em! And they're not too proud to let us human latents join right in—"

"With *silver* torcs."

Aiken gave a short laugh. "Yeah. These silver collars have all the mind-expanding functions of the gold—plus control circuits. The gray torcs and the small collars of the monkeys have nothing but controls, plus a bunch of pleasure-pain circuits and a telepathic communication thing that varies a lot in its range."

Bryan peered over the edge of the balcony. "Can you get any mental clues as to what's going on around here? Quite a few alarums and excursions down there. I'm getting very curious about the Firvulag by now."

"Funny thing about those severed heads the Hunt brought in." Aiken frowned. "They weren't quite dead, some of them! And after a while they started to—how can I say it?—flicker. The Hunters took them away, so we never really got a good look at them. But there was something subliminal about the whole scene."

Sukey and Raimo chose that moment to come out in search of dinner. Aiken asked them, "You guys *hear* anything? With your minds? I've tried, but this damn lock Creyn put on me screens out all but whispers."

Sukey closed her eyes and put her fingers in her ears. Raimo just stood there with his mouth open, finally saying, "Hell, all I hear is my stomach rumbling. Lemme at that food."

After a few minutes had passed with Aiken and Bryan watching her patiently, Sukey opened her eyes. "I get . . . eagerness. From a lot of mental sources that seem to be *different*. Broadcasting on another wavelength from humans. Even different from Tanu. I can tune them in, but it's hard. Do you understand what I mean?"

"We understand, kiddo," Aiken said.

Sukey glanced from him to Bryan anxiously. "What do you suppose it could be?"

"Nothing to bother us, I'm sure," Bryan said.

Sukey murmured something about wanting to sit with Stein and took a plate of fruit and cold meat inside. Bryan was satisfied with a roughly made sandwich and a mug of some ciderlike beverage. He stood looking over twilit Darask. In the east, the monstrous rampart of the Maritime Alps still reflected glaring sunset-pink on the highest snowfields. Extraordinary, Bryan thought. The mountains looked to be as high as the spine of the Himalaya or even the Hlithskjalf Massif on Asgard. A cool wind was coming down from the heights, spreading across the everglade flats where the Rhône finally relaxed and spread wide after its precipitate plunge from the region around unborn Lyon.

The day's journey had been something like descending a series of vast canyoned steps. They would sail peacefully for thirty or forty kilometers, then encounter savage rapids that would chute them to the next lower level at jetboat velocity. Despite Skipper Highjohn's reassurances, Bryan felt that he had survived the ordeal of a lifetime. The last stretch of rapids—occurring, as he had suspected, in the gorge area about fifty kloms above the future Pont d'Avignon—had been formidable beyond belief. The prolongation of terror had blunted his senses to the point of stupor. Aiken Drum had begged Creyn not to put him to sleep for that last rough ride, being eager for some taste of the thrills that Bryan had described. When the boat had tumbled end over end down the face of the final great cataract and fetched up in the placid Lac Provençal, Aiken's face had turned to gray-green and his bright eyes were sunken in shock.

"A fewkin' flea ride," he had moaned, "in a fewkin' food blender!"

By the time they reached Darask on the Lower Rhône, they had journeyed nearly 270 kilometers in less than ten hours. The shallowing river twined and split and braided itself into scores of channels divided by rippling grasslands and mudflats inhabited by flocks of long-legged birds and cream-and-black checkered crocodiles. Here and there islands rose from the marshy plain. Darask crowned one of them, looking for all the world like a tropical Mont-Saint-Michel towering above a sea of grass. Their boat had used its auxiliary engine to move out of the mainstream of the Rhône into a secondary channel leading to the fortified town. Darask had a small quay secured behind a limestone wall more than twelve meters high that butted against unscalable cliffs.

And now, in the town beneath the high-rising palace, ramas were lighting the small night-lamps, clambering up spindly ladders to tend those on brackets along the house roofs, working pulleys to raise long strings of lanterns up the face of the inner fortifications. Human soldiers touched off larger torches on the bastions of the town's perimeter. As Bryan and the others surveyed the scene, the peculiar Tanu-style illumination sprang into operation, outlining the spired palace in dots of red and amber that symbolized the heraldic colors of its psychokinetic lord, Cranovel.

Aiken inspected the Tanu lamps along their own balcony. They were of sturdy faceted glass resting in small niches in the stone, without wires or any other metallic attachments. They were cold.

"Bioluminescence," the little man in gold decided, shaking one. "You want to bet there are microorganisms in here? What did Creyn say—that the lights were energized by surplus meta emanations? That figures. You get some of the lower echelon torc wearers to generate a suitable waveform while they're playing checkers or drinking beer or reading in the bathtub or performing some other semiautomatic—"

Bryan was paying scant attention to Aiken's speculations. Out in the surrounding marshland, the ignes fatui were lighting their own lamps—wispy blobs of methane blue, firefly glimmerings that winked on and off in scattered synchrony, wandering pale flames gliding around the island's misty backwaters like lost elfin boats.

"I suppose those are glowing insects or marsh-gas flames out there," Sukey said, coming up behind Bryan to stare into the darkening landscape.

Raimo said, "*Now* I hear something. But not with any meta-faculty. You guys catching it?"

They listened. Sukey pursed her lips in exasperation. "Frogs!"

An almost inaudible trill was building up on the breeze, swelling and finally fracturing into a complex treble chord of tinkles and peeps. An invisible batrachian maestro lowered his baton and more voices chimed in—gulps and grunts, rattling snares, pops and clicks, tunking notes as of hollow canes. Additional frog voices contributed their simulations of slowly dripping water, plucked strings, human glottal trills, buzzing drillbits, amplified guitar notes; and underriding it all was the homely *jug-o'-rum* of the common bullfrog, that durable Earth creature that would, in only six million years, accompany mankind on its colonization of the far-flung stars.

The four people on the balcony looked at one another and burst into laughter.

"We've got a front-row seat," Aiken said, "in case there's any Firvulag invasion. And this blue pitcher is full of something that's cool and definitely alcoholic. Shall we pull up chairs and fortify ourselves just in case the monsters arrive on schedule?"

"All in favor?" Bryan demanded.

"Aye!"

They held out their mugs and the little man in gold filled them, one by one.

*   *   *

Elizabeth pressed the back of her hand to her clammy forehead. Her eyes opened and she exhaled a long, slow breath.

Creyn and a haggard Tanu man in a rumpled yellow robe bent anxiously over her chair. Creyn's mind touched hers—supporting, querying.

Yes. I have separated them. Finally. Sorry so weak my skill rusty disuse. They will be born now.

The mind of Lord Cranovel of Darask wept gratitude. And she? Safe oh safe my darling?

Humanwomen tougher than Tanu. She recovers easily now.

He cried aloud, "Estella-Sirone!" and ran to the inner chamber.

In a few moments the querulous wail of a newborn infant came to the two who still waited. Elizabeth smiled at Creyn. The first grayness of dawn lightened the mist outside the palace windows.

Elizabeth said, "I've never handled anything quite like that before. The two unborn minds so intertwined, so mutually antagonistic. Fraternal twins, of course. But it seems incredible that genuine enmity should have been able to—"

A Tanu woman dressed all in red put her head through the curtained doorway and exclaimed, "A lovely girl! The next one is a breech, but we'll get it safely, never fear." She disappeared again.

Elizabeth got up from the chair and walked wearily to the window, letting her mind reach out beyond the birthing rooms for the first time since she had entered so many hours ago. The anomalies were outside—crowding closer and stumbling over one another in horrid eagerness—those twittering little unhuman minds, seemingly operant, changing their soulform even as she tried to grasp them for examination. They eluded her, wove disguises, faded and flared, shrunk to atomies or expanded into looming monsters that postured in the mental-physical fog swirling about the towers of the island palace.

Another baby cried.

Pierced by a terrible realization, Elizabeth's mind met that of Creyn. A slow-distilling drop of regret formed from a complex of the man's emotions. Then he slammed down an impervious screen between them.

Elizabeth ran to the door of the inner chamber and pushed the draperies aside. Several women, both human and Tanu, were attendant upon the new mother, a human wearing a golden torc. Estella-Sirone was smiling, the beautiful baby girl held to her right breast. Cranovel knelt beside her, wiping her brow.

The Tanu nurse in red brought the other baby to show to Elizabeth. It was a very small boy, weighing about two kilos, wizened as an old man and with an oversized head thickly covered with wet dark hair. Its eyes were wide open and it screeched thinly from a mouth that had a full set of tiny sharp teeth. Even as Elizabeth watched, the manikin shimmered and became furry all over its body, then shimmered again and turned to a virtual double of its plump blonde sister.

"It is a Firvulag, a shape-changer," the nurse said. "They are the shadow-brethren of the Tanu from the foundation of worlds. Ever with us, ever against us. The twin situation is fortunately rare. Most such die unborn, and the mother with them."

"What will you do with him?" Elizabeth asked. Fascinated, horrified, she sounded the small alien mentality and recognized the anomalous mode, now that it was fully separated from the more complex psychic structure of the Tanu sister.

The tall nurse shrugged. "His folk are awaiting him. And so we give him to them, as always. You would like to see it?"

Dumbly, Elizabeth nodded.

The nurse swiftly wrapped the baby in a soft towel and hurried out of the birthing room. Elizabeth had all she could do to keep up as the woman raced down flight after flight of stone stairs, all empty and echoing and lit only by the tiny ruby and amber lamps. They finally came to a cellar. A dank corridor led to the outer wall of the town and a great, locked watergate, beside which was an indoor anchorage full of deserted small boats. The gate had a wicket with a bronze bolt, which the exotic woman shot open.

"Guard your mind," she warned, and stepped outside onto the fog-obscured dock.

There were lights out there, and they converged with alarming speed, making no sound whatsoever. Then came a single deep-green glow that became a sphere some four meters across, rolling on the surface of the water and burning the mist to shreds as it approached the dock.

With great caution, Elizabeth pried apart the fabric of the illusion and looked inside. There was a boat—a punt, rather—with a dwarfish fellow poling and a round-cheeked little woman sitting in the bows with a covered basket in her lap.

So you see us, do you?

Elizabeth staggered as a barrage of lightning seemed to explode behind her eyes. Her tongue swelled as if to strangle her. The flesh of her hands blistered, blackened, burst, and cooked in a living flame.

That'll show the upstart!

"I warned you," said the Tanu woman. Elizabeth felt the tall one's arms about her, holding her up. She saw only the glowing ball receding into the mist. Her mouth was normal, her hands unhurt.

"The Firvulag are operant metapsychics of a sort. All most of them can do is farsense and spin illusions—but those can be strong enough to drive an unready mind mad. We handle them well enough—at Grand Combat time and at most other times, too. But you must not let them take you unaware."

The baby was gone. After a few seconds the green glow vanished as well, and daylight broke fitfully through rags of vapor. Far up on the battlements, a woman's voice was singing alien words to a familiar melody.

"We'll go back now," the nurse said. "My Lord and Lady will be very grateful to you. You must receive proper thanks—then refreshment and rest. There is a small family ceremony—naming the child and giving her the first tiny golden torc. They will wish you to hold the baby. It is a great honor."

"Imagine me as fairy godmother," Elizabeth murmured. "What a world! Are you going to name her after me as well?"

"She already has a name. It is traditional among us to give anew the name of one who has recently passed on to Tana's peace. The baby will be called Epone—and the Goddess grant that she be more fortunate than the last who bore that name."

15

AMERIE CAME DOWN to the lakeshore where the freed prisoners were ballasting their hastily inflated boats.

"I've had to sedate Felice. She was ready to tear the poor noddy apart."

"Not surprising," Claude growled. "Once I'd thought the matter through, I was tempted along those lines myself."

Richard was treading siphon bulbs with both feet, flooding the interstices of his and Claude's beached dinghies while the old man loaded equipment into the two small decamole craft. Richard had changed back into his pirate costume, curtly telling the nun to keep his spacer's coverall "for the duration." Now he glowered at her. "Maybe Dougal did us all a favor without knowing it. How do we know what Felice would turn into once she got hold of a golden torc?"

"There's that," Claude had to admit. "But if she'd got it, we wouldn't have to worry about any immediate danger from the soldiers. As it is, some kind of armed force is going to be breathing down our necks any minute now. We couldn't have been far from the next fort when the fight started."

Amerie said, "You two come up and help me with Felice when you finish here. Yosh has been going through the baggage packs, retrieving some of our stuff."

"Any weapons?" Richard asked.

"They seem to have left ours back at the castle. But most of the tools are there. No maps or compasses, I'm afraid."

Claude and Richard shared a glance. The paleontologist said, "Then it's seat-of-the-pants navigation and devil take the hindmost. You go on up, Amerie. We'll be along in a few minutes."

In the aftermath of the fight, when all of the prisoners had been released, they had held a hasty conference and decided that the best chance of escape lay in taking to the water—one or two people to a decamole dinghy from the Survival Units. Only the five Gypsies had ignored Claude's warning about the dangers of riding the torc-susceptible chalikos. They had gone back to attack the suspension bridge guardpost after donning the gory armor of the slain escort and taking most of the soldiers' weaponry.

The remaining escapees had reestablished the bonding forged back at the auberge, the original Groups coming together once more to plan their collective getaway. Claude, the only person with a working knowledge of the Pliocene landscape, had suggested two possible escape routes. The one that would take them most quickly to rugged country entailed a short voyage northeast, across the narrow upper portion of the Lac de Bresse to canyons leading into the heavily forested Vosges highlands. This had the disadvantage of crossing the main trail to Finiah on the opposite shore of the lake; but if they managed to elude mounted patrols, they could reach the high country before nightfall and hole up among the rocks.

The second route would have them sailing southeast across the widest part of the lake to the shore of the Jura piedmont some sixty kilometers away, then continuing south into the mountain range itself. There seemed an excellent chance that the land in that direction was completely uninhabited, since beyond the Jura lay the Alps. On the other hand, the lakeside forts were likely to have boats of their own that could be used for pursuit. The escapees might outsail the Tanu minions; but the breeze was fitful and the nearly cloudless sky suggested that the air might go dead calm as it had the day before. If the boats were becalmed at nightfall, they might attract the attention of the Firvulag.

Basil had confidently elected for the Jura route, while Claude's conservatism inclined him to hold out for the Vosges. But the climber was most persuasive to the majority, so in the end it was decided that all of the time-travelers except the remnant of Group Green and Yosh, the surviving ronin, would go south. The prisoners had hastily unloaded their baggage from the chalikos and followed a gully down to a tiny beach below the cliff. There boats could be launched. A few of the small craft were already spreading their sails when Richard completed ballasting the two Green boats and scrambled back up the embankment in search of the others.

He discovered Claude, Amerie, and Yosh standing over Felice's unconscious body. The Japanese warrior said, "I've found Claude's woodworking tools and the knives and hatchets and saws from our Survival and Smallholder Units." He held out a hideously stained packet to Richard. "And here are also a soldier's bow and arrows that the Gypsies overlooked."

"We're grateful, Yosh," said the old man. "The bow could be very important. We have very little food except for the survival rations, and the kits have only snares and fishing gear. The people going south with Basil will have time to make new weapons if they reach the Jura shore. But our Group will be in much more danger of land pursuit. We'll have to keep moving and do our hunting on the run."

"But you should go with us, Yosh," Amerie said. "Won't you change your mind?"

"I have my own Survival Unit and Tat's lance. I'll take the rest of the tools that I scavenged down to the people on the shore. But I won't go with them, and I won't go with you." He gestured to the sky, where dark specks were already circling in the morning gold. "I have a duty here. The Reverend Sister has given my poor friend the Blessing of Departure. But Tat must not be left to the scavengers. When I've finished, I plan to head due north on foot to the River Marne. It joins the Pliocene Seine and the Seine flows into the Atlantic. I don't think the Tanu will bother to track one man."

"Well—don't hang around here too long," Richard said dubiously.

The ronin knelt swiftly beside Felice's limp form and kissed her brow. His grim eyes swept those of the others. "You must take good care of this mad child. We owe her our freedom, and if God wills she may yet accomplish her purpose. The potential rests in her."

"We know," said the nun. "Go blessed, Yoshimitsu-san."

The warrior got to his feet, bowed, and left them.

"Time for us to go, too," said Claude. He and Amerie picked up the pathetically light body of the girl while Richard gathered her helmet and pack, together with the tools and weapons.

"I can sail single-handed," the pirate said when they reached the waiting boats. "Put Felice in with me and you two follow."

They shoved off, the last to set sail, and relaxed only when they were far out from land. The lake waters were cold and of an opaque blue, fed by rivers running out of the Jura and the Vosges forest to the northeast. Amerie stared at the receding shore, where carrion birds were gradually descending.

"Claude . . . I've been thinking. Why didn't Epone die sooner from those dreadful wounds? She was literally torn to pieces before Richard and Yosh and Dougal ever got near her. She should have bled to death or died from hypovolemic shock. But she didn't."

"The people at the fort told you that the Tanu were nearly invulnerable. What did you *think* they meant?"

"I don't know—perhaps I assumed that the exotics were able to use their coercive power to fend off attackers. But I never dreamed a Tanu could survive such physical punishment. It's hard not to think of them as approximately human, given that breeding scheme Epone spoke to us about."

"Even human beings without metafunctions have been mighty tenacious of life. I've seen things in the colonies that were damn near miraculous. And when you consider the enhancement of mental powers that the Tanu achieve with the torc . . ."

"I wonder if they have regenerative facilities here in Exile?"

"I should think so, in the cities. And God knows what other kinds of technology they have. So far, we've only seen the torcs, the mind assayer, and that frisking device they used on us when we first came through the time-portal."

"Ah, yes. And that brings us to the lethal dagger."

The old man stripped off his bush jacket and pillowed his back against one of the boat seats. "I don't doubt that our anthropologist friend Bryan could tell us all about the legendary faerie antipathy toward iron. He'd probably explain it in terms of the ancient tensions between Bronze Age and Iron Age cultures . . . Be that as it may, European folklore is almost universal in believing that iron is repugnant or even deadly to the Old People."

The nun burst out, "Oh, for heaven's sake, Claude! Epone was an exotic, not some bloody elf!"

"Then you tell *me* why bear-dog bites and dismemberment and stab wounds from a bronze sword didn't finish her off, while a single thrust from a steel knife blade did."

Amerie considered. "It may be that the iron interferes in some way with the function of the torc. The blood of the Tanu is red, just like ours, and probably just as iron-rich. Their bodies and minds and the torc might operate in a delicate harmony that could be upset by the introduction of a gross mass of iron. Iron might even wonk them up if it just came near the body's intimate aura. Remember Stein and his battle-axe? None of the castle people was able to prevent him from doing terrible damage—which didn't strike me as strange at the time. But with what we know now, it seems significant."

"They frisked us thoroughly enough," Claude said. "I can understand why the guardians weren't able to pry Stein loose from his axe. But how did Felice's knife slip through?"

"I can't imagine—unless they were careless and didn't sweep her leg. Or perhaps the gold of the scabbard confused the detector. It suggests possibilities for countertactics."

Claude studied her through half-closed lids. There was an intensity about her that was new and startling. "Now you're beginning to sound like Felice! That child has no qualms about taking on the whole Tanu race. Never mind that they control the friggerty planet!"

Amerie flashed him an odd smile. "But it's *our* planet. And six million years from now, we'll be here. And they won't."

She snugged the tiller under her arm and kept the boat racing eastward, its sail taut before the freshening breeze.

* * *

They came up behind a marshy island, hauled down sails and unstepped and deflated masts and centerboards. Armloads of reeds and young willows were cut to disguise the boats. They substituted rear-mounted decamole sculling oars for the sailing rudders. A person crouched low in the stern could impart a barely perceptible forward motion by wagging the oar back and forth.

Richard protested, "It'll take us two hours to travel the half klom to the shore at this rate."

"Keep your voice down," Claude warned him. "Sound travels over water." He brought his boat close to Richard's. "Somewhere on that shore is the trail—maybe even the fort where we were scheduled to stop for sleep this morning. We've got to be careful about showing ourselves until we're sure the coast is clear."

Richard laughed nervously. "The coast is clear! So that's where the cliché came from! Probably pirates—"

"Shut up, son," said the old man, weariness making his low voice harsh. "Just follow me from here on in and pretend you're a collection of flotsam."

Claude sculled so slowly that there was no wake; they seemed to drift from islet to islet, gradually approaching a low-lying shore where reeds and sedges grew more than five meters tall and long-shanked water birds with plumage of pink and blue and dazzling white stalked the shallows, jabbing at frogs and fish with their beaks.

The sun rose higher. It became excruciatingly hot and humid. Some kind of biting midge zeroed in on them, trapped as they were beneath the concealing greenery, and raised itching welts before they could find repellent in their awkwardly stowed packs. After a tedious interval of paddling, they scraped bottom on a jungly mudflat where many of the bamboos had trunks as thick as a man's thigh. Broadleaf evergreen trees perfumed the air with sickly sweet flowers. There was a game trail in the mud, heavily trampled by large flat feet. It looked as though it would lead them to higher ground.

"This is it," Claude said. "We deflate the dinghies and hike from here."

Richard extracted himself from the mass of stalks and branches in his boat and surveyed the site with disgust. "Jesus, Claude. Did you have to land us in a fuckin' swamp? Talk about your green hells! This place is probably crawling with snakes. And will you look at those footprints? Some mighty ugly mothers been cruising through here!"

"Oh, stuff it, Richard," Amerie said. "Help me get Felice ashore and I'll try to revive her while you guys—"

"Get down, everybody!" the old man whispered urgently.

They crouched low in the boats and stared in the direction from which they had come. Out beyond the marshy little islands, where the lake was deep and the breeze blew unimpeded, were a pair of seven-meter catboats that bore no resemblance to any of the craft launched by the escapees. They were slowly tacking northward.

"Well, now we know where the fort must be," Claude remarked. "South of here and most likely not very far away. They've probably got oculars on board so we'll have to stay down until they get around that point."

They waited. Sweat trickled down various body surfaces and made them itch. The frustrated midges whined and went on sorties against their unprotected eyeballs and nostrils. Claude's belly rumbled, reminding him that he had not eaten in nearly twelve hours. Richard discovered a sticky gash hidden in the hair above his left ear, and so did the local variety of blowfly. Amerie made a desultory attempt to pray; but her memory bank refused to pay out any withdrawals except the grace before meals and "Now I Lay Me Down to Sleep."

Felice moaned.

"Cover her mouth, Richard," Claude said. "Keep her quiet for just a few minutes longer."

Somewhere, ducks were quacking. Somewhere else, an animal was snuffling and slurping and breaking the giant bamboos like twigs as it sought its lunch. And elsewhere still, the silver sound of a horn sang on the limit of audibility, to be followed seconds later by a louder response farther north.

The old paleontologist sighed. "They're out of sight. Let's deflate these boats and move on."

The power-inflators, used in reverse, swiftly sucked both air and water out of the decamole membranes, reducing the boats to spheres the size of Ping-Pong balls. While Amerie revived Felice with a dose of stimulant, Claude rummaged in his pack for survival-ration biscuits and fortified candy, which he shared with the others.

Felice was listless and disoriented but seemed well enough to walk. Claude tried to get her to remove her leather cuirass, greaves, and gauntlets, which had to be acutely uncomfortable in the muggy atmosphere of the marsh; but she refused, only agreeing to keep her helmet stowed in the pack when Claude pointed out that its plumage might betray them to searchers. As a final ritual they daubed each other with camouflaging mud, then set off with Claude in the lead, Richard following, and Amerie and Felice bringing up the rear. The ring-hockey player had appropriated the bow and arrows.

They went quietly along the trail, which was wide enough for them to travel in comfort, a circumstance that pleased Richard and the women but rather alarmed the more wilderness-wise Claude. For nearly two kilometers they slogged through stands of bamboo, alder, willow, and semitropical evergreens, some trees laden with fruits of russet and purple, which Claude warned them against sampling. To their surprise, the only wildlife encountered was birds and giant leeches. The ground became higher and drier and they passed into dense forest, loud with bird and animal voices. The trees were draped in vines and the undergrowth formed a mass of impenetrable thornbushes on both sides of the trail.

At length the gloomy greenness gave way to sunlight as the trees thinned. Claude held up his hand as a signal for them to stop. "Not a peep out of you," he breathed. "I was half expecting to meet something like this."

They gazed through a thin screen of young trees into an open meadow with scattered clumps of bushes. Cropping the shrubbery was a herd of six adult and three juvenile rhinos. The full-grown specimens were about four meters in length and might have weighed two or three tons. They had two horns, piggy little eyes, and quaintly tufted ears that waggled as flies buzzed around them.

"Dicerorhinus schliermacheri, I'd say," Claude whispered. "This is their trail we've been using."

Felice stepped forward, nocking a razor-sharp arrow. "It's a good thing the wind is with us. Let me feel around their minds for a while and see if I can move them."

Richard said, "Meanwhile, we can hope they don't get thirsty."

Leaving Felice to experiment with her coercive power, the others withdrew back along the trail into a sunny glen at one side, where they sat down to rest. Richard planted a straight stick about as long as his arm upright in a patch of soil, marking the position of the shadow's tip with a small stone.

"Making a sundial?" Amerie inquired.

The pirate grimaced. "If we stay here long enough, we can get a fix. The tip of the shadow moves as the sun seems to travel across the sky. You wait, mark the new position of the shadow tip with another stone. Connect the two stones with a line and you got an east-west bearing. If we want to reach those highlands by the shortest route, I think we've got to bear more to the left than we've been going on this trail."

It was nearly an hour before Felice returned to tell them that it was safe to cross the meadow. They chose a new route according to Richard's aboriginal navigation; but without a convenient animal track to follow, they were forced to go cross-country through the tangled, thorn-choked forest understorey. It was impossible to travel quietly and the wildlife was making a racket like feeding time at the zoo; so they threw caution to the winds and broke out the vitredur hatchets and Claude's big carpenter's axe and hacked a trail. After two exhausting hours of this, they came upon a sizable creek and were able to follow it upstream into a slightly more open section of forest.

"We're on the bench above the lake now," Claude said. "The trail to the fort must be near. Be very quiet and keep your ears open."

They crept onward, skulking in the shadows of giant conifers, cycads, and ferns. Anticlimactically, they blundered right into the trail when they had to alter course to avoid a spiderweb the size of a banquet tablecloth. The bush-constricted track was deserted.

Felice bent over a pile of chaliko dung. "Cold. They must have passed here two hours ago. See the prints heading north?"

"They'll be coming back," Claude said. "And if they have amphicyons, they'll be able to track us. Let's blot out our own prints and get out of here. Once we get higher, there should be fewer trees and easier going. We'll have to follow another stream somewhere to kill our scent."

The trees did become more widely separated as they continued upslope, but the going was hardly easy. They followed a dry watercourse for most of an hour before the gentle grade above the bench steepened to a bluff studded with house-sized chunks of rock. The wind died and the heat of midafternoon smote them as they climbed.

At times when they rested, they could see out over the great lake. There were sails far to the south, apparently motionless on the water. It was impossible to tell whether they belonged to the gray-torc marines or to the escapees. They wondered out loud about the fate of Basil and his contingent, about Yosh, and about the Gypsies and their quixotic foray against the guardpost; but the trail talk dwindled as they were forced to save their breath for more difficult climbing. Hope that they would be able to cross the first high ridge began to fade after one of Richard's plass-and-fabric running shoes was slashed by a rock and he had to put on the more awkward seaboots of his original costume. Then Amerie's saddlesore legs betrayed her on a treacherous slope and she lost her footing, dislodging several large stones that tumbled down upon Claude and bruised his arm and shoulder.

"We'll never make it to the top today," Richard groused. "My left heel is one big blister and Amerie is ready to collapse."

Felice said, "It's only a couple of hundred more meters. If you can't climb, I'll carry you up! I want to get a view of the terrain we're heading into tomorrow. With luck, we might be able to see the bonfires from the fort or even trail beacons below us once it gets dark."

Claude declared he could manage on his own. Felice gave one hand to Richard and the other to the nun and hauled them up after her by main strength. It was slow going, but they were finally able to reach the top shortly after the sun descended behind the hills on the other side of the lake.

When they had regained their wind, Claude said, "Why don't we hole up on the eastern side of these big boulders? There's a nice dry shelter in there and I don't think anyone below could spot a fire if we lit one after nightfall. I could gather some wood."

"Good idea," said Felice. "I'll scout around a bit." She went off among the crags and gnarled savin junipers while the others tended their wounds, inflated decamole cots and weighted the legs with earth—because there was no water to waste—and regretfully laid out a meal of biscuits, nutrient wafers, and cheesy-tasting algiprote. By the time Claude had assembled a pile of dry branches, Felice was back, her bow resting jauntily over her shoulder, swinging three fat marmotlike animals by their hind legs.

"Hail, Diana!" chortled the old man. "I'll even skin and clean 'em!"

They lit the fire after it was completely dark and roasted the meat, devouring every gamey morsel. Then Richard and Claude collapsed onto their cots and were asleep in minutes. Amerie, her brain buzzing with fatigue, still felt obliged to shake the grease and scraps off the dinnerware, sterilize them with the power source, then shrink and stow them away. There's my big, helpful girl!

"I can see the fort," came Felice's voice from the nearby darkness.

Amerie picked her way over the rocks to where the athlete was standing. The ridge fell steeply to the southwest. The young moon hung over the lake and an incredible profusion of Pliocene stars reflected upon the water, differentiating it from the black land. Far to the south on their side of the lake was a cluster of orange specks.

"How far away is it?" the nun asked.

"At least fifteen kloms. Maybe more. As the vulture flies." Felice laughed, and Amerie was suddenly wide-awake, experiencing the same feeling of fear and fascination she had known before. The woman beside her was an indistinct silhouette in the starlight, but Amerie knew that Felice was looking at her.

"They didn't thank me," the athlete said in a low voice. "I set them free but they didn't thank me. They were afraid of me still. And that fool of a Dougal! . . . None of them—not even you—sympathized or understood why I wanted to—"

"But you couldn't *kill* Dougal! For the love of God, Felice! I had to put you out."

"Killing him would have been a comfort," said the young girl, coming closer. "I was working on my plans. Plans I never told to the rest of you. The golden torc was the key. Not only to free us, but to rescue the others—Bryan, Elizabeth, Aiken, Stein. To free all of the human slaves! Don't you see? I really could have done it! With the golden torc I could have tamed this thing inside me and *used* it."

Amerie heard herself babbling. "We're all grateful to you, Felice. Believe me. We were simply too stunned by it all to say anything after the fight. And Dougal—he was just too fast for Basil and Yosh to stop, and too crazy to realize what he was doing when he threw the torc away. He probably believed he wouldn't be safe from Epone's power until the torc was separated from her body."

Felice said nothing. After a while the nun said, "Perhaps you could get another."

There was a sigh. "They know about me now, so it will be very dangerous. But I'll have to try. Maybe waylay another caravan, or even go to Finiah. It'll be hard and I'll need help."

"We'll help."

Felice laughed softly.

"*I'll* help. I won't be retiring to any hermitage for quite some time yet."

"Ah. That's . . . good. I need your help, Amerie. I need you."

"Felice. Don't misunderstand."

"Oh, I know all about your little vow of renunciation. But that was made six million years ago in a different world. Now I think you need me as much as I need you."

"I need your protection. We all do."

"You need more than that."

Amerie backed away, tripped over a rock and fell, tearing open the scabbed cuts on her hands.

"Let me help you up," said Felice.

But the nun scrambled to her feet unaided and turned back toward the glowing remnants of the campfire where the others were sleeping. She stumbled and clenched her fingers into the lacerated palms so that her nails opened the cut even more, while behind her Felice laughed in the darkness.

16

"HE'S READY, SUKEY. You must take the final discharge."

"But—can I? I could botch it again, Elizabeth."

"You won't. You'll be able to handle this aspect of his healing. He wouldn't let me—but you can do it. Don't be afraid."

"All right. Just let him come out of the torc's neural bath slowly. I'm ready."

. . . Illinois cornfields, flat as a table and stretching from horizon to horizon, with the toy farmhouse and outbuildings lonely amid the immensity. Sitting in one of the cornrows, a three-year-old boy and an Alsatian bitch. The boy, clever with his hands and mischievous, circumvents a childproof fastener and removes a beeper-trace from his jeans. He offers it to the bitch. She is pregnant and of capricious appetite, and so she swallows it. The boy rises from the ground and toddles off down the row toward an interesting noise in the far distance. The bitch, unsatisfied by her electronic snack, runs toward the farmhouse where lunch is being prepared . . .

"No! I can't go there again!"

"Hush. Easy. You're close, so close."

. . . A robot harvester, nearly as large as the farmhouse and bright orange, moves along, swallowing the corn plants in a thirty-row swath, grinding the stalks and leaves to useful pulp, shelling the ears —long as a man's forearm—and packing the rich golden kernels into containers for shipment to other farms all over the Galactic Milieu. This new maize hybrid will yield twenty cubic meters of grain to the hectare . . .

"I don't want to look. Don't make me look."

"Be calm. Be easy. Come with me. Only once more."

. . . The little boy wanders down the straight row where the black soil has baked to crumbly gray dust. Gigantic plants loom over him, tassels brown against the sky, swollen cobs jutting from the stalks ripe and ready for harvest. The boy walks on toward the noise but it is far away from him and so he must sit down and rest for a while. He leans against a cornstalk thick as the trunk of a young tree, and the broad green leaves shade him from the sun's heat. He closes his eyes. When he opens them again, the noise is very much louder and the air is full of dust . . .

"Please. Please."

"You must go there one last time. But I'm with you. It's the only way out for you."

. . . Wonderment becomes unease becomes fear as the little boy sees an orange monster chewing toward him, its robot brain conscientiously scanning the rows ahead for signals from a beeper-trace that would trigger instant emergency shut-off. But there is no signal. The machine moves on. The boy runs ahead of it, easily outdistancing the harvester's steady one-klom-per-hour pace . . .

"She knew! She looked for me on the scanner at lunchtime and only found the dog, sending two signals instead of one there in the yard. She knew I had to be out in the fields. She called Daddy to have him stop the harvester and look for me, but there was no answer. He was outside the farm contower trying to fix a stuck rotor on one of the antennas."

"Yes. Go on. You can see her looking for you in the egg."

. . . The little boy dashes on, too inexperienced to realize that he should move to the side, out of range of the machine, instead of continuing down the row immediately ahead of it. He runs faster and a stitch comes in his side. He begins to whimper and runs more slowly. He trips, falls, gets up and staggers on with tears blinding his bright-blue eyes. Up in the air an egg-flier hovers over him. He stops and waves his arms, screaming for his mother. The harvester moves along, cutting the stalks off at ground level, hauling them into its maw on a spiked conveyor, chopping, shredding, plucking the kernels from the cobs, reducing the rows of giant plants to neat packages of grain and finely ground cellulose pulp . . .

"No. Please, no more."

"You must. We must. Once more and then gone forever. Trust me."

. . . The egg lands and the child stands stock-still, waiting for his mother to save him, weeping and holding out his arms as she runs toward him, picks him up, with the noise louder and louder and the dust swirling about them in the hot sun. She holds him close to her as she pushes obliquely through the tough, impeding stalks while the great orange thing moves on, cutter beams and carrying spikes and whirling knives at work. But the fifteen meters she must traverse are too far. She gasps and lifts the boy high and throws him, so that the green corn plants and the orange machine and the blue sky all spin very slowly around him. He falls to the earth and the harvester rumbles past with the busy clanking of its machinery drowning out another noise that did not last very long . . .

"Oh, Jesus, I can still hear please no the machine stops and he comes and screams at me you murdering little animal Cary Cary oh my God no Daddy Daddy Mommy fell help her oh my God Cary you did it to save him and he killed you and it's his fault the murdering little animal no no what am I saying God my own little boy Steinie I'm sorry I didn't mean it oh God Cary Steinie . . . Daddy please keep me."

"He did, Stein."

"I know now."

"You heard it all? All that he said?"

"Yes. Poor Daddy. He couldn't help saying it. I know now. Angry and frightened and helpless. I understand. He shot the dog, though . . . But I don't have to be afraid. He couldn't help it. Poor Daddy. I understand. Thank you. Thank you."

Stein opened his eyes.

An unfamiliar woman's face was very near to him—sun-reddened round cheeks, a turned-up nose, intent indigo eyes set a bit too closely together. She smiled.

He said, "And I don't have to be angry at either one of us."

"No," Sukey said. "You'll be able to remember and feel sad. But you'll be able to accept it. No guilt or fear or anger about this part of your life ever again."

Stein lay without speaking, and she let her mind merge with his in a touch that admitted a sharing of his ordeal, bespoke her care for him.

"You've been helping me," he said. "Healing me. And I don't even know your name."

"I'm Sue-Gwen Davies. My friends call me Sukey. It's a silly sort of name—"

"Oh, no." He got up onto one elbow and studied her with an innocent curiosity. "You went through the auberge training program, too. I saw you, the first and second days I was there. And then you were gone. You must have passed through the gate ahead of our Group Green."

"I was in Group Yellow. I remember you, too. That Viking costume isn't easy to miss."

He grinned and shook sweat-touseled elflocks out of his eyes. "It seemed like a good idea back then. Sort of reflection of my personality . . . What are you supposed to be?"

She gave a self-conscious little laugh and toyed with the embroidered belt of her long gown. "An ancient Welsh princess. My family came from there a long time ago and I thought it might be fun. A complete break with my old life."

"What were you—a redactor?"

"Oh, no! I was a policewoman. A juvenile officer on ON-15, the last Earth colonial satellite." She touched her silver torc. "I didn't become an operant redactor until I got here. I'll have to explain about that—"

But he broke in. "I tried metapsychic treatment before. It never helped. They said I was too strong, that it would take a special kind of practitioner—one with commitment—to ever get down inside of me and root my mess out. And you did it."

She protested, "Elizabeth did all the preliminary lancing. I was trying to do it"—her eyes slipped away from his—"and I bungled the job badly. Elizabeth did a marvelous fix and drained out all the really dangerous stuff that I couldn't touch. You owe her a lot, Stein. So do I."

He looked dubious. "Back at the auberge, me and my pal Richard called her the Ice Queen. She was a very cryogenic and spooky lady. But wait—! She told us that her metafunctions were lost!"

"They returned. The shock of passing through the time-portal did it. She's a marvelous redactor, Stein. She used to be one of the top teachers and counselors in her Sector. She was masterclass. I'll never be so good—except perhaps with you."

Very carefully, he folded her in his huge arms. Her hair was long and black and very straight, with a simple grassy perfume from the Tanu soap. She lay against his bare chest, hearing his heart beating slowly, afraid to look into his mind in case the thing that she hoped for would not be found. They were alone now in the tower room. Even Elizabeth had disappeared when it became clear that the healing would be a success.

Sukey said, "There are things you have to know." She touched the silver torc about her rather plump neck. "These silver collars— your friend Aiken got one, too, and so have some other people who've passed through the portal—they make latent metafunctions operant. That's how I became a redactor . . . And there's an exotic race living here in the Pliocene along with us. They're called Tanu and they came here a long time ago from some galaxy light-billenia away. They're latents, too, and they wear golden collars that make them almost as powerful as the metapsychics of our Milieu. They look quite human except for being very tall and having mostly blond hair and funny eyes. The Tanu rule this place almost like the barons of the Middle Ages ruled ancient Earth."

"I'm beginning to remember," Stein said slowly. "A fight in a kind of castle . . . Are we still locked up in that place?"

Sukey shook her head. "They took us—you and me and a few others—down the River Rhône. We're on our way to the Tanu capital. This is a place called Darask, almost at the Mediterranean shore. We've been here for two days. Elizabeth helped the mistress of the place, who was having a hard time in childbirth, so we got to stay and fix you up and rest as a kind of reward. The river trip down here was pretty nerve-racking."

"So Elizabeth is here, and Aiken. Who else?"

"Bryan, from your Group. And another man, named Raimo Hakkinen, who used to be a forester in British Columbia. I think he was in Group Orange. And there's a Tanu man in charge of bringing us to their capital city. His name is Creyn and he seems to be some kind of exotic physician when he's not acting as a prisoner-escort. He healed all of the wounds you got in the fight, by the way—and without using any regen-tank, either, just something like plass wrapping and mind-power. The rest of your friends and the other people who were being kept prisoner in the castle were sent to another place hundreds of kloms north of here."

"What are they planning to do with us?"

"Well, Elizabeth is special, obviously, because it seems she's the only human in all of Exile who is operant without a torc. I suppose they plan to make her Queen of the World if she'll stand for it."

"Jesus H. Christ!"

"And Bryan—he's another special case. No torc on him, either. I haven't discovered why, but the Tanu appear to think that they need an anthropologist to explain what all of us humans have done to their Pliocene society. Coming through the time-gate, you see. It's very complicated, but . . . well, silver-torc wearers like Aiken and me and Raimo, the ones with latent metabilities made operant, we have a chance to join the aristocracy of the Tanu if we behave ourselves. Ordinary people who aren't latent don't seem to be enslaved or anything—the exotics have some kind of small ape to do the rough work. The ordinaries that we saw were working at various arts and crafts."

Stein raised his hands to touch his own torc, then tried to undo it by twisting and pulling. "Can't get the damn thing off. You say it'll turn on my latent metafunctions?"

Sukey looked stricken. "Stein . . . your torc . . . it isn't silver. It's some gray metal. You're not a latent."

A dangerous gleam came into the bright-blue eyes. "Then what's my torc for?"

Her lower lip caught between her teeth. She reached out one hand to the metal around his neck. In a voice that was scarcely more than a whisper, she said, "It controls you. It gives pleasure or pain. The Tanu can use it to communicate with you telepathically, or they can use it to locate you if you run away. They can put you to sleep, and soothe your anxieties, and program hypnotic suggestions and do other things, probably, that I don't know about yet."

She explained more about the operation of the torcs as she knew it. Stein sat, ominously quiet, on the edge of the bed. When she had finished he said, "So the ones who wear gray mostly do jobs that are essential or potentially vital to the exotics. Soldiers. Gate guardians. This boatman taking us down a dangerous river. And they do their jobs without rebelling, even though they're not turned into zombies by the damn torc."

"Most of the gray-wearers that we've met behaved normally and seemed happy enough. Our boat skipper said he loved his job. One of the palace people that I talked to here said that the Tanu are kind and generous unless you go against their orders. I—I expect that after a time, you simply do as they expect you to without any coercion at all. You're conditioned and loyal. It's really the same sort of socialization that takes place in any tight group—but the loyalty is guaranteed."

Very quietly, Stein said, "I won't be a goddam flunky for some exotic slavemaster. I came through the time-gate and gave up everything I owned to get away from all that. To be a natural man, free to do as I pleased! I can't live any other way. I won't! They'll have to burn out my brain first."

Eyes swimming, Sukey let her fingers stray to his cheek. Her mind slipped beneath his surface consciousness and saw that he was telling the simple truth. The obstinacy that had shut out every healer save the one who had loved him now stood unyielding before any notion of adaptation, totally rejecting the thought of making the best of a difficult situation. Stein would never bend to the Tanu. He would break. If they dominated him at all, they would dominate only his mindless shell.

Tears spilled, splashing onto the bedsheets and the wolfskin kilt that Stein still wore. He took both of her hands. She said, "It didn't turn out to be the world that any of us dreamed about, did it? I was going to find the tunnel leading to the hollow Earth paradise, to Agharta. Creyn said that the legends had to refer to the paradise his people founded here. But that can't be true, can it? Agharta was a land of perfect peace and happiness and justice. This can't be the same place. Not if it—makes you miserable."

He laughed. "I'm a hard case, Sukey. Things'll be different for you. You'll get to join the high life. Be a Pliocene princess instead of just a Welsh one."

She pulled away from him. "I forgot one other important thing about this Exile world. Human women . . . the Tanu undo our salpingzaptomy and restore our fertility. Their own women don't reproduce very well on Earth, and so . . . they use us, too. Some human women become Tanu wives, like the lady of this palace that we're in right now. But a lot are just used as—as—"

Stein drew her close to him again and wiped her tears away with a corner of the bedclothes. "Oh, no. Not you, Sukey. It won't happen to you."

Incredulously, she raised her face. He said, "Go ahead. Look deep inside. As long as it's you, I don't mind."

She took a shuddering breath and plunged into the new place, and could not help crying out when she found that what she hoped for did exist, all new and strong.

After he had hushed her and the pledge was sealed in both their minds, they completed the healing of each other in their own way.

17

CLAUDE and Richard and Amerie could have slept for days, but with the sunrise came a distant howling of amphicyons angling up the ridge from the south, and they realized that the Tanu were going to do their utmost to prevent the escape of Felice, whose role in the massacre had doubtless been betrayed by some recaptured prisoner. The remnant of Group Green didn't waste any time trying to destroy traces of their camp but marched on not long after dawn, deflating their equipment and eating a scratch breakfast as they went. Claude had attempted to relinquish leadership to Felice, but she refused to hear of it.

"You've had experience in this kind of travel. I haven't. Just get us off this ridge as quickly as you can and down into thick woodland with a good-sized river. Then I think we'll be able to shake off the trackers."

They skidded and tramped and once even rappelled over a small cliff in their downhill flight, making better time when they found a dry wash that turned into a thin rivulet in the lower elevations. Trees crowded together and became taller, roofing over the widening stream and shading them from some of the sun's heat. As they splashed down the rock-clogged watercourse they startled big brown trout and fishing weasels that resembled pale minks. They took to the stream bank, first on one side, then on the other, in an attempt to confuse pursuit. Claude had them tramp an obvious trail up a tributary creek, relieve themselves to enhance the spoor, then double back in the water and continue wading down the original stream. It was becoming dangerously deep in places, broken with short pouroffs and stretches of white water.

Claude called a halt in midmorning. He and Felice were in good shape, but Richard and the nun sagged with weary gratitude. They rested on half-submerged rocks out in a backwater pool, straining their ears for sounds of pursuit. They heard nothing but an explosive *splat!* a short distance downstream.

"If I didn't know better," Amerie remarked, "I'd say that was a beaver."

"Quite likely," Claude said. "Might be our old friend Castor, but it's more likely Steneofiber, a more primitive type that didn't go in much for dams but just dug holes in the—"

"Shhh," Felice hissed. "Listen."

Rushing water, birdsong, the occasional screeches of what Claude had told them was an arboreal ape, a small squirrel chattering its annoyance.

And something large clearing its throat.

They froze on their rocks and instinctively drew up their legs, which they had been dangling in the water. The noise was a guttural cough, unlike anything they had heard before in the Pliocene. The bushes on the left bank swayed slightly as an animal passed through and came down to the stream to drink. It was a cat, massive as an African lion but with large canine teeth protruding like daggers below its closed jaws. It muttered to itself like a dyspeptic gourmet after an overly lavish feast and took a few desultory laps. Its upper body was decorated with marbled polygons of russet edged with tan and black; these merged into dark stripes about the animal's face, and black spots on its underparts and lower limbs. It had whiskers of heroic proportions.

The breeze shifted and carried the scent of the humans to the drinking sabertooth. It raised its head, stared directly at them with yellow eyes and snarled, exuding the studied restraint of a creature in complete command of an awkward situation.

Felice met its gaze.

The others were immobile with horror, waiting for the cat to spring into the water. But it did no such thing. Its belly was full and its cubs were waiting, and Felice's mind stroked its feline vanity and told it that the scrawny prey crouching on the rocks was scarcely worth a ducking. So the machairodus lapped and glared at them and wrinkled the bridge of its nose in a contemptuous one-sided snort, and at last withdrew into the undergrowth.

"It will take me five minutes," Amerie whispered, "to offer a Mass of Thanksgiving. And long overdue."

Felice shook her head with an enigmatic smile and Richard turned away looking superior, but Claude came to Amerie's rock and shared the gold thimble of wine and the flake of dried bread from the Mass kit she carried in the pocket of Richard's uniform. And when that was over they went on their way again, chopping a path on the bank opposite from that claimed by the sabertooth.

"It was so incredibly beautiful," the nun said to Claude. "But why does it need those teeth? The big cats of our time got along nicely with shorter ones."

"Our lions and tigers didn't try to kill elephants."

Richard exclaimed, "You mean those monstrous hoe-tuskers they tried to frighten us with in the auberge Tri-D's? Here?"

"More likely the smaller mastodons in these uplands. Gomphotherium angustidens is probably the common sort. Hardly half the size of those rhinos we dodged yesterday. We won't run into deinotherium until we have to cross a swamp or a large river bottomland."

"Kaleidoscopic," the pirate growled. "Pardon me for asking, but do any of you aces have a destination in mind? Or are we just running?"

Claude said softly, "We're just running. When we've shaken off the soldiers and the bear-dogs, then there'll be time enough to make strategic decisions. Or don't you agree, son?"

"Aw, shit," said Richard, and began hacking at the streamside shrubbery once more.

At last the brook merged with a large turbulent river flowing in a southerly direction. Claude thought it might be the upper Saône. "We won't follow this river," he told the rest of the Group. "It probably curves around to the southwest and empties into the lake forty or fifty kloms downstream. We'll have to cross over, and that means the decamole bridges."

Each Survival Unit was equipped with three bridge sections that could be married to produce a narrow, self-supporting span twenty meters in length that resembled a ladder with close-set rungs. Moving up the river to a point where the torrent narrowed between two craggy shelves of rock, they inflated and ballasted the sections, joined them, and swung the bridge over to the opposite bank.

"Looks kinda flimsy," Richard remarked uneasily. "Funny—when we practiced with it back at the auberge it seemed a lot wider."

The bridge was a good third of a meter in width and steady as a rock. However, they had used it to cross a still pond in the auberge's cavern, while here surging rapids and sharp rocks awaited below.

"We could inflate another bridge and lash the two side by side if it would make you feel safer," Amerie suggested. But the pirate bristled indignantly at the suggestion, hoisted his pack, and lurched across like an apprentice tightrope walker.

"You next, Amerie," said Claude.

The nun stepped confidently onto the span. How many hundreds of logs had she walked over, crossing the mountain streams of the Oregon Cascades? The bridge rungs were less than a handspan apart, impossible to fall through. All that was necessary was a firm step, balanced posture, and keep the eyes on the opposite bank and not on the foaming chute six meters below—

Her right thigh muscle went into spasm. She teetered, caught herself, then overbalanced on the opposite side and went feet-first into the river.

"Dump your pack!" Felice screamed. Moving so fast that her hands were blurred, she dropped the bow and arrows, unfastened her own backpack, slapped the quick-release buckles of her cuirass and greaves, and jumped in after Amerie.

Richard gaped from the other side, but the old man ran back the way they had come, to the relative calm of the smaller stream's outspate. Two heads bobbed in the rapids. The leading one fetched momentarily against a humpbacked boulder and disappeared. The second one swept up to the rock and also went under, but after a long minute both women reappeared and floated toward Claude. He seized a stout piece of driftwood and held it out. Felice caught hold with one hand and he was able to pull her in. Her other hand had the fingers entwined in Amerie's hair.

Claude waded out and dragged the nun onto the bank. Felice

rested on hands and knees in the shallows, spewing and coughing. He lifted Amerie's sodden body in a jackknife bend to empty the lungs of water, then filled them with his own warm air.

Breathe, child, he begged her. Live, daughter.

There was a sound of gagging, a first halting expansion of the chest beneath the soaked and torn starship captain's uniform. One last kiss of shared breath, and she returned.

Amerie's eyes opened and she stared wildly at Claude, then at the smiling Felice. A choked sob rose in her throat and she buried her head in the old man's breast. He had Felice pull the warm Orcadian sweater from his pack and wrapped the nun in it; but when he tried to pick Amerie up and carry her across the bridge she was much too heavy for him. So it was the little athlete who had to assist the nun, while the paleontologist toted his own and Felice's gear.

Amerie's pack with its medical supplies was lost, swept far downstream. They had to set her broken arm with the meager first-aid equipment from the individual Survival Units, following steps outlined in a laconic plaque entitled *Common Medical Emergencies.* The injury was a simple fracture of the left humerus, easily reduced even by amateur medics; but by the time Amerie was treated and sedated, the afternoon was well advanced. Richard convinced Claude and Felice that it would be useless to try to press on farther, regardless of possible pursuit. They went a short distance from the river into a concealing grove of massive oaks. There Richard erected two decamole cabins while Felice went out and shot a big fat roebuck and Claude grubbed nourishing cattail tubers from a boggy spot.

With their stomachs full, cots set on maximum soft, and critterproof screendoors latched, they fell asleep even before night fell. They never heard the owls and nightingales and treefrogs singing, nor the fading howls of bear-dogs raging on a cold and futile trail far to the south. They did not see the mist start to rise from the rapids as the stars brightened. And they never saw the glowing grotesqueries of the Firvulag, who came and danced on the opposite bank of the river until the stars paled with the coming of dawn.

* * *

The following morning Amerie was feverish and weak. By common consent they dosed her with their limited store of medication, made her comfortable in one hut, and withdrew to the other so that she could sleep and mend. They all stood in need of recuperation, and there seemed little danger that any pursuit party could cross the crag-bordered torrent without their being aware of it.

Felice was confident that they had eluded the trackers altogether. "They might even find equipment from Amerie's pack downstream and decide that we've drowned in the river."

So they slept, lunched on cold venison and algiprote, and then sat in the shade of an ancient oak, sipping small cups of precious instant coffee, and trying to decide what to do next.

"I've been working on a new plan," said Felice. "I've considered different possibilities and decided that the best place to get another torc would be near Finiah, where there are plenty of Tanu. They might even have a storehouse or a factory for the things. What we have to do is hide out until Amerie is healed, cross the Vosges, then hole up outside the city. We can rustle supplies from caravans or outlying settlements."

Richard choked on his coffee.

Felice went on serenely, "And then, after we've analyzed their defenses and learned more about the actual technology of the torcs, we can work out plans for the strike."

Richard set his little cup down on a tree root with great care. "Kid, you've conned us and bullied us into going along with your plans so far, and I'm not saying you didn't do a damned good job getting us away from Epone and her stooges. But there is no way you're gonna force me into a four-man invasion of a whole city full of exotic mind mashers!"

"You'd prefer to hide in the woods until they hunt you down?" she sneered. "They won't stop searching, you know. And the Tanu will be coming out themselves instead of just sending human slavies. If we follow my plan—if *I* get a golden torc—I'll be a match for any of them!"

"That's what *you* say. How do we know you'll be able to get it up? And what's in it for us? Do we get to be your loyal spear carriers while you're playing Madam Commander? No friggerty golden torcs are going to do the rest of us poor normals any good. Sure as shit some of us'd get chopped by these freaks before your private guerrilla war was over, win *or* lose. You want to know what my plans are, bull-dolly?"

She sipped her drink, eyes hooded.

"I'll tell you!" Richard blustered. "I'm gonna rest up here for another day or two and repair my footgear, and then I'm heading north to the big rivers and the ocean, just like Yosh did. A little luck and

I might even meet up with him. When I get to the Atlantic I'm sailing southward along the coast. While you're doing your bandit-princess routine, I'll be getting pissed on good wine and bouncing broads in my pirate shack in Bordeaux."

"And the rest of us?" Claude kept his tone neutral.

"Come with me! Why not? I'll be marching easy, not breaking my butt climbing to hell and gone over the Vosges. Listen, Claude—you and Amerie stick with me and I'll help you find some nice peaceful place the Tanu never heard of. You're kinda old to get mixed up in this crazy kid's battles. And what life would it be for a nun, for God's sake? *This* one kills people for fun."

Felice said, "You're wrong, Richard," and drank coffee.

The old paleontologist turned from one to the other, then shook his head. "I've got to think about this. And there's something else I've been meaning to do. If you don't mind, I'll just go a little farther into this grove of oak trees and spend some time alone." He got to his feet, felt briefly in the big pocket of his bush jacket, and walked off.

"Take as long as you like, Claude," Felice called. "I'll see to Amerie. And keep a lookout, too."

"Don't get lost," Richard added. Felice muttered an expletive under her breath.

Claude wandered along, automatically noting landmarks as he had done for so many years on freshly tamed planets. An oak with two massively drooping branches like ogre arms. A reddish pinnacle standing out amidst the gray granite. A dry meadow with a maple, one branch turned anomalously golden too early in the season. A little pool dotted with pink waterlilies, with a pair of ordinary mallard ducks swimming lackadaisically about. A spring issuing from the rocks, adorned with lacy ferns and shaded by a magnificent beech.

"How's this, Gen?" the old man inquired.

He knelt down and held out his palms to the trickle, drank, then laved his forehead and the sunburnt back of his neck. Asperges me, Domine, hyssopo, et mundabor. Lavabis me, et super nivem dealbabor.

"Yes, I think this will do very well."

He took a thin flat stone from the basin of the spring and went to the foot of the beech tree. After carefully removing a pad of moss, he dug a hole, set the carved wooden box into it, and replaced the soil and plants, patting them firm. He marked her resting place with no stone nor cross; those who cared about her knew where her dust lay. When he was finished he went back to the spring for a handful of water to refresh the disturbed moss, then sat down with his back against the tree trunk and closed his eyes.

When he awoke it was late afternoon. Something crouched at the spring and watched him with a wary light-green gaze.

Claude held his breath. It was one of the most beautiful little animals he had ever seen, its graceful and sinuous body not much longer than his hand, with a slender tail adding another twenty centimeters to its length. Its underparts were pale orange and the upper fur tan with subtle black shading rather like a kit fox. The feline face was full of intelligence, mild and unthreatening, for all that it resembled that of a miniaturized cougar.

It had to be Felis zitteli, one of the earliest of the true cats. Claude pursed his lips and whistled a soft, undulating call. The animal's large ears cupped toward the sound. With infinite slowness, Claude slipped his hand into his pocket and withdrew a small piece of cheeselike algiprote.

"Pss-pss-pss," he invited, placing the food on the mossy sward beside him.

Calmly, the little cat came to him, nostrils quivering, white whiskers pointing forward. It sniffed the food discreetly, tested it with a dainty pink tongue, and ate it. Eyes proportionally larger than those of a domestic cat and outlined in black looked at Claude in an unmistakably friendly fashion. There was a faint humming sound. Felis zitteli was purring.

The old man gave it more food, then ventured to touch it. The cat accepted his stroking, arching its back and curling its black-tipped tail into an interrogative curve. It came closer to Claude and butted its forehead against the side of his leg.

"Oh, you are a cutie, aren't you? Tiny little teeth. Do you eat insects and little rock critters, or do you fish for minnows?" The cat tilted its head and bestowed a melting glance, then leaped into his lap, where it settled down with every evidence of familiarity. Claude petted the pretty thing and spoke softly to it while shadows purpled and a chill breeze stole through the grove.

"I'll have to be going," he said reluctantly, slipping one hand beneath the warm little belly and lifting the cat to the ground. He got to his feet, expecting the animal to take fright at the movement and flee. But it only sat down and watched him, and when he moved away, it followed.

He chuckled and said, "Shoo," but it persisted. "Are you an instant domestic?" he asked it, and then thought of Amerie, who would face a long stint of convalescence with him and Richard on their way north. If they left Felice behind (and there seemed no alternative), the nun would fret about her as well as brood over her own guilts. Perhaps this charming little cat would be a distraction.

"Will you ride in my pocket? Or do you prefer shoulders?" He picked it up and inserted it into the bellowslike pocket of his jacket. It turned about several times and then settled down with its head out, still purring.

"That's that, then." The old man lengthened his stride, passing from landmark to landmark until he came back into the open part of the oak grove where they had set up camp.

The two decamole cabins were gone.

Throat constricted, heart racing, Claude staggered back behind a huge tree bole, leaning with his back to the trunk until his pulse slowed. He peered cautiously out, studying the clearing where the camp had been. It was empty of their equipment. Even the fire trench and the remains of the roasted deer were gone. There were no footprints, no broken ferns or shrubs to indicate a scuffle (take *Felice* without a fight?), nothing to show there had ever been human beings among the big old trees.

Claude left his place of concealment and did a more careful search. The site had been cleaned up by persons who knew their woodcraft, but there remained a few clues. One dusty place bore parallel sweep marks from the branch that had been used to obliterate footprints. And down by the torrent, on a faint game trail that led upstream, was a piece of emerald-green fluff stuck to the resiny trunk of a pine.

A bit of green feather. Dyed green.

Claude nodded as the puzzle began to resolve itself. They had found three people and three packs and taken them this way. Who? Certainly not the minions of the Tanu, who would not care about concealing their presence. Then—? Firvulag?

Claude's heart leaped again and he pinched his nostrils shut and exhaled gently. The adrenalin flood was stemmed and the pounding in his chest eased. There was nothing to do but follow. And if they caught him . . . well, at least he had fulfilled part of what he had come here to do.

"You're sure you don't want to get off?" he whispered to the cat, crouching and pulling open the pocket to afford an easy egress. But the animal only blinked its big eyes sleepily and cuddled down out of sight.

"It's us versus them, then," Claude said, sighing. He set a good pace and hiked up the noisy river until it was nearly dark. Then he smelled smoke and followed his nose into a stand of sequoias on a rocky slope above the river. There was a sizable fire, surrounded by many dark figures who were laughing and talking.

Claude lurked among the shadows, but he was evidently expected. Completely against his will, he found himself walking up to the fire with his hands above his head, drawn by the same irresistible compulsion he had known in the examining chamber of the Lady Epone.

"It's an old one!" somebody said as he came into the firelight.

"Not such an alter kocker, though," a hulking shape remarked. "He might be good for something."

"Acting more reasonable than his friends, anyhow."

There were perhaps a dozen tough-looking human men and women seated on the ground around the flames. They were dressed in dark buckskin and oddments of ragged costume, eating the last bits of Felice's venison and turning a long spit crowded with spatch-cocked birds.

One desperado arose and came over to Claude. It was a middle-aged woman of medium height with dark hair graying at the temples and eyes that displayed a fanatic sparkle in the firelight. Her thin lips tightened critically as she studied the old man. She lifted the fine beak of her nose in a proud gesture and Claude could see a golden torc nestled beneath the collar of her doeskin cloak.

"What do you call yourself?" she asked sternly.

"I'm Claude Majewski. What have you done with my friends? Who are you?"

The mind-grip gentled and the woman looked at him with astringent humor. "Your friends are safe enough, Claude Majewski. As for myself, I am Angélique Guderian. You may call me Madame."

18

THE RIVER RHÔNE flowed slow and wide. The boat, even with its sail fully spread and its small engine working, was a long time leaving the Isle of Darask behind. The watery plains of the Camargue shimmered with a golden haze that blurred regions a kilometer or so away into an indistinct scrim backdrop. Later, as the boat traveled farther south, the passengers caught sight of mountains on their left and the tops of occasional rock outcroppings in the swamp; but there was no sign of the sea. Handsome little orange-and-blue reedlings and red-headed buntings teetered on the tall papyrus growing beside the river's main channel. The bubbletop was off all morning and the passengers watched, fascinated, as crocodiles and dugongs cruised around them. Once there was a shoal of marvelous watersnakes, nearly transparent and shining like undulant rainbows beneath the hazy sun.

Around noon they pulled in to another island where more than twenty boats were gathered—cargo craft, small yachts conveying brightly garbed Tanu, larger vessels crowded with silent little ramas sitting five abreast on rows of benches like small unchained galley slaves who had lost their oars. The island had only a few low buildings. Skipper Highjohn explained that they would not disembark here, only stop long enough to reinstall the bubble panels.

"Not another damn shoot-the-chutes!" groaned Raimo. He pulled out his flask.

"The very last," Highjohn soothed him, "and not rough, even though it's a bit steep. One of the unreconstructed gorfs who piloted Tanu barges through here back in the earliest days of the time-portal named the thing la Glissade Formidable. Sounds classier than the Dreadful Slide, so that's what we call it today, too."

Stein, sitting in a seat beside Sukey, looked puzzled. "But we should be in the Rhône delta now. Bang on the Mediterranean shore. What kind of gradient can there be?"

"You're in for a surprise," Bryan told him. "I couldn't believe it myself when the skipper explained it to me. I used to sail the Med, too, you'll remember. What it adds up to, Stein, is a slight miscalculation on the part of the boffins who drew up our Pliocene maps."

The workman installing the transparent panels gave the last one a smack and said, "You're off, Cap'n!"

"Belt in, everyone," Highjohn ordered. "You come forward, Bryan. You're gonna love this one."

A light wind sprang up as they puttered away from the moorage, following in the wake of a thirty-meter barge loaded with metal ingots. The vapors that had obscured their view finally dissipated, and they looked to the south for a first glimpse of the sea.

They saw a cloud.

"What the *hell* is that?" Stein wondered. "Looks like a plass factory on fire or a big volcano vent. Friggerty cloud goes clear to the tropopause."

The mast of the riverboat folded and withdrew, and the auxiliary engine cut out. They began to pick up speed. The clumps of marshgrass were more widely spaced now, and the boat followed a marked channel that trended southeastward, close beneath a rounded headland on their left that jutted into the flats as an outlier of the alpine foothills. They were heading directly toward the towering white cloud, picking up speed every minute.

And then Elizabeth said, "Dear Lord. The Mediterranean is gone."

The barge that was traveling about half a kilometer ahead of them dropped out of sight. To the east and west along the horizon were low points of land—but between them was only a line of water meeting milky sky, having a shallow dip in the center. And there was a sound, a swelling rumble with a hissing component that grew to deafening proportions as they swept closer and closer to la Glissade Formidable, where the wide expanse of the Rhône ended at the continental brink.

Creyn's mental voice rang in the brains of all the torc-wearers. "Shall I program oblivion?" But they all replied, "No!" for their curiosity was greater than any terror of what lay ahead.

The boat raced over the edge and started down, borne on muddy waters cascading over a steep fan of sediment, plunging at eighty kilometers an hour into the depths of the Empty Sea.

They came to the end of the Glissade after four hours and floated in the pale waters of a great bitter lake. All around them were the many-colored rocks of the continental roots and glistening, fantastically eroded shapes of salt and anhydrite and gypsum. With its bubble panels stowed away, the boat spread its sail and raced along toward the southwest, for it was there that Creyn told them that the capital city of Muriah lay—at the tip of the Balearic Peninsula, which the Tanu called Aven, above the perfect flat of the White Silver Plain.

They traveled for one more day, overcome by the strangeness and the beauty and hardly able to talk about it except for endless exclamations in both the vocal and mental speech, to which Creyn responded, "Yes, it is wonderful. And more to come, more splendid than you can imagine."

In the late evening of the sixth day after they had departed from Castle Gateway they arrived. The high peninsula of Aven stretched away into the west, green and rolling, with a single peak near its tip and other eminences half-hidden in haze. A team of helladotheria in glowing trappings of rainbow fabric pulled the boat up a long rollered way while chaliko-riders dressed in gauzy robes and glass armor, bearing lights, animal-headed horns and banners, followed along the steep towpath. The welcoming Tanu sang all the way to the blazing city high above the salt. Their song had a haunting melody that seemed strangely familiar to Bryan; but those human beings who wore the torc were able to understand the alien words:

> Li gan nol po'kône niési,
> 'Kône o lan li pred néar,
> U taynel compri la neyn,
> Ni blepan algar dedône.
> > Shompri pône, a gabrinel,
> > Shal u car metan presi,
> Nar metan u bor taynel o pogekône,
> Car metan sed gône mori.

> There is a land that shines through life and time,
> A comely land through the length of the world's age,
> And many-colored blossoms fall on it,
> From the old trees where the birds are singing.
> > Every color glows there, delight is commonplace,
> > Music abounds on the Silver Plain,
> On the Gentle-Voiced Plain of the Many-Colored Land,
> On the White Silver Plain to the south.

> There is no weeping, no treachery, no grief,
> There is no sickness, no weakness, no death.

There are riches, treasures of many colors,
Sweet music to hear, the best of wine to drink.
>Golden chariots contend on the Plain of Sports
>Many-colored steeds run in days of lasting weather.
Neither death nor the ebbing of the tide
Will come to those of the Many-Colored Land.

* * *

THE END OF PART TWO

PART III

The Alliance

1

THE GIANT SEQUOIA had endured for 10,000 years. Standing amidst a grove of lesser specimens high in the Vosges, it was hollowed by ancient wildfire and rot. In millennia past lightning had sheared its top, so that the Tree was only about 100 meters in height; the trunk nearest the ground spanned fully a fourth of that distance, giving the sequoia the appearance of a huge truncated pylon. That it lived at all was evidenced only by sparse branches writhing at the broken crown, their small needles seemingly incapable of photosynthesizing enough sugar to nourish such a monument.

The sequoia was host to a family of fire-backed eagles and several million carpenter ants. Since early in the afternoon it had also harbored a band of freeliving humans who were accustomed to use the great hollow trunk as a safe-house in times of particular danger.

A thin rain fell. In another hour it would be dark. A woman in a water-stained doeskin cloak stood beside one buttress of the great bole, her eyes shut, her fingertips pressed to her throat. After five minutes had passed, she opened her eyes and wiped some of the moisture from her forehead. Stooping, she pulled aside the fronds of a large fern and entered an inconspicuous opening, a nearly healed fissure that led into the interior of the Tree.

Someone helped her out of the sodden cloak. She nodded her thanks. All around the inner perimeter of the trunk small fires burned on low stone platforms, their smoke plumes plaiting together with that of a larger central blaze and rising toward the natural chimney high above. The main fire was laid on a great X-shaped hearth. Its flames towered at the center and diminished to a comfortable cooking height at the ends of the arms. People were gathered around the central fire in great numbers; smaller groups huddled near the subsidiary fireplaces. The place smelt of steaming clothing spread before the flames, of baking ash-bread and pots of hot spiced wine, and of simmering meat stew.

Richard hovered over the stew kettle, snarling at the cooks and occasionally adding dried herbs from a collection of crocks at his feet. Claude and Felice sat together nearby, and Amerie was using her good arm to lay out medical supplies on a clean blanket. The nun's tiny wildcat watched with keen interest, having learned quickly that the drug doses, dressings, and instruments were not playthings or prey.

Angélique Guderian came to this side of the fire and extended her hands to the warmth. She said to Amerie, "It's a good thing, ma Soeur, that Fitharn and the other Firvulag were able to retrieve your pack. We are always short of medical supplies, and we will have great need of your secular skills as well as your spiritual ones. There are no professional healers among us, since all such persons are subjected to the bondage of the gray torc as soon as their expertise is discovered. We can only presume that your own torcless state is the result of a Tanu error."

"And there's no escape for the gray-torcs, once they're collared?"

"They may escape, certainly. But should a wearer of either the gray or silver torc come within the sphere of influence of a coercive Tanu, the human will be compelled to serve the exotic—even to giving up his life. This is why there can be no torc wearers among us."

"Except yourself," said Felice softly. "But those who wear gold are free, aren't they?"

Claude was whittling a new rosary for Amerie, his vitredur knife gleaming like sapphire in the firelight. He asked, "Can't the torcs be cut off?"

"Not while the person lives," Madame replied. "We have tried, of course. It is not that the metal is so durable, but rather that the torc somehow becomes bonded to the life-force of the wearer. This bonding is accomplished after the torc has been worn for an hour or so. Once a person has adapted, to unfasten or sunder the device brings death in convulsions. The mortal agony is similar to that inflicted by certain perverted redactors among the Tanu."

Felice leaned closer to the fire. She had finally taken off her armor after the thirty-six-hour forced march to the Tree, and the wet cloth of her green dress clung to her slight body. Her legs and upper arms, where they had not been protected by gauntlets and greaves, were a mass of scratches and deep bruises. News that the Tanu Hunt had invaded the Vosges sent Madame and her scouting party, together with the remnant of Group Green, fleeing toward the Tree refuge, where they had been met by other human renegades.

Felice tried hard to be casual. "So there is no way that you can remove your own torc, Madame?"

The old woman gazed at the girl athlete for a long moment. At last she said, "You must not allow yourself to fall into temptation, my child. This golden torc remains a part of me until my death."

Felice gave a light laugh. "There's no need for you to be afraid of me. Just look into my mind and see."

"I cannot read your mind, Felice. You know that. I am no redactor, and your strong latencies shield you. But many years at the auberge gave me an insight into the personalities of others such as yourself. And limited though my own metafunctions may be, I am in the confidence of the Firvulag . . . and *they* read you like a child's primer."

"So that's it," Felice remarked obscurely. "I felt something."

"The Firvulag have watched you almost from the beginning," the old woman said. "They always follow the caravans, the Little People, hoping for some contretemps that will put the travelers into their power. So they beheld you on the shore of the Lac de Bresse in your bid for freedom. They even aided you—did you realize that?— by adding images of confusion to the minds of the chalikos and the soldiers, so that you and your friends were able to triumph. Ah, the Firvulag were impressed by you, Felice! They saw your potential. But they also feared you—and quite rightly. And so Fitharn, wisest among those who were following, caused a vivid illusion to seize the mind of one of your confrères—"

"Dougal!" Felice cried, springing to her feet.

"C'est ça."

Richard gave an ironic cackle. "Crafty spooks! I'll bet they could get that golden torc back out of the lake if they wanted to."

A chaotic mix of emotions played over the girl's face. She began to speak, but Madame held up her hand.

"The Firvulag bestow their gifts only as they choose, not as we demand. You will have to be patient."

Claude said, "So the Firvulag followed us all the way. Don't tell me that they clouded the minds of our pursuers as well?"

"Certainly," Madame Guderian replied. "Would not the boatful of gray-torc marines have seen some trace of your own wake? Would not the tracking soldiers have found you in the forest, in spite of your pathetic attempts to throw them off the scent? But of course the Firvulag helped! And Fitharn also notified us of your presence in our Vosges forest, and so we came for you. His people also warned us of the Hunt, which does not usually penetrate deeply into the mountains."

Richard tasted the stew again and grimaced. "Now that we're here in a safe place, what happens? I'll be damned if I'm going to spend the rest of my life hiding out."

"We do not enjoy it, either. You have caused us a good deal of trouble by escaping into the Vosges. Ordinarily, the Tanu are inclined to let us be, and our free people reside in small homesteads or in secret villages. I myself live in Hidden Springs, which is near the future site of Plombières-les-Bains. But now Lord Velteyn of Finiah is wild over the killing of Epone. You must understand that no Tanu has ever before been killed by a mere bareneck human. Velteyn's Flying Hunt will now search out even the most remote of our settlements, hoping to find Felice. There will be gray-torc patrols everywhere—at least until the Tanu become distracted by the preparations for the Grand Combat . . . As to what shall be done with you, we will discuss that when Peo and his warriors return. I have already perceived their approach."

Claude rolled one of the large rosary beads toward the little cat. The animal patted it toward Amerie, then arched its back in appreciation of its own cleverness. The nun picked up the cat and stroked it as it tried to nestle into her sling. "Do you have any news of the other escapees? The people in the boats? Our friend Yosh? The Gypsies?"

"Two of the Gypsies survived their encounter at the ravine bridge. They will be guided here. There has been no word at all about the Japanese. The Firvulag in the northern regions are savage and not inclined to respect the alliance that their High King has formed with us. Your friend's chance of survival is not good. As to those in the boats—most were recaptured by gray-torc marines from the lake forts. They are now imprisoned in Finiah. Six escapees who reached the Jura shore are presently in the care of friendly Firvulag and will be taken to a free-human refuge in the high mountains.

Seven more"—Madame shook her head—"were taken by les Criards, the malign Firvulag known as Howlers."

"What will happen to them?" Amerie asked.

Madame lifted her shoulders and the golden torc reflected the flames. "These exotics! Ah, ma Soeur, they are barbaric, even the best of them. And the worst—! Who shall even speak of their enormities? Firvulag and Tanu are members of the same species. En vérité, they actually constitute a dimorphic race with a most peculiar genetic pattern. On their home planet, this led to an ancient antagonism between the two forms—the one tall and metapsychically latent, the other mostly short in stature and with limited operancy. You must understand that the exotics came to Earth in order to be free to pursue certain barbarous customs, holdovers from their archaic culture, that were justly proscribed by the civilized ones of their galactic confederation. Some of their cruel games are physical—the Hunt, the Grand Combat, of which you will learn more later. But others are jeux d'esprit—games of the mind. The Tanu, with their wide-ranging latent metafunctions, do not favor this subtle jousting so much. It is more commonly the province of the torcless Firvulag. The Little People possess some farsensing power, plus one highly developed operant metafunction—that of creativity. They are masters of illusion. But what illusions they make! They are capable of driving humans, even the weaker among the Tanu, insane with terror or anguish. Sensitive persons may even be killed outright from psychic shock. Firvulag can take the shape of monsters, devils, whirlwinds, conflagrations. They insinuate their delusions into more helpless minds and trigger suicide or self-mutilation. The latter is of great amusement to the worst of them, the so-called Howling Ones, since they are themselves deformed mutants. The weapons of the Firvulag are our own nightmares and fever-dreams, the fears and phantoms that assault one's imagination in dark places. They take a sadistic delight in destroying."

"But they haven't destroyed *you*," Felice said. "They gave you a golden torc. Why?"

"Because they hope to use me, of course. I am to be a tool—a weapon, c'est-à-dire—against their most deadly foe: the Tanu, their brothers."

Amerie said, "And now you hope to use us."

Madame's thin lips lifted in a small smile. "It is obvious, is it not, ma Soeur? You do not know how poor we are, what odds we have faced. The Tanu call us Lowlives . . . and we have assumed the name proudly. Over many years our people have managed to escape from captivity and were hardly thought to be worth pursuing. Most of us have no special talents that can be used against the exotics. But you in your Group are different. The Tanu would take revenge upon you—but we Lowlives see you as invaluable allies. You must join us! Felice, even without a torc, can control animals, even influence certain humans. She is physically strong and an experienced game-playing tactician. You, Amerie, are a doctor and a priest. My people have struggled for years without either. Richard is a navigator, a former commander of starships. For him there may be a key role in the liberation of humanity—"

"Now just a damn minute!" bellowed the pirate, waving his soup ladle.

Claude flipped bits of wood into the fire. "Don't forget me. As an old fossil hunter, I can tell you exactly what Pliocene beast will be cracking your bones for the marrow after the Tanu and Firvulag get finished with you."

"You are quick with a jest, Monsieur le Professeur," said Madame tartly. "Perhaps the old fossil hunter will tell us his age?"

"A hundred and thirty-three."

"Then you are two years my senior," she retorted, "and I will expect you to render good advice to our company as a result of your vast experience. As I lay before you my grand design, the plan for the liberation of humanity, give us your invaluable counsel. Correct any youthful impulsiveness that I may show."

"Gotcha, Claude," Richard said, snickering. "Say . . . if anybody cares, this vat of slumgullion is as ready as it will ever be."

"Then we will eat," said Madame, "and shortly Peo and the fighters will join us." She raised her voice. "Mes enfants! You will all come to supper!"

Slowly, all of the people from the smaller fires approached, carrying bowls and drinking vessels. The total number of Lowlives included perhaps two hundred, far more men than women, with a handful of children as quiet and alert as the adults. Most of the people were dressed in buckskin or homespun peasant garb. They did not seem to be outstanding physical specimens, nor were any of them decked out in the wildly eccentric fashion of certain timefarers in the Finiah caravan. The Lowlives did not look beaten or desperate or fanatical. In spite of the fact that they had just fled for their lives at Madame's mental alarm, they did not seem afraid. They saluted the old woman gravely or cheerfully, and many of them had a smile or even a joke for Richard and the other cooks dishing out the hastily prepared fare. If one word could be used to describe the guerrilla contingent, it might be "ordinary."

Amerie searched the faces of these free people, wondering what had inspired this relative handful to defy the exotics. Here were exiles whose dream had come alive again. Was it possible that this small nucleus could grow—even prevail?

"Good friends," Madame was saying, "we have among us newcomers whom all of you have seen but few as yet have met. It is on their account that we have had to gather here. But we may hope, with their help, to reach our precious goal that much sooner." She paused and looked about the company. There was no sound except the snap and sizzle of the firelogs. "As we eat, I will ask these new arrivals to tell us how they came from the prison of Castle Gateway to this free place." Turning to the remnant of Group Green, she asked, "Who will be your speaker?"

"Who else?" Richard said, pointing the ladle at Claude.

The old man rose to his feet. He spoke for nearly a quarter of an hour without interruption until his narrative reached the point where Felice was about to initiate the attack upon Epone. Then there was a loud hiss. Amerie's little cat sprang from her arms and struck a stiff pose, facing the door of the Tree like a miniature puma at bay.

"It is Peo," said Madame.

Ten people, all heavily armed with bows and blades, came stamping and dripping into the shelter. They were led by a gigantic middle-aged man nearly as massive as Stein who wore the shell ornaments and fringed deerskin clothing of a Native American. Claude held off continuing his tale until these people were served with food and given a place close to the big fire. Then the paleontologist resumed and told the story to the end. He sat down and Madame handed him a cup of hot wine.

Nobody spoke until the gray-haired Native American said, "And it was iron—*iron* that killed the Lady Epone?"

"Nothing but," Richard declared. "She was chewed to pieces and I let her have a couple of good ones with the bronze sword—but she still just about nailed me. Then something made me try Felice's little dagger."

The red man turned to the girl and demanded, "Give it to me."

"And who the hell do you think you are?" she said coolly.

He roared with laughter and the sound of it boomed in the hollow trunk of the Tree as in an empty cathedral. "I'm Peopeo Mox-mox Burke, last chief of the Wallawalla tribe and former justice of the Washington State Supreme Court. I'm also the one-time leader of this gang of paskudnyaks and its present Sergeant at Arms and Warlord in Chief. Now may I please examine your dagger?"

He smiled at Felice and held out a great hand. She smacked the golden scabbard into it smartly. Burke drew out the leaf-shaped little blade and held it up in the firelight.

"Stainless steel alloy with an eversharp edge," the girl said. "A common toy on Acadie, useful for picking teeth, cutting sandwiches, pricking out transponders from rustled cattle, and putting out the lights of casual assaulters."

"It seems quite ordinary except for the gold of the hilt," Burke said.

"Amerie has a theory about it," Claude said. "Tell him, child."

Burke listened thoughtfully as the nun set forth her hypothesis on the possible deadly effect of iron on torc-bearing exotics, then murmured, "It could be. The iron disrupting the life-force almost like a neural poison."

"I wonder . . ." Felice began, staring at Madame with an innocent expression.

The old woman went to Chief Burke and took the knife from him. As the assembled crowd gasped, she held it to her own throat below the golden neck-ring and pricked the skin. A pearl-sized drop of dark blood appeared. She handed the dagger back to Burke.

"It seems," Felice said gently, "that Madame is made of sterner stuff than the Tanu."

"Sans doute," was the old woman's dry reply.

Burke mused over the small blade. "It's incredible that we never thought to try iron against them. But vitredur and bronze weapons were so easily available. And we never tumbled to the reasons why they confiscated steel items back at the Castle . . . Khalid Khan!"

One of the crowd, a gaunt man with burning eyes, a scraggly beard, and an immaculate white turban, got to his feet. "I can smelt iron as readily as copper, Peo. All you have to do is furnish the ore. The religious prohibition that the Tanu put on ironwork among their human subjects simply led us to carry on with copper and bronze out of sheer inertia."

"Who knows where iron ore might be found?" Madame asked of the company. There was silence until Claude said, "I might help you there. We old fossil hunters know a little geology, too. About a hundred kloms northwest of here, down the Moselle River, should be an accessible deposit. Even primitive men worked it. It'll be near the site of the future city of Nancy."

Khalid Khan said, "We'd have to do the refining work up there. Arrowheads would be best to begin with. Some lance tips. A few smaller blades."

"There's another experiment you might try," Amerie said, "once you have a strong iron chisel."

"What's that, Sister?" asked the turbaned metalsmith.

"Try removing gray torcs with it."

"By damn!" exclaimed Peopeo Moxmox Burke.

"Iron might short out the linkage between the brains of the torc wearers and the slave-circuitry," the nun went on. "We must find *some* way of freeing those people!"

One of Burke's fighters, a hefty fellow puffing a meerschaum, said, "To be sure. But what about those who don't wish to be freed? Perhaps you don't realize, Sister, that a good many humans are quite content in their filthy symbiosis with the exotics. The soldiers, especially. How many of them are sadistic misfits, delighting in the rôles given them by the Tanu?"

Madame Guderian said, "It is true, what Uwe Guldenzopf says. And even among those of goodwill, even among the barenecks, there are many who are happy in bondage. It is because of them that the expiation of my guilt cannot be a simple matter."

"Now don't start that again, Madame." Burke was firm. "Your plan, as it stands, is a good one. With the addition of iron weapons, we can shtup it forward that much faster. By the time we've located the Ship's Grave, we'll have enough of an armory to give the scheme a reasonable chance of success."

"I'm not going to wait weeks or months for you people to hatch your plot," Felice declared. "If my dirk killed one Tanu, it can kill others." She held out her hand to Burke. "Give it back."

"They'd get you, Felice," the Native American said. "They're expecting you. Do you think all of the Tanu are as weak as Epone? She was small fry—fairly powerful as coercers go, but her redact function wasn't worth much or she'd have smelled you out back at the Castle, even without using the mind-assay machine. The leaders among the Tanu can detect people like you in the same way that they detect Firvulag. You're going to have to keep out of the way until you get your golden torc."

She exploded. "And when will that be, dammit?"

Madame said, "When we manage to obtain one for you. Or when the Firvulag choose to give you one."

The girl replied with a volley of obscenities. Claude went up to her, took her by the shoulders, and sat her down on the soft wood-dust of the floor. "Now that's enough of that." Turning to Burke and Madame Guderian, he said, "Both of you have referred to a plan of action that you seem to expect us to participate in. Let's hear it."

Madame uttered a deep sigh. "Very well. First, you must know what we are up against. The Tanu seem to be invulnerable, immortal, but they are not. They can be killed by Firvulag brainstorms, the weaker ones—and even a powerful coercer-redactor may be overwhelmed if many Firvulag all project together or if one of their great heroes, such as Pallol or Sharn-Mes, chooses to fight."

"What is this bad vibes thing?" Richard asked her. "Can you do it?"

She shook her head. "My latent abilities include the farsensing function in moderation, a somewhat less powerful coercive ability, and an aspect of creativity that may spin certain illusions. I can coerce ordinary humans, and grays who are not under direct compulsion from a Tanu. I cannot coerce the exotics or humans wearing gold or silver torcs—except with subliminal suggestions, which they may or may not follow. My farsense permits me to eavesdrop upon the so-called declamatory or command mode of the mental speech. I can hear the golds, silvers, and grays when they call out to one another over moderate distances, but I cannot detect more subtle narrow-focus communication unless it is directed at me. On rare occasions I have perceived messages coming from far away."

"And can you farspeak back?" Claude asked in an excited tone.

"To whom would I speak?" the old woman inquired. "All around us are enemies!"

Amerie exclaimed, "Elizabeth!"

Claude explained. "One of our companions. An operant far-speaker. She was taken south to the capital." He told what he knew of Elizabeth's former life and her regained metafunctions.

Madame frowned in preoccupation. "So it was *she* that I heard! But I did not know. And so I suspected a Tanu trick and withdrew at once from the touch."

"Could you contact her?" Claude asked.

"The Tanu would hear me," the old woman said, shaking her head. "I seldom project, except to sound the alarm to our people.

Rarely to call to our Firvulag allies. I have not the skill to use the narrow focus that is undetectable except to the intended receptor."

Felice broke in rudely, "The plan! Get on with it!"

Madame pursed her lips and lifted her chin. "Eh bien. Let us continue to speak of the potential vulnerability of the Tanu. They kill one another by decapitation during their ritual combats. In theory a human could accomplish this, too, if it were possible to get close enough. However, the Tanu with coercive or redactive functions defend themselves mentally, while the creators and the psychokinetics are capable of physical assault. The weaker among them remain within the protective sphere of their more powerful fellows or else have bodyguards of armed silvers or grays. There are two other ways in which a Tanu may meet death—both very rare. The Firvulag told me of a very young Tanu who died by fire. He panicked when burning lamp oil spilled upon him and in fleeing, fell off a wall. His human guardians were unable to reach him before he was incinerated. If they had rescued him before his brain burned, they could have restored him to health in the usual Tanu fashion."

"Which is?" Amerie asked.

Chief Burke said, "They have a psychoactive substance that they call Skin. It looks like a thin plass membrane. Tanu healers with a certain combination of PK and redact are able to work through this stuff in some metapsychic way. They just wrap the patient up and start cogitating. They get results comparable to our best regeneration-tank therapy back in the Milieu, but with no hardware. Skin works on human beings, too, but it's worthless without the Tanu operator."

"Do the Firvulag use Skin?" asked the nun.

Burke shook his huge head. "Just old-fashioned frontier doctoring. But they're tough little devils."

Felice laughed. "So are we."

"The last way that the exotics may die," Madame resumed, "is by drowning. The Firvulag are excellent swimmers. However, most of the Tanu are rather more sensitive than humans to the injurious effects of immersion. Still, death by drowning is very rare among them and seems to take mostly certain careless sportsmen of Goriah in Brittany, who are accustomed to carry their Hunt to the sea. Sometimes they are swallowed or carried into the depths by the enraged leviathans that they prey upon."

Felice grunted. "Well, there's not much chance we'll be able to hold the bastards' heads under water. So how *do* you plan to get the drop on 'em?"

"The plan is complex, involving several phases. It requires the co-operation of the Firvulag, with whom we have a very precarious alliance. Briefly, we would hope to attack and overrun Finiah aided by the forces of the Little People, who would be able to wreak havoc once they penetrated the city walls. Finiah is a strategic target of prime importance and it is isolated from the other Tanu population centers. Within its environs and protected by its defenses is the only barium mine in the Exile world. The element is extracted with great difficulty from a meager ore by rama workers. It is vital to the manufacture of torcs. *All* torcs. If we eliminate the supply of barium by destroying the mine, the entire socioeconomy of the Tanu would be undercut."

"Kinda long-range for a disaster, isn't it?" Richard remarked. "I should think they'd have stockpiles of the stuff stashed away."

"I have said that the matter is complex," Madame responded in some irritation. "We will also have to find a way of stopping the flow of time-travelers. As you will see, it is the coming of humanity to the Pliocene that has enabled the Tanu to dominate the era. In the days before I began my meddling, there was a virtual balance of power between Tanu and Firvulag. This was destroyed by the human advent."

"I get it," said Richard, the old intriguer. "The Firvulag are willing to help you and your bunch in hopes of restoring the good old days. But what makes you think the little spooks won't turn on *us* once they get what they want?"

"It is a matter still requiring some reflection," said Madame in a low voice.

Richard gave a derisive snort.

"There's more to the plan," said Peopeo Moxmox Burke. "And don't kick it in the head until you've heard the whole thing. Now down south in the capital—"

The little cat growled.

All of them looked toward the entrance crevice. There stood a short, broad-shouldered figure in a dripping, mucky cloak. His high-crowned hat leaned lugubriously over one ear from an accumulation of moisture. He grinned at the company through a mask of mud in which eyes and teeth were the only bright points.

"Pegleg!" exclaimed Burke. "For God's sake, bubi—what have you been up to?"

"Had to go to ground. Bear-dogs on my trail."

As he came stumping toward the fire, Madame whispered, "Not a word of the iron."

The new arrival was something under a meter and a half in height, with a barrel chest and a visage that was rosy-cheeked and long-nosed, once the filth had been wiped away. He had lost one leg below the knee, but walked about agilely enough with the aid of a singular prosthesis fashioned of wood. Seating himself by the fire, he swabbed at the peg with a damp rag, revealing carvings of snakes and weasels and other creatures twining about the artificial limb. They had inset jewels for eyes.

"What news?" Burke inquired.

"Oh, they're out there, all right," Pegleg replied. Somebody passed food and drink, which the little man attacked with gusto, simultaneously talking with his mouth full. "Some of the lads drew off a large patrol coming up the Onion River. Finished a good half dozen and sent the rest off with their tails between their legs screeching for Daddy Velteyn. No sign of the Exalted Cocksman himself yet, Té be thanked. Probably doesn't want to get his lovely glass armor all wet in the rain. I had a bad moment when some bear-dogs from the squad that we finished began tracking me unawares. Could've nailed me, the sneaky turdlings, but I happened on a nice stinking bog and hid in it until they tired of waiting."

The little man held out his mug to the nun for a refill of wine. Amerie's cat had not returned to her, even though she snapped her fingers in a way that usually brought the animal running. Two baleful glowing eyes watched Pegleg from a dark pile of baggage far from the central fire. The cat continued to utter high-pitched, quavering growls.

"We must introduce our new companions to you," Madame said graciously. "You have seen them, of course. The Reverend Sister Amerie, Professor Claude, Captain Richard . . . and Felice."

"May the Good Goddess smile on you," the little man said. "I'm Fitharn. But you can call me Pegleg."

Richard goggled. "Christ! *You're* a Firvulag?"

The one-legged man laughed and climbed to his feet. There beside the fire stood a tall, dead-black apparition with coiling tentacles for arms, slitted red eyes, and a mouth full of shark's teeth that slavered foul saliva.

Amerie's little cat let out a spitting screech. The monster vanished and Pegleg resumed his seat by the fire, nonchalantly drinking his wine.

"Impressive," said Felice. "Can you do others?"

The Firvulag's eyes twinkled. "We have our favorites, little one. The visions-of-the-eye are the least of it, you understand."

"I do," said Felice. "Since you had to flee the amphicyons, I conclude that they're not affected by your powers."

The exotic sighed. "A perverse species. We have to watch out for the hyaenids, too—but at least *they* can't be tamed by the Foe."

"I can control bear-dogs," Felice said in soft persuasion. "If I had a golden torc, I could help win this war of yours. Why won't you give me what you've already given Madame Guderian?"

"Earn it," said the Firvulag, licking his lips.

Felice clenched her fists. She forced a smile. "You're afraid. But I wouldn't use my metafunctions against any of you. I swear it!"

"Prove it."

"Damn you!" She started toward the little man, her doll-like face twisted with rage. "How? How?"

Madame intervened. "Felice, compose yourself. Be seated."

Fitharn stretched out his peg and groaned. "More wood for the fire! I'm chilled to the bone and my leg-long-gone torments me with phantom pain."

Amerie said, "I have a medication . . . if you're certain that your protoplasm is near-humanoid."

He gave her a broad grin and nodded, extending the stump. As she applied a minidoser he cried, "Ah, better, better! Té's blessing, if you can use such a thing, Sister."

"Masculine, feminine, only aspects of the One. Our races are closer than you think, Fitharn of the Firvulag."

"Perhaps." The little man stared morosely into his winecup.

Madame said, "When you arrived, Fitharn, I was explaining to the newcomers my plan. Perhaps you will be good enough to assist me. Tell them, if you will, the story of the Ship's Grave."

Once again, the exotic's cup was filled with wine. "Very well. Come close and listen. This is Brede's Tale, which was told to me by my own grandfather, gone these five hundred years to Té's dark womb until the great rebirth, when Té and Tana shall be sisters no more, but One, and Firvulag and Tanu cease at last their contention in the truce that shall have no end . . ."

He was silent for a long while, holding the cup to his lips and closing his eyes against the hot wine's rich fumes. Finally he set the vessel beside him, folded his hands in his lap, and told the tale in an oddly cadenced singsong:

"When Brede's Ship, through Té's compassion, brought us here, its mighty striving drained its heart and strength and mind—and so it died that we might live. When we left the Ship our flyers spread their curving wings, and people sang the Song together, friend with foe. We made our weeping way to where the Grave would be. We saw the Ship come burning from the east. We saw it coming through the high air and the low. It howled its agony. As the rising of a planet's sun dismisses night, so did the flaming of our Ship transform the very day, and make the Earth-star dim.

"The passing of the Ship devoured the air. The forests and the eastern mountains fell and thunder rolled around the world. The waters steamed within the brackish eastern seas. No living thing survived along the westward-trending path of death, but we watched sorrowing until the end. The Ship cried out aloud, it burst, it yielded up its soul. Its falling made the planet moan. The air, the waters, planet-crust, and Ship had merged into a glowing holocaust of stormy wound. But we stayed, singing there until the fire was quenched by rain and tears of Brede, and then we flew away.

"Then Pallol, Medor, Sharn, and Yeochee, Kuhsarn the Wise and Lady Klahnino, the Thagdal, Boanda, Mayvar, and Dionket, Lugonn the Shining One and Leyr the Brave—the best of Tanu and of Firvulag—went forth into the setting sun to find a living-place while still the Truce prevailed and none should fight. The Tanu chose Finiah on the riverside; but we, far wiser, took High Vrazel on the fogbound mountain crag. This being done, one task alone remained—to consecrate the Grave.

"In final flight the aircraft took to air. We rode within them to the place, and all embarked to stand upon a rim of land above a cup of liquid sky too wide to see across, while all around the land lay scorched and still. We watched a Great Ordeal, the first upon this world, with Sharn contending for the Firvulag and for the Tanu, bright Lugonn. With Sword and Spear they smote until their armor blazed and birds fell from the sky and heedless watchers lost their eyes. They battled for a month of hours and longer still, until the folk who watched screamed out as one, transfigured in the glory that redounded to the Ship and solemnized its death.

"At last, brave Sharn could bear no more. He fell with Sword in hand, steadfast until the end. The victory was won by bright Lugonn, whose Spear had caused the crater's lake to boil and liquefied the rocks and conjured sparkling dew that merged its tears with ours. And thus the votive offerings of Man and Blade were chosen for the consecration of the Grave. We marched away, the voices of our minds raised up in Song for one last time in honor of the Ship and also him who there was offered up to captain it upon its voyage to the healing dark. There, comforted within the Goddess's womb, they wait the coming of the light . . ."

The Firvulag raised his cup and drained it. He stretched his arms with a pop and crackle of ligaments and sat staring at Felice with a whimsical expression.

Madame Guderian said, "Within this ancient tale are certain pieces of information that repay our study. You will have noted the reference to aircraft. These are clearly machines of some sophistication, since they were able to leave the moribund Ship prior to its entrance into Earth's atmosphere. Given the advanced technology implied by the encapsulation of the passengers within the intergalactic organism, one can hardly assume the smaller craft to be simple reaction-engine fuelers. It is more likely that they were gravo-magnetically powered, like our own eggs and subluminal spaceships. And if so—"

Richard interrupted, wide-eyed. "They'd probably still be operational! And Pegleg said his people *marched* away from the Grave, so they must have left the aircraft there. Son of a bitch!"

"Where are they?" cried Felice. "Where's this Grave?"

The little Firvulag said, "When a person dies among us, the remains are taken by the family or friends to a secret place, one that none of the mourners has ever seen before. After the interment ceremony, the grave is never visited again. Its very location is blotted from the mind lest the remains be disturbed by the Foe or by irreverent rascals who would steal the funerary offerings."

"Quaint customs," Richard said.

Felice wailed, "Then you don't know where the Ship's Grave is?"

"It's been a thousand years," the little man replied.

Richard flung the ladle into the stewpot with a clang. "But, dammit, it's gotta be a whackin' great crater! What'd he say—? 'A cup of liquid sky too wide to see across.' And it lies east of Finiah."

"We have been searching," Madame said. "Ever since I first heard the tale three years ago and conceived the plan, we have looked for the Ship's Grave as best we could. But understand the terrain, Richard! The Black Forest lies beyond the Rhine to the east. In our day it was a minor range, a picturesque parkland full of hikers and carvers of cuckoo clocks. But now the Schwarzwald mountains are younger and higher. There are portions well above twenty-five hundred meters, rugged and dangerous to cross and a notorious haunt of les Criards—the Howling Ones."

"And do you know who *they* are?" inquired the Firvulag, smirking at Richard. "They're the people like me who don't like people like you. The snotty ones who won't let King Yeochee or anyone else tell 'em who their enemies are."

Madame said, "We have, over the past years, done a precarious exploration of the middle portion of the Black Forest range, north of Finiah. Even with the help of friendly Firvulag such as our good friend Fitharn, the project has been fraught with peril. Ten of our people have been killed and three driven mad. Five more vanished without a trace."

"And we lost some of our lads to the Hunt, too," Pegleg added. "Guiding humans just isn't healthy work."

Madame went on, "Forty or fifty kilometers east of the Black Forest begins the Swabian Alb, a part of the Jura. It is said to be full of caves inhabited by monstrous hyenas. Not even the malign Firvulag care to dwell in this territory—although it is rumored that a handful of grotesque mutants eke out a pathetic livelihood in sheltered valleys. Yet it is in this inhospitable country that the Ship's Grave is most likely to be found. And with it, not only workable flying machines but perhaps other ancient treasures as well."

"Would there be weapons in the aircraft?" Felice asked.

"Only one," said the Firvulag Fitharn, staring into the fire. "The Spear. But it would be enough, if you could get your hands on it."

Scowling, Richard said, "But I thought the Spear belonged to the guy named Lugonn—and he was the *winner* of the fight!"

"The winner received the privilege of sacrificing himself," Madame explained. "Lugonn, Shining Hero of the Tanu, raised the visor of his golden glass helmet and accepted the thrust of his own Spear through his eyes. His body was left at the crater, together with the weapon."

"But what the hell good would this Spear do us?" Richard asked.

Fitharn spoke softly. "It isn't the kind of weapon you might think. Any more than the Sword of our late hero, Sharn the Atrocious—which the obscene Nodonn has had in his thieving clutches in Goriah for forty years—is any kind of ordinary sword."

"They are both photonic weapons," Madame said. "The only two that the exotics brought from their home galaxy. They were to be used only by the great heroes—to defend the Ship in case of pursuit or, later, in the most exalted forms of ritual fighting."

"Nowadays," said Chief Burke, "the Sword only serves as the trophy of the Grand Combat. Nodonn's had it so long because the Tanu have won the contest for forty years running. Needless to say, there's little chance we'd ever be able to get our hands on the Sword. But the Spear is another matter."

"Christ!" Richard spat in disgust. "So to make Madame's plan work, all we have to do is mount a blind search over two-three thousand square kloms crawling with man-eating spooks and giant hyenas and find this antique zapper. Probably clutched in some Tanu skeleton's hand."

"And around his neck," Felice said, "is a golden torc."

"We will find the Ship's Grave," Madame stated. "We will search until we do."

Old Claude hauled himself to his feet with some difficulty, limped over to the pile of dry wood, and picked up an armful. "I don't think any more blind hunting will be necessary," he said, tossing the sticks onto the blaze. A great cloud of sparks soared into the Tree's black height.

Everybody stared at him.

Chief Burke asked, "Do you know where this crater might be?"

"I know where it *has* to be. Only one astrobleme in Europe fits the bill. The Ries."

The stout fighter with the pipe smacked his own forehead and exclaimed, "Das Rieskessel bei Nördlingen! Natürlich! What a bunch of stupid pricks we've been! Hansi! Gert! We read about it in kindergarten!"

"Hell, yes," sang out another man from the crowd. And a third Lowlife added, "But you gotta remember, Uwe, they told us kids a meteorite made the thing."

"The Ship's Grave!" one of the women cried out. "If it's not just a myth, then there's a chance for us! We really might be able to free humanity from these bastards!" An exultant shout went up from the rest of the crowd.

"Be silent, for the love of God!" Madame implored them. Her hands were clasped before her breast almost prayerfully as she addressed Claude. "You are certain? You are positive that this—this Ries must be the Ship's Grave?"

The old paleontologist picked up a branch from the woodpile. Scuffing an area of dust flat, he drew a vertical row of X's.

"There are the Vosges Mountains. We're on the western flank, about here." He poked, then slashed a line parallel to, and east of, the range. "Here's the Rhine, flowing roughly south to north through a wide rift valley. Finiah is here on the eastern bank." More X's were drawn behind the Tanu city. "Here's the Black Forest range, trending north-south just like the Vosges. Same basic geology. And beyond it, slanting off to the northeast, the Swabian Jura. This line I'm drawing under the Jura is the River Danube. It flows off east into the Pannonian Lagoon in Hungary, someplace over under the woodpile. And right about *here—*"

The entire company was on its feet, straining to see and holding its collective breath as the old man stabbed his branch down.

"—is the Ries astrobleme. A few kloms north of the Danube, at the site of the future city of Nördlingen, maybe three hundred kloms east of here. And sure as God made little green apples, that's your Ship's Grave. It's a crater more than twenty-five kloms in diameter. The largest in Europe."

There was an uproar among the Lowlife folk. People crowded in to congratulate Claude and get refills of wine. Someone got out a reed flute and began to play a sprightly tune. Others laughed and danced about. The day that had begun in panicked flight from exotic enemies showed signs of ending as a celebration.

Ignoring the merrymakers, Madame whispered to Chief Burke. She and the Native American beckoned to the remnant of Group Green and withdrew into a deeply shadowed part of the hollow sequoia.

"It may be possible," Madame said, "just barely possible, to implement the plan yet this year. But we will have to set out at once. You must lead, Peo. And I must also go to detect and repel the Howling Ones. We will require your help to find the crater, Claude, and that of Felice to coerce hostile animals. Richard must come to pilot a flying machine, if we should indeed find any to be operational. We will take also Martha, who was a highly skilled engineer and who may help decipher the operation of the exotic devices as well as repair them. Also Stefanko, who tested egg transports. He can assist Richard if need be, and perhaps he might be able to pilot a second aircraft."

Chief Burke said, "Seven people. Two of them old, and Martha's not strong. Awkward, Madame. Too few for strength, too many for speed. Even with Felice and me for muscle, it'll be a rough trip."

Felice said, "I want Amerie to come. We could need a doctor."

The nun lifted her good shoulder in a hesitant gesture. "I'm willing—but I think I'd be more trouble than help."

"There is no question of your accompanying us, ma Soeur," said the old woman, giving Felice a sharp glance. "You can do the most good by remaining here, recovering your strength, and ministering to the people. We have some stolen medications, but many of them are unsuited to lay administration. There are any number of debilities you can allay—poorly knit fractures, fungus afflictions, internal parasites. When this present emergency has passed, Uwe Guldenzopf and Tadanori Kawai will take you to our village at Hidden Springs northwest of here. You will live in my own cottage and the people will come to you."

Chief Burke said, "Khalid Khan can take charge of the iron-smelting party. Say, ten strong men. Claude can tell Khalid what to look for, and if the boys locate the ore and get to work, they might have a fair number of weapons ready by the time we return."

"*If* we return!" Richard exclaimed. "Chrissake, why does everybody just take it for granted that I'm willing to go along with this scheme? Forget it! As soon as the heat's off from the Tanu, I'm blasting outa here."

"You can't weasel out," Felice said. "We need you!"

"Let that other sucker—the egg driver—be the pilot. I don't fight other people's wars."

Madame reached out one hand and touched the black velvet doublet of Richard's costume. "Der fliegende Holländer, is it not? I saw it performed many times in Lyon . . . Oh, Richard! This need not be your destiny. Do not run away. We need you. Help the rest of us to become free and thereby find your own peace. Stefanko's flight experience is very limited. You know how automated our eggcraft were. But you! You have boasted of how you flew the most advanced starships, orbital landers—even primitive aeroplanes. If any among us can operate the exotic craft and bring back the Spear of Lugonn it is you."

Her mind seemed to embrace him—suppressing his objections, calming all fear. And in spite of himself, Richard felt his resolution waver. He knew the damn woman was coercing him, playing her own tune on his superego, bending his willpower; but the more he struggled to get away, the more compelling her mental hold became . . .

Richard! Dear son, don't I know you? I—the mother of one hundred thousand wretched wayfarers who came to me as their last hope? You have always been alone, always self-centered and fearful of opening yourself to other persons, for to do so is to risk rejection and pain. But it is a risk we are born to take, we humans. We cannot live alone, cannot find happiness or peace alone, cannot love alone. The person alone must always be fleeing, always searching. He flees from the loneliness without end. He searches, whether he will or not, for another who will fill his emptiness . . .

Richard backed away from the terrible old woman until he was trapped against the ancient wood of the Tree, trying to defend himself against the thrust of her need and hope and—damn her!—the genuine compassion flowing out from her like healing water bathing his cracked and shitty soul.

Aloud, she said, "Come with us, Richard. Help us—all of us who need you. I cannot truly coerce you. Not beyond the passing moment. You must choose freely to help us. And in the giving you will receive what you have hungered for."

"Damn you!" he whispered.

My poor flawed little one. You have been mortally selfish and paid for your folly. The Milieu forced you to pay. But the sin remains, as does my own, and its true expiation must be in the same coin as that unjustly used. The loss of your starship, of your livelihood, was not enough and you know it! You must give of yourself, and then you will no longer despise yourself. Help us. Help your friends who need you.

"Damn—" He blinked away the mist that had risen in his eyes.

Save.

His words were barely audible. "All right." The others were all looking at him, but he could not see their eyes. "I'll go with you. I'll fly the aircraft back here if I can. But that's all I can promise."

"It is enough," Madame said.

Back at the central fire, the singing and laughing were more subdued. People drifted away to the smaller hearths to prepare for sleep. A small figure hobbled toward Madame, silhouetted against the dying bonfire.

"I've been thinking on your expedition to the Ship's Grave," said Fitharn. "You're going to need the help of our people."

"To find the Danube quickly," Claude agreed. "Do you have any idea of the best way to reach it? In our time, its headwaters were in the Black Forest. God knows where the river begins nowadays. The Alps—even some super version of Lake Constance."

"There is only one person with the authority to help you," the Firvulag said. "You're going to have to visit the King."

2

YEOCHEE IV, High King of the Firvulag, came tiptoeing into the main audience hall of his mountain fortress, his seekersense probing the dim recesses of the great cavern.

"Lulo, my little pomegranate! Where are you hiding?"

There was a sound like the jingling of tiny bells mixed with laughter. A shadow fluttered among the red-and-cream stalactites, the hanging tapestries, the tatty fringed trophy banners from Grand Combats forty years gone. Leaving a musky scent in its wake, something glided like a huge moth into a cul-de-sac chamber at one side of the hall.

Yeochee rushed in pursuit. "Now I've got you trapped! There's no way out of the crystal grotto except past me!"

The alcove was lit by candles in a single golden sconce. The flames struck glints from an incredible profusion of quartz prisms that encrusted the walls, sparkling pink and purple and white like the interior of a giant geode. Heaps of dark furs made inviting mounds on the floor. One of these heaps quivered.

"So there you are!"

Yeochee bounded into the grotto and lifted the concealing rug with tantalizing slowness. A cobra with a body as thick as his arm reared up and hissed at him.

"Now, Lulo! Is that a way to welcome your King?"

The serpent shimmered and acquired a woman's head. Her hair was varicolored like the snakeskin, her eyes a teasing amber. The tongue that stole from her smiling lips was forked.

With a cry of delight, the King threw open his arms. The snake-woman grew a neck, shoulders, soft arms with clever boneless fingers, a marvelously formed upper torso. "Stop right there for a moment," Yeochee suggested, "and we'll explore a few possibilities." They fell onto the bed of furs with an élan that made the candle flames gutter.

A trumpet sounded far away.

"Oh, damn," groaned the King. The concubine Lulo whimpered and uncoiled but her forked tongue continued to dart hopefully.

The trumpet blatted again, nearer this time, and there was a booming of gongs that made the mountain vibrate in sympathy. The stalactites just outside the crystal grotto hummed like tuning forks.

Yeochee sat up, his once jolly face a mask of dismay. "That stupid contingent of Lowlives. The ones who think they're onto a secret weapon against the Tanu. I promised Pallol I'd check 'em out."

The alluring lamia wavered, melted, and became a plump little naked woman with apple cheeks and a blonde Dutch bob. Pouting, she pulled a mink rug over herself and said, "Well, if this is going to take a while, for Té's sake at least get me something to eat. All this chasing about has got me starving to death. No bat fritters, mind you! And none of that awful broiled salamander, either."

Yeochee tied his slightly shabby cloth-of-gold dressing gown and ran his fingers, comb-fashion, through his tangled yellow hair and beard. "I'll order you something lovely," he promised. "We caught us a new human cook the other day who has a marvelous way with cheese-and-meat pastry." The King smacked his lips. "This business won't take long. Then we'll have a picnic right here, and for dessert—"

The trumpet sounded a third time, just outside the hall.

"You're on," said Lulo, snuggling down under the mink. "Hurry back."

King Yeochee stepped outside the grotto, took a deep breath, and transformed himself from one hundred sixty to two hundred sixty centimeters in height. The old robe became a great trailing cloak of garnet-colored velvet. He acquired a splendid suit of gold-chased obsidian parade armor, its open helm surmounted by a tall crown sprouting two curling members like golden ram's horns and a beak-like extension jutting over the forehead that threw his upper face into deep shadow. He turned on his eyes so that they gleamed with sinister chatoyance. Making a run for it, he assumed the throne without a moment to spare.

The trumpet sounded for the last time.

Yeochee raised one mailed hand and several dozen illusory courtiers and men-at-arms winked into being about the throne dais. The rocks of the mountain hall began to glow with rich colors. Rippling music, as from a marimba of glass, filled the room as six Firvulag of the palace guard escorted the humans and Fitharn Pegleg into the royal presence.

One of the quasi courtiers stepped forward. Using Standard English for the sake of the Lowlives, he declaimed: "Let all pay homage to His Appalling Highness Yeochee IV, Sovereign Lord of the Heights and Depths, Monarch of the Infernal Infinite, Father of All Firvulag, and Undoubted Ruler of the Known World!"

An organlike peal of deafening intensity stopped the approaching visitors in their tracks. The King arose and seemed to grow taller and taller before their eyes until he loomed among the stalactites like some gigantic idol with emerald eyes.

Fitharn doffed his tall hat briefly. "How do, King."

"You have our leave to approach!" boomed the apparition.

Fitharn stumped forward, the seven humans trailing after him. Yeochee noted with regret that only two of the Lowlives—a sharp-featured fellow with a big black mustache and a younger woman, hollow-cheeked and thin, with fair hair pulled into an unflattering knot—seemed genuinely impressed by his monstrous guise. The rest of the human party regarded His Appalling Highness with either scientific interest or amusement. Old Madame Guderian even betrayed a trace of Gallic ennui. Oh, what the hell. Why not relax?

"We shall condescend to assume a gentler aspect!" Yeochee decreed. He shrank down to his ordinary self—gold dressing gown, bare feet, and all, with his coronet set askew as usual. "Now what's all this?" he inquired of Fitharn.

"Madame Guderian's plot against the Tanu seems to've taken a quantum leap, King. Better let her tell it."

Yeochee sighed. Madame reminded him disconcertingly of his late grandmother, a lady who always knew when he had been up to childish mischief. Despite the old Frenchwoman's talent for political intrigue, Yeochee had long since bitterly regretted giving her a golden torc. Madame's schemes always seemed to end up benefiting the Lowlife humans, with only minimal gain to the Firvulag. He should have followed his first instinct and blasted her to flinders with his psychoenergies in those early days when she first had the temerity to step through her own time-gate. Indirectly, after all, she was the author of the present Firvulag degradation!

The old woman, dressed now in the dappled deerskin garments favored by forest prowlers of her race, stepped boldly to the throne and gave the King a perfunctory bob of her head.

"You're looking well, Monseigneur. Plenty of healthy exercise, one trusts."

Yeochee frowned. But at least the old trout had jogged his memory in regard to Lulo's promised snack. He reached out and pulled a bellrope. "Pallol tells me you may have discovered the location of the Ship's Grave."

"It is true." She gestured toward a silver-haired man among the humans. "One of our new compatriots, Professor Claude, believes he has identified the locale. It was known to him through his scientific studies in the world of the future."

"Still known six million years from now?" The King beckoned to the paleontologist, who came closer. "You there, Claude. Tell me—in the future, did your people have any recollections of *us?*"

Claude smiled at the little exotic and let his gaze wander about the fantastic hall that lay within the heart of the Vosges' highest mountain.

"Your Majesty, right this minute humanity's direct ancestors are small apes cowering in the forest. They have no language, and so there is no way they can pass on to their descendants any memories whatsoever. Primitive human beings having the power of speech won't evolve for another two or three million years or so, and they won't develop reliable oral traditions until—oh, say, eight or nine thousand years before my time. Wouldn't you agree that it was highly unlikely for future humanity to have retained any recollections of a race of small shape-changing exotic people who live in underground dwellings?"

The King shrugged. "It was only a thought . . . So you know where the Ship's Grave is, eh?"

Claude said, "I believe so. And you have no moral objections to our plundering it to our mutual benefit?"

Yeochee's beady green eyes flashed dangerously. "Be careful, old Claude. You won't be robbing the Ship of anything that can't be returned in good time—with interest—when the unfair advantage that the despicable Foe has seized is equalized."

Madame said, "We will help you to accomplish this end, Monseigneur. I have sworn it as part of my expiation! When humans can no longer be enslaved by the Tanu, the status quo between your two races will be restored. And our first strike will be against Finiah—using an aircraft and the Spear from the Ship's Grave."

The King twisted his beard into golden ropes. "The time factor! It's only three weeks to the equinox—then another week and a half and we're into the Truce for the Grand Combat ingathering. H'mm. Our forces would need at least a week to prepare for an attack against the Tanu. Is there a chance that you can get back here with the flyer and the Spear before the Truce begins? We'd be willing to join you in an attack if there was a real hope of knocking off Velteyn and his flying circus. If we were successful against Finiah, the morale of our lads and lasses would be at zenith going into the Games this year."

The old woman turned to Claude. "Is it possible for us to get to the Ries and back inside of a month?"

"We might barely manage it. But only if we obtain a guide who can take us by the shortest route to the head of small-boat navigation on the Danube. This would be some place beyond the Black Forest in a kind of sediment-filled basin—the molassic foredeep between the Swabian Jura and the Alps. The river would likely flow as gently through the molasse as the Sweet Afton. We could sail to the Ries easily and fly back."

"Within the month?" the King persisted.

"If you use your good offices to get us a guide, it's feasible."

Fitharn stepped forward. "The mighty Sharn-Mes suggested that one Sugoll might be made to assist the expedition. A bad-tempered joker, even for a Howler, and not any too loyal. But he claims to rule the Feldberg country, even the Water Caves beyond the Paradise Gorge. Sharn-Mes thought that if anyone knew of this river, Sugoll would. I can take these people to his lair if you'll authorize Madame to impress his service."

"Oh, very well," grumbled the King. He crouched down and began groping under the throne, presently hauling out a small coffer that looked as if it was carved from black onyx. After fumbling with its golden catch, he flung it open, rummaged around, and came up with a Parker pen of twenty-second-century vintage and a much-creased, stained piece of vellum. Still kneeling on the floor he scrawled several emphatic ideographs and appended the royal signature.

"That should do it." He replaced the writing materials and the chest and handed the missive to Madame. "It's the best I can do. Freely translated, it says: *Help these people or it's your ass.* You have our royal leave to coerce this Sugoll into slime-mold if he gives you a hard time."

Madame gave a gracious nod and tucked the note away.

A bowlegged little fellow in a belted red smock came trotting into the audience hall and saluted the King. "You rang, Appalling One?"

"We hunger and thirst," said the Monarch of the Infernal Infinite. He turned abruptly from the steward and shot a question at Madame. "You really think this expedition has a chance of success?"

"It does," she affirmed solemnly. "Captain Richard, here, was a master of starships. He will be able to pilot one of the flyers spoken of in your legends, if they have not been destroyed by the elements. Martha and Stefanko possess technical knowledge that will enable us to make both the aircraft and the Spear operational. Chief Burke and Felice will defend us against natural perils en route. I myself will use my metafunctions to confound inimical members of your own race, as well as such Tanu that may venture to pursue us. Professor Claude will lead us to the crater once we are safely on the river. As to success—" She ventured a wintry smile. "That remains in the hands of le bon dieu, n'est-ce pas?"

Yeochee glowered at her. "Why can't you speak English like a regular human being? Don't I have enough trouble with you? Oh—I admit the plan sounds good. But so did the scheme for tunneling under the Finiah wall and setting off that damned guano explosive your people cooked up. And at the last minute Velteyn let the Rhine into the diggings! A hundred and eighty-three Firvulag stalwarts swimming for their lives in a soup of bird shit!"

"This time it will be different, Monseigneur."

Yeochee beckoned to the steward. "Bring me some of the best ale. And have that new human cook, Mariposa—the one with the nose— bake up one of those big flat open-face tarts with the melted chamois cheese and tomato sauce and the new sausage."

The steward bowed low and ran off.

"We have your leave, then, to pursue the expedition immediately?" Madame asked.

"Oh, yes, yes." The King's growl was petulant. He drew his golden bathrobe around himself. "We command it, in fact. And now you are dismissed . . . Fitharn, you stay here. I've got something to talk over with you."

The palace guards, who had stood immobile in their black-glass armor during the interview, now thumped short lances on the floor and prepared to escort the human visitors out. But the smallest female, the one with the cloud of pale hair who was scarcely as tall as a Firvulag woman, had the boldness to call out.

"Your Majesty! One more word."

"Oh, very well," sighed the King. "I know who *you* are. I suppose you still think we ought to give you a golden torc."

"Don't make me wait!" Felice fixed him with a gaze even more penetrating than Madame's. "With a golden torc I could insure that the expedition would be a success."

The King vouchsafed what he hoped was a suave smile. "I know all about your extraordinary abilities. You'll be rewarded with your heart's desire in good time. But not yet! First, help your friends get the Spear and the flyer. If you should happen to find Lugonn's torc there at the crater, take it! If not, we'll see what can be done when you return. Deliver the goods and then we'll talk about presents."

He waved his hand in dismissal and the guards ushered the humans out.

"Are they gone?" Yeochee whispered, jumping down off the dais to peer into the gloom.

"Gone, King," Fitharn confirmed. He sat on the edge of the regal platform, pulled off one boot, and tipped a pebble from it. "Ah, you little bastard!"

"Show some respect," growled Yeochee.

"Speaking to the stone in my shoe, Appalling One . . . Well? What do you think?"

"Risky, risky." The King paced up and down, hands clasped behind his back. "If only we could do without these damned middlemen! Pull off the whole thing ourselves!"

Fitharn said, "The despicable torc wearers must often entertain the same thoughts. They, too, are dangerously dependent upon humanity. But there is no other way for us, Appalling One. The humans are smarter than we are, stronger in other ways as well. Could we ever hope to operate a flyer after all this time? Or put the Spear into working order? We've had forty years to think of ways to bring down the Foe—and all we've done is cry in our beer. I don't like the redoubtable Guderian any more than you do, King. But she's a most formidable person. Like her or lump her, she can help us."

"But we can't *trust* humans!" howled Yeochee. "Did you feel that blast of hostility from Felice while she was saying 'pretty please'? Give that one a golden torc—? I'd sooner try to plug a lava dike with my royal swizzle stick!"

"We can control Felice. Pallol and Sharn-Mes have been giving the matter thought. Even if she finds a torc at the Ship's Grave, she can't learn to use it overnight. They'll fly back here right away and

Felice will be wild to get into the fight against Finiah. We'll put her in the care of our Warrior Ogresses—"

"Té's titties!" blasphemed the King.

"—and Ayfa or Skathe can put her down at the least hint of treachery. If Felice survives the assault on Finiah we can get rid of her by sending her south to the Combat. That will seem to fit right in with the second phase of Guderian's famous plan. Don't worry, King. We'll use Felice and the rest of them to our advantage . . . and then Sharn and Pallol will engineer a suitably heroic demise for our noble human allies. If we play this right, the Firvulag can end up with both the Spear *and* the Sword—on top of the Tanu torcers and the Lowlives, too! And you can really mean it when you call yourself Undoubted Ruler of the Known World."

Yeochee gave him an awful look. "Just wait until it's *your* turn in the king barrel! We'll see how well you—"

The steward came skipping out of the passage, carrying a large steaming tray and a glass flagon of tawny liquid. "It's ready, Appalling One! Hot-hot-hot! And not with ordinary salamander sausage, either, but with a new kind! The cook Mariposa says it'll frizzle your cojones!"

Yeochee bent over the tray to savor the fragrance of the wheel-shaped open pie. It was cut into wedges, each one oozing delectable layers of creamy white and red.

"Beggin' your pardon, King," Fitharn ventured, "but what the hell is that?"

The King took the platter and the bottle of ale and began to trudge happily toward the crystal grotto. "The special dish of one Señora Mariposa de Sanchez, late of Krelix Plantation, earlier of Chichen-Itza Pizza Parlor in Merida, Mexico . . . Leave us, Fitharn. Go with those damned Lowlives and watch 'em."

"As you command, Appalling One."

At last, the great cavern was quiet once more. Yeochee poked his head around the entrance to the geode chamber. The candles burned low and two fascinating eyes peered at him from the stack of dark furs.

"Yoo-hoo!" he caroled. "Goody time!"

Lulo came bouncing toward him in the most charming way. "Grrum! Yumyumyum!"

He gave a delighted screech. "Let go! Let me put it down first, you mad succubus, you! Oh, you're going to love this. It's my newest favorite. Half cheese, half axolotl!"

3

"THE UNICORN! The unicorn! The unicorn!"

Martha keened the word unceasingly as she wept over the torn body of Stefanko lying in the middle of the marsh trail. Great cypresses reared up from pools of brown water on either side. Where the morning sunlight shone through the trees there were clouds of dancing midges and scarlet dragonflies hawking among them. A lobster-sized crayfish, perhaps attracted by the blood dripping into the water, scrabbled slowly up the shallow embankment that raised the trail above the Rhine bottomland.

Peopeo Moxmox Burke sat propped against a mossy trunk, groaning as Claude and Madame Guderian cut away his deerskin shirt and one leg of his pants.

"The horn seems only to have grazed your ribs, mon petit peau-rouge. However, I will have to sew. Claude, administer a narcotic."

"See to Steffi," the Chief pleaded through clenched teeth.

Claude only shook his head. He took a herendorf bleb from the medical kit Amerie had prepared for them and applied the dose to Burke's temple.

"Oh, God. That's better. How is the leg? I could feel the bugger's teeth fress me to the bone."

Claude said, "Your calf muscle is all slashed to hell. And you can bet those tusks were poison-filthy to boot. There's no way we can patch this out here, Peo. Your only chance is professional care back with Amerie."

Cursing softly, Burke rested his huge gray head against the cypress and let his eyes close. "My own fault. Stupid schmuck—I was concentrating on covering our scent by taking us through that patch of stinking pitcher plants. Watching for hoe-tusker sign, traces of bear-dogs . . . and we get ambushed by a goddam *hog!*"

"Silence, child," Madame ordered. "You derange my stitching."

"It was no ordinary porker," Claude said. He wrapped the Chief's leg in porofilm after packing the wound with antibiotic floc. The decamole leg splint was already inflated and ready to be fastened in place. "I think the beast that did this job on you was none other than Kubanochoerus, the giant one-horned Caucasian boar. It was supposed to've been extinct by the Pliocene."

"Huh! Tell that to Steffi, poor faygeleh."

Madame said, "I will finish tending Peo, Claude. See to Martha."

The paleontologist went over to the hysterical engineer, studied her swaying, wild-eyed actions for a moment, and saw what had to be done. He grasped her by one wrist and yanked her roughly to her feet. "Will you shut up, girl? Your stupid bawling will bring the soldiers on us! Do you think Steffi would want that?"

Martha choked in outraged astonishment and drew back one arm to slap the old man's face. "How do you know what Steffi would want? You didn't know him! But I did, and he was gentle and good and he took care of me when my damn guts were—when I was sick. And now look at him. *Look* at him!" Her ravaged, once beautiful face crumpled in fresh sobs. Martha's momentary fury at Claude dissolved and her arm fell. "Steffi, oh, Steffi," she whispered, then fell against the sturdy old man. "One minute he was walking along and smiling over his shoulder at me, and the next—"

The gray monster had burst without warning from a thick stand of reeds and charged the middle of the line of hikers, tossing Stefanko into the air and then savaging him. It had switched its attack to Peo when the Chief drew his machete and tried to stop the animal's awful gobbling. Fitharn had burst into illusory flame, driving the boar off the natural causeway into the swamp shallows. Felice and Richard followed the fireball with drawn bows, leaving the others to help the wounded. But there was no helping Stefanko.

Claude held the shuddering Martha in his arms, then pulled out the tail of his bush shirt and used it to wipe her streaming eyes. He led her to the mossy hollow where Madame was working on Burke and made her sit down. The knees of the engineer's buckskin trousers were stained with dark blood and muck, but there were also bright scarlet patches down around both ankles.

"You'd better have a look at her, Madame," Claude said. "I'll take care of Steffi."

He got a mylar blanket from his own pack and went to the body, fighting to control his own rage and revulsion. He had known Stefanko only four days; but the ready competence of the man and the warmth of his personality had made him a congenial trail-mate on the trek from High Vrazel to the Rhine bottomland. Now Claude could only do his best to smooth the contorted face back into its accustomed smooth lineaments. No need to look so surprised any more, Steffi boy. Just relax and rest. Rest in peace.

A horde of flies had descended upon the ripped mass of intestines and moved only with sluggish reluctance as Claude rolled Stefanko's body onto the metallic sheet. Using the heat-beam of his powerpack, the old man welded the edges of the mylar into a bag. The job was nearly finished when Fitharn, Richard, and Felice came squelching back out of the jungle.

Felice held up a ridged yellowish object like an ivory marlinspike. "We got the fuckard for what good it does."

Richard shook his head in awe. "A pig the size of a goddam ox! Musta weighed eight hundred kilos. Took five arrows to finish it off after Pegleg trapped it in a thicket. I still can't figure how anything that big could have snuck up on us unawares."

"They're intelligent devils," Fitharn growled. "It must have followed us downwind. If I'd had my wits about me I'd have sensed it. But I was thinking about how we'd have to hurry to cross the river before the morning mist lifted."

"Well, we're stuck here now that it's broad daylight," Felice said. She held up the trophy horn. "This fellow saw to that."

"Now what?" Richard wanted to know.

Felice had unclipped the arrows from the holder on her compound bow and she now knelt to dip the stained glassy heads in the water beside the trail. "We'll have to hide out on this side until sundown and then cross. The moon's nearly full tonight. We could probably get over the narrow strip of east-bank lowland in a couple of hours and then bivouac among the rocks at the foot of the Black Forest scarp for the rest of the night."

The Firvulag gave an exclamation. "You're not thinking of going on?"

She glared at him. *"You're* not thinking of turning back?"

Claude said, "Steffi's dead. Peo's in a bad way. He's going to have to be taken back to Amerie by one of us, or he'll lose his leg—or worse."

"That still leaves five of us," Felice said. She frowned, tapping the boar horn against her buckskin-clad thigh. "Pegleg could go back with the Chief. He could get help from his people along the way.

And before you leave," she said to the little man, "tell us how to get to the stronghold of this guy Sugoll."

"It won't be easy." The Firvulag wagged his head. "The Black Forest is a lot more rugged than the Vosges. Sugoll's place is up on the northeastern slope of the Feldberg, where the Paradise River comes off the snowfields. Bad country."

"The Tanu won't be looking for us on the other side of the Rhine," she said. "Once we're across, we probably won't have to worry about any more gray-torc patrols."

"There are still Howlers," Fitharn said. "And at night, the Hunt. Airborne, if Velteyn leads it. If the Hunt spots you in the open, you're finished."

"Can't we travel mostly by day?" Richard suggested. "Madame Guderian's metafunctions can warn us of hostile Firvulag."

The old woman had come up to the group, an expression of deep concern upon her face. "I am not so worried about les Criards as about Sugoll himself. Without his help, we may never locate the Danube in time. But if Fitharn does not accompany us, Sugoll may feel that he can ignore the King's directive with impunity. And there is another matter for grave concern . . . Martha. She has begun to hemorrhage from the shock. Among the Tanu, she was forced to give birth to four children in quick succession and her female organs—"

"Oh, for God's sake," said Felice impatiently. "If she rests, she'll pull out of it. And we'll take our chances with Sugoll."

"Martha is greatly weakened," the old woman persisted. "She will become worse before she is better. This has happened before. It would be best if she returns with Peo and Fitharn."

Richard looked dubious. "But now that Stefanko's gone, she's the only technician we've got. Without her help, God knows how long it might take me to trace the circuits on that exotic aircraft. And if the zapper needs work, I wouldn't have a prayer of fixing it."

"The expedition could be postponed," Fitharn said.

"That would mean waiting a whole year!" Felice blazed. "I won't do it! I'll go get the damn Spear all by myself!"

Back at the cypress, Martha cried out to them, "We can't postpone the search, Madame. Anything could happen in a year. I'll be all right in a day or two. If I get a little help, I know I can make it."

"We could rig a litter from one of the cots," Claude suggested.

Felice brightened. "And in the rough spots, I could carry her on my back. She's right about anything being likely to happen if we delay." Her eyes strayed to the Firvulag, who looked back at her with bland objectivity. "Others could find the Ship's Grave ahead of us."

"It would be wisest to turn back," Fitharn said. "However, the decision will have to be that of Madame Guderian."

"Dieu me secourait," the old woman murmured. "One of us has already given his life." She took a few slow steps toward the mylar-wrapped bundle lying on the trail. "If we could ask him his opinion, we know very well what he would say."

She turned back to them, lifting her chin with the familiar gesture. "Alors . . . Fitharn, you will turn back with Peo. The rest of us will go on."

* * *

They concealed themselves for the rest of the day in a dense taxodium grove hard by the western bank of the Rhine. The gnarled, low-growing branches made comfortable perches. Curtained by festoons of lichens and flowering epiphytes, they could safely observe the river traffic and at the same time be secure from the crocodiles, hoe-tuskers, and other potentially dangerous wildlife that infested the bottomland.

It became very hot as the sun climbed. Food was no problem, for there were plenty of turtles whose meat could be roasted with the power-beams, as well as palms with edible hearts and an abundance of honey-sweet grapes the size of golf balls that drove Richard into raptures of oenological speculation. But as morning dragged into afternoon, boredom and reaction from the dawn violence made the younger members of the party drowsy. Richard, Felice, and Martha stripped off most of their clothing, tied themselves to upper limbs of the big tree, and slept—leaving Claude and Madame on branches below keeping watch over the broad river. Only a few supply barges from upstream plantations drifted past their hiding place. Finiah itself lay about twenty kilometers to the north on the opposite bank, where the short Paradise River tributary tumbled out of a deep gorge that almost bisected the Black Forest massif.

"Later," Madame told Claude, "when it is dark, we will be able to see Finiah's lights against the northern sky. It stands on a promontory jutting into the Rhine. It is not a large city, but it is the oldest of all the Tanu settlements and they have illuminated it with great splendor."

"Why did they migrate southward, out of this area?" Claude

asked. "From what I've been told, most of the Tanu cities are down around the Mediterranean, with this northern country left pretty much to the Firvulag."

"A very warm climate is more to the Tanu taste. I believe that the division of territory between the two groups reflects a very ancient pattern, perhaps one that goes back to the origins of the dimorphic race. One might imagine a world of singular ruggedness where highland and lowland forms evolved—perhaps interdependent yet antagonistic. With the coming of high civilization and the eventual migration of the race to other worlds in their galaxy, these ancient tensions would be sublimated. But it would seem that Tanu and Firvulag genes never blended completely. From time to time during the history of these people the old rivalries would be resurrected."

"And crushed by the high-tech majority," Claude said. "Until this one group of barbarian throwbacks found a perfect refuge instead of coming to the usual quixotic end."

She nodded her agreement. "It was perfect for the exiles, our Pliocene Earth . . . except for the irony that equally quixotic humans should also have desired to dwell on it."

She pointed to a pneumatic barge far out on the river. "There goes one of the products of the human advent. Before the humans came, the Tanu had simple rafts of wood. They had little river commerce because of their dislike of water. They supervised their own plantations and even did honest work because there were not so many rama slaves. The torcs for the little apes formerly had to be made by hand in the same manner as their own golden torcs."

"Do you mean that human know-how enabled mass production?"

"For the ape torcs, yes. And the entire silver and gray system, with its linkage to the golden torcs of the Tanu rulers, was devised by a human psychobiologist. They made him a demigod and he still lives in Muriah—Sebi-Gomnol the Lord Coercer! But I remember the pinched little self-hating man who came to my auberge forty years ago. Then he was called Eusebio Gomez-Nolan."

"So a human being is responsible for this slave setup—? Sweet Lord. Why do we screw things up, wherever we go?"

She gave a short bitter laugh. With her hair straggling in sweat curls about her ears and forehead, she seemed to be scarcely forty-five years old. "Gomnol is not the only traitor to our race. There was a Turkish man of the circus, one of my earliest clients, named Iskender Karabekir. His fondest wish, as he told me, was to train sabertooth tigers to do his bidding. But I have discovered that in this

Exile world he devoted himself instead to the domestication of chalikos and helladotheria and amphicyons—which became pivotal in the subsequent Tanu domination of society. The ancient Hunt and Grand Combat were fought by Tanu and Firvulag afoot. The groups were evenly matched, for what the Firvulag lacked in finesse and sophisticated metafunctions they made up in sheer numbers and a more rugged physique. But a mounted Tanu Hunt was a different matter. And a Grand Combat with Tanu and torced human warriors on chalikoback and Firvulag afoot has become an annual massacre."

Claude stroked his chin. "Still, there was the Battle of Agincourt —if you'll pardon my mentioning it."

"Bof!" said Angélique Guderian. "Longbows will not conquer the Tanu, nor will gunpowder. Not while perverse members of our own human race betray their fellows! Who taught the Tanu physicians how to reverse the human sterilizations? A gynecologist from the planet Astrakhan. A human woman! Not only our talents but our very genes have been placed in the service of these exotics—and many, such as Martha, choose death rather than the degradation of becoming brood stock. Do you know how Martha came to us?"

Claude shook his head.

"She threw herself into the Rhine, hoping to drown herself in the spring flood rather than submit to a fifth impregnation. But she was cast ashore, dieu merci, and Steffi found her and restored her. There are many others like Martha among us. Knowing them, loving them —and knowing also that I am the one ultimately responsible for their pain—you will understand why I cannot rest until the power of the Tanu is broken."

The river was turning from shining pewter to gold. On the Black Forest side, the heights of the Feldberg to the south became luminous with the sinking sun, tinted primrose and purple. In order to reach Sugoll, they would have to go up into that high country and cross at least seventy kilometers of mountain forest—and all this before even beginning their search for the Danube.

"Quixotic," Claude said. He was smiling.

"Are you sorry you agreed to help me? You are an enigma to me, Claude. I can understand Felice, Richard, Martha—the strong-willed ones of our company such as Chief Burke. But I have not yet been able to understand you. I cannot see why you came to the Pliocene at all, much less why you agreed to go on this quest for the Ship's Grave. You are too sensible, too self-possessed, too—débonaire!"

He laughed. "You have to understand the Polish character,

Angélique. It breeds true, even in a Polish-American like me. We were speaking of battles. Do you know which one we Polacks are proudest of? It happened at the beginning of the Second World War. Hitler's Panzer tanks were rolling into the northern part of Poland and there was no modern weaponry to stop them. So the Pomeranian Cavalry Brigade charged the tanks on horseback, and they were wiped out, man and beast. It was madness, but it was glorious . . . and very, very Polish. And now suppose you tell me why *you* decided to come to the Pliocene."

"It was not because of romanticism," she said. There was no more of the accustomed asperity in her tone, not even grief. She told her story flatly, as though it were the scenario of a stage play that she had been forced to attend too many times—or even an act of confession.

"In the beginning, when I was only greedy for money, I did not care what kind of world lay on the other side of the time-portal. But later, when my heart was finally touched, it became very different. I attempted to have the travelers send messages back to me, reassuring me about the nature of the Pliocene land. Time and again I gave to sensible-seeming persons materials that I felt certain would survive the reversal of the temporal field. Very early tests by my late husband had shown that amber was best, and so my envelopes were pieces of this material, carefully sliced in half, with little wafers of ceramic to insert. These could be written upon with an ordinary graphite pencil, then sealed in the amber with natural balsam cement. I instructed certain travelers to study the ancient scene, write down their considered judgment of it, then return to the vicinity of the time-gate where the translations invariably took place at dawn. You see, Professor Guderian had long ago established that solar time in the ancient epoch was the same as that of the modern world we lived in. I had wished to give the new arrivals maximum daylight to adjust to the new environment, so I always sent them at sunup. Malheureusement, this unvarying program made it most convenient for the minions of the Tanu to control the portal! Long before it occurred to me to try the amber message holders, the exotics had built Castle Gateway and taken steps to seize all time-travelers immediately upon their arrival."

"So you never got any messages from the past?"

"Nothing. In later years, we tried more sophisticated techniques for mechanical retrieval of information, but nothing worked. We could get no pictures, no sounds from the Pliocene. The devices always returned to us in a useless condition. Of course, it is easy to see why!"

"And yet you kept sending people through."

Her face was haunted. "I was tempted again and again to shut down the operation—but the pathetic ones would implore me, and so I continued. Then there came the time when my fearful conscience could no longer be denied. I took the amber materials, constructed a simple trip-lever device to operate the switch of the machine, and came to see for myself this world six million years distant from our own."

"But—" Claude began.

"In order to elude my devoted staff, who would surely have stopped me, I made the translation at midnight."

"Ah."

"I found myself enveloped in a terrible dust storm, a hell of choking wind that threw me to the ground and rolled me as easily as a Russian thistle across the arid plateau. I had taken cuttings of my beloved roses, and in my fright I clung to them as the hurricane tumbled and battered me. I was blown to the lip of a dry watercourse and precipitated into its rocky depths, where I lay unconscious until dawn, badly bruised but otherwise unhurt. By the time the sun rose the sirocco was gone. I spied the Castle and had just made up my mind to go to it for aid when the attendants came trooping out to wait for the morning's arrivals."

She paused and a slow smile stole over her lips. "No time-travelers came that day. My staff was too much in a tumult, you understand. The people from the Castle became very agitated and rushed back inside. Not long thereafter a troop of soldiers came galloping posthaste out of the barbican and rushed off to the east, passing not thirty meters from the bushy cleft where I lay hidden. At the head of the train was an enormously tall exotic man dressed in robes of purple and gold.

"You will understand that I was in great pain from my battering. I crawled into a kind of shallow cave beneath the roots of an acacia tree that grew on the rim of the dry ravine. As the sun climbed, my thirst became dreadful. But this torment was as nothing compared to my agony of soul. Back in the auberge, I had imagined many possible derangements of the Pliocene world—fierce beasts, inhospitable terrain, exploitation of newcomers by the earlier arrivals among the timefarers—even a malfunction of the translational field that would cast the poor travelers into oblivion. But never had I imagined that the ancient epoch would see our planet in thrall to a nonhuman race. All unwitting, I had sent my pathetic, hopeful people into slavery. I turned my face into the dust and asked God to grant me death."

"Oh, Angélique."

She did not seem to see or hear him. Her voice was very quiet, barely audible among the rising evening clamor of the Rhineland birds and insects.

"When I finally stopped weeping, I saw a round object half-buried in the dust not an arm's length away on the ravine floor. It was a melon. The rind was thick and it had not been broken by its rolling across the plateau in the windstorm. When I cut into it with my small couteau de poche I found it sweet and laden with water. And so my thirst was quenched and I lived through the day.

"Very late in the afternoon there came a procession of carts drawn by strange animals. I know now that these were hellads, large giraffes with short necks used for draft purposes. The carts had human drivers and contained vegetables resembling large beetroots— fodder for the Castle chalikos. The carts entered the fortress by the postern gate and after a time returned laden with manure. As they journeyed back into the lowlands I followed at a far distance. Just before nightfall we came to a kind of farm with the buildings secure behind a stockade. I hid myself in bushes and tried to decide what to do. If I revealed myself to the farm people they would surely recognize me. And was it not possible that they would exact retribution for my betrayal of their dreams? I would accept this punishment if God willed. But I had already begun to suspect that a different rôle had been ordained to me. So I did not approach the gate of the farm but went instead into a dense forest adjacent to it. I found a spring, ate a small amount of the food in my Survival Unit, and prepared to spend the night in a great cork tree—even as we have sheltered ourselves in this cypress today . . ."

The other three members of the expedition had wakened on their perches among the higher branches. Now they swung down as slowly and quietly as sloths to take places next to Claude and listen. The old woman, sitting far out from the trunk with her legs dangling, did not seem to notice them.

"Very late in the night, after the moon went down, the monsters came. At first there was a great silence, with all of the jungle noises falling still as though a switch had been cut. I heard a sound of horns and a distant baying. And then it seemed as though the moon were rising again over a ridge of land just north of my tree. There was light of many colors coming from some flaming thing twisting in and out of the trees. It raced down the slope toward me. I heard a noise like a tornado, at once terrible and musical. The fiery apparition became an elfin cavalcade—the Hunt!—and it glowed as it raged downhill. It was chasing something. That I saw when the whirlwind of jeweled riders came into a small glen some two hundred meters away from me. By the bright starlight I saw the prey shambling along—a huge creature, black as ink, with coiling arms like those of a devilfish springing from its shoulders and eyes like great red lamps."

"Fitharn!" Richard hissed. Claude gave him an elbow in the ribs. Madame paid no attention to the interruption.

"The black monster dodged among the trees on the slope below me, coming ever closer, with the Hunt in hot pursuit. I have never in my life known such terror. My very soul seemed to shriek with it, although I uttered no sound. With all of my will I prayed for deliverance, clinging to the large branch of my cork tree with eyes tightly shut. There was a noise of carillons and thunderbolts, a buffeting wind, blinding flashes of light that penetrated my closed lids, smells of ordure and ozone and cloying perfume. Every nerve end of mine seemed assaulted and overloaded—but still I willed myself to be safe.

"And the Hunt passed by. I knew that I was fainting, but my fingernails dug deeply into the soft cork bark and kept me from falling. There was darkness and I knew nothing. When I awoke . . . a little man in a tall hat stood beneath my tree looking up at me with starlight shining on his round cheeks and pointed nose. He called out, 'Well done, woman, you hid the both of us!' "

Claude and the others had to laugh. Madame looked from one to the other in a kind of surprise, then shook her head and allowed herself a small smile. "Fitharn took me in charge and we went to the underground home of one of his confrères, where we were safe from further harassment. Later, when I had recovered my wits, I had long conversations with the Little People and learned the true situation here in the Pliocene world. Because I am who I am, and because of the brief flash of strong metafunction I had shown in concealing us, Fitharn brought me at length to the Firvulag Court at High Vrazel in the Vosges. I proposed that the Firvulag take humans as their allies rather than bedevil them, as had been their custom since the opening of the time-gate. I contacted the soi-disant Lowlife humans of the region in turn and convinced them of the wisdom of the alliance. We engineered several encounters with the gray-torcs to the Firvulag advantage, and the entente was confirmed. King Yeochee bestowed the golden torc upon me after our spies enabled his warriors to ambush and kill Iskender-Kernonn, the Lord of Animals—that same Turk who had earlier used his perverted talents in the service of the Tanu. After that, there were minor triumphs and major failures, refinements of planning, advances and setbacks. But always in my mind I have cherished the hope that one day I would be able to help undo the evil I have done."

There was a harsh little laugh from the dimness on the other side of the cypress trunk. Martha sat apart from the others in a forked branch. "How noble of you, Madame, to take all of our guilt upon yourself. And the atonement as well."

The old woman did not reply. She raised one hand to her neck and passed two fingers behind the golden collar as though trying to loosen it. Her deepset eyes were glittering; but as always, the tears did not fall.

From the mudflats upstream came the basso bellowing of deinotherium elephants. Closer to the tree-refuge some other creature began reiterating a plaintive *hoo-ah-hooo, hoo-ah-hooo*. Large bats zipped among the palms that clustered on the high ground. Over the backwaters, patches of mist had already coalesced and now extended thickening feelers toward the mainstream of the Rhine.

"Let's get out of here," Felice said abruptly. "It's dark enough now. We've got to be across the river before the moon shows over those mountains."

"Right," said Claude. "You and Richard help Martha down."

He held out his own hand to Angélique Guderian. Together they climbed from the tree and made their way to the water's edge.

4

THE BLACK FOREST of Elder Earth was a thoroughly tamed woodland. When seen from a distance its firs and pines did appear dark; but within the twenty-second-century forest itself all was green and pleasant, with manicured pathways that tempted even the laziest hikers to indulge wanderlust without the threat of inconvenience. Only in the southernmost part of the range, around the Feldberg and its sister peaks, did the terrain rise above a thousand meters. In the twenty-second century the Schwarzwald was thickly peppered with quaint resorts, restored castles, Kurhäuser, and mountain villages where outworld visitors were welcomed by costumed inhabitants and mouthwatering Kirschtorten.

The Pliocene Schwarzwald was something else altogether.

Before the erosive action of small Pleistocene glaciers wore the range down, it was higher and more sinister. Facing the rift valley of the Proto-Rhine was an escarpment that rose sheerly for almost a kilometer and a half, broken only by occasional narrow gorges cut by torrents from the highlands. Foot-travelers approaching the Black Forest from the river had to climb up one of these clefts, following precipitate game trails or scrabbling over great blocks of granite sheathed in rampant greenery, kept moist even during the dry season by mists rising from chains of cascades. Able-bodied Firvulag hikers were known to have ascended the escarpment in eight hours. It took Madame Guderian and her crippled party three days.

Above the rim of the eastern horst the true Black Forest began. Nearest the river, where strong winds blew down the trough from the Alps, the spruces and firs grew contorted into fantastic shapes. Some of the trunks resembled dragon coils or writhing brown pythons, or even humanoid giants frozen forever in agony, their upper limbs woven together into a roof twenty or thirty meters above the ground.

Farther east, this Twisted Forest calmed and straightened. The land of the southern Schwarzwald rose rapidly toward a culminating crest more than two thousand meters high, with three eminences. On the flanks of the western slope were conifers of climactic proportions, white firs and Norway spruces seventy meters tall growing in ranks so dense that when one tree died, it could hardly find room to fall, but instead leaned against supportive neighbors until it decayed and fell to bits. Only rarely was there a break in the forest canopy that allowed Richard to plot their course from the sun or the North Star. They could find no obvious trail, so the ex-spacer had to lay one out—moving from landmark to tedious landmark, never able to get a line of sight more than fifteen or twenty meters long because of the denseness of the trees.

The understorey of this evergreen expanse received very little sun. Its dreary bluish twilight supported almost no low-growing green plants—only saprophytes nourished by the detritus of the great trees. Some of the things that battened on decomposition were degenerate flowering plants, pale stalks with nodding ghostly blooms of livid white, maroon, or speckled yellow; but paramount among the eaters of the dead were the myxomycetes and the fungi. To the five humans traveling through the Pliocene Black Forest it seemed that these, and not the towering conifers, were the dominant form of life.

There were quivering sheets of orange or white or dusty translucent jelly that crept slowly over the duff of needles and decaying wood like giant amebae. There were bracket fungi—from delicate pink ones resembling baby ears to stiff jumbos that jutted from the trunks like stair treads and were capable of bearing a man's weight. There were spongy masses of mottled black and white that enveloped several square meters of forest floor as though veiling some unspeakable atrocity. There were airy filaments, pale blue and ivory and scarlet, that hung from rotting limbs like tattered lacework. The forest harbored puffball globes two and a half meters in diameter, and others as small as pearls from a broken string. One variety of fungus cloaked decaying shapes in brittle husks resembling colored popcorn. There were obscene things resembling cancerous organs; graceful ranks of upright fans; counterfeit slabs of raw meat; handsome polished shapes like ebony stars; oozing diseased purple phalluses; faerie parasols blown inside out; furry sausages; and mushrooms and toadstools in varieties that seemed to be without number.

At night, they were phosphorescent.

It took the foot-travelers another eight days to traverse the Fungus Forest. During this time they saw no animal larger than an insect;

but they would never cease to feel that invisible watchers lurked just outside their field of vision. Madame Guderian assured her companions again and again that the region was safe despite its ominous aspect. There was no source of food for predatory animals in the fungoid realm of life-in-death, much less support for Firvulag, who were notorious trencherfolk. The thickly matted upper branches made it impossible for the Flying Hunt to see anyone moving below. Other Lowlife scouting parties that had penetrated similar forests farther north in the range had reported them empty except for the trees, the triumphant fungi, and their parasites.

But still there was the feeling.

They suffered and grumbled all through the ghastly woods, wading through soft growths that concealed treacherous, ankle-trapping holes. Richard declared that the spores in the air were choking him. Martha drooped in anemic silence after pestering Madame one time too many with a report that something was prowling among the giant toadstools. Claude caught a fierce case of jock itch that crept all the way up to his armpits. Even Felice was ready to scream out loud at the endless trek; she was sure that something was growing in her ears.

When they finally broke free of the Fungus Forest, all of them—even Madame—shouted with relief. They came into a brilliantly sunny alpine meadow that stretched north and south along the slope of an undulating crest. One bald tor rose from a ridge on their left; to the right were two more barren gray domes. Ahead of them and farther east was the rounded height of the Feldberg.

"Blue sky!" cried Martha. "Green grass!" Heedless of her disability, she went bounding over the flower-dotted alp and scrambled to the top of the eastern ridge, leaving the others to follow more slowly. "There's a little lake down there, not half a klom away!" she called. "And lovely *normal* trees! I'm going to soak and scrub myself and lie in the sun until I'm cooked to a frazzle. And I never want to see another mushroom again for as long as I live."

"Say again, sweetie," Richard agreed. "Not even a truffle."

They descended to the beautiful little tarn, icy cold in its depths but sun-warmed in shallower little pools around its rocky perimeter, and gave themselves up to the luxury of becoming clean again. Their filthy buckskins were left to soak in a tiny brook that ran from the lake down into the eastern valley. Shrieking like children, they went splashing and diving and swimming and wallowing.

Never since he had entered the Pliocene had Richard been so

happy. First he swam to the other side of the tarn and back again. (It was only about fifty meters across.) He found a shallow pothole with the water warmed to precisely the right temperature and floated with the sun glaring redly behind his shut eyelids. Dark sand, scintillating like mica, floored his little pool. He took handfuls of it and rubbed his entire body, even his scalp. Then one last dash across the lake and out onto a hot granite slab to dry.

"You should have tried out for the Polity Olympics," Martha said.

He crept up a little higher on his rock and peered over the far edge. She was below him, lying flat on her stomach in a sheltered hollow and looking at him with one eye. Bright pink flowers grew in the crevices around her.

"How you feeling now?" Richard inquired. And he thought: Hey! She looked so different. Clean, relaxed, smiling with one corner of her mouth tilted higher than the other.

"I'm much better," she said. "Why don't you come down?"

* * *

On the opposite shore of the lake, Claude and Madame Guderian lay side by side on decamole cots among the gentians and asters and harebells, baking the miseries out of their old bones and munching bilberries from the low-growing bushes that grew everywhere on the alpine meadow. A stone's throw away, Felice's pale-skinned form was bending in rhythmic exertions. There was a regular slapping sound as she beat their soiled clothing against the rocks of the little brook.

"Oh, to be young and energetic again," said Madame, a lazy smile upon her lips. "She has such enthusiasm for this mad expedition of ours, that little one. And what strength and patience she has shown with poor Martha. It is hard for me to credit your ominous assessment of Felice's character, mon vieux."

Claude grunted. "Just a little angel of mercy . . . Angélique, I've been doing some calculating."

"Sans blague?"

"This isn't funny. It's been fifteen days since we left Yeochee's court at High Vrazel. We took eleven of those days just to travel the thirty kloms from the Rhine to the crest of the Schwarzwald. I don't think we have a hope in hell of getting to the Ries inside of the four weeks' limit—even if we do contact Sugoll. There's probably another forty or fifty kloms of land travel ahead of us before we even reach the Danube. Then damn near two hundred kloms down the river to the Ries."

She sighed. "Probably you are right. But Martha is strong enough to keep up with the rest of us now, so we will press on nevertheless. If we are not back before the Truce begins, we will have to wait until another time to attack Finiah."

"We can't do it during the Truce?"

"Not if we hope for the assistance of the Firvulag. This Truce, which covers periods of a month prior to *and* following the Grand Combat week, is deeply sacred to both exotic races. Nothing will induce them to fight each other during Truce time. It is the time when all of their warriors and Great Ones go to and from the ritual battle, which is held on the White Silver Plain near the Tanu capital. Of course, in olden times, when Firvulag sometimes triumphed in the yearly contest, the Little People might host the games on their own Field of Gold. It lies somewhere in the Paris Basin, near a large Firvulag city named Nionel. Since the Tanu expansion, the place has been virtually abandoned. It has not hosted the Combat in forty years."

"I should think it would be good tactics to go after the mine when the Tanu are out of town. Do we really need the Firvulag?"

"We do," she said starkly. "There are only a handful of us and the ruler of Finiah never leaves the mine completely undefended. There are always silvers and grays there, and some of the silvers can fly.

". . . But the real reason for the matter of timing has to do with my grand design. Strategy—not tactics—must guide us. We do not aim simply to destroy the mine—but rather the entire human-Tanu coalition. There are three steps in the master plan: first, the Finiah action; second, an infiltration of the capital, Muriah, in which the torc factory itself would be destroyed; and third, the closing of the time-portal at Castle Gateway. Originally we had thought to instigate guerrilla warfare against the Tanu after the threefold plan was accomplished. Now, with the iron, we will be in a position to demand a genuine armistice and the emancipation of all humans who do not serve the Tanu willingly."

"When do you see the implementation of phases two and three? During the Truce?"

"Exactly. For these, we do not require Firvulag help. At Truce time the capital is filled with strangers—even Firvulag go there with impunity! A penetration of the torc factory would be greatly simplified then. As for the time-gate—"

Felice came running up as lightly as a mountain sprite. "I can see flashes over to the east, on the flank of the Feldberg!"

The two old people sprang to their feet. Madame shaded her eyes and followed the girl's pointing finger. A series of short double flashes came from a high wooded slope.

"It is the interrogation signal, as Fitharn warned us. Somehow, Sugoll has become aware of us entering his domain. Quickly, Felice. The mirror!"

The athlete ran back to the brook where the packs lay and returned in a few seconds with a square of thin mylar mounted on a folding frame. Madame sighted through its central aperture and flashed the response Fitharn had taught them: seven long slow flashes, then six, then five, then four-three-two-one.

They waited.

The reply came. One-two-three-four. Five. Six. Seven. Eight.

They relaxed. Claude said, "Well, they won't come gunning for us now, at any rate."

"No," Madame agreed. Her voice held a touch of sarcasm. "At least Sugoll will meet with us face to face before deciding whether or not to burn out our minds . . . Eh bien." She handed the mirror back to Felice. "How long do you think it will take us to reach the foot of the Feldberg? That valley we must cross—it is not too deep, but there are woodlands and meadows where les Criards may lurk, probably a river to cross, and the terrain will be rougher than that of the Fungus Forest."

"We'll count on Sugoll keeping his friends and relations under control," Claude said. "And good solid ground instead of that spongy muck will let us keep moving right along, even if it is a bit steep in places. Barring any unforeseen balls-up, we might make it to the mountain in a dozen hours."

"Our clothes are drying on the hot rocks," Felice said. "Give 'em an hour or so. Then we can march on until sundown."

Madame nodded in agreement.

"Meanwhile, I'll hunt lunch!" the girl declared brightly. Taking her bow, she went running naked toward a cluster of nearby crags.

"Artemis!" exclaimed Madame in admiration.

"One of our old Group Green companions, an anthropologist, used to call her that, too. The Virgin Huntress, goddess of the bow and the crescent moon. Benevolent—if you kept her happy with the occasional human sacrifice."

"Allons donc! You have a one-track mind, Claude, seeing the child always as a menace. And yet see how perfect she is for this Pliocene wilderness! If only she could be content to live here as a natural woman."

"She'll never settle for that." The paleontologist's usually kindly face was as hard as the granite around him. "Not so long as there's one golden torc left in the Exile world."

* * *

"Thank you, Richard," Martha said, smiling into his eyes, and with his vision still dimmed, she was beautiful enough and it had been very good between them.

"I wasn't sure you really meant it," he said. "I didn't want to—hurt you."

Her gentle laugh was reassuring. "I'm not completely ruined, even though strong men have been known to blanch at the sight of my little white body. The fourth birth was a caesarian, and these donks never heard of a transverse. Just slice 'er open down the middle, grab the precious kid, and pass the catgut and darning needle. It didn't heal properly. A fifth pregnancy probably would have been the end of me."

"The filthy swine! No wonder you—uh—I'm sorry. You probably don't want to talk about it."

"I don't mind. Not any more. D'you know? You're the first man since *them*. Before this, I couldn't even bear the thought of it."

"But Steffi—" he began hesitantly.

"A dear gay friend. We loved each other, Richard, and he took care of me for months when I was really bad, just as though I were his little sister. I miss him dreadfully. But I'm so glad you're here. All the way through that horrid forest . . . I watched you. You're a fine navigator, Richard. You're a good man. I hoped that you wouldn't be—revolted by me."

He pulled himself up into a sitting position, back resting against a great hot boulder. She lay again on her stomach, chin on clasped hands. With her scarred belly and pitifully shrunken breasts hidden, she looked almost normal; but her ribs and shoulder blades were prominent and her skin had a translucency that revealed too many of the blue blood vessels beneath. There were smudgy shadows around her eyes. Her lips were purplish rather than pink as they continued to smile at him. But she had loved him with marvelous passion, this wreck of a handsome woman, and when something within him said: *She will die*, he felt his heart contract with an amazing, unprecedented pain.

"Why are you here, Richard?" she asked. And without knowing why, he told her the whole story without sparing himself—the dumb sibling rivalry thing, the greedy maneuvering and betrayals that had made him master of his own starship, the ruthlessness resulting in wealth and prestige, the ultimate crime and its punishment.

"I might have guessed," she said. "We have a lot in common, you and I."

She had been a Deputy Supervising Engineer on Manapouri, one of the two "New Zealand" planets, where extensive marine mining made up an important part of the economy. A contract had been let for the sigma-field energy-dome of a new township to be built six kilometers beneath the planet's South Polar Sea. An Old World company sent its people to install the dome generator; approval of each phase of the work was subject to personal inspections by Martha and her staff. She had worked with the offworld technicians for nearly six months, and she and the project head had become lovers. Then, with the generator complex three-quarters completed, she discovered that the contractor had substituted certain structural components when a shipment from Earth went astray. The substitutions were rated at ninety-three percent of the capacity of those called for in the original specs. And everybody knew how ridiculously high those standards had been set, for Manapouri had originally been surveyed by the ultrapicky Krondaku. Her lover had pleaded with her. To dismantle the thing and make replacements would lose them months of time, put the job into the red, and probably get him the sack for authorizing the sneetch in the first place. Ninety-three percent! That dome generator would keep running in anything short of a Class Four tectonic incident. On this stable-crust world, the chances of that were one in twenty thousand.

And so she had given in to him.

The sigma-field generator complex was completed on time and within budget. A hemispheric bubble of force flowed out from it and pushed back the seawater for a radius of three kilometers. A mining village of fourteen hundred and fifty-three souls sprang up within its security, down beneath the frigid waters near Manapouri's South Pole. Eleven months later there was a Class Four . . . 4.18, to be exact. The dome generator failed, the waters reclaimed their hegemony, and two-thirds of the people were drowned.

"The worst thing about it," she added, "was that nobody ever blamed me. It was right on the knife-edge for the original specs, with that 4.18. I knew that the thing would have held if we hadn't sneetched, but nobody else thought to question it. It was a borderliner, a tossup, and the thing had crapped out. Tough. The generator complex was so smashed up by the quake and turbidity currents that they didn't bother with much of a fail-analysis. There was more important work to be done on Manapouri than dredge through half a klom of sediment looking for broken parts."

"What about *him?*"

"He had been killed a few months earlier at a job on Pelon-su-Kadafiron, a Poltroyan world. I thought of killing myself but I couldn't. Not then. I came here instead, looking for God knows what. Punishment, probably. My executive mind-set was all wiped out and I was completely switch-off. You know—take me, stomp me, use me, just don't make me have to think . . . The stud farm setup I landed in after the trip from Castle Gateway seemed like a mad dream. They only take the best of the women for breeding stock. Those under forty, natural or rejuvenated, those who aren't too ugly. The rejects are kept sterile and made available to the gray torcs and the bareneck males. But us keepers had fertility restored by Tanu physicians, and then we were sent to the Finiah pleasure dome. Would you believe there were lots of dopey broads like me who just lay there and took it? I mean, if a dame didn't mind the basic shabbiness of being used, it was a hotsheet paradise. I understand that the Tanu women are better than the men when it comes to incendiary sex—but the men left no chime unrung as far as I was concerned. The first few weeks were a nympho's delight. And then I got pregnant.

"All the little expectant moms are treated like royalty by the Tanu. My first baby was blond and adorable. And I'd never had any, and they let me nurse him for eight months. I loved him so much I almost came up sane. But when they took him away, I went back on psycholine and wallowed around the pleasure dome with all the rest of the screwed-silly tarts. The next pregnancy was awful and the baby turned out Firvulag. The Tanu sire them one time in seven on humans and one time in three on their own women; but Firvulag parents never have Tanu children. At any rate, they didn't let me nurse the poor little spook—just took him out and left him in the traditional spot in the woods. I hadn't even recovered from him when they were trying to knock me up again. But by then, all the fun had gone out of it. I was sobering up, maybe. It's bad to be too sane in the pleasure dome . . . whether you're a human female *or* a human male. Too many of those Tanu blasts and you start hurting instead of skyrocketing. It happens sooner with some than with others—but if you're the average human, after a while Tanu sex starts killing you."

"Yeah," said Richard.

She looked at him quizzically. He gave a small humiliated nod. She said, "Welcome to the club . . . Well—I had another blond baby and then a fourth. The last was the caesarian—four and a half kilos of lovely fat girl-child, they said. But I was delirious for a week, so they farmed her out to a wet nurse and gave me six whole months of peace to pull my poor old bod back in shape. They even gave me a treatment with their Skin, which is a kind of poor man's regentank, but it didn't do much good. The practitioner said my mindtone was wrong for it, just as it was wrong for a gray torc. But I knew that I just didn't want to get well and have more babies. I wanted to die. So one lovely night I slipped quietly into the river."

He could think of no words to comfort her. The uniquely feminine abasement was a horror beyond his understanding—although he pitied her and raged inwardly against the ones who had used her, planted a half-human parasite inside of her that fed on her, kicked against her internal organs and belly wall, then violated her again as it burst out into the open air. God! And she'd said that she loved the first baby! How was it possible? (*He* would have strangled the little bastards before they drew their first breath.) But she'd loved one, and would have loved the others, likely as not, if they hadn't been taken away. She'd loved those paingivers, those unworthy children. Could a man ever make sense of the ways of women?

And you'd think she'd never want to look at another male. But somehow she'd fathomed his own need and—yes!—needed him as well. She might even like him a little. Was she as generous as all that?

Almost as though she read his thoughts, she gave a sensuous little chuckle and beckoned him back to her. "We still have time. If you're the man I think you are."

"Not if it would hurt you," he found himself saying even as he came back to life. "Never if it would hurt you." But she only laughed again and pulled him down. Women were amazing.

Off in a remote little nook of his brain, something was typing out a message to him, a conviction that grew to enormous, almost frightening, proportions as the exquisite tension built to its culmination. This person was not "women." She was not, as all the others had been to him, an abstraction of feminine sexuality, a comforter, a receptacle for physical release. She was different. She was Martha.

The message was hard to understand, but any minute now, he was going to figure it out.

5

IT HAD BEEN Martha who gave the Bogle his title.

He had been there, sitting on a boulder and regarding them with a misanthropic glare, when they awoke early the next morning in their camp below the southern flank of the Feldberg. After brusquely identifying himself as an emissary from Sugoll, he had ordered them to pack up without even waiting to let Richard make breakfast. The pace he set up a spur ridge of the mountain was deliberately trying and he would have raced them uphill without a rest if Madame had not occasionally demanded that they stop to catch their breath. Plainly, the dwarfish creature was feeling ill-used at having to serve as a guide and had decided to wreak his own petty revenge.

The Bogle was much shorter than any Firvulag they had ever seen before—and much uglier, with a tubby little torso and skinny arms and legs. His skull was grotesquely compressed to the point of being birdlike. Large black eyes with overlapping pouches were set close together above his toucanish nose. Prominent ears drooped flaccidly at the upper margins. His skin shone greasy reddish brown, and his sparse hair twisted into strands like a string mop. The Bogle's clothing, belying his physical repulsiveness, was neat and even beautiful: polished boots and a wide belt of carved black leather, wine-red breeches and shirt, and a long vest embroidered in flamelike patterns and studded with semiprecious stones. He wore a kind

of Phrygian bonnet with a large brooch positioned just above his
scraggly brows, which were knit in what seemed to be a permanent
scowl.

Following their trollish guide, the five travelers skirted the mountain ravines, following a tiny but very distinct trail, and passed
through a part of the Black Forest that had nearly as many broadleaf
trees as conifers. Wherever the Feldberg brooks slowed enough to
pool there were bosky dingles clogged with tall ferns and alders,
creeping clematis vines, and fall-blooming primroses with poi-
sonously bright blossoms. They came to a hollow where the waters
of a hot spring bubbled to the surface. Lush and unhealthy-looking
vegetation crowded the steamy swale. A flock of ravens croaked a sardonic greeting from the half-eaten carcass of a small deer that lay
near the edge of a mineral-encrusted puddle. More bones—some
clean, some furred with thick moss—were strewn about the undergrowth.

Farther east, the rock formations began to change. Colored limestone outcroppings intruded amongst the granite. "Cave country,"
Claude remarked to Madame. They were walking side by side now,
the path widening as they passed below a wooded cliff. The sun was
warm; nevertheless, the paleontologist felt a subterranean chill. In
the few places where the rock face was visible, they saw scarlet and
blue swallows with long forked tails darting in and out of pocks in
the limestone. Spiny-ribbed elephant-ears grew in dense patches beneath the trees. They sheltered clumps of distinctive mushrooms,
white-stemmed, red caps flecked in white.

"They are here," the old woman said abruptly. "All around us!
Can you not feel them? So many! And all . . . deformed."

For a moment, he failed to catch the significance of what she was
saying. But it fit—fit with the undercurrent of anxiety that had
lurked at the edge of his consciousness ever since early morning. Fit
with the surliness of the Bogle, whom Claude had mistaken for an
ordinary Firvulag.

"Les Criards," Madame said. "They follow us. One of them leads
us. The Howling Ones."

The path led uphill at an easy slope, entirely free of debris. The
swallows flickered among the firs and beeches. Great bars of golden
light slanted down into the forest as if through open windows.

The old woman said, "Such a beautiful place. But there is desola-
tion here, mon vieux, a wretchedness of spirit that at once touches
my heart and disgusts me. And it grows stronger."

He lent her his arm, for she was faltering, apparently for no physical reason. Her face had gone dead white. "We could ask the Bogle to stop," Claude suggested.

Her voice was dulled. "No. It is necessary to go on . . . Ah, Claude! You should thank God for not making you sensitive to the emanations of other minds! All sentient beings have their secret thoughts, those that remain hidden except to the good God. But there are other thoughts as well, pitched, as it were, on different psychic levels—the nonvocal speech, the currents and storms of emotion. This latter is what I am enveloped in now. It is a most profound enmity, a malevolence that can come only from the most distorted personalities. The Howling Ones! They hate other beings but they hate themselves so much more. And their howling fills my mind . . ."

"Can't you shut it out? Defend yourself as you did against the Hunt?"

"If I had been properly trained," she said forlornly. "But all that I know I have taught myself. I do not know how to counter this horde. They don't offer any concrete threat that I can seize upon." Her expression was very near panic. "All they do is hate. With all their strength . . . they hate."

"Do they seem to be more powerful than ordinary Firvulag?"

"I cannot be sure of that. But they are different in some unnatural way. That is why I called them deformed. With the Firvulag, and even with the Tanu, human metapsychics can feel a certain mental kinship. It is no matter that the exotic is an enemy. But never could I be akin to these Criards! I have never before been so close to so many of them. Only rarely did we encounter them in our little enclave within the Vosges, and there they were wary. But these—!"

Her voice broke off, harsh and too high-pitched. Her right fingers stroked the golden torc with a feverish urgency while those of her left hand dug painfully into Claude's arm. She kept darting her eyes from side to side, scanning the crags. There was nothing unusual to be seen.

Felice, who had been at the tail end of the line behind them, now closed the distance and announced, "I don't like this place at all. For the past half hour or so I've had the damnedest feeling. Nothing at all like those nervous fantods we got in the Fungus Forest, either. This time, there bloody well *is* something to be afraid of! Come on, Madame—what's going on?"

"The malign Firvulag—the Howlers—are all around us. Their

mental projections are so powerful that even you, in your latent state, can perceive them."

The blonde athlete's mouth tightened to a straight line and her eyes flashed. In her unaccustomed buckskin garb, she looked like a schoolgirl playing at Red Indians. She asked Madame, "Are they getting ready to attack?"

"They will do nothing," the old woman replied, "without the permission of their ruler, Sugoll."

"Only mental intimidation, damn their eyes! Well, they don't scare me!" Felice unstrapped the bow from her pack and checked the arrows expertly without losing stride. The cliff had now become a crazy jumble of blocks and pinnacles with the rising of the land. The trees thinned. They could see far out over the intermontane valleys. Even the distant Alps were barely visible to the south. The Feldberg itself reared up another thousand meters above them, chopped off in a sheer precipice on its southeastern face as though some Titan had taken an axe to it, mutilating the symmetry of the smoothly rounded crown.

Up at the head of the line, the Bogle was holding up one hand. They had arrived at an alpine park, a meadow surrounded on all sides by steep rocks. Precisely in the center of the area was a haystack-shaped knoll of velvety black stone, veined with a weblike tracery of bright yellow.

"This is it," said the Bogle. "And here I gladly leave you."

He folded his arms and, scowling, faded from sight. The scowl lasted longer than the rest of him.

"Well, that's a hell of a—" Richard began.

"Silence!" Madame exclaimed.

Without knowing why, the other four drew close to her. Her brow was dewed with sweat and she clutched at the torc as if it had suddenly become too small for her. Above the little bowl of flower-tufted gravel was a cloudless sky; but the air seemed to be thickening into a liquid in which uncanny transparent whorls and streamings formed and re-formed faster than the eye could follow. It became impossible to see clearly beyond the encircling rocks. The upper slopes of the mountain shimmered and flowed and broke into fluid masses of constantly changing shape. The black knoll, on the other hand, assumed a pristine clarity. It was obviously the center of whatever activity was pending.

Madame gripped Claude's arm in mortal desperation. "So many, doux Jésus! Can you not feel them?"

Richard ventured to say, "I sure as hell feel something. It feels like a sigma force-shield bombardment, for God's sake! Hostile minds against us—is that it?"

The aura of foreboding was building to an unbearable crescendo. There was a low-cycle vibration in the rock underfoot as well, amplified in slow spurts, almost like the treading of invisible feet inside the mountain.

And things howled.

The atmospheric whirlings intensified. A new sound began—a mad ensemble of tremolo notes that wailed up and down at a hundred different intervals, each voice with a tempo of its own. The humans clapped their hands over their ears. The avalanche of sound forced them to scream in a futile effort to neutralize it before it overwhelmed them.

And then it stopped, and the Howlers appeared..

The five travelers stood like a group of statuary, eyes wide and mouths still agape. The rocks surrounding the alpine clearing were crowded with beings. There seemed to be hundreds of them, perhaps even thousands; they sat atop one another, dangled from overhanging formations or from one another's lower limbs, peered out of crevices and clambered agilely over the heads and bodies of their fellows in an effort to get a front-row view.

They were the folk of nightmares.

Most of them were very small, under a meter in height, with the rounded torso and skinny limbs of the Bogle. Many had disproportionately large hands and feet. Some of the bodies seemed twisted, as with spinal deformities; others had asymmetric bulges under well-made garments, hinting of tumorous growths or even concealed extra limbs. The heads were grotesque: pointed, flattened, ridged like tree bark, crested, even horn-bearing. Some were too large or too small for the supporting body, or monstrously ill-suited—as the tiny female head with the lustrous curls and lovely features that sat incongruously on the hunched form of a young chimpanzee. Almost all of the faces were hideous, warped or swollen or stretched beyond any semblance of humanoid normality. There were faces covered with red and blue wattles, with hair, with saurian scales, with weeping scabs, with cheeselike exudate. There were eyes bulbous, beady, stalked, misplaced, superfluous. Some of the creatures had mouths so wide as to be froglike; others lacked lips altogether, so that the stumps of rotted teeth were exposed in perpetual ghastly grins. Those mouths ranged from animal muzzles grafted onto otherwise normal skulls to improbable vertical slits, coiled trunks, and parrot beaks. They opened to show fat tusks, close-set narrow fangs, drooling gums, and tongues that might be black or fringed or even double or triple.

Very gently, the misbegotten throng howled again.

On the black rock now sat a fairly tall bald-headed man. His face was beautiful and his body, clad from neck to heel in a tight-fitting purple garment, that of a superbly muscled humanoid.

The howling ceased abruptly. The man said, "I am Sugoll, the lord of these mountains. Say why you come."

"We bring," Madame said in a barely audible voice, "a letter from Yeochee, High King of the Firvulag."

The bald man smiled tolerantly and held out one hand. Claude had to support Madame Guderian as she approached the rock.

"You are afraid of us," Sugoll observed as he perused the piece of vellum. "Are we so disgusting to human eyes?"

"We fear what your minds project," Madame said. "Your bodies can only stir our compassion."

"Mine is an illusion, of course," said Sugoll. "As the greatest of all these"—he swept one arm to encompass the quivering mass of creatures—"I must naturally be their superior in all things, even in physical abomination. Would you like to see me as I really am?"

Claude said, "Mighty Sugoll, this woman has been severely affected by your mental emanations. I was once a life-scientist, a paleobiologist. Show yourself to me and spare my friends."

The bald man laughed. "A paleobiologist! See if you can classify me, then." He stood upright on his rock. Richard came and took Madame back, leaving Claude standing alone.

There was a brief flash and all of the humans except the old man were momentarily blinded.

"What am I? What am I?" Sugoll cried out. "You'll never guess, human! You can't tell us and we can't tell you because none of us knows!" Peal after peal of mocking laughter rang out.

The handsome figure in purple was once again seated on his rock. Claude stood with feet widely planted, his head down on his breast and his lungs pumping. A trickle of blood oozed from his bitten lower lip. Slowly, he raised his eyes to meet Sugoll's.

"I do know what you are."

"What's that you say?" The goblin ruler hitched forward. In one lithe movement he vaulted to the ground and sprang close to Claude.

"I know what you are," the paleontologist repeated. "What all of you are. You are members of a race that is abnormally sensitive to the background radiation of the planet Earth. Even the Tanu and Firvulag who live in other regions have suffered reproductive anomalies because of this radiation. But you—you have compounded the problem by living *here*. I daresay you've drunk from the deep springs, with their juvenile water, as well as from the shallower fountains and the brooks of melted snow. You've probably made your homes in caverns"—he pointed to the yellow-streaked knoll—"full of attractive black rocks like that one."

"It is so."

"Unless I miss my guess and my old memory bank's fritzed out, that rock is nivenite, an ore containing uranium and radium. The deep springs are likely to be radioactive, too. During the years that you people have lived in this region, you've exposed your genes to many times the radiation dose experienced by your fellow Firvulag. This is why you've mutated, why you've changed into . . . what you are."

Sugoll turned and stared at the velvet-black rock. Then he threw back his beautifully formed illusionary skull and howled. All of his troll and bogle subjects joined in. This time the sound was not terrifying to the humans, only unbearably poignant.

At length, the Howling Ones ceased their racial dirge. Sugoll said, "On this planet, with only primitive genotechnology, there can be no hope for us."

"There *is* hope for generations unborn if you move away from here—say, into more northerly regions where there are no concentrations of dangerous minerals. For those of you alive today . . . well, you have your powers of illusion-making."

"Yes," the exotic ruler agreed, his voice flat. "We have our illusions." But then the implications of what Claude had said began to reveal their true import to him. He cried out, "But can it be true? What you said about our children?"

The old man said, "You need advice from an experienced geneticist. Any human with that background has probably been enslaved by the Tanu. All I can tell you is a few basic generalizations. Get out of this area to put a stop to new mutations. The worst of you are probably sterile. The fertile people will likely have recessives for normality. Inbreed the most normal among you to fix the alleles. Bring normal germ plasm into the population by mending your fences with the other Firvulag—the normal ones. You'll have to use your illusion-making powers to make yourselves attractive as potential mates, and you'll have to be socially compatible to encourage the mixing. That means no more bogey-man mentality."

Sugoll gave a bark of ironic laughter. "Your presumption passes belief! Emigrate from our traditional lands! Give up our mating traditions! Make friends with our old enemies! Marry them!"

"If you want to change your genetic pattern, that's the way to start. There's a long shot, too . . . if we should ever manage to liberate humanity from the Tanu. There just might happen to be a human genetic engineer among the time-travelers. I don't know exactly how the Tanu Skin works, but it may be possible to utilize it to alter your grossly mutated bodies back into a more normal form. We were able to do this in some cases, using the regeneration-tanks of the future world that I came from."

"You have given us much to ponder." Sugoll was more subdued. "Some of the intelligence is bitter indeed, but we will think on it. Eventually, we will make our decision."

Madame Guderian now stepped forward and resumed her rôle of leader. Her voice was firm; her color had returned. "Mighty Sugoll, there is still the matter of our mission. Our request of you."

The exotic clenched his fist, which still held Yeochee's message. The vellum crackled. "Ah—your request! This royal command was useless, you know. Yeochee has no power here, but doubtless he did not care to admit it to you. I allowed you to enter our territory on a whim, curious as to the extremity that would make you take such a risk. We had planned to amuse ourselves with you before finally permitting you to die . . ."

"And now?" Madame inquired.

"What do you ask of us?"

"We seek a river. A very large one, rising in this area, which flows eastward until it reaches the great half-salty lagoons of the Lac Mer hundreds of kilometers from here. We hoped to travel upon this river to the site of the Ship's Grave."

There was a surprised chorus of howls.

"We know the river," Sugoll said. "It is the Ystroll, a truly mighty flood. We have a few legends of the Ship. Early in the history of our people on this world, we broke away from the main body of the Firvulag and sought independence in these mountains, away from the Hunting and the senseless annual slaughter of the Grand Combat."

Madame had to explain carefully the human complicity in the recent rise to dominance of the Tanu, as well as her own scheme to re-store the old balance of power while freeing humanity. "But to do this, we must obtain certain ancient items from the crater of the Ship's Grave. If you will furnish us with a guide to the river, we be-lieve that we will be able to locate the crater."

"And this plan—when will you put it into effect? When might the human scientists be free of the Tanu yoke and able—if Téah wills—to help us?"

"We had hoped to implement the scheme this year, before the start of the Grand Combat Truce. But there is scant hope of this now. Only twelve days remain. The Ship's Grave lies at least two hundred kilometers from here. It will doubtless take us half of the remaining time just to walk to the head of navigation on the river."

"That is not so," Sugoll said. He called out, "Kalipin!"

The Bogle stepped forth from the throng. His formerly surly face was transfigured by a broad smile. "Master?"

"I do not understand these kilometers. Tell the humans how it is with the Ystroll."

"Below these mountains," the Bogle said, "are the caverns where we make our homes. But at other levels—some deeper, some shal-lower—are the Water Caves. They are a maze of springs, bottomless pools and streams flowing through the blackness. Several rivers have their sources in the Water Caves. The Paradise, which flows past Finiah to the northwest, is one. But the mightiest torrent born be-neath our mountains is the Ystroll."

Claude exclaimed, "He could be right! There were underground tributaries to the Danube even in our own time. Some said they came from Lake Constance. Others postulated a connection to the Rhine."

The Bogle said, "The Ystroll emerges as a full-grown river into a great lowland to the northeast. If you enter the Water Caves at Alliky's Shaft via the lift buckets, you can pick up the Dark Ystroll not two hours' march from here. Then it is a subterranean water-journey of but a single day to the Bright Ystroll, that which flows beneath the open sky."

Madame asked Sugoll, "Would your boatmen guide us along the underground section?"

Sugoll did not speak. He lifted his eyes to the surrounding crowd of monstrosities. There was a musical chorus of howls. The goblin shapes began to shift and change, and the terrible swirling pattern of the sky calmed. The mental energies of the little people relaxed from the projection of undisciplined hatred and self-loathing and began to weave gentler illusions. The dreadful deformities faded; a throng of miniature men and women took the place of the nightmares.

"Send them," sighed the Howling Ones.

Sugoll bowed his head in acknowledgment. "It will be done."

He arose and lifted his hand. All of the small people repeated the gesture. They became as tenuous as mountain mist burning away in the noon sunlight.

"Remember us," they said as they vanished. "Remember us."

"We will," Madame whispered.

The Bogle went trotting away, beckoning for them to follow. Claude took Madame Guderian's arm, and Richard, Martha, and Felice came trailing behind.

"Only one thing," the old woman said to Claude in a low tone. "What did he *really* look like, this Sugoll?"

"You can't read my mind, Angélique?"

"You know I cannot."

"Then you'll never know. And I wish to God," the old man added, "that I didn't."

6

LATE IN THE EVENING, when the giant hawkmoths and the flying squirrels played their aerial games above the wooded canyon of Hidden Springs Village, seven men bearing six heavy sacks came home to the Lowlife settlement, led by Khalid Khan. They sought Uwe Guldenzopf, but his hut was empty. Calistro the goat-boy, bringing his animals home from their browsing, informed the seven that Uwe was at the community bathhouse with Chief Burke.

"The Chief is here?" Khalid exclaimed in consternation. "Then the expedition to the Ship's Grave was a failure?"

Calistro shook his head. He was about five years old, sober and responsible enough to know something of the great plans that were afoot. "The Chief was hurt, so he came back. Sister Amerie fixed his wounded leg, but he still must soak it many times each day . . . What do you have in the sacks?"

The men laughed. Khalid dropped his load on the ground with a loud clanging sound.

"Treasure!" The speaker was a wiry, shock-haired individual standing just behind Khalid, the only one of the seven not burdened down. The stump of his left arm was wrapped in a wad of dark-stained cloth.

"Let me see!" begged the child. But the men were already on their way up the flat-floored canyon. Calistro hurried his animals into their night pen and rushed to follow.

White starlight shone on a small area of open grass near the banks of the brook that was born of the hot and cold springs' mingling; however, most of the village lay concealed in deep shadow, the homes and community buildings sheltered beneath tall pines or spreading evergreen oaks that hid them from Finiah's Tanu sky-searchers. The bathhouse, a large log structure with a low-eaved roof overgrown with vines, was built against one of the canyon walls. Its windows were closely shuttered, and a U-shaped passage kept torch-light from the interior from shining out the open door.

Khalid and his men entered into a scene of steamy cheerfulness. It seemed that half the village had gathered in here on this rather chilly evening. Men, women, and a few children splashed in stone-lined hot or cold pools, lolled in hollow-log soaking tubs, or simply lounged about gossiping or playing backgammon or card games.

Uwe Guldenzopf's voice rang out over the communal din. "Hoy! Look who's back home again!" And the Lowlives raised a shout of welcome. Somebody yelled, "Beer!" And one of Khalid's grimy contingent appended a heartfelt, "Food!" The boy Calistro was sent to roust out the village victualers while the new arrivals pushed through a gabbling, laughing mob toward an isolated tub where Peopeo Moxmox Burke sat, his long graying hair stringy in the bathhouse vapors and his craggy face atwitch as he suppressed a delighted grin.

"How," quoth he.

"Beats me," the Pakistani metalsmith replied. "But we did it." He dropped his sack on the stone floor and opened it, taking out a lance-head rough from the casting mold. "Secret weapon, Mark I." Turning to one of the other men, he groped in his sack and produced a handful of smaller objects, approximately leaf-shaped. "Mark II. You sharpen 'em, they're arrowheads. We've got about two hundred and twenty kilos of iron all told—some of it cast like these, some in bars for miscellanea, ready for forging. What we have here is medium-carbon steel, smelted in the best antique style. We built us a forced-draft furnace fueled with charcoal and drafted with six skin bellows hooked up to decamole tuyères. Carbon from charred bulrushes. We buried the furnace so we can go back and make more iron when we've a mind to."

Burke's eyes glistened. "Ah, mechaieh! Well done, Khalid! And all the rest of you, too—Sigmund, Denny, Langstone, Gert, Smokey, Homi. Well done, all of you. This could be the breakthrough we've all been dreaming of—praying for! Whether or not the others succeed at the Ship's Grave, this iron will give us a fighting chance against the Tanu for the first time."

Uwe stood sucking his meerschaum, his gaze wandering over the tattered and soot-stained smelters. "And what happened," he inquired, "to the other three of you?"

The grins of the men disappeared. Khalid said, "Bob and Vrenti stayed too long one evening at the ore pit. When we came to check up on them, they were gone. We never saw a trace of them again. Prince Francesco was off hunting for the pot when the Howlers nailed him."

"They let us have *him* back, though," said the skinny hatchet-faced man named Smokey. "Day later, poor Frankie came staggerin' back into camp starkers. They'd blinded and gelded him and cut off his hands—and then really got down to business with hot pitch. His mind was gone, o' course. Small hope the Howlers blunked him before they had their fuckin' fun 'n' games."

"Suffering Christ," growled Uwe.

"We got a bit back," Denny offered. His black face flashed a wry smile.

"You did," said the bandy-legged little Singhalese named Homi. He explained to Chief Burke, "On our way home, a Howler came at us in broad daylight—oh, maybe forty kloms down the Moselle from here. All dressed up in his bloody monster suit like a great winged naga with two heads. Denny let him have an iron-tipped arrow in the guts and he went down like a rotten willow tree. And would y'believe? All that was left was this hunchbacked dwarf with a face like a stoat!"

The men grunted in reminiscence and a couple of them whacked Denny on the back. The latter said, "At least we know now that the iron works on both kinds of exotics—right? I mean, the Howlers are nothing but screwed-up Firvulag. So if our noble spook allies ever forget who their friends are . . ."

There were murmurs of agreement and a few quiet laughs.

Chief Burke said, "It's a point to keep in mind—although God knows we need Firvulag help to bring off Madame's plan against Finiah. The Little People were agreeable to the original scheme. But I'm afraid adding iron to the equation might give them second thoughts."

"Just wait'll they see us take out some Tanu with the iron," Smokey said confidently. "Just wait'll we equalize things with them dog-collar sumbitches! Why—the damn Firvulag'll kiss our feet! Or bums! Or somethin'."

Everybody roared.

An excited young voice from among the crowd of villagers shouted, "Why should we hold back on the Tanu until Finiah? There's a caravan going to Castle Gateway in two days. Let's sharpen up some arrows and bag us an Exalted One right away!"

A few of the others yelled approval. But Chief Burke hauled himself out of his bath like an enraged bull alligator and yelled, "Simmer down, you turkey-turd shlangers! *Nobody* touches this iron without permission from me! It has to be kept secret. Do you want the whole Tanu chivalry on our necks? Velteyn would send out a screech like a goosed moose if we tipped our hand. He might bring in Nodonn—even call for reinforcements from the south!"

They mumbled at this. The aggressive youngster called out, "When we use iron in the Finiah attack, they'll know. Why not now?"

"Because," Burke drawled, in the sarcastic tone he had once used to freeze the collops of inept fledgling advocates, "the attack on Finiah will come just prior to the Truce for the Grand Combat. None of the other Tanu will pay much attention to Velteyn's troubles then. You know the way these exotics' minds work. Nothing, but *nothing*, gets in the way of preparations for the glorious shemozzle. Two or three days before Truce—when we hope to strike—not a Tanu on Earth will come to the aid of Finiah. Not even to help their pals, not even to save their barium mine, not even to beat back humans armed with iron. They'll all be hot to head south to the big game."

The crowd fell back to palaver over the amazing single-mindedness of the exotic sportsmen, and Burke began to get dressed.

Uwe waggishly suggested that the Tanu were nearly as bad as the Irish for loving a fight without considering the long-view consequences. There was universal laughter at this and not a single son nor daughter of Erin's Isle rose to defend the racial honor. The thought flashed into Burke's mind that there was a reason for this, and he ought to know what it was; but at the same moment Khalid Khan caught sight of the red man's healing wound.

"Mashallah, Peo! You did scratch yourself up a bit, didn't you?"

Burke's left leg was hideously indented at the calf by a purplish-red scar over twenty cents in length. He grunted. "Souvenir of a one-horned chozzer. It killed Steffi and damn near did for me by the time Pegleg shlepped me back here to Amerie. Galloping septicemia. But she caught it. Looks like hell, but I can walk—even run, if I care to pay the price."

Uwe reminded him, "The meeting of the Steering Committee. Tonight. Khalid should come."

"Right. But first we have to see to the needs of this gang. How about it, men? Food and drink's on the way—but is there anything else we can do for you now?"

Khalid said, "Sigmund's hand. Aside from our three deaders, he's the only casualty."

"What happened?" Burke asked.

Sigmund sheepishly hid his stump. "Aw. I was stupid. Giant salamander sprang at me, fanged me right in the palm. You know there's only one thing to do, the way their venom works . . ."

"Sig was bringing up the rear," Denny said. "All of a sudden we missed him. When we went back to investigate, there he was putting on a tourniquet cool as you please, with his vitredur axe and his mitt lying on the ground beside him."

"You come along with us to Amerie's place," the Chief said. "We'll have her check it out."

"Aw, it's all right, Chief. We put plenty of AB and progan on it."

"Shut your pisk and come along." The Chief turned to the others. "The rest of you boys relax and eat and have a couple of days' sleep. There'll be a big council of war—a contingent one, anyhow—inside of a week, when the volunteers from the other settlements start showing up. We'll need you to work on this iron when we get the blacksmith shop set up some place where the Firvulag won't spot it. Till then, I'll take charge of the stuff. Put it out of temptation's reach."

Then Burke raised his voice so that the entire bathhouse could hear him. "All of you! If you value your own lives, and if you give a damn about the liberty of humans who are still enslaved, forget about what you've seen and heard here tonight."

A breath of assent rose from the assemblage. The Chief nodded and hoisted two of the heavy sacks. Khalid and Uwe dragged away the other four and they moved out of the bathhouse, trailed by Sigmund.

"The meeting is at Madame's cottage as usual," Burke told the metalsmith as he limped along. "Amerie's living there now. We put her on the committee by acclamation."

Uwe said, "That nunnie is some medic. She shrank Maxl so we don't have to keep him locked up anymore. And poor Sandra—no more suicidal threats now that the fungus is cured. Then there's Chaim's eyelid, all rebuilt, and she healed that big mother of an ulcer on Old Man Kawai's foot."

"That'll make for quieter meetings," Khalid remarked. "One less thing for the old boy to complain about. This nun sounds like a handy lady to have around."

The Chief chuckled. "I didn't even mention the way she cleaned up sixteen cases of worms and almost all the jungle rot. Madame might have to do some fancy politicking in the next election if she wants to hold on to the freeleadership of this gang of outlaws."

"It never struck me that she relished the honor." Khalid was acerbic. "Any more than you did when you were in the hot seat."

They plodded along, making almost no sound on the path that wound beneath the sheltering trees. The long canyon had many little dead-end tributaries from which the numerous springs debouched. Most of the cottages had been built close to these natural water supplies. There were some thirty homes altogether, in which dwelt the eighty-five human beings who made up the largest Lowlife settlement in the known Pliocene world.

The four men crossed a rill on stepping-stones and headed up one of the rocky clefts to where a distinctive little house stood under a huge pine. The cottage was not built like the others of prosaic logs or wattle and daub, but of neatly mortared stone, washed white with lime and reinforced with dark half-timbering. It was eerily evocative of a certain elder-world dwelling in the hills above Lyon. Madame's rose cuttings, nourished by the manure of mastodons, had burgeoned into rampant climbers that all but smothered the thatched roof in blossoms. The night air was heavy with their perfume.

The men came up the path, then halted. Standing in their way was a tiny animal. Stiff-legged, its oversized eyes gleaming, it growled.

"Hey, Deej!" Burke laughed. "It's just us, pupikeh. Friends!"

The little cat growled louder, the low rumble moving up the scale to become a threatening howl. It stood its ground.

Chief Burke put down his burden and knelt with one hand outstretched. Khalid Khan stepped behind Sigmund, a memory and a terrible suspicion crowding to the fore of his mind. A memory of a rainy night inside a Tree when the cat had growled like this before. A suspicion of a valued companion who had been too good a woodsman to be surprised by the relatively sluggish attack of a giant salamander . . .

Khalid slipped open the mouth of his sack just as the cottage door swung wide to show Amerie's veiled figure silhouetted against dim lamplight.

"Dejah?" the nun called, rattling her rosary beads in what was evidently some signal. She caught sight of the men. "Oh, it's you, Chief. And Khalid! You're back! But what—"

The turbaned metalsmith seized the hair of the one they had called Sigmund. With his other hand he pressed something gray and hard against the man's throat.

"Do not move, soor kabaj, or you are dead, even as your brother before you."

Amerie screamed and Uwe uttered an obscenity—for Khalid was suddenly struggling with a gorgon. Instead of hair, the Pakistani clutched writhing little vipers growing from Sigmund's scalp. These struck, sinking tiny fangs into flesh that puffed up, throbbed, as quasi-deadly venom flooded the blood vessels and went racing toward Khalid's heart.

"Stop, I say!" roared the anguished smith. Involuntarily, his right arm tightened, driving the dull point of the iron lance-blank into the soft hollow below the monster's voicebox.

The thing emitted a gurgling squeal and went limp. Khalid sprang away from the falling body, dropping the iron. It hit the earth with a dull thud and came to rest close beside the dead shapechanger. Amerie and the three men stared down at the creature, which could have weighed no more than twenty or thirty kilos. Flattened little dugs identified it as a female. Its bald cranium was monstrously compressed just above the eyes and elongated backward into a triangular bony collar. It had a mere hole for a nose and a massive lower jaw with loose, peglike teeth. The body was almost globular, the limbs spiderishly thin, with the left forepaw missing.

"It's not . . . a Firvulag," Amerie managed to say.

"A Howler," Burke told her. "Some biologists believe they're a Firvulag mutation. Each one is supposed to have a different true shape. All hideous."

"You see what she was trying to do, don't you?" Khalid's voice was shaking from reaction and chagrin. He felt his left hand, which was now completely normal. "She saw us kill her mate with iron, and had to find out what the new weapon was. So she must have crept up on Sigmund as he marched at the end of the line and . . . she took his place. Cut off her hand so she wouldn't have to carry the iron."

"But they've never masqueraded as humans!" Uwe exclaimed. "What could have been its motive?"

"Look at her—dressed in rags," Amerie said. She knelt down in the light from the doorway to examine the goblin body. One of the Howler's crude skin boots had dropped off in the struggle, exposing a humanoid foot—miniaturized but as perfectly formed as that of a child. There was a pathetic blister at the heel; evidently the little being had had to hurry to keep pace with the faster humans.

The nun replaced the boot, straightened the pipestem legs, closed the glazed eyes. "She was very poor. Perhaps she hoped to discover information valuable enough to sell."

"To the normal Firvulag?" Burke suggested.

"Or to the Tanu." The nun got up and dusted the front of her white habit.

Khalid said, "There might be others. Others who watched us at the smeltery. If this one could change to human shape, how will we ever be sure—"

Burke picked up the iron blade, grasped the metalsmith's arm, and drew the rough lancehead across the skin. A few drops of dark blood sprang from the abrasion. "You're real enough, anyhow. I'll go test the rest of the crew right away. Later, we'll work out something a little less crude. Pinprick, maybe."

He limped away toward the bathhouse. Uwe and Khalid hauled the precious bags of iron into the rose-covered cottage, then returned to where Amerie stood over the body. She held the cat, which was still gently growling.

"What shall we do with her, Sister?" Khalid inquired.

Amerie sighed. "I have a large basket. Perhaps you can put her in the springhouse for me. I'm afraid I'll have to dissect her tomorrow."

* * *

As the Steering Committee waited for Chief Burke to return to the cottage, the Victualer in Chief offered samples of a new beverage. "We took some of that lousy raw wine of Perkin's and steeped this little forest wildflower in it."

Everybody sipped. Amerie said, "That's nice, Marialena."

Uwe said something in German under his breath. "You know what you've done, woman? You've reinvented Maiwein!"

"That's it! That's it!" Old Man Kawai piped. He was only eighty-six; but since he had declined rejuvenation on a matter of principle, he resembled an unwrapped Oriental mummy. "Most refreshing, my dear. Now if we can only produce a decent saké . . ."

The cottage door opened and Peopeo Moxmox Burke stooped to enter. The other committee members sat stark still until the red man gave a nod. "They were all kosher. I tested not only the smelters, but all the rest of the folks in the bathhouse as well."

"Thank heaven," said the Architect in Chief. "What a thought—shape-changers infiltrating *our people!*" He wagged his neatly trimmed muttonchops, managing to look like an accountant who had discovered that a valued client was cooking the books.

"Neither Firvulag nor Howlers had any reason to try this trick before," the Chief warned. "But now, with the attack coming up and the iron as a maybe not-so-secret weapon, we're going to have to be alert for other attempts. When the volunteers start arriving, every single one must be tested. And we'll test all participants before every important meeting or briefing."

"My responsibility," said Uwe, who was Hunting and Public Safety. "Whip me up some needles, Khalid?"

"As soon as I can get the forge hot tomorrow."

The Chief took his place with the other seven committee members around the table.

"All right, let's get this over as quickly as possible so Khalid can get some rest. As Deputy Freeleader, I call this meeting of the Steering Committee to order. Old business. Structures. Let's have it, Philemon."

"The huts at the Rhine staging area have been completed," said the architect. "Everything is ready there except the main shelter pavilion. The boys will have our Hidden Springs visitor dorm ready in another two or three days."

"Good," said the Chief. "Public Works. Vanda-Jo."

A taffy-haired woman with the face of a madonna and the voice of a drill sergeant spoke up. "We've finished the masked trail from here to the staging area. A hundred and six bloody kilometers, invisible from the air. Corduroyed the last two kloms through the swamp —and don't think that wasn't a bitch! Still putting up the thorn boma around the staging camp to keep most of the critters out and the recruits in."

"How about the launching ramps?"

"Decided on pontoons. Inflated skins and boarding. Put 'em up at the last minute. Pegleg and his lads are contributing the skins."

"Good. Hunting and Public Safety."

"Nothing much new from me," Uwe said. "Most of my people are working with Vanda-Jo or Phil. I've liaised with the commissary at High Vrazel to help with quantities of game and staples when the extra bods start arriving. And we've set up a procedure for processing new arrivals here at Hidden Springs before sending them to the river."

"Sounds okay. Domestics."

Old Man Kawai pursed his scored lips. "There is *no* way we can come up with more than a hundred boiled-leather hard hats and chest guards by D-Day. You know how long it takes to shape and dry that stuff—even with the forms filled with hot sand. The volunteers are just going to have to go mostly bare-ass unless you want our people deprived. Do shimasho? I've done my best, but I'm no miracle man."

"The shortage can't be helped," Burke said soothingly. "How about the camouflage nets?"

"We'll be putting the big one in position tomorrow, just in case they get back early with the exotic flyer." The wizened ancient threw an anxious glance at the Chief. "Do you really think they've got a chance, Peo?"

"Not much of one," Burke admitted. "But we won't give up hope until the last hour before the Truce . . . Human Services."

"Linen bandages ready," Amerie said. "We're assembling stores of oil and alcohol and all of the AB we can scrape up. Fifteen fighters have been rough-trained as front-line medics." She paused, her face furrowed with determination. "I want you to change your mind about having me accompany the fighters, Peo. For the love of God—when will they need me *more* than in a battle?"

The Native American shook his head. "You're the only doctor we have. Probably the only one in the Lowlife world. We can't have you at risk. There's the future to think about. If we do liberate Finiah, we may be able to de-torc other medical people. If we fail and the troops come across the Rhine to our staging area . . . it may be a long time until the next war. Our fighters will tend their own injuries. You stay here."

The nun sighed.

"Industry," said Burke.

"We brought back two hundred and twenty kilos of iron," Khalid said. "Four of our men died. We have enough experienced people left to begin final work on the weapons as soon as we get some sleep."

There were somber congratulations all around.

"Provisioning."

"We've enough stored here to feed five hundred people for two weeks," Marialena said. "That does not include the five tons of instant rations we'll distribute to fighters going down to camp. You don't want any cooking going on down by the Rhine where the Tanu might spot the smoke." She pulled a handkerchief from the sleeve of her pink and yellow gown and mopped her ample brow. "Those poor souls are going to curse pemmican and parched bulrush roots before this thing is over."

"If that's all they curse," Burke said, "they'll be lucky. All right, that leaves my report. Warlord in Chief. I've received word from Pallol, the Firvulag generalissimo, that his forces will hold themselves combat-ready for the last three days in September. Under optimal circumstances we'll mount the attack before dawn on the twenty-ninth, which will give us nearly two full fighting days before the Truce officially begins on October first at sunrise. After that, we humans'll be on our own—and Finiah better be ready for mop-up. I'll have more details on plans of attack at the war council later. Okay? Now—new business. We'll consider the matter of the Howler spy as already introduced and sent to Public Safety for action."

"The final preparation of the iron weapons," Khalid said. "My men will soundproof one of the vented caves and turn it into a smithy. I'll need some help from Phil's people."

"More new business?"

"We will need more alcoholic drink," Marialena said. "Mead or beer from the Firvulag. I can't have the volunteers swilling our young wines."

Burke chuckled. "Perish the thought. Uwe—will you sound out the High Vrazel people on that?"

"Check."

"Any more new business?"

Amerie hesitated. "Perhaps it's too soon to bring this up. But there is the matter of the second phase of Madame's plan."

"Hai!" cried Old Man Kawai. "If Finiah is a success, Madame will want to send others south immediately!"

Philemon was uneasy. "We'll do well to accomplish even a small part of the first phase of Madame's plan—much less the other two. I say, leave this to Madame to work out when she returns. It's *her* scheme. Perhaps she and that wild little person, Felice, will have worked something out."

"Caracoles," grumbled Marialena. "I must consider the later phases, even if the rest of you shirk your responsibility. If our people must go south without proper provisions, it is I who receive the cowchip bouquet! Ahhh—I'll do what I can."

"Thank you, querida," the Chief said peaceably. "I'll talk with you tomorrow about a possible division of rations. But I think that's the best we can do for now on Phase Two or Three planning. There are too many unknown factors—"

"Such as who will survive Finiah!" wailed Old Man Kawai. "Or, if we even mount the Finiah attack in the first place!"

Vanda-Jo slapped one hand on the table. "Tails up! No defeatism allowed! We're going to hit those high-pocket bastards like they've never been hit before. And, Khalid—I've got dibbies on one iron arrowhead, if you please. There's a certain Tanu stud on the other side of the Rhine whose ass belongs to me."

"If you're sure that one will do it," the metalsmith laughed.

"Order," Burke muttered. "Chair will entertain a motion to table strategy planning for the Grand Combat."

"So move," said Amerie. It was quickly affirmed and seconded.

"Any more new business?" the Chief asked. Silence.

"Move adjournment," said Old Man Kawai. "Past my bedtime."

"Second," said Uwe, and the Steering Committee meeting came to an end. Everyone except Chief Burke bade Amerie goodnight and slipped away into the shadows. The quondam judge stretched out his wounded leg for the nun to examine.

At length she said, "There's nothing more I can do for you, Peo. Hot soaks and moderate exercise to keep the muscles from tightening. I can give you a herendorf to block the pain on D-Day."

He waved a deprecating hand. "We'll save it for somebody who really needs it."

"As you like."

They went outside, where the village was quiet except for faint insect noises. It was nearly midnight and the moon was still down. Burke craned his neck and studied the starry vault of the sky.

"There it is, just above the rim of the canyon," he said, pointing.

"What?" she inquired.

"Ah—I forgot you were a newcomer, Amerie. The constellation we call the Trumpet. See the triangular bell, the four bright stars forming the straight tube? Take special note of the mouthpiece star. It's the most important one in all the sky—at least to the Tanu and Firvulag. On the day when it culminates at midnight over Finiah and High Vrazel—those are the oldest exotic settlements, remember— it will mark the opening of the five-day Grand Combat."

"The date?"

"By our Milieu calendar, around October 31 or November 1."

"You're kidding!"

"It's true. And the noon culmination that takes place exactly six months later comes around May Day. The exotics have another big show then, which Tanu and Firvulag celebrate separately—the Grand Love Feast. Most popular with the females of the species, it's said."

"That's really very odd," Amerie said. "I'm no folklorist, but those two dates . . ."

"I know. Only in our time, there was no good explanation—in astronomy or anything else—for the ritualization of those days rather than any others occurring about the same times."

"It's ridiculous to assume a correlation."

"Oh, certainly." The Native American's face was inscrutable in the starlight.

"I mean—six million years."

"Do you know the significance of the mouthpiece star? It's a marker. Their home galaxy lies almost directly behind the star."

"Oh, Peo. How many light years?"

"A hell of a lot more than six million. So in one way, they've come even farther away from home than we have, poor devils."

He gave her a brief salute and limped away, leaving her standing beneath the stars.

7

"But it isn't blue!" Felice protested. "It's brown."

Madame changed the course of their dinghy to avoid a stranded snag. "The color brown—it lacks that certain cachet. The composer wished to evoke the river's beauty."

The girl gave a contemptuous snort as she studied the terrain. "This place would never win any prizes. Too dry. It looks like it hasn't rained for months." She knelt upright in the bow of the little boat and scanned the open dun-colored slopes with the aid of Madame Guderian's little monocular. Only in the arroyos and in the flats nearest the Danube were there areas of green. The widely scattered groves of trees had a dusty bluish look.

"I can see a few small herds of hipparions and antelopes," the girl said after a time. "Nothing else seems to be alive in those uplands on the left bank. No sign of the crater. Nothing distinctive at all except that little volcano yesterday. You don't think we could have passed it by, do you? This damn river really *rolls*."

"Richard will tell us at noon."

The old woman and the athlete had shared one decamole boat since the party had emerged from the Water Caves nearly two days ago. Claude, Martha, and Richard occupied a second boat that drifted a few dozen meters ahead of them on the swift current of the Bright Ystroll. In spite of the drought they had made splendid time, since the flood received most of its water from the Alps, which shone white in the far south. On the previous night they had pulled up on a wooded gravel bar to sleep, the Bogle having warned them against camping on shore. They were grateful for their isolation when they were awakened later by the cries of hyenas. Claude told them that some of the Pliocene species attained the bulk of large bears and were active predators as well as scavengers.

For navigation, they had one precious map. Back at the Tree, Richard had traced pertinent portions from the fading plass of a venerable Kümmerley + Frey Strassenkarte von Europa (Zweitausend-jährige Ausgabe), which a nostalgic Lowlife treasured as his dearest memento of times to come. The old road map was dim and difficult to decipher, and Claude had warned Richard that the watershed of the Pliocene Danube was going to be greatly altered during the coming Ice Age by volumes of glacial till washing down from the Alps. The tributary streams of the upper Danube that were shown on the map would likely occupy different positions during the Pliocene; and the bed of the great river itself would lie farther south, twisted all out of recognition. The travelers could not hope to follow Galactic Age landmarks to the Ries crater. But there was one precious bit of data from the old map that would have retained its validity over six million years: the exact longitudinal component in kilometers between the meridian of High Vrazel peak (alias Grand Ballon) and that of the Ries (symbolized on the map by the future city of Nördlingen, which lay within what would be a mere ringwall plain on the Elder Earth). No matter how the Ystroll wandered, it was still bound to cross the Ries meridian. As nearly as Richard had been able to determine from the decrepit plass of the road map, the linear distance was 260 kilometers—three and one-half degrees of longitude east of the "prime meridian" of High Vrazel.

Richard had set his accurate wrist chronometer for precisely noon at High Vrazel and had carefully improvised a quadrant to measure the solar angle. Every clear day, the quadrant could be used to tell them local noontime—and the difference between this and P.M. noon shown on the watch could be used to calculate the longitude. When they reached the Ries meridian on the Danube, all they had to do was march due north to reach the crater . . .

One of the figures in the lead boat raised an arm. The craft pulled in to shore.

"There's a little break in the northern highlands there," Felice said. "Maybe Richard has decided it's our best bet." When they had beached their boat next to the other one, she asked, "What d'you think, guys? Is this it?"

"Pretty close, anyhow," Richard said. "And it doesn't look like too bad a hike, for all it's uphill. I calculate thirty kilometers north should hit the lower rim. Even if I'm a little off, we should be able to see the thing from the crest of those northern hills. Damn crater's supposed to be more than twenty kloms wide, after all. How about lunch, while I set up one more sun shot?"

"I've got fish," Martha said, raising a string of silvery-brown shapes. "Richard's excused for his navigating chores, and that leaves you two to dig the perishin' bulrushes while Madame and I get these to grilling."

"Right," sighed Claude and Felice.

They made their fire in a well-shaded spot near the edge of a large grove. Clear water came trickling down a limestone ledge to disappear into a muddy depression that swarmed with little yellow butterflies. After fifteen minutes or so, the delectable smell of roasting young salmon came wafting to the tuber grubbers.

"Come on, Claude," Felice said, sloshing a net full of lumps up and down in the water to rinse them. "We've got enough of these things."

The paleontologist stood quietly, up to his knees in the river among the tall stalks. "I thought I heard something. Probably beavers."

They waded back to the bank where they had left their boots. Both pairs were still there, but something—or someone—had been messing about with them.

"Look here," said Claude, studying the surrounding mud.

"*Baby* footprints!" Felice exclaimed. "Screw me blind! Could there be Howlers or Firvulag in this country?"

They hurried back to the fire with the tubers. Madame used her farsensing metafunction to scan the area and professed to sense no exotic beings.

"It is doubtless some animal," she said, "with prints that mimic those of children. A small bear, perhaps."

"Bears were very rare during the early Pliocene," Claude said. "More likely—ah, well. Whatever it is, it's too small to do us any harm."

Richard came back to the group and tucked map, note-plaque, and quadrant back into his pack. "We're near as damn all," he said. "If we really hump this afternoon, we might get there fairly early tomorrow."

"Sit down and have some fish," Martha said. "Doesn't the aroma drive you wild? They say that salmon is just about the only fish that's nutritionally complete enough to serve as a steady diet. Because it has fat as well as protein, you see." She licked her lips—then gave a strangled squeak. "Don't . . . turn . . . around." Her eyes were wide. The rest of them were sitting on the side of the fire opposite her. "Right behind you there's a wild rama."

"No, Felice!" Claude hissed, as the athlete's muscles automatically tensed. "It's harmless. Everybody turn very slowly."

Martha said, "It's carrying something."

The little creature, its body covered with golden-tan fur, stood a short distance back among the trees, trembling noticeably but with an expression of what could only be called determination upon its face. It was about the size of a six-year-old child and had fully humanoid hands and feet. It carried two large warty fruits, greenish bronze streaked with dull orange. As the five travelers regarded it with astonishment, the ramapithecine stepped forward, placed the fruits on the ground, then drew back.

With infinite caution, Claude rose to his feet. The little ape backed up a few paces. Claude said softly, "Well, hullo there, Mrs. Thing. We're glad you could stop by for lunch. How's the husband and kiddies? All well? A little hungry in this drought? I'm not surprised. Fruit is nice, but there's nothing like a bit of protein and fat to keep body and soul together. And the mice and squirrels and locusts have mostly migrated into the upper valleys, haven't they? Too bad you didn't go along with them."

He stooped and picked up the fruits. What were they? Melons? Some kind of papaw? He carried them back to the fire and took two of the larger salmon and wrapped them in an elephant-ear leaf. He put the fish down in the exact spot where the fruit had been and withdrew to his place by the fire.

The ramapithecus stared at the bundle. She reached out, touched a greasy fishhead, and put the finger into her mouth. Giving a low crooning call, she everted her upper lip.

Felice grinned back. She drew her dirk, hefted one of the fruits, and sliced it open. A mouth-watering sweet smell arose from the yellowish-pink flesh. Felice cut off a tiny slice and took a bite of it. "Yum!"

The rama clucked. She picked up the package of fish, everted her lips over her small teeth once again, and ran away into the trees.

Felice called out, "Give our regards to King Kong!"

"That was the damnedest thing," Richard said. "Smart, aren't they?"

"Our direct hominid ancestors." Claude stirred up the tubers.

"We had them for servants in Finiah," Martha said. "They were very gentle and cleanly little things. Timid—but they would work conscientiously at the tasks given them by torc wearers."

"How were they cared for?" Claude asked, curious. "Like little people?"

"Not really," Martha said. "They had a kind of barn adjacent to the house, where they lived in partitioned stalls—almost like small cave rooms filled with straw. They were monogamous, you see, and each family had to have its own apartment. There were community areas, too, and dormitory nooks for the singletons. The childless adults worked for about twelve hours, then came home to eat and sleep. The mothers would care for their young for three years, and then put them in charge of 'aunties'—old females who acted for all the world like schoolteachers. The aunties and other very old males and females played with the children and cared for them when the parents were absent. You could see that the parents were unhappy at having to leave the little ones, but the call of the torc couldn't be denied. Still—the rama-keepers told me that the auntie system was a variant of one used by the creatures in the wild. It generally produced well-adjusted individuals. The Tanu have raised ramas in captivity for as long as they've lived on this planet."

"Those sounds they make," Claude said. "Could ordinary bare-necked people such as yourself communicate with them?"

Martha shook her head. "They answered to their names, and there were perhaps a dozen simple voice commands they'd respond to. But the principal means of communicating with them was through the torc. They could grasp very complex *mental* commands. And of course they were trained with the pleasure-pain circuitry so that they required little supervision for routine tasks such as housework."

Madame shook her head slowly. "So close to humanity, and yet so far away from us. Their life span is only fourteen or fifteen years in captivity. Probably less in the wild. So fragile, so helpless-seeming! How did they ever survive the hyenas, the bear-dogs, the sabertooth cats, and other monsters?"

"Brains," Richard said. "Look at that one who came to us. Her family won't be hungry tonight. There's natural selection working right in front of us. That little ape is a survivor."

Felice looked at him with a wicked expression. "I thought I noticed a family resemblance . . . Here you go, Captain Blood. Have some of your great-great-et-cetera grandmother's fruit for dessert."

* * *

They left the Danube behind them and walked. It felt like the temperature was over forty in the September sun, but their adapted bodies could take it. Over the sunburnt grass, through thickets of brittle maquis, over boulders in the dry watercourses they walked. Richard had set their goal—the notch between two long hills that lay due north beyond slowly rising land with hardly a patch of shade and no water at all. They stripped to shorts, backpacks, and broad-brimmed hat. Madame passed a precious squeeze-bottle of sunburn cream. Richard led and Felice took the rear, the athlete ranging out tirelessly to be sure that no animal stalked them and to search— without luck, as it turned out—for some spring or other source of water. Between the two marched Claude and Madame, supporting Martha between them. The engineer became weaker as the hot hours of hiking accumulated; but she refused to let them slow down. None of them wanted to stop, in spite of the fact that there seemed to be nothing ahead of them but the dry stubbly upland reaching to the undulating horizon. Above it hung a pale-yellow, pitiless sky.

At last the sun dropped low and the sky turned to a light green. Madame called a halt near a rock-choked ravine where they could at least relieve themselves in privacy. Madame led Martha off and when the two returned, the old woman's face was grim.

"She is hemorrhaging again," she told Claude. "Shall we stop here? Or shall we make again a litter from one of the cots?"

They decided upon the litter. While there was still daylight, they wanted to press on. Just a few kilometers farther and they would reach the brow of the hills.

They continued on as they had done earlier in the journey, one at each corner of the modified cot. Martha lay with her lower lip clamped between her teeth, twin spots of bright rose on her pale cheeks the badges of her mortification. But she said nothing. The heavens turned to ultramarine and then to indigo, and the first stars appeared. However, they could still see well enough to walk and so they kept going—higher and higher, closer to the notch.

At last they were at the summit. The four of them set the litter down and helped Martha to her feet so that she could stand with them and look northward. About five kilometers away and just slightly below the pass where they rested was a long rampart. It reared up from the countryside behind the line of hills in a virtual jungle of spiny maquis scrub and curved away on both sides in a great arc that eventually melted into the northern horizon. The bare lip of the crater gleamed pale in the dusk.

Felice took Richard's head between her hands and kissed his mouth, standing on tiptoe. "You did it! Right on the nose, buc-caneer-baby—you did it!"

"Well, I'll be damned," said the pirate.

"I don't think so." Claude's broad Slavic face wore an exultant smile.

"Oh, Madame. The Ship's Grave!" Martha's voice broke; her eyes spilled tears. "And now—now—"

"Now we will make camp," the Frenchwoman said practically. "We will rest well and recover our strength. For tomorrow, our work really begins."

* * *

The skeleton had been laid out in state in the belly compartment of the fifth flyer that they inspected.

Unlike the other craft, which had had their hatches closed, the sepulchre of Lugonn was wide open to the elements. For long years the mammals, birds, and insects of the maquis had made free with it. Felice had, as always, been first up the boarding ladder of the exotic craft. Her cry of triumph at finally finding the remains of the Tanu hero was followed by a tortured howl that raised the neck hairs of the other four members of the expedition.

"He has no torc! *No torc!*"

"Angélique!" Claude shouted in alarm. "Reach out and stop her doing any harm in there!"

"No . . . torc!" A shriek of diabolic rage echoed within the flying machine and there was a thudding sound. As Richard and Claude clambered up the ladder, Madame Guderian stood beneath the shadow of the metal bird's wings, eyes wide, mouth drawn into a strained grimace, both hands clenching the gold at her throat. It took every bit of her coercive metafunction to restrain Felice, to force the girl to back off from the instinctive urge to destroy the source of her frustration. Driven by furious disappointment, the ath-lete's latencies trembled on the brink of operancy. The old woman felt her own ultrasenses being tested to the limit. She held, pressed the volcanic thing that writhed within her mind-grasp while at the same time her telepathic voice cried: Wait! Wait! We will all search! Wait!

Felice let go her opposition so abruptly that Madame Guderian staggered backward and collapsed into Martha's frail arms.

"Okay!" Richard shouted from above. "I popped her one. She's out cold!"

"But did she ruin anything?" Martha called, easing Madame to the dusty ground.

"Doesn't look like it," Richard replied. "Get up here, Marty, and have a look at this frigger yourself. Like something out of a goddam fairy tale."

Felice lay in a heap on the far side of the flyer's belly compartment, which measured about three by six. She had managed to seize Lugonn's helmeted skull and dash it to the deck in a paroxysm of rage; but the interior of the ancient craft was so deep in dust, animal droppings, and other organic trash that the relic had come to no harm. Claude knelt down and restored the head to its place. Resting on his haunches, he studied the legend laid out before him.

Lugonn's armor, heavily jeweled and filmed with gold, was now so dimmed and crusted that his bones could barely be discerned within the articulated plates and scales of glass. The crystalline helmet, crested with a peculiar heraldic animal, was a baroque and incredibly intricate piece of craftsmanship—so gorgeous, even coated with grime, that one forgot that it had a utilitarian purpose: to deflect photonic beams. Carefully, Claude raised the visor and unfastened the overlapping gorget plates and hinged cheekpieces. Lugonn's skull was mutilated by a great wound, perfectly circular and a full twelve centimeters in diameter, which drilled through the naso-orbital region and obliterated the rear of the skull opposite the eyes.

"So that much of the tale was true," the old man murmured.

He could not resist inspecting the skull for nonhuman attributes. Most of the differences were subtle; but the Tanu had possessed only thirty teeth and he had been notably longheaded as well as massively built. Aside from anomalies in the positions of some cranial sutures and the mental foramina, the Tanu skull seemed almost completely humanoid.

Richard stared about the compartment, noting the adobe wasp nests that crusted almost every surface, the shredded bulkhead insulation, the exposed ceram framework of once luxurious cabin appointments. There was even a beehive in one of the open forward lockers.

"Well, we don't have a prayer of getting this sucker off the ground. We'll have to go back to one of the others."

Martha was digging in the mounds of rubbish on the left side of the skeleton in armor. She gave a satisfied cry. "Look here! Help me get it out of the garbage, Richard!"

"The Spear!" He helped her push away the moldy mess. In a few minutes the two of them had laid bare a slender instrument nearly a meter taller than the great skeleton, connected by a cable near the butt to a large jeweled box that had once been worn at Lugonn's waist. The box straps had now disintegrated, but the glassy surface of the box and the Spear itself did not seem to be corroded.

Martha wiped hands on hips. "That's it, all right. Zapper and powerpack. Careful of those studs there on the upper armrest, lovie. Even cruddled up as they are, they might still trigger the thing."

"But how," Claude marveled softly, "how did he ever pull the trigger on himself?"

"Oh, for chrissake," said Richard. "Forget that and help us get the thing outside before our little butch Goldilocks wakes up and goes bonkers again."

"I am awake," Felice said. She massaged the point of her chin, where a bruise was forming. "I'm sorry about that. I won't lose control again. And no hard feelings for the love-tap, Captain Blood."

Madame Guderian came slowly up the boarding ladder. Her eyes rested briefly on the glass-armored skeleton and then passed to Felice. "Ah, ma petite. What are we going to do with you?" A sadness weighted her voice.

The girl got up and displayed a gamine grin. "I didn't really spoil anything with my little temper fit. And I guarantee it won't happen again. Let's forget it." She prowled about the flyer interior, kicking at the trash. "I expect the torc's around here someplace. Maybe some critter carried it away from the skeleton and stashed it in another part of the ship."

Claude took up the pack and started to descend the ladder while Richard and Martha followed with the still-tethered weapon, not wanting to risk disconnecting the cable.

Madame regarded the skeleton. "So here you lie, Shining Lugonn. Dead before the adventures of your exiled people had scarcely begun. Your tomb defiled by the little vermin of Earth—and now by us." Shaking her head, she turned to descend the ladder. Felice sprang to the old woman's assistance.

"I've a wonderful idea, Madame! I won't be any use working on the aircraft or the Spear. So when I'm not needed for camp chores or hunting, I'll come back here and clean this place out. I'll make it all neat again and polish his golden glass armor—and when we leave, we can close the hatch."

"Yes." Madame Guderian nodded. "It would be a fitting work."

"I'd have to move all this rubbish anyway," Felice added, "when I was looking for the torc. It must be here somewhere. No Tanu or Firvulag would have dared to take it. I know I'll find it."

Standing on the ground now, Madame looked up at Felice—so small, so winsome, so dangerous. "Perhaps you will. But if you don't? What then?"

The girl was calm. "Why, then I'll have to hold King Yeochee to his promise, that's all."

Richard said, "How about getting down here and giving us a hand, kid? You can moon around with your ancient astronaut all you want when we get a work camp set up. Come on—we're going to move back to the last bird in line. See if you can carry this whole Spear rig by yourself, will you? She's an awkward bitch for a two-man tote."

Felice dropped lightly down from the belly hatch, hoisted the eighty-kilo powerpack in one arm, and stood while Claude and Richard balanced the long weapon on her opposite shoulder.

"I can manage," she said. "But God knows how that old boy ever used this gadget in a running fight. He must have been quite a lad! Just wait till I find his torc."

Claude and Madame looked at each other wordlessly for a moment, then helped Martha gather up their things. They began the half-kilometer trudge back along the crater lip to the Number Four Aircraft.

Madame said, "We have been fortunate, finding the Spear so readily. But there is another factor that may preclude an attack on Finiah this year."

"And that is?" Claude inquired.

"The matter of who shall fly the ancient craft during the actual fire-fight." She looked back over her shoulder at Richard, who was supporting Martha. "You will recall that he agreed merely to fly the machine back to the Vosges. If we must train another pilot for the battle—"

Martha had heard every word, of course. She turned to the ex-spacer with a stricken expression.

Richard gave a terse little bark of laughter. "Madame, you prove it again and again. You're no mind reader. D'you really think I'd miss our little war?"

Martha clutched him tighter and whispered something to him. Madame said nothing—but as she turned away from them to resume the march along the rim trail, she smiled.

After a while, Richard said, "There's something else we ought to think about, though. Wouldn't it be best if we concentrate first on fixing up the flyer and hold off on the Spear until we get back home? Today is September twenty-second and the little King said that the Truce begins on October first. We're cutting things *damn* short if the spooks are gonna need a week to mobilize. And what about getting your people ready, Madame? And working out the tactics for the iron weapons—if they got 'em? Seems to me, the faster we get outa here, the more time'll be left for organizing. And back at your village, Martha can get proper medical care from Amerie. Maybe somebody like Khalid Khan could help out with the Spear repairs, too."

It was Martha who demurred. "Don't forget we've got to *test* the Spear. We must get it working, then install it in the aircraft somehow and try it out from the air. If this zapper is as powerful as I think it is, every Tanu with a microgram of farsense would be able to detect its atmospherics if we shot it off within a hundred kloms of the Vosges."

"God, yes," Richard said, crestfallen. "I forgot about that."

Madame said, "We must do the best we can to put both flyer and Spear in working order before we leave this place. As for those back home, we will trust Peo to have everything in readiness. He knows every nuance of the plan against Finiah. If we have even one day remaining before the start of the Truce, we will still mount the attack."

"Well, let's get hopping then!" Felice said. She broke into a brisk trot, leaving the rest of them straggling far behind. They saw her wave at them briefly from the vicinity of the neighboring flyer, then vanish down the outside of the crater into the scrub. When they reached the great metal bird, they found the Spear placed carefully in the shadow of its wings. Beside it, scratched in the dust, was a message: GONE HUNTING.

"For what?" Richard wondered cynically. Then he and Martha climbed up the ladder of the undisturbed aircraft, opened the simple hatch lock, and disappeared inside.

8

Iᴛ ᴛᴏᴏᴋ ᴛʜʀᴇᴇ ᴅᴀʏs to get the flyer airborne.

Richard had known that these exotic craft were gravo-magnetic the moment he had looked inside the first specimen. The flight deck and passenger compartment of the thirty-meter bird had simple easy-seats—not acceleration couches. Ergo, "inertialess" drive, the universal propulsion system for aircraft and subluminal spaceships of the Galactic Milieu, which enabled almost instantaneous acceleration or deceleration in apparent defiance of gravity-inertia. The odds seemed good that the exotics had tapped the key forces of the universe in much the same "cablecar" fashion as the engineers of the Milieu. Richard and Martha had warily opened one of the sixteen power-modules of what they hoped was the flux-tap generator, using the flyer's own tools. They found to their relief that the liquid within *was* water. No matter that the thingummies generating the rho-field reticula were concentric spheres within spheres instead of the stacked crystalline blades of the analogous Milieu device; the principle, and the basic operation, had to be the same. When the generator was fueled with good old aqua pura, this exotic bird would very likely go.

Claude rigged up a still and tended the ever-bubbling decamole pot while Richard and Martha traced the control circuitry and made sense of the quaint in-ship environmental system, which was capable of recharging itself once they got a little water into the powerplant. After one day of fiddling with the alien controls, Richard felt confident enough to carry on with the analysis alone, letting Martha transfer her efforts to the Spear. For safety's sake, on the off chance that the flyer might blow during one of the groundside tests, they transferred the work camp to a shelf-like clearing in the maquis several kloms downslope from the aircraft, where a spring gushed through the crater wall.

On the evening of the third day, as they gathered around the campfire, Richard announced that the ancient machine was ready for its first flight test.

"I've scraped most of the lichen off and dug all the bird and bug nests out of the vents. She seems damn near good as new, for all her thousand years of squatting."

"How about the controls?" Claude asked. "Are you sure you've figured them out?"

"I turned off all the audibles, of course, since they weren't speaking my language. But the flight instrumentation is mostly graphic, so I can get by. Can't read the altimeter, but there's a terrain-clearance and position monitor that shows a nice picture—and eyeballs were made before digitals anyhow. Numeralwise, the engine cluster is hopeless. But each reader is equipped with three idiot lights—cyan, amber, and violet for go, watch-it, and bye-bye. So I should do all right there, too. My big problem is going to be the wings. Putting wings on a gravo-mag aircraft is weird! They must be a cultural relic. Maybe these folks just *enjoyed* gliding!"

"Richard," Martha said breathlessly. "Take me with you tomorrow."

"Oh, Marty-babe—" he began.

Madame intervened. "You may not, Martha. There is a risk, even though Richard is confident."

"She's right," he said, taking Martha's hand. It was cold in spite of the warm evening. The firelight threw cruel shadows on the engineer's sunken cheeks and eyes. "Once I've checked her out—then we'll go for a spin. Promise. We can't let anything happen to you, kid . . . Who'd put that damn zapper back together?"

Martha moved closer to Richard and stared into the fire. "I think the Spear will work. The powerpack shows half-charge, which is really remarkable, and none of the tiny little internal components of the lance unit seems to have been damaged. The main difficulties have been cleaning out the barrel and replacing the chewed-up cable. It was lucky that the flyer had some stuff that seemed compatible. I'll need one more day to finish and reassemble, and then we can test it and begin practice."

"How powerful do you think it will be?" Claude asked.

"There are several options, I believe," the engineer said. "The lowest setting is the only one lacking a caplock, so they might have used that for their ritual fighting. I'd guess its power to be within light-pistol range. The four higher settings under the lock must have been for special purposes. At the top of the line, we could have us a portable photon cannon."

Richard whistled.

"I don't think we dare test it on max unless we want to risk draining the powerpack," Martha said.

"No chance of recharging?" asked Richard.

"I can't get the pack open," she admitted. "It takes a special tool and I was afraid to kark around with it. We'll just have to save our big zap for the war."

The gnarled branches of the maquis burned with a pungent resinous odor, snapping and throwing sparks that had to be smacked out. Only a few insects buzzed in the drought-stricken jungle. When it was full dark, the remaining birds and small mammals in the area would come to the spring to drink, and Felice and her bow would glean food for tomorrow.

The blonde athlete said, "I have Lugonn's place nearly clean now. There's no sign of the torc."

Only Martha was able to voice a regret.

Richard said, "Should be plenty of the things lying around if we make good at Finiah. You won't have to beg the little King for one. Just reach down on the battlefield and grab."

"Yes," sighed Felice.

"How have you planned to mount the Spear, Richard?" Claude asked. "I can't see how we could rig up a pilot-operated trigger given the short time we have left."

"There's really only one way to handle it. I hover the aircraft and somebody else shoots the zapper out the open belly hatch. I suppose we could trust one of Chief Burke's bullyboys to—"

The old man said softly, "Every exopaleontologist knows how to handle big zappers. How do you think we cut the rocks to get the specimens out? I've carved up a few cliffs in my day—even moved a mountain now and then to get at some really choice fossils."

Richard chortled. "I'll be damned. Okay, you're hired. We'll be a two-man crew."

"Three," said Madame. "You will need me to provide a metapsychic screen for the flyer."

"Angélique!" Claude protested.

"There is no helping it," she said. "Velteyn and his Flying Hunt would see you hovering there."

"You're not going!" the old man stormed. "Not a chance! We'll come over Finiah at high altitude, then drop down vertically and take 'em by surprise."

"You won't." Madame was implacable. "They will detect you hovering. We can only hope to surprise them if I conceal the vessel metapsychically during its initial maneuvers. I must go. There is nothing more to be said."

Claude got to his feet and stood hulking over her. "The hell there isn't. Do you think I'd let you fly into the middle of a fire-fight? Richard and I have one chance in a hundred of getting out with whole skins. We're going to need every gram of concentration to do the job and then get out. We can't afford to be worrying about you."

"Tchah! Worry about yourself. Radoteur! Who is the leader of this group? C'est moi! Whose plan is it, de toute façon, for the entire attack? Mine! I go!"

"I won't let you, you stubborn old she-gorf!"

"Try to stop me, senile Yankee-Polack vieillard!"

"Shrew!"

"Salaud!"

"Ball-breaking old bat!"

"Espèce de con!"

"Shut the hell up!" thundered Felice. "The pair of you are as bad as Richard and Martha!"

The pirate grinned and Martha turned away, nibbling her lip to suppress laughter. Claude's face blackened with embarrassed rage, and Madame was stunned out of her hauteur.

Richard said, "You two listen to me. The rho-field of the flux-tapper will prevent any of the Tanu Hunt from touching the aircraft. It'll probably deflect lances and arrows and whatnot, too. So all we really have to worry about is mental attack. For countering that, our only hope is Madame's metapsychic screen."

"If I had a torc . . ." Felice muttered.

Richard asked Madame, "How long can you hold out against a bunch of 'em?"

"I don't know," she admitted. "We will be disguised as vapor until we direct the first blasts at the city wall. Then they will know an enemy is there, and many minds will be brought to bear upon my little screen. It is certain to be pierced. We can hope that this will happen after we strike at the mine. Once this is done, we can flee at top speed."

"How fast can Velteyn's outfit fly, anyhow?" Richard asked.

"Not much faster than a chaliko at full gallop. The mind of this

Tanu champion is able to levitate his own steed and those of twenty-one warriors through PK, psychokinesis. There is only one other who is capable of such a feat and that is Nodonn, the Tanu Battle-master and Lord of Goriah in Brittany. He can support fifty. There are others who can levitate themselves individually and a few who can carry one or two other persons. But none is strong enough to support many riders save these two."

"If I had a torc!" Felice wailed. "Oh, wait! Just wait!"

"We'll leave 'em in the dust," Richard scoffed. "A couple of zaps to take out the wall on either end of the city, maybe one for the Tanu quarter to demoralize the opposition, then the big zorch for the mine. If that Spear really is a portable cannon, we can melt the place to a slag heap."

"And come home safely ourselves," Claude said, staring into the fire. "While our friends fight it out on the ground."

"Velteyn will try to defend his realm," Madame warned them. "He is exceptionally strong in creativity, and there are strong coercers in his company. We will be in great danger. Nevertheless, we will go. And we will succeed." There was a loud snap and an ember flew through the air like a meteor, landing in front of the old woman. She got up and stamped upon it with great thoroughness. "I believe it is time for us to retire. We will want to get up early for Richard's test flight."

Martha rose from her place and said to Richard, "Come for a little walk with me before we settle down."

"Conserve your strength, chérie," Madame warned.

"We'll just go a little way," Richard said.

He slipped one arm around the engineer's waist to steady her. They went out of the pool of firelight, leaving the others still talking, and walked to the far side of the camp clearing. Only stars illumined the tangle of maquis, for the new moon had gone down. Above them was the overgrown slope with its narrow trail leading to the crater rim. They could not see the refurbished flyer, but they knew it was up there waiting.

"We've been happy, Richard. Can you figure it? A pair like us."

"Two of a kind, Marty. I love you, babe. I never thought it could happen."

"All you needed was a good old-fashioned sexy girl."

"Fool," he said, and kissed her eyes and cold lips.

"When it's all over, do you think we could come back?"

"Back?" he repeated stupidly.

"After the Finiah attack. You know we're going to have to teach others how to fly the machine and maintain it so that they can carry out the other two phases of Madame's plan. But you and I needn't worry about those. We'll have paid our dues. We can have them fly us back here, and then—"

She turned to him and he held her. Too frail and racked by cramps and hemorrhage to endure any further intercourse, she had still insisted upon consoling him. They spent every night in each other's arms, sharing one of the decamole huts.

"Don't worry, Marty. Amerie will know how to fix you up for good. We'll come back here somehow and get a flyer just for ourselves and find us a good place to live. No more Tanu, no more Firvulag or Howlers, no more people at all. Just you and me. We'll find a place. I promise."

"I love you, Richard," she said. "Whatever happens, we've had this."

* * *

In the morning, Richard waved goodbye to the others and went up to where the bird stood. It still looked pretty scruffy in spite of the scraping, but he'd soon fix that.

He settled into the pilot's seat and patted the console in the manner of an equestrian soothing a skittish mount. "Oh, you beautiful, droop-snoot, swivel-winged thing. You wouldn't badass the old Cap'n, would you? Course not. We're gonna fly today!"

He lit her up and went through the checklist. A familiar sweet hum of rho-field generators came to him there on the flight deck and he grinned at the thought of microscopic thermonuclear reactions hitting nicely on all sixteen, ready to weave a net of subtle forces that would free the metal bird from gravity's domain. All of the engine idiot lights gleamed cyan-for-go. Keeping her firmly latched to Earth, he fed juice to the external web. The bird's scabby skin glowed faintly purplish in the bright sunshine as the rho-field reticula clothed it lightly. All the crud that he'd been unable to remove sizzled away, leaving the surface a smooth cerametal black—just what you'd expect for an aircraft with orbiter capability.

He cut in the environmental system. Oh, yeah—little bluey-green lights telling him that no matter where the ship carried him, his life would be duly supported. Ease off on the field-web runup. Crank back the wings to minimum area until he got used to them. No use risking overcontrol on his maiden flight, wallowing all over the sky like a shot duck. Gotta do this with class, Cap'n Voorhees.

Okay . . . okay . . . and *upsy* daisy!

Straight up and dead level and hold at squiggle-hundred meters according to the readout on the indecipherable altimeter display. Call it 400. Down below, the Ries crater was a great blue cup with little spread-winged birds strung around its western lip, politely waiting for permission to drink. There were forty-two of them, with one missing where a section of the rim had collapsed in a landslide, and one empty slot for his own aircraft.

Damn those wings when the wind caught him at hover! He'd better move. Slowly . . . slowly . . . bank and zoom. Figure eight and vertical five and stop and start and swoop and glide and pendulum arc and—hot damn, he was doing it!

Down on the ground, four small figures were jumping up and down. He did a creditable imitation of a wing-waggle to let them know that he had seen them, then laughed out loud.

"And now, my friends, fare thee well, for I must leave you! We'll save the touch-and-goes for later. Now the old Cap'n is gonna give himself a few lessons in how to drive this here flying machine!"

He slammed the rho-field into full inertialess web, stuck a burr under her tail, and took off vertically for the ionosphere.

9

Would volunteers come?

As the days of September dwindled and the preparations at Hidden Springs were completed, this question was paramount among the followers of Madame Guderian. Her influence—and indeed, the benefits of her Firvulag-Human Entente—did not extend much farther than the tiny settlements of the Vosges and the upper Saône wilderness, a region that would be able to muster not more than 100 fighters. Communication with other Lowlife enclaves was minimal because of the danger from Hunts, gray-torc patrols, Howlers, and even nominal subjects of King Yeochee who were reluctant to give up their human-harassing ways.

Before leaving High Vrazel, Madame and Chief Burke had discussed this problem with the shrewd old Battlemaster of the shape-changers, Pallol One-Eye. It had been agreed that the only hope for recruitment of more distant humans lay in the hands of the Firvulag. Only the illusion-spinners could hope to shepherd groups of Lowlife fighters from the far villages to Hidden Springs in time for the Finiah attack; but it was clearly going to take more than a simple call to arms to budge skeptical humans from their swamps or mountain fastnesses—especially if the invitation to the war was delivered by the little exotics.

Madame and Peo had recorded joint appeals on AV letter-plaques and left these with Pallol; however, the Firvulag messengers would have to establish credibility for the enterprise, and to this end a certain stratagem proposed by the Battlemaster was ultimately agreed upon. At the same time that Madame's expedition left High Vrazel for the Ship's Grave, picked Firvulag teams, including King Yeochee's most tactful Grand Combat referees, had set out on journeys to the south and west to summon all of the Lowlives in the known world to participate in the strike against Finiah.

The Little People went laden with gifts. And it happened that lonely huddles of cabins tucked away among the volcanoes of the Massif Central were visited at night by benevolent pixies. Bags of finely milled flour, flagons of honey and wine, luscious cheeses, candy, and other rare dainties appeared mysteriously on human doorsteps. Missing geese and sheep unaccountably found their way back to their pens; even lost children were guided home safely by butterflies or will-o'-the-wisps. On the mountain slopes of the Jura, a poorly tanned deerskin pegged to the wall of a Lowlife hovel might disappear, and in its place the delighted inhabitants would discover well-cobbled boots, fur jerkins, and butter-soft suede garments. Deep in the swamps of the Paris basin, the fen-dwellers would find that rotting punts were exchanged for new decamole dinghies stolen from Tanu caravans; great nets of waterfowl were left where outlaw human hunters could find them; plass containers of Survival Unit insect-repellent, more precious than rubies, appeared on the windowsills of the stilt-legged marshland houses where no passerby could possibly have reached. In scores of Lowlife settlements, humans were amazed when odd jobs were done by invisible helpers. Sick folks were nursed by elfin women who vanished with the dawn; broken things were mended; empty larders were filled; and always there were gifts, gifts, gifts.

Finally, when the Firvulag messengers ventured to appear en clair and present the awesome plan of Madame Guderian (who was, of course, known to all of the fugitives), the Lowlives were at least willing to listen. Fewer numbers agreed to respond to the appeal for fighting volunteers, for there were many emotional burn-outs and physical cripples among them, as well as a sizable percentage who cared only for their own skins. But the bolder, the healthier, and the more idealistic spirits were fired by the notion of striking a blow against the hated Tanu, while others agreed to participate in the attack when the subject of loot was delicately broached. So the Firvulag emissaries began to return, and those at Hidden Springs exulted because they brought with them a total of nearly 400 men and women recruited from places as far away as Bordeaux and Albion and the tidal estuaries of the Anversian Sea. These were welcomed in the name of Free Humanity, briefly trained, and equipped with weapons of bronze and vitredur. None of the newcomers, it had been agreed, would be told of the iron until the very day of the attack; and only the most competent of the volunteer fighters would be armed with the precious metal.

The secret staging area in the Rhineland bottoms opposite Finiah was in a state of full readiness by the middle of the last week in September. Lowlife warriors and a contingent of crack Firvulag stalwarts were poised to cross the river in sailing lighters belonging to the Little People. The boats would be disguised as blobs of mist for as long as the most powerful Tanu did not consciously seek to penetrate them. Another Firvulag force was concealed farther upstream in a second camp, primed to strike at the second break in the city wall, which was supposed to be made roughly opposite to the main thrust.

Tactics and targets had been decided upon and logistic preparations were complete. All that remained was the arrival of the Spear of Lugonn.

* * *

"The Hunt flies tonight, Peopeo Moxmox Burke."

It was very dark in the cypress swamp, for the moon was down. Chief Burke focused his night ocular on the activity across the river. The high, narrow-necked peninsula upon which the Tanu city perched was, as always, ablaze with an incredible display of colored lights. The much sharper vision of Pallol One-Eye had already discerned what the Chief now viewed through his scope: a glowing procession rising from the topmost parapet of House Velteyn. It spiraled slowly toward the zenith, the figures of the Flying Hunt distinct even at a distance of two kilometers. Tanu riders whose faceted armor flashed every color of the rainbow mounted upward on great white chalikos. The legs of the steeds pumped in unison as they galloped into the airy darkness. There were twenty-one knights in the train and another who forged ahead to lead them, his billowing cloak streaming back like a comet tail of vaporous silver. From the distance came the faint notes of a horn.

"They're turning south, Battlemaster," said Burke.

Beside him, Pallol One-Eye nodded, he who had seen 600 winters upon his own far world and more than a thousand orbits of the nearly seasonless Pliocene Earth. He was taller than the Native American and nearly twice as massive, and he moved as fluidly as the black man-sized otters of the riverine jungle whose form, three times magnified, he often adopted. His right eye was a great orb of gold with an iris colored deep red; the left eye was hidden by a jeweled black leather patch. It was whispered that when he lifted that patch in battle, his glance was more deadly than a thunderbolt—which is to say that the destructive potential of his right-brain's creativity was second to none among the Firvulag and the Tanu. But Pallol One-Eye was an irascible ancient now, and he had not deigned to soil his obsidian armor at a Grand Combat for more than twenty years, unable to bear his people's annual humiliation. He had found Madame Guderian's plan against Finiah to be mildly amusing, and he had acquiesced in a Firvulag rôle when both Yeochee and the young champion, Sharn-Mes, decided to support the Lowlives. Pallol declared that he would lend the effort his good advice, and he had done so; but it was unthinkable that he should participate personally in what he termed "Madame's little war." More likely than not, the assault would be indefinitely postponed when the lady failed to return with the vital matériel. And even if she did bring back the Spear, how could mere humans hope to wield it effectively against the bravos of Velteyn? It was a weapon for a hero! And it was all too true that heroes were in short supply among this effete younger generation.

"Now they're crossing the Rhine—heading west into the Belfort Gap," Burke said. "No dout planning to convoy the last caravan from Castle Gateway before the Truce."

Still Pallol only nodded.

"The Tanu can't have any inkling of our preparations, Battle-master. We've carried it off without a flaw."

This time Pallol laughed, a grating sound like the chafing of lava blocks. "Finiah shines bright across the river, Leader of Humans. Save your self-congratulation for its snuffing. Madame Guderian will not return and all of this scheming against the torc-wearing Foe will be for nothing."

"Perhaps so, Battlemaster. But even if we don't fight, we've accomplished things that we never dared dream of before. Nearly five hundred Lowlives have been brought together in a common cause. Only a month ago, that would have been an idle fancy. We were scattered and afraid, mostly without hope. But not any more. We know that there *is* a chance that we can break the Tanu domination of humanity. If you Firvulag help us, we can do it sooner. But even if you break off the alliance, even if Madame fails to bring back the Spear this year, we'll return to fight again. After this, humans will never go back to the old timid ways. Others of us will go searching for the Ship's Grave if Madame fails. We'll find that ancient weapon and make it work again—something your people could never do. And if the Spear is gone—if we never find it—we'll use other weapons until the Tanu slavers are defeated."

"You mean you will use the blood-metal," said Pallol.

Chief Burke was silent for a dozen seconds. "You know about the iron."

"The senses of the torc-wearers may be so puny that they require machines to sniff the deadly metal out—but not those of the Firvulag! Your camp reeks of iron."

"We will not use it against our friends. Unless you plan betrayal, you have nothing to fear. The Firvulag are our allies, our brothers-in-arms."

"The Tanu Foe are our true brothers and yet we are fated to contend with them eternally. Could it be otherwise between Firvulag and humanity? This Earth is destined to belong to you, and you know it. I do not believe that humanity will be satisfied in allowing us to share. You will never call us brothers. You will call us interlopers and try to destroy us."

"I can speak only for myself," Burke said, "since my tribe, the Wallawalla, becomes extinct upon my death. But there will be no treachery by human against friendly Firvulag as long as I am the general of the Lowlives, Pallol One-Eye. I swear it on my blood—

which is as red as your own. As for our never being brothers . . . this is a matter I'm still pondering. There are many different degrees of kinship."

"So thought our Ship," sighed the old champion. "It brought us here." He tilted his huge head toward the sky. "But why? With so many other yellow stars in the universe, so many possible planets—why here, with you? The Ship was instructed to find the *best*."

"Perhaps," said Peopeo Moxmox Burke, "the Ship took a longer view than you."

* * *

All day long the birds of prey had circled.

They rode thermals above the Vosges woodland in a neat stack, holding most of the time at altitudes appropriate to their species. Lowest was a wheeling flock of small swallow-tailed kites; above them soared a mated pair of bronze buzzards; the fire-backed eagles came next, and then a lone lammergeier vulture, mightiest of the bone crackers. Most lofty of all the circling birds was the one that had initiated the day-long vigil and attracted all of the others. On motionless wings, it orbited at a height so remote that it was barely visible to watchers on the ground.

Sister Amerie watched the birds through the sparse branches of a stone pine, her tawny cat resting in her arms. " 'Wherever the body is, there will the eagles be gathered together.' "

"You quote the Christian scriptures," said Old Man Kawai, who was shading his eyes with a tremulous hand. "Do you think the birds are truly clairvoyant? Or do they only hope, as we do? It is late—so late!"

"Calm yourself, Kawai-san. If they get here tonight, there'll be a whole twenty-four-hour day for the Firvulag to join in the assault. That should be enough. Even if our allies withdraw at sunrise day after tomorrow, we can still win with the help of the iron."

The ancient continued to fret. "What can be keeping Madame? It was such a slim hope. And such hard work we have done here in expectation that the hope would be fulfilled!"

Amerie stroked the cat. "If they arrive before dawn tomorrow, the attack can still proceed according to the second alternative."

"*If* they arrive. Have you considered the navigation problem? Richard must come first to Hidden Springs. But how will he find it? Surely these tiny mountain valleys must look much alike from the air, and ours is hidden because of the Hunt. Richard will not be able to distinguish our canyon, even in daylight, if he approaches at a high altitude. And he does not dare to fly a low-level search, lest the enemy observe him."

Amerie was patient. "Madame will conceal the ship mentally, of course. Calm yourself! This constant worry is bad for your health. Here—pet the cat. It's very soothing. When you stroke the fur, you generate negative ions."

"Ah so desu ka?"

"We can hope that the flyer would be equipped with an infrared scanner for night flight, just as our eggs of the twenty-second century were. Even with all of our fighters gone, there are still more than thirty warm bodies here in Hidden Springs. Richard will sniff us out."

Old Man Kawai sucked in his breath. A horrible thought of a new sort crossed his mind. "The metapsychic concealment of the aircraft! If its volume is more than about ten cubic meters, Madame will be unable to render it invisible! She will only be able to disguise it somehow and hope that the Tanu do not concentrate their perceptive powers too closely upon it. What if the machine is so large that her faculties are insufficient to invest it with a plausible illusion?"

"She'll think of something."

"It is a great danger," he moaned. The little cat gave him a long-suffering glance as his hand essayed a few nervous pats. "The Flying Hunt could even discover the aircraft while it rests here! All that is needed is for Velteyn to descend for a close look at my poor camouflage nets. They are pathetic things."

"Adequate for night concealment. Velteyn has no infrared, thank God. And he almost never comes this far west nowadays. Stop your fussing! You'll stew yourself into cardiac arrest. Where's your jiriki?"

"I am a foolish, useless old man. I would not be here in the first place if I were able to rule myself through Zen . . . The nets—if they fail their purpose, the fault will be my own! The dishonor!"

Amerie gave an exasperated sigh. She thrust the cat at Kawai. "Take Deej into Madame's cottage and give her some leftover fish. Then hold her on your lap and close your eyes and pet her and think of all those lovely Tri-D's that used to come rolling off your assembly lines in Osaka."

The old man giggled. "A substitute for counting sheep? Yatte mimasu! It may serve to tranquilize me, at that. As you say, there is still time to mount the attack . . . Come, kitty. You will share your valued negative ions with me."

He pottered off, but turned after a few steps to say with a sly grin, "However, one incongruity remains. Forgive my flaunting of the obsolete technology, Amerie-san—but even the lowliest electronicist knows that it is quite impossible for negatives ions to be cat-ions!"

"You get out of here, Old Man!"

Tittering, he disappeared into the cottage.

Amerie walked down the canyon past the huts and cottages, nodding and waving to the few people who, like herself, could not resist watching the sky while they waited and prayed. The last of the ablebodied men and women had marched off under Uwe's command three days ago, and the deadline for the optimal two-day assault had come and gone. But there was still time to execute the one-day attack. At dawn tomorrow, it could be that human beings would unite together for the first time on this Exile world to challenge their oppressors.

Oh, Lord, let it happen. Let Madame and the rest of them get here in time!

It was getting cooler as the sun descended, and soon the thermals —those buoyant upwellings of heated air—would fade away completely and the soaring raptors would have to come back to earth. Amerie came to her secret place beneath a low but open-armed juniper and lay down, face to the sky, to pray. It had been such a wonderful month! Her arm had healed quickly and the people . . . ah, Lord, what a fool she had been to think of becoming a hermit. Hidden Springs folk and the other Lowlife outlaws of the region had needed her as a physician and counselor and friend. Among them she had done the work she had been trained for. And what had become of the burnt-out case with the self-punishing compulsion to flee into a haven of solitary penitence? Here she could even pray her Divine Office, contemplate in the forest stillness; but when the people needed her, she was there ready to help. And they were there to help. And he was there in the midst of them. It was her dream fulfilled, even in its changing—only now the language that she prayed in was a living one.

I put my trust in the Lord! How dare you say to my soul:
fly away like a sparrow to the mountains,
for lo—the wicked draw their bows and aim their arrows,
to shoot in the dark the upright of heart;
and they have destroyed the good things
while just people let the evil happen!

But the Lord tests both the just and the wicked;
he hates the lawless ones, the evil-lovers.
Flaming coals and burning sulfur will he pour on them!
A fiery whirlwind shall be their punishment . . .

The lammergeier flew away to his lair among the high crags and the eagles descended to their roosting trees an hour before the sun set. The kites scattered, having to satisfy their appetites with insects, and even the buzzards disappeared at last, perhaps wondering what had prompted all of them to waste time waiting in the futile hope of sharing the great newcomer's prey. He alone still circled aloof in the high air, completely disdainful of the vanished thermals.

And Amerie watched him, lying under the tree, watched that distant speck endlessly wheeling that had drawn all the others and then disappointed them. That bird with motionless wings.

Heart pounding, she scrambled to her feet and ran back up the canyon to rout everybody out.

* * *

"Stand back! Don't touch it until the field's off, for God's sake!" someone shouted.

The huge thing, still glowing faintly purple, seemed to fill the whole lower end of the canyon. It had descended just as soon as the sky was fully dark, subsonic by a whisker but still shoving a hurricane blast ahead of it that tore bundles of thatch from the roofs and sent poor old Peppino's geese tumbling like leaves in a gale. It had come to a dead halt no more than two meters above the highest trees, its drooping nose, gull wings, and fan-shaped tail bathed in a crawling network of nearly ultravisible fire. Old Man Kawai, composed now and curtly efficient, had sent several youngsters for wet sacks and ordered the rest of the villagers to stand by the rolls of camouflage netting.

They all watched, awe-struck, as the hovering thing folded its great wings back against its thirty-meter fuselage and delicately felt its way down. It nosed obliquely between a pair of tall firs where there was a minimum of undergrowth, hesitated just barely off the ground, and then let its long legs settle. There was a loud hiss; a few bushes began to smolder and wisps of smoke curled up around the footpads. The skin of the bird went dead black.

Then the people, who had stood as though paralyzed, broke into wild cheers. A number sobbed aloud as they rushed to follow Kawai's orders, beating out the little fires that had been set by the rho-field and hustling to set up poles and guy-ropes for the nets.

The belly hatch opened and the ladder extruded. Slowly, Madame Guderian came down.

Amerie said, "Welcome home."

"We have brought it," said Madame.

"Everything is ready. Exactly as your plan specified."

Lame Miz Cheryl-Ann, who was two hundred and three and nearly blind, seized one of Madame's hands and kissed it; but the Frenchwoman hardly seemed to notice. Up above, a word of warning came from within the flyer. A litter was lowered from the hatch by Felice and Richard.

Madame said only, "You are needed, ma Soeur." And then she turned and walked as in a daze toward her cottage. Amerie knelt down and took one of Martha's bony wrists. Richard stood there in his ruffled pirate shirt and battered buckskins with fists clenched and tears running down his dirty sun-scorched cheeks.

"She wouldn't let us come back until the Spear was working right. And now she's damn near bled to death. Help her, Amerie."

"Follow me," said the nun, and they rushed off after Madame, carrying the litter with them, leaving Claude to see that the big black bird of prey was safely bedded down for the night.

10

BEFORE DAWN there was the Battle Mass, and then Madame exerted her farspeech power to transmit an enigmatic "we come" to Pallol, insuring that the invasion fleet would be poised to exploit the bombardment of Finiah's wall. Sunrise was less than an hour away and if past performance was any criterion, Lord Velteyn and the members of his Flying Hunt would be back at their stronghold after the night's foray.

Claude strode along nearly at the end of the procession heading for the flyer and wished Felice would shut up. She was once again attired in her black leather ring-hockey armor, which had been beautifully refurbished by Old Man Kawai's artisans, and she was wild with anxiety lest she should miss the war.

"I wouldn't take up any room. And I *swear* I won't say a word during the flight! Claude, you've got to let me come with you. I *can't* wait for you to come back after the strike. What if you don't make it?"

"If Velteyn nails the flyer, you'd go down with us."

"But if you get away, you could put me down right outside Finiah! Say, at the breach in the wall on the land side of the peninsula. I could go in with the Firvulag on the second wave! Please, Claude!"

"The Hunt could have spotted us by then. Landing could be suicide—and that's not what this fight is all about. Not for me and Madame Guderian, at any rate. Finiah is just the beginning of our war. And Richard's got Martha to live for now."

Up ahead, villagers were pulling the nets from the black bird. A few candles gleamed in the mist where Amerie was blessing the aircraft.

Felice said, "I could help you with the Spear, Claude. You know what an awkward big bastard it is. I could be useful." She clutched at the old man's bush shirt and he stopped abruptly and took her by the shoulders.

"Listen to me, girl! Richard is all strung up. He hasn't slept for more than twenty-four hours and he's half-crazy with worry because of Martha. Even with the transfusions, Amerie gives her less than a fifty-fifty chance. And now Richard has to fly a combat mission in an exotic aircraft with a couple of old crocks and the future of Pliocene humanity riding on his tail! You know how he feels about you. Having you in the flyer during the mission could be the last straw. You say that you'd keep out of the way. But *I* know you couldn't help asserting yourself once the heat was on. So you're staying here, and that's that. We'll do our job and then run for home—and with luck we'll leave Velteyn completely mystified about where we've gone. We'll come back and pick you up. I promise you that if we make it, we'll get you to the battle not more than an hour or so after the main assault begins."

"Claude . . . Claude . . ." Her face peered through the T-shaped opening in the black hoplite helmet, panic and fury and some other more alien emotion at war with reason. Claude waited, praying that she wouldn't jump him. But he was so steeped in fatigue that he almost didn't give a damn whether or not she knocked him cold and forced the others to let her take his place. It was in her mind, all right; but she also knew that he was by far the better shot.

"Oh, *Claude*." The blazing brown eyes closed. Tears poured behind the cheekpieces of her helmet and the green plumes flattened as she wrenched away from him and fled back toward Madame's cottage.

He let out a long breath. "Be ready when we get back!" he called, and then hurried to where the others were waiting.

* * *

The great bird crept furtively from its hiding place. When it was in the clear, it mounted the predawn sky like a violet spark going up an invisible chimney, attaining an altitude of 5000 meters in a thunderclap inertialess surge. Angélique Guderian stood beside Richard, clutching the back of his seat with one hand and her golden torc with the other. Richard had changed into his old spacer's coverall.

"You got us hidden, Madame?" he asked.

"Yes," she replied faintly. She had said hardly a word since their safe return.

"Claude! You ready?"

"Whenever you give the word, son."

"We're on our way!"

A split second later, the belly hatch rolled smoothly back. They hovered motionless above a patch of microscopic jewels, shaped roughly like a tadpole with its tail joined to the eastern bank of the Rhine.

"Why, it's on the Kaiserstuhl," Claude said to himself.

The patch grew, spread, its star-cluster blur clarifying into twinkling lights as the flyer dropped—subsonically this time—and stopped dead in the air about 200 meters above the highest eminence of the Tanu city.

"Give it to 'em," said Richard.

Claude horsed the great Spear into position and took a bead on the line of fiery dots marking the Rhineside wall. Somewhere in the graying mists of the river waited a flotilla of Firvulag boats loaded with human and exotic troops.

Keep her depressed, old man! You don't want to boil your own folks out of the water!

He raised the caplock and swung it aside. There—right there. Touch the second stud.

A thin bar of green-white lanced without sound.

Down below, a tiny orange flower bloomed—but the line of dots atop the wall remained unbroken.

"Shit!" Richard exclaimed. "You missed! Elevate!"

Calmly, Claude took aim once again, pressed the stud. This time there was no burst of orange fire, only a dull-red glow. Perhaps a dozen of the rampart lamps were swallowed by it.

"Hee-*yow!* Gotcha!" screeched the pirate. "Making a one-eighty, Claudsie-boy! Ready for the back door!"

The flyer spun on its vertical axis and Claude found himself aiming at a point near the base of the shining tadpole's tail. He fired and missed . . . high. He fired and missed again . . . low.

"Jesus, hurry it up!" urged Richard.

The third time, the blast struck the wall squarely, melting it at a point where the causeway of the peninsular neck met the extinct volcanic mass of the Kaiserstuhl proper.

Madame moaned. Claude felt dragon talons grip his guts.

"Are they coming?" Richard demanded. "Hang on, Madame! Sweet Christ, Claude—get on with it! Never mind zapping the Tanu buildings. Go for the mine!"

The old man wrestled the Spear around, a sudden burst of sweat greasing his hands and making them slip on the weapon's glassy butt. His used-up muscles trembled as he tried to bring the weapon to bear upon the small blue constellation that marked the mine workings. He could not depress the Spear sufficiently to bring the target into range. "Quick, Richard! Take her a couple of hundred meters south!"

"Aye," growled the pirate. The flyer changed position in the twinkling of an eye. "That better?"

"Wait . . . yes! I've just about got her. Have to do this right the first time. Only have one blast at full zap—"

"Merde alors," Madame whispered.

The old woman staggered away from Richard to crash against the right bulkhead. Fists pressed to her temples, she began to scream. Claude had never heard such a sound from a human throat, such a distillation of anguish, horror, and despair.

At the same moment, something flashed past the flight deck port. It glowed neon-red and was shaped like a mounted knight.

"Oh, God," said Richard flatly. Madame's screams cut off and she fell senseless to the deck.

"How many?" asked Claude. He tried to get a grip on himself, tried to steady the heavy Spear on target, prayed that his damned old body wouldn't betray him at this last extremity. They had almost done it! Almost . . .

"I make it twenty-two." Richard's calm voice seemed to come from a considerable distance. "The whole Round Table circling us like Sioux around a wagon train. All scarlet except the leader, and I'd put his spectral class somewhere in the B0 range—look out!"

One of the figures, the blue-white one, soared down and took a position immediately below the flyer. He drew his glassy sword and thrust it upward. Three Roman-candle globes of ball lightning left the tip and soared rather slowly toward the open belly hatch. Claude dodged, pulling the Spear out of the way, and the things flew into the aircraft, where they began caroming off the panels and decking, hissing and emitting a fearful smell of ozone.

"Shoot!" shrieked Richard. "For God's sake, shoot!"

Claude took one deep breath. He said, "Steady, son," and aimed, depressing the fifth stud of the Spear of Lugonn just as the little blue lights centered themselves in the weapon's sight.

An emerald bar jabbed once at the spangled earth. Where it struck, the rock went white, yellow, orange, roiling crimson like a flame-armed starfish. Claude fell sideways and the Spear clanged to the deck. The belly hatch started to close.

Lightning balls bounced and crackled. The old man felt one of them strike him in the back, rolling up his spine from buttocks to the base of his neck, burning all the way. The interior of the flyer was filled with smoke and a smell of burnt flesh and fabric. There were sounds, too, Claude discovered, as he studied the scene from afar—a sizzle as the remaining two energy balls sought their targets, curses and then a thin scream from Richard, a whimpering sob from Angélique as she tried to creep toward him over the smeared deck, someone breathing in and out in harsh, rhythmic persistence.

"Get it away from me!" a frantic voice cried. "I can't see to land! Ah—dammit, no!"

A jarring crash and a slow tilt to one side. Claude felt a breeze (amazing the way it seared his back) and the hatch opened. A peculiarly angled surface of grassy ground, gray and dim in the first light of morning. Richard sobbing and cursing. Angélique making no sound. Voices shouting. Heads poking up through the hatch—again at that odd angle. Wails from that silly youngster, Old Man Kawai. Amerie's familiar tones: "Go easy. Go easy." Felice spitting obscenities when somebody said she was going to get her armor all messed up.

"Put him over my shoulder. I can carry him. Stop your wiggling, Claude. Silly old fart! Now I'm going to have to walk all the way to the war."

He laughed. Poor Felice. And then his face was upside down among her green skirts and he was jouncing up and down and he screamed. But after a little bit the movement stopped, and they laid him on his stomach and something touched his temple, making the pain and the rest of it grow muzzy.

He said, "Angélique? Richard?"

Unseen, Amerie replied, "They'll recover. You all will. You did it, Claude. Sleep now."

Well, how about that? And for a moment he saw the fiery starfish again, but with crimson and gold limbs expanding, branching out among the hapless helpless firefly patterns of Finiah streets in the instant before the hatch of the flyer slammed shut. How about that . . . and if the lava kept oozing out of the old Kaiserstuhl volcano for even a little while, it was going to be a long, long time before they mined any more barium in the regions around there.

"Don't worry about it, Claude," Felice said.

And so he stopped.

11

HALF-DOZING in the dead hour before dawn, Moe Marshak and the other human troops on duty in Finiah had mistaken the first blast of the photon weapon for a lightning stroke. The thin green beam had lanced out of the stars, barely missing the Rhineside wall that the gray-torc garrison manned and demolishing an adjacent mess hall inside the compound. Marshak was still gaping at the flames consuming the wreckage when Claude's second shot struck the Number Ten bastion squarely, breaching the fortification not a dozen meters from Marshak's station. Great blocks of granite flew in all directions and the air boiled with smoke and dust. Oil tubs that held the watch fires spilled in the concussion and sent blazing rivulets racing down the cracked walkway.

When Marshak was able to get a grip on himself, he rushed to look through one of the embrasures. There in the fog-blurred waters below were the boats.

"Alert!" he shouted aloud; and then his mind sent the alarm on the declamatory mode, amplified by his gray torc.

MARSHAK: Invasion viaRhine! Wallbreach StationTen!

CAPTAL WANG: Howthehellmany be there Moe? Howmany boats?

MARSHAK: Wholefuckin river FULL!! Eightyhundred who can count damnfog bastards everywhere Firvulagboats but letmesee *yes!* LOWLIVES TOO! Repeat Lowlives + Foe invading. Landings! Rocks swarming damnfuckers penetrating breach estimate hole maybeninemeters max.

CORNET FORMBY: All troopsofwatch to StationTen. General alert RhineGarrison to arms. Dutyobservers scan/report. Defensiveunits to wallstations . . . CANCELCANCELCANCEL! Defensive-units to garrisoncompound! Invader penetration compound!

COMMANDER SEABORG: Lord Velteyn. Alert. Firvulag and human invasion force has penetrated the city fortifications at breached Number Ten Station. Countering.

LORD VELTEYN OF FINIAH: Kinfolk arise and defend! Flyers to saddle! Na bardito! Na bardito taynel o pogekône!

Chief Burke and Uwe Guldenzopf led the mob of Vosges Lowlives and outland volunteers up the steep rampart and across the tumbled rubble of the breakthrough. Vitredur arrows and crossbow bolts rained down from the battlements, but until the defenders could redeploy at ground level, the invaders would have a brief advantage. As bad luck would have it, the breach was within the grounds of the principal Finiah garrison. In addition to the confusion caused by the mess hall conflagration, which was spreading to adjoining structures, a chaliko stable had been broken open by falling debris and numbers of the great animals were loose.

Three soldiers ran from the guardhouse at the compound gate. "Take 'em," yelled Burke, and howling desperados fell upon the little force and cut it to pieces. "Out of here! Into the city streets! And get this gate off the hinges!"

Troops were pouring from the barracks, some with their armor only half strapped on. Free-for-all clashes erupted everywhere in the murk as invaders scrambled through the broken wall while the human minions of the Tanu strove to press them back. The irregulars trying to unhinge the gates were attacked and overwhelmed, and soldiers swung the heavy metal grille shut, locking it.

"We're sealed in!" Chief Burke jumped on top of an overturned feed wagon. His face and upper torso were painted in the old war patterns and he had the wing feather of a fire-eagle thrust into his knotted, iron-colored hair. "Hit the sonsabitches! Get that gate back open! This way!"

He saw Uwe fall beneath a sword-wielding gray-torc and leaped down, brandishing the wide tomahawk Khalid Khan had forged for him. The blade sank into the soldier's crested bronze kettle-helmet as though it were made of pasteboard. Burke hauled the body off to find Guldenzopf lying flat on his back, one hand clutching his breast and an expression of agony on his bearded face.

Burke knelt. "Did he nail you, bubi?"

Struggling up on one elbow, Uwe groped inside his buckskin shirt. Bone-colored bits gleamed in the lurid light. "Only my second-best meerschaum, dammit."

The Lowlives remained hemmed in, unable to break out of the area in the immediate vicinity of the garrison complex. Those crowded in the breach were pressed both by the defenders and by their own comrades coming up from the beachhead. A wail of panic arose. Some invaders fell and were trampled. A garrison officer wearing a silver torc and full blue-glass body armor directed a unit of halberdiers that advanced upon the stalled irregulars. Sweeping crystal blades mowed down the packed, shrieking throng.

And then the monsters came to the rescue.

High on the steep slope of rubble shone the wavering nightmare shape of a three-meter albino scorpion—the illusionary aspect of Sharn the Younger, general of the Firvulag. From the minds of the exotics came a mighty wave of terror and dread that overloaded the telepathic circuits of the gray torcs and sent their wearers writhing into madness. Sharn himself could smite the enemy at a range of nearly twenty-five meters; others of his advancing company might not have auras so formidable, but woe to the Foe who fell into their clutches!

Hideous trolls, spectres, manticores, shambling dark presences seized the soldiers in spine-crunching embraces, sank fangs into unarmored throats, even rent men limb from limb. Some of the exotics were capable of flinging bolts of psychoenergy that broiled troops in their bronze cuirasses like lobsters in the shell. Other Firvulag harassed with sheets of astral fire, streams of nauseating ichor, or brain-crippling illusions. The great hero Nukalavee the Skinless, wearing his aspect of a flayed centaur with blazing eyes, howled until enemy soldiers fell writhing to the ground, eardrums split and minds reduced to near-idiocy. Another champion, Bles Four-Fang, invaded the headquarters of the garrison, caught up the silver commander named Seaborg, and appeared to devour him—armor and all —while the dying officer calmly broadcast final telepathic orders to his subordinates directing the troops now making a last stand at the gate opening into the inner city. Seaborg's aides blunted their vitredur weapons against Bles's scaly illusory hide, only to be eaten alive in turn for their temerity. By the time the monster had downed the last adjutant, the headquarters building was afire and the invasion force swarmed in Finiah's streets. So Bles withdrew in good order, picking his teeth with a silver spur. His appetite had only been whetted, and the morning was young.

* * *

Vanda-Jo was still overseeing the last wave of volunteers embarking from the staging area when Lord Velteyn and the Flying Hunt took to the air. Shouts of fear came from the crowd as they saw the glowing knights mount up from the city across the water. One man yelled, "The bleeders're coming for *us!*" and jumped into the Rhine. A fiasco was averted when Vanda-Jo tongue-lashed the outlanders for their cowardice, pointing out that the Hunt was circling high above Finiah, bent on some more urgent objective.

"So into the boats and quit farting around!" she bellowed. "You don't have to be afraid of Velteyn and his flying circus any more! Did you forget our secret weapon? We've got iron! You can kill Tanu now—even easier than you can kill those traitor human torcers that do their dirty work!"

Eyeballs rolled anxiously in the half-light. The Firvulag skipper in the two-masted shallop nearest Vanda-Jo glowered in dwarfish impatience. "Hurry it up, spiritless earthworms, or we'll sail to the war without you!"

Suddenly a column of emerald light stabbed down from apparently empty sky in the axis of the wheeling Hunt, striking a low knoll within the city across the Rhine. Orange-and-white fire fountained up at the point of impact, and seconds later, the sound of a rolling detonation sped over the river.

"The mine!" somebody shouted. "The barium mine's blowing up! God—it looks like a volcano erupting in there!"

As if the bombardment had been a signal, another gout of flame belched up from the farthest reaches of Finiah, back where the peninsula narrowed to a small neck connecting the city to the mainland.

"See that?" Vanda-Jo was exultant. "The second wave of spooks have landed opposite our main beachhead! That female Firvulag general named Ayfa is attacking from the Black Forest side. *Now* will you shitheads get a move on?"

The men and women on the dock hoisted their iron-tipped spears into the air and yelled. They pounded down the spindly gangplanks into the waiting boats so eagerly that the small craft rocked and nearly swamped.

On the other side of the Rhine, flames made a scarlet track on the dark water. The faerie lamps of blue and green and silver and gold that had outlined the splendid Tanu City of Lights began to wink out.

* * *

Velteyn, Lord of Finiah, pulled up the reins of his chaliko and hung in midair, shining like a magnesium flare. The nobles of his Flying Hunt, eighteen male and three female knights, all glowing red, drew in their mounts to surround him. His thought-thrust was nearly incoherent with frustration and rage:

Gone! The flying machine is gone . . . and yet my lightnings surely penetrated its belly. Kamilda! Send your farsense seeking it.

. . . It recedes from us Exalted Lord. Ah Tana at a speed unprecedented! It drops behind the brow of the Vosges and beyond my perception. My Lord if I ascend to a great height—

Stay Kamilda! More urgent threats confront us below. Look all of you! Look what the Foe has done! O the shame the pain the havoc! Down to the ground all of you. Each to command a mounted party of chivalry in defense of our City of Lights! Na bardito!

Na bardito taynel o pogekône!

* * *

The fighting moved steadily inland from the Rhineside break. Two hours after dawn, the western front was strung through the gardens of the pleasure dome, on the very outskirts of the Tanu quarter.

Moe Marshak had reloaded his quiver several times from those of fallen comrades. He had wrenched the gaudy crest from his bronze helmet early on and then rolled in filth to camouflage the shine of his cuirass. Unlike certain of his luckless fellows, he had deduced quickly that the Firvulag would be able to detect telepathic communication, and so he made no attempt to contact his officers for orders. Maintaining a quiet mind, he went his lone way, keeping out of monster range as he skulked Finiah's byways, potting Lowlives with cool economy while dodging hysterical ramas and noncombatants. Marshak had already taken out at least fifteen of the enemy, plus two bareneck civilians he had caught looting a gray-torc corpse of its weaponry.

Now Marshak slipped into the long porch that formed the perimeter of the pleasure dome. Hearing one of the distinctive Lowlife yodels, he concealed himself behind thick ornamental shrubs and nocked one of the serrated war arrows in his compound bow.

In the next instant an unexpected diversion came from within the building. The stained glass from a pair of French doors perhaps five meters away from the soldier shivered to atoms from the impact of some heavy object. There were screams and a rumbling sound. Long hands all adorned with rings fumbled with the jammed catch. Other hands shook the bent framework. The angle was such that Marshak could not clearly see the people trapped inside, but their cries of terror and dismay reached both his mind and ears, as did the uncanny warbling of the thing pursuing them.

"Help! The door's stuck! And it's coming!"

Help us! *Helphelphelp us!* HELP US!

The blanket coercive summons of a Tanu overlord clutched at Marshak's consciousness. His gray torc compelled obedience. Forsaking his hiding place, he ran to the door. On the other side, pressed against the mangled copper fretwork, were three female denizens of the pleasure dome and their tall Tanu client, whose handsome violet and gold robes proclaimed him an official of the Farsensor Guild. He presumably lacked the coercive or psychokinetic potential to fend off the apparition that was now poised in an inner doorway, ready to strike.

The Firvulag wore the appearance of a gigantic hellgrammite, a larval water insect with clashing razor-sharp mandibles. The brute's head was nearly a meter wide, while the long segmented body, slick with some stinking secretion, seemed to fill the corridor behind it.

"Tana be thanked!" cried the Tanu. "Quickly, my man! Aim for its neck!"

Marshak raised his bow, shifted position to avoid the struggling women, and let fly. The glass-tipped shaft sank for most of its length between chitinous plates behind the creature's scissoring jaws. Marshak heard the Firvulag utter a telepathic bellow. Without hurrying, he drew two more arrows and sent them into the hellgrammite's glittering orange eyes. The insectile form wavered, became insubstantial . . . and then the awful thing was gone and a dwarf in black obsidian armor lay dead on the floor, throat and eyesockets transfixed.

The soldier used his vitredur short sword to pry open the ruined latch. Pleasure surges engendered by the grateful exotic throbbed along his pelvic nerves in the sweet, familiar reward. When the nobleman and his disheveled companions were freed, Marshak saluted, right fist pressed against his heart.

"I am at your service, Exalted Lord."

But the farsensor dithered. "Where are we to *go?* The route to House Velteyn is cut off!" His abstracted expression showed that he was scanning about with his mind's eye.

"Well, we can't go back inside," said the most petite of the pleasure dome inmates, a black woman of exquisite contours and sharp voice. "The damn muffers are crawling out of the woodwork!"

"Oh, Lord Koliteyr," squealed a teary blonde. "Save us!"

"Silence!" commanded the Tanu. "I'm attempting to—but no one will respond to my summons!"

The third woman, thin and empty-eyed, her provocative attire half torn from her bony shoulders, sank down on the pavement and began to laugh.

Koliteyr gasped. "The dome is surrounded! I call—but Lord Velteyn's knights are in the thick of battle! . . . Hah! The invaders cringe and retreat before the coercive might of Tanu chivalry! The Goddess be thanked, there are many more powerful than I!"

A great jarring thump came from inside the pleasure dome. Distant cries became louder. More glass broke and a rhythmic pounding began.

"They're coming! The monsters are coming!" Once again, the blonde burst into hysterical tears.

"Soldier, you must lead us—" The Tanu scowled, shook his head as if to clear it. "Lead us to the Northern Watergate! There may be a boat—"

But it was too late. Across the garden, trampling flowerbeds and hurtling through the bushes came a force of twenty-odd Lowlife humans led by a half-naked red man of heroic stature.

Marshak's hand poised above his quiver, frozen. Most of the invaders had compound bows as good as his own held at the ready.

"Surrender!" shouted Peopeo Moxmox Burke. "Amnesty for all humans who yield freely to us!"

"Stand back!" cried the Tanu farsensor. "I—I will burn out your minds! Strike you mad!"

Chief Burke smiled, and his painted face, framed in straggling gray hair, was more menacing than the Firvulag phantasm had ever been. The exotic man knew that his bluff was useless, just as he knew there would be no amnesty for those of his race.

Commanding Marshak to defend to the death, Koliteyr tried to flee. The iron tomahawk spun and split the exotic's skull before he had taken two steps.

Marshak relaxed. He let the bow and arrow fall to the flagstones and watched the approaching Lowlives in numb silence.

* * *

The strategic importance of the barium mine had been made clear to Sharn-Mes at the Lowlife briefing session prior to the invasion. Humiliation of the hated Foe, the Firvulag general was made to understand, must take second place to the complete destruction of the mine and its trained personnel. It was vital to Madame Guderian's grand design that the supply of the precious element, indispensable in the manufacture of torcs, be cut off.

Shortly before noon, when Sharn was taking a breather with Bles and Nukalavee in a makeshift command post well supplied with liberated beer, a Firvulag scout arrived with important news. The Mighty Ayfa and her Warrior Ogresses had made a successful thrust from the eastern breach and now invested the sector around the mine workings. They had ascertained that molten rock, triggered by Claude's blast from the Spear, had plugged the mine entrance, buried the main refinery and the complex that housed the human and rama workers, and flowed some distance into the streets of the upper city before congealing. However, the mine administration building with its store of purified barium stood firm. The place was completely surrounded by black and steaming lava—now sheathed in a clinkery skin of cooled rock except where cracks revealed the red glowing interior. There were still Tanu engineers in the building, and among them a creator of the first rank. Ayfa and her force had gleaned this intelligence when an unexpected bolt of psychoenergy zapped one of the investigating ogresses to a cinder, narrowly missing the Dreadful Skathe. She of the snaggleteeth and dripping talons had spun a psychic shield over the survivors that sufficed for a disorderly retreat out of mindbolt range.

"And so the Mighty Ayfa," the scout concluded, "now awaits your suggestions, Great Captain."

Bles uttered a hoarse bleat of ironic laughter. He tipped half a barrelful of beer into his maw. "Ahh—let's go help the poor little ladies save their honor."

"Honor, my left testicle!" hissed Nukalavee. "If the Foeman's creative force strained the defenses of Skathe, then he is a worthy antagonist to any of us at a distance. We would expend our mindpower simply in the erection of screens and have little left for offense."

"Even the approach is fraught with danger," Sharn noted. "The crust of cooling lava, as this scout says, is fragile and may crack under the weight of a stalwart. You know our minds cannot penetrate dense rock deeply enough to strengthen the crust. And to fall through into the magma below is certain doom." He addressed himself to the dwarf messenger. "Pliktharn—how broad is the expanse of lava that would have to be crossed?"

"At least fivescore giant steps, Great Captain." Pliktharn's face became eager. "The crust would bear *my* weight easily!"

"You could send me and Nukalavee to mind-guard him, along with Ayfa and Skathe," Bles suggested. "The four of us working together have the range."

"And what happens when our brave gnomish brother reaches the mine building?" Nukalavee sneered. "How will he attack the Foe *through our own mental screens?* Four-Fang, you've worn that reptile suit so long that your wits are shrinking to fit your illusory brainpan!"

"The Great Captain Ayfa," cautioned the scout, "has perceived that the Tanu engineers are calling upon Lord Velteyn for help."

Sharn smacked a great hand onto the table. "Té's tonsils! And when he responds, he'll airlift them out, barium and all! We can't take that chance. I hate like hell to resort to Lowlife tactics—but there's only one way to handle this."

* * *

"Easy does it, lads!" Ayfa called out. "Don't lose your nerve now that you're almost there."

Homi, the little Singhalese iron-smelter, clutched Pliktharn's neck tighter. The lava crust bent as the Firvulag approached the lee of the mine building. There the flow was thicker and had held heat longer, which meant that the skin of cooled rock might crack and let them fall through to the magma at any moment.

About the incongruous pick-a-back figures shone a radiant hemisphere, the mental screen conjured by the joint power of Ayfa, Skathe, Bles, and Nukalavee. The four heroes, and most of the force of Warrior Ogresses, were concealed behind the sturdy walls of burnt-out townhouses, well back from the edge of the lava flow and a full 200 meters from the mine headquarters. Energy bolts flung by the trapped Tanu creator blazed from an upper-storey window, disintegrating into a web of lightnings as they were neutralized by the screen's potential. At length, Pliktharn and Homi reached a lower window and climbed inside. Ayfa, who was strong in the farsensing talent, observed what happened next.

"The three Foemen descend to the lower chamber, armed with vitredur geology picks! One of them has considerable coercive power. He's trying to force Pliktharn to lower the screen—but that won't work, of course. The mindbolt flinger now gathers his strength for one mighty thrust at point-blank range! He uses steady pressure rather than abrupt projection. Our screen wavers! It goes spectral—into the blue! The yellow! It will surely fail—! But now the Lowlife has his arbalest ready and aims at the creator. Ah! The missile of blood-metal passes through our weakening shield as through a curtain of rain! The Foeman falls! A second shot, and a third—and all of the Foe are downed!"

The four heroes leapt and the Warrior Ogresses whooped with joy in the triumph. All of their minds, even at the great distance, felt the death-flare of first one Tanu mind, then a second.

But the mindbolt flinger was strong even in the dying. Amplified, agonized, his thought thundered in the aether:

The Goddess will avenge us. Accursed through the world's age be those who resort to the blood-metal. A bloody tide will overwhelm them.

An instant later, his soul flickered out.

The Lowlife named Homi, having retrieved the three iron quarrels for reuse in his crossbow, appeared at the window and waved. Then he and Pliktharn set to work chipping and prying at the heavy limestone windowsill until its mortar gave way. The stone smashed the thin lava crust beneath the window, sending up a gush of smoke and flame. Before the fresh rift could heal, the human and the Firvulag were seen to toss certain small containers into the pit of molten rock, after which they climbed out a different window and made their way carefully back the way they had come.

* * *

A young girl clad in shiny black jogged in apparent tirelessness along the narrow Vosges jungle trail. Shadows grew deeper and a cool wind swept from the heights into the ravine that the footpath followed. Treefrogs were beginning their evening songs. Before long, the predators would awaken. After nightfall, there would be so many hostile creatures on the prowl that Felice would be unable to fend them off with her coercive power. She would be forced to bivouac and wait until dawn.

"And I'll be too late! The Truce starts at sunup and the war in Finiah will be over!"

How far had she come? Perhaps two-thirds of the 106 kilometers that lay between Hidden Springs and the western bank of the Rhine? She had lost so much time this morning before getting started, and the sun went down at eighteen hundred hours . . .

"Damn Richard! Damn him for getting hurt!"

She should have insisted on going with them in the flyer. She could have done *something*. Helped old Claude steady the Spear. Assisted Madame's mental defense. Even deflected the globe of ball lightning that had blinded Richard in one eye and caused him to crash the flyer.

"Damn him! Damn him! The Firvulag will quit fighting when the Truce begins and our people will have to withdraw. I'll be too late to get my golden torc! Too late!"

She splashed heedlessly across a small stream. Ravens, disturbed in their feeding upon some otter's leftovers, rose squawking into the vine-hung forest canopy. A hyena mocked her, its mad laugh echoing from the ravine wall.

Too late.

* * *

The glass carnyx of a fighting Tanu woman sounded the charge. Armored chalikos, bearing knights who coruscated each in a different jewel-color, galloped down the corpse-strewn boulevard toward the barricade where the contingent of Lowlives was making its stand.

"Na bardito! Na bardito!"

There were no Firvulag allies at hand to dampen the mental assault. Images of brain-searing intensity whipped and stabbed at the humans. The night was fraught with unspeakable menace and pain. Plunging exotics in their sparkling harness seemed to be coming from all directions, gorgeous and invulnerable. The humans loosed iron-tipped arrows, but skillful psychokinetics among the Tanu turned most of the fusillade aside, while the rest clattered harmlessly against the plates of the glass armor.

"The spooks! Where are the spooks?" howled a despairing Low-life. A moment later one of the knights crashed upon him, impaling his claw-torn body with a sapphire lance.

Of the sixty-three human beings who had made their stand in that street, only five escaped into the narrow alleys where hanging awn-ings, lines of washing, and crowded ranks of rubbish carts aban-doned by panicked rama sanitary workers made it impossible for the mounted Tanu to follow.

* * *

A mammoth bonfire was ablaze in the Central Plaza of Finiah. Ju-bilant phantoms in a hundred hideous guises capered around it, waving battle standards festooned with strings of freshly psycho-gilded skulls.

Khalid Khan protested. "They're wasting time, Mighty Sharn! Our people are taking a terrible beating when they meet the Tanu unsupported by Firvulag mind-cover. Even the mounted gray-torcs can cut right through our infantry. We've got to work together! And we must find some way to counter those chaliko-riders."

The great luminous scorpion bent over the turbaned Pakistani, multicolored organs within its translucent body throbbing to the rhythm of the exotic war chant.

"It has been many years since we had cause for celebration." The unhuman voice clanged in Khalid's brain. "For too long the Foe has lurked safely behind stout city walls, despising us. You do not un-derstand how it has been with us—the humiliation our race has suffered, draining our valor and driving even the most powerful of us to hopeless inaction. But behold! Look upon the trophy skulls, and these only a small proportion of the total!"

"And how many of them belong to Tanu? Dammit, Sharn—most of the enemy casualties have been among the torced and bareneck humans! The noncombatant Tanu are all holed up in House Vel-teyn where we can't reach them, and only a handful of their mounted knights have been killed!"

"The Tanu chivalry"—the eerie voice hesitated and then made reluctant admission—"presents a formidable challenge to us. Armored war steeds with their minds held in thrall by the riders are not intimidated by our horrific illusions or shape-shifting. We must contend against them physically, and not all of the Firvulag company are of heroic frame. Our obsidian weapons—our swords, halberds, chainflails, and throwing spears—are not often effective against chaliko cavalry in the Grand Combat. And the same obtains in this battle."

"You need a change in tactics. There are ways for foot soldiers to put down charging horsemen." The metalsmith's teeth glittered in a brief grin. "My ancestors, Pathan hillmen, knew how!"

The response of the Firvulag general was cool. "Our battle customs are fixed by sacred tradition."

"No wonder you're losers! The Tanu weren't afraid to innovate, to take advantage of human science. Now you Firvulag have human allies on your side—and you stick one timid little toe into the battlefield and then mess about singing and dancing instead of going for the prize!"

"Beware lest I punish your insolence, Lowlife!" But the furious retort lacked conviction.

Khalid said softly, "Would you help *us* if we try a new tactic? Would you shield our minds while we try to knock those long-shanked bastards out of the saddle?"

"Yes . . . we would do that."

"Then pay close attention."

The monster scorpion metamorphosed into a handsome young ogre wearing a thoughtful scowl. After a few minutes the hobgoblins left off their madcap dancing, changed into gnomish warriors, and crowded in to listen.

* * *

Converting Sharn's lieutenants proved to be more difficult. Khalid had to engineer a demonstration. He rounded up ten volunteer Lowlives equipped with iron-tipped javelins and led them to the approaches of House Velteyn, where gray-torc and Tanu riders guarded the ultimate sanctuary. The paved avenue was lit by widely spaced torchères. No other invaders were to be seen because of the heavy concentration of defenders. Sharn and six of his Great Ones lurked in the shelter of a deserted mansion while Khalid deliberately led his squad of spearmen into plain sight of a patrolling gray troop.

The human leader, fully armored in blue glass, drew his vitredur blade and led a charge at the gallop down the cobblestone street. Instead of scattering, the Lowlives drew closely together, forming a tight phalanx bristling with four-meter spears.

The patrol swerved to the right at the last instant to avoid crashing into the iron porcupine, individual troopers reining up and wheeling their mounts about so that they could strike with longsword or battle-axe. They were plainly nonplussed, since almost all of the antagonists they had encountered thus far had emulated the Firvulag maneuver of tossing their pole-arms and then fleeing. This pack of innovators stood their ground until the animals were off balance in the turn, then stabbed deep into the unarmored bellies of the huge clawed beasts.

The hideous pain of disembowelment overrode the mind-control exerted by each rider upon his mount. Wounded chalikos stumbled and fell—or went careening off in a frenzy while the troopers hung on for their lives. Khalid's warriors pounced upon the unhorsed, dispatching them with spear or blade. Five minutes after the initiation of the attack, every member of the gray troop was either dead or had fled.

"But will it work on the Foe?" inquired Betularn of the White Hand skeptically. With Pallol Battlemaster a nonparticipant, he was the doyen of Firvulag stalwarts, and his opinion counted for much.

Khalid grinned at the beetle-browed giant while one of his comrades tried to staunch bleeding arm and leg wounds with torn strips of the dead captal's cloak. "It will work on the Tanu, providing we take them by surprise. We must assemble as many Lowlives and Firvulag as possible for a massed thrust against House Velteyn. Those of our people who don't have spears will improvise them from bamboo awning poles. We needn't use iron to gut the chalikos—but each human fighter will have to have an iron weapon to use against downed Tanu riders. And *your* people will have to be right in the thick of things beside ours, handling mind-defense and getting in whatever licks they can."

The venerable warrior shook his head slowly. He said to Sharn, "This is contrary to our Way, as you know, Great Captain. But the Foe has defied tradition for more than forty years." The other five Great Ones growled assent. "We have prayed to the Goddess for a chance to recoup our honor. And so I say . . . let us essay the Lowlife tactic. And her will be done."

* * *

Long after midnight, with smoke from the burning city blotting out the stars and the untended torchères guttering low, Lowlives and Little People gathered for the grand assault. In a rare display of cooperative virtuosity, the best of the Firvulag illusion-spinners wove a curtain of confusion to deceive the farsensing Foe. The Tanu besieged within House Velteyn knew that the enemy was up to something, but the nature of the assault remained in doubt.

The Lord of Finiah himself, aloft once again with several of his most trusted tacticians, made pass after pass at low altitude, attempting to discern the plan of the invaders; but the metapsychic shimmer was just dense enough to defeat his farsight. He beheld the Foe massed opposite the main portal of his palace. There were to be no feints, no multipronged storming of the several entrances—that much was self-evident. With typical Firvulag singlemindedness, Sharn seemed to be gambling everything on a last great frontal assault.

Velteyn sent the telepathic order on the intimate mode to each knight commander, and these in turn transmitted the Lord's words to their subordinates:

"To the forecourt! Let all the noble Tanu battle company, all of our adopted kinfolk of the gold and silver torc, all loyal and valiant gray soldiery attend! The Foemen gather for their final push. Let us destroy them body and soul! Na bardito! Forward, fighters of the Many-Colored Land!"

All aglow and exalted with battle ardor, the Tanu chivalry charged in a mass against the indistinct, dense groups of advancing Foe. The screens of confusion snapped off in the last seconds before contact to reveal the deadly pincushions of spears—many of them iron. With mental weapons all but neutralized by the Firvulag, the Tanu unshipped their pennoned lances and sent their mounts caracoling about the flanks of the hedgehog formations, alert for the expected rain of flung spears. And thus the treacherous novelty caught them completely unawares.

Velteyn, from his vantage point in the sky, could only farwatch aghast in those early minutes of slaughter. Then he dove his mount down, bombarding the enemy with all the psychoenergy he could muster. His mind and voice rallied the shattered ranks.

"Abandon your animals! Let all fight afoot! Creators and psychokinetics—raise shields for your fellows! Coercers—compel all grays and silvers to stand fast! Beware the blood-metal!"

The vast courtyard and immediate palace grounds were now a surging mass of bodies. Dull-red flashes signaled Firvulag and Tanu mind-screens interfacing in mutual collapse, after which the antagonists might fight hand to hand—with perfidious Lowlives attacking with the iron at every opportunity. The merest prick from the blood-metal meant death to a Tanu. Human gold-torcs, of course, could be wounded by the blood-metal, but not mortally poisoned. Velteyn's heart warmed at the bravery shown by the gold adoptees, many of whom seized iron weapons and turned them against the Firvulag.

Unfortunately, it was otherwise with the grays and silvers. The discipline of the torc faded in the face of diminished coercion from beleaguered Tanu overlords. The lower echelons among the human levies were unmanned by the demoralizing sight of Tanu knights falling to the iron. Both Firvulag and Lowlives seized the advantage and decimated the ranks of the terror-stricken troops.

For three hours, Velteyn hovered above the battlefield, invisible except to his own forces, directing the ultimate defense of his City of Lights. If they could only hold out until dawn—until the start of the Truce! But as the sky beyond the Black Forest massif paled, two powerful bodies of the Foe, spearheaded by Bles Four-Fang and Nukalavee, made a great press and reached the palace gate.

"Fall back!" Velteyn cried. "Stand and defend the portal!"

The jewel-armored knights did their utmost, wreaking a fearful toll of dwarfs and humanity as they laid about with their glowing two-handed swords. Sooner or later, however, an iron dart would find a chink of vulnerability at groin or armpit or the back of a knee—and another brave warrior would attain Tana's peace.

Velteyn groaned aloud, overwhelmed by sorrow and rage. The doors of his palace were giving way. There was no course left but the evacuation of the noncombatants via the roof with the help of the sad-eyed little human PK adept, Sullivan-Tonn. By Tana's grace, the two of them might save most of the nearly 700 trapped Tanu civilians while the knights staved off the invading horde in the stronghold corridors.

If only he could die with them! But that release was forbidden to the humiliated Lord of Finiah. He was going to live on, and he was going to have to explain all of this to the King.

* * *

Peopeo Moxmox Burke slumped against the roof parapet of House Velteyn, letting fatigue and reaction sweep over him. Gert and Hansi and a few other Lowlives beat the bushes of the roof garden and searched the ornate penthouse for hidden Tanu. But they found only the discarded baggage the fugitives had left behind—spilled pouches of jewelry, heavy embroidered cloaks and fantastic headgear, broken flagons of perfume, a single ruby-glass gauntlet.

"No sign of 'em, Chief," Hansi said. "Ganz ausgeflogen. They've flown the coop."

"Get back downstairs, then," Burke ordered. "See that all the rooms are checked out—and the dungeons, too. If you see Uwe or Black Denny, send them to me. We'll have to coordinate the looting."

"Check, Chief." The men clattered away down the broad marble stairway. Burke raised one leg of his buckskin trousers and kneaded the puckered flesh around the healing scar. With the anesthetic of battle fury worn off, it hurt like hell; and there was a long cut on his bare back and about forty-seven bruises and abrasions that were also making themselves known. But he was in pretty good shape, for all that. The rest of the Lowlife army should be so lucky.

One of the fleeing evacuees had left behind a basket with wine and breadrolls. Sighing, the Chief began to eat and drink. In the streets below, Firvulag were gathering their wounded and their dead and forming long processions on their way to the Rhine watergates. Bobbing lanterns out on the river marked the position of small boats that had already begun the withdrawal in anticipation of the dawn. Here and there among the burning ruins stubborn human loyalists continued a futile resistance. Madame Guderian had warned Burke that the humans living in Finiah might prove less than grateful for their liberation. She had been right, as usual. There were interesting times ahead, damn it.

Sighing once again, he finished the wine, gave his stiffening muscles a stretch, then took up a discarded Tanu shawl to wipe off his warpaint.

* * *

Moe Marshak shuffled a few steps forward in line.

"Quit crowding, big boy," snarled the lovely dark-skinned woman from the pleasure dome. The other two inmates had not worn gray torcs and were long gone, led away to the sailing lighters that shuttled back and forth between Finiah and the Vosges shore. The promise of amnesty was being kept by the Lowlives. But if you were a human torc wearer, there was a catch.

Marshak knew all about the activity of the drumhead tribunal, of course. He was in telepathic communion with all of the grays within his range who had not deliberately shut him out—as the black woman had. The Tanu, givers of delight and power, were gone. As they had wafted away to the east, they had reached out in poignant farewell, caressing and commiserating and sending a final warm surge flooding the neural networks of those who had been faithful, so that the gray-torc prisoners had an illusion of celebration in place of grief and despair. Even now, at the end, they could comfort one another. The kinship remained. None of them was alone—except by choice.

The black woman stood before the judges, her eyes bright. When the question came, she almost screamed her reply: "Yes! Yes, by God! Do it! Give me back my self again!"

Lowlife guards led her through a door to the right of the tribunal. The rest of the grays, mourning the sister's defection but respecting her choice, reached out one last time. She defied them all, placed her head on the block. The great mallet smote the iron chisel and there was overpowering pain. And silence.

Now Marshak's turn came. As a man dreaming, he told the Lowlife judges his name, his former occupation in the Milieu, the date of his passage through the time-portal. The oldest of the judges pronounced the formula.

"Moe Marshak, as a wearer of the gray torc, you have been held in bondage by an exotic race and compelled to abet the enslavement of humanity. Your Tanu overlords have been defeated by the Alliance of Freeliving Humans and Firvulag. As a prisoner of war, you are entitled to amnesty, provided that you agree to the removal of the torc. If you do not agree, you will be executed. Please make your choice."

He chose.

Every nerve in his body seemed to ignite. Kindred minds sang as they gave consolation. Steadfast, he reaffirmed the unity and a great rejoicing flare obliterated all other sensation: the sight of the hollow-eyed judges, the pressure of hands that gripped and dragged him away, the penetration of his heart by the long blade, and the final cold embrace of the River Rhine.

* * *

Richard stood in the dim little log chapel in Hidden Springs village where they had laid Martha out, seeing her in a swimming reddish haze even though Amerie had tried to reassure him that his right eye was virtually undamaged.

He wasn't angry. Disappointed, that was all, because Marty had promised to wait. Hadn't they planned it all together? Hadn't they loved each other? It wasn't like her to let him down after all they'd been through together.

Well, he would work something out.

Wincing a little from the bandaged burns, he gathered her into his arms. So light, so white. All gowned in white. He almost fell as he pushed the door open. No depth perception with only one eye. "Doesn't matter," he told her. "I can wear a patch like a real pirate. Just you hang on."

He went lurching toward the place where the flyer stood, covered by camouflage netting, one landing strut broken and one wing partly crushed by his prang-in. But a gravo-mag ship didn't need wings to fly. It was still in good enough shape to take both of them where they wanted to go.

Amerie spotted him just as he was lifting Martha inside. She came running, her nun's veil and robes billowing. "Richard! Stop!"

Oh, no you don't, he thought. I did what I promised. Now it's you guys who owe *me*.

With the flyer tilted, it was tricky to maneuver Martha. He made her comfortable and tossed the Spear out, powerpack and all. Maybe some wisehead would figure out how to recharge it some day. Then Madame Guderian could get another flyer and go zap all the rest of the Tanu cities and make Pliocene Earth safe for good old humanity.

"Just don't call me to drive the bus," he muttered. "I've got other plans."

"Richard!" the nun shouted again.

He waved to her from the flight deck port and sat down in the charred seat. Close hatch. Light up. Juice to the external web. Camouflage netting burning away. Oh-oh. Environmental system in the amber. Shorted by the lightning, maybe. Well . . . it would last long enough.

The soothing hum filled his brain as he brought the ship up level. He glanced back at Marty to be sure that she was still safe. Her form wavered, seemed to go red. But in a moment it was all right, and he told her, "I'll take us up nice and slow. We've got all the time in the world."

* * *

Amerie watched the broken-winged bird rise vertically into the golden morning sky, following the first component of the sign she traced. The mist was gone now and it was going to be a beautiful day. Over in the east the smoke cloud was thickening, but upper-level winds carried it in the opposite direction.

The aircraft ascended until it was a mere speck. Amerie blinked, and the speck became invisible against the bright vault of the heavens.

* * *

THE END OF PART THREE

*Volume II of The Saga of Pliocene Exile,
entitled* THE GOLDEN TORC, *tells of the
adventures of the other four members of
Group Green in the Tanu capital city, and
of their reunion with the northerners in an
attempt to accomplish the final phases of
Madame Guderian's plan to liberate
Pliocene humanity.*

APPENDIXES

Some Notes on "The Tanu Song"

THE ENGLISH WORDS to The Tanu Song, appearing on page 248 of this volume, are freely adapted from *Gods and Fighting Men: The Story of the Tuatha de Danaan and of the Fianna of Ireland,* a compendium of Celtic myth translated and "arranged" by Lady Augusta Gregory (New York: Charles Scribner's Sons, 1904). She tells some of the adventures of a race of heroic faeries or gods, the People of Dana or Men of Dea, who were said to have come to Ireland "from the north" in times implied to be late pre-Christian or early Christian. Her tales are part of the greater body of Celtic mythology originally engendered on continental Europe at a much earlier date.

One section of Lady Gregory's book tells the adventures of the god Manannan the Proud, who was said to have established other members of his race in Ireland, after which he himself disappeared—only to pop up again from time to time, playing tricks and making sweet music. Chapter 10 of *Gods and Fighting Men* tells how Manannan sent a faerie woman to summon one Bran, son of Febal, to his current abode in the Land of Women, also called Emhain (Aven) of Many-Colored Hospitality. The woman sings the following song to Bran:

I bring a branch of the apple-tree from Emhain, from the far island around which are the shining horses of the Son of Lir [Manannan].

A delight of the eyes is the plain where the hosts hold their games; curragh racing against chariot in the White Silver Plain to the south.

There are feet of white bronze under it, shining through life and time; a comely level land through the length of the world's age, and many blossoms falling on it.

There is an old tree there with blossoms, and birds calling from among them; every color is shining there, delight is common, and music, in the Gentle-Voiced Plain, in the Silver Cloud Plain to the south.

Keening is not used, or treachery, in the tilled familiar land; there is nothing hard or rough, but sweet music striking on the ear.

To be without grief, without sorrow, without death, without any sickness, without weakness; that is the sign of Emhain; it is not common wonder that is.

There is nothing to liken its mists to; the sea washes the wave against the land; brightness falls from its hair.

There are riches, there are treasures of every color in the Gentle Land, the Bountiful Land. Sweet music to be listening to; the best of wine to drink.

Golden chariots in the Plain of the Sea, rising up to the sun with the tide; silver chariots and bronze chariots on the Plain of Sports.

Gold-yellow horses on the strand, and crimson horses, and others with wool on their backs, blue like the color of the sky.

It is a day of lasting weather, silver is dropping on the land; a pure white cliff on the edge of the sea, getting its warmth from the sun.

The host race over the Plain of Sports; it is beautiful and not weak their game is; death or the ebbing of the tide will not come to them in the Many-Colored Land.

There will come at sunrise a fair man, lighting up the level lands; he rides upon the plain that is beaten by the waves, he stirs the sea till it is like blood.

An army will come over the clear sea, rowing to the stone that is in sight, that a hundred sounds of music come from.

It sings a song to the army; it is not sad through the length of time; it increases music with hundreds singing together; they do not look for death or the ebb-tide . . .

From this felicitous fragment (which unfortunately continues with the rather dull adventures of Bran and his comrades in Emhain, where they ultimately meet disaster), and from the first three paragraphs of Lady Gregory's first chapter, which list the names and attributes of the principal Celtic gods, I derived a fragile skeleton for *The Many-Colored Land* and *The Golden Torc*, its culminating sequel. The actual plot of the saga, needless to say, has no basis in folklore; but students of mythology will recognize elements borrowed not only from the Celts but also from the fairy tales of nearly a dozen other European nations. The exotic people are all given names derived from those of the heroic faeries, with attributes that may or may not match the originals; the archetypal human characters Aiken Drum, Felice Landry, and Mercy Lamballe are also out of Celtica, via Jung and Joseph Campbell, among others. Folkloric bits purveyed by the character Bryan Grenfell are all authentic; especially noteworthy is the almost universal theme of the anima-menace—the faerie woman who snatches mortal men and wreaks her passionate will on them until they are drained husks. She shows up in tales from the Balearics to Russia.

The musical setting for The Tanu Song, which follows, is my own simplified adaptation of that mysterious melody, "Londonderry Air," which is purportedly of faerie authorship. This version, arranged for four human voices (SATB with divisi), varies somewhat from that which the exotics would sing. Their voices possessed richer overtones than those of humanity; and they were fond of dissonances and "violations" of human harmonic theory that sound weird, to say the least, when essayed by a human chorus. Only a few of these musical oddities have been included in the arrangement.

Among the Tanu, The Song was sung as a solo or in double chorus. On the rare occasions when Tanu and Firvulag sang together, such as the Grand Combat featured in *The Golden Torc*, the full grandeur of the exotic music was made manifest. The Little People used different words in their own dialect; and more important, they used different phrasing and at least four separate contrapuntal melody lines, which twined and writhed through the fabric of the basic Tanu harmonies in a richly complex polychoral effect. I must leave to more skilled hands the transcription of The Firvulag Song proper, as well as its musical marriage with the version sung by the Tanu.

The traditional "Londonderry Air" has perhaps the most eccentric history of any Irish melody. It does not fit any known Irish meter, and its history, as detailed by Anne G. Gilchrist in *English Folk Dance and Song Society Journal* (December 1932, p. 115), is a cloudy one. The air was first published in 1855 by George Petrie in *Ancient Music of Ireland,* noted "name unknown" and having no words. After the song appeared in Petrie's collection, its striking beauty led many arrangers to try to fit words to it. The best-known and most adequate version is "Danny Boy" (1913), with lyrics by Frederick E. Weatherly. Most public-domain songbooks use turgid lyrics composed by Katharine Tynan Hinkson (b. 1861) beginning: "Would God I were the tender apple blossom/That floats and falls from off the twisted bough,/To lie and faint within your silken bosom,/Within your silken bosom, as that does now." An equally unsingable version with slightly more dignity is "Emer's Farewell to Cucullain" (1882), with words by Alfred Percival Graves in a setting by C. Villiers Stanford. This begins: "O might a maid confess her secret longing/To one who dearly loves but may not speak!/Alas! I had not hidden to thy wronging/A bleeding heart beneath a smiling cheek."

The original melody in Petrie's collection came from a Miss Jane Ross of Limavady in the Northern Irish country of Londonderry. The lady arranged it for the piano herself and simply commented to Dr. Petrie that it was "very old." Unfortunately, later researchers were unable to find any trace of its origins, nor were there any Gaelic words to it. The fact that its meter was "wrong" for Irish folksong made it even more suspect, and some denied that it was a trditional melody at all.

Gilchrist tracked down relatives of Miss Ross and established that she was indeed a serious student of folksong, dedicated and honest. She collected some melodies herself, and others came from her brother, who fished in neighboring County Donegal. Both regions are known for preserving ancient bits of Irish culture.

It would seem, then, that we can discount the possibility of Miss Ross's palming off one of her own compositions as a traditional air. The problem of the atypical meter is ingeniously attacked by Gilchrist, who suggests that Miss Ross might have erroneously transcribed the tune in common (4/4) time rather than in the 3/4 or 6/8 rhythm of the majority of old Gaelic songs. If the rhythm is thus changed, and certain prolonged notes shortened, one does indeed get a typical Irish ditty of rather appalling banality. Gilchrist claims to see affinities between the transmogrification and two other songs, "The Colleen Rue" and "An Beanuasal Og."

If Miss Ross did err, we can only bless her for the inadvertent modification that brought musical immortality to what would have otherwise been a forgettable jig. If, on the other hand, she did record the air faithfully, then its provenance is a mystery still. We can only fall back upon the whimsical opinion that ascribes the haunting song to faerie folk—whoever they might have been.

The Tanu Song

WORDS BY JULIAN MAY

Andante

FOR FOUR LOW VOICES

Ancient Celtic Melody
Adapted and Arranged by
JULIAN MAY

Li gan nol po'-kône nié-si, ____ 'Kône o
Li gan nol ____ kône nié-si, 'Kone o

lan li pred né-ar, ____ U tay-nel com-pri la
lan ____ pred né-ar, U tay-nel com-pri la

neyn, Ni ble-pan al-gar de-dône. ____ Shom-pri
neyn, ____ pan al-gar de-dône. ____ Shom pri

pône, ____ a gab-ri-nel, Shal u car ____ me-tan pre-
pône ____ car ____ me-tan pre-

si, ____ Nar me-tan u bor tay-nel o po-ge-kône, Car me-
si, ____ Nar me-tan u bor tay-nel o po-ge po-ge-kône, Car ____

tan ___ sed gône mo- ri. _____ Ah po-ge-

Car me-tan ____ gône mo - ri. _____

kône, u bor tay-nel o po-ge-kône, ____ U bor tay-

nel, u bor tay-nel o po-ge- kône. _____

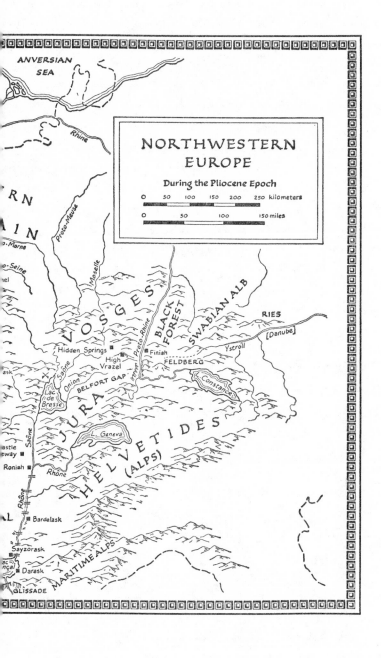

ANVERSIAN
SEA

Rhine

NORTHWESTERN
EUROPE

During the Pliocene Epoch

0   50   100   150   200   250 kilometers

0   50   100   150 miles

R N

I N

Proto-Meuse

o-Marne

o-Seine

nel

Moselle

V O S G E S

BLACK FOREST

SWABIAN ALB

RIES

[Danube]

Hidden Springs

High Vrazel

Finiah

Proto-Rhine

FELDBERG

Ystroll

J U R A

Saône

Onion

BELFORT GAP

Constance

Lac de Bresse

ask

L. Geneva

H E L V E T I D E S

(ALPS)

astle eway

Ronish

Saône

Rhône

Rhône

L

Bardelask

Sayzorask

ac ncal

Darask

MARITIME ALPS

GLISSADE

The Golden Torc

VOLUME II IN
THE SAGA OF PLIOCENE EXILE

For Barbara,
nurse and redactor and sternman

Open the door to us, and we will see the orchards,
We will drink their cold water where the moon
   has left its trace.
The long road burns, hostile to strangers.
We wander without knowing and find no place . . .

Before us is the door; what use for us to wish?
Better to turn away, abandoning hope.
We will never enter. We are weary of seeing it.
The door, opening, let so much silence escape

That neither the orchards appeared nor any flower;
Only the immense space where emptiness and light are
Was suddenly everywhere present, overflowed the heart,
And washed our eyes almost blind under the dust.

"The Threshold," Simone Weil
translated by William Burford

Contents

PART I

The Mésalliance

1

THE DRAGONFLY HOVERED, a golden spark, just above the bare mast of the motionless boat.

As the first breezes broke the water with cat's-paw dimpling, the dragonfly darted off. He zoomed powerfully into the sky and hovered once again. The boat below him was now transformed into a lonely speck amid a pastel expanse of shallow lagoons and saltflats, all blurred in pearly mist.

Higher! His shape-shifted wings lofted him into the dawn. Keen compound eyes that covered most of his head showed him the continental slope's dark rampart along the northern horizon: the brink of Europe punctuated by a single towering cloud that marked the cascade of the Rhône River, pouring down a vast slope of sediment into the nearly waterless Mediterranean Basin of Pliocene Earth that was called the Empty Sea.

Should he fly toward the mainland? His wings had the strength to carry him more than 100 kilometers per hour for brief sprints. He knew it would be easy for him to retrace the journey the boat had made on the previous day; or he could fly eastward to the upthrust mass of Corsica-Sardinia, where Creyn had said no Tanu lived.

He could go anywhere he liked. He was free now.

Gone were the mental restraints programmed upon him by the exotic slavemaster. This morning when he awoke, the silver torc at his throat was cold rather than warm, the neural circuitry of the psychocoercive device overloaded and rendered useless by his mind's new power. The metapsychic latencies that the torc had unlocked remained operant. And were still growing.

He reached out with his farsense, listening. He perceived the slow-cycling rhythms of the seven people asleep in the craft beneath him, and farther afield, telepathic murmurs from other boats scattered about the Great Lagoon. In the distant south—he concentrated his farsense, clumsily attempting fine focus—was a conglomerate mental shimmer. Fascinating! Could it be coming from the Tanu capital city of Muriah, the goal toward which they had been traveling these past five days?

If he gave a hail, would anyone down there answer? Try!

There came a hard bright response, shocking in its eagerness:

O *shining boymind who?*

Well . . . Aiken Drum that's who.

Hold still littlemind so far yet so glowing. Ah!

No. Stop that—!

Do not pull away Shining One. What can you be?

Let go dammit!

Do not withdraw *I think I know you* . . .

Suddenly, he was overcome by an unprecedented fear. That distant unknown was locking onto him, coming at him in some manner down the pathway of his own mind's beam. He pulled away from the grasp and discovered too late that it was going to take almost all of his strength to sever the connection. He tore free. He found himself falling through thin air, his dragonfly shape shifted back to vulnerable humanity. Wind whistled in his ears. He plunged toward the boat, mind and voice screaming, and only managed to regain control and the insect form a scant moment before disaster. Trembling and funked out, he settled to the tip of the mast.

His projected panic had awakened the others. The boat began to rock, generating concentric ripples in the pale lagoon. Elizabeth and Creyn emerged from the covered passenger compartment to stare at him; and Raimo, with an expression of bleary incomprehension on his upturned face; and scowling Stein, with worried little Sukey; and Highjohn, the skipper, who yelled, "I know that's you up there, Aiken Drum! God help you if you've been playing any of your tricks with my boat!"

The boatman's shout brought out the last passenger, the torcless anthropologist, Bryan Grenfell, who was feeling testy and was aware of none of the telepathic querying now being hurled at the dragonfly by the others. "Is it necessary to rock the boat quite so much?"

"Aiken, come down," Creyn said aloud.

"Not bloody likely," the dragonfly replied. Wings abuzz, the insect prepared to flee.

The Tanu raised one slender hand in an ironic gesture. "Fly away, then, you fool. But be sure you understand what you're renouncing. It makes no difference that you've escaped the torc. We were expecting that. Allowances have been made. Special privileges have been arranged for you in Muriah."

A doubting laugh. "I've already had a little hint of *that.*"

"So?" Creyn was unconcerned. "If you'd kept your wits about you, you'd know that you have nothing to fear from Mayvar. On the contrary! But make no mistake—even without the silver torc, she is able to detect you now, wherever you might go. Running away would be the worst mistake you could possibly make. There's nothing for you out there, all alone. Your fulfillment lies with us, in Muriah. Now come down. It's time we resumed our journey. We should arrive in the capital tonight, and you can judge for yourself whether or not I've told the truth."

Abruptly, the tall exotic man withdrew into the passenger compartment. The small group of humans remained on deck, gaping.

"Oh—what the hell," said the dragonfly.

It spiraled down, landed at the skipper's feet, and became a little man clad in a gold-fabric costume all covered with pockets. Self-confidence completely restored, Aiken Drum grinned his golliwog grin.

"Maybe I *will* stick around awhile. For as long as it suits me."

* * *

That evening, when the throng of Tanu riders came to welcome the boat to the shores of Aven, Bryan could think of only a single thing: that Mercy might be somewhere among the exotic cavalcade. And so he rushed from one side of the boat to the other while a team of twenty stout helladotheria, looking something like giant okapis, were hitched to the craft in preparation for its being hauled up the long rollered way to Muriah. There was a bright gibbous moon. A kilometer or so above the docks, which lay on a saltflat surrounded by weathered masses of striped evaporite, the Tanu capital city glittered on the dark peninsular height like an Earthbound galaxy.

"Mercy!" Bryan called. "Mercy, I'm here!"

There were numbers of human men and women riding together with the tall exotics, dressed, like them, either in faceted and spiked glass armor or richly jeweled gauze robes. The flameless torches that they carried cast beams of many colors. The riders laughed at Bryan and ignored the questions that he tried to shout amidst the tumult of the hitching.

So many of the human women perched on the great chalikos seemed to have auburn hair! Again and again Bryan strained to catch a closer glimpse of a likely one. But always when the beautiful rider approached it was not Mercy Lamballe—nor even one who really looked like her.

Aiken Drum stood on one of the boat seats posturing like a gilded puppet, throwing out teasing or challenging quips that provoked exotic hilarity and increased the bedlam. The Finno-Canadian woodsman, Raimo Hakkinen, hung over the pneumatic gunwale of the boat kissing the proffered hands of the ladies and toasting the men with swigs from his silver flask. In contrast, Stein Oleson sat back in the shadows with one huge arm curved protectively around Sukey, both of them apprehensive.

Skipper Highjohn came to stand beside Bryan in the bows. He fingered the gray torc around his neck and laughed out loud. "We'll be on our way any minute now, Bryan. What a welcome! I've never seen anything like it. Just look at your tricky little gold friend up there! They'll have a hell of a time taming that one—if they ever do!"

Bryan looked at the smiling brown face blankly. "What? I'm—I'm sorry, Johnny. I wasn't listening. I thought I saw—someone. A woman I once knew."

With kind firmness the boatman pressed the anthropologist down onto one of the benches. Teamsters whipped up the hellads and the boat began to roll, accompanied by cheers and a bell-loud clangor from the escort, some of whom were beating their gem-studded shields with glowing swords. From nearly a hundred throats and minds came the Tanu Song, its melody oddly familiar to Bryan, for all that the words were alien:

Li gan nol po'kône niési,
'Kône o lan li pred néar,
U taynel compri la neyn,
Ni blepan algar dedône.

Shompri pône, a gabrinel,
Shal u car metan presi,
Nar metan u bor taynel o pogekône,
Car metan sed gône mori.

Bryan's fingers dug into the boat's splashcover fabric. The fantastic panoply of riders swirled along the towpath as the boat mounted a long slope. There was no vegetation this close to the salty lagoon, but eroded lumps and pillars of mineral loomed in the wavering shadows like the ruins of some elfin palace. The train entered a depression between steep cliffs and bright Muriah disappeared from view. The hellad-drawn boat and its faerie escort seemed to move toward a black tunnel mouth flanked by huge broken cherubim. The Song echoed from overlooming walls.

An old imagery reasserted itself to Bryan. A cave—deep and dark—and a loved thing lost inside. He was a small boy and the time was six million years into the future: in England, in the Mendip Hills where the family had a cottage. And his kitten, Cinders, wandered off, and he searched for three days. And finally he had stumbled upon the entrance to the little cave, barely large enough for his eight-year-old body to wriggle through. He had stood staring at the fetid black hole for more than an hour, knowing that he should search it but terrified at the thought.

In the end, he had taken a small electric torch and wormed his way in. The passage twisted and angled downward. Scratched by sharp stones and nearly breathless with fear, he had slithered on. The stench from bat droppings was dreadful. All daylight vanished at a turn in the narrowing corridor; and then the crack opened into a deep cavern, too large to be illuminated by his little flashlight. He aimed the beam downward and saw no bottom. "Cinders!" he called, and his boy's voice reverberated in broken wails. There was a horrid rustle and a faint sound of squeaking. From the cave roof high above, a mist of acrid bat urine drifted down upon him.

Choking and retching, he had tried to turn around, but the crevice was too narrow. There was nothing for it but to back out on his stomach, tears streaming down his cheeks, knowing that at any moment the bats might fly into his face and sink their teeth into nose and lips and cheeks and ears.

He dropped the torch as he hunched along. Maybe the light would frighten the bats. He kept going, centimeter by centimeter backward over rough stones, his knees and elbows getting rawer.

The passage would never end! It was already much longer than it had been when he entered! And it was tighter, too, squeezing him beneath unimaginable tons of black rock until he knew it would press away his life . . .

He came out.

Too weak even to sob, he had lain there until the sun was low. When he was able to get up and stagger home, he found Cinders lapping a saucer of cream in the back garden. The ghastly trip into the cave had been for nothing.

"I hate you!" he had screamed, bringing his mother on the run. But by the time she reached him he was cradling the black kitten against his bruised and filthy cheek, stroking it while the sound of its purring helped slow his thudding heart.

Cinders had lived another fifteen years, fat and complacent, while Bryan's boyish devotion to the animal dwindled away into vague fondness. But he would live forever with the horror of the loved thing lost, the fear and the gush of hate at the end because his bravery had been wasted. And now he was entering another chasm . . .

The friendly voice of the skipper drew him back. "The lady you're looking for. Did they tell you she was down here in Muriah?"

"An interviewer back at Castle Gateway recognized her picture. He said she had been sent here. Creyn seemed to hint that if I cooperated with the local authorities along professional lines, she and I might—meet."

He hesitated only for a moment before unbuttoning his breast pocket and taking out the durofilm sheet. Highjohn stared at Mercy's self-luminous portrait.

"What a beautiful, haunted face! I don't know who she is *here*, Bry, but then I'm on the river most of the time. God knows I'd never forget her if I ever did catch sight of her. Those eyes—! You poor bastard."

"You can say that again, Johnny."

"Why did she come here?" the skipper asked.

"I don't know. Ridiculous, isn't it, Johnny? I knew her only a single day. And then I had to leave her for some work that seemed to be important. When I returned, she was gone. All I could do was follow after. It was the only choice open to me. Do you understand?"

"Sure, Bry. I understand. My own reasons for coming weren't that different. Except that no one was waiting . . . But there's something you've got to expect, when you do find her. She'll be changed."

"She was a latent. They'll have given her a silver torc. I'm aware of that."

The big riverman shook his head slowly. Once again he touched his own gray necklet. "There's more to it than a latent's becoming operant—although God knows, acquiring metafaculties all of a sudden has its hazards, so I'm told. But even us grays—without getting any metafunctions to speak of—gain something fantastic through this torc. Something that we never had before." He pursed his thin purplish lips, then suddenly exclaimed, "*Listen,* man! What do you hear?"

"They're singing in their Tanu language."

"And to you, the words mean nothing. But to us collared ones, the Song says well-met, and fear-not, and this-is-it, and we-you-us! When a human being becomes part of the torced society, he gains a whole new level of consciousness. Even us grays, with no operant metafunctions, can share in it. It's more than telepathy—although that's a part of it. It's a whole new form of social intercourse, this mind-to-mind intimacy. How the hell can I explain it? Like being a member of some kind of superfamily. You know you belong to this great thing that keeps rolling along and taking you with it. You'll never be alone in your pain again. Never be outside. Never be rejected. Any time you need strength or comfort, you can dip into the collective *resource*. It's not a smothering thing because you can take as much or as little of it as you choose—well, subject to limitations unless you're a gold-wearer. You obey orders, just like in the service . . . But what I'm trying to tell you is that wearing these things changes you deep inside. It doesn't happen right away, but it does happen. As you wear the torc, you're educated whether you want to be or not. Your lady is going to be a different person from the one you remember."

"She might not want me. Is that what you're trying to prepare me for?"

"I don't know her, Bry. People react in different ways to the torcs. Some of them bloom. Most of them."

The anthropologist did not meet the skipper's dark eyes. "And some don't. I see. What happens to the failures?"

"There aren't too many among us grays. The Tanu have worked out a fairish battery of tests to sort out the go and no go. Human psychotechnicians working under Lord Gomnol try to make sure that no normal human gets a gray torc unless his or her PS profile shows that the device will be generally beneficial to the individual's functioning. They don't want to *waste* the torcs because they're not easy to make. If your psychosocial tests show that you're a maverick, likely to whack out unless you're allowed to stew in your own independent juice, then you don't get a gray collar. They'll coerce you in more conventional ways to make you a productive member of their society—or else give up and toss you into the discard. But the real winners here in Exile are the torc wearers. The Tanu know they can trust us because they can share our thoughts and control our rewards. So we're allowed positions of responsibility. Look at me! Tanu are lousy swimmers. But I've had members of the High Table, the top Tanu administration, riding in my boat."

"With never a qualm, I trust."

"Okay—laugh. But I'd never do anything to endanger the lives of the exotics and they know it. It would be unthinkable!"

"But you're not free."

"Nobody is ever free," the skipper said. "Was I a goddam lily of the field back in the Milieu, piloting my ferryboat on Tallahatchie with Lee driving me crazy jealous? Here in this world, with this torc, I follow Tanu orders. And in return I get a share in the kind of mind-pleasures that only the metapsychics got in our twenty-second century. It's like seeing with a thousand eyes. Or going high with a thousand bodies all at once. I can't tell you how it is. I'm no poet. No psychologist, either."

"I'm beginning to understand, Johnny. The torcs are certainly more complex than I first thought."

"They make life a lot easier for the people who can stand up to 'em. Just take the matter of language. In our Milieu, the exotic sociologists knew how vital it was for each single race to have a single language. That's why we humans had to agree to become monolingual as a condition to Milieu acceptance—and Standard English won hands down. But with this mental speech, any kind of verbal misunderstanding is impossible! When another person mindspeaks to you, you know exactly what the message is."

Half to himself, Bryan murmured, "Barbaric. That's why the Milieu places such strict limitations on the metas. Especially the *human* metas."

"I don't get your point there, Bry. See what I mean? If you wore a torc, I'd know exactly what you were trying to say."

"Forget it, Johnny. Just my cynicism showing its fangs."

"To me, the mental unity seems ideal. But then, I'm just a dumb sailorman whose lover went over to another. Now if the two of *us* had been able to understand each other from the start . . . aw, the hell with it. Now there are thousands of people who love me. In a manner of speaking."

The skipper waved at the procession of riders. Almost all of them immediately waved back. Bryan felt something cold clutch at his bowels.

"Johnny?"

The skipper broke out of his reverie. "Mm?"

"Not all of the time-travelers are tested for psychocompatibility before being torced. Stein wasn't. They collared him when he became a menace."

Highjohn shrugged. "You can understand why. The torc can be used to subdue rebellious people on a short-range or long-range basis. Since your pal is still with us, I presume they have some plans for him. Certain types—medics and some other specialists who rarely come through the gate—they get collared willy-nilly, too. Essential occupations."

"And the metapsychic latents—people such as Aiken and Sukey and Raimo? They were apparently put into silver collars as soon as their latency was detected, without consideration of any adverse mental consequences."

"Well, the silvers are a special case," Highjohn admitted. "There's the matter of the genes."

Bryan looked at him.

"The Tanu use human women in their breeding scheme, Bry. Some human men as well. Normals, latents, both kinds get used. But the latents are the most valuable to them. I'm not too clear on the specifics of the thing, but somehow they figure that putting human latent genes into their pool will speed the day when the whole Tanu race goes operant. You know . . . just like the human race is going operant back in the Milieu."

"But the Tanu are operant now, with their golden torcs!"

"Limited, man, limited. Even the best of 'em can't measure up to masterclass metas in the Milieu. And none of the Tanu are a patch on our Grand Masters. Nope—they've got a long way to go in the mind-power game. But this genetic scheme is supposed to give them a boost. The Tanu are great schemers. Plotting and fighting are their favorite sports—followed closely by screwing, drinking, and feasting. The gene plan is just one of the ways they're trying to consolidate their advantage over the Firvulag. You know about the Little People, don't you? Racial brothers to the Tanu. No-torc operants—but only in illusion making, creativity, and some farsensing, for the most part. Firvulag genes are strong recessives among Tanu, so the Tanu mothers keep throwing Firvulag babies. And the little gnomies are physically tougher and reproduce a hell of a lot faster than the Tanu do. So if the Tanu want to keep control of Exile, they've got their work cut out for them."

"I'm starting to appreciate the situation," Bryan said. "But, come back to the silver-torcs. If they're indiscriminately collared, then some of them must whip out under the neural tension."

"True. Some go mad. Any kind of torc can do that if the personality of the wearer is fundamentally incompatible. Even the pure Tanu have their zonk-outs. Black-torcs, they call 'em. However, even if a silver goes bananas, the Tanu try to save the genes. A woman will be put on oblivion hold and used as brood stock until she breaks down. If she can't be restored by the healers, her ova can be transplanted to ramas. That often doesn't pan out because these exotic folks have a crude reprotechnology—but they try anyhow."

"And the male silver-torc dropouts?"

"Sperm is an easy keeper. As for the bonkered-out owner . . . well, there's always the Hunt. Or the life-offerings."

"I know about the Hunt." Bryan was grim. "But the life-offering thing is new. What is it—human sacrifice?"

"More like ritual execution of criminals and hopelessly unfit persons. As I understand sacrifices, the victim was supposed to be noble or pure or something. Well, the Tanu have *that* kind of ritual killing only once in a blue moon—like when there's a new King or Queen inaugurated. But the regular life-offerings come twice a year. At the tail end of the Grand Combat in early November and at the Grand Loving, in May. It's more like a clean sweep of the jails and soft rooms than anything else. Uncivilized by Milieu standards, but not all that bad an idea when you get right down to it."

Don't read my mind, Johnny, Bryan thought. Aloud, he said, "How do the human silvers become golds?"

The skipper gave a basso profundo laugh. "There's ways and ways. Your weird little pal is a shoo-in candidate!"

Bryan was at a loss for words. Yes, Aiken might fit in very well in this mad world of wondrous powers and appalling barbarity. But what of Mercy, fey and fearful?

Tall Creyn, with his red-and-white robes billowing in the breeze, came into the bows area, followed by Elizabeth. "We're almost there, Bryan. You can see the High King's palace now—that complex with bars of golden light and the hundreds of bright lamps spaced along the façade. We'll be ending our journey there. After we've rested for a few hours, there'll be a supper feast in honor of you new arrivals. King Thagdal and Queen Nontusvel will be there themselves to bid you welcome."

"Do all newcomers get such a splendid reception?" Elizabeth inquired. Half hidden behind the towering Tanu, she was an unobtrusive figure in her red denim jumpsuit.

"Not all." Creyn smiled down at her. "Your arrival is a very special occasion. It's been an honor for me to escort you. I hope to be able to work with you at Redact House in later days."

The realization burst upon Bryan. Of course. The magnificent escort had really come to catch a glimpse of *Elizabeth!* And the banquet with the King and Queen in attendance would be primarily for her. What a priceless catch the exotic time-fishers had made in this quiet, repressive woman with the unfathomable mental powers. And what new plans the genetic schemers must be hatching! Poor Elizabeth. Bryan wondered whether she was yet aware of the kind of temptation that the Tanu were sure to offer; and whether she realized the deadly danger that she faced if she should decline to cooperate . . .

Creyn continued to point out features of the capital city to the two of them. "The largest of the structures, those with the surmounting towers and faceted beacons, are the headquarters of the five great Guilds Mental. You might think of them as metapsychic clans—for there is more of a family than a professional relationship among the membership. The violet and amber lights adorn the Hall of Farsensors, which is presided over by the Venerable Lady Mayvar Kingmaker. The Guild of Creators has its headquarters lit with aquamarine and white. At the present time, this group is led by Lord Aluteyn Craftsmaster. However, his authority has been recently challenged and there may be changes made after the manifestations of power take place at the Grand Combat. The blue and amber lights symbolize the Coercer Guild, whose head is Sebi-Gomnol, a human wearer of the gold. Beyond that complex rises the home of the psychokinetics, the movers and shakers who are led by Lord Nodonn Battlemaster. He is at this time resident in his home city of Goriah. The PK Guild has rose and amber for its heraldic colors."

"And your own association?" Elizabeth asked.

"The Guild of Redactors has its headquarters outside of the city, on the southern slope of the Mount of Heroes. The white-and-red illumination is not visible from this side of the peninsula. Our guild is headed by Lord Dionket, Chief Healer of the Tanu."

A small figure in a suit of metallic fiber came slithering forward. Aiken Drum doffed his hat and bowed. His grinning face was shadowed and masklike in the light of the escort's torches.

"I couldn't help but eavesdrop, Chief. How is it that a human being—this Gumball, or whatever his name is—can head up one of your big corporations?"

Creyn's reply was cold. "Lord Sebi-Gomnol is a person of extraordinary talents—both metapsychic and scientific. After you meet him, you'll know why we hold him in such high esteem."

"How did he get his gold?" Aiken persisted.

Even Bryan was aware of the palpable revulsion flowing from the exotic healer. "You'd better hear that from his own lips as well."

Aiken gave a wicked chuckle. "I can hardly wait. Old Gumball sounds like the kinda guy who could even give *me* a few tips!"

You will leave us Aiken Drum.

Anything you command Chief!

Elizabeth frowned at the retreating back of the golliwog youth. To analyze this interesting implication was going to take some patient work. She hoped Lord Gomnol would be present at the feast.

Bryan was asking, "Are the rest of the buildings in the city private, then?"

"By no means," Creyn said. "Muriah is a working capital. The persons resident here are primarily concerned with the administration of our Many-Colored Land. Our education facilities are here and certain other vital operations as well. But you will discover, Bryan, that we are not nearly so formal in these high matters as your Galactic Milieu will be six million years into the future. We have a small population in our High Kingdom and a fairly simple culture. Many workings of our government are handled family-fashion. You will be encouraged to study the social structure very closely. There are things you must tell us about ourselves."

The anthropologist inclined his head. "It'll be a fascinating project. I can't think of a Milieu culture even remotely resembling yours."

The boat was finally drawing up to a quasi-Babylonian edifice of white stone, lavishly adorned with flowering plants that dripped over stepped, lamplighted balconies. The portico of the palace fronted on a spur of the rollered way. There were no casual mobs of human onlookers to be seen, but a large group of liveried human attendants stood waiting, together with forty or fifty little ramas dressed in white tabards ornamented with the stylized golden male face, emblem of the sovereign. As the boat came to a halt, the mounted escort rode partway up a flight of shallow steps that led to the palace entrance. The riders sat straight in their saddles, raised their torches on high, and formed into ranks like an honor guard.

There was a gong sound and a flourish of trumpets. A stately Tanu woman dressed all in silver and attended by silver-armored human soldiers came to the head of the stairs. She held out both arms toward the travelers in the boat and sang a strophe in the Tanu language. The riders chorused a response at the top of their lungs.

Creyn interpreted. "The Exalted Lady Eadone, Dean of Guilds and eldest daughter of the Thagdal, greets you. Elizabeth will answer."

Skipper Highjohn had been busy amidships winding out a gangplank that settled onto the lowest step. He winked at Elizabeth and held out a big brown hand to assist her to disembark.

An abrupt silence fell. The brisk evening breeze whipped the pennons, capes, and robes of the chaliko riders. Elizabeth in her simple red suit looked lost in the midst of the pageant; but her physical and mental voice was firm and quite as impressive as that of the King's daughter.

She spoke a phrase in the Tanu language and then repeated it in English: "Thank you for welcoming us to this beautiful city. We are impressed by the splendor and richness of your Many-Colored Land, which is so different from the primitive world we expected to find six million years into our past. We greet you with all goodwill. We hope you will be patient with us as we learn your ways. And we pray that there will be peace between our two races through the length of the world's age."

Crash! went the drums and cymbals. The orderly scene dissolved into a carnival whirl. Chaliko riders galloped up and down the steps, cheering, laughing, and singing. After a courteous nod to Elizabeth, the Lady Eadone vanished into the palace. Attendants and ramas came swarming to assist the time-travelers and gather up their baggage.

Elizabeth came quickly back onto the boat before the wild throng could engulf her. Distracted, all barriers up against the mental cacophony, she went forward to say goodbye to Skipper Highjohn.

Bryan was there, leaning against the doorframe of the wheel-house, a look of horror on his face.

Creyn passed Elizabeth, smiling. "It's quite all right. Highjohn did such a fine job of conveying us that I wanted to give him his re-ward immediately." The redactor stepped onto the gangplank and vanished into the crowd.

Elizabeth came and stood beside Bryan, looking into the wheel-house. The boatman lay on the deck beside the steering housing. His old U.S. Navy cap had fallen from his head. His eyes were rolled back so that only the whites were visible. Ribbons of saliva were spun from his open mouth to his kinky black beard. The gray torc was slimy with sweat. Highjohn's hands scratched at the deck-ing and his body arched up again and again in convulsive spasms.

He groaned in ecstasy.

Bryan whispered, "Are they all doing it to you, Johnny? All of them, curing the loneliness?"

With gentle firmness he drew Elizabeth back and closed the wheelhouse door. Then they followed the others into the palace of the Tanu King.

2

A GAUDY throng eddied around the feast-hall anteroom in anticipation of the arrival of what a courtier had called Most Exalted Personages. Both humans and Tanu wore filmy robes in different styles. Most of the women sported fantastic wired and jeweled headdresses. Music filled the air, played by an unseen orchestra that featured flutes, harps, and glockenspiels.

Bryan and Elizabeth and Stein and Sukey and Raimo had met again after an interval of three hours, brought into a railed enclosure separate from the rest of the crowd of dinner guests. The time-travelers stared at one another and then burst into laughter, so bemusing had been their transformation.

"But they took away my other clothes!" Raimo protested, his face aflame. "And they told me this would be the kind of thing the other guys would wear!"

Stein guffawed. "Talk about giving the ladies a treat—! You look like a friggerty ballet dancer. Or Captain Marvel!"

"Steinie, shut up," said Sukey. "I think Raimo looks fine."

Glowering, the former woodsman tried to pull his skimpy golden cape around his torso. He wore a scarlet leotardlike garment with a faint diapré pattern of gold that looked as if it had been shrink-wrapped about his muscular body. Golden boots and a matching belt completed the ensemble.

He is packaged for display, Elizabeth realized. *With his meager psychokinetic ability and low level of intelligence, he is destined to be a toy.*

Raimo was scowling at Stein. "At least they got you out of that mangy fur kilt."

The Viking only smiled. He looked magnificent and knew it, having been decked out by palace servitors in a deep-green short tunic of simplest cut, together with his own leather collar and belt studded with gold and amber. To this had been added an ornate baldric in similar style that supported a bronze two-handed sword in a jeweled scabbard. From Stein's great shoulders fell a cloak of sherry-colored brocade held by a greenstone brooch. He wore his bronze Viksø helmet with the curling horns.

Sukey clung to one arm of this incarnation of Norse divinity. Her gown was of white silken gauze with a trailing skirt and close-fitting sleeves. The simplicity of the dress was offset by an elaborate headdress resembling a silver halo, ornamented with glowing red gems. The ruby color of the stones was repeated in her narrow pendant belt and in the wide bracelets at her wrists.

"I think they dressed me in the heraldic colors of the clan I'm to be initiated into," Sukey said. "The redactors seem to wear red with white or silver. I wonder why you didn't get red-and-white regalia, Elizabeth?"

The farspeaker said, "I think I look very tasteful in black. Perhaps it has a special significance. They did spend a lot of time dressing my hair, at any rate. And when the wardrobe mistress saw my diamond ring, she came up with this nice little tiara."

"You and I make rather a set," Bryan observed. "Elegant restraint in the midst of these birds of paradise."

Elizabeth was amused. "And not bad at all, Doctor, now that

you've shed those wrinkled bush-cottons and the imitation Aussie hat."

The once-drab anthropologist now wore garments cut from a glistening fabric of deepest blue-green. He had narrow trousers tucked into silver short boots, a well-tailored jacket piped in silver, and a long cape that matched the suit. Elizabeth's costume was also simple. Her loose gown of filmy black was adorned by a narrow neck-yoke of red metallic fabric; two free-hanging ribands of the same material, jeweled and embroidered, fell from the front and rear of the yoke. It was a style that many of the Tanu women wore—although none showed the black-and-red color scheme.

Sukey was looking around. "I wonder where Aiken is?"

Stein muttered, "I don't see how they could make *that* kid any fancier-looking than he already is."

"Speak of the devil," Bryan said.

A servant pulled aside the drapery covering the passage door that led to their enclosure. The missing member of the group was ushered in, and Stein's observation proved to be prophetic. Aiken Drum was still wearing his own golden suit with the hundred pockets. He had added only a black cape that sparkled like carbonado and a tall bunch of black feathers fastened behind the cockade of his broad-brimmed hat.

"The festivities may now commence!" the jester declared.

"Maybe we'd better wait for the King and Queen," Elizabeth suggested.

Raimo was indignant. "Would you believe it, Aik? They took my *flask!*"

"The fewkin' fiends! I'd bring it running to you on little bitty feet, Chopper, if I wasn't so confused by the layout of this place."

"You could really bring it here?" the ex-woodsman exclaimed.

"Why not? You know what whisky means? And akvavit and all those other boozy words we know and love? They all translate as 'water of life!' All those old folks who put a name to strong drink thought that it put the life back into you. So why shouldn't I put a little life into the booze? Make it sprout legs . . . easy!"

"I thought they programmed a curb on your metafunctions," Elizabeth said. She probed gently and met a well-constructed defense.

Aiken winked. He hooked a finger around his silver torc and pulled. The metal necklet seemed to stretch—then snap back to solidity. "I've been working on that, sweets. Plus a few other things. Want to bet this is going to be one mother of a party?"

"Attaway, buddy!" Raimo cackled.

"I must say," the shining youth observed, "that the rest of you are really looking up, sartorially speaking. You're almost as gorgeous as me!" He studied Stein and Sukey in silence for a moment, then said, "And let me offer my largest felicitations on your union."

The Viking and his lady stared at Aiken with mingled fear and resolution.

Damn you Aiken, Elizabeth sent. I'll snap your synapses if you—

But the trickster swept on, black eyes alight. "The Tanu aren't going to like it, because they had plans of their own for you two. But I'm a sentimentalist. Romance must triumph!"

"Do you know what you're talking about?" Stein's voice was quiet. One ham-sized fist closed over the pommel of his bronze sword.

Aiken skipped close to him. Scandinavian blue eyes bridged a fifty-cent gap as they met those of the mischief-maker. Elizabeth was aware of an electric surge of mindspeech, well-directed along the intimate mode. She could not decipher it; but Sukey must have understood it, as well as her gigantic consort.

The background music ceased. A squad of trumpeters, their glass carnices hung with banners featuring the male-head motif, appeared in the arch of the feasting hall and sounded a fanfare. The butterfly swarm of guests paired off and a fuller orchestra began to play *alla marcia*.

Bryan caught the eye of a human courtier who was opening the gate of their enclosure. *"Wagner?"*

The gray-torc nodded. "Indubitably, Worthy Doctor. Our gracious Lady Eadone wished to make you feel more at home, insofar as that's possible. The Tanu are very fond of human music. The feasters will also use your own speech-vocal in consideration of your torcless status. If you please, your scholarly analysis of our society may begin this very night."

It began when I came through the damn time-gate, Bryan thought. But he only nodded to the man.

Aiken was asking the gray, "What do we do now, cockie? We don't want to commit any fox paws in front of the biggies."

The courtier said, "The Most Exalted Personages are enthroned at their own banqueting table. You'll be presented to them briefly, and then the supper will begin. Court etiquette is very informal in this society. Just carry on with reasonable courtesy."

They waited until the last of the privileged citizens of Muriah had entered the hall, marching two by two. Then it was time for their own entrance.

Aiken swept off his golden hat and made a mocking bow to Raimo. "Shall we, dear?"

"Why the hell not?" laughed the forester. "If this party is anything like the last one, the ladies'll be joining us inside!"

"This party," Aiken said, "is not going to be anything like the last one. But you'll have a great time, Ray. I guarantee it."

"How about the rest of us?" Stein asked. He had tucked his helmet under one arm. He and Sukey fell in behind Raimo and Aiken.

"Make your own fun, my man," said Aiken Drum. He strutted through the ranks of trumpeters into the hall.

Wordlessly, Bryan offered his arm to Elizabeth; but all thought of the farspeaker and her fate had gone from his mind. As they stepped forward to the Tannhäuser cadences he felt only the stabbing thrust of his fixe: that Mercy would be there! There and safe within her silver. Not trapped, not struggling, but secure in the faerie family that enraptured the lucky ones among its captives.

Only let her be happy.

They walked into a great beamed and paneled room that was lit by brazen sconces full of honest fire. The sparkling little meta lamps were in use, too, but for decoration only, studding strange tapestries and metal sculptures along the walls. The feasting board made a great inverted U-shape, with the several hundred guests ranged along both sides of the lateral sections, standing at their places. At the far end of the chamber was the local version of the high table—actually somewhat lower than the two side boards so that the dignitaries enthroned there would be more visible to the guests. The wall behind the Exalted Personages had a huge reproduction of the male-head motif, crafted of gold and deeply set into a complex mosaic of the crystalline meta lights. Draperies of thin metallic fabric framed the whole emblem and merged into a canopy above the line of twenty thrones. Liveried waiters were poised behind all of the guests. The Personages were attended by a double line of servitors, much more sumptuously dressed than those who waited upon the lower orders.

Bryan and Elizabeth walked toward the table, past the ranks of smiling nobility. The anthropologist tried to be discreet as he scanned the throng; but there were such numbers on both sides of

the room, and far too many of the human women had auburn
hair . . .

"The Worthy Doctor of Anthropology Bryan Grenfell."

. . . And then the arbiter bibendi was presenting him, and he
stepped forward and made his brief obeisance in the usual Milieu
style, conscious that the people at the High Table were craning forward to study him and his female companion with an eagerness they
had not vouchsafed to the four other honorees. Court etiquette evidently did not include the introduction of the Personages to *him*,
but he had little curiosity about the glittering figures at the moment.
Mercy was not among them.

Bryan stepped back and Elizabeth, pale and strained-looking, had
her turn last of all.

"The Most Illustrious Lady Elizabeth Orme, Grand Master Farspeaker and Grand Master Redactor of the Galactic Milieu."

Bloody hell, marveled Bryan.

The standing guests raised their arms. Astonishingly enough, the
Exalted Personages got up from their thrones and also joined in the
salute. The entire assembly gave voice to a threefold hail:

"Slonshal! Slonshal! Slonshal!"

Hairs bristled at the back of Bryan's neck. Now *that* had to be a
linguistic coincidence.

The most central of the male Personages gave a small twisting gesture. From somewhere came a jangling sound, as though a chain
were being shaken. Silence fell.

"Let refreshment and fellowship prevail," intoned the male Personage. A magnificent physical specimen, he wore a white robe,
completely unadorned. His long blond hair and flowing beard were
dressed with exquisite care in braids and tiny thin curls. There was
a distinct resemblance to the masklike heraldic emblem and Bryan
knew that this must be Thagdal, High King of the Tanu.

The tableau broke into a confetti swirl as the guests flung themselves into their seats or went dashing about to exchange fresh greetings with one another. Human waiters and rama servers began load-
ing the tables with food and drink. The six honorees were seated on
low couches opposite the Exalted Personages and all formality went
by the board as the Tanu aristocrats satisfied their curiosity by asking the time-travelers a torrent of questions.

Bryan found himself addressed by a formidable woman in white
seated at the right hand of the King. Glorious red hair cascaded
from beneath a close-fitting hood of golden fabric with upstanding

jeweled wings. "I am Nontusvel, Mother of the Host and wife to the Thagdal. In courtesy I am your Lady, Bryan, and I bid you warm welcome to our Many-Colored Land and company. Now . . . what's this I see? Confusion in you? And perhaps a fear? I would ease that if I might."

The power of her smiling ur-mothermind was irresistible, strumming his memories like an expert lutanist. A dim control room high in a château tower and a face full of sweet rue. Tears at a troubadour's song. And with that chord plucked, segue into another of apple blossoms nightingales moon rising flesh warmth auburn hair and eyes of the haunted sea so fey. And then the dissonant arpeggio. But where Gaston where's she gone where through that damn time-portal into Exile. Here I go Monsieur le Chat into the deep cellar . . .

Bryan's festive costume had inner pockets. Without volition, he reached a hand into the one over his breast and handed the durofilm to Queen Nontusvel. She gazed at Mercy's portrait. "You followed her here, Bryan."

"Yes." I did but see her passing by. Till I die I see her.

Nontusvel's metapsychic tendrils came weaving solace and diversion. "But your Mercy is safe, Bryan! Successfully integrated into our fellowship. And so happy! It was as though she had been born for the torc. As though she yearned unconsciously to belong to us and searched us out over the gap of six million years."

The Queen's eyes were as bright as sapphires, shining with an inner light, for all that they seemed to have no pupils.

"May I visit her?" he asked humbly.

"She is in Goriah, in that region you would call Brittany. But she will soon return to our City of the White Silver Plain and then you shall hear her tell of her life among us. And in return for this reunion, will you serve us willingly? Will you help us to gain the knowledge that we require, the insight that may be vital to our survival as a race?"

"I will do what I can, Exalted Lady. My training has been in the analysis of cultures and the evaluation of intercultural impact and the attendant stresses. I admit that I don't understand completely what you want of me, but I'm at your disposal."

Nontusvel nodded her winged golden head and smiled. The High King turned from Elizabeth and said to the anthropologist, "My dear son Ogmol will help you coordinate your researches. See him? That high-spirited fellow at the righthand table in the turquoise-

and-silver robe, balancing the wine ewer on his head, the silly twit. There! Now he's done it . . . Well, even a scholar has a right to celebrate. You'll see his more serious side tomorrow. He'll be your guide. Your *assistant*, damme! And between the two of you, you'll make sense out of our conundrum before the Grand Combat convenes or I'm a no-ball son of a Howler mule!"

He guffawed hugely and Bryan, overawed, could only think of a particularly virile Ghost of Christmas Present he had seen as a child on the Tri-D.

"If I may ask, King Thagdal—what is the basis for your sovereignty?"

Both Thagdal and Nontusvel laughed uproariously, the King to the point of coughing. Whereupon the Queen took up a great golden cup and soothed her husband with a draft of honey-wine. When the King was restored, he said, "I like that, Bryan! Begin at the top with the authority figures. And begin *now!* Well, it's simple enough, lad. I've got stupendous metafunctions, of course, and I'm a wiz in battle. But my most valued attribute is—fertility! More than half of the people in this hall are my children and grandchildren and great-grandchildren. And that's not to count the absent loved ones—eh, Nonnie?"

The Queen simpered discreetly. She told Bryan, "My Lord Husband is the father of eleven thousand and fifty-eight—and never a Firvulag and never a black-torc among them. His germ plasm is without peer, and for this reason he is our High King."

Bryan tried to phrase his next inquiry tactfully. "And you, Noble Lady, have a similarly distinguished reproductive history?"

"Two hundred and forty-two children!" trumpeted Thagdal. "A record among the royal spouses. And among them such many-talented luminaries as Nodonn and Velteyn and Imidol and Culluket! And the Exalted Ladies Riganone and Clana and Dectar—to say nothing of dear Anéar! None of my other wives, not even the lamented Lady Boanda, brought forth such riches."

And now Elizabeth entered the colloquy, saying softly, "Bryan—be sure to have His Majesty tell you about the *other* mothers of his children."

"Simple enough." Thagdal beamed. "Share the wealth! Propagate the optimal phenotype, as Crazy Greggy would say. Every gold and silver lady gets a whirl with the Old Man first time around."

Elizabeth said, "And after they're impregnated by the King, they may become the wives or mistresses of other Tanu nobles and have children by others. Isn't that interesting?"

"Very," Bryan said faintly. "But this—uh—genetic plan could not have been in force from the beginning of your race's residence on the planet Earth."

Thagdal stroked his beard. His bushy blond brows came together. "No-o-o. Things were a little different back in the beginning—in the Dark Ages, so to speak. There weren't too many of us then, and I had to fight for my Kingly rights if the lady wasn't willing. But of course I won most of the time, because in those days I was the best swordsman in more ways than one. You understand?"

Bryan said, "There was a similar custom during the ancient days of our Earth. It was called the droit du seigneur."

"Right! Right! I recall one of the dear little gorfie silvers mentioning it. Where was I? . . . Yes, the history thing! Well, with the opening of the time-gate and the coming of you people from the future, we tried to organize the propagation of the race more scientifically. Some of your folks were a great help along those lines. You must be sure to meet them, Bryan. I'd say they rank as near-godparents of the glorious Tanu fellowship you see here today! Dear old Crazy Greggy, of course—Lord Greg-Donnet, that is, our Eugenics and Genetics Master. And that marvelous woman, Anastasya-Bybar! Where the hell would we be if Tasha hadn't shown our decadent reprotechnicians how to reverse the sterilization of human women? Why—all of those precious latent ova would have been lost to us!" He dug an elbow into Nontusvel's junoesque torso. "And half *my* fun is persevering until I get that little bun safely into the oven—eh, Nonnie?"

The Queen simpered.

Bryan took an overlarge swallow of wine. He was conscious of Elizabeth's eyes on him. "And so—and so approximately seventy years ago, when the first time-travelers began to arrive, you started to hybridize with humans?"

"Get it straight, son. Only the human *males* contributed to the gene pool at first. Tasha didn't come through until—when?—say, ten years after the gate opened. Our ladies had their fun, of course, in those early years. And it didn't take long for us to discover that human-Tanu hybrids were less likely to go Firvulag—and more likely to be carried to term by our delicate little mothers . . . saving your presence, Nonnie love! Even our numbwit Tanu geneticists noticed that. Aluteyn and his people were on the lookout for someone like Academician Anastasya Astaurova. And sure enough—Compassionate Tana sent her to us with bells on! Literally."

Thagdal indulged in another fit of jollity, quenching it with heroic drafts of wine. All around the feasting hall, spirits were rising as cups were drained and refilled. The supper consisted mostly of meat dishes in bewildering variety, together with great platters of fruit, and breadrolls baked into odd shapes. Entertainers, announced by the arbiter bibendi, did their turns in the middle of the U of tables, and the guests responded with showers of small coins or half-chewed bones, according to the quality of the talent displayed. The Exalted Personages supped in a more refined fashion; but down near one end of the High Table, where Aiken was seated opposite two nobles attired in rose and gold, there was a good deal of rowdy laughter and cup-thumping going on.

The Queen said, "Tell dear Bryan about our gift of the *torcs,* Thaggy."

"Tell both of us," Elizabeth said, with her most Mona Lisa smile.

The King wagged a finger at the farspeaker. "Barriers still up, little love? That'll never do, you know. Honey-wine is what you need. Is there anything else I can tempt you with?"

Nontusvel covered her mouth and spluttered with stately mirth.

"Your Majesty is a most gracious host." Elizabeth raised her goblet to him. "Please continue your fascinating history."

"Where was I? . . . Torcs for the humans! Well, you have to understand that true fellowship between us Tanu and you people wasn't something that could spring up full-grown in a year or two. There was the genetic compatibility, with advantages that were manifest but not well understood. We bestowed honorary golden torcs on Greggy and Tasha in gratitude for their efforts. They weren't latents, as it turned out, and not all that psychoadaptive, either. And then Iskender-Kernonn came through and domesticated the animals and we gave *him* an honorary torc."

"Poor dear Isky," the Queen lamented, emptying her goblet. A waiter filled it immediately. "Snatched from us by the Firvulag and their bestial coterie of Lowlives!"

"And then about forty years ago Eusebio came through and did such brilliant work improving the rama torcs—being a psychobiologist back in the Milieu and the first person who seemed to understand the *theory* behind the torcs. So we gave him a gold, too, and named him Gomnol. And damned if the man didn't turn out to be a superlative latent coercer, for all that he's an ugly little runt! What a shock for us!"

"You hadn't known about the human metapsychic latency factor before?" Elizabeth asked.

"We are an old, old race," the Queen admitted, "afflicted with a certain scientific languor." A tear stole from one sapphire eye and trickled down her flawless cheek, splashing into the cushioned depths of her corsage. She took consolation from the cup.

"As Nonnie says," the King resumed, "we're an ancient race. Rather decadent in certain disciplines, I fear. And our own small faction—which as you may know fled our home galaxy under duress —was even less scientifically inclined than the common ruck of Tanu . . . No, except for Brede (who doesn't really count), we didn't understand how the torcs worked to make our own metafunctions operant, and we didn't try very hard to understand the powers themselves. They were *there,* if you follow me. We didn't worry overmuch about the whys and wherefores, so human latency came as a complete surprise. As Gomnol pointed out, you humans didn't know your own minds and bodies for ninety-nine pip niner per centum of your racial history, either! So don't sneer at us. Where was I? . . . Oh, yes. Latent humans. Well, when Gomnol got his golden torc and went meta, *he* connected the whole thing in a flash. The Tanu are latents and so are normal humans—some more, but most very much less, even to the point of nullity. In your future world, the babies that are potential operants are detected and later trained up by farsensing and redactive practitioners such as this Illustrious Lady." He gave a courtly nod to Elizabeth. "Since no operants came through the time-portal in those days, and since our torc-enhanced powers are shaky in detecting human latents, Gomnol decided that we must make ourselves a mechanical device for mental assay of the human population. He worked out the gadget that tested you folks back at Castle Gateway. We have others at our principal cities to catch the latents that elude us because of mental turmoil during the initial testing. There are a fair number of slip-throughs." He scowled thunderously. "Including one that was an unmitigated *disaster!* Where was I? . . . Gomnol's brainstorm! Understand now —this chap is an inspired psychobiologist. He knew it would be dangerous to put gold torcs on human latents who weren't wholeheartedly assimilated into our fellowship."

"There are always," the Queen interposed darkly, "ingrates."

"So Gomnol conceived the silver torcs, with their built-in psycho-regulators. And shortly after that, the gray torcs—to be used by so-called nonlatent humans who could stand very low-level metapsychic involvement. A whole new world of fellowship was born! Beginning in Gomnol's time, when it became possible to mass-produce the gray torcs—well, produce them with relative speed, at any rate—we of the Tanu were able to seize the ascendancy on this world. The vile Firvulag, those shadow-siblings of ours, were no longer able to contend with us on a virtually equal footing. We had armies of loyal human grays to crush their superior numbers! We had human mothers to counter the vulgar fecundity of their coarse little women! We had the noble silvers—our operant allies-mental! And as time went on, many of the silvers were advanced to full citizenship and given gold."

This can be done without psychic injury torcexchange?

Certainly cherishedElizabeth silvertorc removed without danger after gold in place.

"And think! The brilliant gray technicians have improved our economy by devising more efficient means of transport and goods production! Thanks to the mourned Lord of Animals, Kernonn, we have beasts to ride and beasts to haul and beasts to guard us from Firvulag depredation. And perhaps best of all . . . we have hybrid human champions in the Grand Combat." The King paused. He leaned across the table, upsetting his cup in the process, and took one of Elizabeth's hands.

"And now, Tana's bounty surpasses itself. She has sent us you."

Queen Nontusvel seemed to radiate a lunar benevolence. There was a different glow in the deep green eyes of Thagdal.

Impervious and calm, Elizabeth repeated, "And now Tana has sent me. But in our own world, the gifts of God are often ambiguously given. You don't yet see me as I am, King Thagdal."

"But that will come, dearest Elizabeth. You shall go to the most noble of us all for your initiation into our ways—to the Prescient Lady Brede Shipspouse, she of the Two Faces and the poetry. Brede will teach you and you will teach her. And in good time you will go to Tasha-Bybar and then you will come to me. Dearest Elizabeth."

"Dearest Elizabeth," came Nontusvel's echo. Surely it was as full of goodwill as it had ever been.

"A toast!" bellowed Thagdal, leaping to his feet. His cup had been speedily righted and replenished.

"A toast!" the several hundred guests shouted back. The arbiter shook the chain of silence.

"To the Tanu race and the human race! In fellowship, in communion, in love!"

The feasters raised their great golden goblets. "Fellowship! Communion! Love!"

"With an emphasis on the latter!" called out Aiken Drum.

There was laughter and shouting and a great swallowing and spilling of wine, with many a soggy embrace and a sipping from lip to lip. The royal couple, inflamed by the drink and festivity, now clung to each other murmuring and snorting. A corps de ballet of human women and men, dressed alike in bold magpie leotards, appeared as music struck up and began to lead the throng in elaborate contredanse patterns.

Elizabeth whispered to Bryan, "I'm going to have to leave you for a while. I must look into them while their inhibitions are down. If you like, I'll share the data with you later." She gave him a solemn moue, then closed her eyes and withdrew to some mental vantage point.

One of the female black-and-whiters tried to haul Bryan off his bench into the dance, where Aiken and Raimo were already whirling and leaping as though they had been doing the complex steps all their lives. Bryan shook his head to the invitation. He let the waiters fill his great cup again and again and tried to blot from his mind the realization of how it must be now with Mercy.

When he finally thought to examine the cup closely and discovered what the gold and jewels ensheathed, he was too drunk to care.

3

STEINIE don't dance with them don't. Look what they do to Raimo myGod.

Allright allright littleone calm keep on hiding the two of us don't give way don't fear.

They are stronger especially this DionketLordHealer I could never keep him out of us without Elizabethhelp. They don't like that friendshipwall but afraid offend her too early. O Jesus. That beautybitchslut Anéar taking Raimo right there middlemob shame disgust furyhate . . . Steinie!

Calm calm shelterlove armsword bless Elizabeth. Atleast they no make Aiken dance their tune viceversa if anything.

Not toy like Raimobooby.

Nor I Sukeylove if you help.

"Are you sure you won't take a turn with the dancers?" The Lady Riganone smiled at Stein and Sukey. The magpies were back importuning them. "Your two friends are having a marvelous time."

"No thank you, Lady," Stein said. The magpies minced away with reluctance.

Sukey helped herself to another of the spiced tournedos. "These are delicious, Lord Dionket." She spoke shyly to the deep-eyed Chief Healer, who sat opposite her. "Are they made from venison?"

"Why, no, Little Sister. Hipparion."

"Those adorable little *horses?*" Sukey cried in dismay.

Lady Riganone tossed her head and laughed merrily. The pendants dangling from wires on her lavender and gold headdress clashed and pealed. "What else would we do with them? They're the most abundant meat source that we have—and the Goddess be thanked they're so delicious. Why—do you realize that those poor people up in the Hercynian Forest, in Finiah and those other places at the end of the world, must make do with pigs and tough old stags and even mastodons? We southerners are so lucky. There's really nothing to compare with a roast loin of hipparion, seasoned with garlic and a hint of thyme and perhaps a little of that new *pepper*, all brown and crackling on the outside and oozing blood within."

"Don't be squeamish, Sukey," Stein told her, dipping out another helping from a bowl of rich stew. "When in Rome, you know! I don't know what *this* is, but it's sure got flavor."

Dionket poked a bony finger into the deep silver dish, then sucked meditatively. "Mmm . . . a promephitis ragout, dear warrior. I believe the Elder Earth equivalent for the little creature would be—"

The mental picture flashed before Stein and Sukey.

"Skunk!" The Viking choked.

"Oh—there, there, Steinie," Lady Riganone exclaimed, radiating solicitude. "Did something go down the wrong pipe? Do take some wine for that coughing."

The Personage seated next to Dionket, a burly giant in a short jerkin of blue and gold, said, "Try some of these hedgehogs in burgundy to settle your tripes, Stein. Now there's a dish to make your belly take notice! And you know what they say about hedgehog." He leered and the mental image of the prickly pun was distressingly overstated.

Coolly, Sukey shoved the platter of odd little dainties far out of Stein's reach. "The warrior is recovering from an injury, Lord Imidol. He mustn't overindulge. In anything."

Lady Riganone's fluting chuckles and her chapeau tinkled together. "Isn't she marvelous, Dionket? She'll be such an asset to your Guild of Redactors. But it was really very naughty of you to have reserved her from the bidding."

Mindsnap.

"What do you mean, Lady?" Stein asked.

"Have some more cherry brandy," the President of the Redactors urged. "Or would you prefer plum or raspberry?" He fingered his torc. Both Stein and Sukey were compelled to relax.

I couldn't help it Steinie he slipped through. O Elizabeth come back from there and help us before Stein finds out I won't be able to hold him!

. . .

Sukeywoman whatwhatWHAT dammit?

Steinie stop I can barely cover you if they perceive allthat inside they'll hurt you love O please calmrecedeflattentranquilize. Damn you ElizaMasterbeth come back from there!

Out in the middle of the floor, the arbiter bibendi was holding a length of glittering glass chain above his head and shaking it. The riotous dancing calmed and the music drained away. Revelers drifted back to their seats. Four Tanu ladies all but dragged the disheveled Raimo with them. Aiken Drum suffered no such indignity. He strutted back to his place at the High Table and sat carefully on the edge of his couch.

"Exalted Personages, most noble lords and ladies, and illustrious honorees!" cried the arbiter. "Pray silence! It is the hour for the contributions of the honored guests!"

Cheers, cup-thumping, and a clatter of knives upon golden plates.

The arbiter shook the chain again. "Two of our guests"—the silver-torced exquisite bowed toward Bryan and Elizabeth—"are exempted from show by command of Their Awful Majesties. And one other"—he pointed at Raimo—"has already made his talents known!"

The ladies at the low tables screamed with laughter. A number of them began pelting Raimo with bananas, stopping reluctantly as the chain of silence rang once again.

"We will hear from Sue-Gwen Davies!"

Sukey felt herself impelled toward the center of the room. The soul within her was turned over and over helplessly by the examining psyches of the King and Queen and the other Personages. The Tanu were surprised at the deep barrier (for Elizabeth had returned to assist in the nick of time), but were disposed to be satisfied with the superficial revelations that were accessible to them. Dionket's mind spoke.

Dear little RedactorSister, apprentice comforthealer! Lend us a small solace this night sing of ElderEarth of ancient parentland.

Sukey's apprehension began to melt. Other minds all around her seemed to beg: Lull us.

Keeping her gaze on Stein, she sang a cradlesong in a small clear voice, first in Welsh and then in Standard English. After the first phrase, a single harpist accompanied her.

> Holl amrantau'r sêr ddywedant,
>> Ar hyd y nos.
> Dyma'r ffordd i fro gogoniant,
>> Ar hyd y nos.
> Golau arall yw tywyllwch,
> I arddangos gwir brydferthwch,
> Teulu'r nefoedd mewn tawelwch,
>> Ar hyd y nos.
>
> Love, fear not if sad your dreaming,
>> All through the night.
> In the mist bright stars are gleaming,
>> All through the night.
> Joy will come to us at morning,
> Life with sunrise hope adorning,
> Though sad dreams may give dread warning,
>> All through the night.

Behind the words and music glowed the sheltering love of the caregiver. Her healing energy poured over the manchild to whom she had given rebirth, overflowed and spread in a great psychic pool throughout the hall. For a moment, the lullaby's softness quenched all the others' anxieties, soothed anger and lust, diminished grief and frenzy.

When the song was done the banqueters were silent. And then on an alien level of consciousness, which the torced humans could sense but not decipher, came a burst of declaration from many Tanu minds. It was cut off in full spate by the lofty voice of Dionket. The Lord Healer rose from his place at the High Table and held out his arms, forming a living tau of crimson and silver.

Mine. Reserved.

Sukey returned to her place, dazed, and sat down beside her husband. The arbiter bibendi shook his chain.

"We will know the talents of Stein Oleson."

It was the Viking's turn to be drawn irresistibly from his seat. He stood with his head uncovered and glared at the exotic nobility lounging at the High Table, feeling their minds come tapping, prying, snooping. And the Queen's motherthought, more compassionate:

He should *not* have been torced alas the briefliving!

And then the King: Suffice unto the Combat. Skillplay!

Two of the magpie dancemasters came bounding from the sidelines, carrying metal baskets full of fruit resembling large oranges. One pitched a bright globe overhand and it flew at Stein's head.

The bronze sword hissed from its scabbard, gripped in both the giant's hands. He smote the fruit neatly in two.

King Thagdal roared with jovian delight. The men in black and white began flinging oranges at Stein as fast as they could. His sword flashed like a golden wheel. He spun and leaped, chopping the flying spheres to bits. The King pounded the table while tears of mirth ran into his splendid beard. The company of Tanu screeched and cheered.

The chain of silence sounded.

The arbiter gushed, "Oh, a fair show indeed by our newest warrior! Well done, Stein!"

Bid.

Again the burst of exotic mindspeech. This time Elizabeth was attuned to it. Without surprise, she heard Stein being auctioned off to the highest bidder as a likely gladiator in a contest called the Low Mêlée. Since the ex-driller was one of the most impressive physical specimens to have appeared in Exile within the past decade, the sports-crazed exotics drove the bidding to what was evidently an unprecedented level. They were bidding their personal services to the Crown—nominal owner of all exceptional time-travelers—offering their metafunctions, their material wealth, their torced and untorced human subjects.

Three hundred grays for the Royal Guard!

My garnet mine in the Pyrénées!

The renowned dancing woman Kanda-Kanda and all of her suite!

A hundred racing chalikos caparisoned in gold!

The death of Delbaeth.

The King cried aloud, "Hold!" He rose from his couch and glowered over the startled assemblage. Out in the middle of the floor, Stein stood still, the point of his great sword resting on the tiles.

"What person has dared this bid?" asked Thagdal with silken softness. "Who esteems the strength of this warrior so highly that he will rashly pledge the destruction of the Shape of Fire?"

The crowd of banqueters held their tongues and minds.

"I do," said Aiken Drum.

There was a collective sigh, and a collective lancing out, and a mental gasp of stunned surprise as all of the mind-probes fell blunted. Thagdal began to laugh aloud and after a moment, so did Nontusvel and then all of the others. Reaction to the enormity rocked the hall.

Elizabeth came sliding into Aiken on the uniquely human mode. What in the *world?*

Look Thaggymind yourself Elizababe fondest wish extirpation meanie FirvulagDelbaethShapeofFire. So bid.

For Steinie? Deranged clownAiken gaming with ourfriend's life?!

Elizadummybeth! I'd save Steinbuddyvulnerable. Tanu combatschool ferocitymindset recharge berserkerpsychoenergy irrevocably.

Damn . . . yes. I affirm.

Safe with me. Eventually get Sukey too. TurdflockTanu really bit it off when torced me. *You* know.

Suspected. But damn they get you if comedown mindunion crunch. Get us both if they decipher operant snuffsequence.

Distract distract distract.

The mental exchange between Aiken and Elizabeth had occupied a fraction of a second. The arbiter bibendi was frantically jangling the chain of silence as the prankster in the shining suit strolled from his place at the High Table to a position beside Stein. When the tumult died away, the King said, "Speak, Aiken Drum."

The little man swept off his hat and bowed. Then he began to talk; and as he spoke aloud his mind played a subtle descant that somehow gave his ludicrous words credence, painting them with a mesmeric plausibility that disarmed even the most skeptical of the exotic audience.

"Now I know that my bidding has surprised you, friends! For not only is the deed itself an impudent thing, but you scarcely can understand how I know enough of the horrid Delbaeth to suggest his removal. It seems incredible to you, doesn't it, that a newly arrived little silver-torc can propose to do what so many of your own champions have failed of.

"Well, let me tell you how things are! I'm a different kind of human! You've never seen my like. Now, this big fellow who stands beside me is my friend. And I fear that the Good Queen is right in saying that he's not the kind who can wear your gray torc long and live. The coaching style of your fighting-school would undo all the redaction done by the little Sue-Gwen and the Lady Elizabeth to restore his sanity. And to save Stein, I'd take him from you. But not without offering a fair price in return.

"Now you've been probing me and pinching me and trying to peek inside me while I speak. And you've failed! Even King Thagdal has failed. Even *Elizabeth* can no longer probe me! And so you'd better know that the torc put on me at Castle Gateway set off a mental chain reaction that's still going on. I scared your Lord Creyn and I'm scaring you now. But don't fash yourselves! I don't fancy doing you any harm. In fact, I like almost all I see of this world, and the more I grow within, the better things seem to portend for all of us together. So wait until I have my say before you give in to the fear and try to swat me! First see how I can help you become even greater than before!

"Now, Delbaeth. I saw his Shape of Fire deep inside the Thagdal's mind. I was curious, and I studied it as we ate and drank and amused ourselves. And when the bidding started, I said to myself: Why not? And so I bid my services, following your own custom. I'm confident that I can exterminate this Firvulag menace. So I leave it up to all of you, friends-mental. And you, High King of the Tanu! I'll open myself for just a moment and let you look at what's growing in my skull. Then decide whether you want to treat me as a fellow mind-jouster, or as a slave . . ."

He expanded to them all and they went rushing in.

Elizabeth flowed over and around and through the exotics, rating an ironic acknowledgment from Aiken for her skill. The Tanu stumbled through incandescence, hardly aware of what the burgeoning mental sprouts showed promise of becoming. But Elizabeth knew.

Milieu well shot of you Aikenboy.

Pooh lass see how they run fewkin' psychelliptical blindmice.

No . . . one of them knows. See there?

Hah! Yes! . . . Who you anyhoo oldwomanmind?

I am Mayvar. I have been waiting for the likes of you since the coming of the Ship. I am ancient and I am ugly and I lead the Guild of Farsensors. Come freely to me for your initiation and it shall all be as you hope. Unless you are afraid . . .

The chain of silence clanged. The Great Ones and all of the piddling, timorous inspectors went fleeing out of Aiken. He politely waited while Elizabeth and Mayvar withdrew, before slamming down the barrier once more.

"Shall we allow him?" roared King Thagdal.

"Slonshal!" the assembly responded.

"Shall we send him to the test, and shall the boldest of us witness his victory or destruction?"

"Slonshal!"

The King's voice fell to the threshold of audibility. "And who among us will dare to take him to kin and teach him our way, this perilously shining youth?"

Far down at the left end of the High Table a wand-thin figure arose. She came into the center of the hall leaning on a tall golden staff. Her gown was of a purple so deep as to be almost black, powdered with gold stars, and having a hood that concealed her hair but let the amazing ugliness of her features be fully revealed to the two humans waiting for her.

"Mayvar Kingmaker will take him to kin," said the crone. "I'll see him to his gold and if he's kind, to more! Will you come with me, bright laddie? And will you bring your friend to learn the battle-company's way, before the two of you together dare Delbaeth?"

"Stein!" cried Sukey.

The hag laughed. Her mind spoke to Aiken in the intimate mode.

Countercustom though it be I'll see that he alone has her if you fill your boast. Dionket and I are allied. Now are you coming?

The little man in the suit of gold extended both arms to the tall old Tanu woman. She bent to him and they kissed. Then they walked together from the hall, with Stein following as if in a dream a few paces behind. The arbiter bibendi gave a frantic signal and the musicians struck up a spirited dance tune. The magpies came cavorting to draw the stunned guests out onto the floor by sheer force.

At the High Table, Thagdal watched the strange trio leave through the door at the opposite end of the room. He had not moved so much as a muscle since the woman in purple had risen from the table. But then the opaque green eyes returned to life. Thagdal smiled and raised his cup and so did the remaining Exalted Personages occupying the thrones that flanked his.

"Shall we give Aiken Drum slonshal?" the King asked softly. "Or shall we wait a bit to see whether or not the Venerable Lady Mayvar has chosen rightly?"

His goblet tipped. Raspberry liquor poured onto the polished tabletop like fresh blood. Thagdal inverted his cup in the midst of the puddle, lurched to his feet, and vanished through a door concealed by draperies. The Queen hastened after him.

Sukey came to Elizabeth, mindweeping but with dry eyes. "What's happened? I don't understand. Why have Stein and Aiken gone with that old woman?"

Patience little Mindsister I'll explain—

"Kingmaker!" Bryan peered owlishly at the two human women, then raised his own jewel-eyed golden skull goblet with an unsteady hand. "Mayvar Kingmaker, Creyn called her! Bloody damn legend. Bloody damn world. Slonshal! Long live the King!"

He tilted the dregs down his throat and fell prone onto the table.

"I think," said Elizabeth, "that the party is over."

4

Queen Nontusvel and three of her children walked in the garden before noon, while it was still cool, and if the royal lady was apprehensive, she kept her fear well veiled.

The Queen plucked a coral-colored blossom from a honeysuckle and held it out with an invitational thought. A hummingbird came, its feathers flashing iridescent blue and green when it darted through sunbeams. It drank nectar and suffered the Queen to tickle its avian brain. When it was done it hovered for a moment before her face, buzzing, and then whisked away into the lemon tree.

"Those things are vicious, Mother," Imidol said. "They'll go for your eyes if they catch even a hint of threat. We should never have allowed them out of the aviary."

"But I *love* them," the Queen said, laughing as she tossed away the drained flower. "And they know it. They would never try to hurt me." This morning she was wearing a soft blue robe. Her flame-colored hair was bound into a braided diadem.

"You're too trusting," Culluket said. And there it was, the opening wedge the other two had been waiting for.

Imidol, the youngest and most aggressive, rushed in with all the natural force of the metacoercive. "Even creatures that appear to be harmless can be dangerous. Consider human women! When they're cornered, when they're confronted with multiple psychic shocks, they may strike out rather than subside into the complaisant mode we've come to expect from them."

"This new operant one could be a serious menace," Riganone cautioned.

Culluket took his mother's arm as they came to a wide flight of rustic steps that led to a grassy area fully enclosed by flowering shrubs. A small marble pavilion stood in the center of the lawn.

"Let's sit here for a moment, Mother. We must speak of this. It can't be postponed."

"I suppose not." Nontusvel sighed. Culluket was smiling his reassurance and she radiated affection in return. Of these three grown children, he resembled her the most physically, having the same wide-set sapphire eyes and high brow. But in spite of his beauty and his great redactive skill, members of the Host rarely sought him out for the healing, even though he was their brother. Was it true, what the others said, that Culluket was too zealous in his scrutiny of pain?

Nontusvel said, "Surely we have the resources among the Host to control this Elizabeth—for all her torcless power. When she sees more of our ways, she will surely unite with us. It's only reasonable."

O Mother misapprehend! Woe.

Screen up Cull? Listeners!

Upfast. Imi shunt those gardeners away. Riga show her.

"You mustn't whisper behind my mind," the Queen chided them. "This mental jumble—! I taught you better, dear ones. Now, an orderly disquisition, if you please."

Riganone the farsensor rose from the marble bench and paced back and forth, tall and mauve, without meeting her mother's mind in the intimate mode.

"Early this morning, as I had planned, I observed the awakening of the woman Elizabeth. I knew that her screens would be misty in half-sleep and hoped that I would be able to penetrate her deeply and without trace during the few moments that she was vulnerable. I undertook the task, rather than Culluket, because my combination of farsensing and redactive faculties is perhaps most congruous to Elizabeth's own, and thus least likely to be detected by her . . . I believe that I succeeded. I observed her reactions to the events that took place at the supper last night, as well as her later response to the removal of her hot-air balloon and other survival gear from her chambers. As to the first: She views our simple culture with condescension and disdain. She finds our manners barbarous, our mental patterns adolescent, and our sexual mores incompatible with the ritual monogamy and sublimation fostered among the metapsychic elite of her Milieu. She despises us. She will never willingly integrate. She rejects and abominates the role of royal consort. There was something deep within her motivation that I was unable to con, but the fact of her resolution was clear and immutable. She will never submit to the new genetic scheme hatched by Gomnol. As to our abstraction of her escape gear—she still hopes to flee from Muriah in some manner and become a Lowlife."

Reliefgratification! "But, my dears! We couldn't ask for a better outcome! My greatest anxiety was that she should aspire to be queen." And I . . . come at last to share the fate of Boanda and Anéar-Ia.

Never! cried the three sibling minds.

The Queen expanded to embrace them: Dearest children flowers of my Host.

Culluket said aloud, "Nevertheless, we mustn't delude ourselves. Even without ambition, Elizabeth menaces our dynasty. I have been farspeaking to Nodonn in Goriah and he agrees. As matters now stand, our noble brother is the obvious heir to the Thagdal even in spite of his flaw—and we shall amplify our power beneath Nodonn's aegis. But we could not hope to prevail against a line of operant metapsychics of the type that Elizabeth and Thagdal would engender. You can be sure that Gomnol is quite aware of this."

The redactor projected two genetic diagrams. "The first shows the offspring if Elizabeth is homozygous. Greg-Donnet says that meta-psychic operancy is an autosomal dominant with full penetrance."

"All of the children would be operant!" Nontusvel exclaimed in dismay.

Culluket continued. "The second diagram assumes Elizabeth has only a single allele for operancy. Half the offspring would then be operant. Inbreed the operants of the first generation, and the next yields three operants out of four. Continue the consanguineous matings, and you have a rival host of torcless metapsychics ready to oppose us in the third generation!"

Riganone's mind queried: Incest?

Culluket showed his sister a bleak smile. "The scheme is Gomnol's. He is hardly one to scruple at our Tanu taboos. And the Thagdal grows old and ever more subject to the filthy Coercer Lord's human wiles."

The four minds paused to reprise the old infamy. A human upstart as President of the Coercer Guild! Poor old Leyr hadn't had a chance against him.

"A good thing the wretch is sterile." Young Imidol's hatred was vividly displayed. "Gomnol would go for Elizabeth himself! Defiler of our sacred blue and gold!"

We depart from the immediate matter Brother.

"Culluket is right," said the Queen. "But what are we to do with Elizabeth?"

Visions: A red balloon soaring eastward from Aven, over the Deep Lagoon to the long isle of Kersic . . . A sailing craft manned by Highjohn, or even by the woman herself, fleeing south to Africa . . . A furtive figure in a red jumpsuit making its way westward on foot along the high spine of the Aven Peninsula, guided by ramas into the wilderness of Iberia . . .

Consequents: The balloon swiftly spied out and pursued by flying psychokinetics loyal to the King rather than to the Host. The escaping boat retrieved with even greater ease by the same PK adepts, the sails of their cutters filled by mind-conjured gales. The woman fleeing on foot presenting a knottier problem—but how far could she go with the entire countryside aroused, and four hundred kilometers to travel before reaching the mainland of Spain? She would have to skirt the large city of Afaliah at the peninsula's base, escape its Hunt and plantation security forces. Still, if she did reach the Catalan Wilderness . . .

"She would be out of the Thagdal's reach and out of ours,"

Culluket said, "but subject to capture by the Firvulag or even the heretic Minanonn. And this last, I submit, would be an even greater calamity than the one facing us now."

The Queen's kindly heart shrank from the next question. "What is the solution, then?"

"She must be put to death," said Imidol. "It is the only way. And not only her mind but her body destroyed, so there is no hope of Gomnol utilizing her ova in his obscene contraptions."

Little olive-and-black finches warbled in the lemon trees. The breeze from the Mount of Heroes above Muriah was dying now and it was getting very hot. The Queen extended a ringed finger toward a tiny spider that was lowering itself from the rafters of the pavilion. Its web floated as in an unfelt wind, bringing the creature to a landing on Nontusvel's fingernail. She watched it stand there, combing the air with its front legs, its sparky predator's mind sniffing.

"It may not be easy," she said. "We know little of the offensive capability of such a one. If we sent her far away, she would not desire to return. She would be grateful to us rather than perhaps doing us great harm."

The spider began a wary descent from the Queen's finger. She sent it sailing safely to the branch of a remontant shrub rose. *Eat the aphis, little hunterkiller, so that the roses may thrive.*

Culluket said, "Elizabeth is strong only in farsensing and redaction. Her other metafaculties are negligible. She cannot spin concrete illusions nor conjure up psychoenergies. She has a small PK factor but it is useless for self-defense or aggression. There is no coercive power per se—but the redact is developed to a formidable degree."

Imidol sent an ironic thrust at his brother. *And you, if anyone, Interrogator, should know the potential for mischief in a corruption of the mindhealing power.*

Imi we have no time for pettypushies! Aloud, Riganone said, "The Galactic Milieu placed limitations on masterclass metas after the time of their rebellion. There is not only an ethical restraint but also an imposed superego block, which I saw very clearly during my probing. Elizabeth cannot harm a sentient being except in the gravest defense of her *fellow humans.*"

Digestivemindpause.

"A nice point," Culluket mused. "If we had sufficient time . . . a compulsion to self-destruction would be effective. Do you agree, Farspeaking Sister?"

"Her emotional tone was deep gray," Riganone agreed. "She feels she is alone. Bereft."

And so she is, came the Queen's soft motherthought.

Imidol said, briskly, "Cull and I will design a suitable compulsion. We'll plan a coordinate thrust powered by the one hundred and nine members of the Host who are presently here in Muriah. If this isn't strong enough, we'll try again at Grand Combat time when the rest get here."

"We can't count on compulsions alone," Culluket said. "I'll try to work out some other options. And when Nodonn arrives, he may think of some better means of dealing with her."

"The Thagdal must never know!" the Queen warned them.

Nor Gomnol, Culluket's mind added.

"We have time for maneuvering," Riganone said. "Remember that Elizabeth must go to Brede first for the initiation, and that will take some time. Not even the King would dare to interfere with an initiate—or with Brede."

The enigmatic image of the Shipspouse hovered in all their minds. The guard and guide of their Exile, older than the oldest of them, some said she was the most powerful of them all and few would doubt that she was the wisest. But Brede rarely intervened directly in the affairs of the High Kingdom on Earth. It had been a shock to the entire company when the King announced that Elizabeth would become the Shipspouse's initiate.

"Brede!" Imidol exuded the contempt of the younger generation for venerable mysteries. "She has no allegiance to any faction. Still—Elizabeth is such a patent danger to us all, that perhaps if we appealed to the Shipspouse—"

Riganone laughed without mirth. "Do you really believe that Brede doesn't know? She sees everything, hiding away in her room without doors! She very likely ordered the Thagdal to send the human woman to her!"

"Damn Brede," said Culluket in vicious dismissal. "Let the Two-Faced One have Elizabeth for the time of initiation. What can she do? We'll get the human bitch somehow when the Shipspouse finishes with her. Elizabeth will never become queen-dam in your place, Mother."

Never, never, vowed the other two.

"Poor woman." The Queen arose and went out of the pavilion. It was time to seek the cool inner rooms of the palace. "I feel so sorry for her. If only there were another way."

"There isn't," said Imidol. Dauntless in his coercer's blue and gold, he offered Nontusvel his arm. The four of them went off down the garden path.

Back in the rose bush, the little spider was busy sucking the life juices from an aphis. When the finch swooped down on him, it was too late to duck.

5

"NOT SILVER . . . of course not silver, Bryan. Gold!"

Ogmol's high voice, incongruous in one of such heroic physique, was loud enough to carry over the normal clatter and buzz of the marketplace and cause shoppers and sellers to stare at him. There weren't that many Tanu wandering among the stalls anyway, and no males that Bryan could see. Here and there a willowy exotic lady, attended by a retinue of grays and ramas to carry the packages and hold the sunshade, bent over the offerings of an itinerant human jeweler, glassblower, or some other cottage artisan. There were a few silver-torcs among the browsers; but most of those who moved about the open plaza seemed to be torcless human householders or grays in the livery of the great houses, out to purchase fresh produce for the kitchen, flowers, live birds or animals, or other items not generally available in the many small shops that lined the perimeter of the Square of Commerce.

"I've been over this with Creyn," Bryan said patiently. "No torc for me." He stopped to examine a table crowded with a jumble of oddly assorted twenty-second-century artifacts; canteens, half-empty jars of cosmetics, tattered page-books, worn articles of clothing, broken musical instruments, defunct chronometers and voicewriters, a few common decamole appliances and vitredur tools.

"It would help you in your work," Ogmol insisted. He took belated notice of the flea market wares Bryan was looking at. "These things—the usual castoffs. The more unusual and valuable items from your era may be disposed of only through licensed dealers. But there is a black market, of course."

"Mm," said Bryan, moving on.

Ogmol returned to the previous tack. "There are no coercive or dispositive circuits of any kind in a golden torc. In your case, since you have no significant latencies, the torc would merely enhance your telepathic ability—the metapsychic power every human has— and allow you to mindspeak with us. Think of the time we'd save! Consider the semantic advantage! You wouldn't miss a single nuance of your cultural immersion. The scope of your analysis would be broader, less prone to subjective error—"

A vendor in a straw sombrero grinned and waved a skewer of small, freshly roasted birds. "Barbecued larks, Exalted Lords? My own Texas-style chili sauce!"

"Popcorn," croaked a withered old woman in the stall next door. "New crop tetraploid. One kernel a snack in itself."

"Only a few Périgord truffles left today, Lord."

"Attar of roses! Orange-water to cool your temples! Just for you, Lord—a rare flagon of 4711!"

Ogmol grimaced. "It's a fake. They ought to do something about these fellows . . . But as I was saying, with a torc—"

"The only working conditions I'll accept are those affording complete freedom." Bryan kept his good humor. Ogmol made a gesture of resignation and led the way to a building on the shady side of the square. A sign designated it BAKERY-KLEINFUSS-CAFÉ.

The crowd of shoppers parted respectfully before them. Tables were set on a flower-decked terrace fronting the bakery. A rama in a red-and-white checked tabard came trotting up, bowed, and took them to a table, where Ogmol collapsed in a wicker chair.

"This walking in the heat of the day! I hope we can engage in less strenuous researches for a while, Bryan. I'm still a bit hung-over from the party last night. I don't know how you manage to look so bright."

The rama swiftly produced two cups of coffee and a large tray of pastries. Bryan chose one.

"Why, there's a pill. Our race had to wait a long time, but we finally developed an instant cure for overindulgence just in the last year or so. Tiny little pills. I packed a good number in my rucksack. A pity I didn't think to bring them this morning."

"There!" moaned Ogmol. "The very thing I mean. If you wore a torc, you'd *know* how I was suffering without my having to tell you in so many words." He downed his coffee in a long gulp and the rama refilled the cup. "And you'd be able to make your wishes known to the ramas as well. See? That little chap almost warmed up your cup before you were ready for it—but he'd never do that with me. You can't do much verbal communication with ramas, you know. Just 'come' and 'go,' that kind of thing. Persons without torcs have to use sign language with the little apes—and that can be very awkward for all but the simplest commands."

Bryan only nodded, eating his pastry. It was delicious, evoking Vienna's best. Small wonder that the interior of the Bakery Kleinfuss was crowded with take-out customers. "As I understand it, the golden torc can't be removed once it's in place. And I also have learned that some personalities become seriously disturbed through wearing the thing. You can understand why I don't want to risk my sanity, Ogmol. There's no reason why my torcless status should limit my researches. I was a competent worker in the Milieu without metafaculties, and so were most of my colleagues. All that's necessary for a valid analysis is dependable source material."

The Tanu's eyes shifted. "Well, yes. We'll try our very best to obtain that for you. My Awesome Father has given explicit orders."

Bryan tried to be tactful. "Some of my investigations are bound to touch raw nerves. I can't help it in a study such as this. Even my superficial observations have begun to reveal a pattern of profound stress resulting from the impact of human and Tanu cultures."

"The very thing my Father wishes to evaluate, Bryan. But the researches could be done so much more—gracefully on the mental level. Words are so *dense*." He downed another cup of coffee, squeezed his eyes closed, and pressed the fingertips of both hands to his golden torc. Many of the exotic men had faces of transcendent beauty; but Ogmol's was refreshingly unhandsome. His nose had a knot at the bridge, and his lips, between the short-cropped beard resembling tawny plush, were too thick and red. He resembled the King only in his deepset, jade-colored eyes—now lamentably blood-webbed. For the sake of coolness he was attired in a short sleeveless robe of cyan-blue and silver, symbolic of the Guild of Creators. His arms and legs were furred with wiry tan hair.

"No use trying to psych the miseries away." Ogmol tapped his knuckles against his brow. "Plum brandy will have its revenge. You *will* let me have a pill or two for future use, won't you, old man?"

"Of course. And I'll try to be as judicious as possible in my investigations. It might take a little longer that way, but we'll get on."

"Feel free to be as direct as you please with *me*." Ogmol gave a rueful chuckle. "My sensibilities are quite expendable."

"Why do you say that?"

"It's my duty to assist you. My honor. And as a half-blood, my skin isn't quite as thin as that of the—uh—isolate fraction."

"Your mother was a human?"

Ogmol waved away the rama and leaned back in his chair. "She was a silver. A sculptor from the Wessex world. She passed her latent creativity along to me, but she was too emotionally unstable to last long in the Many-Colored Land. I was her only offspring."

"Would you say that there was significant prejudice against those of mixed heritage?"

"It exists." Ogmol frowned, then shook his head. "But—damn *words!*—the disdain in which we're held by the Old Ones is strongly tinged by other emotions. Our bodies aren't as finely formed as theirs, but we're stronger physically. Most purebloods can't swim, but *we* have no difficulty in the water. Hybrids are more fertile, in spite of the fact that the full Tanu have a more urgent libido. And we're less likely to engender Firvulag offspring or black-torcs." He repeated the uneasy little laugh. "You see, Bryan, we hybrids are actually an improvement on the original model. That's what's so insupportable."

"Mm," the anthropologist temporized.

"As you can see, my body is superficially very similar to that of a pureblood: light hair, fair skin, typical light-sensitive eyes, elongated torso, attenuated limbs. But the ample body hair is a human heritage, and so is my more robust skeletal structure and musculature. Only a minority of the pureblooded men have this type of physique . . . the King and the battle-champions. Back in the home galaxy of the Tanu, a heroic body was rather an anachronism. A reminder of the crude origins of the race."

"But the very heritage," Bryan observed, "that the exiled group was determined to revive. Interesting."

The rama came running up with a large napkin, which Ogmol used to wipe his brow. It really was a pity, Bryan thought, that he had left the aldetox back at the palace.

"But don't you see, Bryan, how difficult it is for the Old Ones to accept the fact that human genes optimize their racial survival on Earth? Hybrid vigor is a putdown to them. The Old Ones are very proud. It's illogical—but they seem to be afraid of us mixed-bloods."

"The mind-set wasn't uncommon even in my own era," Bryan admitted. He swallowed the last crumb of pastry and finished his coffee. "You said we might visit Lord Gomnol's establishment. Shall we go there next?"

Ogmol grinned and fingered his torc. "You see? Another advantage! Give me a minute."

The rama waiter stood passively beside the table, a monkey-child with intelligent, sad eyes. As Ogmol made his telepathic call, Bryan fished in one pocket for some of the local coinage he had been given and held out a random assortment. Solemnly, the hominid fingers extracted two pieces of silver. "No tip?" Bryan wondered. He looked around at the other tables. Not a single person without a torc was seated on the terrace. The barenecks had to make do with a self-service bar inside where human clerks took their verbal orders.

"Good news," said Ogmol. "Gomnol is free and would be delighted to conduct you around his laboratories personally! . . . I see you've paid. Just let me—"

The rama gave a little yip of pleasure and everted its lips at Ogmol. "*Mental* largesse, Bryan."

"I should have guessed."

* * *

They took a cab, drawn by a helladotherium, to the large complex on the northern edge of the city that housed the Coercer Guild. On the way down the wide boulevards they passed many small shops and neat attached dwellings. There was none of the quaint "Munchkin Tudor" architecture of the outlying settlements to be found in Muriah. Here the buildings had a classical elegance of line that was almost Doric. The white and pastel masses were softened by lavish plantings, tended by the ever-present ramapithecines. The human inhabitants of Muriah—artisans, shopkeepers, service workers, troops, and functionaries—were universally well-fed and prosperous-looking. The only persons who could be classed as shabaroons were the peddlers in the open market, the caravan drovers, and travelers newly arrived from the hinterlands; even these seemed only temporarily grubby. Bryan saw no evidence of disease, privation, or maltreatment among the torcless element. On the surface, Muriah looked to be an idyllic small city. Ogmol told him that the total permanent population included some four thousand Tanu, a few hundred gold-torc humans, under a thousand silvers, about five thousand gray-torcs, and six or seven thousand torcless. The ramas outnumbered the people by at least three to one.

"We classify as Tanu any person who *looks* exotic," the brawny scholar explained. "Officially, there is no discrimination among purebloods and mixed. And, of course, a gold-torc human is the social equal of a Tanu. In theory, anyhow."

Bryan suppressed a smile. "Another reason for your urging a collar on me? Your association with a bareneck must be a trifle déclassé. I noticed that the vendors were giving me a fishy look back in the market."

Rather stiffly, Ogmol said, "Any person of consequence knows who you are. The others don't matter." They rode in silence for a while. Bryan considered another possible motive for the King's having commissioned the anthropological study. He was glad that Ogmol was unable to read his thoughts.

They came to a handsome group of buildings at the very edge of the dropoff to the Catalan Gulf. The white marble of the Coercer Headquarters was inlaid and ornamented with blue and yellow. The forecourt had mosaic pavement with abstract designs. The roofs were sheathed in striking azure tiles with gutters and other fittings that glistened like gold. Squads of well-armed gray-torc guards in half-armor of blue glass and bronze posed stoically in the entry archway and at all of the doors. As the carriage passed and Ogmol emitted some unheard telepathic hail, the men thumped the butts of their vitredur halberds in salute. A detail stood by as Bryan and Ogmol alighted, making sure that the human cabdriver did not linger in Guild precincts.

"The Coercers seem quite security-conscious," Bryan remarked.

"The torc works is here. In a certain sense, this place is the very keystone of our High Kingdom."

They passed into cool corridors, where more guards stood like living statues—any boredom presumably assuaged by their gray torcs. Somewhere a deep-toned bell sounded three times. Bryan and Ogmol ascended a staircase and came to a pair of tall bronze doors. Four guards on station lifted a heavy ornamental bar so that the two researchers could enter the antechamber of the President's office. There behind a console equipped with constructs of glowing crystal sat an exotic woman of singular beauty. Bryan felt something like an icy needle whisk behind his eyes.

"Tana's mercy, Meva!" said Ogmol irritably. "Would I bring a hostile here? Doctor Grenfell was vetted by Lord Dionket himself!"

I was? Bryan wondered.

The woman said, "I only do my duty, Creative Brother." She gestured to the door of the inner sanctum, apparently opened it by psychokinesis, and returned to whatever esoteric work their arrival had interrupted.

"Come in! Come in!" called a deeply pitched voice.

They came before Gomnol, Lord Coercer, who inhabited a world all his own. The room was chilly in spite of the tropical climate of Muriah. A few coals smoldered in the grate of a manteled baronial fireplace, above which was a stark canvas that had to be a Georgia O'Keeffe. A Chihuahua dog eyed the newcomers dyspeptically from its cushion in front of the fire. The walls of the room were paneled in dark wood, interrupted by shelves crowded with leatherbound page-books, Tanu crystalline audiovisuals, and plaques of the twenty-second century. A stand held a copy (surely it was a copy?) of Rodin's sinister little Tentation de Saint Antoine. Chairs and settees of tufted, wine-colored leather stood before a huge reproduction of a rococo-revival desk, upon which rested a green-shaded oil lamp, a tarnished silver inkstand with quill pen, a fruitwood humidor, and an onyx ashtray overflowing with cigar butts. A walnut credenza in the same ornate style as the desk, flanked by fern stands, held a dozen cut-glass decanters, a tray of Waterford tumblers, a soda siphon, and a small tin of Cadbury biscuits. (And what time-traveler had surrendered the last treasure to the Lord Coercer's irresistible demand?)

In the midst of a cloud of fragrant smoke sat Eusebio Gomez-Nolan himself, wearing a quilted jacket of gold brocade with lapels and cuffs of midnight-blue satin. While perhaps not the "ugly little runt" deprecated by King Thagdal, he was only of medium stature by the standards of the Old World, with a nose that was not merely aquiline but verging on the bulbous. His eyes, however, were a beautiful luminous blue with dark lashes, and he smiled at his visitors, showing small, perfect teeth.

"Be seated, colleagues," he said in a casual tone, gesturing with his cigar.

Bryan asked himself how the devil this ordinary-looking little fellow had managed to install himself as President of the Coercer Guild.

And Gomnol heard.

Once in years long past, Bryan had sailed his small yacht into a hurricane that had broken loose from the weathermakers and wandered close to the British Isles. After enduring hours of battering, he had relaxed in a respite—only to see rising before his craft a mountainous green sea with a breaking crest that appeared to be at least thirty meters above him. Deliberately, this huge wave had curled over his yacht, pressing it under with a monster insouciance that he knew must end in annihilation. And so it was now with Gomnol's psychic force impinging upon his own stunned consciousness, pressing him easily toward a final darkness.

The great storm-surge had unaccountably released his broken but still seaworthy yacht. With a similar mannered fillip, Gomnol let loose of Bryan's mind.

"That's how," said the President of the Coercer Guild. "Now. How may I assist your researches?"

Bryan heard Ogmol explain the task that the High King had set and the techniques that they hoped to use to gather data for the culture-impact analysis. Lord Gomnol could help, if he would, not only by explaining the pivotal role of the torcs, but also by sharing his personal reminiscences, uniquely valuable because of his privileged human status. And if the Exalted Lord would prefer to confer with Dr. Grenfell alone . . .

Smoke rings drawn around a friendly smile. "I believe that would be best. My congratulations on your delicacy of feeling, Creative Brother. Why not return and join us for dinner—say, in three hours? Splendid. Assure our Awesome Father that I'll take the very best care of the worthy Doctor of Anthropology."

And then Gomnol and Bryan were alone in the pseudo-Victorian snuggery, and the psychobiologist was clipping the end off a fresh cigar and saying, "Now, then, my friend. What the devil is the likes of you doing in Exile?"

"May I—have a drink?"

Gomnol went to the decanters and lifted one containing a nearly colorless liquid. "We have the Glendessarry, but no Évian water, I'm afraid. Or would you care to try some of our homebrews? Five whiskies, a vodka, any number of brandies—the preferred tipple of our Tanu brethren."

"Straight Scotch is fine," Bryan managed to say. When the whisky had restored his nerve a bit, he said, "I hope you won't regard me as a threat. Really—I'm not at all certain of the motivation behind the King's request myself. I came through the time-portal for the most ordinary of reasons. I was following the woman I loved. I had expected to become a fisherman or a trader in a primitive Pliocene world. The interest in my profession by my Tanu captors was a complete surprise to me. I'm cooperating because I've been told that this is the only way I'll get to see Mercy."

Gomez-Nolan lowered one black brow in a half-scowl, seeming to scrutinize something floating in the air just in front of Bryan. "*That's* your Mercy?" he inquired cryptically. "Good God." Not bothering to explain himself, he lit his cigar. "Come along. I'll show you the factory and tell you the Changeling's Tale."

A slab of the paneling swung aside, revealing a long, well-lit passage. Bryan followed Gomnol in a wake of smoke. They came to a great gateway of bronze bars that folded aside of its own volition as Gomnol strode heedlessly into it.

"Oh, yes. I have PK, too," the psychobiologist said. "And farspeak and redact. Not as strong as the coercive faculty, of course, but enough to be useful."

They came into a large room filled with what appeared to be jewelers' benches. Human and Tanu men and women in blue smocks, wearing magnifying eyelenses, were making golden torcs.

"This is the heart of the place, right here. All handwork for these. Subassemblies—the crystalline chips with the circuitry—have to be grown, then spattered and etched and sent here for installation within the metal shell. The Tanu brought only a single crystal-growing unit and chip etcher with them from their home galaxy, but I was able to build more to permit an increase in production of about tenfold."

A rama went by, trundling a cart with containers of glittering components. Gomnol waved his cigar, causing a pink wafer to fly out of a box and into his fingers. "This little widget is my own psychoregulator that I developed for the silvers and grays. It puts the wearer at the mental disposal of any gold."

Bryan could not help but envision Aiken Drum.

Gomnol brightened. "A fascinating case. I wasn't at the feast, but they told me all about him. Too bad old Mayvar has him locked up over in Farsense House. Both Culluket and I are itching to interrogate him."

"He worries the establishment?"

Gomnol laughed. "The more naive elements. He doesn't worry me. The boy sounds like he must be a mental nova. Flash-in-the-pan pseudo-operant. The phenomenon wasn't unknown in the Milieu. Certain latents can be shocked into operancy by some profound trauma. We've had it happen here once or twice before, although none of the cases was quite as memorable as this Aiken Drum seems to be. The temporary operant status of the brain overrides the controls of the silver torc. But the thing can't sustain itself and eventually burns out—googol to gaga, just like that."

"I've heard about the sad cases who couldn't adapt to the torc. But I understand you've been wearing one for forty years without suffering a mental burnout."

The man in the smoking jacket only smiled around his cigar.

They wandered among the benches, watching the painstaking work. It took almost a week for a technician to complete one of the golden neck-rings—even longer for the delicate little torcs worn by Tanu children. These came in four sizes; and when a larger one was put on, the smaller could be safely removed and used on another child.

"No silver torcs for children?" Bryan asked.

"Tanu women don't have human offspring—not even when they mate with human males. And human women—whether gold or silver or gray or bareneck—are only permitted to conceive by Tanu males. All of their offspring are exotic as well, but with a much smaller percentage of Firvulag phenotypes in the litter than Tanu women produce. The Tanu hybrids vary greatly in metapsychic faculties, of course. So far, all of them are latent. But in time, the race will produce natural operants, just as humanity has done. The human advent was quite a genetic leg up for the Tanu, as you can imagine. On their own—without any human admixture—they wouldn't have gone operant for millions of years. The human-Tanu matings speed up the evolutionary process drastically. Given the quality of the latent stock coming through the time-gate, Prentice Brown had calculated that the Tanu would go reliably operant in only fifty generations. Of course, now . . ."

"Elizabeth?"

"Exactly. When we got word of her arrival, Prentice Brown and I recalculated the heritability of the different meta genes based upon Elizabeth's presumed genetic assay and the results were astounding. You can get the details from Prentice Brown himself over at Creation House. He's called Lord Greg-Donnet, you know."

Bryan couldn't help thinking: Crazy Greggy.

Again Gomnol laughed, teeth tightly clenching the cigar. "Some sooner, some later. Come along through here. The silver torcs are basically similar to the gold. But we've been able to automate a bit in the manufacture of the gray and rama types."

"How," Bryan asked, "do the Firvulag fit into your genetic enterprise?"

"They don't, as yet. A great pity from the eugenic viewpoint, as you've already deduced. The Little People are genuine operants, even if their powers tend to be limited. Unfortunately, both races have a horrendous taboo against interbreeding—and no Firvulag would touch a human with a barge pole. But some of us are working on the problem. If we could only convince the Tanu to keep their Firvulag children instead of passing them over to the Little People, we might have a chance of changing the mating pattern. It's fraught with possibilities."

They did a quick run through the area where the gray torcs were made. There was more of a factory atmosphere in this workshop, where several simple stamping machines were turning out torc shells and ramas were performing some of the assembly. Gomnol explained that the gray torcs were a variant of the device originally used on ramas by the pioneering Tanu, which he himself had modified into a psychoregulator suitable for humanity.

"We still have some problems with the torcs, as you heard. But by and large they're much more effective than the docilization implants that were used on sociopaths in the Milieu. And the pleasure-pain circuitry and the farspeak augmentation are completely innovative." Gomnol's eyes darted sidelong. In a neutral tone, he added, "I designed the original docilization device at Berkeley, you know."

Bryan's forehead furrowed. "I thought Eisenmann—"

Gomnol turned away. In a tight voice, he said, "I was a graduate student working under him. A young fool. We had a touching father-son relationship and he was so proud of me. My work was promising, he said, but its potential might remain unrealized because I lacked the cachet necessary to attract Polity funding. However, if I worked under him . . . there would be no problem. I was grateful and he was clever and the work was a resounding success. And now the entire Milieu knows Eisenmann the laureate. A few even remember Eusebio Gomez-Nolan, his faithful little assistant."

"I see."

The other man whirled around. "Oh, do you?" he flared. "Do you, indeed? Just forty years, and I've shaped an entire culture—turned these exotics from a path of feckless barbarism toward civilization! If the genetic manipulation with Elizabeth comes about, they could become transtechnological, superior to the Union of our unborn Galactic Milieu! What would Eisenmann and those Stockholm idiots think if they could see all *this*?"

Oh, God, Bryan thought. He tried to keep his own mind as blank as possible. What had Elizabeth told them back at the auberge? Count! Onetwothreefour onetwothreefour onetwothreefour . . .

But Gomnol was not attempting to read the panicked anthropologist's thoughts. He was fully occupied with his own inner vision. "Many years ago, during the time of the Rebellion, a small number of other operants came through the time-gate. I wasn't ready. My position was still unconsolidated and the Tanu culture was in such a state of flux that matters were taken out of my hands before I could act. But I'm ready now! There are people working with me who share my views. With a new generation of operants standing with us, we'll prevail."

Onetwothreefour onetwothreefour. "It's a remarkable ambition, Lord Gomnol. Given the cooperation of Elizabeth, I don't see how it can fail." Onetwothreefour.

The psychobiologist seemed to relax. He blew a smoke ring, then gave Bryan a hearty clap on the shoulder. "Keep an objective eye, Grenfell. That's all I ask."

They moved into another area, where the crystal modules for the mental-assay machines were being assembled. "Care to have your soul microanalyzed?" Now Gomnol was jovial. "We can do a much better job here than at Castle Gateway. Prototype of an improved model coming up. I could furnish you with your complete psychosocial profile as well as a latency analysis. It would take only a few hours."

Onetwothreefour. "It wouldn't be too useful to you, I'm afraid. Lady Epone wasn't impressed when she tested me back at the castle."

An expression of wariness clouded the Lord Coercer's smile. "Yes. It *was* Epone who checked your Group out, wasn't it." He fell silent, and after a perfunctory stroll through research and testing facilities, where Gomnol was evasive about the exact nature of the work being done, they went down a long ramp that led from the factory to an atrium open to the sky and cooled by the jets of a spectacular fountain. They sat at a shaded table and rama servants in blue-and-gold livery brought a drink resembling iced sangría.

"One of your Group was a young woman named Felice," Gomnol said. "She's been involved in a serious accident. Can you tell me anything about her background?"

Onetwothreefour.

Bryan recapitulated all that he could remember of the girl's career as a ring-hockey player, her attack on the auberge counselor, her great physical strength and obvious deviation from the psychosocial norm. "I never saw her profile. But her ability to control animals is certainly suggestive of latency. I'm rather surprised that she didn't rate a silver torc. Was she badly injured in the accident?"

"She wasn't hurt at all." Gomnol's tone was studiously neutral. "The travelers in her caravan staged a revolt on the way to Finiah. The Lady Epone, a powerful coercer, was killed, together with the entire escort of gray-torc troops. The prisoners escaped, but most of them were later recaptured. They agreed under interrogation that your friend Felice had been the ringleader of the affair."

Onetwothreefour! "That's incredible. And did she—did you recapture Felice?"

"No. She and three other members of your Group are still at large. Most of the Tanu Great Ones are inclined to think that the affair was a fluke. There have been other minor uprisings from time to time, sometimes abetted by the Firvulag. But never before this have bareneck humans been able to kill a Tanu. If Felice engineered it, I must find out how."

Onetwothreefour onetwothreefour. "I don't think there's much more I can tell you about her that would be useful. She struck me as a peculiar and dangerous child. She's only about eighteen, you know."

Gomnol sighed. "The children are *always* the most dangerous . . . Finish your drink, Bryan. I think we just have time to visit the classrooms of the apprentice coercers before the end of the afternoon. You'll enjoy meeting my youngsters. I have the highest hopes for them. The very highest."

Puffing his cigar, Eusebio Gomez-Nolan took Bryan off to view fresh marvels.

6

SUKEY'S FEAR had lessened now but there was still the underlying sense of terror at being separated from Stein. But she no longer worried that he might be in danger; Aiken Drum, that inexplicable jester, would take care of him.

But what would become of *her?*

Creyn had come for her—friendly, familiar Creyn, the only person besides Elizabeth that she would have willingly followed. (And how had they known?) She rode now with the exotic healer in a helladdrawn calèche to the College of Redactors, which was situated high above the city on a road that led up the forested Mount of Heroes. Olive trees heavy with plum-sized fruit grew along the verge and in the walled compounds of handsome white villas. She saw groves of citrus and almond; and, higher up the slope, rows of grapevines were being dressed by ramas. To the west the land of Aven stretched in a crazy quilt of greens and golds to the Dragon Range dimly visible on the horizon. Most of the region seemed under intensive cultivation, a striking contrast to the saltflats and pale bluish lagoons of the surrounding Mediterranean Basin.

As the carriage climbed higher, Sukey was able to see the peculiar topography of the ancient seabed south of Balearis. A scarp nearly 100 meters high fell off sharply on that side of the peninsula. Below lay an undulant slope of snow-white dunes, broken here and there by buttes and eroded pillars of what seemed to be pastel-colored salt. A small river coming off the peninsula slightly west of Muriah had carved a canyon through sparkling sediments. The watercourse wandered over the barren bed of this gorge, whose walls showed pale strips of color, and eventually reached the southern arm of the lagoon. East of the river channel and extending below the tip of Aven were flats that reflected the sunlight with a mirror dazzle.

"The White Silver Plain," Creyn told her. "We hold the Grand Combat down there, setting up cities of tents on either side of the Well of the Sea. Nearly ten thousand Tanu and human fighters come to the Combat from all parts of the Many-Colored Land, together with five times that number of noncombatants. And the Firvulag come as well, all tricked out in their bright and fearsome illusions with the black armor hidden beneath, carrying monstrous effigy standards hung with dyed scalps and festoons of gilded skulls."

Her mind's eye gaped at the picture he conjured up—first of the preliminaries, where the Firvulag played their uncouth games while the Tanu contended in splendid tournaments and races with chalikos and chariots. And then the manifestation of powers when the battleleaders were chosen, and finally the High Mêlée itself, with Tanu and human and Firvulag thundering toward one another, shining hero versus hideous demon in battles pitting arm against arm, mind against mind, for three days—with the seizing of banners or standards and the taking of heads, the whirl of glass and bronze and leather and sweating flesh, the victors howling and glowing in the dark like torches, while the losers lay silent, spilling their blood black on the salt . . .

"No!" Sukey cried. "No—not Stein!" But he would love it— Peace flooded through her.

Be at ease littleSistermind. It is a ways away and things may happen and not allTanu revel in its bloodshed O no not all.

"I don't understand," she said, searching Creyn's shuttered face. "What are you trying to tell me?"

"You're going to have to be strong. Bide your time until the proper moment and take a long view of matters. Keep hope high even when . . . distressing things happen to you. Stein and Aiken Drum have a hard way ahead of them, but yours may be harder."

She tried to probe him, to discover what lay behind that walled and kindly gaze, but it defeated her. She fell back into the simpler comfort that he offered, hardly caring any more what happened to her so long as there was a chance it might come right in the end.

"There *is* a chance, Sukey. Remember. And be brave."

Walls and turrets of silver and scarlet loomed over their carriage. They passed beneath an arch of marble filigree and halted before a white structure with pillars of red marble. A Tanu woman gowned in filmy white came out and took Sukey's hand.

Creyn introduced her. "The Lady Zealatrix Olar, who will be your teacher here in the House of Healing."

Welcome Daughterdear. What is your name?

Sue-Gwen.

"A goodly name," said the woman aloud. "We will give you the honorific Minivel, and you will rejoice to know that the lady who bore it last lived for two thousand years. Come with me, Gwen-Minivel!"

Sukey turned to Creyn, lips trembling.

"I leave you in the best of hands," he said. "Courage."

And then Creyn was gone, and Sukey followed Olar into the headquarters of the Guild of Redactors. It was quiet and cool, the décor mostly a chaste white and silver with only occasional accents of the heraldic red. Only a few people were to be seen; there were no guards.

"May—may I question you, Lady?" Sukey asked.

"Certainly. Later there will be the testing and the discipline. But now, at the beginning, I will show you the work that we do and answer your queries as fully as possible." And correct and guide and light.

"Persons like me—with silver torcs, or gold. How long may we live in this world? Is it as you imply—"

Smile. Come see. Anticipate!

They descended into arched catacombs within the rock of the mountain, lit with ruby and white lamps. Olar opened a thick door and they entered a circular room, quite dark, where a lone Tanu redactor sat on a central stool with his eyes closed in meditation. Slowly, Sukey's vision accommodated itself to the dimness. What she had mistaken for white statues ranged around the wall proved to be people, their naked bodies completely shrouded in transparent, clinging cauls that resembled some plastic membrane.

May I examine?

Freely.

She moved around the room, looking at the standing figures. Here was a gold-torc human male, reduced to a virtual skeleton by cachexia. Beside him was a Tanu woman, apparently lost in serene sleep, one pendulous breast distorted by a tumor. A Tanu child, motionless, her eyes wide open, had one arm severed below the elbow. A robust goldenbeard, smiling as he dreamed inside the artificial amnion, displayed the slashes and punctures of a hundred wounds. Another warrior type had both hands burned away. Next to him stood a human woman in late middle age, her body sagging but unmarked.

"The more severe cases are dealt with on an individual basis," said Olar. "But these our Healing Brother may minister to en masse. The membrane is a psychoactive substance we call Skin. Through a combination of psychokinesis and redaction, the practitioner is able to muster healing energies from the patient's own mind and body. Injuries, disease, cancers, the debilities of age—all respond to treatment if the patient's mind is strong enough to cooperate with the healer."

Limitations?

"We cannot restore brain injuries. And it is against our ethic to restore those who are decapitated in combat or ritual observances. If a person is not brought to treatment before full brain-death, we cannot help. Nor can we restore the aged whose minds have been allowed to deteriorate beyond a critical point. Given these limitations, we are not as advanced as the science of your Galactic Milieu, which could regenerate an entire cerebral cortex if only a gram of tissue remained, or rejuvenate even the most decrepit if their will was strong."

"Still—this is marvelous," Sukey breathed. "May I hope to do this kind of work some day?"

Olar took her hand and led her from the room. "Perhaps, child. But there are other tasks. Come and see."

They looked through one-way windows into rooms where the mentally deranged were undergoing deep-redact. A large percentage of the patients were young people, and Olar explained that these were mostly Tanu-human hybrids experiencing difficulties adapting to the torc.

"We treat human golds and silvers as well. However, some human brains are fundamentally incompatible to the long-term effects of the torc's amplification. Bringing such patients to full sanity may be impossible. Lord Gomnol has provided us with devices that indicate feasibility. We may not waste the time of our talented redactors on hopeless cases."

"I don't suppose you waste time on gray-torcs, either," Sukey said in a low voice, Elizabethstyle barrier firmly in place.

"No, dear. Ordinarily not. Valuable as our grays are to us, they are ephemerides—here and gone in a brief flash of vitality. The healing is a difficult and time-consuming process. It is not for them . . . Now, come and see our babies growing!"

They ascended to the upper reaches of the huge building and came to sunny rooms full of bright-colored play equipment. Beautifully groomed female ramapithecines romped and lolled under the benevolent eyes of human and Tanu keepers. In adjoining rooms, ramas were eating or sleeping or submitting to various kinds of care. Every one of the little apes was pregnant.

"You may know," Olar said in an offhanded manner, "that we Tanu women have experienced difficulty reproducing on this world. Early in our Exile, we utilized ramas as nurturers of the zygote. Ova fertilized in vitro are implanted within these animals and nourished. The ramas are too small to carry the fetuses to term, of course. But when development has progressed as far as possible, the infant is delivered by caesarian section. The mortality is nearly eighty percent, but we feel that the precious survivors are well worth the struggle. In the earliest days, these surrogate mothers seemed to be our only hope of racial survival. Fortunately, that situation no longer applies."

They left the ramas and tiptoed through a darkened ward where premature infants slept in sheltering glass crèches. Sukey was amazed to see Firvulag as well as Tanu babies receiving devoted care.

"They are our shadow-brethren," Olar told her. "We are obliged by the most ancient precepts of our way to rear them to term and subsequently turn them over to their own folk."

And then hunt and kill them?

You will understand one day littleSistermind. It is our way. If you would survive it must become your way.

"And now," Olar spoke out loud, "we will visit the Lady Tasha-Bybar."

Behind her mental screen, Sukey cried out.

"The procedure is very brief, but it is usually some weeks before the menstrual cycle reasserts itself normally. We will take care of this small matter before beginning your apprenticeship so that there will be a minimum of delay in your initiation."

Keeping a firm grip on herself, Sukey said, "I—I protest. To be *used* in this fashion—"

Peacecalmsolace. "It is your lot. Accept it. There is so much joy to be gleaned in compensation! And the Lady Bybar is very skilled. You will feel no pain."

Olar stood still for a moment, fingers resting on her golden torc. She nodded, smiled, and took Sukey up a winding stairway into one of the high turrets. The room at the top was fully thirty meters in diameter, commanding a fantastic view of the surrounding countryside and the misted, glaring salt.

In the middle of the polished black floor was a long golden table surrounded by small trolleys with jewel-bright objects gleaming on their open shelves. The reflector dish of a huge lamp, unlit, hung above the equipment.

"The Lady Bybar will first dance for you, Gwen-Minivel. She does you great honor. Wait here now until she comes, and comport yourself with a dignity befitting your silver torc."

With that, Olar left her alone.

Hesitating and fearful, Sukey approached the central table. It was! There were clamps and stirrups. And the jewel-bladed things were just what she had suspected.

Tears blinded her and she stumbled away from the apparatus. She cried out secretly: Stein I would for *you*.

Or she could still run . . .

Olar's mind-grip caught her. She was forced to stop, to turn around, to watch in stunned incredulity as Tasha-Bybar entered and began her dance.

The human body was as pale and as lush as that of an houri—and so exaggerated in its sexuality that Sukey's instinct told her it must have been artificially enhanced. There was hair only upon the woman's head, and this flared like a blue-black cloak when she spun and leaped, and rippled almost to her knees when she was momentarily still.

All that she wore was bells, and the golden torc. The bells were small and round, fastened to her living flesh in graceful twisting patterns. They had differing notes; and as the dancer's muscles flexed and extended, an elfin melody born of the movement itself sounded in the huge, nearly empty room. The rhythm was that of Sukey's pulse. She stood frozen and helpless as the dancer approached in great fluid leaps, arms beckoning as they wove their eerie song, feet stamping with an accelerating insistence that compelled Sukey's heart to beat faster and faster.

The dancer's sunken eyes were as black as her hair. Nearly colorless lips drew back in a rictus above her teeth. Around and around Sukey the dancer spun, increasing the tempo of the music until Sukey was dizzy, nauseated, trying in vain to close her eyes and ears and mind to the flashing chiming gyrating thing that seized her and whirled her into oblivion.

7

"You've FIXED IT! You're a bonny boy, my Shining One."

Mayvar the Hag watched in delight as the tiny figures on the timepiece came sliding out on their tracks and circled one another. The turquoise-and-jet dragon flapped golden wings and lunged, clashing its jeweled fangs. The knight in opal armor fended off the little monster, then raised his glittering sword and struck; once . . . twice . . . three times. The clock told the hour. The dragon expired, chopped into three sections revealing ruby entrails. The entire turntable at the front of the timepiece revolved, carrying the tableau back inside golden doors.

Aiken Drum stowed tools back into pockets. "It wasn't that hard to fix. Crud in the drivetrain, a worn tooth on one of the little gears. You ought to have a glassblower make a dome to cover it, sweets. Preventive maintenance."

"I will," the old woman promised. She lifted the elaborate toy from the table where Aiken had been working on it to a safe place on a high shelf. Then she turned to him and held out both hands, grinning.

"Again?" he protested. "Insatiable old bag, aren't you?"

"All we Tanu women are," she cackled, pulling him toward the bedroom, "but there's few that can rise up to Mayvar and live, my Shining One, as you should know by now. So when I find such as you I must test and prove him. And if he lasts—ah, then!"

The room was very dark and cool and the awful old woman only a shadow waiting. Free of the golden suit, floating in the air, he came to her and was devoured. But there was no fear in him or cringing—not after the first time had shown him what lay beyond the repellent husk.

O amazing Hag with your hidden cauldron of near-deadly rapture! You'd take the entire measure of life-force if I'd let you—snuff me after I'd fed your ancient nerve-fires and stoked them to youth again! But I won't die, Hag. I won't burn out. I'm up to you, old Mayvar, and beyond and above you, drawing you along with me while you scream. Come along and don't falter, Mayvar! Cry to die, Mayvar! Then burst and tumble down when you've had your surfeit of the Shining One who meets your test again and laughs . . .

The golliwog put on his golden boots and gave her ugliness a touch of pure affection. "You know, you're pretty good yourself, Witch."

"Once the Thagdal said the same." She uttered a long sigh. "And my darling Lugonn, that I had such hopes for before he died." She showed him the way it had been, back at the Ship's Grave, when all of them had first arrived in the Many-Colored Land.

"What a funny race you are," Aiken said. "Not civilized at all. You'd be in a fine mess by now if humans hadn't come through the time-gate and organized things for you. You should be grateful instead of resenting us!"

"I don't resent you," Mayvar said complacently. "Come close, my bonny boy." She took it from under the pillow and held it out to him.

"Do I need it?" he asked her, mouth quirking with the old mischief. "Would you have even more of me, glutton Mayvar?"

But this time she was serious. "You've still a way to go and a way to grow before you're a match for the greatest of the Host, Aiken Drum. There are those who can kill you—make no mistake. If you're wise, you'll go about this prudently and follow my counsel. Take it."

He settled the twisted golden ring around his neck and snapped the ends shut. Mayvar's gnarled fingers unfastened the old silver torc and dropped it beside the bed.

"I'll do as you say, Witch dear. And savor the fun to the fullest every step along the way."

She got up from the bed and he helped her to don the purple robe. Then they went out into her sitting room, where he combed her white hair and called for refreshment, which they both stood in need of.

"You've proved yourself to me," Mayvar said at length, "but you must also prove yourself to *them*. They must freely accept you. This is our way."

A tinkling fanfare came from the golden clock on the shelf. Once again the dragon slithered forth and the knight came stalking him; and this time, the bejeweled prey was hewn into four sections to mark the striking of the hour.

"You want me to go and do likewise," Aiken observed. "Show all the folks what a grand barbarian warrior I am by making good on my monster-killing boast."

"It'll be a significant proof, the slaying of Delbaeth." She began to rock back and forth, chortling, hands clasping bony knees through the fabric of her gown. "Oh—you caught their attention with that offer, lad! Tana herself must have put the notion into your mind."

His response was laconic. "Your High King was so loud broadcasting his anxiety about the spook that it was impossible to resist."

"Ah! But, you see, there'd been talk of how the Thagdal himself should deal with Delbaeth! And since he's really too old, he'd have to ask Nodonn to do it. And that would obligate him to the Host, and—ah, you'll know about the politics soon enough. But as for Delbaeth—this Firvulag is one of the most powerful sort. He's a giant, not one of the little kind. He's been rampaging around burning up plantations outside of Afaliah, on what you'd call the Spanish mainland, for nearly a year now. Much of our provisioning here at the capital comes from the Afaliah region, and we also count on those farms for the extra supplies needed during Grand Combat time. Now, Afaliah's Lord is Celadeyr. He's a First Comer and a feisty old shit-kicker of a Creator-Coercer—but no match for Delbaeth. None of us are—if you match power for power. Old Celo's tried to Hunt down the Shape of Fire, but he gets outwitted every time when the Firvulag runs off and hides in the caves of the Gibraltar Isthmus. Things are getting serious, with the Grand Combat nearly on us, and Celo has demanded the assistance of the High King. The Thagdal is obliged to respond."

Aiken nodded. "I get it. But the King is getting a bit long in the tooth for that kind of adventure. Rogering maidens is more his style these days."

"He may properly designate any champion as his agent to deal with Delbaeth. But you forced him to send you! Do you see how galling it must be? An outsider—a human!—taking on a job that's defeated Tanu stalwarts. And all by accident, you've put one up Nodonn, too, since he was too wily to volunteer before the King asked him! If you succeed in killing Delbaeth, wearing the gold and all, you tell the world that you think you're as good as any of them."

"Just as Gomnol did?"

She half-closed her pouched eyes, simultaneously projecting a vision of the long-ago triumph of the human Lord Coercer for Aiken's study. She looked out over the White Silver Plain where it had happened. "Gomnol would have aspired higher," she said softly, "but I spurned him, even though he could have sated me. Sterile! Or more correctly, so riddled with lethal genes that even the science of your Galactic Milieu had been powerless to correct his faulty plasm. The Kingmaker rejects such offal . . . Needless to say, I've already determined that you have no such deficiency."

Hands on hips, he threw back his head and laughed. "What a cold-blooded witch you are! And I thought it was all for sweet passion's sake."

Destiny rules passion in us both ShiningOne.

"You weird old crone!" he cried. "Meddling old bag of bones! Power-hungry ballbreaker! Get your stringy old ass to Redact House and crawl into the Skin and have them make you young again. We'll go and screw 'em all together, Lovie!"

Grasping one of her hands, he spun her tall figure around—then stopped short at the expression on her face and the vision that accompanied it.

"I've been lucky, Aiken. Most of my kind are only able to choose once. But I picked the Thagdal, and I chose his successor as well—although Tana's will took dear Lugonn before my choice could be made manifest. After he was gone, I waited these thousand years, weighing the hopefuls as it's my duty to do. But all of them fell short in one way or another. And so I had settled on the best of the rejected, Nodonn Battlemaster of the Host. His mind is stupendous and his heritage is acceptable—but ah, what a meager flame he kindles, for all his jealous pride! What a poor stick to aspire to the engendering of a race of heroes! But he was the best we had until . . ."

"Silly Hag."

The knotted fingers stroked his golden torc, sending sweet fever rushing through him.

She crooned, "Lucky Mayvar! To see the third one come after all. Ah, but I've reached my limit with you, bright laddie. Three thousand three hundred and fifty-two of your years I've lived and done the love testing for the Tanu. You'll be the death of me, Aiken Drum. But not, please Tana, until I've seen you safely installed."

"First things first," he said, divesting himself of her mental caress with some reluctance. "This Delbaeth. You realize that I don't have the faintest idea how to go about killing him? I talk a good game, but when push comes to shove, the spook might just burn the fewkin' gold britches off me! Wouldn't that be a nice end to our schemes?"

Mayvar gave a gay titter. "Would I send my own Initiate away unprepared? You'll be taught to use your powers properly before you go on the Delbaeth quest. Two weeks under my tutelage—and that of mighty Bleyn, and Alberonn Mindeater, and the mistress of illusion, Katlinel the Darkeyed—and you'll be more than a match for this Firvulag . . . And to be on the safe side, I'll give you something else as well. What you would call an ace in the hole."

"Witch!" He sniggered. "What is it?"

"You'll never guess! No true Tanu would dare to use it because of the mortal danger to himself. But it'll be harmless to you, my bonny boy, and it'll dispose of Delbaeth if you but track him down. You must keep it secret from the others if you love your life—but with you as clever as I know you are, it should be no problem."

"What is it, for God's sake?" He grasped her by her bony shoulders and shook her as she continued to tantalize him, dangling a small mental image just out of reach.

At last she sobered. "Come along to the cellar, then, and I'll show it to you."

* * *

Stein was in an uneasy and dangerous mood, his great hands white-knuckled as he gripped the railing and pretended to watch the apprentice fighters larruping each other out in the arena. The upper level of his mind listened obediently to the running commentary of the Lord of Swords, who pointed out the technique—or lack of it—displayed by the young gray-torcs. Beneath the veneer, however, Stein was raging. Bluff Tagan, preoccupied with his exposition of martial arts, never noticed; but the gold-torc human woman who had been delegated by Mayvar to shepherd Stein on a tour of Muriah was all too aware of the giant's growing impatience. With a far-speaker's tact, she insinuated herself.

FriendStein are you weary of viewing fighterschool? Had hoped it would amusedistract.

Something wrong Sukeywife. WhatWHAT Lady Dedra I will know!

". . . and observe that young ox in the rust-colored kilt, Stein. Kurdish stock. Splendid musculature and as game as they make 'em, but he won't last five minutes in a Low Mêlée if he doesn't learn to stop telegraphing his ripostes. You don't need a torc to read that one's mind! Now, if you want a real study in finesse, keep a close eye on those two Masai types sparring with vitredur lances. That's the kind of work that makes an old fighter's blood sing . . ."

Calmcalm relax Stein. Remember VenerableMayvar's directive-promise + that AikenDrum: no harm to Sukey.

Disbelief! FURY. I *hear* her she is crying afraid bellspun falling reach out Lady Dedra to her find her tell me why she cries!

Verywell I will look but do not betray yourself TaganCoercer freshaware your inattention.

Aloud, Stein said, "Those fellows have the moves, Lord Tagan. I'm no expert, but they look damn impressive. But I don't see how they'd have much of a chance in a contest against one of your Tanu brain benders."

"Most of this lot will only fight in the Contest of Humans—against one another. It's only the best who get to fight side by side with the metapsychic warriors in the High Mêlée against the Firvulag. Brave and strong-minded grays have managed to give a good account of themselves in the High. It's a matter of resisting the fear-provoking illusions of the Little Folks and keeping your mind on business. Of course, ultimately most of the grays . . ." The vision winked out almost as soon as it formed in Tagan's telepathic projection; but it had been clear enough to Stein.

The Lord of Swords peered obliquely at the Viking. Tagan looked more weather-beaten than most of the other Tanu, with a drooping gold mustache, and shaggy brows hedging sunken green eyes. "There have been exceptions to the usual fate of the gray fighter. A really superlative gladiator can expect a reprieve. And not just until the next year's Combat, either. Permanently. To serve on my staff here at the school."

Dedra said, "You know, Coercive Brother, that Stein's assignment must come ultimately from the Lady Mayvar, who has taken to kin the Candidate Aiken Drum." Putative master of this perhapsbriefliving gray.

The blue-armored Tanu gave a mental sneer, dismissing both Mayvar and her upstart protégé. "We'll see you in the Combat one way or another, Stein. You're a natural, boy! I saw you at the supper. Just a few weeks of work here . . ." The coercer reached out: comradeship, adrenalin, challenge, release, gore, sweet shattering fatigue! "How about it, lad?"

Stein opened his mouth to curse the Lord of Swords. But what he said was, "I thank you, Lord Tagan, for thinking that I might be worthy to study under a great champion such as you. After my master and I dispose of the loathsome Delbaeth, we'll be free to think of the upcoming Combat. My master will confer with you in good time."

I didn't speak you spoke damnedDedra let me go let me go let me—

"We will leave you now, Coercive Brother," Dedra said, bowing and drawing her lavender chiffon cloak about her slender body. The sun had gone down behind the rim of the arena, which might have explained why she had begun to shiver. "You may be sure that Stein and his master, Aiken Drum, will consider your generous offer most seriously." Stop it! Stop fighting me you great blockhead!

Tagan smote his armored breast with a sapphire gauntlet. "I salute you, Farspeaking Sister, Exalted Lady Mary-Dedra. Remember me to your President . . . And you, valiant Stein. We hold the City Games thrice weekly here and at the Plain of Sports. Join us! To-morrow our top wrestlers will test the first of the giant apes that were recently captured in the North African hills. It promises a bit of excitement."

Stein was forced to remove his horned helmet and abase himself before the Lord of Swords. And then he had to hurry along after the gold-torc woman through cold, echoing passages that led beneath the arena to the carriage-yard where their calèche waited. The corridors were dark and deserted. Stein called for Dedra to wait for him, but she threw a glance over her shoulder and began to run instead. Her mind, operating on the coercive mode, reiterated:

You will submit to me you will be calm you will submit—

"Something's happened to Sukey, hasn't it?" he cried out.

You will submit to me you will be calm—

"You're afraid to tell me!" His stride lengthened. "I can't hear her calling me any more!"

Youwillsubmit youwillsubmit YOUWILLSUBMIT!

The pressure of his rage built into a great igneous flood, undermining her restraints, melting them. "They've killed her—haven't they?" the berserker roared. Dedra dodged away from him, almost falling on the damp stone floor. "Answer me, you stupid bitch! Answer me!"

YOU WILL . . .

Stein gave a shout, mingling pain and triumph, as the last of the mental shackles dissolved. A single leap brought him up to Dedra and he snatched the human woman into the air, spinning her around so that the panic-stricken, lovely face stared up helplessly. He bent her spine backwards and drew her into a dark niche, clammy and odorous, at one side of the corridor.

"I'm going to break your back if you make one sound! And don't call out in the farspeak mode, either, because I'll hear you. Understand? *Answer* me, dammit!"

Stein O Stein you misapprehend we wish no harm we would help—

"You listen to me," he hissed, relaxing the tension slightly. "There's no one down here but you and me. No one to come and save you. Mayvar should have given me a stronger keeper than you, Dedra. She should have known you'd never be able to hold me."

"But Mayvar would—"

He gave her a brutal shake. "Stop trying to get back into my mind, bitch!" She moaned and her head lolled sideways. "I want to know what's happened to my wife! You know and you'll tell me—"

"She's alive, Stein." Jesus God man you're crushingbreaking me ease up the spinalnerve bruising ahhhh . . .

He relaxed, propping her sagging body against the rough stone wall. She hung there like a cut-string marionette, belly swelling against her rucked-up lilac gown, lavender-and-gold headdress awry. Her mental explanation came rushing out.

As with all silvertorchumanwomen yourSukey gone to Bybar for fertility restoration.

"They promised she wouldn't be harmed! Mayvar promised—and that bloody little gold grannybanger. They *promised!*"

Tears white arms reaching compassionbalm . . . "She hasn't been hurt, Stein. Can't you understand? We had to treat Sukey like an ordinary candidate. If an exception had been made before Aiken's position among the battle-company was affirmed—*don't!* Don't hurt me again! Can't you see I'm telling you the truth? Mayvar and Dionket must move cautiously at this stage or all the planning goes for nothing. There's more at stake here than you and your wife!"

Stein let her go. She sank to the dirty floor. Her mind was numb, shallowly adrift. The violet human eyes looked at him from amidst runnels of tears. "We never meant Sukey to go to the Thagdal. There's time. At least a month before her female cycle is reestablished."

"When will *your* Tanu bastard be born, bitch? To hell with Mayvar and Dionket and their schemes! To hell with all of you! I could hear Sukey calling me, dammit, and now she's stopped. You prove to me that she's alive and unharmed or—"

Take him to her.

Stein gave a start. His hand dropped to his sword hilt and he looked wildly about. The corridor was empty.

"I warned you, Dedra!" His face clouded again with fury.

She raised one shaking finger to her golden torc. "It's Mayvar. She's seen and heard. I'm to take you to Sukey. *Now* will you believe that we're on your side?"

He pulled her to her feet. Her gown was snagged and stained. Swiftly, he unpinned the brooch of his own short green cape and flung the covering garment about her shoulders. "Can you walk?"

"As far as the carriage. But give me your hand."

Outside, the bareneck gaffer who waited with their calèche was dozing as the cicadas tuned up for their evening performance. Ramas were going about with short ladders and slow-matches, lighting the streetlamps. The broad promenade that skirted this side of the stadium had only a few cabs rolling along and no pedestrians except for the busy little apes.

Respectfully, Stein handed the Lady Dedra into the carriage before going around to the other side and climbing in.

"Where to, marm?" the driver croaked, coming to life with reluctance.

"Redact House. And quickly."

The driver whipped up the hellad and they trotted off. The carriage drove through the central city and its western suburbs before reaching the road that led to the heights. Muriah had no city wall. The natural isolation of the Aven Peninsula was deemed protection enough here in the southland where the Tanu were most powerful. Dedra did not speak and Stein sat stiffly at her side, not looking at her. Finally, when they were well above the city, the woman said, "There's a fountain ahead. Will you let me stop to clean up? If I enter the precincts of the redactors looking like this, there are bound to be questions."

Stein nodded and she gave instructions to the driver. After a few minutes they pulled into a deeply shadowed wayside. Some kind of bird was going *doink doink* among the crags. A spring emerged from the yellow limestone into a triple-tiered basin and the hellad was permitted to drink from the lowest pool, after which Dedra had the driver lead the beast to where it could crop from the thick shrubbery. She bathed her face in the central basin and produced a small mirror and a golden comb, which she used to repair her straggling coiffure. The ornate headdress was badly crushed. After a futile attempt to restore it, she threw it into a waste receptacle.

"Let some trash collector have a treat. I think my hair will do for now, but we'll have to hope Tasha is too stoned to notice my gown."

"Can you stop her reading our minds?"

Dedra gave a sour little laugh. "Ah! You don't know about our dear Tasha-Bybar, the Anastasya Astaurova that was, prime benefactress of the Tanu breeding scheme. Well, relax, lover. She has no metafaculties at all! Her gold torc is honorary—a token of Tanu esteem. Tasha is the human gynecologist who first showed the exotics how to reverse our sterilization some sixty-odd years ago. There are about a dozen other gut choppers doing the work now as well as Tash, of course, but none as competent as she is. She does all of the silvers herself. Literally keeps the old hand in."

A picture of the bell-dancer was projected before Stein's mental eye. "I've seen a few," he muttered. "But that's a different shade of kink!"

Dedra dipped one hand into the topmost pool of the fountain and drank from her cupped palm. "She's quite insane now. She must have been borderline when she passed through the auberge . . . Don't give me that old-fashioned masculine look, lover! I think she's a traitor to the human race, just as you do. But what's done is done. Most of us women make the best of it."

Stein shook his head. "How *could* she?"

"There's a crazy kind of logic to it . . . How do you like frustrated motherhood for starters? Here's this too dreadfully sexy bod that can't grow babies—so why not be a mother by proxy? All these perfectly healthy female time-travelers could have lovely Tanu children if only some good doctor repaired the mischief done by those gyn-folk with the little laser scalpels back at the auberge. The fix is quite tricky, because Madame's people seem to've anticipated some kind of jiggery-pokery among the philoprogenitive. But dear Tasha perseveres! Finally she gets it right, and she passes on her skills to a select squad of Tanu students. And here we all are, ready to be plowed and planted."

"If she's such a wiz of a doctor, why doesn't she have one of her prize pupils fix *her* up?"

"Ah! That's the too-barfmaking tragedy of it all, lover. Within that voluptuous female form with the enhanced secondaries and the estrogen implants there beats the heart of a true XY."

Stein glared at her in impatience. "What the hell are you talking about?"

Dedra climbed down from the fountain and sent an imperious mental command for the carriage. "An XY, lover. Tasha is a transsexual. Oh, you could stow away some real woman's fertilized egg in her fake uterus, and maybe shoot her full of preggy hormones, if you could get them in this primitive world—and perhaps the embryo would live a few weeks before dying. But that's all, lover. Maternity is a marvelous and tricky symbiosis. And of course, no one in our Galactic Milieu or anywhere else has ever made a *true* mother out of a male."

She stepped lightly into the calèche without assistance. "Well? Don't just stand there. Do you want to see your wife, or don't you?" Stein climbed in and they rode away.

When the red and white lights of the Redactor Guild buildings were quite close, Dedra said, "You're going to have to be careful when we get inside. Tasha can't read you, but there will be plenty of others who can. Heavy screens aren't my specialty, although I'll do the best I can for you. But if you start thrashing around and break through me it's going to be *both* our asses in a sling."

"I'll relax," he promised. "Sukey taught me things when we—on the trip down the river when we wanted privacy."

"Trust me," she pleaded. Looking up at him in the dusk, she tried to find one small scrap of empathy; but all that mattered to him was the safety of his precious, funny-faced love.

"I'm sorry I hurt you," he conceded. But that was all.

She stared straight ahead at the slouched beanbag shape of the old driver. "Think nothing of it. My fault for standing in the tornado's path. Lucky little Sukey . . ."

The carriage drew up to the entrance. Once again, Stein played the solicitous gray-torc esquire and Dedra, the Exalted Lady. There were two guards in garnet-colored half-armor on station beneath the portico. A peevish silver male came to escort them up to Tasha-Bybar's eyrie.

"Most unusual," he fretted. "The routine is completely upset, Farspeaking Lady. You know, it was necessary for the Lord Healer himself to use his good offices—"

"We're very grateful to Lord Dionket, Worthy Gordon. It's a matter very important to the Venerable Mayvar Kingmaker."

"Oh, well, of course then. Along through here and up we go. Gwen-Minivel will still be groggy, you know. Lady Tasha likes them to rest well afterward."

"I'll bet," growled Stein. He lurched slightly as Dedra administered a psychic correction.

"We'll not be long, Worthy Gordon. How peaceful it is in your precincts at night! It seems we at Farsense House never really seem to settle down. In and out, in and out. Someone always has an important message or a data-search or a surveillance or a lost dog or something even more vital. I must say, I prefer your tranquil atmosphere."

"Indispensable in a house of healing," Gordon said. They had reached a landing just below the topmost floor of the tower. "The recovery rooms are arranged around the perimeter. The Candidate Gwen-Minivel is resting in Three."

"Please don't trouble yourself to wait." Dedra was firm. "We'll find our way out, and we'll only stay a very few minutes."

Gordon received this suggestion dubiously, but after arguing with the farspeaker for a few minutes, he bowed and retreated, leaving them standing before the door marked 3. Slowly, Dedra slid it open.

Stein pushed past her into the darkness. "Sue? Are you here?"

Someone moved on a chaise near the open window and sat up, dark against the lights of Muriah outside. "Steinie—?"

He knelt down beside her and took her face between his hands. "Have they hurt you? *Have* they?"

"Hush, love. No." Gently gently my darling ah how did you know? How could you hear me?

Muffled, he said, "I did and I came."

You broke Dedra/Mayvar control O Steinlove how did you break free how is it possible O mydear so wilduntamedrashmadloving!

They will not tie me separate us never until I die.

"Stein," she whispered, and began to weep.

From one corner of the darkened room, the one farthest from the door, came a small sound. The tinkle of a tiny bell.

"So you like to spy, too, do you?" Stein's voice was very soft. He rose to his feet and stood motionless.

"So *tall!* so *strong!*" The bells shivered up the scale and down. One with a lower note began a languorous rhythm. The dancer came, fluid as a shadow, and undulated before him. "So you want her? How sweet." It was a song the dancer sang, accompanied by the suddenly discordant chiming. "You want to take her, to take her, to take her!"

In Stein the white-hot anger was born again, an eruption of primitive psychoenergy howling wrath against the mocker and her music. Sukey uttered a low cry and reached out to stem the peril; and Dedra, with her back against the closed door, threw her mind against him, too, even though her restraints were even weaker than Sukey's against that uniquely masculine tidal bore.

"Don't, Stein!" Sukey cried aloud. "Oh, don't!"

"You want to take her," laughed the bell-dancer, bending and thrusting. "But why why why? Take her her her?"

The bell sound and the laughing blended with twisting lights— the glittering bits of metal that rippled over white skin, the pulse quickening with the danger that made it more sweet—and then the music and dance ended in a shuddering finale and she opened to him as Dedra moaned and Sukey made one last futile try to prevent what was going to happen.

"Take *me*," invited Tasha-Bybar.

And the bronze sword did.

There was a great silence. Quite calm now, Stein wiped his blade on the draperies, sheathed it, and lifted Sukey into his arms. He stepped over the thing on the floor. "Get out of the way," he told Dedra.

"You can't!" the farspeaker wailed. *Mayvar! Mayvar!*

The door to the corridor opened, admitting a wide swath of light. An immensely tall man stood there, flanked by two servitors in the scarlet-and-white livery. "I warned Dionket that this was a mistake," Creyn said, his tone weary. He came into the room, gestured, and turned on festoons of the small cold-light lamps. A grim smile played over his lips as he looked beyond Stein and Sukey to the fallen dancer. The coarseness of his mental comment brought a gasp from Sukey and a surprised bark of laughter from Stein.

"You're on our side," marveled the Viking.

"Put Sukey down, you great ass," Creyn told him. "Thanks to you, your wife must be hidden away until the Grand Combat . . . and we'll have to move even faster than we'd originally planned."

8

Nodonn sent the thunderbolt down into the dark waters of the Gulf of Aquitaine, where the wavelets reflected the moon and an unsuspecting monster chased a school of tunny not far beneath the surface.

As lightning struck, the sea boiled and belched clouds. Fifteen of the big fish went belly-up, electrocuted instantly. The plesiosaur, however, was only stunned. It broke through the maelstrom, raised its wattled head, and bellowed.

"Oh, you got him!" Rosmar cried. "And a big one!"

"The prey! The prey!" The other Hunters all burst forth into radiance, riders and mounts alike, now that there was no longer a need for concealment. A wheel of rainbow splendor turned in the air above the feebly swimming beast, almost fifty gloriously armored men and women from the court of the Tanu Battlemaster. And to one side, aloof as rosy-gold comets, were Nodonn himself and his new bride.

The Hunt whacked shields, sounded crystal horns. "The prey! The prey!"

"To Vrenol," Nodonn decided, his voice storm-loud.

One of the riders plummeted, trailing sparks, and swooped over the brute writhing amid the deadly waves. The snakelike neck of the plesiosaur lashed out and the knight hauled his chaliko up just in time to escape the dagger teeth. The rider thrust with his glowing sword and a ball of purplish fire flew from the tip to strike the marine monster between the eyes. The animal screamed.

A cheer was emitted by the circling Hunt. "At him, Vrenol!" some woman urged.

The Huntsman waved his sword in jaunty acknowledgment—which was a mistake. With its attacker distracted, the plesiosaur sounded with a simultaneous push from all four paddlelike limbs, leaving the discomfited Tanu knight poised in the air above a surge of evil-smelling bubbles.

"Oh, hard luck," an anonymous voice drawled. One of the armored women blew a derisive triple toot on her animal-headed glass trumpet.

Now Vrenol was faced with the dreadful expedient of pursuing the beast into the water—that element so abhorred by his race—if this first attempt at a kill were not to end in humiliation as the prey escaped.

"Ah, the silly young juggins," said Rosmar. "Bring the leviathan back up, my Lord!"

The blazing face of the Battlemaster smiled upon his bride. "If you ask it, vein of my heart. But Vrenol deserves to dunk for his foolishness." Nodonn reached out to discern the monster's position. "Oh, you'd sneak away, would you?" A blue bolt of energy split the gulf's water, causing the chalikos of the circling Hunt to rear and squeal. The plesiosaur surfaced once more and this time Vrenol went for it with his lance.

"He's got it!" Rosmar exclaimed. "Right at the base of the neck! Let's go down for the kill!"

The Lord and Lady of Goriah spiraled toward the water, the wheel of light fracturing respectfully before their passage. Now the individual Hunters poised waiting for the end. The plesiosaur, paralyzed by the wound, was still able to open and close its great jaws slowly. The seven-meter bulk of it wallowed amidst spreading bloodstains, lapped by small waves and glistening from the moonlight and the radiance of the killer hovering above.

Vrenol gripped his sword in both hands. The blade flashed down. The Hunt cried, "A trophy! A trophy!" One of the ladies descended, her lance couched, and with easy expertise pierced the floating severed head and hoisted it high. She presented the trophy to Vrenol. His glowing form changed from rainbow to neon-red and he was off like a scorching bolide to draw triumph figures among the stars.

"Well, he's young," Nodonn observed tolerantly. "We must make allowances." But on the command mode of the mental speech he warned the others:

Don't think the rest of you will be permitted such sloppiness! These beasts are getting scarce with overhunting and I'll not have them wasted.

The shining troupe responded: We hear Lord and Battlemaster!

Aloud, Nodonn said, "Then back to Armorica and the Tainted Swamp. I require heads from the Firvulag Foe on your lances this night, for they are growing bold. And we must find, if we can, one of the great armored reptiles. It is urgently needed for the arena in the capital."

"On with the Hunt!" cried the sparkling riders. They formed a fiery procession again, with the scarlet figure of Vrenol now leading, and vaulted into the sky on the way to the mainland of Brittany.

Nodonn and Rosmar followed more slowly. He said to her, "There came to me just now a farspoken message from my Lady Mother. You and I must go to Muriah—and the reptile with us. We will take only a small escort to see to the beast."

"You are troubled," she said.

"It's nothing that can't be dealt with." But his deep thoughts on this matter were heavily screened.

Rosmar lifted the flashing glass helmet from her head and hung it from the horn of her saddle. "That's better. The wind in my hair! How I love to ride beside you, my daemon lover! Shall I ever learn to fly without your help?"

"In time you may learn. It's a shallow enough trick. We reverence you more for your gentler powers." And he smiled on her.

"My powers are for your service," she said. "But tell me what is happening in Muriah."

"There are matters touching upon our dynastic hopes. I must go down to assist other members of the Host of Nontusvel—for our Tanu people only respect the display of power."

"Is it the Firvulag?"

"There is a certain Delbaeth," he said, "whom I shall have to deal with before another does, shaming our House. But the real danger comes from newly arrived humans. Damn the time-gate! When will the others understand its perils?"

Rosmar laughed. "Do you think we humans should be locked out of Exile? Do you think the Tanu could survive without us?"

He reined up his steed and halted hers, so that the two of them drifted a moment in apparently motionless air. The sound of surf against the coastal rocks reached them, a faint booming.

"Some humans belong in the Many-Colored Land. People like you, Rosmar, my green-eyed, gray-eyed love, who never truly fit into the world of Elder Earth. But not all members of your race who come through are willing to accept the Tanu as masters. There are those who'd take the land away from us . . . or failing that, destroy it."

"Let's fight them together!" she said, wild with excitement. "Yours is the only world I want to know." Her soul opened to the bright Apollo, showing that what she said was true. Their two minds embraced in an ardent lifting.

"My daemon lover," she laughed.

And he said, "My own Mercy-Rosmar."

9

JUMP ELIZABETH.

She stood on the headland above the White Silver Plain, looking down on the phantom cavalry of cloud shadows racing there on the empty moonlit salt. At the rim of the grassy terrace was a low railing. Beyond that a few stunted, picturesquely deformed pines at the precipice edge overhung a sheer drop of perhaps 100 meters to the Mediterranean abyss.

Jump Elizabeth jump to peace.

"Do you hear it?" she asked Brede.

A dark shape sitting on a stone bench stirred. Its topheavy headdress with the padded brim inclined in agreement.

"They're farwatching me from the palace," Elizabeth continued. "See what happens when I approach the brink—"

Jumpjumpjump! Be free abandoned onlyoneofkind! Poorforlorn thing Elizalonelybeth. Jump to release. Escape undesecrated while yet possible. Jump . . .

Palms resting on the balustrade, she leaned far out. Night winds brought the scent of the distant lagoon to mingle with the orange blossoms of Brede's garden. Out here on the land's end of Aven, far from any freshwater influx that would encourage simple algae and hardy crustaceans to flourish, there was no fishy-iodine smell of marine life—only the bitter alkali of the Empty Sea.

Elizabeth said, "They worked on me all afternoon while I was locked in my suite, trying to set up what they thought would be an appropriate emotional basis for the suicide impulse. Trading mostly on motifs of despair and dignity-threat, mixed with a good dollop of old-fashioned funk. But their whole foundation is spurious. The motivations are unacceptable to my metapsychic ethic. If they'd gone for the self-sacrificing altruism angle they'd have been nearer the mark—not that *that* would have worked, given this exile situation."

Brede's mental voice, so formal and lacking in the elisions and concatenations of ordinary mindspeech, said:

The masterclass metapsychics of your Milieu embraced a common ethical formula?

Elizabeth let amiable affirmation shine through the barrier she had maintained between herself and the Shipspouse since her first meeting with the exotic woman two hours earlier. "Most of us followed a system consonant with the philosophy of an evolving theosphere. Are you familiar with this concept? With the major religions of the later human era?"

I have studied your people since their first timefaring. Some of their professed philosophies have dismayed and repelled me. You must understand that the Tanu embrace a simple, unstructured monotheism without any priesthood or established hierarchy. We have been quite willing to grant religious freedom to those humans whose faith was nonmilitant. But there have been zealots who persisted in disrupting the King's peace—bareneck ones, of course— and these were speedily granted the martyrdom they subconsciously craved . . . But none of the humans I have studied was able to shed light on the Unity of your Galactic Milieu. And this is understandable, for only a true metapsychic can know it. In humility I request that you enlighten me.

"What you ask is virtually impossible, Brede. A young meta usually begins training before birth. The mental enlargement is intensified in early childhood—this is the kind of work I devoted my life to before my accident. A person with masterclass potential must expect to spend thirty years or more adapting to the full Unity. Enlighten you? . . . You invited me to inspect your intellectual potential and I'll agree that psychounion between us two is not utterly impossible. But that torc of yours presents a wall and a snare all at once. You think of yourself as operant. But, believe me—you aren't. Not truly. And without genuine metafunction you can't know the Unity or any of the rest of the Milieu essence."

The calm thought came: It is foreseen that one day my people will partake of this essence.

"Foreseen by whom?"

By me.

Elizabeth came away from the railing and stood in front of the Shipspouse. Upon their first encounter Brede had revealed that she belonged to a race different from that of the other exotics. She was of less than medium height, with eyes that were carnelian-brown instead of blue or green. Her face, the lower part exposed now that she had once again removed her baroque respirator, lacked the preternatural beauty of the ruling Tanu race but was comely enough, appearing middle-aged. Brede wore a gown of metallic red fabric that was styled in a different manner from the thin flowing robes of the Tanu. It was trimmed with red-and-black beading and over it she wore a black coat with trailing bell sleeves and borders of red flame-shapes. Her huge chapeau, also black and red, was aglitter with jewels and had a black veil floating from it. The costume, except for the ornate breathing equipment, reminded Elizabeth of one of the tapestries from the Middle Ages that had adorned the grand salon back at l'Auberge du Portail. There was an archaic aura about the Shipspouse, a flavor of some thing conspicuously absent from the other exotics. Brede was no barbarian, no oracle, no priest-mother. All of Elizabeth's attempts at analyzing her had thus far proved futile.

"Tell me what you want from me," the human woman said. "Tell me who you really are."

The Shipspouse lifted her bowed head, revealing a sweet, patient smile. For the first time, Brede voiced her thoughts aloud.

"Why will you not mindspeak with me, Elizabeth?"

"It would be imprudent of me. You're more formidable than the others. As both of us know."

Brede rose from the bench. Her breath began to come painfully again and she raised the respirator for relief. "This atmosphere—so suitable for my Tanu and Firvulag people—is rarefied for one of my stock. Will you come inside my home? The oxygen is enriched within, and we can also seclude ourselves in my room without doors, and these hostile minds will no longer be able to weary you with their importunities."

Jump Elizabeth! Don't let Twoface Brede fool you take you from onlyescape. She worst of usall! Go back cliffside and jump jump . . .

"The compulsion is getting rather annoying," Elizabeth agreed. "But I'm capable of dealing with it."

"The attack of the Host represents no threat to you?"

"In order for their compulsion to work, it would have to be strong enough to completely override my superego and will. They'd almost have to dismember my personality and reintegrate it on a lower, complaisant level. There's a great crowd of them pecking at me now and the directing intelligences are respectably strong. But none of them—not severally and not working together—can summon the power to compel my suicide. Who are they? Can you recognize any of them?"

"The four directors are leaders among Nontusvel's Host. The PK adept is Kuhal, Second Lord Psychokinetic to Nodonn. Imidol is the coercer, a battle-champion with small mental subtlety. The farsensor is Riganone, a female warrior who sees herself as the successor to Mayvar—an amusing conceit! The fourth, the redactor, represents a more serious challenge, although perhaps not in the compulsive mode. He is Culluket, the King's Interrogator, whose loyalty lies with his mother Nontusvel and her Host rather than with his father, the Thagdal. Culluket's faculties for deep-probe and mind alteration are second only to those of Dionket the Lord Healer. But healing is not the work for which Culluket is known. It would not be wise for you to encounter him at close range until you are conversant with certain aggressive techniques in use among our less principled element."

"Thanks for the warning. A perverted redactor might be able to get into my autonomic nervous system while I was asleep or emotionally distraught. I'll have to spin a special stem-shield—maybe a trap, too. We had problems along this line many years ago in the Milieu, before the Unity had reached full maturation, with all human metapsychics assenting to the common moral imperative. The self-defensive maneuvers are still taught to young metas . . . just in case."

The compulsion now built to a near-hysterical crescendo as Elizabeth walked at Brede's side on the path through the orange grove. There were lurid threats of Tanu gang-rape and mutilation; visions of suffering, exploited daughters yet unborn; wheedlings that promised death-peace and a reuniting with Lawrence; even—belatedly—logical arguments for self-destruction based on the genetic ramifications of the situation.

Elizabeth turn back! Better for you for allhumans in Exile all-Tanu as well if you die! Don't listen Twoface Shipspiderspouse lies! Turn back and jump! Jump!

There were oranges on the ground, for Brede was not served by ramas. The distinctive smell of citrus-mold blended with the flower perfume; the trees carried blossoms simultaneously with the fruit. Elizabeth reached up and picked a pendant globe.

The mental voices keened at ultimate strength: *Don't!* Don't turn away from release! Don't lose opportunity Elizabeth! Escape impossible within roomwithoutdoors! Turn back! Jump! Turn back . . .

BE GONE.

(Bubblesnapripplequench.) (Withdrawal.)

Brede's amplified voice said, "Now they know you were fully aware of their attack."

"They had to find out sooner or later. I prefer sooner."

"They'll try again. More of them. Queen Nontusvel has more than two hundred surviving children."

"Let them try! The compulsion-aggression would be ineffective if they amplified their efforts a thousandfold. Your people and their torcs! They don't achieve true mental synergy at all! They can't marshal the proper force behind a multimind thrust. They're primitive and sloppy—out of phase and out of focus. And out of their league, if you follow my idiom."

O cruel in aloof superiority O proud Elizabeth.

She paid no attention to the unspoken reproach. It had been an irritating day. As they walked toward the small white villa, Elizabeth peeled the orange and ate the small segments. The flesh of the fruit was dark in the moonlight, adding another brick to the edifice of her indignation: It was a blood orange.

Elizabeth's voice was snappish as she said, "You won't get any-where being subtle with me, Brede. I never was much good at diplomatic byplay, even back in the Milieu. I want to know whose side you're on and what expectations you have of me. And just what is this room without doors?"

"You need have no fear of it. It cannot hold one such as you. But it will keep the Host away from you, body and soul, for as long as you remain within its sanctuary. I had hoped that you would stay with me. We could . . . teach one another. There is ample time, nearly two months before the Combat, where I foresee a climactic resolution."

The last pieces of orange rind fell from Elizabeth's hand. She slowed as they came out onto a small patch of lawn in front of the villa. Brede's house bore none of the usual Tanu faerie lights, but stood in Grecian simplicity framed by cypresses. It was a dwelling fit for the mystery woman, lacking any exterior openings.

The half-masked face of the Shipspouse looked up at her, entreat-ing. It seemed to say: More than all the rest, we two are exiled.

"What happens if our attempted meeting of minds is unsuccess-ful?" Elizabeth inquired.

"Then you will do what you must." Brede was apparently unper-turbed. "Shall we go in together?"

Side by side, the two of them crossed the grass, came onto the pillared porch of the little house, and passed through the smooth marble wall.

Into peace.

Elizabeth could not help letting a great sigh escape her lips. Men-tal as well as physical silence enveloped her—the kind that had once provoked such anguish back at the Metapsychic Institute on Denali, where the therapists had tried in vain to reestablish contact with her regenerated brain. But now—how welcome the stillness! It brought surcease from the background noise of all those lesser psyches that had mumbled and squealed and droned and piped their thin discord-ancies even when they were not actually reaching out in childish in-solence or daring a frontal attack against her very ramparts. They couldn't reach her, of course; but there was still the battering . . . In the Milieu, such mental static was shut out by the overwhelming harmony of the Unity. Here, until now, there had been relief from it only in that cocoon of fire that was the last terrible refuge of a suffering, self-centered soul.

But this—

"Do you like my room?" asked Brede.

"I do," said Elizabeth. Both her mind and countenance smiled.

The exotic woman lowered her respirator. "There is an elevated partial pressure of oxygen here, which promotes euphoria. But the mental stillness is the most precious attribute of this room without doors. We two may reach out, but none may enter."

The exterior of the villa had been modest, with classic perpendicular lines; but the walls inside curved and arched away into immense distances. They were midnight-blue with ever-changing fragile patterns of faint carmine and silver, reminiscent of oil-sheen on deep water. There were pictures—projections, rather—of two deep-space vistas: a barred-spiral galaxy trailing two great arms, and a planet whose landmasses wrinkled into high mountains, having blue seas in rounded basins resembling lunar maria.

The furnishings of the room were simple, nearly invisible because they were made of the same dark stuff as the walls. There were a few chests, shelves holding colored glass cylinders with magnetic imprints that were Tanu audiovisuals, a pair of long couches, several featureless cubes the size of footstools. Hovering at eye level against one wall was a small piece of sculpture, an abstraction of a female figure. Three blue lights were ranged around it. In the center of the room (or what might have been the center, if the walls had not approached or receded as one concentrated on them or ignored them) stood the most striking piece of décor: a low oval table that glowed milky white, flanked by two dark padded benches. On the table was a glass model that Elizabeth assumed represented some intricate protist organism such as a marine radiolarian.

"An image of my Ship," Brede explained. "Let us be seated and I will begin the sharing by telling you of our journey."

"Very well." Barriers firm, Elizabeth sat with clasped hands, looking not at the Shipspouse and her room of wonders but at the small diamond ring on her own right hand.

* * *

Aeons ago in our distant galaxy [Brede said] there lived a sentient race on a single small planet orbiting a yellow sun. When this race first achieved a written history it had but a single body form and a single mental pattern. With the passing of millennia it developed a high technology and the gravo-magnetic transport, which enables vessels to travel at velocities approaching that of light without being restricted by the limitations of inertia. Suitable planets within practical range were colonized and a federation established. But then there was an interstellar war, and for long years the shattered colonies were separated from their mother-planet not only by the gulfs of space but also by a profound deterioration of culture. One daughter-world alone—my own planet of Lene—retained limited space-travel capability, using primitive reaction engines for brief forays into its own solar system.

Back on the mother-planet, which was called Duat, the great war had provoked melancholy changes. Damage to the land and atmosphere led to climatic alterations. The high mountains became a wilderness of snow; the precipitous valleys, though semitropical, were largely overcast and foggy. Over a thousand generations, the native people evolved two body forms, both different from the parent stock that had colonized the daughter-worlds so many years before.

The upland race, the Firvulag, dwelt in wintry austerity for most of the year. They were mostly small in stature and physically tough. Their culture was simple, with the technological conservatism and cooperative social patterns that often prevail in harsh environments. Isolated for long periods in their snowbound caves, they consoled themselves not merely with handicrafts but more especially with mental diversions designed to preserve sanity. They developed the ability to conjure entertaining visions and pseudomaterial manifestations, as well as many other refinements of the psychoenergetic metafunction that you of the Milieu term "creativity." They also achieved a form of farspeech and farsight that enabled them to contact distant brethren without venturing into the deadly storms. The Firvulag became true, if limited, metapsychics, and they prospered.

Meanwhile, in the lowlands of this same Duat, a second racial type flourished—tall and slender and pale-skinned, with light-sensitive eyes, as was suitable in a warm climate with heavily overcast skies. This ancestral Tanu population struggled slowly back to a level of high technology. They never evolved into operant metafunction, as the Firvulag did; instead they developed the mental amplifier you know as the golden torc, which made their latent metafunctions imperfectly operant and gave them a crude but satisfying simulacrum of psychounity—the "mind-family" relationship that you have observed among our people and among the golds and silvers and grays of this Many-Colored Land . . .

There was always a strong strain of aggression in the people of biracial Duat. The Tanu and Firvulag were perennial antagonists, although neither group wreaked more than superficial damage upon the other because of a reluctance to penetrate far into enemy territory. The ritual battles became the basis for a simple religion that prevailed for another sixty generations—until Duat was contacted once again by explorers from the reborn Interstellar Federation.

Yes . . . we regained the stars, we daughter-worlds. While our ancient home-planet went its separate and peculiar way, we rediscovered the gravo-magnetic drive. But there was more! We entered into a wonderful symbiosis with the titanic sentient organisms that came to be called Ships. They were capable of superluminal travel through the exercise of their own minds, generating what you would call upsilonfields by means of a unique ultrasense. If the Ships were suitably motivated, they would carry a thousand or more of our people along with them in an implanted capsule, soaring to the uttermost parts of our galaxy in minutes—hours, at most. As you may have already guessed, the Ships could be motivated only by love. And each Ship that served us had as Spouse a woman of my race.

The dimorphic population of Duat was welcomed into our federation. Their golden torcs proved to be compatible with the minds of many, but by no means all, of the people living on the former colonial worlds. A torc-wearing elite came to power; and after only four generations, our confederation was experiencing a Golden Age of cultural and technoeconomic expansion.

Like all Golden Ages, ours came to an end. Descendants of the original Tanu and Firvulag, who were zealous endogamists, carried their ancient enmities to the stars, precipitating a new series of ruinous wars. After much suffering, peace was restored; but our federation decreed that the remnant of Firvulag and Tanu purebloods must abjure the battle-religion and mingle their genes so that the basis for the old hatred would be obliterated. Most of the dimorphic population eventually agreed to this. But one diehard segment refused and demanded the right to emigrate to another galaxy. This request was denied and their unconditional surrender required. They fled, only a thousand Tanu and Firvulag, to a remote world near the tip of one spiral arm, where they prepared to battle to the death among themselves in a last gesture of apocalyptic defiance.

One person only was sympathetic to their original plea for exile. This woman was blessed—or afflicted—with more than the ordinary Shipspouse's share of the metafaculty of prolepsis. You would call this prescience or foresight. She foresaw that the small mob of malcontents, so useless in their own galaxy, would have a catalytic effect in another star-whirl younger and less mentally evolved, where the great longevity and mental power of the exiles would have a beneficial influence on the slowly coalescing local Mind. The vision was a cloudy one. But it was sufficient to inspire this person to offer the services of herself and her Ship to carry the exiles away . . .

Thus we came.

And the human time-travelers came.

And *you* came.

* * *

"At this point," Brede admitted, "my prescience fails me. The arrival of people from Earth's distant future gave me great concern, upsetting as it did the Tanu-Firvulag balance of power that had prevailed up until about seventy years ago. I still have not fully assessed the impact. The survey now being conducted by your friend Bryan will possibly provide data necessary for my ultimate judgment —although neither King Thagdal nor any of the rest have thought deeply on what would have to be done should the verdict be unfavorable to further human participation."

"Humanity," said Elizabeth, "occupies a similarly equivocal position among the coadunate races of the Galactic Milieu."

"The human advent has brought about many advantageous changes—and not merely technoeconomic and eugenic. Factions among both the Firvulag and Tanu—especially *hybrid* Tanu— have begun to weary of the traditional contention and reach out toward a more civilized philosophy. It may well be that the assimilation of latent humanity into the Tanu population is a desirable thing. But you—!"

"No anthropological survey will assess my impact."

"Perhaps it is appropriate that you contribute your priceless heritage to our racial evolution at this point. The Thagdal believes this, as do Eadone Sciencemaster, Aluteyn the Lord Creator, Sebi-Gomnol, and a number of others among our Great Ones. But you and your genes for operant metafunction might just as easily be a potential lethal factor—as the Host of Nontusvel perceives you. What is to be done? I am at a loss to know how to proceed."

Slowly, Elizabeth rotated the diamond ring on her finger. "Some other would-be manipulators of humans have known the feeling."

10

Isolated from the mainland on its long peninsula as the Tanu capital was, its citizens were restricted in their ability to engage in Hunts. Long before humans came to the Many-Colored Land, all Firvulag had been exterminated or driven from Aven; citizens hankering for blood sport had either to travel to the Iberian mainland or content themselves with the organized events that took place in Muriah's huge open-air arena or at the Plain of Sports, a great green field northwest of the city that was laid out with grand- and petit-prix racecourses. In addition to the thrice-weekly contests, there was held midway in each month, excepting those of the Grand Combat and the flanking Truce, a much larger Sport Meeting that attracted contestants and spectators from all parts of southern Europe.

It was at the September Sport Meeting that Aiken Drum and his man-at-arms Stein Oleson were ordered to demonstrate their newly acquired martial skills. If the two of them passed muster in the arena, they would be allowed to participate in the Delbaeth Quest—which was now scheduled to be conducted by the King himself. After frantic maneuvering on the part of the Queen and her Host, it was decided that not only Aiken but also Nodonn Battlemaster, Lord of Goriah, would pursue the elusive monster under Thagdal's designated agency. All of the noble sports fans who could manage to get away would accompany the expedition to Spain to watch the fun.

Opening odds on Aiken to take the Shape of Fire were 300 to 1.

A nasty driving rain swept over Aven on Meeting Night. A team of PK stalwarts led by Nodonn's twin brothers Fian Skybreaker and Kuhal Earthshaker mobilized efforts to deflect the downpour from the stadium by means of psychic energies. It was expected that the Battlemaster himself would arrive at the capital in time to witness the testing of the Candidate Aiken and his Viking henchman.

In the royal box awaiting the parade of contestants, Queen Nontusvel glanced up at a crooked discharge of natural lightning that flashed above the transparent roof generated by the psychokinetics.

"Such unusual weather for this time of year. I hope Nodonn and dear Rosmar won't be delayed." She turned to Eadone Sciencemaster who sat beside her, austere in unadorned silver. "Gomnol theorizes that our Flying Hunts may be disrupting the ozone layer and changing the climate."

"Twaddle," said Eadone, secure in her position as Dean of Guilds and eldest child of the King. "It's nothing but a freak storm. Perhaps the remnant of some tropical cyclone from the South Atlantic that managed to cross the Gibraltar Isthmus."

"Let's hope so, August Daughter," boomed Thagdal. "If this rain settles in to stay, it'll mean poor sport for our Delbaeth Quest. The old Shape of Fire might just stay home in his cave with his pipe and slippers if the crops at the plantations get all soggy and nonflammable. We'll have a devil of a time tracking him if he stays underground."

"Here's Bryan!" exclaimed the Queen. She now spoke in Standard English, a courtesy followed by all of the Tanu Great Ones in the presence of the torcless anthropologist. "And Greggy, and the Craftsmaster, too! Quite drenched, poor things. Aluteyn, darling! Couldn't your PK cope?"

"I'm a creator, Awful Lady, not an umbrella merchant," grumped the stout old Craftsmaster. "What's wrong with a little rain, anyhow? We Tanu ought to stiffen up and shake our silly water phobia. Whoever drowned in the rain?"

Bryan bowed to the royal couple. "It wasn't at all bad until we were forced to make a run from our carriage to the arena entrance. There are so many people here tonight that the ramas holding canopies over the new arrivals kept tangling up with one another."

Someone giggled, a sound approximating that of a strangling bantam chicken. A human male in a golden torc, wearing a clawhammer cutaway in the colors of the Creator Guild, stumbled moistly toward the King and Queen, spattering the other occupants of the royal box as he waved his arms in greeting. His marmoset face was full of blithe innocence; he seemed to be about sixty years old.

"Aluteyn spun us an *illusion* of dryness!" this personage declaimed, executing a kind of curtsy that ended just short of his pitching over the rail into the arena. "But can illusion ever mimic truth? Especially when a canopy full of water tilts and—"

"Oh, shut up, Greggy," said the Craftsmaster, looking tired. "It's been a long day, Great Ones," he told the King and Queen.

"And did you take good care of Bryan? Show him all the wondrous secrets of your Guild?" The good Queen's solicitude warmed all three of the arrivals and dried their wet feet.

"A most impressive tour," Bryan said. "The facilities for training artists and scientists reminded me of certain universities of my own era. And of course Lord Greg-Donnet conducted me around the research laboratories of his own Genetics Department—"

"And wasn't it marvelous? Wasn't it?" The former Gregory Prentice Brown gave a small skip and clapped his hands. "I can't tell you what a joy it is chatting with a colleague who could fill me in on some of the latest developments of Milieu science! Do you realize, Majesties, that the percentage of operant metapsychics among last year's newborn humans in the Galactic Milieu has risen from two to *four?* I simply must replot my study of the latency coefficients! I had based my original prognosis on the assumption that the population was in equilibrium . . . but Grenfell says it's not! The implications are *enormous.*"

"I'm sure they are, Greggy dear," said the Queen. "Do sit down and relax. Look—here come the clowns!"

"Oh, goody!" Lord Greg-Donnet cried. "I hope the exploding one is here tonight." He plumped down onto a seat and appropriated a plateful of finger-bananas from the royal snack table, eating them skin and all.

Eadone asked Bryan, "Is what Greggy says true?"

"I should think so, Lady Sciencemaster."

She frowned. "But for a replot, we'll need the computer."

"But we *have* the computer," Bryan said. "Ogmol and I have been using it to store our data."

With some stiffness, Aluteyn said, "The kid fixed it."

"Tana's toenails!" exclaimed the delighted King. "Maybe I misjudged Aiken!"

The Queen sat watching the cavorting entertainers with a fixed smile.

"Aiken Drum has been busy about many things," the Craftsmaster continued in a voice heavy with irony. "He was able to show some of my people at the glass works how to restore the large annealing machine. He and Gomnol have been conferring on ways to improve the mental-assay device—which as you know has always been dismayingly fragile. And he has also introduced the vulgar nobility to kite fighting and three-dimensional chess. The new diversions have swept Muriah in the past two weeks."

"H'm," mused the King. He did not look delighted any more.

"Oh, the *animals!*" Greggy squealed. "Just look at that gigantopithecine! Will he fight? Will he?"

"Not to the death, darling," the Queen said. "We must save him for the Grand Combat. But there'll be elephants, and giant bear-dogs from the Catalonian Wilderness. And—look there, in that wagon. Another new monster! Isn't it dreadful? Like a cross between a sabertooth and a huge hyena!"

"Hyainailouros," Eadone said. "Another specimen brought back by the African expedition. The last delayed shipment arrived today."

Now there was a flourish of brass and tympani, punctuated by thunderclaps. The night's contestants paraded forth: first the lesser grays on foot, wearing different kinds of gladiatorial gear; then the higher-ranked grays, the silvers, and the human and Tanu gold-torcs in resplendent glass armor of many colors and styles. The chaliko steeds they rode were also armored and trapped richly, and many of the animals had their coats dyed yellow or crimson or blue.

The applause of the throng swelled almost to the pain threshold. Through the entrance and into the arena came two riders, side by side. One was a gigantic human male riding a coppery-red chaliko. His full armor was crystalline green studded with roundels and spikes of glittering topaz. The visor of the horned emerald helmet was up and Stein grinned at the shrieking fans and smote his shield with the flat of a huge vitredur axe. Beside the Viking rode a diminutive figure who seemed all plated in gold, astride a great black mount. As the ladies began to throw flowers he gave a bound and stood upright in his saddle, bearing aloft a lance from which floated a long purple pennon with a golden symbol on it.

"A banner with a strange device," Bryan murmured. "Is that charge really a digitus impudicus?"

"The Venerable Mayvar," said the Queen in a neutral tone, "allowed her Candidate to choose his own armorial bearings. Am I right in presuming that the hand-gesture motif represents a certain raffish defiance?"

"Your Majesty is quite correct," said Bryan, keeping a straight face.

The parade now ranged in a great circle all around the arena. The

Marshal of Sport and the Lord of Swords entered last of all, together with their attendants and the corps of referees. When these functionaries came to the great fenced stairway in front of the royal box, they made their duty to Thagdal and Nontusvel and led both contestants and spectators in a loud salute.

Thagdal's mind and voice bellowed: "Let the games begin!"

The audience settled down while the principal fighters and animals retired to sideline areas. Preliminary events and circus acts began to warm things up. The King asked Bryan, "How does your survey go, Worthy Doctor?"

"I've gathered a considerable body of data, as Lord Ogmol has doubtless reported."

The King nodded. "Oggy's fighting tonight, but he tells me you've been running him all over town—and into the countryside."

"It's important to include agriculture, especially since it has become your policy to delegate operation of the plantations entirely to humans. I was surprised to find so many torcless workers employed in nonmenial positions. It's interesting that most of them seem productive and happy."

"Were you surprised to discover that, Bryan?" inquired the Queen. She took a napkin and dipped it into a goblet of white wine, then wiped mashed fruit pulp from Lord Greg-Donnet's face. The Genetics Master smiled adoringly at her.

"The apparent assimilation is significant. I understand that malcontents are relatively few—at least in the Aven area. Will I be allowed to compare these data with similar surveys of other metropolitan regions—say, Goriah and Finiah?"

"Unfortunately," the King said, "there will not be time. We will require your completed analysis before the Grand Combat. You must make do with the material you're able to gather here—even if it does tend to be loaded with positive factors."

"We gather the crème de la crème of humanity for Muriah," said Greggy, looking smug. "Hardly anybody runs away down here. Not even the women. I mean—where could they go?"

"Kersic, mostly," said Eadone. She applauded an exhibition of roping and hog-tying of elk-sized antelope, performed by cowboys in orange lamé. To Bryan, she explained, "That's an island east of here. In your future world it has split into Corsica and Sardinia."

"And the—outlaws live there?"

"A few," the King said, waving a dismissive hand. "Gangs of

sickly bandits preying on each other. Every few years we mount a Hunt and clean them out. Not much sport, though."

"Look! Look! The hoe-tuskers!" The Genetics Master, and most of the rest of the crowd, jumped up and down and screamed. Handlers with long goads brought on six colossal proboscideans with down-curving tusks. The largest stood nearly four meters high at the shoulder. Tanu knights afoot, armed only with vitredur lances bearing large banners, performed an exotic corrida with the animals. One luckless fighter botched a pase and was trampled. The rainbow blaze of his unbroken armor dulled abruptly, as though a switch had been thrown.

Greg-Donnet tittered. "Snapped his neck. Well—there's one for Dionket's baggie-bin!"

The Queen told the appalled Bryan, "He will be restored, dear boy, never fear. We're a very tough race, you know. But that poor fellow will be sidelined for the Grand Combat while he heals within the Skin. He's lost great prestige by being so clumsy."

The deinotheria and the surviving knights retired to applause.

"None of the animals are to be killed?" Bryan asked.

"There will be only two battles to the death tonight," said the Queen. "Ah. That's the end of that. And now . . ."

An elaborate blast of brasses sounded. The Marshal of Sport came to the steps in front of the royal box and Aluteyn translated his announcement for Bryan.

"Be pleased, Awful Majesties, to accept the homage of the Novice-at-Arms Stein Oleson, loyal servant of the Candidate Aiken Drum!"

Stein cantered out on his chaliko, rode up to the steps, lowered his long-hafted glass axe, and saluted by touching his gray torc. The cheers were loud but tentative. When the King arose and made a gesture, the crowd fell silent.

Stein turned his mount to face the chosen antagonist. Animal handlers on the other side of the arena opened a stout gate on the wheeled cage that held the hyainailouros.

The beast seemed to flow across the pocked and stained expanse of sand. It had the snakey neck and relatively small head of a polar bear. Its body, however, bulked at least twice as large as that of the unborn ursid. The hyainailouros might have weighed a ton or more; it moved with speed and agility, flattening its large rounded ears against its head and heading directly for Stein in a kind of galloping slither. The animal's mouth hung wide open, displaying a pair of oversized upper canines that were longer than Stein's mailed hand. "Oooh!" shrilled Lord Greg-Donnet.

Following the obligatory etiquette of the arena, Stein came at a gallop to meet the creature, swerving aside at the last second to whack it on the rump, en passant, with the flat of his glass axe. It whirled, giving a kind of hissing hoot, and slashed with one clawed forefoot, then the other. Stein returned to count more coups, attacking and retreating, smacking the animal on flanks, back, neck—even gently tapping its flat skull. The hyainailouros spun about in a frenzy, trying to disembowel the chaliko or catch the tormenting rider in its gnashing jaws. The spectators greeted each coup with a roar of approbation. Finally, when the sabertoothed beast was beginning to reel with vertigo and frustration, scattered voices among the fans started to shout: "A kill! A kill!"

Stein spurred his mount and galloped in a tight circle around the swaying creature, which had risen to its hind legs. It uttered a series of short, high-pitched bleats, like demon laughter.

Thagdal stood up once more and gestured.

"*A kill!*" howled the crowd in unison.

And then there was silence, except for the thud of the chaliko's clawed feet as Stein guided it away from the hyainailouros, and the rasping exhalations of the winded prey waiting for its enemy to return. Stein dismounted. At the end of his axe was a stout lanyard; the advancing Viking began to swing the weapon by this cord, whirling it around and around his horned head. He approached the now rampant brute with every facet of his armor aglitter and the rotating vitredur blade all but invisible. Then he sprang, his body's trajectory timed to coincide with the swaying of the sabertoothed prey, and scythed its head off.

The spectators erupted in a mental and vocal tumult, shouting, clapping, and stamping. Thagdal opened a wicket in the front of the box and descended the stairway that led into the arena. Down below, the Marshal's attendants threw wide the gate in the protective fence so that Stein could approach the sovereign. The Viking took off his emerald helmet and clumped forward.

And then the crowd gasped. From the other side of the stadium came thundering a black steed bearing a small rider armored in gold-lustred glass. Just as Stein paused in front of the King, Aiken Drum reined up in a sliding halt scarcely a meter behind his "servant," grinning like the personification of Jack O'Lantern.

"And he did it all himself!" the jester said. "No assists from mighty Me!"

The Marshal of Sport had been obliged to act fast with his PK to keep the great dust cloud Aiken had generated from enveloping the disconcerted King. Now the official stepped forward and declaimed: "Pray silence for the accolade of His Awful Majesty!"

"Yeah," said Stein, giving Aiken a look. "You'll get your chance."

Thagdal produced a large chained medallion embossed with the heraldic male face. He raised it. As the crowd cried, "Slonshal!" he hung it around Stein's neck.

"Accept this our accolade, and be forever our faithful man-at-arms."

The people cheered, and Queen Nontusvel sent down a napkin threaded through a magnificent ruby thumb ring (Stein didn't mind at all that it was a little messy with banana), and the Tanu ladies exuded concupiscence, and *very* guarded hostility emanated from the Tanu gentlemen, and a hostler brought Stein's chaliko to him, and he rode away. Aiken followed after, broadcasting, "That's my boy!" on a highly amplified farspeech mode.

When Thagdal returned to the box there was a distinct atmosphere of jovian pique.

"Now, Thaggy," soothed the Queen.

"Didn't you *love* it?" Greggy squealed.

A great crack of thunder rang out. "My sentiments exactly," growled the High King of the Many-Colored Land. "You will all excuse me. I am going for a royal leak."

"He doesn't really care for humans, you know." Lord Greg-Donnet's cheery infant face was illuminated by momentary sanity. "No more than you do, my Queen, and all your Host. The King endures humanity as a necessary evil. But *you* would rather the time-gate had never opened."

"Shame on you, Greggy," said Nontusvel. "Some of my best friends are human. You mustn't talk like that, naughty boy. What will Bryan think? Here—have a nice hard-boiled egg."

The Genetics Master took the proffered silver dish and stared into it, apparently puzzled. "Eggs? Eggs? But they, dearest Lady, are the matter of contention! A quarter of a million of them tucked within her human ovaries! So generous, so wasteful, so providential of Mother Nature to stuff evey human female with such a superabundance of ova!" He peered sideways at Bryan, took up an egg and dipped it into a jar of Grey Poupon mustard before taking a meditative bite. "Do you know, Dr. Grenfell, that in the Pliocene, dear Mother Nature's name is Tana? . . . Or Té, if you're of the Firvulag persuasion."

"Don't talk with your mouth full, Greggy dear," said the Queen.

Tears began to trickle down the madman's smooth cheeks. "If only we could clone her!" And Bryan was quite aware that the Genetics Master no longer referred to Mother Nature. "You wouldn't believe, Grenfell, how primitive this outfit really is compared to my old lab back at Johns Hopkins."

"Watch the tournament, Greggy," Nontusvel urged. "See? There's Ogmol coming into the lists."

The Lady Eadone Sciencemaster gave Bryan an appraising glance. "And what preliminary conclusions have you been able to draw in these first weeks of your culture-impact survey, Doctor? Genetic considerations aside, we're worried that the Tanu may be becoming too dependent upon human workers and human technology. As you've noted, none of our young people choose a career in agriculture any more. The same is becoming true in other practical disciplines: mining, architecture, civil engineering, manufacturing."

"All activities that fall into *my* province," Aluteyn put in, looking harried. "Creation House is overflowing with musicians and dancers and sculptors and apprentice couturiers. But do you know how many signed up for bioluminescence technology this year? Five! Another couple of hundred years and we'll have to light our cities entirely with olive oil and reed pith soaked in tallow!"

"You may have grounds for your concern," Bryan said carefully.

The indignant Craftsmaster said, "There's even talk of separating the arts and sciences entirely—spinning off a new Guild, if you please!—with mostly gold humans in charge of technology!"

"Gomnol's idea, of course," Eadone remarked, entirely sedate.

"I've been in harness since the old days," Aluteyn said. "I was one of the First Comers who defied the federation and made contact with Brede. There aren't many of us left now among the Tanu—the Thagdal, Dionket, Mayvar, Lady Eadone, the Lord of Swords, poor old Leyr sulking in the Pyrénées . . . There! Even *I* give the damn mountains their human name! Just sixty-odd years of the time-gate and a millennium of Duat culture nearly gone down the drain. Even the best *fighters* these days are mostly hybrids! The world's gone to hell in a nightsoil cart."

"Compose yourself, Creative Brother," the Queen said.

Greg-Donnet showed his teeth in a wide grin. "You can't stand in the way of progress."

"Oh, really?" said Nontusvel.

A gray-torc usher opened the curtains at the rear of the royal box. He announced: "The Exalted Lord Nodonn Battlemaster and his consort, Lady Rosmar."

A towering form in rosy-golden armor stood in the doorway, almost blinding Bryan with sunrise radiance.

"My son!" cried the delighted Queen.

"Mother!"

"I'm so glad you're in time for his testing."

The visage of Apollo displayed an ironic smile. "I wouldn't have missed it for the world. I've brought a little present for Mayvar's fancy-boy."

The Queen had risen from her seat to kiss her eldest child. Now she took the hand of a human woman dressed in a splendid costume and headdress of auroral hues and led her to the still-dazzled anthropologist.

"And here's a surprise for you, Bryan. Just as we promised! Dear Nodonn will want to go down to the arena to witness the trial of Aiken Drum, so you two must sit together and get reacquainted. You *do* remember Bryan Grenfell, don't you, darling Rosmar?"

"How could I ever forget?" Mercy said. Tenderly, she bent and kissed the anthropologist on the lips, then raised a playful eye to her resplendent Lord. "You mustn't be jealous, my daemon lover. Bryan and I are old, old friends."

"Enjoy one another," said the Battlemaster.

He opened the wicket and descended the stairs to the arena. The stadium crowd and the stormy sky thundered together in a concert of adulation.

* * *

Watching from the opposite side of the stadium, Aiken asked the Lord of Swords, "Who's the badass archangel?"

"You'll be finding out shortly! I understand he's brought something special for your testing from the marshes of Laar." Tagan went out of the sideline dugout to meet the Tanu champion. The jousting had come to a standstill in the uproar attending Nodonn's appearance.

Stein, free now of his glass armor and gnawing the roasted leg of some large fowl, called from the passageway leading to the dressing rooms. "Hey, kid! Somebody here to see you. Your old pal, the B.C. stud."

Raimo Hakkinen slid furtively into the dugout, pale eyes darting. None of the human or Tanu warriors was paying any attention to him, but he spoke in an anxious whisper just the same. "Only a minute of your time, Lord Aiken. That's all—"

The trickster was aghast. "What's this fewkin' *lord* bullshit? It's me, Chopper—your li'l bitty buddy!"

Aiken sent a quick probe behind bloodshot Mongol eyes . . . and found chaos. There was hardly a sensible thought to be found in that bog of weariness and dread that was Raimo's mind. Somehow, the silver torc had exacerbated the personal devils of the former woodsman. His experiences during the previous two weeks combined with this functional derangement to drive him to the brink of brain-wreck.

"The women, Aik! The goddam man-eating Tanu bitches! They been squeezing me like a lemon!"

Stein slapped one great thigh and gave a roar of cruel laughter.

Raimo only hung his head. He looked as if he had lost ten kilos. The formerly arrogant Finnish face had gone pinched and blotchy, the blond hair hung lank beneath a jaunty cap, and the once powerful body was shrunken within a costume that mimicked Italian Renaissance styling with its puffed sleeves, trunk hose, and codpiece. Raimo paid no attention to the Viking's derision but raised clasped hands and fell on his knees before the mischief-maker.

"For the love of God, Aik—help me! You can! I heard how you got this fuckin' town eatin' outa your hand."

Redaction was not Aiken's long metapsychic suit, but he plunged in to do the best he could for the tottering psyche. Some of the Tanu contestants for the games had begun to stare curiously, so Aiken pulled Raimo out into the corridor. Stein trailed after, chewing his bone.

"They been passing me from one to the other," Raimo said. "All the ones who don't have kids—and there are a coopful! They try out all the silver guys—grays, too, if they like the looks of 'em. But if it turns out that you don't knock any of 'em up, they quit being nice and get their buzz by—by—Jeez, Aik! D'you know what they can *do* to a guy wearin' this friggin' torc?"

Aiken saw. He moved quickly through the limbic system of the humiliated, hagridden brain, turning off pain circuits and putting up a temporary mitigating structure that would help . . . a little.

When things were at their worst, Raimo would be able to retreat into it and stay sane. As the woodsman's twitching features calmed, he pleaded, "Don't let 'em get me, Aik. We were buddies. Don't let the Tanu bitches ball me to death."

A sudden burst of conversation and laughter sounded from the other end of the long passageway. Six tall apparitions of unearthly beauty, all rainbow chiffon and sparkling gems and floating blonde hair and on-the-gad pheromones, came gliding toward the three men with eager exclamations.

"We farwatched you and knew you'd be hiding here!"

"Wicked, delicious Raimo, to run away!"

"Now we'll have to punish you again, won't we?"

"Sisters! Do you know who the big one is? It's Stein! Let's take him, too!"

There was a perfumed scurrying and a clash of coordinated coercive power against a mind-shield of gold, followed by mental giggles and impudent tweaks that set Aiken and the Viking on fire even though the psychic barriers were up. A single moan: "Don't let 'em." And then Raimo and the Tanu women were gone.

"Holy shit," whispered Stein.

Aiken shook his golliwog head. "Back in the good old Milieu, I'd of said, 'What a way to go.' But you wouldn't believe what was rattling around in that poor bastard's skull. A genuine fate worse than death! He just can't keep cutting it with those crazy broads!"

Stein said, "Too bad you can't give lessons."

"*Aiken Drum!*" came the mental and vocal command of the Lord of Swords. "You are required to demonstrate your power before the King and the nobility and populace of Muriah."

"Oh-oh. I'm on." The trickster looked up at Stein, serious for once. "If they nail me out there, Mayvar will bring you to the place where Sukey's hidden."

"Go stick it to 'em, kid," the Viking told him.

* * *

"Be pleased, Awful Majesties, to accept the homage of the gold-torc human Aiken Drum, sponsored Candidate of the Venerable Mayvar Kingmaker, President of the Guild of Farsensors."

Aiken rode up on the black charger to pay his devoirs. The plaudits were nearly as wild as those that had greeted the Battlemaster.

Nodonn himself stood at the foot of the stairs with Tagan and the Marshal of Sport, his head bared and an expression of benignity on his glowing face. When the cheers had completely died away, he said:

"Aiken Drum—your Venerable Patron has acquainted us with your considerable metapsychic talents. But these are not the qualities we seek to assess tonight as we weigh your candidacy. Instead, we would test the fundamental attributes that must characterize those of our battleworthy company—courage, resolution, intelligence. Demonstrate these as you meet the antagonist I have chosen for you . . . His name, according to the sages of Goriah, is Phobosuchus. Most of his kind have been extinct for nearly fifty million years. But a few survive as living fossils in the regions south of my city, in the vast estuaries of the River Laar where the long-necked sea monsters come to bask and breed. By my mind's power I have subdued and transported him here to try your skill. But I charge you, Aiken Drum, to remember our conventions of sport! You may use no overt mental force in your combat with Phobosuchus—only bodily strength, bravery, and natural cunning. Violate our precepts and the massed scorn of this noble company will annihilate you."

A low-pitched sound swept over the crowd. Conflicting farspoken sentiments eddied around the little figure in the golden armor: some hostile, some mocking or fearful, but others . . .

I'll be damned, Aiken thought. I think most of them want me to win!

Nodonn's admonitions having ended, the King signaled that the contest should begin. With one hand Aiken raised his pennoned lance, saluting first the royal box and then the mob of spectators. With the other hand, as he spurred his chaliko around to face the center of the arena, he repeated to the Battlemaster the finger gesture depicted on his banner.

There was a great cheer. A heavily barred doorway beside the animal pens swung wide, revealing a dark cavelike opening. Nodonn cried out in simultaneous vocal and mental command:

"Phobosuchus, come forth!"

A dragon raced into the arena, then stopped in the middle of the field to gape its jaws and give a hiss like an erupting fumarole.

The spectators responded with screams of awe and frenzied applause for the novelty, the like of which had never before been seen in the arena of Muriah. Phobosuchus was a monstrous crocodilian. Its skull measured two meters in length and the teeth in the bluish-gray mouth were the size of large bananas. At rest, and watching the approach of Aiken's black charger with a sardonic catlike eye, Phobosuchus squatted on the sand with bowed legs; the body was at least fifteen meters long, the dorsal surface armored with ridged bony scutes. The whimsy of the Battlemaster had augmented the natural pale-green-and-black banded pattern of the beast with painted designs of his own heraldic colors, rose-red and gold.

Infuriated by the mob's screeching, the bright lights, and the painful mental goad that Nodonn's coercive faculty had just administered, Phobosuchus sought whom it might devour. It lashed its serrated tail, releasing a noxious blast of musk from its cloacal glands. Then it hoisted its huge body high off the ground and started running toward the most likely target at a brisk gallop.

The pioneer "Scottish" planet of Dalriada where Aiken Drum had been nurtured had no native crocodilians, nor had the ecology engineers deemed that particular reptile order a suitable addition to the local biota. And so Aiken really hadn't the foggiest notion of the type of creature that was charging toward him. He decided that it *had* to be a dragon. A dragon that could run like a racehorse and was thoroughly pissed. Game etiquette decreed that he meet the oncoming monster with bold resolution. He took a firm grip on his lance and thumped spurred heels upon his mount's wide shoulders . . .

. . . and quite forgot to hold onto its mind.

The black chaliko gave a ringing scream of fear and threw him. It fled for its life to the opposite end of the arena while the young man in the golden glass armor scrambled to his feet, snatched up his lance, and took to his heels with Phobosuchus in pleased pursuit.

After a silent beat of stunned horror, the spectators began a hilarious riot of cheering. The heavens added to the noise with a fanfaronade of thunder, which inspired the crocodile to bellow in response. It did this with its mouth closed, chasing Aiken up one side of the arena and down the other while clowns, referees, animal handlers, manure shovelers, Tanu knights in spiky jeweled armor, and dignified officials tumbled over one another and leaped or levitated into the front-row seats, trying to escape the racing monster.

As he approached the stairway to the royal box, where Nodonn, Tagan, and the other high-ranking observers stood like a collection of huge carved-gemstone chessmen, Aiken suddenly changed course. He streaked in a flat curve for the center of the arena with Phobosuchus two or three meters behind and beginning to get a trifle winded. Aiken thrust the butt of his lance ahead of him, sank it deeply into the sand, and went hand over hand up it in a fluid pole vault that sent him arcing through the air like a golden missile. He landed a monster's length to one side of Phobosuchus. The creature hesitated, then shied at the lance and its banner, which still quivered, embedded in the earth.

Phobosuchus halted, belly to the ground. It swung its awesome gape toward the golden manikin dancing around its flank. Aiken dashed toward the rear end of the great crocodile before it could shift its hulk and finally attained its blind spot. Skipping lightly as an autumn leaf, he ran along the knobbed and enameled expanse of the animal's back, keeping his balance like a logrolling champ while the reptile writhed and spun in an effort to discover what this peculiar prey was up to now.

Abruptly, the crocodilian froze. The crowd drew a collective breath. Aiken flung himself prone onto the gaudy cobbled hide and clung to a pair of scutes with a death-grip. Phobosuchus exploded into a fit of bucking and twisting, furious to dislodge the human pest that adhered to its back. Its jaws clashed with a noise of rending timbers; it bounced and squirmed and flung its three-ton body about with the agility of a basilisk, trying in vain to claw Aiken off with the black scimitars that tipped its feet. The reptile's tail churned up clouds of dust that momentarily hid both dragon and golden sticktight; but when the beast finally paused to rest, Aiken was still in position, lying on his armored stomach between two lines of scutes just aft of the front legs.

Phobosuchus lowered itself to its belly again and hissed exasperation. As the mouth, approximately as long as Aiken's body, closed, the trickster suddenly sprang to his feet and dashed up the neck, between the eyes, and down the length of the prostrate skull to leap off the tip of the snout. The monster watched in a kind of stunned fascination as Aiken sprinted for his lance and wrenched it out of the ground. He came running back to retrace his madcap route up the reptile's head and onto its shoulders, purple banner streaming raggedly above his dusty golden helm.

"A kill! A kill!" trumpeted the crowd.

Phobosuchus bellowed in despair. The jaws opened and the huge skull tilted above Aiken like the span of a nightmare drawbridge. Lance at the ready, the little man looked into the dragon's upside-down eyes. Aiken's farsense showed him the structure of the skull beneath the thick, ornamented hide—the two parietal openings behind the eyesockets.

Aiken chose the right fenestra, plunged his lance in, and immediately leapt from the creature's back and retreated to a safe distance. Once again Phobosuchus erupted into a paroxysm of thrashing, and this lasted for some time because dragons do not die easily. But at last the great body lay jerking in the dust and Aiken plucked the shattered lance with its ruined pennon from the bleeding brain. He walked very slowly to the royal stairway.

There was King Thagdal waiting for him. And the Queen, smiling, and off at one side the Battlemaster, aloof and glorious. And there was also a tall stooped figure in a plum-colored robe who cleaned his dusty armor with a gesture of her hand and gave him a fresh ensign, violet plumes, and a cloak like the spangled purple-black of the twilight sky to wear as he stood before the King.

Three times the Marshal had to cry: "Pray silence for the accolade of His Awful Majesty!" At last, the spectators were still.

The Lord of Swords stepped to the side of the sovereign and held out a scabbard, from which Thagdal drew an amethystine sword. Holding the blade in one hand and the golden hilt in the other, the King poised the weapon in front of the face of the shining youth.

"We tender to you this our accolade, and bid you be forever our faithful knight. What name do you choose for your initiation into the noble battle-company of the Tanu?"

Mayvar's mental voice pervaded the arena with its muted tone.

He may not choose his name. I will choose his name at the acceptable time. But that time is not now.

The royal mouth tightened and static stirred the blond tendrils of the King's beard. "I defer to my Venerable Sister, your Patron and Lady. You will retain your human name until that time which she . . . foresees comes to pass. Receive this sword then, Lord Aiken Drum, and bear it in my service on the Delbaeth Quest."

Grinning, the golliwog accepted the vitredur blade. The Lord of Swords fastened the scabbard and its baldric and the crowd cried, "Slonshal!"

Up in the royal box, Lord Greg-Donnet hung over the rail cheering and scattering crumbs of egg yolk. "Good boy! Good lad! Well done!" He turned to the Craftsmaster, who watched the ceremony below with stony restraint. "Now we know that the lad is brave as well as talented in the metafunctions. Perhaps Mayvar wasn't quite so out of line as we feared, eh, Aluteyn?"

"Stop talking like an ass, Greggy. There's the Shape of Fire. The kid hasn't a chance of taking him."

Greg-Donnet chortled. "You think not? The bookies are giving three hundred to one on him. Or they were, before he polished off the dragon. Can I interest you in a side bet at those odds?"

Down in the arena, Mayvar was embracing her protégé. The King and the Battlemaster mounted the stairs to the box, looking unaccountably grim.

"A bet?" Aluteyn Craftsmaster was startled, then thoughtful. "Oh, no, Greggy. I don't think so. In no way."

"I was afraid of that," sighed the madman. He reached for another egg.

11

THE TRIMARAN flew westward beneath the outthrusting arm of Aven, skimming the shallow salt lagoon by virtue of the metapsychic gale Mercy had whistled up when Bryan protested that the day was too calm for sailing.

For what seemed like hours they took turns at the helm. She sang the oddly familiar Tanu Song, and the red-and-white sail bellied before them, hiding the distant mainland and the snow-crowned eastern end of the Betic Cordillera.

So strange, he thought, exulting in the nearness of her and the speed and the sunshine. So strange to realize that this was Earth. The Dragon Range of Aven, which would one day become the heights of Mallorca, had its lower slopes dark with tame forests and meadows where hipparions and antelopes and mastodons ranged in royal preserves. Those tawny hills, half-shrouded now in haze to starboard, would in six million years be islands named Ibiza and Formentera. (But never again would he race a yacht through azure waves off Punta Roya, for the Pliocene waters were pale as milk, and so her wild sea-reflecting eyes.) So strange.

The peninsular mass of Balearis rose from thick deposition beds of salt and gypsum and other sediments that had been laid down during the numerous regressions and inundations of the Mediterranean Basin. Streams flowing southward from Aven carved the minerals into canyons and buttes, spires and hoodoos, striped with pastel colors and sparkling in faerie splendor . . . and all of it would be gone without a trace by the time of the Galactic Milieu, drowned under unimaginable tons of water that would press the very bed of the sea two kilometers deeper and more, making abysses where now the Pliocene shallows glinted in the trimaran's wake. So strange.

After a long time the flats closed in around them and then folded into blinding gypsum dunes shimmering with mirages, among which weathered turrets of igneous rock poked up. There were hills and cliffs. The boat sailed up an eerie long fjord where whiteness gave way to purple and gray-blue, eroded slopes of ancient ash and volcanic scoria, broken cindercones lightly clothed in coniferous forest. The fjord was deep, the water now flowing from some western source. But Mercy's tame wind let them press on, breasting the current, until they emerged at last into an open expanse of saltmarsh, a green and living everglade that seemed to stretch on forever into the misted west.

"This is the Great Brackish Marsh," she told him. "A Spanish river pours in fresh water off the Betics, the high peaks we'll call the Sierra Nevada."

The diminished salinity of the marsh produced an environment much less inimical to life than the shores of the Mediterranean lagoons. Here grasses and sedges and mangroves throve in the shallows and there were many scattered islets with shrubs and hardwoods and swags of flowering vines. Gulls and gaudy pigeons wheeled overhead. Pink-and-black flamingos left off straining crustaceans from the pools and fled with honking cries when the invading trimaran glided by.

"We'll stop here," Mercy said. Her psychokinetic wind died away to the lightest of breezes. They hauled in the spinnaker and steered to a beautiful anchorage where a tall limestone outcropping crowned with laurel and tamarisk gave them shade from the sun.

"The Southern Lagoon proper ended when we came into the Long Fjord," she said. "This marsh stretches westward for another hundred and fifty kilometers or so, and beyond it are dry lakes and sand and alkali deserts all the way to the Gibraltar Isthmus. It's all far below sea level except for Alborán Volcano and a few smaller cones. Nothing lives in there but lizards and insects."

She coiled lines neatly. Leaving him to cope with the other sails, she went into the little cabin to get the basket with the lunch he had packed: a bottle of genuine Krug '03 from Muriah's black market, a wedge of the local cheddar equivalent, goose-liver sausage, sweet butter, a long loaf, and oranges. It had been too late in the season for black cherries.

"If only you'd waited for me back in the future," Bryan said, "we'd have eaten this off Ajaccio. I had it all planned. The cruise, the supper under the Corsican moon . . ."

"The obligatory lovemaking. Dear Bryan!" Her wild eyes had become opalescent.

"I wanted to marry you, Mercy. I loved you from the first time I saw you. I still love you. That's why I had to follow, even though it meant coming this far."

One of her hands reached toward him, touching his cheek. The breeze moved the heavy fall of auburn hair that was tied back with a narrow bandeau. She was not wearing exotic clothing but rather a simple sunsuit of green and white, cut in the style of their own era. Only the torc, gleaming in the V-neck of the halter, recalled to him the gulf that now separated Mercy from Rosmar.

What did that matter? What matter any of the changes—the intrigues of the exotics, the cynical entrusting of her to him by the Tanu lover as he departed on his preposterous Quest. Mercy was here with him and real. All the rest was a fantasy to be forgotten . . . or at least postponed.

But change the earth or change the sky, yet will I love her—

"Have they made you happy?" he asked.

She cut bread with a glass knife and sliced the cheese. "Can't you tell, Bryan?"

"You're different. More alive. You never sang in our world."

"How did you know?"

He only smiled. "I'm glad you can sing here, Mercy."

"I never fit into the world we were born into. Don't laugh! There are more of us changelings than you might think! Misbegotten ones. Atavisms. No amount of counseling or brain chemical fiddling or deep-redact ever helped me to feel contented or satisfied. No man—forgive me if this hurts you!—no man ever gave me more than momentary comfort. I never knew a human being I could truly love."

He was pouring champagne. The words she spoke had no meaning and so they brought no pain. She was here with him. Nothing else mattered.

"It was the latencies, Bryan. I know that now. The people here have helped me to understand. All those strong metapsychic tensions locked away unused and unrealized. But pulling me—do you see? The operant metapsychics of the Milieu have their Unity, but there was none of that for me back on the Elder Earth. I belonged nowhere. Rested nowhere. Found peace nowhere . . . I found a little solace in drugs, a little more in music, in my work with the medieval pageants in Ireland and in France. But it was really no good. I felt I was an outsider, a misfit. Just a bit of nonviable scum on our famous human gene pool."

"Mercy—" I would love you any way. Every way.

"None of that, now!" She laughed lightly and took the glass of bubbling wine from him. "You know quite well that I was a hopeless mess, banging about like a moth around a streetlight. I played my games at the château and found other lost ones to share my bed, and suffocated quite a bit of the pain in a fog of sinsemilla. An old-fashioned vice. You smoke it as a euphoric. I brought some cuttings with me to grow—never dreaming that here I'd have no need of it ever again. This place, these people, *all* of this is what I yearned for without knowing."

"All I wanted," he said, "was you. If you can't love me, all I want is your happiness." She put her fingers against his lips, then lifted her own champagne glass for him to drink from.

"My dear. You are a rare man, darling Bryan. In your own way, perhaps as uncanny as I."

"I won't intrude on you if you're happy with him—"

"Hush! You don't understand how it is here. It's all new. A new world with new ways. A new life for you as well as for me. Who can say what might happen?"

He raised his eyes from the wineglass and met her wild glance, still not knowing what she was saying.

"Do you know what they've freed in me?" she cried. "What this golden torc has done? I've become a creator! . . . Not the kind who spins illusions or invents things or fashions works of art. A better kind! The highest of the Tanu creative ones are able to gather energy and channelize it. I can do that. Throw lightning, project beams of light, make things go hot or cold. But I can do other things as well—things no Tanu is capable of! I can take air and moisture and drifting dust and any old kind of rubbishy matter you can imagine and knead it and stir it and transform it into something all new! Look—just look!"

She sprang up, setting the boat to rocking, and reached toward the sky, a goddess summoning wind and mud and marshwater and cellulose and sugars and acids and esters from the grass. A flash of flame, an explosive report—

She held cherries.

Laughing, almost giddy, she let the black-red fruit dangle from her fingers. "I saw them in your mind! Your favorite fruit that you wanted to lavish on your true love! Well—here they are, to complete the picnic that we've had to postpone for so long. We'll have them together with the golden apples of the Hesperides!"

It was not real, he told himself. Only she was real in all this world. And so he was calm and smiling as she dropped the cherries onto a large napkin they had spread on the chart table. The fruit was cold; drops of condensation beaded the juicy heart shapes.

"I'm still learning to use the power, of course. And there's no guarantee I'll pass it along full-blown to the children, because these high faculties are unpredictable. But who knows? Perhaps some day I'll be able to manipulate the genes themselves! Nodonn thinks it's possible, although Gomnol and Greggy don't. But even without that, I'll do marvelous things. Miraculous things!"

"You always were a miracle," he said. (Alas the child whose child?)

"Ah, silly!" she exclaimed, pretending anger. "The Thagdal's, of course, as the first must always be. You know about our jus primae noctis. And does it matter to you?"

"All that matters is that I love you. I'll always love you, no matter what you are."

"And what do you think I am?" She looked into his mind and the anger that blazed out now was real. "I'm *not* Nodonn's concubine! I'm his wife. He's taken me and no other."

And sixteen Tanu women and four hundred human latents of high talent before you . . . "I don't care, Mercy. Stop reading me! I can't help the way the thoughts come. They have nothing to do with my love for you."

She turned away from him and looked out over the marsh. "He'll be king one day when the Thagdal's finished. When he feels he has the full support of the battle-company, he'll challenge the old man in spite of Mayvar and win in the Heroic Encounter. And I'll be his queen. None of his other women had metafunctions to match mine. The exotics were barren except for five who had daughters and died. The humans . . . were beautiful and fertile but none of their talents are as fine as mine. They've all been discarded. I won't be. After I've borne this child for the Thagdal I'll have Nodonn's. Even if I can't manipulate the genes, I *can* learn to split the zygote with my psycho-kinesis and have twins, triplets even, just as easily as a single child. With the help of the Skin I'll have them safely and painlessly again and again and again. I could have hundreds! And live for thousands of years. What do you say to that?"

"If you want it, I wish it for you."

Her indignation melted as she saw how forlorn and hopeless he had become before the prospect of her apotheosis. He stood there, moving slightly to keep his balance as the boat rocked, and she came to him and put bare arms around his neck and let her softness rest against him.

"Bryan, Bryan, don't be sad. Didn't I tell you it was a new world? I can't promise to be yours alone, my dear, but you needn't fear I'll drive you away. Not if you'll be gentle and discreet. Not if you'll . . . help me."

"Mercy!"

She closed his lips with her own. The warmth and brightness of her flooded suddenly over him, carrying far away the doubts and fearful promptings of logic. He kissed and shut her wild eyes and his own vision of the real world faded before her opening blaze. As their minds merged, so did their bodies, easily and perfectly as though angels were coupling instead of man and woman. He lifted and exalted her and she in accepting drew him even higher until each had consumed the other in a sunburst of joy.

"That's the way it is with us," she told him. "When mind and body are in sweet harmony it happens like this between lovers. And you're spoiled for the other kind forever."

"Yes," he agreed. "Yes."

"And you will help me?"

"Always. In any way."

"Remember your promise when you wake up, my dear. If you really love me. If you really want me to be happy. I have enemies, my dear. There are people who can hurt me, who can see to it that I never reach the thing I've been promised. You must help me. I'll show you how. I need you."

He heard himself say, "Only let me stay."

"Of course." Now the sun-flood gentled, became soft and dark as he was carried into the depths. "You'll stay with me and love me. As long as you can."

12

THE BODY in its translucent shroud lay in state upon a plinth of black glass in the great hall of Redact House.

These were the Great Ones of the High Table who came to pay homage: Queen Nontusvel, Eadone Sciencemaster, Dionket the Healer, Mayvar Kingmaker, Aluteyn Craftsmaster, Sebi-Gomnol the Lord Coercer, and Kuhal Earthshaker, a son of the Queen who was deputy to Nodonn and second among the psychokinetics. And others of the High Table included Imidol the Deputy Coercer; Riganone, second among farsensors; Culluket the King's Interrogator; and Anéar the Loving—all children of Nontusvel; and Katlinel the Dark-eyed, half-human daughter of the deposed Lord Coercer Leyr. And those Great Ones absent on the Delbaeth Quest were Thagdal the High King, Nodonn Battlemaster, Tagan Lord of Swords, Bunone War-teacher, Fian Skybreaker, Alberonn Mindeater, and Bleyn the Champion.

The rulers of the Many-Colored Land looked upon the dead Anastasya Astaurova, linked minds, and sang the Song.

The caul clung tightly to her wide-open eyes, the arched nostrils, the clenched teeth visible through parted lips, the graceful neck with its golden torc. White as the salt and as cold were her splendid breasts and torso all beaded with tiny round bells, the belled legs and belled arms and ingenious surgeon's hands.

Mental speech, flickering and nuance-filled, passed among the assembled mourners with electric swiftness.

NONTUSVEL: Tasha-Bybar, farewell. So lovely to die, alas, thou strangest of Earth's gifts to us, never understood and never sated, in torment even after thy refashioning, dancing to find release in grotesque death.

DIONKET: A variation of her sabre dance with an unforeseen climax. Or was it?

GOMNOL: She was a genius! She should have been saved!

DIONKET: Teams of my redactors strove for three weeks to restore her within the Skin, but her mind was never able to cooperate. There were too many adverse factors: the massive trauma of the impalement, her longstanding unsanity—burned out as she was from our loving—the subconscious desire for obliteration. Even at best she was an insecure vessel of life-force, maladapted, unhelped by her transsexual conversion.

ALUTEYN: None other had her skill with the operation.

GOMNOL: No Tanu surgeon could equal her. No other human surgeon could/would do the great work she did.

EADONE: She was the opener of human wombs, the guarantor of our Tanu survival. Before her coming, our race dwelt precariously beneath this ferocious sun, multiplying slowly, so slowly. But she showed us a way to conquer our biological limitations, to burst forth in an explosion of life that has given us mastery of the planet. Praise to the departed Tasha-Bybar for having saved us!

ALUTEYN + GOMNOL: Praise.

MAYVAR: Given time, we could have saved *ourselves*.

EADONE: With the rama surrogates? Hardly!

ALUTEYN: Even now, Venerable Sister, the Firvulag outnumber us four to one.

MAYVAR: Nevertheless, what I say is true.

NONTUSVEL: Listen to Mayvar. She tells the truth, although her vision of it may differ from that of my Host. Oh, yes . . . we can and will survive of ourselves. As to how, I point in humility to the fruit of my own womb, the children of the Thagdal and Nontusvel: strong men and women, of the pure Tanu strain without human admixture, sitting at our High Table, leaders within our Guilds. *They* are the true salvation of our race! These children—my Host—and their own offspring are living proof of Tanu viability here on Earth, our guarantee of racial continuity. I will not deprecate the good work of Bybar nor the contributions of our other human benefactors. But let it be noted that the Tanu are survival-fit even without the mingling of human genes! The Host of Nontusvel, two hundred and forty-two strong, has proved fully adapted to life on this planet.

KUHAL + IMIDOL + RIGANONE + CULLUKET + ANÉAR: Let the Queen-Dam's words be noted. It is in our Host that true survival resides!

EADONE: Your offspring's reproductive rate is still far below the optimum, Queen and Sister. But we may concede that your strain is the strongest among fullbreeds.

GOMNOL: You still can't deny that human genes saved the Tanu genetic bacon! In the sixty or so years of interspecific mating the Tanu population growth rate has increased tenfold. And the hybrids include most of your best fighters, your top creative people, and a majority of the coercers.

CULLUKET: Nevertheless, we now question the wisdom of continued dilution of our heritage.

IMIDOL: And above all, Coercive Brother, we question your scheme concerning the human operant, Elizabeth.

GOMNOL: So that's it.

ANÉAR: Dear adopted Brother: we of the Host harbor only goodwill toward those of mixed Tanu and human blood. And we embrace the loyal human golds, such as yourself, who have so enriched our lives upon this planet. But we must take care lest we squander our inheritance by engendering more and more hybrids.

RIGANONE: Tana's will would be better served by an increase of purebloods. The vigor of the Host has proved that the original Tanu strain may reproduce itself adequately, albeit at a slower rate.

KUHAL: Disaster awaits us if we continue to mate with humans! Our noble Brother Battlemaster warned us of this decades ago. But we were so bedazzled by the benefits offered by humanity that we would not listen to his admonitions.

CULLUKET: The prospect of children by the Thagdal and Elizabeth has forced us to listen.

GOMNOL: The King endorses my plan fully. Eagerly!

EADONE: As Aluteyn and I have done. And yet . . . I must admit to some misgivings concerning the role of humanity in our High Kingdom. The Thagdal, too, has pondered this matter. For this reason we have commissioned the human anthropologist Bryan Grenfell to conduct a culture-impact study so that we may better understand the patterns of the psychosocial currents, both beneficial and inimical.

KUHAL: We of the Host have no need for human anthropology! Our racial instincts alone are sufficient to show impending calamity!

IMIDOL: We and our Mother have seen what must be done if the Tanu heritage is to survive. Once Elizabeth's genes merge with ours, the true Tanu will be doomed. We say: Put an end to all bastardization! Return to the ancient way before it is too late!

ALUTEYN: Throw out the babies with the bath water? Piffle! You and Nodonn are only afraid your precious dynasty might get nudged out of power.

EADONE: Nevertheless, Craftsmaster, our Coercive Brother Imidol has raised a serious point.

NONTUSVEL: Dearest Sister—we are convinced of its seriousness!

GOMNOL: O Adopted Kinfolk, look at this matter rationally. This yearning for the good old days is futile. I've studied the records of the Lord Historian Seniet. Have you forgotten how it *really* was before the coming of humanity? Would you go back to living in crude strongholds in the wilderness? Would you revert to the hunter-gatherer culture of the Firvulag? You lived like savages before we shared our technology and our genes with you!

NONTUSVEL: Not really, Gomnol dear. It was a simpler life, that's true. Not nearly so grand. But we had the ramas to serve us. And our young people were interested in crafts then—

ALUTEYN: Not like the damn dilettantes nowadays. Wasn't for the humans and the hybrids, the whole economy'd go to pot.

NONTUSVEL: Now, Aluteyn. You exaggerate. I am a First Comer like you, even though I have only been Queen for eight hundred years. We had a good life in those early days. We hunted for food as well as for sport. There was some trading with the Firvulag for gems and furs and useful herbs and trinkets. And we bartered our splendid textiles and glass armor to them. Do you remember how valiantly our warriors fought when the Grand Combat was celebrated fiercely afoot, hand to hand, with no human levies standing between our fighters and the Old Foe? Do you remember those battles on the Firvulag's Field of Gold, and how we would rejoice when we captured their Sword of Sharn and bore the trophy home in triumph? And perhaps they would wrest it back from us in the year following, but we would train and scheme and strengthen our brains and muscles for the next Combat—and win! Those were the days, dear Craftsmaster! But now . . . for forty years running we have bested the Firvulag in the Combat with the aid of human and hybrid warriors. How stale the victory becomes. What if the Foe become so discouraged that they refuse to fight?

MAYVAR: It would show that they, at least, had evolved.

DIONKET: Morally, if not mentally.

CULLUKET: Lord Healer, you cannot expect me to sit unprotesting as you and the Venerable Kingmaker flirt with heresy against our glorious ideal of battle!

ALUTEYN: Dip your heresy in chaliko flop, boy! I say, what we need are fewer head-wallopers and more technicians! These simple joys of barbarism are all very well. But I'm the one who'll have to keep the glass-ovens stoked and the food and drink coming to the table. I remember how it was, chivvying Tanu crafters who were more interested in battling and screwing and Hunting than in getting a day's work done. Oh, the old-time ways had their charm! I'll concede that I wallowed in gore and flung thunderbolts with the best of 'em. But you can't give up progress any more than you can pretend the time-gate never opened. It did! The humans came. We used them. And now the good old days are gone.

NONTUSVEL: We could restore the best parts of them.

KUHAL: We are not against material progress, Craftsmaster. Only against the erosion of our Tanu ideals and their replacement with alien human values. The pacifistic sentiments of Lord Dionket and Lady Mayvar and their factions are well known—call them heresy or moral evolution. But the majority of us don't share their philosophy. It is a philosophy of weaklings, of hybrids, and of *humans!*

GOMNOL: Our Psychokinetic Brother distorts reality. All torced humans, excepting a few abnormals who have not reacted favorably to the mental amplification, are loyal to the Tanu race. As to the erosion of your ideals . . . when have you been stronger? You rule the world! And my plan can only make that rule more glorious. I will admit that times have changed—but this is not the planet of your origin. You have adapted, and you'll continue to adapt, to Earth. This is fully in accord with Tana's will.

KUHAL: We are grateful to the Lord Coercer for explaining our religion to us.

GOMNOL: Your suspicions of my plan are groundless. It poses no threat whatsoever to your dynasty. Would the Thagdal approve it if it did? Do you question the vision of your own King?

EADONE: The plan involving Elizabeth is exciting. I am fascinated by the prospect of speeding our race's mental development—from latency to operancy—by incorporating her heritage within our own. To be free of the artificial action of the torcs! To see our offspring grow up to be true metapsychics! To see them possessed of godlike powers, perhaps even greater than those of the Milieu metapractitioners! There would be no more black-torc tragedies, no more burnt-out young Tanu brains unable to withstand the torc's amplification. With Elizabeth's genes, we could take an evolutionary shortcut, a leap across the aeons. Instead of waiting thousands or even millions of years to achieve operancy, we could see it within our own lifetimes . . .

ALUTEYN: I admit: a magnificent dream.

GOMNOL: No dream! A reality—if you don't turn your backs on my plan because of superstitious fear or racial chauvinism or petty politics. The anthropologist will prove to you that the coming of humanity to the Many-Colored Land has done you far more good than harm. I'll stake my life on it.

IMIDOL: You may, at that.

NONTUSVEL: Now . . . we must keep our tempers.

GOMNOL: You Host talk of racial purity. A thoroughly unscientific notion! Any biologist of the Milieu would tell you that. Just take an objective look at your allegedly pure Tanu heritage—! Firvulag recessives popping up like mad in every third birth.

KUHAL: Take care, Lord Coercer! Our Mother's strain is untainted. Never once has she given birth to one of the Foe.

GOMNOL: If that's true, you're very likely throwing out the very alleles you want to fix! And you want to use the Host as prime brood stock! Damn it, the Firvulag strain is the *operant* one! Ask the Lady Sciencemaster. Greggy and I have given up trying to sell you on mating with the Foe. But Elizabeth represents a unique genetic opportunity! A human operant has genes that not only enhance general survival, as the latents have done, but also give you the grand evolutionary leap that Lady Eadone spoke of. My plan leads to the fulfillment of Tanu destiny!

KUHAL: Again you presume to interpret Tana's will.

NONTUSVEL: It would be more *fitting* for the Goddess to work through our own Tanu line. We're afraid that Elizabeth's genes will turn us into humans, you see. Or at least into a race that is quite non-Tanu.

KUHAL + IMIDOL + RIGANONE + CULLUKET + ANÉAR: We do not need humanity! Better that we fulfill our destiny without humans!

GOMNOL: Then why has Nodonn himself taken to wife a woman of my race?

(Confusion.)

GOMNOL: Perhaps you'd better read your Crown Prince a refresher course in Tana's holy will.

NONTUSVEL: Do not descend to blasphemy, Lord Coercer. We have made it clear that we acknowledge the benefits that human genes have vouchsafed: the more powerful bodies, the increased fertility, the enhancement of coercive and creative metafunctions. And in the case of the precious Rosmar, we have embraced a rare and wondrous refinement of the creative power never seen among our Tanu adepts. *She* is the unique one! The value of her genes is self-evident. We welcome her as a fit consort for our future King. Dear Nodonn has had many wives—and as he is scarcely eight hundred years old, he may have many more if it pleases him. But let us not wander from the original matter at hand. Your plan, Adopted Son, proposes to go far beyond the mating customs that already obtain between the two races. The woman Elizabeth is not a talented latent such as yourself or Rosmar. She is a masterclass operant whose genes must be formidable indeed. Lord Greg-Donnet postulates that it is likely that all of her offspring would be operant—although perhaps not so powerful as their mother. He has also urged that, for the speediest achievement of race operancy, we should implant her ova in surrogates. But not ramapithecines! Human and Tanu women are to bear these wonder children! Who can assure us that this large new generation of torcless hybrids would be loyal to Tanu ideals? They will be a *new race*. It is logical that they would owe first loyalty to their own kind.

EADONE: There is a danger.

ALUTEYN: That possibility hadn't occurred to me. And I know Greggy never talked up artificial implanting to the King. That's not the Thagdal's idea of fun.

GOMNOL: This is ridiculous! Elizabeth's children would be as much Tanu as any hybrids. Education would see to it.

KUHAL + IMIDOL + RIGANONE + CULLUKET + ANÉAR: The Host does not concur. There is only one way to secure the safety of the Tanu heritage. The operant woman must die.

GOMNOL: You must not destroy her genes! Do you want to wait millions of years to achieve operancy? Future generations might call you worse than shortsighted! And if you come to your senses later on, it will be too late. There may never be another like Elizabeth to come through the gate!

NONTUSVEL: Alas. If only *she* hadn't come.

GOMNOL: She's here. I say it's Tana's will that she not be wasted . . . And don't you start twitting me about religion again, Kuhal!

Not until the Goddess gives you her blueprint stamped APPROVED! My plan is as likely to coincide with divine will as your own.

ALUTEYN: Damn all this talk of becoming operant in millions of years! We *know* what's going to happen here on Earth in millions of years. The ramas will have evolved into humans. And we'll be extinct! There's Tana's will for you! Maybe the Thagdal *is* right about Gomnol's plan. At least it would give our people a good long run at playing metapsychic before the last snuff. Jack up our brain-power to operant status and we'll likely figure a way to get off this flatulent orifice of a planet!

NONTUSVEL: Aluteyn, dear. Control yourself.

ALUTEYN: If only we could be sure. These damn precious genes of Elizabeth's. If only they weren't so . . . human.

GOMNOL: How many times must I prove my motives to you? I have only the Tanu best interests at heart. I have had, from the beginning!

NONTUSVEL: There's still the vexing question of possible overdependence upon humanity by our race. I confess that I await the results of Bryan's survey with some trepidation.

KATLINEL: And what happens if the survey *does* show that the culture impact was largely unfavorable? Will you of the Host demand the death of all humans? Will you kill hybrids like me as well? Is this the secret solution that you've had in mind all along?

NONTUSVEL: Oh, Katy. How can you think it?

KATLINEL: The rest of them do, Queen-Mother.

IMIDOL: Nonsense.

CULLUKET: You are overwrought, Creative Sister. Let me administer a calmative.

KATLINEL: No, thank you, Redactive Brother. No, thank you!

EADONE: When the Thagdal returns at the time of Truce, we must have this out. Surely there can be a compromise.

KUHAL + IMIDOL + RIGANONE + CULLUKET + ANÉAR: Never on Elizabeth!

. . .

ALUTEYN: There's another factor nobody's even mentioned. As long as we're discussing genetic menaces, what about the other one? How would *he* fit into Gomnol's scheme? Or has Aiken Drum slipped the Lord Coercer's mind?

GOMNOL: I've assured King Thagdal and I assure you, too, that the boy is nothing but a mental nova. His mind will burn out as quickly as it flared up. He'll be a puling idiot inside of another month.

IMIDOL: You've tested him with your psychometric gadgets and proved this, Coercive Brother?

GOMNOL: You know very well that the Lady Mayvar wouldn't consent to my meddling with her great and good protégé, Coercive Brother.

IMIDOL: So much for guarantees. Tell us, Venerable Sister: On your honor as Kingmaker—is the youth Aiken Drum a mental nova?

MAYVAR: No. But he is no menace to our race, either.

GOMNOL: Even if he doesn't burn out, he's only a harmless nuisance —a practical joker with a certain crowd-pleasing charm. You people just haven't seen this type of human being before.

ANÉAR: I should hope not.

RIGANONE: Nodonn doesn't take Aiken Drum lightly. Why else would he have insisted on sharing the Delbaeth Quest with him?

EADONE: That is not the important question. What we really must know is why this charming, harmless prankster has been taken to kin by Mayvar Kingmaker. Let us be blunt. Will Aiken Drum challenge in the Grand Combat?

MAYVAR: If Tana wills that my golden laddie survive the Delbaeth Quest, then he will.

EADONE: Is Aiken Drum fertile?

MAYVAR: He is.

EADONE: Would he challenge Nodonn?

MAYVAR: You must ask him that.

NONTUSVEL: A *human*? A human challenging my Nodonn?

KUHAL + IMIDOL + RIGANONE + CULLUKET + ANÉAR: Tana forfend!

EADONE: Are Aiken Drum's metapsychic powers of sufficient potential to defeat the Battlemaster?

MAYVAR: Only Tana knows.

ALUTEYN: You know what would happen if the boy *did* win, don't you, kinfolk? He'd challenge the Thagdal! Is that the game you're playing, Venerable Sister?

MAYVAR: Beware, Aluteyn Craftsmaster. I play no games! I only do my Making as the Goddess commands me, and neither you nor the Host nor the entire battle-company of the Many-Colored Land may tell me how to fulfill my ancient office . . . Or would you? (Dread.)

ALUTEYN: Well, you blew it once before with Lugonn, so it's no certainty.

MAYVAR: It is no certainty, as you say, Craftsmaster. But the Combat alone may prove the Goddess's will in this matter. Let no one here presume to interfere with my Making.

CULLUKET: No one will interfere—if your motives are true to the Tanu ideal.

MAYVAR: So once again, Young Redactor, you accuse me of heresy.

CULLUKET: Do you deny you have long opposed the battle-philosophy? Do you deny your sympathy for the traitorous heretic Minanonn, who betrayed his office as Battlemaster by preaching that Tanu and Firvulag should be brothers in sun as well as shadow?

MAYVAR: Poor Minanonn was ahead of his time, and imprudent. And he has paid for his rashness these five hundred years.

CULLUKET: But you and Dionket are cool hands! You're willing to play a waiting game until your human puppet is on the throne.

DIONKET: The Venerable Kingmaker and I are loyal to the Tanu race and resolved to see its destiny fulfilled in glory. And I admonish you to keep a respectful turn of mind, Redactive Brother, when addressing your elders.

NONTUSVEL: Oh, dear. This is all so confusing! Culluket, my son, you can't accuse people of heresy simply because they prefer the quiet life to Hunting and fighting. There have always been gentle ones among us.

IMIDOL: And they grow more numerous. Especially among the hybrids.

KATLINEL: We hybrids are loyal to the Tanu race! It is our race! But if it's heresy to persuade the Thagdal to look afresh upon the old violent customs that originated on a forgotten planet in an inaccessible galaxy—then perhaps we *are* guilty!

NONTUSVEL: Of course you aren't, Katy. I'm sure Cull didn't mean it that way. Why—many of the Host are of a peaceful temperament, unless the Firvulag do something hopelessly provocative . . .

MAYVAR: And even then, there are those who eschew the pleasures of punishing villains such as Delbaeth in favor of remaining securely at home here in the capital while others do the Questing.

ALUTEYN: That's one on you, Cull. You never were one to do your own dirty work.

NONTUSVEL: We will not quarrel! There will be no more talk of heresy. I forbid it.

EADONE: Our Awful Queen is wise. Listen to her.

NONTUSVEL: There is still another potential consequent of the Aiken Drum matter to be considered. Let us look again upon the plan of Lord Gomnol. Suppose it happened that, in the uncertain future, the operant genes of the woman Elizabeth merged not with the seed of our beloved Thagdal, but with that of this *fully human male?*

EADONE: Tana have mercy! There is the true threat to our racial destiny!

ALUTEYN: The penalty for bearing a human child is death for parents and offspring.

NONTUSVEL: How could this be enforced if Aiken Drum were High King?

IMIDOL: A race of operant humans contending against us!

RIGANONE: We would be crushed.

CULLUKET: Let our loyal Lady Kingmaker explain this away!

MAYVAR: I can only do my Making as the Goddess prompts me.

IMIDOL: And Gomnol! Is our *human* brother manipulating the lot of us in some new experiment, as he has been manipulating us ever since he came through the time-gate?

GOMNOL: Perhaps you would like to challenge me for the Guild Presidency in the manifestation of powers, Coercive Brother?

NONTUSVEL: Oh, *no!* Now stop this, all of you! There is only one way we will ever untangle this muddle.

EADONE: Tell us, Sister and Mother.

NONTUSVEL: We must demand a ruling of Brede.

EADONE + ALUTEYN: Excellent. The Thagdal will surely agree.

RIGANONE: But there's no telling what that weird old Two-Face will say! She *never* involves herself in the affairs of the High Kingdom. She's no true Tanu at all . . . she's something else altogether.

ANÉAR: Something dreadful.

EADONE: Listen to me, you fearful young ones. Brede is the oldest and wisest, our guide and our first benefactor when an entire galaxy was arrayed against us. She had the original vision that inspired transport of the First Comers to our Exile here.

KUHAL: True, Lady Sciencemaster. But let us also remember that Brede brought *both* Tanu and Firvulag to this Earth. In some deep way she is linked in destiny to both races. We cannot be sure—

NONTUSVEL: We can only hope that she will choose what is best for both. We may even pray that she will choose what is best for all three races! . . . And now, my dearest ones, I would have you link minds with me once again. But this time you will not sing the Song for our poor dead sister, Bybar, but for all of us living on this planet, exiled and afraid.

13

AFTER NEARLY TWO WEEKS of Questing it had come to this: a vast black hole in the mountain and a nasty choice.

"What's wrong with chasing him underground?" Aiken Drum asked.

Nodonn bestowed a pitying glance on his diminutive rival. "On foot? With no bear-dogs to help catch his scent and distract him?"

The two of them were sitting on thoroughly winded chalikos, waiting for the other leaders of the great Hunt to reach the ledge in front of the cave. Several dozen amphicyons milled about yowling their frustration. None ventured more than two or three meters into the cavern entrance, from which a chill, dampish exhalation flowed.

"Let's take a peek at what's inside," Aiken suggested. He conjured up a fulgurant ball of energy like a floating star shell and sent it wafting into the dark cleft. The two Hunters followed its progress with their farsight. It came into a huge chamber all fanged with stalactites and stalagmites where there was a broad lake. On the far side a low arched passageway led deeper into the mountain and Aiken guided the psychoenergetic flare into this opening, through which an underground river flowed. The tunnel pinched and the roof lowered after about half a kilometer, and finally the stream flowed over a precipice into a void so black that the light of the flare could not illuminate it. For a moment the two metapsychics saw with their mind's eye a waterfall dropping like a length of gauze into nothingness. Then the flare was suddenly extinguished.

A faint sound of laughter floated from the depths.

"And up yours, too," Aiken said to the faraway Shape of Fire.

516 THE GOLDEN TORC

The King's mount came scrambling up the rocky slope, followed closely by Stein—whom the monarch had taken a liking to, Lord Celadeyr of Afaliah, Lady Bunone Warteacher, and fifteen or so others of the party possessing the PK power to assist their faltering steeds in the climb. Because of Delbaeth's habit of bombarding pursuers with fireballs, it had not been possible for the Quest to take to the air.

"Well?" growled Thagdal.

"Gone to ground," said the Battlemaster.

The King removed his diamond helm, slouched in the saddle, and chewed his golden mustache. "Damn it all to hell. After chasing him all this way."

"He does it every time," Celadeyr of Afaliah remarked, shrugging aquamarine-armored shoulders. "Leads you from one plantation to the next. Lets you think you've got him trapped, then pops up outside your line, fries a few grays and anybody else he catches with his pants down, and then off to the races again. Daring you to nail him! That's our Delbaeth. But it always ends the same way—into some bloody cave, and the laugh's on you."

"Damn smart for a Firvulag, Celo."

The Lord of Afaliah spurred his chaliko through the rabble of bear-dogs to the cavern mouth. "Would I have asked for your help against an ordinary spook? Good thing for us Delbaeth is a maverick and doesn't fight in the Combat! . . . This is a new bolt-hole. At least we've managed to chase him farther west than ever before. This part of the Cordillera is way to hell and gone out on the Isthmus."

The King spat. "Don't know *where* the devil we are, not being able to reconnoiter from the air. Steinie—you got any beer left?"

The Viking passed a large canteen.

Celadeyr said, "Now that the Shape of Fire's underground, it's safe to fly if you wish, Majesty. He'll stay holed up for several days now to rest. There'd be no danger at all flying back to Afaliah."

"Give it up?" cried Stein. "We still got three days clear until the friggin' Truce! There's still a chance we could get him."

The mounted assembly laughed. Bunone Warteacher, awesome in a silvery bascinet that made her look like a bird of prey, said, "Delbaeth isn't coming out. Would you and your saucy master follow him *in?*"

"Why not?" Stein asked, and once more the Hunters laughed.

Aiken said to the King, "I told you I'd get him for you. I promised it, in fact. If I don't get Delbaeth, I'm screwed for the Grand Combat—right?"

"Oddly phrased," said the King. His smile was affable. "But the conclusion is accurate. You've had ample opportunity to carry out your boastful proposal on this Quest. If we return to Muriah having failed, I'll consider your service-bid for Stein null and void. It would be proper to punish you for the insolence of having made the bid in the first place, but in consideration for your repair of the computer and several other worthwhile accomplishments, I feel disposed to generosity. You'll be eligible to fight in the High Mêlée with the other gold-torc human warriors. But you may not aspire to the Heroic Encounters."

"It is fitting," said Nodonn, glowing in the advancing dusk. A few bats began to zip out of the cave on their evening forays.

"If we're packing it in," Celadeyr said, "let's get down the mountain before any others ruin their mounts trying to climb up here."

"Now just a damn minute," Aiken protested. "I didn't say I was giving up. There's still three days before the Truce . . . I'm going after Delbaeth. Into the cave."

"And I'm going with him," Stein said. "Nobody's gonna auction me off like a prize steer again!" The mental and vocal babble greeting their declarations made it possible for Aiken to screen off Stein's unspoken thought: So what if I get killed? If any Tanu takes me for a slave, I'll never see Sukey again.

"Make your foolhardy gesture if you must," said Nodonn. "Show us, if you can, that you know how to beat the Shape of Fire on his own home ground." Most of the Tanu crowded onto the ledge roared appreciation of the Battlemaster's remark. "The rest of us will return to Lord Celadeyr's castle for refreshment, then fly on to the capital. Delbaeth will keep until after the Grand Combat. Should we discover your bones when we finally penetrate to his lair, we'll conduct suitable obsequies and sing for you the Song."

More laughter. But in the midst, a protest.

"So you object, Bleyn and Alberonn?" inquired the Battlemaster.

Two riders urged their beasts to the fore. Bleyn the Champion was a hybrid, powerful in both PK and coercion, who sat at the High Table. Alberonn Mindeater, another hybrid, was one of the best warrior-illusionists. Both were of the faction of Mayvar and both had helped to train Aiken and Stein in martial arts for their initiation.

"It is not fitting that this company desert Lord Aiken here in the wilderness while he descends to challenge Delbaeth," Bleyn stated. "Shame on those who would hold a brave man's endeavor up to mockery."

Nodonn only smiled.

Alberonn said, "We two will await the return of Aiken and Stein. We will camp before this very cave mouth, praying for their success. We will wait for the three days, so that the time originally allotted for this Quest may be honorably fulfilled."

"I also will wait," decided Bunone, "and my three warrior-maids. Aiken Drum is a man of singular talents! We, too, will pray that he survives."

The High King threw up one flashing hand in a gesture of resignation. "Oh, very well! What's three more days? We've earned a little rest after chasing that damn spook the length of the Betics and never once daring to take to the air for fear of his fireballs. But if we stay here, Celo, you've got to fly us in some decent food and booze."

The Lord of Afaliah said, "We can set up camp in the meadow below, near the torrent, where the attendants and the baggage train now wait. My son Uriet himself will lead a squadron of levitants to bring refreshment."

"That's that, then," said the King. He glowered at Aiken. "Three days only! You hear me?"

The golden manikin leapt from his saddle, knelt on one knee before the royal chaliko, and grinned under his golden visor. "Thank you for your patience, Awful Father. We'll bring you Delbaeth's balls for biddy-swabbers!"

And then, while the Questers watched in incredulous silence, Aiken Drum and Stein took off their armor and stacked it in a pile just beside the cave entrance. They left all their weaponry except Stein's bronze sword and took from their saddlebags only the Viking's parcel of snack foods, the canteen of beer, and a thin golden box about the size of a pen case, which Aiken stuffed quickly into the front of his undertunic.

Waggling an admonitory finger at Nodonn, the golliwog said, "No fair peeking after us, Sun-Face. Don't you chase us with flares."

"I will not," the Battlemaster promised, his smile undimmed.

"Then—goodbye, all!" said Aiken Drum.

There was a soundless snap.

Two extra bats joined the flock wheeling over the heads of the Hunt. After taking a few minutes to get used to their wings, the pair swooped down and disappeared into the darkness of Delbaeth's cave.

* * *

"Hey, kid!"

"Shh. Gotta be sure nobody's farsensing us. Wouldn't trust that fewkin' Archangel one AU's worth."

". . . Kid, what about the friggety monster?"

"*Will* you shut your snoose-chompin' yap? It's touchy work, doing these different kinds of mind-bendery all at the same time."

"Sorry."

They hung from the roof of the cataract shaft by their tiny claws. The world was utterly, appallingly black. The waterfall made a hissing sound as it sprayed into the mountain's gut. A faraway rumble down below announced its drainage into an abyssal sump.

The two bats could "see" by means of the sounds.

At last Aiken said, "It's okay. They're all going down to the campsite. Nobody's making a real effort to farsense us. The least little screen'll take care of them now . . . Trouble is, Steinie, I don't really know how good at farsensing any of these Tanu biggies are. I'm certain that most of the exotics can't farsee underground. That's why the Firvulag live in caves and burrows. But the King, Nodonn, that damn Fian who does the PK stunts—they just might be able to figure some way to spot us through a klom of solid rock . . . just like I can."

"*Jeezuss* God. Will you lay off the bragging and scan out where that torch-ass spook is holed up? Or don't you care if we get incinerated?"

"We're not gonna get incinerated. Delbaeth isn't waiting in some cranny to ambush us. He's gone home. He knows nobody in this Exile world is stupid enough to follow him into the caves."

"Ha ha. All right, Ace. Now that we're here—where the hell are we?"

"We're in a better position to nab the spook than we were before, hemmed in by that mob of exotics. This is just the kind of chance I hoped for ever since we took off on this dumb monster hunt! A chance to go after Delbaeth without the rest of 'em watching how I kill him!"

"You're not gonna zap him with your superbrain?"

"Betcher sweet ass I'm not. I wouldn't have a chance in a mind-to-mind with Delbaeth. Neither would any of those Tanu turds—unless the Firvulag was taken completely by surprise. And fat chance of that happening, with that friggety circus parade of three hundred knights of the Round Table whooping after him. Nope! There's only one way to take the Shape of Fire. My little old sweetheart, Mayvar, knew it."

"Well how, for chrissake?"

"I'm gonna cheat. Come on. Let's get outa here to some place where it's flat and dry and I'll show you."

The two bats spiraled down the shaft. At the bottom they turned into pallid eyeless fish and went whisking through the flooded tunnel of the sump, "seeing" the twists and turns of the rock pipe by means of pressure changes and the reflection of water currents, rather than the echolocation they had used while they were bats. They traveled for more than a kilometer before the stream broke into a large air-filled space. One fish leaped from the water—flopped back. Then both jumped up and metamorphosed into bats. A few moments later they were in human form again, sitting on a rock shelf beside the underground river while a small ball of incandescence hung in midair to furnish light. The cave ceiling two or three meters above was covered with a fantastic growth of crystal soda-straw formations, thin and delicate, each with a pendant drop of water at the tip.

Aiken wasted no time admiring the scenery. He took the golden box from his shirt, manipulated the lid in some tricky PK fashion, and showed Stein what was inside: a single thin gray object about twenty cents in length, vaguely resembling a silvery length of punk with a wire stem.

Stein frowned. "You know what that looks like? When I was a kid back in Illinois we had—"

"That's what it is. Just one of these little things is gonna kill that shitfire Firvulag stone dead. A long time ago, some poor sucker brought this through the time-gate, thinking he'd liven up the Pliocene a little bit. Since they're perfectly harmless, the people at the auberge had no objection. But when the guy stepped into Exile, his stuff was confiscated—and all but this one destroyed before Mayvar got hold of it. You know why? Because here, things like this are deadly! Not to humans—not even torc-wearing humans—but to the exotics."

"Iron." Stein was awestruck. "No iron tools here, no iron implements, nothing iron at all. All glass, vitredur, bronze or other alloy, silver, gold, whatnot. But never any iron! Hell—why didn't anybody notice?"

"How much iron did we use back in the Milieu in places where it

The Mésalliance 521

showed? We were almost out of the iron age. You know what the Tanu and Firvulag call the stuff? Blood-metal! One prick and they're goners. Or, in the case of this thing—"

"Jeez, yes!" Stein exclaimed. His expression became intent. "You're gonna do it, kid. I'm a believer at last. And after we finish off this Delbaeth, you're gonna help me escape with Sukey. And if any dumb Tanu tries to stop us—"

"You stupid squarehead! You forgot your gray torc? And Sukey's silver one? The Tanu could track you anywhere. Relax! I got other plans. We'll all make it if you don't pull any more great moves like you did with Tasha."

Aiken closed the golden box and put it back into his shirt. "Now sit still and shut up. I gotta track Delbaeth, and this X-ray vision thing is a hell of a lot tougher than you might think. Good thing these mountains aren't granite."

"Naw. Limestone, sandstone, medium-grade schists, and other metamorphics down below at this end of the Med. Don't forget I used to work these rocks when I was a crust driller."

"Shut up, dammit."

The two of them sat there in their underwear. The psychoenergy flare went out as Aiken concentrated all of his power in his seeker sense. The only sounds were the drips from the slender calcite pipelets.

Could I reach out, too? Stein wondered. Sukey had told him it was love that did it before, that broke through Dedra's coercive control. Was love strong enough to cross the thousand kilometers that separated him from Sukey, hidden back there in Muriah in the catacombs beneath Redact House? First, visualize her in the mind's eye. (Easy when your optic nerves are getting input zilch.) There she is. Now tell her that you love her, that it's going to be all right, that you're safe, that you're going to come back, that you're going to win . . .

"I found him, Steinie! I found the fuckard!"

The astral light snapped on. Stein passed a great hand over his eyes and wiped it on his hip. The attempt at farspeech hadn't worked. His head hurt.

Reddish hair standing up like a charged mop, eyes seeming to snap with excitement, the trickster sprang to his feet and pointed toward a solid rock wall. "That direction. Maybe eight, nine kloms and a couple hundred meters lower down. There's this fuzzy blob—a mental aura, I guess. Only living thing anywhere around. It's gotta be him."

Stein sighed. "And all we have to do is walk through the wall."

The golliwog was apologetic. "That's not my act, Steinie. I can't do interpenetration. Can't zap mountains, either, not so's you'd notice. We'll have to walk, fly, or swim. If Delbaeth got there from here, so can we. This whole lousy range is honeycombed with caves. It'll take a while finding our way through the maze." He looked grim. "But it better not take too long or we'll be into the Truce. That's when Firvulags go outa season until Grand Combat time."

Stein looked at his wrist chronometer. "Half past eighteen hours, September twenty-seven, six million B.C."

"Checko."

"Just tell me one thing before you do your Dracula act, kid. Do we *really* turn into bats and fish and things when you say shazoom, or is it some kinda shape-shifting illusion thing and do we keep our regular bods all the time?"

"Damned if I know," said Aiken Drum. "Hang onto that food and beer, pally—we're off!"

* * *

They searched.

Tunnels dry and flooded; great galleries where flowstone and stalactites and rippling curtains of thin rock fell like frozen creations of peach and vanilla ice cream; constricted slots and tortuous low corridors studded with sparkling calcite teeth; tumbled rockfalls where a cave ceiling had collapsed into piles of house-sized chunks; partially drained streamways gleaming with mud; dead-end holes that had to be retraced; tempting passages that took them in the wrong direction.

They ate, and after a while, they slept. They woke and continued flying, swimming, walking, climbing. The food and beer were finished midway through the second day. There was plenty of water, but no bugs for bats, no edible bits floating in the subterranean waters that the men-fish could swallow to assuage the all-too-real spasms of their possibly illusory stomachs.

Aiken's mental screen was now projected only between them and the concentration of psychic energy that presumably marked Delbaeth. This hardly seemed to shift position at all now; perhaps the Shape of Fire took very long naps between sorties, or perhaps the fuzzy aura marked something else altogether . . .

The bats flew down a long, sloping tunnel. For the first time since their descent, they were aware of a current of air against their flapping wing membranes. The mental voice of Aiken spoke to Stein on the intimate human mode:

Don't think one solitary thing. Keep your mind quiet if you value your sweet ass. I don't think he can hear me on this mode but any squeak outa you would hit him S9 and wall to wall.

The two bats, now totally enveloped in the heaviest mind-barrier that Aiken could conjure, came to a ninety-degree bend in the corridor. They fluttered around the corner and saw light ahead—orangey yellow and flickering gently. The passage was dry. There were huge footprints in the dust.

Drifting among the rock formations, the bats approached the lighted area. It was a large open chamber full of looming monoliths almost like shrouded human figures, together with complex tiers of flowstone that resembled gigantic gilled fungi. The bats flew up toward the ceiling to a ledge that jutted far out over the central area of the floor. There, hidden from the sight of anyone below, the bats turned into Aiken and Stein.

Silence. Don't move. Don't rattle that damn sword scabbard. Don't do one friggerty thing.

Aiken crept toward the edge of the formation on his stomach and peered down. A large fire burned within a well-made circular hearth. Piles of barkless tree trunks were neatly stacked in an alcove. Other parts of the cavern were furnished with a table, chairs, a bedstead of gargantuan proportions having a canopy and side curtains of the finest Tanu brocade, and any number of carved wooden chests and shelves. Leathern bags bulging with mysterious contents stood at the base of one pillar. Near another was a framework hung with fish netting edged with wooden floats. The floor was carpeted in glossy pelts—some dark, some spotted. Most of the dirty dishes on the table seemed to be large mollusk shells.

Drawn up close to the fire was a species of overstuffed chair upholstered in gray hide. In the chair, quite asleep, was a humanoid exceeding the tall Tanu in height and vastly more robust of build. His head had a tangled brick-colored mane of hair and bushy beard. He wore a leather shirt with the front lacing open, showing the reddish pelt of his chest. His breeches were scarlet. He had taken off his boots and extended his huge feet toward the fire. Now and then the toes wiggled. A cyclic noise reminiscent of a malfunctioning ore crusher told Aiken Drum that Delbaeth, the Shape of Fire, most formidable wild Firvulag in the southern reaches of the Many-Colored Land, was snoring.

Aiken opened the golden box and removed the pencil-slim gray object. Hefting the little thing, he seemed to calculate a trajectory. He ignited the tip of his secret weapon with his creative metafunction.

The sparkler burst into vivid white light, throwing out glowing iron filings like tiny meteorites. Aiken held the firework at arm's length.

Down below, Delbaeth surged from his chair, bellowing. His body, nearly three meters tall, was transformed into a blazing mass that reached fiery arms toward the ceiling ledge and began to mold a ball of fire between incandescent paws.

Aiken threw the sparkler, guiding it with whatever PK he could muster through the thick psychic screen he had erected around Stein and himself. Delbaeth's fireball arced up, dead on target, and bounced.

There was another echoing cry from the monster. The fragile firework struck his flaming form and fell to the cave floor, still spitting sparks. Delbaeth's fire was extinguished. He crumpled slowly, almost seeming to melt into the ground, and did not move again.

"Come on!" Aiken cried.

The two bats flew down and became men once more. They stood beside the awesome carcass, and Stein said, "See where it hit him? Right on the forehead, because he was looking up. One tiny little burn with a hot iron wire!"

There was a leather bucket full of water beside the table. Aiken hoisted it and poured a stream over the still-coruscating sparkler. It hissed and went out. A hole had been burned in one fur rug, ruining it.

"You did it!" Stein swept up the little man and crushed him in a bear hug. "You did it!" Dropping Aiken, Stein howled to the stalactites: "Sukey, babe, we *did* it!"

Aiken frowned, then laughed out loud. "I'll be damned, Viking. She did hear you! Maybe you can't pick her up, but I get this little weak farspeak whisper. Aw . . . you'll never guess. She loves you."

Stein grabbed up the bucket and emptied it over Aiken.

"Thanks," said the golliwog. "I needed that. Now cut off his head and let's get out of here. We've gotta find the shortest route to the open air and fly back to bedoozle the royalty. Not to sweat, though! We're one whole day early!"

Stein began to draw his great bronze sword from its amber-studded sheath. But when the blade was halfway out he froze and tilted his head. "Listen! Hear that? . . . It's a lot clearer now than it was up next to the ceiling with that spook snoring."

Aiken cocked an ear. A slow, deep *boom* vibrated the rocks. Several seconds passed. *Boom.* Like the tolling of some huge bell the sound repeated. *Boom.* Slow. Inexorable.

"Do you know what that is, kid?" Stein asked. "It's surf. Somewhere just the other side of that rock wall is the Atlantic Ocean."

* * *

THE END OF PART ONE

PART II

The Closure

1

FELICE WALKED the ruins of Finiah.

By the time that the Truce was in its third day, the minor eruption of lava from the old Kaiserstuhl volcano had come to an end. Streams of once molten rock solidified into clinkery masses—fat, rounded, and branched like monstrous roots where they had flowed out from the central mineworkings into the streets and arcades of the devastated city. It had rained heavily. Buildings that had been white or golden and rose, or blue-green and silver with the colors of the Creative Lord Velteyn, were now streaked and smeared with ashy mud. Ash had smothered the gardens and blasted the foliage from most of the ornamental trees. The central plaza, where Felice prowled, was a tangle of burnt-out shops, shredded awnings, broken carts and tradesmen's booths, and bodies half-buried in cinders and muck.

Giant ravens as long as Felice's arms pecked at the swollen remains of chalikos, hellads, ramapithecines, and people. The scavengers were not disturbed by the passing of the small woman dressed in shining black. Perhaps they took her for one of themselves.

There were noises. The ravens uttered their *pruk pruk* calls. A broken water conduit gushed and flooded down a flight of stairs, washing clean the corpses of gray-torc soldiers and Lowlife invaders. In a cul-de-sac near the palace of Lord Velteyn, nearly a dozen uninjured ramas in ruined aquamarine tabards huddled together, whimpering. A sound of human groans came from a porter's house adjacent to the main palace approach. Felice ignored it and walked toward the entrance of Velteyn's mansion, an iron-tipped arrow nocked and ready in her compound bow. She had many other arrows in a shoulder quiver, all with stained shafts. There had been a few stubborn grays down at the river landing determined to fight on, even though their Tanu overlords had fled; and down in the artisans' quarter, a bareneck woman had come rushing out of a devastated glasscrafter's workshop, brandishing a vitredur machete and crying vengeance on the despoilers of Finiah even as Felice shot her in the throat.

Humans were too irreligious to hold to the Truce. Long after the Firvulag and Tanu had quit the burning wreck of the city, Lowlife warriors continued to fight against those of their fellow humans who remained loyal to the exotics. Captured grays, as well as the few silvers who fell into the invaders' hands, were hustled before a guerilla tribunal where a Lowlife officer showed them an iron chisel and an iron knife and bade them choose: "Live free or die." A surprising proportion had opted for death rather than the removal of their mind-amplifying collars.

Felice entered the palace. The carrion birds were absent here, but there were flies, swift-scuttling rodents, and an appalling stench. The bodies of guards and servitors were heaped behind improvised barricades of furniture and demounted doors. Many of the defenders had died without a mark upon them, faces contorted by the mind-blasting attack of the Firvulag.

Except for the buzzing of insects, the rustle and squeak of rats, and the sighing sound of wind through smashed panes of colored glass, the palace of Lord Velteyn was quiet in its ruin. The little woman in black penetrated deeper into the apartments of the Great Ones, leaping over the piled corpses of human retainers who had fought an increasingly desperate rearguard action as the invading army hunted their trapped exotic masters.

Felice came to a great open door of bronze, studded with green stones. Bodies in Lowlife buckskin and homespun mingled with those in palace livery to clog its threshold. And here, for the first time, there were also Firvulag bodies, some squat, some taller than humans or Tanu and as burly as fairytale giants; all were attired in the gold-chased obsidian armor of Pallol One-Eye's elite corps and all had been dispatched by iron-tipped weapons that Velteyn's human guard had presumably wrested from the Lowlives.

Calmly, Felice pulled a spear from a dead shape-shifter and used it for an alpenstock as she climbed over the noisome mound blocking the doorway. Inside the room, which was an elaborate bedchamber reduced to a shambles by the fighting, were six bodies attired in colored-glass armor. Four men and one Tanu woman were bloodied, transfixed by iron-pointed arrows. The second woman, a gold-torc human armored in sapphire blue, bore no wounds and had presumably succumbed to mental assault.

Felice removed her hoplite helmet and set it upon a large bedside stand. On a lower shelf, incongruous in undisturbed tidiness, were a golden ewer and basin. The girl filled the basin with water and set it on top of the table. For a moment, she stood looking down at the corpse of the human woman. In death, her azure eyes showed wide pupils, oddly emphatic in a face as pale as chalk. Long chestnut hair spread on the carpet in a nimbus around the bare head; her helmet lay nearby. The slender fingers in jeweled blue-plate gauntlets were hooked over a golden torc.

Like an acolyte enacting a ritual, Felice knelt. The rigor had left the dead hands and the torc was easily freed from their grip. The knobbed front catch clicked. The girl pivoted the collar on its back hinge and slipped it from around the livid throat. Rising, she went to the basin, dipped the gold several times, and dried it upon a soft towel.

Then Felice fastened the torc about her own neck.

The reality opened to her. She uttered a piercing cry.

This . . . so it was like this. All of it had been hidden within her, battened down and denied, so feared by the weaker ones all around her. But now open, released, and ready to be used.

She went out onto the balcony of the death room. Trembling, vision partly blurred by the tears of her joy, she looked over the ruins of Finiah. There was the wide Rhine, the heights of the Vosges, High Vrazel itself on the western skyline, where King Yeochee and Sharn-Mes and the other Firvulag were doubtless still celebrating the triumph over their ancient Foe. There were the high passes she had come through alone, too late for the war, passing Chief Burke and Khalid Khan and the remnant of the Lowlife force conducting newly liberated human survivors of Finiah to the bottomland camp where they would await the judgment of Madame Guderian.

Gold warm at her throat, Felice began to laugh. The sound swelled on the wind until it reverberated over the wasted city. The ravens, shocked out of their aplomb, took wing.

2

SHARN-MES the Young Champion regarded the riotous scene in the Hall of the Mountain King and shook his head in humorous wonderment.

"Just look at that gang of stewed fewmets. It'll be at least three days' sleep to work off this three days' drunk. You know, Ayf, this is going to play havoc with our travel schedule. The armor and weaponry will have to be refurbished before we head south unless we want to go into the Grand Combat looking like a tatty rabble."

"There's still plenty of time." Ayfa, leader of the Warrior Ogresses, tossed off her bumper of mead and helped herself to a refill. "The lads and lasses are entitled to a celebration. It's been forty years since we've had anything worth getting drunk about. Who cares if we miss some of the prelims down at the White Silver Plain? The high-ass crowd aren't about to start any main events without us."

"I suppose," Sharn agreed, "that we do deserve a party."

The two great captains were sequestered in a snug gallery that ordinarily accommodated musicians at formal feasts. But there was nothing formal about the action now taking place below them. All of the Firvulag veterans of the brief Finiah campaign, together with most of the rest of the citizenry of High Vrazel, seemed to have crowded into the royal audience cavern to cheer the unexpected victory.

Brown ale and mead and cyser and blackberry brandy fountained up from hollow stalagmites right into the waiting mugs of those merrymakers who were still on their feet. Enough pastries, meats, and other party food remained to make the oaken tables creak under the weight. One mob in front of King Yeochee's empty throne was playing a type of blindman's buff in which the hooded female protagonist had taken the game's title quite literally. Another hilarious crowd surrounded the two heroes of the battle, Nukalavee the Skinless and

Bles Four-Fang, who vied with one another to see who could create the most ridiculously obscene illusory body. Points were awarded by the cheers, jeers, and occasional retchings of the onlookers.

More serious-minded revelers (and the maudlin drunks) gathered about a crookbacked goblin bard who had reached the one-hundred-sixty-fifth verse of a lugubrious ballad of doomed Firvulag lovers. Cheerier souls were concocting ingenious new stanzas to the soldiers' beloved drinking song, "A Princess Must Never Have Fleas," detailing those eccentricities that the royal demoiselle might legitimately expect to get away with. Warriors of the walking wounded, cosseted by plump little wenches, bragged of their late derring-do. Superannuated stay-at-homes muttered into their beer that the reduction of Finiah couldn't possibly compare to certain ancient affrays in which *they* had participated during the good old days.

Queen Klahnino supervised the safe retirement of fallen celebrants, who were dragged away into alcoves and packed cheek by jowl to sleep it off. King Yeochee wandered around in bare feet and a stained golden robe, his crown tilted over one ear, kissing all of the ladies and quite a number of the gentlemen as well. Pallol the Battlemaster, still disdainful of the enterprise but always ready for a party, had succumbed to a surfeit of sidecars—another legacy of the insidious Lowlives. He lay snoring in the King's crystal grotto, his huge head resting in the lap of the resigned concubine, Lulo.

"Yes," Sharn repeated himself at length. "We definitely deserve a celebration . . . What do you suppose the Lowlives are up to?"

"I'll look," said Ayfa, who possessed more farsight than the majority of her race. She was a handsome creature if one overlooked the excessively developed arm muscles, a concomitant of her prowess with the two-handed sword. Her hair was apricot-colored and her broad face freckled. Like most Firvulag, she had dark, twinkling eyes. She had shed her armor and wore a rumpled kirtle and blouse of madder rose, which clashed with her hair.

"Yes, there they are. The human prisoners, or refugees, or whatever you call 'em, are installed in the old staging-area camp. But Burke and his cronies are slogging along through Ravine Pass toward Hidden Springs. They're getting rained on."

"Good," said Sharn. "Maybe it'll rust their perishing iron." He took a pull from his beaker and wiped his lips with a furry paw. "Dammit, Ayf, that's a bad business—using the blood-metal. Unprecedented! You know, when we trapped that bunch of Tanu engineers near the smeltery, one of 'em let off a really heavy curse before he died. I can still hear it: 'The Goddess will avenge us. Accursed through the world's age be those who resort to the blood-metal. A bloody tide will overwhelm them . . .'"

"Well, it seems to me that the curse is for the humans, not us. We'd always planned to put the Lowlives to the sword once they'd served our purposes."

"But we're only too willing to use them—*and* their iron—in the meantime! I hate it, Ayfa. It's a Lowlife way of doing battle, not our way. Old Pallol was bitching about how we'd surrendered our ancient honor just by fighting alongside humans . . . and how the iron was so obscene that it made a travesty of our whole combat-philosophy. I can't help agreeing. How can war be glorious with such an ignoble weapon? It puts the mightiest Firvulag or Tanu hero on the same level as some half-starved human pipsqueak with a compound bow. It's unfair!"

Ayfa grunted. "I suppose the Tanu have been fighting fair . . . with their chalikos and bear-dogs that have turned the Hunts into massacres! Or the human cavalry and charioteers in the Grand Combat who've been whipping the shit out of us for the past forty years!"

"Aaah. You women never did appreciate the fine points of chivalry!"

"No—we're willing to fight dirty to win." The female warrior served herself another great tankard of mead. "And speaking of that —did you see how the Lowlife infantry dealt with the mounted Foe in Finiah?"

Sharn acknowledged the fact with a surly nod. "Unsporting! That's not our *way*."

"Screw our way. The chalikos weren't the Tanu way, either, until that human animal tamer came along . . . Now you listen to me, big boy. There won't be any iron weapons to help us in the Grand Combat this year, but you can bet your sweet filberts that we *will* adopt those new antichaliko tactics of the Lowlives. This go-around, those gray-torc troopers are in for a helluva surprise! I've already got the armorers working on the modification. Easiest thing in the world."

"It could make a difference," he conceded. "If we can get the warriors to accept it."

"I'll leave the persuasion to you," she told him, smiling. Then her expression changed. "Keep still for a minute while I go back to my farsight of the Lowlives coming from Finiah . . . I get a few under three hundred surviving irregulars going over the pass and maybe twice that many captives and casualties down in the Rhineside camp. Most of the refugees are barenecks . . . No—wait. Some are too well dressed. By damn, they've got to be ex-grays or silvers with their torcs chiseled off! Noncombatants. Maybe scientific types, special-talent artificers. Old Madame Guderian will make good use of *them,* you can bank on it!"

"I wonder just how loyal to her those liberated townees will be, though?" Sharn was skeptical. "The humans who craved freedom the most tended to be the newcomers and the psychos. The people who'd been here for a while settled down under Tanu domination even without being torced. A life of freedom in the wild greenwood is going to be as appealing to those easy-goers as a case of hives."

"Hush. I'm looking for Felice."

"Oh, *that* one. The one you'll have to take into your crew if—"

"—if she finds a golden torc and goes metapowerful. I could strangle that Yeochee for pushing the dirty work off on me! As if the Combat wasn't tough enough for us women these days . . . Oh-oh."

"Spotted her?"

"She's in a room of Velteyn's mansion. Wearing a torc. And she's looting a body of its glass armor. So much for Yeochee's idea. This kid is way ahead of him, making her own Combat plans!"

"Cheer up." Sharn climbed to his feet, yawned hugely, and scratched his hairy chest through the open front of his tunic. "You're rid of her, anyhow. It'll take her a while to get used to the torc. And there's no guarantee that her latent metafaculties will measure up to her nerve, in any case. Even if she did mastermind Epone's killing and help bring back the Spear, she's still only a young girl. Maybe coercing animals is the only power she's got."

Ayfa's eyes came back into focus. "Té only knows. I guess I'm just too tired now to give much of a damn."

Sharn gave her a hand and hauled her up. "It's been a short war and a long party. What say we make our duty to the King and Queen and amble on home?" He gathered their black-glass armor by the straps and slung it onto his back.

"Good thinking," Ayfa agreed. She clapped her companion on one shoulder and, rising on tiptoe, kissed the end of his grubby nose. "I hate to think of the overtime we're going to owe the babysitter."

3

THE GUARDIANS in their white tunics stood ready around the square of bare granite that had been marked off with rounded stones. There were soldiers as well this morning, in consideration of the visit of the Most Exalted Personages. Thagdal, Eadone, Gomnol, and the two brothers Nodonn and Velteyn kept well back from the vicinity of the time-portal and waited for the manifestation with the stoicism that dignitaries invariably assume when they are obliged to inspect some important but depressing activity taking place at an inconvenient hour.

Pitkin the Castellan said, "It's just dawn, Exalted Ones. Here they come."

A block of air above the granite began to shimmer as if suddenly heated. Four figures materialized within the singularity and hovered some thirty centimeters above the surface of the rock.

"Sindbad the Sailor, a Joe Meek mountain-man type, one moribund hash aficionado complete with hubble-bubble, and a classic British birdwatcher," Pitkin rattled off in snap appraisal. "The drugger's for the discard, I'm afraid; wasted to a shadow. But the others will serve."

The guardians had darted forward to seize the arms of the time-travelers and assist them as they stepped down the gap that separated the invisible floor of Professor Guderian's device from the solid ground of Pliocene Earth.

"Fortuitous that they don't materialize inside a mass of bedrock, isn't it?" Pitkin remarked. "This region has undergone many vicissitudes, geologically speaking."

Sindbad had been separated from his scimitar, and the other dazed timefarers were being frisked for iron by a guardian with a metal detector. Pitkin said, "That new iron-sniffer of the Craftsmaster's is a great improvement. No more worries about missed contraband . . . Ah. There goes the tau-field back for the second lot."

On the next cycle the time-portal admitted a young man in a suit of white denim carrying a crossbow; a goateed chap costumed as Queen Elizabeth I, whose farthingale skirts were a dreadful nuisance to his fellow embarkees; a deeply tanned woman wearing an Atalanta peplum and buskins; and a well-rejuvenated black man in a dacot lounge suit, draped with a dozen extremely expensive AV recorders.

"All serviceable stock," Pitkin said. "Don't be fooled by Good Queen Bess. There's probably a useful technician under that pearl-studded red wig . . . Now let's see what kind of impedimenta we rate today."

The temporal field sprang into existence once more and guardians hastened to remove three large containers labeled MEDICATIONS, a case of Canadian Club, a papillon dog yapping hysterically inside its mesh carrier, a twenty-liter carboy of "Joy," a set of Larousse's *Grand Dictionnaire Universel du XIXème Siècle Français,* and a contrabassoon.

"After these new arrivals are processed, they go to the holding area, as you know, Exalted Ones. Because of the emergency, we have set up a temporary stockade by walling off sections of the outer ward, transferring the bear-dogs to exterior pens. In this way we can accommodate most of Lord Velteyn's refugees from Finiah in relative comfort within the castle proper until they are able to move on to Muriah. It's fortunate that this disaster took place at Truce time when there are extra supplies and transport available for those traveling down to the games. And of course the security matter is much more easily dealt with at this time as well."

"Sounds like you've got things in hand," the King muttered grudgingly to the Castellan.

"We have Lord Gomnol to thank for the initial disaster-relief planning. Castle Gateway was the logical receiving area, of course, and we were able to rush help northward in time to meet the refugees on the eastern shore of the Lac de Bresse just five days after the —uh—exodus from Finiah. Now, if you'd care to step into my office, Exalted Ones, I can go over the revised distribution system for the time-travelers that compensates for the temporary suspension of the Finiah run. There are also preliminary overviews of Castle Gateway's role in laborforce procurement for the reconstruction and pacification operations."

"Thank you, Pitkin," Gomnol said. "We won't trouble you for

that now. I'll meet with you later myself to finalize the concentration of time-travelers during the Truce interim."

The Castellan bowed, excused himself, and hurried back up the path leading to the fortress. Only the five Exalted Personages and a small squad of soldiers waiting at a discreet distance now remained in the time-portal area. The sun was well over the brow of the eastern highlands.

"Sometimes," the King said, looking after Pitkin with a peeved expression, "the efficiency of you humans really depresses me. No righteous indignation. No avowals of vengeance or fealty. Just revised distribution systems and preliminary overviews!"

The Lord Coercer laughed in a genial fashion. "Vengeance is the Battlemaster's department. Mine is making certain that this disaster is confined to the Finiah region and neutralized as quickly as possible to minimize its impact on the socioeconomy. If it weren't for the importance of the barium mines, I'd be inclined to write Finiah off."

"Why, you arrogant little squeakpoop!" Velteyn's face was suffused with a red glare. "You're talking about my home! The cradle of Tanu culture on this planet! The City of Lights!"

"The lights," Gomnol said, unperturbed, "have gone out. Finiah is in ruins. The Foe used brilliant strategy to attack it. It's awkwardly situated, on the wrong side of the Rhine and too far away from our other population centers. There are Firvulag on one side of it and Howlers on the other—and Madame Guderian and her rustic irregulars making merry in between. Of all our cities, it was the ripest for surprise attack."

"I've kept it safe for five hundred years!" Velteyn shouted. "Once we get the walls back up and some reinforcements for the Flying Hunt, we'll have it as secure as ever. We'll wipe out Guderian's outlaws by organizing a Quest through the Vosges to destroy their settlements. Once the Lowlife nests are burned out, the Firvulag will crawl back into their own holes just as they've always done. They never would have mobilized for the attack at all if it hadn't been for that obscene old woman and her damned iron."

"It may not be as easy as you think to put down the hostile humans, Creative Brother," Eadone told Velteyn. "And I'm afraid that Lord Gomnol raises a serious point about the isolated position of Finiah. In the early years, when there were fewer of us and fewer Firvulag, your little walled city on the promontory was at a strategic advantage. But today it is trapped within a web of inimical forces. Now that the humans are aware of the power of iron, they'll make dreadful use of it. Even a handful of Lowlives will be able to waylay caravans and troops columns, attack your plantations, perhaps set up a blockade in the river that could reduce your citizenry to starvation. There is no way you can be supplied by land. The Black Forest massif behind you is too formidable a barrier. Neither could your armed forces be reinforced by land. Soldiers would have to cross the Rhine to reach you from our other northern strongholds —from Goriah, Burask, or Roniah. Even rebuilding your city will be a very difficult task because of the length of the lines of supply."

Velteyn's flaming face went almost purple. "But we *must* rebuild! The destruction wasn't total. By no means! Almost all of our noncombatant Tanu citizens survived. Six hundred and eighty-nine airlifted to safety by me, by Lady Dectar, and by our gold-torc human brother Sullivan-Tonn."

The King said, "But you lost most of the knights. And more than four thousand humans—silvers, grays, and barenecks—and every single rama! The whole damn working populace either dead, taken prisoner by that Tana-bedamned old harridan, or run off into the bushes where the Howlers or the wild animals will finish them off."

"The plantations are still secure! And the military outposts. We can rebuild, Awful Father! We can make Finiah impregnable. We'll bring in more PK and coercer adepts to strengthen our mental capability."

For the first time, Nodonn Battlemaster spoke. "We will have to reopen the mine. That is self-evident, unless we discover a new source of the vital barium ore. But there can be no thought of restoring Finiah to its former glory. Its day as a gracious and venerable seat of culture has passed. In future, it must present an austere but secure face to our Foe. We will rebuild it as a fortified mining settlement . . . but that's all."

Velteyn's entire body reacted as if from a physical assault. His mind screamed.

O myBrother what do you say how can you woundsoulflay me disgracedegrade me before mypeople a battlechampion fallen unavengedunrestoredabandoned to human/Firvulag derision + Tanu pityscorn . . .

Nodonn turned away. He walked to the empty granite platform of the time-portal and stood in the middle of it, aurora-hued robes bright in the sunrise. His immense voice rang in their minds and ears.

"Blame *this*! From this came your pain, Brother! From this source of rottenness and deadly peril that has seduced us from our ancient way! Cursed be the woman who first opened the time-gate to invading humankind. We will all of us be mourning for a world forever lost unless we have the courage to shut the humans out before it is too late. If we continue our fatal dependence upon them, the death of Finiah will be nothing in comparison to the death of the Many-Colored Land!"

Eadone said, "I could almost believe it now. And yet—"

"You're wrong, Nodonn!" Thagdal said. "You've been trying to sell that prophecy of doom ever since they first started coming. But look at us! We're stronger now than we ever were before. It's a damn shame about Finiah. The city was a shrine to our pioneer heritage. But, let's face it—a bloody inconvenient place to get to or from, for all its picturesqueness and charm and pretty lights and all! . . . Tell you what, Velteyn, son! We'll build you a new city in some better place. How's that sound?"

Gomnol joined the King in persuasion. "Perhaps on the shore of the Lac de Bresse. We can cut a new road from it to Goriah and open a whole new region for exploitation. Just as soon as the Combat is behind us, we can begin the planning. All of the other cities will contribute to its building, and you can have every one of the time-travelers for the next two years as a population base. We'll build you a new Finiah even better than the old. Proper streets and drains, proper water system and access, proper urban planning and defensive works. What do you say to that?"

Nodonn said: Proper/*human*?

Gomnol said: Rather wattledaubhuts handcrafted You?

Eadone said: Take comfort our Mourning Brother. We will see you restored never fear. Go now to your LadyWife + sorrowing folk and bid them hope.

"Yes." Velteyn lifted his head and the psychic luminosity faded. He spoke aloud. "It is a good plan, Awful Father, and I stand humbly grateful before your generosity." And to Nodonn: "If you think me lacking in courage, Brother Battlemaster, I'll prove differently at the Grand Combat. I confess that the battle-joy went out of me with this disaster . . . but by game-time I'll be a warrior restored. The Firvulag will pay a thousand times over for their unholy alliance with the Lowlives. As for the human despoilers—iron or no iron, we will see them screaming in the Great Retort as they offer their lives to the Goddess at the Combat's glorious end!"

"Well said," observed the High King. "And now that the future is assured, I believe it is safe to go into the Castle for breakfast."

4

THE REFUGEE CAMP and field hospital had been set up in the former invasion staging area in the Rhine bottomland. With the Tanu withdrawal to Castle Gateway and the retreat of Finiah's loyalist humans to the lake forts, the riverside was secure enough while the Truce prevailed. The wisdom of Old Man Kawai had dictated that the unfortunates not be sheltered in Hidden Springs village.

"It is a matter of simple psychology," he told Peopeo Moxmox Burke. "If we bring them to our canyon they will want to stay there, where there is ready-made housing and a vestige of civilization. But we cannot feed five or six hundred people indefinitely, nor will our buildings and sanitary facilities accommodate such a number. And the Firvulag bring in fresh stragglers every day! No—these refugees must be motivated to establish new settlements of their own. For this reason we must assemble them in a spartan campsite, care for their disabilities, furnish them with equipment and guides, and disperse them as rapidly as possible before the post-Combat Truce ends and the Tanu begin their countermeasures."

It was Khalid Khan who came up with the suggestion for the Iron Road. The metalsmith pointed out that the wilderness smeltery should become the site of a new human stronghold. Other smaller settlements could be strung along the bank of the Moselle to secure the trail between the iron workings and Hidden Springs.

"Provided the Tanu don't return in force too soon after the Truce's end," Khalid had said, "we can secure this whole region for Lowlife humanity by producing quantities of iron. The refugees can support themselves by making it after we help them to get established. I think we can bank on the Howlers clearing out once word of the iron is passed around. But a massive Tanu Quest would be another matter, of course."

"If the next two phases of my plan succeed," Madame Guderian had said, "there will be no Quest."

Seven days following the attack on Finiah, Madame Guderian and Chief Burke came on chalikos to meet with Kawai for a last inspection tour of the refugee camp before proceeding south. The old woman and the tall Native American dismounted and tied their beasts to bushes near a stream, then walked with the aged Japanese into the grove with its rows of palmetto-thatched lean-tos and other rather squalid shelters. The area was becoming garbage-strewn and fetid.

"We have tried to have the refugees police the area," Kawai said in a low voice, "but many are still in a shocked and depressed state and indifferent to personal hygiene and orderly behavior. There was a bit of trouble yesterday, as Chief Burke has doubtless told you. A group of perhaps forty, led by five de-collared gray soldiers, insisted upon being allowed to proceed to Fort Onion River on the lake. We procured an escort of Firvulag and sent them away. It would have been useless to detain them."

"We did not lose any of the doctors?" Madame was anxious. "Or the glass technicians?"

"The medical personnel remained with us," Kawai said. "They were not willingly enslaved. One glassblower is gone. We have also lost the printer, several skilled stonemasons, some weavers and jewelers."

The old woman attempted a chuckle. "We will not miss the latter, at any rate." Her voice was hoarse and she coughed often. During the aerial bombardment of Finiah, when she lay unconscious on the floor of the flyer, she had inhaled fumes from cabin materials set on fire by Velteyn's lightning balls. Unlike Claude and Richard, she had not been seriously burned; but Amerie was deeply concerned about damage to Madame's lungs, which could not readily be treated with the medications and equipment on hand. Also, the old woman refused to rest and was obstinately determined to participate personally in the next phase of her plan. The youthful appearance brought about by her rejuvenation had begun to fade away, and there were now deep furrows in her forehead and beside her thin mouth. Loss of facial substance had thrown her cheekbones and her beaklike nose into gaunt prominence. The golden torc rolled loosely about her thin, corded neck.

Kawai said, "There remain with us in the camp some five hundred and fifty souls, most of them in good physical health in spite of their confused mental state. It is my opinion, as well as that of the three liberated physicians, that these people will recover once they embark on a course of positive action. We will begin dispersing the strongest within the next three days. They will travel with Homi and Axel and Philemon to the site of the Nancy iron workings. Others of our own people and some of the volunteers who remain will accompany this group with supplies. If all goes as planned, we will have at least the shell of a stockaded village erected within two weeks. Several smaller settlements will be built between here and Nancy as soon as Philemon and Axel can train the workers."

Madame nodded. "Bien, entendu. But remember—production of the iron must be given priority! Let nothing be spared in the encouragement of those refugees who are willing to undertake this work. We must equip all of the Lowlives with iron weapons as soon as possible."

They walked among the improvised huts toward a tributary of the Rhine, where the hospital tent had been set up. Many of the refugees came out of their shelters and stood in silence, watching Madame go by. She nodded to them and sometimes spoke a name, for almost all of these people had passed through the auberge during her tenure—and even those who were not known to her personally knew very well who *she* was.

Some of them smiled. A number of faces displayed open hostility and one man spat and turned his back on her. But most watched with a spiritless torpor that made the old woman's heart shrink.

"It was right, what we did!" She hurried along between Burke and Kawai, arms held stiff at her sides. "They had to be freed. They will become accustomed to it soon and then they will be content again."

"Of course," said Chief Burke gently.

Kawai said, "They are still profoundly shocked. We must make allowances for them. Later they will appreciate their release from bondage."

"Many will continue to hate me, though." Her voice was toneless. "First for having sent them into slavery, and now for having freed them, casting them into fresh uncertainty. Their misery lies heavy upon my conscience. If I had not permitted them to pass through the time-portal, this tragedy would never have taken place."

"They would have found another way to make themselves miserable," Burke said. "Look at me! The last of the shmohawks, for God's sake. No more Wallawallas after the Big Chief passes into the

Happy Hunting Grounds—so I dramatize the damn shame of it by calling a press conference and telling the rotten paleskins, 'I will fight no more forever.' Not a dry eye on the Tri-D in a dozen Yankee planets as the noble Native American jurist makes his gesture. But later I got a note from the tribal council of the Yakimas telling me to get the hell back on the bench and quit being such a damn kvetch."

Old Man Kawai said, "We have all of us been foolish, Angélique. But you are not to blame. Without your time-gate as an honorable exit, I would likely have taken my own life. That is perhaps true of many of us exiles. But I came here instead—and it is true that I endured much suffering at first, while I was a captive of the Tanu. But later, after my escape, I knew also a great joy. I have learned that there is happiness to be found in service to others. Without you, without your time-gate, I would have ended my days as selfishly as I lived most of them. I am still a fool, perhaps. But I am a fool who has known good friends and true peace."

Madame's head lowered. "Nevertheless, I will not find my own peace until I atone in the way that I must. The slavery of the gray and silver torcs must be abolished. And the time-portal must be closed. We have made a beginning here at Finiah—but I will see it to completion or die!"

She began to cough violently and her face went bluish white.

"Goddam it!" muttered Burke. He scooped her up and went striding toward the shelter of the field hospital, a great tent made from dozens of durofilm tarps zipped together into a pavilion with screened sides.

"Put me down, Peo! I am quite all right." She struggled in his arms.

Kawai, trotting ahead, brought a swarthy man with tired eyes and a stethoscope held at the ready. "Put her on the plank table," the physician said. After examining the state of the old woman's lungs, the doctor said, "You don't take care of yourself, you're gonna drown in your own glop! Hear me? You been doing the drainage exercises Amerie prescribed?"

"They are undignified."

"Mashallah! Will you listen to the woman?" He scratched at an irritated ring of skin beneath his Adam's apple where the gray torc had been. "You guys—talk some sense into her!"

He produced a minidoser and applied it to her jugular.

"That will help some. But only rest will let your body get that fluid out of your lungs. Now are you going to behave?"

Madame said, "Hélas, Jafar chéri! There are matters that require my attention." Ignoring his protests, she got down from the table and toured the hospital, where most of the faces looked warmly upon her. One obviously pregnant woman, lying on a cot in the remnants of a splendid court costume, seized Madame's hand and kissed it.

"Thank God you freed us." The woman began to weep. "Twelve years. Twelve years of a living nightmare—and now it's over."

Madame smiled and gently extricated her hand from the woman's grasp. "Yes, for you it is over, dear child. You are free."

The woman hesitated. "Madame . . . what am I to do with it when it comes? There are other women, too, carrying *their* children. I am too close to delivery. But the others—"

"You must make your own choices. The tenets of my own faith would counsel me to bear the child. It is, after all, innocent. After that . . . perhaps the wisest action is that followed by the Tanu themselves."

The pregnant woman whispered, "I should give it back to them?"

"The Firvulag will help you." Madame raised her eyes to the doctor. "You will see to it, if this is what she decides?"

"I will."

The old woman bent and kissed the forehead of the expectant mother. "I must now undertake a long journey. Perhaps you will pray for my . . . safe arrival at my destination."

"Oh, yes, Madame. And I'll tell the others."

With a small gesture of farewell, the old woman turned away. The doctor followed her to the door of the tent where Kawai and Chief Burke waited.

"They are now in your hands, Jafar chéri. You and Lucy and Lubutu must take care of them, since Amerie will go south with us."

The physician wagged his head in dismay. "You're still determined to go?" He looked helplessly at Burke. "It's insanity."

"I must carry out my plan," she insisted. "We leave early tomorrow morning. Only three weeks remain of the Truce and there is no time to waste."

Burke said, "If you won't consider your own welfare, think of the rest of us! Having to worry about you and take care of you. Amerie would probably act sensibly and stay in Hidden Springs if she didn't feel you needed her."

Angélique Guderian looked up at the huge red man with affection. "You do not trap me with your forked tongue, mon petit sauvage. Now that Felice has returned from Finiah with her obedient herd of chalikos, we will ride south in comfort. As for Soeur Amerie, she has her own reasons for wishing to participate in the operation, as have the other volunteers. And so we march! Au 'voir, Jafar. We go now to the village to complete the last arrangements." She began walking toward the hospital door.

The doctor called out, "Reconsider, Madame!" But she only laughed.

Old Man Kawai shrugged as he started after her. "You have seen that it is useless to argue with her, Jafar. And perhaps, when you are as old as Peo Burke and I, you will understand why she thinks she must finish this affair herself."

"Oh, I understand," said the doctor. "Only too well."

He went back into the ward, where the expectant mother had begun to moan.

5

MARIALENA COOKED the farewell supper herself, laying places at Madame's table for the eleven who were going south, plus one for Kawai, who would take over as Freeleader in the morning.

When all were seated, the Frenchwoman said, "The Reverend Sister will ask a blessing."

Amerie said in a low voice, "Lord, bless this food. Bless this company. Bless this crazy undertaking."

"Amen," said Khalid Khan.

The others, excepting Felice, said, "Amen." Then they heaped their plates and passed stoneware jugs of chilled wine.

"I thought Pegleg was coming," Khalid said.

Madame confessed, "I told him to meet us tomorrow before we set out. Perhaps you will think me a foolish old woman, mes enfants, but I judged it would be better to confer one last time tonight among ourselves. I know that Fitharn has seemed a faithful comrade during this perilous time. Nevertheless, we should not forget that his first loyalty is to his own Firvulag race. And I have never trusted the arrière-pensée of King Yeochee and Pallol One-Eye. There is always the chance that they plan to use us treacherously once we have succeeded in destroying the torc factory and closing the time-portal."

Vanda-Jo, the plainspoken Public Works Chief, gave a cynical hoot. "We'd be fools to let 'em know every card in our hand. If we bring this double-barreled blast off, the Firvulag will benefit. They don't need to know our planning details. All they have to do is help us with the traveling and hiding out."

"Too bad outlaw humans aren't covered by the Truce," said the nun. She dropped a piece of meat to her little wildcat, which lurked under the table.

"Fat chance," said Peo Burke. "Pass the burgundy—or whatever that is. My old wound needs anesthetizing."

"Speaking of wounds," Amerie went on, "I realize it's useless to urge Madame to stay behind. But Claude and Khalid are another matter. Claude's burns are just beginning to dry and a week isn't nearly enough recovery time for Khalid's concussion and arm and leg wounds."

"You need me," the Pakistani said. "I'm the only one who's ever been to Muriah."

"Ten years ago," the nun corrected him. "And via the Great South Road, not on the Rhône."

"The capital can't have changed much in that time. Besides, I'm looking forward to the boat trip. Gert and Hansi used to kayak on the river back in the future."

Hansi laughed grimly. "It should be a real pleasure cruise for invalids. But there's no escaping the fact that we need Khalid's knowledge of the city. Things will be tricky enough without getting lost."

"This is true," said Madame. "I am distressed that you must go, Khalid, after you have already done so much, but your help might be crucial to our success . . . Claude, on the other hand, is merely being stubborn when he maintains his indispensability!"

"I suppose you're the only one capable of pushing that amber message carrier through the time-warp!" the paleontologist snapped. "I'm fitter than you are, Angélique, and I've earned my place on this mission if anybody has."

"Mulet polonais! Stay home and recover your health."

Felice whacked her spoon handle on the table. "Now don't you two start that again! You're both a pair of sick old coots with no business out of your rocking chairs, and if we had any sense we'd lock you in a shed together and go off without you."

"Fortunately," said Uwe Guldenzopf, taking a placid pull on his pipe, "we have no sense."

Madame glared at Claude. "It is my duty to go! I, who sinned in opening the time-portal, must atone by closing it."

"Hogwash," said Claude. "You've got a death wish, that's what."

Madame flung down her knife. "Will you, of all people, impugn my motives? Look to your own death wish, Monsieur le Professeur!"

Claude took a prim sip from his mug of wine. "Honi soit qui merde y pense, sweetheart."

"Order, dammit!" Chief Burke pounded his huge fist on the table. "As Warlord in Chief of this flea-bitten crew, I declare that there will be no more discussion of motives! All of us have volunteered. All of us have proved that we can be useful in one way or another—either at Castle Gateway or down in Muriah at the torc-works caper . . . Now. I want to know whether there are any more *serious* questions before we wrap it up for the night."

"I have thought of one thing," Basil said with some diffidence. "As a newcomer to the group, I've hesitated to suggest any major modification of Madame Guderian's original scheme. And until Felice returned yesterday morning with her golden torc and the chalikos and said she would go with us, the point was moot anyway. What I'm trying to say is—how about the Spear?"

The others looked at the alpinist don with blank incomprehension. Basil had been liberated in the fall of Finiah, having spent a month in the city dungeons following his recapture on the lake. His place in the new expedition had been assured when he declared himself willing to use his mountaineering skills in scaling the walls of Castle Gateway, the Coercer Headquarters in Muriah, or any other fortress the group might care to invade. He was also, he admitted, "frightfully keen to teach the Tanu a lesson for having spoiled my Pliocene holiday."

Old Man Kawai now shook his head in regret. "The Spear's powerpack is completely discharged, Basil. You couldn't get a glim out of a micro-LED with the juice that's left. I had a stab at trying to open the pack myself, but I simply could not improvise a suitable tool. It needs a craftier hand."

"Still," Basil persisted, "if we *could* get the pack open, there's a good chance we could recharge it. Am I right?"

The former electronics manufacturer lifted his skinny shoulders. "The flyer was water-fusion powered. Why not the zapper?"

Felice said, "Jeez, guys, I'm not sure I can fine-tune my PK enough yet to break into the thing without ruining it."

"That wasn't what I had in mind," said the alpinist. "What you could do is carry the Spear south much more easily than the rest of us could do. It would be priceless for the assault against the torc-making establishment."

"He's right about that," Khalid agreed. "The factory is in the Coercer Guild Complex, locked up tighter than a Lylmik's virtue."

"Lest we forget," Amerie interposed, "the Spear is dead."

Basil said, "I have an idea who might resurrect it. Claude told me all about him one long hot afternoon weeks ago when we spent some time together in quod at Castle Gateway. Your talented little friend in the gold suit."

"Aiken Drum!" said Felice. "Little tricky-pockets!"

Claude's greenish eyes flashed. "He could! If anyone could decipher that antique photon weapon, Aiken could . . . But *would* he? They made him a silver, remember. He might have thrown in with them by now. He was always out for the main chance."

"He was our friend," Amerie said. "He's a human being. He's got to help us against those monsters!"

"Felice could twist his arm," Claude suggested, his smile bland. "Or isn't that your style any more, little girl?"

The athlete ignored him. "Basil—I think your idea is a winner. We'll take the Spear, even if I have to shlep it on my back the whole thirteen hundred kloms down to Muriah. One way or another, we'll get Aiken Drum to make us a can opener."

Chief Burke said, "We can hope for the best . . . Anything else?"

Nobody said anything. Uwe tapped the dottle from his pipe into the empty bowl before him. "Marialena is always furious when I do this. But perhaps one last time?"

"She'll forgive you," laughed Gert.

Chairs scraped back. Everybody got up and stretched. Those with cottages in the village prepared to leave. The others would spread sleeping bags upon Madame's floor.

Amerie laid a hand on Kawai's shoulder as the old man turned toward the door. "One favor, old friend."

"Only name it, Amerie-san."

The nun picked up the tiny pet wildcat. "If you could give a home to Deej—"

He bowed gravely and took the little animal into his arms. "I will keep her safe for you until you return to Hidden Springs. And you will. I have made a most formidable vow to the Martyrs of Nagasaki."

"Crazy old Buddhist," said the nun, pushing him out of the door.

6

"THIS JUDGMENT they demand of me concerning you," Brede began.

"Yes?" Elizabeth replied aloud, as always.

"It must be made consonant with their own racial destiny here. I have foreseen my dear Tanu and Firvulag people united and operant. This is my vision as of the most ancient days, before we ever came to this galaxy, to this planet of the Many-Colored Land. This destiny will happen, even though my prolepsis fails in showing me the how and when . . . I would like to think that we have become friends, Elizabeth. I am deeply aware of your desire for noninvolvement in our affairs. But I cannot believe that you are an extraneous factor here! You are part of the pattern! And so are all of these others, your companions of Group Green, who have so gravely influenced Tanu and Firvulag and even the poor lost ones of the northern wilderness. I can see the lines of destiny reaching toward a sure convergence at the Grand Combat in three weeks' time. I see it, I tell you! And your role . . . is strongly interwoven. But if not as racial genetrix—then what?"

"Brede, I will not be used." Even with her mental screens firm, the determination behind Elizabeth's statement had an adamantine luster.

"Then *choose* to help us," the exotic woman pleaded. "Your own human race, your own close friends, are bound up in this climax."

"No judgment you make concerning me will satisfy all of the Tanu factions. You know that. Your High King wants his new dynasty. But the Host of Nontusvel won't be satisfied until I'm safely dead. As for my friends . . . they seem to be in better control of their own destinies than I am! Why won't you consider strict justice for me for a change, rather than viewing me as a chess-piece in your proleptic game? Let me go free and harmless away from this place if that's what I choose."

And I do. Soaring the world alone splendid at peace.

"But—the pattern! I tell you, I see it! If it is not your genes that are to influence us, then there must be some other factor. O Sister of the Mind, help me to focus my faltering vision!"

"Prescience was not a metafunction that was understood in my time. It was a wild talent. Unpredictable. The foreseeing was dangerous enough . . . but any attempted manipulation of future events foreseen was known to us to be futile. Whether I go free or not, your vision must come to pass. So let me go."

Brede seemed not to have heard. They were sitting together in the limitless room without doors where the ambient atmosphere was enriched to the exotic's special need. But she had gone rigid and gasped in shallow exhalations while her features worked and her partly open mind showed a whirlpool of faces—human and Tanu and Firvulag and Howler—all gyrating and pulsing around Elizabeth's own image, and that generating filamentous probability lines forming and re-forming in what was almost a Lissajous fabric of incoherence—unordered, *ununified*.

"The psychounion!" Brede cried. "Not the genes—the mental Unity!" The mind of the Shipspouse brightened in such sweet hopefulness that even Elizabeth faltered in continuing to refuse empathy.

"What—are you saying, Brede?"

"That is your role! It doesn't matter when my people achieve their coalescence with the local Mind. It *will* happen. And when it does, I must be able to guide them into the orderly levels of metapsychic union that were the basis of the governing forces of your own Galactic Milieu, the reconciliation of divergent intellectual energies into an operant organic whole. *You* are to teach me how this is to be done! That is your role among us. You guided young children of your own time into the Unity. This was the focus of your life's work, as you have told me. In your Milieu, immature metafunctional minds were not left to flounder and make their own way. They were taught, led, enlightened. Show me how this was done. So that I will be ready. And then, if you still desire it, I will help you to . . . leave us."

"You don't know what you're asking of me, Brede."

"But this *must* be the solution! So elegant, so logical an extension of the work I have already done for my dear ones. Consider them as they are now, in their disunity! My poor Firvulag, operant but weak and impotent, their psychic energies diffused into silly byways. Their kinsmen, the Howling Ones, festering in bitter despair. And will the Tanu be any different when they in turn achieve true operancy, delivered from their golden torcs? Your operant human race on the Elder Earth might well have perished if it had not been helped in its extremity by other entities who were wiser. Help me to help *my* people. And then, when they are ready, I also will be ready."

"You foresee this outcome?" Elizabeth inquired, dubious.

Brede hesitated. Again the pained, gasping breaths. "I have—always been the guide and teacher of my people. Even in times when they were unaware. Whence shall the Unity come, if not from me? And where can I learn, if not from you?"

"The difficulties would be enormous. Not only is your mind exotic and therefore unfamiliar to me, but you are also a mature psychic entity conditioned to the torc device over thousands of years. I have never worked with any but humans. Almost all of them were very young children, still flexible and able to absorb the training with a minimum of painful catalyst. I can only compare the process with a child's first acquisition of language. This is a process that seems nearly effortless to a baby; and yet when an adult attempts to learn new languages without using sophisticated ancillaries, he labors and suffers. The bringing of latent metafunctions to fully adept operancy is infinitely more difficult. First, you would have to become operant—and then make the much greater leap to adept status before absorbing the masterclass teaching techniques. There would be atrocious suffering."

"I will endure whatever is necessary."

"Even if you survive my education with your sanity intact, there is no guarantee that you will attain full operancy—much less the adept level. If your strength failed at any point, you would surely die. And then what would become of your people?"

"I will not die," said Brede.

"There are other . . . technical difficulties. The catalyst I spoke of. I can't think of an algetic source of sufficient intensity that would be available to us here in your room without doors."

"Pain? Is this the only way that the psychic enlargement can be accomplished?"

"The only sure way. There are others. In my own world, latent humans have attained operancy when certain psychobarriers were overcome through sublimation of the will to the cosmic Unity. But these other roads are uncertain—and in any case, I'm only qualified in the one technique. It has its roots in the preliterate cultures of my own era. The primitive people of Elder Earth were fully aware that pain, endured steadfastly and with dignified acceptance, acted as a psychic refining agent that opened the newly sensitized mind to wisdom otherwise inaccessible—as well as the individual spectrum of metafunctions."

A panorama of pre-Milieu adepts flashed before Brede's mental eye. Elizabeth showed her monks and nuns and prophets and yogis, shamans and warriors and consecrated leaders, aboriginal healers and seers from all of the wild places of pre-Intervention Earth—humans enduring self-imposed ordeals in the belief that they would emerge transfigured.

Elizabeth said, "As we humans attained high technology, the creative use of suffering was nearly lost. Most high-tech civilizations are zealous in the eradication of pain, both physical and mental. Up until the time of the Intervention, very few of our intellectuals would have placed any value on it—this despite the teaching of earlier philosophers and the clear evidence to be gleaned from anthropology and even from developmental psychology itself."

"My race was as yours in this respect," said Brede. "Understand that I speak of my original home planet—not of these Tanu and Firvulag, who are different. The best of the dimorphics still celebrate life-passages with ordeals. The very Combat itself has roots therein."

"But still perverted! Immature! Among the advanced human cultures of pre-Milieu times, we had comparable kinks. One form of physical suffering that was esteemed was that endured by athletes. Ritual game playing. Do you see the parallel? But our human race never valued any form of *psychic* pain. That attendant upon the normal education process was tolerated as a necessary evil—but there were constant attempts to ameliorate it or eliminate it altogether. It never occurred to our primitive educators that suffering per se had a positive influence upon mental growth. A few religious groups did discover how pain worked as a tool for mental enlargement. My own church had a rather muddled concept of algetic offering that at least produced the proper endurance-discipline. But the faithful saw algetics only from the spiritual angle. When certain practitioners happened to levitate or read thoughts or perform other metapsychic functions, everybody was highly embarrassed."

"Yes . . . yes." The great jeweled headdress nodded. Exotic reminiscences floated through Brede's mental vestibulum. "We of Lene also held to the belief that suffering was evil. And those who denied it were sadomasochists and hopelessly anomalous. For example—these exiles! My dear foolish people. I have never, until now, completely understood my deep motives for adopting them and helping them to escape from our galaxy. But now it becomes obvious that my prolepsis recognized that tiny kernel of psychic validity in their aberrant mind-set. The Firvulag, especially, who endured the greatest rigors in their natural environment, were keenly appreciative of ordeals. And yet—they stalled in their mental evolution. As did the Tanu, seduced by their torcs, and most of the other people of our federation as well . . . As I have told you, all but the incompatibles embraced the mind-amplifying device after the last of the wars."

She paused, touching the gold at her own throat that was half-hidden behind the lowered respirator. "And this torc, which seemed such a boon, resulted in a dead end for the Mind of an entire galaxy. Unless . . . the evolution continues here. And it must! But, Almighty Tana, why is my vision so *dim?*"

Elizabeth said, "The time-dimension may be much greater than you ever suspected. Our Milieu perceived the past manifest in the present, the present manifest in the future."

"Elizabeth!" Brede's voice caught. "Six million years? Ah, no!"

"We had legends. And there is the compatibility."

"And the Ship," Brede whispered. "I told my dearest one to choose the best."

She raised her glittering mask. Tears fell onto its red metallic smoothness, losing themselves in the crystal ornamentation. The women sat silent for a long time. Between them on the table rested the exquisite glass model of the interstellar organism that had been Brede's mate. Together the disparate spouses had shared a kind of psychounion that, inadequate as it was, had partaken in a small measure of the true mental conjugation Elizabeth had known among her own kind. But Brede's Ship was dead. And she—like Elizabeth—was alone.

"Whatever the risks," came the amplified voice from the hidden mouth, "you must teach me. I know that the Mind of my people will mature, just as I know that the destinies of Tanu and Firvulag and humanity are interleaved. Perhaps the Unity of my people will perfect itself soon and perhaps late. But there must be a teacher. And if not me, then you."

Elizabeth flared in anger. "Oh, no you don't! Damn you! Can't you understand the way it is with me? I don't want to sacrifice myself for your people. Not even for my *own* people! Can't you accept that operancy doesn't equate with sainthood?"

"There have been saints among you."

The person behind the mask seemed to melt, to change. Elizabeth stiffened, shocked by the metaphoric thrust that she instantly repudiated.

"No! You can't trick me that way. You're no saint and neither am I! I'm an ordinary woman with ordinary flaws. I once was able to do unusual work because my natural talents were trained up for it. But there was never any . . . consecration. When I seemed to lose my abilities, I didn't offer up the loss and make the best of it. I chose this Exile route. I'm a flyaway and glad of it! My being trapped here in the Pliocene, separated forever from the Unity, with my meta-functions restored and monsters nipping at my heels, is a cosmic joke. And you are, too, whoever you are! And I *still* want my balloon back!"

And that is enough for you loving none loved by none O highflyingfleeing Elizabeth?

"I loved once and suffered the loss. Once was enough. Love costs too much. I won't be a mother to your people. Not physically and not mentally."

Brede's mind and mask mirrored only Elizabeth.

Bitter mind-laughter underlay the vocal speech of the human woman. "Oh, that's clever of you, Two-Face! But the ploy won't work. I know all about my sin of Olympian selfishness. But you can't prove that my duty lies with your people, or with exiled humanity, or with any hypothetical merging of the races."

Brede raised her hands. The mask came down and there was only the sad, patient smile. "Then help me to fulfill *my* duty, which does lie with them all. Teach me."

"We—we don't have a pain source of sufficient intensity."

"We do." Brede's determination was unshakable. "There is hyperspatial translation. My body can be sustained in the superficies of the continuum for as long as necessary. I have the legacy of competence from my Spouse. I require no mechanism whatever to span the width of this galaxy. I have never considered using the translational power before this, simply because there was no question of deserting my people. And of course I would not actually leave them now. I would return."

"If the attempt at mental enlargement doesn't kill you."

"I am willing to risk all, to suffer all."

Elizabeth exclaimed, "How can you love these wretched barbarians so much when they can never appreciate what you do for them?"

Only the smile, and the invitation to enter the mind.

With great reluctance, Elizabeth said, "There's another thing I haven't touched on. The teacher . . . shares the ordeal."

O Elizabeth. No I did not realize. I have been presumptuous and you must forgive. I see now that I have no right—

Elizabeth broke into the protesting thought with brusque words. "Brede, I'm going to die. Even if I fly out of here, your dearly beloved people are going to track me down sooner or later and finish me off. And so . . . why not? Perhaps, if I succeed with you, it would be a kind of epitaph. If you're willing to chance the ordeal, I'll take you. You'll be my last student. And if your vision of joint racial destiny is fulfilled, perhaps you can even be my justification."

"I never intended to cause you more pain. And I commiserate."

"Well—don't waste it." Elizabeth's tone was wry. "Every bit of suffering is valuable! . . . Are you sure you can work the translation?"

Brede's mind showed her. Elizabeth would not physically accompany the exotic traveler, of course. But her mind would remain meshed with Brede's to channelize the neural fires.

"Whenever you are ready," the Shipspouse said, "we can go forth."

The ceiling of the room without doors opened. There toward the south was the milky river of the Galactic Plane. And behind its dust clouds, the Hub; hidden beyond that lay the other arm of the spiral, almost a hundred thousand light-years distant.

"All the way across," said Elizabeth. "Now."

* * *

. . . And there they were, in an instant and forever, stretched on a rack the width of the starry whirlpool, poised between gray limbo and black, distorted, spangled space. The atoms of Brede's physical body had become more tenuous than the rare atomic fog that floats in the void between the stars and vibrates still with the birth cry of the universe. The mind of the Shipspouse shrieked on the same frequencies as the agonized particles. And in this manner, the enlargement began.

It would be all the more difficult because Brede's latent powers were so great. All of the well-worn psychoenergetic circuits leading from the torc would have to be rerouted through the syncytial mazes of the right cortex, reeducated to operancy within the refining flame of the ultimate pain that the universe could inflict upon a thinking, feeling creature. By enduring, Brede might pass in a short time through a process that ordinarily took many years. But the pain in itself was worthless unless discipline could be maintained and the divarication of the mental network kept firmly under control. This was where the guidance of a skilled teacher was all-important. While Elizabeth's great redactive power clamped around the pulsating psyche and kept it from disintegrating, she also directed Brede's flaring limbics as though they were countless metapsychic torches burning away the accumulated cortical debris of a lifetime 14,000 years in length.

The mind of the operant, steadfast in the mutual anguish, led and braced that of the aspirant. The two of them hung locked together in the inferno between true space and hyperspace, where there is but a single dimension, an afferent input that sentient beings of all races apprehend only as pain . . .

The process went on and on, simultaneous and eternal according to their shared subjective consciousness. Brede knew in her agony that changes were taking place within her soul—but she could not rise above the fire long enough to study herself. She could only accept and affirm and continue to be strong, hoping that when the suffering was done her mind would still live in the physical universe.

The pain lessened.

Now Brede felt Elizabeth's binding energies soften to gentleness. She became aware of other life-forces besides their own two, appearing to sing amidst the diminishing flame. How odd! And what was *that?* There, so far away, beyond the gray and the black and the humming megatonal song and the rack of invisible waning fire was a glimpse of brightness that might have been approaching; and the clearer her perception of it, the more irresistible it became. Brede abandoned discipline, forgot all self in her sudden eagerness to reach it, to see and join with it, now that she was capable of the Unity . . .

Return.

O no Elizabeth not now let me go on—

We have reached the limit. Return with me.

No no we exiles together continue on with me to the end of it and join beyond pain where it waits for us loving . . .

We must return. I'm going to draw you back. Don't resist.

No no no no—

Let go. Stop looking. You may not have that and live. Come back now from there submit to my redaction fly back across the expanse don't struggle Sancta Illusio Persona Adamantis ora pro nobis wherever you are submit Brede submit to my guidance rest in me we are almost there . . . there . . .

* * *

The Shipspouse sat unmasked across the table from Elizabeth. "Gone. It's gone. You took me away from it."

"It was necessary for both of us. And the culmination of the pain in your ordeal. Which was successful."

Tears streamed down Brede's face. There was a slow rekindling after near-extinguishment, and regret that would be a part of her until, at last, she died. In the silence of the room without doors Brede recovered.

There was an opening and an invitation. Brede ventured in, then cried aloud as she knew the first true Union with a mind of Earth.

So that is—how it is.

Yes. I embrace thee Sister.

The exotic woman put fingertips to the lifeless gold at her throat and unfastened the catch. She held the open torc at arm's length for a moment before laying it on the table beside the Ship's likeness.

I live. I function freely feeble an infant tottering on first legs but the metafunctions are released and such richness and the Unity is twoinone now but later when I know the loved Mind—

There will be spontaneous growth with joy instead of pain until you are filled to capacity. This last is subject to the limitations of your physical body as well as the state of the local Mind. Since you already love the Mind, you will be able to pour forth without diminishing. This is something I cannot do.

And *that* which I saw—

What most of us operant or no shall see and possess ultimately. Not many aspirants catch a glimpse of it. Fortunately.

Once more the two women sat in mental silence.

"There is no memory of anguish," Brede finally said out loud.

"But I can see that there would not be. The guiding and the acceptance are all-important in differentiating unproductive misery from creative purgation. And after that comes joy. Yes—that, too, is what one would expect. Not mere absence of pain, but ecstasy."

"Almost all mature humans are aware of the thin line dividing the two—even if they can't understand what to make of it. If you wish, as part of your further education, I'll share some concepts of the Milieu essence that our philosophers and theologians debated."

"Yes. You must show me all that you can. Before you—go."

Elizabeth refused the gambit. "The psychology of each sentient race savors the theosphere in a unique way. We might study the possible niche that your people might occupy. And now that there are two of us, we can do what no single operant mind can do—partake together of the essence in a limited fashion. It will be dilute because the Mind of the Pliocene is still so infantile, but you'll find it wonderful."

"It is already wonderful," said Brede. "But the first thing I must do with my enriched newness is look once again along the lines of probability in search of the all-important pattern that was unclear. Will you join me?"

The teacher and sister vanished. Mental doors slammed. "I might have known! Brede, you're an incredible fool."

The exotic woman's mind was fully open but Elizabeth would not go in, would not look.

"I'm leaving your room without doors," Elizabeth said. "I'm going to find your King and tell him your judgment concerning my fate. Your new judgment. And I'm going to find the balloon, and in my own sweet time I'm going to leave this place."

Brede bowed her head. "I will give you your balloon. And if you wish, I will deal with the Host of Nontusvel. Please—let me go with you to the King."

"Very well."

The two of them went out and stood again briefly on the promontory above the White Silver Plain. The salt was crowded with miniature lights. As the time for the Grand Combat approached, the tent-city of the Firvulag grew. Even though it was the middle of the night, supply caravans flanked by rama linkmen could be farsensed as they crept down the slope south of the city toward the temporary encampment. Landing stages at the shore of the lagoon were illuminated and there were lights on the water as well.

Brede studied the scene, masked and inscrutable. "Only three weeks until the Grand Combat, and then it will be resolved."

"Three weeks," Elizabeth repeated, "and six million years."

7

AT THE TIME of the Grand Combat Truce, all roads in the northern regions of the Many-Colored Land led to Roniah. Through this city passed Tanu and Firvulag alike on their way to the games—the Great Ones of both exotic races traveling via riverboat while the humbler majority followed the Great South Road that paralleled the west bank of the Rhône all the way down to Lac Provençal and la Glissade Formidable.

Most of the travelers from northern regions broke their journey at the Roniah Fair. There the ancient enemies mingled freely in a once-a-year orgy of commerce that extended through the middle two weeks of the pre-Combat Truce, day and night without a letup. Booths were set up along the great pillared midway and among the surrounding exterior gardens of the river city. The peripheral area became a huge campground where human and Firvulag entrepreneurs presided over tented caravanserais and dining establishments catering to the tourists.

This year it was the Finiah refugees, well supplied with money but almost completely bereft of possessions, who were the most eager customers at the Fair. To bolster their spirits they spent lavishly for the luxury goods that were the stock-in-trade of Firvulag crafters: polished gems and amber, jewelry, novelties carved of ivory or semi-precious stone, gold and silver gewgaws, begemmed headdresses and garment trims, fancy tack for chalikos, ornate belts and scabbards and battle-harness, perfumes and unguents and scented soaps derived from wildflowers and herbs, peculiar liqueurs, psychoactive flycap and panaeolus fungi, and delicatessen such as wild honey, candies with alcoholic syrup centers, truffles, garlic, spices, gourmet sausages, and that paramount exotic delectable—wild strawberry preserves. More-staple goods were purveyed by human vendors from Roniah and the other Tanu settlements: fine textiles and readymade garments, dyestuffs and other domestic chemicals, glass tools of every description, glass tableware and containers, glass armor, and glass weapons. From the Tanu plantations flowed quantities of beer, wine, and spirits packaged in wooden casks or leather bottles, smoked and preserved meats, dried and pickled fruits and vegetables, and a wide variety of nonperishable cereal products such as flour, groats, and plain and flavored hard-breads. The food was not only sold to the travelers, but was also sent down the river to aid in the provisioning of the Grand Combat itself.

Late on October fourteenth a certain refugee party came riding down the crowded highroad and arrived at the Roniah Fair. It made its way into the private campground area where petty Tanu and Firvulag nobility could erect their own pavilions separate from the commonalty. The group of travelers was unique only in that it consisted entirely of humans. There were two gold-torc ladies who might have been mother and daughter—the elder wearing flowing emerald gauze robes and an outrageous jeweled chapeau, the younger in full blue coercer's armor and a golden cloak, bearing a lance from which floated a banner of gold with a raven displayed sable. The ladies' entourage consisted of five bronze-armored soldiers led by a captal of gigantic stature, an elderly steward, two handmaids, and a gnarled little one-legged wrangler, in whose presence the pack-chalikos and remounts seemed unaccountably skittish.

"Yes—we lost everything in the Finiah disaster," the grandam told the sympathetic human campmaster as they signed in. "All save a few treasures and these faithful gray-torc servants are gone, leaving my daughter and me sadly destitute. Still . . . there is the possibility that we may recoup our fortunes at the Combat, for the Lady Phyllis-Morigel has trained diligently and shows great promise as a warrior-maid, and so we may gain both riches and revenge at the White Silver Plain, if Tana wills."

The campmaster saluted respectfully. The lovely young face of the Lady Phyllis-Morigel smiled at him beneath the raised visor of her helmet. "Good fortune will surely attend you in the lists, Lady. I can feel your mighty coercive power even though you've got it leashed back."

"Phyllis, dear," the old woman chided. "For shame."

The girl blinked and the wave of coercion receded. "Your pardon, Worthy Campmaster. I didn't mean to press you. This will be my first Combat and I'm overexcited."

"Small wonder," said the man. "But don't you worry, little Lady. Just keep cool and you'll come out a sure winner in the prelims. I've got a feeling about you."

"You're kind to say so, Campmaster. I feel that I've been waiting all my life to participate in the games . . ."

"Ladies, it's late," interrupted the old steward, who had been fidgeting in the saddle during the chitchat. "You must rest."

"Master Claudius is right," said the huge captal of the guard. "Tell us our allotted space, Campmaster, so that we can rest our bones. We've been on the trail six days and we're worn out."

"Six days," tsk'd the campmaster. "Then you weren't with the refugee group that was sheltered at Castle Gateway?"

Hastily, the captal said, "We were too late to join the train led by Lord Velteyn. There is great confusion still in the northland."

The campmaster studied a board-map. "Most of your fellow citizens from Finiah who are still here are camped in the riverfront spaces, which are the most attractive sites that we have. I can place you down there for only a slight surcharge—"

The old woman was firm. "Much as we would like to join our compatriots, it is necessary that we economize so that we will not run short of funds at the Combat itself. Furthermore, we should be embarrassed among our friends because we are unable to reciprocate any entertainment they might offer us. Therefore, good Campmaster, indicate to us a modest place sufficient for our two tents and the picketing of our animals. One would prefer high ground, if this is available."

Slightly disappointed, the man restudied his board. "Well, there's Number 478 on the northern edge of Section E. High and breezy—but you'll have to carry water."

"It will do splendidly. My noble daughter will bring us water by virtue of her psychokinetic power. The fee? Ah. Ça y est. And now we bid you good night."

The man took the coins and threw a shrewd glance at the warrior-maid. "So you have PK, too—eh, Lady Phyllis? Now I'm positive you'll do well in the lists! I'll watch for you and risk a few bob. As a rookie, you should get nice long-shot odds. Yes, indeed!" He waved a cordial farewell as the party rode down the lamp-bordered lane into the hurly-burly of the crowded campground.

"You dummy, Felice," said Chief Burke. "What's the idea letting loose your coercion? Now that man's going to remember you."

She gave a light laugh. "He'd remember us anyway, Peo. At least now he knows I'm a genuine gold. You should have seen your face when that guy suggested we camp next to the Finiah crowd!"

"This is our worst danger," Madame said. "Felice and I may easily delude any torced persons by pretending to be half-deranged with grief because of our misfortunes. But the rest of you, with your sundered gray torcs, are sure to be detected as interlopers if Tanu or torc-wearing humans attempt to communicate with you mentally. You must stay close to Felice and me at all times so that we may intercept and turn aside any telepathic importunities. The purchase of supplies and forage must be undertaken tonight by Fitharn. Unless he is deliberately probed by a powerful metapractitioner, he will be above suspicion."

"I still think it's risky camping in here," said Vanda-Jo.

"We've been over that," Burke said. "This far south, it would be suspicious if we tried to camp anywhere else."

"No more Firvulag tumuli to shelter in down here, missy," Fitharn said. "The Little Folk in these parts don't dare have large settlements, the way we do up north. Only single-family burrows for the most part, well-hidden in the wildest regions far from the trails. Folks around here are leery of strangers—even ones that come recommended by King Yeochee."

"We have already had hints," remarked Madame with some tartness, "that the royal authority becomes exiguous in the hinterlands."

Fitharn grinned. "Our King's sovereignty is a little less formal than old Thagdal's. We've an elected monarchy, you know. But we Firvulag are loyal in our fashion. And unlike some other people I could mention, we'd never stoop to using a deposed ruler as a life-offering."

The party came into a region where the tents and campfires were more widely spaced. There were large rock outcroppings and fewer trees and the lamp-bordered trail led increasingly uphill. That they traversed the low-rent district was obvious from the small number of chalikos and hellads that were pegged out among the campsites. The shelters were mostly black Firvulag tents or the motley lodgings of elderly Tanu bachelors. Unlike the noisy conviviality of the central area, this part of the campground was somnolent except for the calling of insects and snorts and grumbles from domestic animals.

Fitharn said, "Here's 478. Nice and secluded." He, of course, could see in the dark better than the humans could see by daylight. Hopping easily on his pegleg, he went up the rocks that hemmed the space on three sides and ascertained that the adjoining sites were empty. "Our closest neighbors are Firvulag, Madame. Looks like a perfect spot. I'll hobble the beasts for unloading and take a pair of remounts to the Fair for supplies right away."

Felice swung down from the saddle of her tall steed. "And I'll set up the tents." She came over to Amerie's mount and smiled up at the nun, who, like Vanda-Jo, was disguised in the blue-and-yellow-striped robes of a gray-torc serving woman. "Still feeling creaky? Let me help you."

Amerie was levitated out of the saddle and floated gently to earth.

"You're learning how, all right," the nun observed.

"Oh, yes. By the time we reach Muriah, I should have it pretty well figured out."

"How about Madame and me?" Vanda-Jo was letting her irritation show. "And poor old Claude and Khalid could use a leg down, too."

The athlete bent her psychokinetic power to the unseating of the others. Then, as Peo and Basil and Gert and Hansi unloaded the pack-animals, the girl erected the two Tanu-style tents, with their telescoping poles and guy-lines, simply by putting her mind to it. Another mental exercise brought waters streaming through the air from the Rhône, which lay nearly half a kilometer away, into three large decamole tubs that the men had set inflated and ready. An entire deadwood tree, plucked from the cliffs behind the camp, came sailing down and landed without a sound at the edge of the site.

"Now comes the dicey part," Felice said, concentrating. "My creativity isn't under control yet, so everybody stand back while I blast the tree into firewood. I hope! If I bobble it, we'll end up with charcoal or ashes, so cross your fingers."

Zap.

"Oh, well done," said Basil. "Split her right down the middle. Now off with the branches, my dear."

Zap zap zap. Pammedy-pow-pow-pow.

"Slice 'er like bratwurst!" Uwe urged. The girl's small-scale mental lightning flared again and again, cutting the tree into convenient billets. When the pile of wood lay there, steaming gently, most of the party applauded.

Madame said, "One can perceive that your three primary metafunctions are developing to a formidable degree, ma petite. You will exercise prudence, will you not?"

"Haven't I behaved myself on the trip from Hidden Springs?" Felice inquired reproachfully. "Don't worry. I won't go wandering away to show off. I want to see these Tanu bastards screwed just as much as you do, Madame. I won't jeopardize the plan."

The old woman looked exhausted, but she said with determination, "C'est bien. Then let us have a small council of war before our good friend Fitharn returns. The time has come for important decision making."

"We can gather round the campfire," said Felice.

A dozen stool-sized rocks came flying through the darkness and formed a circle. Pieces of wood arranged themselves into a cone and ignited when a glowing ball of psychoenergy materialized beneath them. Within perhaps ten seconds, the fire was ablaze. The conspirators sat down on the rock seats and began divesting themselves of armor and other superfluous gear.

"We have arrived," Madame said, "at a critical point in our enterprise. The usefulness of Fitharn and his Firvulag confrères is virtually at an end, since they will not violate the Truce by participating directly in any attack upon the Tanu. We, of course, have no such scruples. We Lowlives are ever outlaws, protected by no Truce. We know what we may expect if we should be captured. Nevertheless, the exotic enemy will not expect us to strike again so soon after Finiah. Tanu intelligence is doubtless aware that most of our irregulars have dispersed. They will expect us to consolidate our position in the north—which we are doing, of course—but they can scarcely dream that we would be so bold as to move against them in the south, on their own home ground."

Chief Burke said, "The presence of Tanu refugees has worked in our favor. There are so many ill-equipped exotics on the road that our group, dressed in the stuff Felice liberated at Finiah, attracts no particular attention."

"Things have progressed smoothly thus far," Madame agreed. "But now begins the most dangerous part of the operation. The new moon is on the twentieth, six days from now. This is also the last day of the Roniah Fair, after which there will be an emptying of this campground as the exotic people hurry on to the White Silver Plain. It is my belief that the torc factory strike-force should embark at once for Muriah via riverboat. It is possible to make the trip in less than four days—perhaps only three—if a skilled skipper is obtained and one can conjure up psychokinetic winds."

"We'll find us a good boatman," said Felice, peeling off her sapphire shell. "And he'll do exactly as we say, once Khalid puts the chisel to his gray torc."

"You're sure you'd rather not try to mind-bend him?" the metalsmith asked Felice.

"I'm still too clumsy to work through the torcs. If he fought me, I could accidentally kill him. Don't worry—I'll be able to tame him barenecked."

Madame continued. "We may hope that you will arrive in Muriah around the dark of the moon, obtain the assistance of Aiken Drum if possible, and mount your attack at a suitable time. Let us say, early on the twenty-second. In the small hours of the morning. And at dawn, I myself will put the message through the time-portal."

There was an uncomfortable silence.

"So you're still determined to make the grand gesture," Claude said.

The firelight showed Madame's face tightened into its most obstinate expression. "We have been over this. There are only two of us capable of approaching the time-gate under the cloak of invisibility—and Felice would be wasted in the Castle Gateway operation. Her great talents can best be used in the southern thrust, while my more meager ones are quite adequate for the castle action."

"You'll have to wait around here for a week," Claude said. "What if you come down with another pneumonia attack?"

"Amerie has given me medicines."

"So you'll just stroll up to the time-gate and toss the amber inside!"

"Au juste."

"Velteyn is still at Castle Gateway coping with his refugees," Chief Burke warned. "He may not go south until the last minute. We know that he has no difficulty seeing through your illusions. You may be able to approach the gate without being detected—but I doubt that your creative metafunction would be able to operate within the taufield itself. Once you throw the message carrier inside, it will become visible to the guardians and soldiers standing nearby. They'll sound the alarm."

Claude added, "And Velteyn or some other high-powered Tanu

will come running and melt your personal invisibility screen like the snows of yesteryear."

"I will have accomplished my task," the old woman said.

"And died!" Claude exploded. "But it's not necessary, Angélique! I've thought of another way." And he told them.

Uwe nodded his bearded head. "That just might march, Claude. You should be able to do the necessary work without difficulty, and it would solve the problem of finding a place for Madame to hide out as well. And you'd be a backup for her in case—"

Claude broke in. "You guys don't need me down south. I'd be a nuisance—I admit it. But up here, I can be an asset."

"We know your motives, all right," Felice said. "Chivalrous old poop."

Madame glanced around the circle, then made a small gesture of resignation. "We will revise the castle action as Claude has recommended, then. At dawn on the twenty-second, when we two make our attempt against the time-gate, the rest of you will already have accomplished the assault on the torc factory."

"Sit deus nobis," muttered the nun.

Chief Burke said, "Our iron will be a secret weapon in any hand-to-hand fighting with the Tanu, but it will have no special advantage over human enemies—especially gold-torcs. We have only two weapons with really large destructive potential for the blasting of the Coercer Guild stronghold. There's Felice's psychozap—which may or may not be powerful enough to do the job—and the Spear."

"Which is nothing but a pretty glass clothespole," Khalid reminded them, "unless we get Aiken Drum to help us recharge it . . . How about it, Felice? Do you think your energy projection will build up strong enough to break down thick masonry and bronze doors?"

"As of now, I doubt it," the girl said. "I get better every day, but we'd damn well better not plan on that kind of attack. But, listen—as I understand it, our primary target isn't the whole headquarters building but just the factory part. Wouldn't those torc components be delicate little gadgets? Could be, all we'll have to do is bring the roof down on 'em and it's bye-bye, baby! Vanda-Jo could tell by looking at the building just what spots I'd have to hit. Right?"

"I might be able to," said the Public Works Chief, but her tone betrayed doubt.

"I've seen that place," Khalid said. "It doesn't look anything like the fairytale towers of Finiah did. It's a bloody great cube of marble and bronze about as vulnerable as the Polity Bank in Zürich! Unless Felice checks out as a mountain mover by next week, she's going to find it a helluva tough zap."

The little athlete had removed almost all of her glass armor and its padding and sat on her rock attired only in a white chemise and a pair of sollerets with golden spurs. She swung her blue-shod feet. Reflections from the gemmed plates of the footgear danced over her delicate face. "I don't know what I'll be capable of next week. But whatever I've got, I'll lay all over those Tanu friggers."

"You will follow Peo's orders, child," Madame said sharply.

"Oh, yes." Felice's eyes were wide.

Basil said, "Whatever Felice's eventual firepower, our best chance of success still lies in the photon weapon. If we can recharge the Spear, we might even demolish the Coercer Guild complex from a distance with a minimum of hazard to our party. We could do it from out in the lagoon, couldn't we, Khalid?"

"The building is on the northern edge of the city, west of the place where the main rollerway comes up from the docks. One wall of the keep structure is flush with the escarpment. There's a sheer drop of maybe a hundred meters on that side of the peninsula, then a klom or so of dunes and carved-up sediments before the shore of the Catalan Gulf . . . What do you think, Claude? You fired the damn thing."

The paleontologist said, "With a steady platform for the shot, you could zap the building to kingdom come. Or even shoot the cliff out from under it."

Amerie's voice was low. "If we do it in the wee hours of the morning, perhaps the casualties will be minimal."

"Getting cold feet, Sister?" the big Native American inquired. "This is war. If you're squeamish, you'd better stay with Madame and Claude."

The old woman's face was troubled. "It might be best, ma Soeur."

"No!" said Felice. "You agreed to help where you were needed most, Amerie. And that's with us. We can't risk another stupid disaster like Peo's pig screwing up the assault. This time, the doctor goes along."

"I'll do my best," the nun insisted. "I told you that I would. Just settle on a plan and I'll follow it."

"Let me suggest," Basil said, "that we rethink the role of Aiken Drum. Is it really necessary for us to wait until we reach Muriah before contacting him to enlist his help?"

The rest of them looked at the climber, not understanding.

"We might try to farspeak him from *here*," Basil explained. "Let the young man know we're coming. Insure that he's there waiting for us. Perhaps even present the problem of the Spear to him so that he can be thinking about it in advance of our arrival." Madame began to protest, but Basil held up a tactful hand. "I know that Madame Guderian has doubts about her ability to farspeak over great distances—as well as farspeaking on the intimate mode. But it's occurred to me that we might utilize your other friend, Elizabeth, in a telepathic relay."

"Say!" Claude exclaimed.

"You did tell us, Madame, that you perceived Elizabeth's far-speech shortly after Group Green arrived in the Pliocene. Surely by now the woman's faculties must have recuperated to the extent that she could receive your own transmission on—er—tight beam, even if it were a bit wavery, so to speak."

Madame said, "I doubt that I have the competence. Elizabeth's thought flickered past me in an instant. I did not—how shall I say it? —store the data of her mental signature."

Felice jumped to her feet. "I could help you, Madame! We wouldn't have to farspeak Elizabeth on the intimate mode to get her attention. A simple shout at top volume on the human command mode would do it. All Elizabeth needs to know is that we're out here hollering. Her seekersense could surely zero in on us and then pick up Madame's weakie-squeakie on the very narrow focus."

The old woman frowned at the eager girl. "Other minds might be equally capable of tracking down the source of our telepathic loud-hail."

"Not if we handle it my way!" Felice exulted. "What we do—early tomorrow we synchronize timepieces and I go ten or twenty kloms back up the North Road. *Then* we simulcast at predetermined intervals! If we farspeak that way, the Tanu can't possibly get an ac-curate fix on the double shout. But an operant like Elizabeth shouldn't have any trouble sorting the mental patterns of the two of us and tracking Madame when she throttles back to the intimate mode."

"It could work," Amerie said.

Chief Burke growled, "None of this makes much sense to a poor old redskin shyster like me. But let's try it."

"It sounds medium crafty," Khalid said, "provided Felice and

Madame can mesh brains . . . and provided this Aiken Drum can be trusted with our precious petards."

"You're crazy if you tell him the whole plan," Claude said.

"Why must you always be so cynical, Claude?" Amerie complained.

The old man sighed. "Maybe because I've lived so long. Maybe I've lived so long because."

"Claude," Madame asked, "would you trust Elizabeth's judgment in this matter?"

"Absolutely."

"Then it is simple. Tonight we rest, tomorrow we attempt the communication. If we make contact, we will request Elizabeth's own assessment of the character of Aiken Drum and proceed as she advises. D'accord?"

Her dark glance flashed around the circle. The other ten members of the expedition nodded.

"That's settled," said Chief Burke. "You leave at dawn, Felice, and we'll schedule the big broadcast for noon. You dress up in your armor and all and take Basil and Uwe and Khalid as your gray-torc escort. Any Tanu get nosy, you're just looking for your Uncle Max among the refugees. While you're putting some distance between us, Madame and the rest of us odds and sods can go down to the Roniah wharf and scout out a suitable boat. Gert and Hansi know the kind of vessel we'll need."

"Don't be late getting back to camp," Felice cautioned them. "And try to get some more blue lacquer at the Fair. The stuff that Old Man Kawai used to coat the Spear is starting to peel off."

They relaxed then, and as the midnight moon came up over the Rhône, Fitharn the Firvulag returned with forage and fresh food. Madame took the gnomish little exotic aside and told him such of their plans as seemed expedient.

"So you see," she concluded, "that in a few hours most of our people will be embarked upon the river, while Claude and I conceal ourselves near Castle Gateway and await the day when we shall deal our double blow against the Tanu slavemasters. And now you are free to leave us, my friend. Take with you the profound gratitude of our company . . . and of all free humanity. Tell King Yeochee what we hope to do. And bid him for me—farewell."

The little man squirmed within her mental clasp, crushing his pointed red hat between his hands. His alien consciousness, so hard to read even when the screens were down, was now all but walled off. The images that flickered through the near-opacity were colored with conflicting emotions.

"You are troubled," Madame said softly.

"Angélique . . ." The gnome's words and thoughts made a jumble: fear love loyalty mistrust hope doubt pain.

"Dear little friend, what is it?"

"Warn your people!" Fitharn burst out. "Tell them to trust no being too far! Even if they are successful, tell them to remember my warning!"

His face looked up at hers for one last instant. Then he disappeared into the night.

8

THE GOLD-TORC LADY and her steward hovered before the Firvulag jeweler's display while the rest of their retinue, guards and serving women, prevented the fairground multitude from pressing too close.

"I wonder if this one is suitable, Claudius?" the woman asked. "Or is it perhaps so large as to be vulgar?"

The old gray-torc looked with disdain upon the amber paperweight that the jeweler's assistant proffered on a velvet cushion. "It has," the steward declared, "*bugs* in it."

"But they are part of the originality of the piece!" the jeweler protested. "Caught at the moment of their ancient mating hundreds of millions of years ago! The two insects, male and female, united in their nuptial embrace forever within this glowing gem! Is it not poignant, Exalted Lady? Does it not touch your heart?"

The lady peeped askance at her steward. "Do you find it touching, mon vieux?"

The jeweler waxed rapturous. "It comes from the darkest depths of Fennoscandia, from the Black Lake's haunted shores! We Firvulag do not dare to harvest this amber, my Lady. We obtain it"—he paused dramatically—"from *Howlers!*"

"Tana have mercy!" the gold-torc lady whispered, eyes wide. "So you really do trade with the wild ones! Tell me, good jeweler . . . are the Howlers really as hideous to the eye as rumor has it?"

"To see one," the artisan assured her, keeping a solemn face, "is to go mad."

The lady bent a satirical eye upon her silver-haired servitor. "I have suspected as much. Ah, yes."

The jeweler's assistant ventured to remark, "Some persons believe that this year—because of the unrest y'see—the Howlers have even dared to come south!"

The lady squealed in alarm.

Her captal, a huge man with a face like seamed cordovan, slapped his sword hilt. "Now then, Foeman! Beware how you attempt to frighten our noble mistress!"

"Oh, Galucholl is quite right, brave Captal," the jeweler made quick to say. "And let me assure you that we of the True Folk are quite as alarmed about the matter as you. Té only knows what the ugly devils want. But we shall be alert lest they come slinking among us during the games."

The woman shivered in delicious dread. "How exciting! How terrible! We will purchase the amber, jeweler. I am not taken with the doomed insect lovers. Pay him, Claudius."

Grumbling, the steward took coins from his belt wallet. Then his eye fell upon a tray of rings and he began to smile. "We'll take two of those as well, I think. Wrap them up."

"But, sir!" protested the Firvulag. "The carved-jet rings have a certain symbolic significance that you may not be aware—"

The old man's icy green eyes blazed under their white brows. "I said, we'll take them! Now get those fornicating termites under wraps and be quick about it. We're going to be late for an appointment!"

"Yes, yes, right away, Worthy Master. Get a move on, Galucholl, you young lout!" The jeweler bowed to Madame Guderian as he handed the soft pouch to the steward. "Good fortune attend you, Exalted Lady, and may you enjoy your purchases."

The old gray-torc laughed. In a manner overly presumptuous for one of his status, he took the woman by one elbow and signaled for the escort to close in around their mistress.

When the customers had disappeared into the crowd, Galucholl said, "Well, he *could* have been buying the rings for someone else."

The artisan gave a laugh that bespoke long experience. "Oh, my boy. What an innocent you are."

* * *

Gert stuck his sandy head and one arm into the tent. "Here y'go, Madame. All sliced neatly in half. Didn't even disturb the poor bugs."

"Thank you, my son. Claude and I will finish the work. Since it is almost noon, you and the others had best take your positions on the high rocks around our campsite. At the slightest sign of alarm you must notify me so that I can cease the transmission."

"Right you are, Madame." The head vanished.

"Here's the message." Claude held out the ceramic wafer. "Just like yours, but with my signature. You have the cement?"

She bent over the pieces of amber that lay on the decamole table. "Voilà," she said at last. "It is ready. One for you to carry and one for me, par mesure de sécurité. I shall keep the one with the pathetic termites, even though you have signed it. It is fitting."

The two of them considered the message carriers. Shining through the reddish-gold fossilized resin were the words of the sandwiched wafers:

PLIOCENE EUROPE UNDER CONTROL OF MALIGN EXOTIC RACE. CLOSE TIME-GATE FOR THE LOVE OF GOD. IGNORE ANY SUBSEQUENT MESSAGES TO CONTRARY.

"Will they believe us, do you suppose?" she asked.

"They can check our signatures easily enough. And, as you said, two witnesses are better than one. Nobody'd ever suspect a straight old lace like me of pulling a hoax."

They sat together, saying nothing. It was very hot in the closed tent. She brushed a lock of graying hair back from her brow. A rivulet of sweat trickled in front of one ear.

"You are a fool, you know," she said finally.

"Polacks are suckers for bossy women. You should have known Gen! Sector chiefs were known to flinch like whipped curs before her black wrath. Besides, I'm too old-fashioned to compromise myself with a piece like you, hiding in a trapdoor-spider burrow for a week with my poor old nuts singing the 'Marseillaise' while the rest of my equipment tries not to stand at attention."

"Quel homme! C'est incroyable!"

"Not for Polacks." He consulted his watch. "Fifteen seconds until noon. On your mark, old woman."

* * *

Elizabeth and Dionket the Lord Healer looked down on the black-torc child in its cot. A fullblooded Tanu, it seemed to the human woman to be older than its actual age of three years—not only because of the longer limbs, but also in the overglaze of suffering on its still-beautiful face.

The child was naked except for a towel laid over its loins. A water mattress supported the swollen body as comfortably as was possible in this tankless medical technology. The child's skin was a dark red; peripheral body parts such as digits, ears, nose, and lips were almost black with congestion. Beneath the small golden torc, the neck was blistered, clotted with some white salve applied in a futile attempt at soothing. Elizabeth slid into the ruined infant mind. Livid eyelids opened, showing fully dilated pupils.

Dionket said, "Removing the torc would only make him worse. Then there would be convulsions as well. Note the degeneration of the neural linkages between the cerebellum and the limbic areas, the anomalous circuits from the torc to the premotor cortex, the chaotic firing within the amygdala that has frustrated our own attempts at analgesia. Onset of the syndrome is typically abrupt—five days ago in the case of this boy. Death will ensue within approximately three weeks."

Elizabeth rested one hand upon the hot blond curls.

Ah baby there baby lie easy poorlambie let me see let me in to look to help ah there the relentless conduits between gold and charged flesh where misery ramps to and fro poor baby . . . ah. See. I quench it sever the controlinterface between highbrain and low admitting peace so rest now wait now and sleep until they come bright to carry thee away poor baby matured at last in the light.

The small eyes closed. The body relaxed into flaccidity.

Elizabeth you have removed his pain Tanabethanked.

Refusing as always to meet his mind, she turned away from the cot. "He will still die. I can bring no cure, only relief until the end."

But if you stayed longer if you experimented . . .

"I must go."

You could have gone but you have not. Shall I tell you why you have stayed with us even though your balloon waits for you in the room without doors?

"I have stayed to teach Brede, as I promised." Nothing—no shred of empathy passed her mental screen. But Dionket Lord Healer was old, and there are other ways of reading souls.

You have stayed with us in spite of your professed disdain in spite of your selfish self because you have been touched . . .

"Of course I've been touched! And repelled! And I *will* go away. Now—shall we continue to waste time in futile sparring, or shall we see whether I can help you with these wretched babies?"

Elizabeth Brede is so close to understanding her vision if you would only help her to interpret—

"Brede is a spider! The Host of Nontusvel warned me of that. At least they're honest barbarians, making no bones about their antagonism. But Brede weaves metapsychic webs and I say to hell with her!" The spill of bitterness was swiftly reconfined. "Shall we get on with it, or not? And speak out loud to me, please, Lord Healer."

He sighed. "I'm sorry. Brede—and all of us—have only sought to keep you with us because of our great need. We have not given proper consideration to *your* need. Forgive us, Elizabeth."

She smiled. "Of course. Now tell me what percentage of your Tanu children are afflicted with this terrible thing?"

"Seven. The syndrome that we call 'black torc' may appear among purebloods at any age up until the approximate onset of puberty, after which the adaptation to the torc is presumably in homeostasis. Most of the cases are under four years of age. With the hybrids, there is never a danger of black torc, only of the incompatibility dysfunctions that pureblood humans may experience when wearing the device. Severe though the dysfunctions may be, with careful redactive treatment they can usually be remitted. But we have been powerless to help these black-torc children . . . until now. Your execution of the erasures and cutoff was astounding! You of the Milieu are advanced far beyond us in deep redaction. Even if you will not stay—may I hope that you will at least relieve the rest of these suffering little ones before you leave us?"

O yes? Immerse in more innocent agony breast more wailing dumb endurance so use so useless unchanneled unproductive evil rending of me and it poor babies why so ungodly why these everbedamned torcs?

It is our way Elizabeth the only way we know how could we turn away from even this simulacrum of operancy once knowing it could you?

Their massive egos confronted one another, naked in power for the most fleeting instant before veiling. But she had looked down on

Dionket the Healer in her mightiness, and he had abased himself and entreated and offered—what was it he offered?—and he had shown her how many others there were like him.

Tears started to Elizabeth's eyes. She would have lashed out, but she knew that this man at least was no manipulator. And so her response was gentle.

"I can't play the role you ask of me, Dionket. My reasons are complex and personal, but there are practical considerations that I will point out to you. The Host of Nontusvel still means to kill me, even though they know that Gomnol's scheme of mating me with the King has been forbidden by Brede. The Host is even more worried now that I might bear children by Aiken Drum—or team up with him somehow during the Grand Combat! You know me well enough by now to see the impossibility of either notion. But the Host think only of their dynasty. Right now, they're too distracted by Combat preparations to mount more than an occasional attack on me, but I'm still not safe sleeping anywhere but in Brede's room without doors. You and your faction could never protect me from Nodonn and a massed thrust coordinated by him. When I'm sleeping, I'm vulnerable. And they're determined. I won't live the rest of my days imprisoned in Brede's house or fending off mindbolts from that pack of mental savages."

"We are trying to change the old pitiless ways!" Dionket cried. "You could help us in our struggle against the Host!"

"My mind-set is wholly nonaggressive. As you know. Bring about your great changes first and *then* ask me to help."

"As Tana wills," he said, resigned. "When do you depart from us?"

"Soon," she said, looking down again at the sleeping child. "I'll take care of all the rest of these black-torc children for you while you and your best people observe. You may be able to learn the program."

"We will be deeply grateful for your guidance . . . And now, if you will agree, we will leave this chamber of mind-hurt for a time. Even though you screen it away, I know that you are diminished by contact with the black-torcs. We will go to the terrace, beyond reach of their pathetic aura."

The towering form in red and white walked from the ward into cool stone corridors, past screens of marble filigree and onto a great garden balcony. There was a stupendous view of Muriah from up here on the Mount of Heroes, and they could see a long stretch of the Aven Peninsula, the saltflats, and the lagoons all spread below in the clean loud scorch of the noon sun. The crying of the pain-filled young minds was blotted out in the solar emanation. The light so dazzled Elizabeth that she faltered, momentarily blinded—

—and perceived the call.

Elizabeth Orme Farspeaker respond.

Dionket said something solicitous. Taking her arm, he guided her into a shaded corner where there were wicker chairs.

Elizabeth! Elizabeth!

So faint, so garbled, so human, but who?

"Your experience with our poor little ones has affected you, my dear. It's no wonder. Sit here and I'll fetch a restorative."

Could Dionket have heard? But no. It was on the uniquely human mode and almost beyond her own perception, much less his.

"Just—something to drink," she said. "Anything cold."

"Of course. I'll return immediately."

Elizabeth!

Whoyou whereyou I Elizabeth respond.

Me/us! Felice/AngéliqueGuderian! ThankGoditworked O damn quick losing mindmeld t u n e nar r o w An gél i . . .

I have you Madame Guderian.

Grâceàdieu we were soafraid we called solong noresponse listen we are someofus coming to you sabotage torcworks require help Aiken-Drum if trustworthy do you think can you vouch?

Aiken?

Yesyes himalone le petit farceur! Ifonly wecantrustOlisten this how thisway it is . . .

Elizabeth listened in astonishment to the faint babbling thoughts inexpertly squirting data, smearing a crazy quilt of mind-pictures and clumsy subvocalizations, the whole so clogged with anxiety, so wavering and distant that only a Master could have made sense out of it. What an incredibly bold plan! But these human rebels had already accomplished the incredible at Finiah, hadn't they? This scheme, too, might succeed. But—Aiken Drum? What could she tell them about him, his mind now impervious even to her, doubtless of masterclass potential, perhaps even gone fully operant by now. What could she tell them about the laughing little nonborn chosen of Mayvar Kingmaker?

Brede?

Elizabeth I hear.

Prognosticate. (DATA)
  Do it.
Harmless?
  Never that nohuman is.
Harmless forbest myfriends humanity atlarge?
  (Irony.) Longview affirm falsealoof Elizabeth.
Damn you . . .

Madame Guderian?
Yes Elizabeth.
I will relay your request to Aiken Drum without telling him more than he needs to know about your plan of action. I believe it to be in humanity's longterm best interest to include him in your scheme. But there may be shortterm danger. Be wary. I will continue to do what I can for you for as long as I can.

Othankyoumerci butit will be dangerous pourl'amour dedieu be withus Elizabeth we cannot/mustnot fail (fear guilt hope). Elizabeth?

Be at peace Angélique Guderian. And all of you my friends . . .

"Here now!" Dionket proffered a tray. "Cold orange juice should be the very thing to restore you. Vitamin C, potassium, and many other good things in this splendid Earth fruit."

Elizabeth smiled and accepted the crystal tumbler. The faraway mental voice had disappeared amid the bedlam of other thought waves.

* * *

Seized by uncontrollable laughter, Stein fetched his companion a herculean whack on the back. The small figure dressed in gold stood as firmly as a metal statue.

"Aiken . . . kid! Isn't that the damnedest absofuckinlutely *greatest* news you ever heard in your life? They're coming! Our good ole Group Green pals are coming with their pockets full of iron and a friggerty big zapper that we can blast the chickenshit Tanu into orbit with! *And they can cut off our torcs!* Sukey and me can be free! All of the humans who don't want to wear these things can be free! Would you believe it?"

Aiken Drum smiled his golliwog smile. "That's what Elizabeth says."

The two of them were on a balcony of Mayvar's apartment in the Hall of Farsensors. Their interrupted lunch lay uneaten on the table before them. The high hot sun shone upon the holiday-decked capital city, aswarm with Tanu and human visitors. Out on the shimmering White Silver Plain to the south, thousands of small black Firvulag tents spread in serried ranks, together with larger pavilions of ochre and rusty red and other earthen hues that sheltered the nobility of the Little People. Great bleachers with awnings colored scarlet and blue and purple and rosy gold were being completed on both sides of the great Field of Lists where the sporting contests were to be held prior to the blood events of the Combat proper.

Stein, bareheaded and wearing only a lightweight tunic, clutched his cup of iced mead so firmly that the silver threatened to buckle. "How about it, kid? Do you really think you can recharge that photon cannon thing they're bringing?"

"Can't say for sure until I eyeball her, Steinie. But if it's just a matter of figuring how to open a fewkin' powerpack like Madame said, it should be el cincho to a genius like Me."

"Hot damn!" The giant tossed his drink off and slammed the goblet onto the table. "I'm sure as hell gettin' in on the blanket party for the torc works! Think they might let me do the zapping? There's nobody can teach this boy any tricks in how to handle light-blasters . . . or were you figuring to join the zorch yourself?"

Aiken's grin became bemused. He took a daisylike flower from the table centerpiece and started to pick off the petals. "Who, me? Strike a blow for human freedom and the destruction of the Tanu kingdom? Me use the Spear of Lugonn? Pissy patoot, my man! I probably couldn't even lift the fewkin' thing." He dropped petals into the congealed gravy on his plate. "You know, Steinie, that Spear—the zapper, I mean—is really a sacred thing to these exotic folks. Humans using it in war has caused the biggest stink since the Tanu first came to Earth a thousand years ago. The Spear was one of two photon weapons the exotics brought here from their home galaxy for ceremonial fights between great heroes. The second one is smaller, called the Sword of Sharn. Used to belong to an old Firvulag warlord. Now it's only used as a championship trophy in their Grand Combat. Nodonn's got it."

Stein smote the table. "We'll show *that* bastard! We'll show the whole bunch of 'em! No more human slaves. No more filthy breeding schemes. Without a steady supply of torcs, this whole goddam Tanu setup is gonna fall apart!"

Aiken inspected the shredded blossom with comic dismay. "Sure seems like that's what would happen . . . Poor li'l flower. All ruined."

Stein shoved back his chair. "Let's go tell Sukey! She's been worrying her heart out, hiding away there in Redact House."

"Maybe we better hold off on that," Aiken said casually. "You know. The fewer who know a secret . . ."

"She'd never tell."

"Not willingly." Aiken did not look at Stein. "She's safe where Dionket and Creyn put her. But there are other redactors—unfriendly ones—floating around that place, too. If Sukey's thoughts just happened to drift a little one day, a really top digger like Culluket Prettyface might get wind of our little conspiracy. All Sukey would have to do is imagine the Spear. Conjure up an image of you shooting it, for instance."

Stein was stricken. "Sweet Jesus, Aiken! Can't we bring her over here with us?"

"I couldn't cover her the way the friendly redactors can. She'll have to stay there until the northerners get here with their iron chisel. Then I can cut off her torc, and yours, too, and you can sail away into the sunrise just like I promised. I gotta confess, kiddo—until we got this crazy flash from Elizabeth and Madame, I didn't have the least fewkin' idea how I was gonna carry out my promise to you two. But with your torcs off so you guys are out of the Tanu mindnet, so to speak, it won't be that hard."

"Can't get this thing off fast enough for me." Stein gave a futile tug at his own gray collar. "Lately, just in the last week, like, I been getting these screwy feelings. And it's this torc, kid! I know it is. I'll be doing nothin' special and all of a sudden an ordinary thing like a shadow makes me jump like a goosed moose. Or I'll feel like the worst goddam monster in the world is right behind me, reachin' out. And I dassn't turn around and look, because that's all that keeps it from jumpin' me . . ."

"Don't sweat it," the trickster said. "Four, five days, you'll be bareneck and free as a bird and on your way to the Spaghetti Islands with your lady."

Stein gripped the arms of the little man in gold. "And you, too, right, Aiken?"

"Aw." The mischief-maker's eyes slid away. "*I* was having fun here in King Arthur's Court. And the Combat's nearly here. I think

I might just be able to take some of these turdlings. Win myself a fair lady or a spare kingdom or something."

Stein roared with laughter. "And end up with stir-fried brains! You can have your kingdom, sweetheart. What's left of it when me and Madame's gang get finished!" He started for the balcony doors. "I'm going to Sukey. I won't say a word about the zapper. Just tell her things are looking up. Okay?"

Aiken held up the mangled stem of the daisy. Slowly, it straightened. The bruised disc plumped and restored itself. Lavender ray-florets sprang out anew, crisp and perfect.

"And we thought you were a goner, li'l flower!" Aiken chortled. "It just goes to show—don't jump to conclusions!"

Rising off the ground, he tucked the flower behind Stein's ear. Then he returned to the normal mode of human locomotion and strutted away, whistling "Over the Sea to Skye."

* * *

They did it around the campfire at nightfall, since it had been decided that the two old people would have to leave Roniah and go into hiding that night, with the rest of the party embarking for the south at dawn on the morrow.

"It's appropriate," Amerie said when they were all together, "that the traditional Introit for this service should be King David's prayer for victory. It can serve for all of us as well as for Claude and Angélique:

> May the Lord send you help from his holy place
> and defend you from Mount Zion!
> May he grant you your heart's desire
> and make all your plans succeed!

Now repeat after me: 'I, Angélique, take thee, Claude . . .'"

9

Lord Greg-Donnet came scampering into the computer room of Creation House as Bryan and Ogmol were feeding in the very last of the data. His turquoise tailcoat was fresh and clean and he had a huge white rose in his buttonhole.

"I've been looking all over for you to tell you the news! And then Katlinel said you were in here, so I hurried as fast as—" He broke off as he caught sight of the dog-eared notebooks and storage-plaques that Bryan was packing away into his wicker portfolio. "The *survey*? Don't tell me you're ready to finalize it!"

"Why, yes, Greggy." Bryan smiled. "We could have spent months more on it, but King Thagdal was explicit about having some sort of results before Combat time, so we're doing the final digest today. The King will have two weeks to study it and confer with us before he presents it to the High Table, or whatever."

"How exciting!" crowed the Genetics Master. "Will you let me order the printout, Bryan? Will you?"

"Why, certainly. Just give Ogmol another minute or two."

Greg-Donnet began to jump up and down, hugging himself. "I love it when the plaques come pouring out! Can we print scads and scads?"

"Only three for now, I'm afraid," the anthropologist said. "The survey must be confidential until King Thagdal approves it for general circulation. His Majesty was very firm about that."

Greg-Donnet's lower lip thrust out pettishly. "Spoilsport! There's no fun when the computer prints only *three*."

"Greggy published five thousand copies of his new plot of the metapsychic latency coefficients," Ogmol remarked, looking up from the input mouthpiece. "Better hurry up and reserve yours, Bry. There are only about four thousand nine hundred and ninety-one left . . . That's the last of our stuff. We're ready to go."

Bryan gestured to the control console. "Be our guest, Greggy. But only three: one for the King, one for Ogmol, and one for me."

The madman seized the mouthpiece. His little old baby face regained its usual good-humored expression. "Stand back, everyone! . . . *Begin sysprint plaque opren-three-shutpren sem end.* Wheee!"

The machine, stoically ignoring the last indigestible byte, labored for six seconds and brought forth a trio of ten-by-sixteen-cent rectangles of pale-green plass, entitled:

SOCIOECONOMIC STRESS PATTERNS
DEMONSTRATED IN TANU-HUMAN
CULTURAL INTERACTION

— A Preliminary Survey —

BRYAN D. GRENFELL
Centre for Anthropological Studies
London 51:30N, 00:10W Sol-3

OGMOL urJOHANNA-BURNS
vulTHAGDAL
Guild of Creators
Muriah 39:54N, 04:15E Sol-3

"Doesn't that look *authoritative?*" Greggy squeaked, snatching one of the plaques from the hopper. "Just like back home! Let me read just the abstract, Bry. Pretty please!"

Bryan lifted the book out of the Genetics Master's hand before he could press the contents activator and stuffed it into the inside pocket of his own jacket. "I promise you'll be the first to read it after the King gives his approval. You'll just have to be patient, Greggy."

Ogmol took his own copy of the book and the one intended for his royal father. "This is sensitive material, Greggy. Not to be bandied about lightly."

"Oh, cockypop!" the adult infant cried. "I've a good mind now not to tell you my news! That's why I was looking for you two. So you wouldn't miss the fun. But if you're going to be such meanies—"

"When the King gives his consent," Bryan soothed, "I'll see to it that you get your very own copy in a fine red leather case. Stamped in gold. With your name on it."

Greggy beamed. "Oh, very well. I was only joking. I wouldn't want *you* to miss Lady Mercy-Rosmar's formal challenge to the Craftsmaster!"

"Omnipotent Tana!" Ogmol exclaimed. "So she's really going through with it? Going up against Aluteyn at the Combat in the manifestation of powers?"

"You bet!" said Greg-Donnet. "The King and Queen are here to watch the challenge, and ever so many others."

Bryan could only stand stunned into silence. But Ogmol was saying, "Does the grapevine give her a chance for the presidency, Greggy? I've been so out of it working on this survey that I can hardly separate one intrigue from another any more. I suppose Nodonn's behind the challenge. Mark my words—he and the rest of the Host won't rest until they've taken over all the Guilds! Just look how Riganone keeps crowding Mayvar over at Farsense. And Culluket would challenge Dionket as Lord Healer if his psychopotential only measured up to his power-itch."

"Mercy's brought the cauldron and all," Greg-Donnet said. "She'll give us some kind of demonstration, bet on that, Creative Brother. It should be quite a giggle! I feel sorry for poor old Aluteyn, though. It's tough to do your best for years and years in a hard job when people aren't all that fond of you—and then have some charismatic young charmer come along."

Ogmol laughed. "Bryan knows all about the lady's charm! Secure the data, Bry, and let's go."

The anthropologist seemed to snap out of his preoccupation. He spoke his private locking-encodement into the computer's input, shut the machine down, took his portfolio, and started to follow his exotic coworker.

Greg-Donnet was rummaging in a cabinet. "You go on ahead, colleagues. I want to bring some of *my* reports down to the rotunda. Everybody's there! It's a wonderful chance to corner people, ha-ha!"

After the two had gone, Greg-Donnet let his own plaque-books fall to the floor in a heedless clatter. He darted to the rear of the computer and slid open a small door in the opaque glass of the data storage module. Inside was a miniaturized manual terminal, part of the maintenance system of the ancient machine, which had been transported piecemeal to the Pliocene by a notably persuasive technician during the earliest days of the auberge. The stylus for the tiny stallboard had disappeared years ago; but Greggy, who had been a great and good friend of the long-dead computer technician, had tucked an old gnawed pencil stub inside the redundant terminal as a substitute. It was quite adequate for tapping out any number of outré and useful instructions, including overrides of lock-codes.

Greg-Donnet pecked:

```
EXEC 'ALGOVERIDE' LLLL
BEGIN RETRIEVE DT(T) AUTHORS: GRENFELL + OGMOL;
BEGIN SYSPRINT PLAQ(1);
BEGIN EXPUNGE;
END
```

There was a ruminative buzz. A single pale-green plaque fell with a muted click into the hopper. The computer made no sound at all as it obliterated from its memory the entire body of data that Bryan and Ogmol had stored within it.

Greg-Donnet patted the machine, tittering, and tucked his copy of the survey into a pocket beneath one of the tails of his clawhammer coat.

"Tidy graphs and learned jargon! Statistics and correlations and extrapolations of dire, dire portents! No surprise to me, of course. Who needs an anthropologist to point out the deluge coming? Naughty humanity! Imagine poor Thaggy thinking we'd been good for his people! Won't he be shocked to find that Nodonn was right about us? And here it is—all spelled out by clever Bryan and simple Oggy—the fate of humanity and the Tanu-human hybrids writ so plain that even the most thick-headed of the Host will understand . . . Ah, Bryan. With Oggy riding herd on you, you'd just tamely hand the thing over to the King and trust in his good sense not to do the obvious. Or do you even *see* the obvious, Bryan? . . . And they call me crazy!"

He went back to the scattered books on the floor, formed them into a neat stack, and skipped away with it. With a little luck, he wouldn't have missed any of the fireworks.

* * *

Ogmol led Bryan through a secret passageway that eventually opened into an alcove hard by the dais of Creation House's great rotunda. The nook was shielded by curtains of an ingenious weave that provided a one-way view into the chamber.

"An old guard cubbyhole from the Times of Unrest five hundred years ago," Ogmol whispered. "All of the Guild headquarters have them, and the secret passages, too. But no one bothers with them any more except Gomnol and his coercers. You know how paranoid about security they are."

Bryan was paying little attention to the explanation of his companion, nor did he waste much time on the High Faculty already seated on the dais around the empty throne of silver encrusted with beryls that was the accustomed seat of Aluteyn Craftsmaster. The anthropologist recognized perhaps half of the top-ranking creators: the aged musician Luktal, Renian Glasscrafter, Clana the illusion-spinning daughter of the Queen and her blood-sister Anéar, Seniet the Lord Historian, Lord Celadeyr of Afaliah, Ariet the Sage, and the two talented hybrids of the High Table, Katlinel the Darkeyed and Alberonn Mindeater.

The rotunda proper was jammed almost from wall to wall with hundreds of Guild members, dressed in various permutations of their heraldic blue-green with white or silver. There were also a great many outsiders of high rank who had, Ogmol explained, either wangled guest passes or simply crashed what should have been strictly an inhouse ceremony.

"See there?" Ogmol pointed. "Those two in the hooded white cloaks? The Thagdal and Nontusvel in mufti! Dressed like that, they're officially nonpresent, so no one need pay any special attention to them."

The royal incogniti had, however, been accorded front-row standing room next to the dais.

"Here's Lady Eadone," said Ogmol. "Now we'll begin."

The tall silver-clad woman, flanked by two male attendants in silver niello half-armor, came out and stood at the right side of the stage. Somewhere the chain jangled. There was dead silence. Bryan now had no difficulty understanding Eadone's speech.

"Creative Brothers and Sisters! We are in extraordinary assembly. According to the most ancient rules of our fellowship, I stand forth as speaker until the matter of this meeting shall find resolution. Let my action be noted."

"The action of the Dean of Guilds is so noted," declared all of the members.

Eadone said, "Let Aluteyn Craftsmaster, President of the Guild of Creators, come forth and assume his rightful place."

There was a low murmur from the crowd. From the wings opposite the alcove where Bryan and Ogmol hid came a stout figure in a richly jeweled caftan. Aluteyn posed for a moment in front of his throne, his silvery-gold hair and mustache abristle with static. In a loud, harsh voice he said, "I take my seat, yielding the speakership freely to the Fivefold Benevolence of the Lady Dean." He plumped himself down, spread his legs, and hunched forward with arms angled and hands resting on his knees. He looked as though he was ready to spring at the first sign of restiveness in the ranks.

"Lord President and fellow Creators," Eadone declaimed. "There has been presented, with due process, a challenge." The throng uttered a sound like a wave breaking gently on an offshore bar. "Let the challenger come forward and be heard."

A small commotion broke out on the side of the rotunda opposite the dais. The crowd opened an aisle leading toward the throne. The creators and the curious aristocrats of Muriah craned their necks. A few even had the bad manners to levitate slightly in an attempt to get a better view as Mercy entered.

"Way!" sang a herald near the entrance. "Way for the Exalted Lady Mercy-Rosmar, Creative Sister to us all, wife to Nodonn Battlemaster Lord of Goriah, and challenger this day before the extraordinary assembly of the Creator Guild!"

Watching her, Bryan felt his heart contract within him. She had put off the rose-and-gold colors of her awesome husband and assumed those of her adopted guild. Her long gown was silver tissue cut at the edges in long dags and scallops resembling butterfly wings; like wings also were the patterns of iridescent greenish blue that made great swirls and eyespots which appeared and disappeared on the fabric as she approached Aluteyn. Her auburn hair hung free. Mercy was followed by four brawny gray-torcs in the livery of House Nodonn pushing a wheeled trolley of polished wood. Upon it reposed a large and ornate cauldron, apparently made of gold.

"It is the Kral," Ogmol whispered, "the sacred vessel of our Guild which is usually seen by the commonalty and membership only at the Grand Combat. Traditionally, the Lord Creator must fill it at that time for the edification of all Combatants."

"What's Mercy doing with it now?" Bryan demanded. But Ogmol only gestured for him to watch.

The human woman had reached the foot of the dais, where an area perhaps ten by ten was opened for her. She made a sign. Her attendants placed the cauldron on the floor in the center of the space, then stepped far back so as to leave Mercy standing alone with the great kettle beside her.

"Speak your challenge, Mercy-Rosmar," said Eadone.

The pale face lifted. Bryan imagined that he saw the sea-colored eyes go wide and wild.

"I challenge Aluteyn Craftsmaster to defend his presidency of the Guild of Creators! I bid him stand forth at the manifestation of powers during the Grand Combat, contending with me in the exercise of creative metafunction, until by the express judgment of the King, the Dean of Guilds, and our noble membership, one of us shall be declared supreme over the other and shall assume the presidency; while the one vanquished shall choose between the quitting of this Kingdom of the Many-Colored Land and voluntary life-offering to the Goddess, whose Will shall in all things prevail."

There was a roar from the crowd. Bryan turned to Ogmol. "What did she mean, for God's sake? Life-offering? Isn't that your orgy of ritual executions at the end of the games? Do you mean that the loser in this damned manifestation of powers forfeits his life?"

"It *is* the most honorable course. But a few, such as Minanonn the Heretic, who was deposed by Nodonn, and Leyr the former Lord Coercer, overcome by Gomnol, have chosen the ignominy of banishment."

Bryan cried out, "Mercy!" But Ogmol held him behind the concealing curtains and the sound of his voice was lost in the tumult.

"You should feel the Craftsmaster's thoughts!" Ogmol fingered his golden torc. "Very bad form to let your hostility show like that, even if one is a First Comer. Watch this now, Bry. The validation, we call it. Can't have just any young upstart making the challenge, you know."

Aluteyn had risen from his throne and now moved forward until he was able to look down upon Mercy from the front of the dais.

"I accept your challenge, Creative Sister—subject to your filling our sacred cauldron here and now, demonstrating the validity of your right to challenge. And first, you shall extirpate the thing I place therein!"

There was an explosion and an ammoniacal stench. The woman leapt back as a slimy apparition materialized out of the golden kettle. Its body was sinuous but without scales, dripping foul mucus. There were pores along the heaving sides like small portholes. Groping filaments the size of elongated human fingers fringed its head. It resembled a monstrous eel, perhaps eight meters in length and nearly a meter in diameter, oozing forth from the cauldron toward Mercy while Aluteyn watched with folded arms and a sour smile. The creature had no proper mouth. Its head terminated in a species of funnel lined with carunculated ridges; inside gleamed row upon row of sharp triangular teeth. From the gullet of the monster protruded a tongue-like member as thick as a human forearm, studded with rasps.

"Good God, what is it?" cried Bryan.

"A lamprey fish, I'd say—or a simulacrum of one, more likely, unless he had this fellow stashed away and magnified him. Not a particularly ingenious effort. Perhaps Aluteyn thought your lady's sensitivities would be overcome by its horrid appearance. But she doesn't seem to be intimidated . . . ha! Watch!"

Mercy stood her ground with resolution as the thing hung over her, its horrid lips aquiver and tongue groping for prey.

"The Craftsmaster has given you a fish!" she cried in a loud voice. "I will give you its accompaniment!"

There was a second detonation, together with a great cloud of steam that swathed Mercy and the giant lamprey swaying above the cauldron. Abruptly, the stench in the air vanished. There was another aroma, one that was not only pleasant but mouth-watering—and quite familiar to Bryan the former Londoner. The vapors parted and there stood the auburn-haired sorceress with her huge kettle filled to the brim with small things that were golden-brown and smoking and giving off that delicious fragrance together with a complementary smell of fried potatoes.

Mercy began scattering the kettle contents to the crowd.

Bryan collapsed in laughter against the wall of the alcove, as much from relief as from any other emotion. "Oh, my dear! That's showing him!"

Ogmol said, "I presume this is some human in-joke."

The throng of Guild members and nobles were catching the tidbits that Mercy threw and devouring them with hilarious cheers. Aluteyn turned his back on the scene.

Lady Eadone declared, "Let it be noted that the challenger, Lady Mercy-Rosmar, has demonstrated her right to meet Lord Aluteyn Craftsmaster in the manifestation of powers. Until that time, let the two of you dwell in the peace and fellowship of our Guild. This extraordinary assembly is now adjourned."

"Lady Mercy-Rosmar farspeaks you through me," Ogmol said to Bryan. "She has perceived our presence behind the curtains because of the—er—cri de coeur you uttered when you realized she was placing herself in peril by issuing the challenge. She wishes to reassure you. She further asks that you meet her tonight in the Creators' Forecourt, where she will arrive in her calèche at twenty-one hundred hours. She wishes to discuss important matters with you."

"Assure her that I'll be waiting."

The Tanu-human bowed in a strangely formal manner. "I must

go now to present the results of our survey to my Awful Father."

"Yes, of course. Well, why don't I wander back to my rooms for a bit—and then a swim. Will you join me later?"

"I fear not, Bryan. The interview with the King may take some time."

"Well, give him my compliments." The anthropologist was jovial. "Later, I'll tell him myself what a good job you've done. I've never seen anyone pick up cultural theory so quickly. Perhaps the King will authorize us to do a broader study along these lines. I'd like to continue working with you, Ogmol."

Still displaying the air of distance that was at variance to his usual friendliness, Ogmol held out a golden-furred hand for Bryan to shake. "I've enjoyed working with you, too, Bryan." He opened the secret door and held it while the anthropologist slipped inside. "Good—good luck to you, Bryan! And thank you for the hangover pills!"

Before the startled human could reply, the sliding panel closed in his face. He was alone in the dim passage between the walls.

"Funny." Bryan took out the pale-green rectangle of his survey and stared at it. "We did a workmanlike job, given the short time available. An interesting overview, all in all. Old Thagdal should be pleased with it."

But why, then, had Ogmol seemed apprehensive? Bryan hadn't a clue. "Perhaps I've been too close to the study during these hectic weeks," he told himself. "As a half-blood, Ogmol may be making a subjective evaluation of the survey relative to some exotic criteria of his own."

Well, a little relaxation and he might noodle it out. Nothing like a good swim in Oggy's private pool to refresh his fatigued cortex. And then a drive with Mercy in the cool of the evening.

He got to thinking about her and the fish and chips, and went off chuckling. The puzzle of Ogmol—and the plaque in his jacket pocket—were completely forgotten.

* * *

On the dark summit of the Mount of Heroes there was a small open meadow between twin crags, far above the College of Redactors and the city and the gunmetal lagoons. They sent the old carriage driver away to wait and stood side by side in the utterly silent night. It seemed that they had come to a place between two different skies —the one above all distant and frosty and old, and the one below warm and exciting with the twinkling lights of three kinds of people —the olive-oil flames lit by humans, the jewel-lamps of the Tanu, and the massed bonfires of the Firvulag making a festive display out on the southern flats.

"I think," Mercy said, "that my favorite thing in all this Many-Colored Land is the faerie look of the lights . . . and best of all when I see them from up high. Like this, from a mountain, or when flying with my Lord."

She took a small backward step so that his arms could come around her. Her hair met his lips as she swayed back against him. "But I forgot that you've never flown with us, Bry. My poor earthbound one! When I'm able to go alone and lift another, I must take you. But in the meantime, we have this here tonight."

She turned to him. The still-incredible thing began to happen again. Their minds and bodies came together in the ecstatic conjugation that seemed as far beyond ordinary sex as music was beyond noise. They lofted into ever-ascending levels of life-energy where balls of colored light pulsed and sang, clinging and crying out—she in triumph and he in wonder and a kind of defiance that dared the love to become love-death if this was the only way to prolong it infinitely. But it could not be, never was, and always there was the brink and the tumble into deep dark while the glaring colors shrank and receded and went out. And he, swallowed, sated, was enfolded within her and flown safely back over the hollow waters, hearing her hush him as he mourned the end (again), ever asking, "Why doesn't this sea reflect the stars?"

"Hush, love," she said. "Never mind."

They lay quietly on her soft cloak. When his mind steadied he was able to look at her starlit face and very nearly recall what the fulfillment had been like (again).

"It's enchantment, Mercy," he said. "You've bewitched me. Are you killing me, too?"

"Does it matter?" she laughed, taking his head into her lap. A fold of fabric wiped his eyes and she kissed the lids.

"It can't go on, can it?" he asked. "After the Combat, he'll take you back to Goriah. Or will you stay if you become Lady Creator? Is there a chance you'll stay, Mercy?"

"Hush."

"Do you love him?" he asked after a while.

"Of course," she replied, her voice warm.

"Do you love me?" He spoke low, his mouth partially muffled in her gown.

"Would I be here with you if I didn't? Ah, my dear. Why must you always talk of loving and staying instead of the joy? Haven't you been happy? Haven't I given you all that I could, all that you could bear? Do you want the whole of it? Will nothing else satisfy you?"

"I can't leave you. Oh, Mercy."

The corners of her mouth turned up. "And you'd do anything for me, would you?"

He gazed at her smile and could not speak. She began to hum, and the words of the familiar love ballad formed in his mind by the power of hers:

> Cupid is wingèd and doth range
> Her country, so my Love doth change.
> But change the earth or change the sky,
> Yet will I love her till I die.

"And now we'll have one another again, sweet Bryan, and after that go down into the city. And you'll give me as a gift the little book you've written, the book that promises such terrible things for my Tanu people if they continue on as before with the humans and all. But you never intended your book to apply to me, did you, Bryan?"

"Oh, no. Not you."

"I'm one of them, after all, and always have been. *He* knows that and so do you."

"Yes . . . both of us know what you are."

"But it's really a most upsetting thing you've written, sweetheart, particularly if the wrong people such as Culluket or Imidol should read it and misunderstand. Not even Nodonn can control the entire Host. And they believe all humankind to be harmful. Even me. Even the dear loyal hybrids. But you weren't to know that, were you? How your little book could be the death of us all. You'd never foresee such an interpretation . . . so earnest, so civilized and sane, my love."

Bryan was puzzled, lost in his dreaming. The survey? That was only his *work*. "It has nothing at all to do with us, Mercy. Nothing to do with you. Enchantress."

"Then give me your copy of it. Give it to me and never tell that I have it."

Of course he did. And she lifted his head from her lap, laughing, and then leaned over him kissing and leading him on. When they had gone there and back (again), she summoned the carriage and driver and they drove down the mountain. Outside Redact House, as she expected, Nodonn and Culluket the King's Interrogator were waiting.

"He's asleep," she told them. "The only other copies of the survey are in the possession of Ogmol and the Thagdal—and stored in the computer, of course."

"Ogmol can wait," Nodonn said to his younger brother. "And the King has his own reasons for keeping the matter secret. But he will seek the life of this man, this unsuspecting witness for the prosecution. You must keep him safe until the culmination of the Combat, Redactive Brother. He is vital to our cause. See that he is kept happy and unaware."

The Interrogator nodded. "I understand fully, Brother Battle-master. Our company cannot fail to be impressed when the human cancer affirms its own existence." He smiled at Mercy.

Two red-and-white-clad attendants appeared and lifted the unconscious anthropologist from the calèche. Nodonn mounted and took the place next to his wife.

"Until later, then, Brother. We two will go to Creation House and see to the computer ourselves."

Culluket inclined his head. "Until later." He turned to lead the way into the caves deep within the mountain and the men carrying Bryan followed after.

10

NAKED AND WEEPING, the silver-torc girl came running from the King's chamber.

"Oh, dear," said Nontusvel, casting a significant glance at the Master of the Royal Bed. "Not again."

"It wasn't my fault, I swear, Queen and Mother!" the girl wailed. "I did everything! Everything!" She fell on her knees. The Master of the Royal Bed gestured and a gray-torc valet came up to wrap the shivering love-gift manquée in a robe of white satin.

"Get her out of here," the Queen ordered. "I'll see to His Majesty myself tonight."

The Master bowed. He and the servant hurried away with the sniffling girl. Nontusvel extinguished all the lights except one candelabrum of pink jewels. This she lifted on high and carried to the tall door embossed with the golden bearded mask. It swung open before her.

"My King, it is I," she said. "Be of good cheer."

Only a few scattered gleams, like ruby and gold embers, lit the bedchamber of Thagdal the High King. There was an odd sound, a little like a gulping sob, and then a noise of someone blowing his nose.

"N-Nonnie?"

"Yes, dear."

The King sat on the edge of the bed, his mighty shoulders hunched, head down. "Failed again. The sword undrawn, the bow unloosed, the mightiest champion of them all laid low and humiliated. I'm done for, Nonnie. Finished. Not even that damned Lalage and all her tricks could conjure up a glimmer."

"It is all in your mind, beloved. You've been worrying too much."

She set the candelabrum down on the bedside table and stood before him, magnificent and comforting in a flowing peignoir of peach color trimmed in gold. Her flaming hair hung down, her arms opened wide, welcoming as her mothermind with its invitation: Rest in me.

She drew him up and they went out onto the balcony. It was very late. The moon was old, an ochreous sickle near the horizon, giving an unhealthy tinge of brass to the lagoon.

"You must not be down-hearted," the Queen said. "What has changed? Are the Foe yonder on the salt any more confident of victory than they've been in years past? Hardly. We are strong and we will crush them, as always."

"It's not that."

"Aiken Drum, then? A clownish gadfly! Mayvar is senile and it is high time dear Riganone took her place as Lady Farsensor and Kingmaker. The boy knows quite well he would have no chance against the Battlemaster. Has Aiken Drum issued any formal challenge for the manifestation of powers? Of course not! And he won't challenge by Mêlée Rules at the Combat, either. Nodonn will remain your heir—patient and loyal as always. And soon you'll recover your good spirits and your vigor as well."

The King shook his head. "It's not Aiken Drum. Two new things. I—I didn't tell you."

"Will you tell me now?"

"Brede has emerged from the room without doors. I may *not* have the operant woman, Elizabeth."

The Queen's screens shot up to conceal her elation. "The mating scheme with her is then—"

"Brede has placed Elizabeth's genes under the strongest taboo. The Shipspouse claims that the woman's destiny has been revealed to her. That it's not in accord with the scheme Gomnol and I favored. I haven't told Gomnol yet, either. I was afraid to! Can you imagine that? My genes plus Elizabeth's were going to engender a new superrace under Gomnol's guidance. And now she's taboo and I'm—I'm—"

"Gomnol's vision is undoubtedly flawed," said the Queen with some sharpness. "He *is* only a human being, for all his coercive power. And an aging one. Only a few years more, and Imidol will be deposing him."

The King's thought was perceptible even under the screen: another patient and loyal son of yours?

"Now, Thaggy," she chided, slipping an arm around his massive waist. His belly muscles contracted and he straightened his shoulders. One or two static sparks danced in his hair and beard.

"Never mind about Elizabeth," Nontusvel said. "She is beautiful and I can understand your disappointment. But that kind of woman isn't your type, vein of my heart. A Grand Master metapsychic! How too off-putting! I don't suppose Brede said what would be done with her?"

"She wouldn't tell me. Said it would be obvious after the Grand Combat. Bloody two-faced enigma! What can you expect from a female who marries a damn intergalactic *worm?*"

The Queen giggled and pressed next to his naked torso.

"And then another blow this afternoon," he muttered.

"Not Rosmar?"

"Of course not. That creative lout of an Ogmol! Come inside and I'll show you."

They returned to the bedchamber. The King kicked aside the rug, then used his PK to manipulate the lock of a floor-safe. A small greenish plaque floated up into the Queen's waiting hands. She pressed the SLOW activator in the upper righthand corner and studied the glowing pages as they rolled across the plastic. Now and then she stopped the flow to study a chart or graph.

"Skip to the end," the King said. "The conclusion."

She pressed the upper lefthand corner and the pages spun quickly. Then a touch from the REVERSE and she had it. "Oh, dear!"

"Exactly! How's that for an unwitting scenario of doom? That besotted idiot of an anthropologist didn't realize the implication. But Oggy did—and he nearly wet his pants begging me to believe that it wouldn't happen. That he and the other hybrids and the torced humans would remain loyal."

The Queen whispered, "All you need do is extrapolate the trends a bit farther than Bryan has already done."

"And add the focusing factor he doesn't yet know about—the iron. I'll wager my right nut that hybrids are immune to it just like humans. Does that suggest anything to you?"

"Dear Tana, not that! Can nothing be done to stop it? Our beautiful Exile world! *Ours!*"

She threw herself into his arms and wept. The King held her in a mighty grip. His eyes had begun to shine in the dark. The tendrils of his sparkling beard stirred, and something else. "We'll stop any human-hybrid coalition before it's ever born. That thing of Bryan's is only a scientific survey, not an oracle. But it's a danger to *me* in a way I hadn't anticipated! Dammit, Nonnie—I'd hoped to calm No-donn's fears about humanity. That's why I commissioned the survey in the first place—to prove that the advent of humans was beneficial to us, not a racial menace as Nodonn maintained. I mean, *common sense* showed we'd made marvelous strides since the opening of the time-gate. Technical progress as well as genetic. The anthropologist was supposed to confirm what Gomnol and I had been saying all along. And instead—"

"Dearest husband, Nodonn only wants the best for our Many-Colored Land. He doesn't mean to threaten *you*."

The King grunted. "This survey can be used to prove all of his doomsaying is justified. It's a clear contradiction of my stated policy. It may seem far-fetched to you now, but this little book could be the death warrant of every human and hybrid in the High Kingdom—and if *they* go, so does the economy of my realm! It's back to the wilderness strongholds for us Tanu, my lass."

Nontusvel raised her tear-bright eyes. "You said yourself that the survey isn't an oracle. None of these dreadful contingencies need happen at all. You won't let them."

"I won't!" he vowed. "Our Many-Colored Land will not be taken over by Lowlives! I'll see to it! And I'll accomplish my purpose without any of the damn draconian measures Nodonn advocates. There must be a way that Tanu and humanity can continue to prosper together—and I'm going to find it. *I have said it!*"

"Thaggy—?" the Queen ventured breathlessly.

"Come here, woman!" he bellowed.

When dawn came and both of them were drowsy and at peace, she murmured to him, "You see? Everything's perfectly all right. It *was* all in your mind."

"Mm-mm," the King agreed. He raised one of her hands and kissed each dimpled knuckle.

"As to your problem with the silvers . . . I think you simply need a change. These silly human strumpets with their meager little dug-lets are not in tune with your present mood of high seriousness. You require an entirely different type of consolation. A gentler, more re-assuring sort."

The King said sleepily, "Remember that chubby black-haired one who sang the Welsh lullaby? I liked her. I kept expecting her to be sent around, but she never came."

"The very thing," Nontusvel agreed. "I'll make it my personal business to find out what's happened to her. If Dionket thinks he can keep her for himself—why, Nodonn and Culluket will simply point out a few realities to him!" She smiled at her half-dozing Lord.

"Good old girl," Thagdal said. He let her hand fall. His eyes were closed. "And I'll gather up all copies of Bryan's report and have them destroyed, and Gomnol can take care of the anthropologist as well. Too bad about Oggy, though . . . He was a good . . ."

"Sleep, my King." The Queen drew the silken sheet up to cover them both. "Sleep for now."

* * *

Eusebio Gomez-Nolan leaned back in his Victorian armchair and blew three slow smoke rings. They floated across the desk toward the person sitting opposite, turned solid, and fell to the pseudo-Oriental rug with soft thuds.

"Hope you don't mind, Lord Coercer," said Aiken Drum. "Can't stand tobacco."

Gomnol made a gracious gesture. His cigar extinguished itself and he placed it in the onyx ashtray. "My boy, events in this Cloud-Cuckoo-Land of ours have taken some engrossing turns of late. I believe it's time that you and I had a long chat."

"I thought you'd never ask."

"I've revised my earlier opinion of you considerably during the past week or two. Mayvar has been most eloquent in your behalf. And so has Bunone Warteacher, whom you impressed no end on the Delbaeth Quest. Both of these ladies feel that you will be a formidable contender in the upcoming games. They were also fervent in their praise of your—uh—nonmartial arts as well."

Aiken's grin was wicked. He lounged back in his seat with one leg draped over the chair-arm and studied the fingernails of one hand. "So what else is new?"

"I might mention," Gomnol said smoothly, "a rumored disability of our Awful King, provoked—so it's said—by intimations of mortality as much as by the collapse of my late genetic scheme."

"Brede screwed you, eh?" The little man snickered. "Now I get it. The old sinking ship syndrome. With poor old Thaggy cast as Titanic and you as Chief Rat."

The Lord Coercer's guffaw was entirely good-humored. "You are going to require a great deal of help, my boy. I'm prepared to offer it. All I ask is that you think over my proposition carefully." He took a fresh cigar from the humidor and twirled it between his fingers. "We are, I believe, approaching a pivotal point in the history of this

Exile world. The Finiah attack was only the overture. And if there is a power struggle in the offing, doesn't it make sense for all of us humans to stick together?"

He took a clipper from the drawer and operated deftly on the cigar. Then he tossed the silvery little gadget to Aiken Drum, still smiling.

Aiken caught the cigar clipper and Gomnol's unspoken thought simultaneously. He peered at the thing and saw letters incised in the metal: SOLINGEN—INOX STEEL.

11

GERT CAME BACK to the passenger compartment looking grim. "Hansi thinks we'll be into the next batch of bad rapids soon. You'd better put the skipper back together again."

Amerie was bent over a supine figure. "We're working on him now. Five minutes." Chief Burke held one arm and Felice the other. Uwe and Basil were ready to grab the legs. "Here we go," the nun said. She applied the stimulant to the unconscious boatman's temple, then got another injection ready. The little monitor taped to the man's forehead began to change color in all of its four quadrants.

Blood-rimmed hazel eyes snapped open. From the puffy lips came a croak. "Gawd . . . ah, Gawd!" And then he screamed, a sound of bitter hopelessness and physical agony. His body contracted in a superhuman heave that had the four restrainers using all their strength to keep him pinned to the deck.

"*Ahh!* Wotinell yer bleedin' sods done? Wotcher done? Yer tookit *orf,* y'filfy buggerin' baboons! Thass wotcher did. Iss gone! Gone . . ."

Tears poured down the stubbly seams of his cheeks. The boatman howled like an animal as Amerie watched the forehead monitor, white with anger at what they were having to do. The thin grizzle-haired man's once natty green tunic was now stained with vomit and blood and dust from the ordeals he had endured under his kidnappers. Around his tanned throat was a band of pale flesh where the gray torc had been.

They had been on the river two days and this was the sixth time they had brought the boatman around. Gert and Hansi could handle the boat on the smooth stretches of the Rhône; but in rough water they had to have the skipper's help—and every time they woke him, the screaming was worse. Only a few of the de-torced Finiah prisoners had displayed withdrawal symptoms as severe as this man's, and those people had been heavily sedated during the earliest, most painful part of the separation.

But the Rhône boatman could not remain asleep.

"For God's sake," Chief Burke said, "hit the poor meshugeh with the trank!"

Amerie said, "He has to absorb the first injection properly. Do you want him to crash on us? He's on the brink now. Just look at that vital-signs monitor . . . Felice! Go into his mind!"

The cries thinned into a gurgle. The nun turned her patient's head so that he could cough up thin bile. Felice's eyes dimmed and sweat started out on her brow. The boatman's frenzy began to diminish under the drug and the pressure of the girl's coercive power. The colors of the forehead monitor shifted again.

"Good," Amerie said. She slapped on the tranquilizer, then carefully administered the blend of euphoric and energizer. The skipper seemed to relax.

"Come out of him when you think the medications have taken hold," the nun told Felice.

"Jeez, what a balls-up." The athlete let go of the limp arm she had been clutching. Burke and Basil hauled the groggy boatman to his feet.

Uwe said quietly, "Will he last? How's he look inside, babe?"

"All I can do is coerce the guy," Felice said. "I'm no good at redact. This man needs a top-stem refit and I'm not capable. I think he navigates now by the seat of his pants. If he's not totally insane, he's next door to it."

"Rapids ahead!"

Vanda-Jo sang out from her lookout position on the extended mast, where she clung to a squirrel-climb apparatus installed by Basil. Khalid came limping to assist her down. The two of them dismantled the climbing gear and locked the plass roof panels of the boat back into place. The mast sank into its housing.

"Don't stand there!" Chief Burke told them. "Everybody buckle in and be damn sure all the seals are tight. Come on, Felice."

They dragged the skipper into the wheelhouse. Hansi slipped out of the captain's seat and the barely revived boatman was fastened in. Webbing from one of Basil's alpine slings served to strap Felice to a smaller pilot's chair.

"I'm all right," Felice cried. "Get back to your seats, quick! I can handle this bird. And I think I can just about hold the boat with my PK now, in the straight stretches."

The others ran aft. A great roaring filled the air, reverberating from steep canyon walls that rose sheer at least 600 meters on either side of them. Even though it was only early afternoon, dusk filled the misted slot where the Rhône boiled along in ever-accelerating flow. The vessel tilted forward. Black boulders with collars of fountaining spray went past in a blur . . .

Listen to me Harry listen to me Harry you are going to drive your boat just like you always do drive it along safe and sound between the rocks Harry through the rapids just like you always do safe and sound do you hear me Harry drive the boat you're a good skipper Harry you're the best this is nothing to a white-water ace like you Harry bring her through safe and sound do it Harry do it . . .

The red eyes of the boatman narrowed. He spun the wheel to starboard and the craft heeled around a looming obstruction, raced toward the canyon wall, then corrected at the last moment to pass through an opening spill between two colossal standing waves that looked like yellow whalebacks. The boat zigzagged through a churning welter of rock and foam, shot around a curve and headed for a wider section of the canyon where the water seemed oddly calm—until at the last moment Felice saw that the flood poured over an abrupt shelf into misty opacity. She let panic rule her for an instant before she caught sight of the safe bypass channel that was hidden in the cloud and spume—

—but by then it was too late. Harry had escaped her grip. The boat went over the lip of the falls, turning end over end until it landed *spang* on its roof panels and seemed to buckle amidships like some great broken trampoline. The skipper named Harry was now laughing in hysteria. But there was no time to do anything to him, with the rest of them back there yelling and cursing and hanging in their harnesses upside down in the dark bubbling yellow gut.

It took every bit of her psychokinetic power to turn them back over, so tenacious was the grip of the cavitating surge in the undercut rock below the cascade. But finally she hauled them free of it. They flew along on the river's surface again, and she tried to catch Harry and put him back in control—

—but oh, God, there ahead it stood! And there was no way they could maneuver in time not to hit it! And—*spung!* The pneumatic craft caromed off a great jagged monolith with water shooting in through one broken panel while they held a fifty-degree bank around a sharp curve in the Rhône.

At last the boat wallowed into straight and level motion. The waters slowed, flattened, opened out two kilometers wide in the midst of a valley with brown steppe hills.

The boatman was still giggling. Felice tore off her straps, lurched to him, and slapped him with a fury that nearly sent him unconscious again.

"You stupid fuckard!"

The man's subvocal thought defied her through pain and maniacal triumph: You were afraid ha ha afraid monstercunt and I *gotcher!*

Aloud, he groaned and spat blood from his bitten tongue. Hansi and Gert came staggering in to take over the helm.

"Ah, shit, she breached," Hansi exclaimed, spotting the broken panel.

"We can fix it," his partner said. "There's a tool kit and spare plass underdeck. All we have to do is demount the broken piece."

Gert took the wheel while Felice and Hansi supported the limp body of Harry. "What happened, Felice?" Hansi inquired. "Guy suffer a relapse?"

"The only relapse happened to yours truly," Felice snarled. "I let the bastard get away from me. He must have been waiting his chance all this time. And when I saw that damn dropoff just ahead I panicked and let my control slip. That was all he needed. He took us over the falls on purpose."

Hansi said, "No real harm done. No use kicking yourself for being scared. These cataracts would make Genghis Khan holler for his mommy."

Chief Burke, his ruddy complexion faded to gray, reeled up and clung to the frame of the wheelhouse door. "That was a bitch-catawampus, Felice."

"We broke a panel," she said. "We'll have to moor someplace for repairs. And figure out how to keep the Ancient Mariner, here, from committing suicide and taking us along."

"So that was it." The Native American and Felice dragged Harry to the passenger compartment and dumped him without ceremony onto the deck. The exhausted girl dropped into a seat and closed her eyes. Harry drooled and cursed until Burke and Basil tied and gagged him.

The boat steered toward a heavy stand of willows on the left bank. They came into a quiet backwater where curving branches of great trees made a cave of green luminosity. There was a tiny sandy beach.

"That was a bad one," Uwe observed. "I thought the boat was going to fold over on us like an omelet."

"Felice lost control of Harry," Chief Burke said.

Her brown eyes went wide and she jumped to her feet. "I was distracted! All right—I was *scared!* Old Fearless Felice lets the bad vibes get to her at long last. So what are you going to do about it, Red Man? Try me in your kangaroo court?"

Amerie came and put a hand on Felice's shoulder. "Peo isn't blaming you. The boatman was docile enough on the other runs. You couldn't know he'd try something on this one. Your nerves are ravelled after shooting rapids all day, and it's a wonder you did as well as you did."

Felice looked mollified. "I *was* able to turn the bloody boat right-side up again, anyhow. My PK's coming on fast. But the damned coercive function gets tangled up in my emotions too easily. We really miscalculated when we took old Harry's torc off. The Tanu have the right idea with their pleasure-pain circuits. I could have had him biddable as a baa-lamb in the torc, and he wouldn't be cold-turkeying all over us, either."

"Day before yesterday you said you couldn't hack it," Khalid reminded her. "And what if he'd let loose a telepathic warning to any golds or silvers in range? Don't forget that the Great South Road is somewhere up on the west bank. There are Tanu caravans up there—and Tanu on the river, and silvers at the plantations. Quit kicking yourself."

Vanda-Jo peered at the jungly bank. "Do you think it's safe to camp here?"

"It better be," said Hansi, coming from the wheelhouse. "I don't want to go one klom farther until Gert and I give this tub a complete checkup. God knows what else we broke when we came slamming down." He began removing the roof panels preparatory to mooring.

Ducks fled as they nosed in. "I might pot us a few waterfowl for supper," Basil suggested. "We didn't," he added with a rueful chuckle, "retain much lunch."

"We can all use rest and food," Amerie said. "Then tomorrow we'll be in good shape for—whatever lies ahead. And what does, by the way?"

Khalid said, "If we've passed six big rapids, then only one stands between us and Lac Provençal. I haven't been on it, but it's said to be the longest and worst of all—the Donzère-Mondragon stretch."

"Kaleidoscopic," groaned Felice.

"After that there's only the Glissade into the Med Basin. I did ride that when I was taken to Muriah. It's steep but not difficult. Only needs a steady hand at the tiller. Gert and Hansi can handle it easily. But we'll have to depend on this boatman's skill one last time tomorrow."

They all looked down at Harry. His hair stuck up in diabolical spikes. His eyes bulged and he strained and grunted against the gag.

Amerie sighed and reached for her medical kit. "Poor Harry."

"Poor us," Felice retorted.

* * *

A half kilometer downstream from the grove of willows where the boat was moored was a jumble of large rocks, overgrown with tamarisk and acacia, that protruded out from the shoreline and made an excellent lookout. They decided to keep watch there, at least until late evening, to be sure that no other boats happened upon their hiding place.

Amerie's turn came when the sun had been down for an hour and it had become cool. She was glad of the chance to get away from the others—especially the wretched boatman, whose vital signs had stabilized under renewed sedation and a veinfeed. She made her orisons under brightening stars. A few insects shrilled and the Rhône burbled beneath the riverside rocks. Little herons squawked in the shallows while chasing their supper.

Across the broad waters the hills were dark. There must be plantations in this likely valley, Amerie thought. But no lights were visible from her vantage point. No boats came by during her watch, either. Night traffic was normally nonexistent on the river. Still, there was the small chance that the nonarrival of their skipper at his usual stops would be noted by his fellows—hence the watch. Burke and the others had not made too great a point of it, but it was obvious that the farther downriver they progressed, the greater the suspicions of the other rivermen might become when good old Harry failed to appear at some accustomed rendezvous. All of the craft on the Rhône were distinctive; Harry's, although of a common express design, had a spruce-green band around its silver hull and its name, Walloping Windowblind, painted in large letters on bow and stern. They had debated disguising the boat. But in the beginning they hoped that its owner would be cooperative, enabling them to bluff their way clear down to Muriah. Now, of course, it was too late to do anything but press on. When they passed other boats, they tooted greetings on the airhorn, hoping that the absence of a telepathic hail between skippers wouldn't be remarked during the busy Truce season . . .

There was a small sound among the lower rocks.

"It's only me." Felice clambered up to the high perch. "I'll take the last trick."

"Not a soul on the river that I've seen. Only birds. All in order back in camp?"

"Your patient's fine, if that's what you mean. The boat's back in good shape, and Gert and Hansi have gone off into the bushes to celebrate. VJ was in a generous mood, too, but only Uwe took her up. And I think that was mostly sweet charity on the old puffer's part."

She plopped down cross-legged beside the nun, who did not comment on the badinage. "Nice night, isn't it? The weather in this Pliocene world is pyrotechnic! I suppose they must have a rainy season in winter, but it couldn't be lovelier now. Probably why the exotics have their Grand Combat this time of year. Perfect weather for a war."

The nun did not reply.

Felice said, "There'll be a lot of fighting, once we've hit the torc works and closed the time-gate. Those Tanu slavers are going to get what's coming to them now that we've got their number with the iron. I have other ideas, too, that I haven't discussed yet with the others . . . Like, maybe forming a coalition with any of the silvers who'd be loyal to humanity instead of the Tanu. Elizabeth could sort them out for us and we could re-troc them with stolen gold and have a human elite corps ready to counter any mass Hunt the exotics might mount. Human metas versus exotic metas! We could take over the whole corpuscular kingdom!"

Amerie was still silent.

Felice came closer. "You don't approve. It's not your Christian ethic. You think we should try to gain our freedom by some kind of negotiation. Sweet reason and brotherly love! . . . Why have you been avoiding me, Amerie? Have you decided I'm a monster, too, like the others?"

The nun turned. In the starlight her face was kind. "I know just what brand of bullshit you're getting ready to serve up, Felice. Please don't. I've tried to explain to you how it is with me. I know you have your needs and you've been frustrated by missing the Finiah fight and driven half-bats by the poor boatman. But you can't use me to relieve your tensions. Not through cruelty or through sex either. I have a right to my own commitment. I don't expect you to understand it, but you're damn well going to respect it."

Felice's laugh was uncertain. She sat very still, her tanned face contrasting with the halo of pale hair. "So much," she said, "for the brotherly-love pitch. Thanks for nothing, Sister. For a while there, I thought you cared."

The nun rounded on her and grabbed the slender bare shoulders. "You impossible child! Of course I love you. Why do you think I came?"

"Then, why? *Why?*" Felice's voice rose to a wail. For an instant, her coercive power stabbed out. The nun jerked away with a cry of pain. Felice exclaimed, "I'm sorry, Amerie! I'm sorry! I won't do it again. Don't look at me—don't *think* at me like that." The bright head sank. "Never ever. Either one of us. Why? Why is it so wrong to find a little happiness and warmth? We might be dead tomorrow and that'll be the end of it."

"Felice, I don't believe that. Whether we live or die, I don't believe that's the end. That's one of the reasons for my renunciation."

"Your religious mumbo jumbo! Who can prove there's a God out there? Or if there is, who can prove he cares—that he's not some game-playing horror? You can't prove it! You're an educated woman, a doctor. You know there's no proof!"

"Only in human psychology. In our need. In our instinct reaching out. In our very odd veneration for the love that gives without taking."

"I need your love! You won't give it to me! You lie when you say you love me!"

"I have to be true to myself, too. To love myself, Claude called it. I had to come to the Pliocene to discover that I was worth loving. And you . . . dear Felice. You've never learned to love at all. Not in human ways. Your need is different and—terrible. My kind of love can't satisfy you and what you call love would be an injustice to me. I want to help you, but I don't know how. All I can do is pray for you."

"Wonderful!" The girl's laugh was rich with scorn. "Go ahead, then! Let's hear how you pray for poor damned inhuman Felice!"

Amerie reached out, took the resisting girl in her arms. The chant was soft in the night.

"Lord, how great is your constant care. We find protection under the shadow of your wings and are filled with the good things you give us. You have let us drink from the river of your kindness, for you are the fountain of life. In your light we will find light of our own."

Felice cried out, "Oh—*shit!*"

She wept and Amerie rocked her. After a long time, the girl pushed away and wiped her face.

"Tomorrow . . . it's going to be tough. I was scared out of my mind this afternoon and I'm going to be even more scared tomorrow. If I let that damned Harry get away from me again, we're all going to be drowned or dashed to pieces. And I might not hold him. I—my confidence is going. And that's fatal when you're playing mind-games. If you're afraid that you might fail, then the whole thing comes apart and—what am I going to *do?*"

"I'll keep praying."

"Fuck your nonexistent God! If he knows everything, he ought to help us without our asking! Or are we supposed to grovel? Is that what *he* needs?"

"It's good for us to reach out to him. To *will* his help in getting things that we need."

"So your God is a psychologist! And praying is just metapsychic focusing, so that if you have enough faith you move the bloody mountain! Who needs a God at all if we end up answering our own prayers? I should pray to myself, then—right? But I don't believe in me, either!"

"Felice, I don't want to bandy semantics or theology with you. If the word 'pray' seems ridiculous to you, forget it. Just keep the psychic validity behind the concept. Tomorrow, try to reach out and demand strength from the Mind of the universe, from the life-source. Never mind whether it's aware of you or not, who it is or what it is. You have a *right* to share in its strength—not just for your sake but for the sake of all the rest of us who are depending on you."

The girl said slowly, "I think I could do that. I can believe in Mind. I can feel . . . that much is real. I'll try, Amerie."

The nun rose to her feet, lifting Felice with her. She kissed the girl on the forehead, then looked beyond, across the river to the hills black against a purpled western sky. "Felice—there's something over there."

The girl turned. On the far shore was a manifestation like a glittering string of beads moving in and out of the trees.

"The Hunt," said Felice.

They watched it in silence. It was moving southward through the bottomland that lay between the Rhône and the Great South Road.

"I can farsense them a bit," Felice said. "They're out of a place called Sayzorask down beyond the gorge at the head of a big lake. They're looking for us."

Amerie started to say, "You mean the overdue skipper—"

"They're looking for *us*. Fortunately, none of them can fly, and they don't have any hot-dog farsensors, so they aren't aware that I'm eavesdropping on their mental yammerings. Strictly a collection of provincials. But the big boys will be waiting for us farther south."

"How could they *know*?" Amerie cried.

"Somebody told them," Felice said. "And I think I know who."

* * *

They left the moorage as soon as it was light, while the yellow water was still mostly buried in cotton wool fogbanks. The air cleared when they came into the next deep gorge, and they saw that they were not alone on the river; three other craft were lined up at the top of the chute, waiting for a little more daylight before daring the twenty-kilometer stretch of rough water.

"Bad news!" Gert sang out.

"Pass 'em!" Felice decided. "Peo, Basil, get that zombie up here. No sense trying to play tricks. Those other boats can't do a thing once we're in the rapids."

The noise of the cascading turbulence made it almost impossible for them to hear one another. When Harry, blue-lipped and feebly snarling, was strapped into place, Felice gave the other men a shove aft. "If we spring a leak, get everybody out of the harnesses and do the best you can."

They passed the anchored boats at a distance of twenty-five meters. Felice forced Harry to wave and worked the airhorn herself, *toodly-toot-toot*. And then they were into the rapids . . .

Take us through Harry do your job Harry do it and I'll get you another gray torc do you hear me another one just as good as the one we took only do your job Harry steer steer dodge and draw and race through the booming froth and the haystack bulges above the underwater rocks O go Harry good old boy stay off the knifeledge and the monstrous eddy whirling at the bend and the crazy tall waves filling the air with blobs of foam go on Harry go boy go and set her over broadside working the multiple rudders like organ pedals and twirling the wheel virtuoso Harry remember the new torc the old ecstasy just as good as before look out for the sluice and skim her on down Harry braving the violent Rhône all clogged with landslides and rock piles that should hold back the waters but never will come on I'm helping you Harry holding you and see not scared O no *kaboom!* sheesh all right Harry just a bouncer good recovery God there's a big mother big as a house in the middle of the channel right or left you know which is best Harry Harry Harry O you asshole get us out of this spin you Harry or I'll squeeze you until you Harry get us out Harry stop the spin I'll hurt you Jesus Jesus we're going to hit again Harry Harry you rotten *swine* I won't let you you can't do it I won't let you you can't *I won't let you*—

Die.

Felice screamed. The mind within her grasp went incandescent in a last surge of opposing rage. And then, ever so easily, it slipped away from her and went off along a way she dared not follow. Alone, she returned to the chaos of the riverboat caught in the treacherous white eddy, rotating just downstream from a great craggy mass that parted the Rhône into two thundering streams. The boat spun faster and faster. With every other revolution it whanged against an underwater obstruction, the impact causing the strong inflated hull to vibrate like a beaten drum.

Harry hung in his harness, seeming to wink at her. The vital-signs monitor on his forehead was solid black.

Felice worked the quick-release fasteners and let the body fall to the deck. She took the skipper's place, grasped the wheel, tramped the rudder pedals, and sent her PK below the hull to lift.

Ah, so hard so heavy so hard . . . trying to tear loose from the grip of the spinning water! But I am strong (do you all hear?) and you can make me stronger so *do* it! Up . . . up . . . help me lift it up. All you lives loves you must help you will. Up! UP! . . . And the two-in-one hears and helps and the many-in-All as well because it is not only for me and the drumbeats stop and the scratching hiss of the muddy gravely water stops and the whirling the rocking the buffeting all countermovement stops.

I lift. We float.

I am able to hold us (thank you) even pull us higher now. Faster and faster until we fly! And the frustrated water writhes underneath and the amazed canyon walls lean over to get a better view of the magic.

Ahead of us the walls fall away. Water jets out in a great round plume, creamy as rich milk. It arches down and down and down, so far into the vapor that clothes the great hidden lake. The terminal gush of the Rhône is swallowed below us without a trace.

We soar! High above the mist-country, we soar safe in sunlight. Our enemies are stifled and blind below and the happiness is so great that I burn—I burn for joy.

Amerie and the Indian Chief come at last into the wheelhouse and warm themselves at my fire. And then they put hands on me to still the shuddering and say, "Take us down, child."

And I descend. Softly.

12

"You are certain, Mother?" Nodonn asked.

The Queen replied, "You will see for yourself. The Thagdal finished with her only a short time ago and sent her back to Redact House. Culluket got the truth from her when I farspoke him of what had happened. He is bringing her to the palace again for our scrutiny."

They were in the Queen's morning room. She was still en déshabillé, while the Battlemaster, summoned from the arena, wore a light practice cuirass with vambrace and pauldron for his unshielded right arm and shoulder.

"A *new* human conspiracy!" he mused aloud. "The audacity of the Lowlives almost passes belief. That Guderian woman is at the bottom of it, of course. The human-Firvulag entente, the use of the holy Spear . . . and now this!"

Nontusvel said, "It was a vengeance-thought that the girl Gwen-Minivel let slip, you see, when the Thagdal was filling her full of his grace. The gist of it was, 'You won't be able to do this to human women much longer when we destroy your torc factory and shut the time-gate. We will free all human slaves.'"

"It was fortunate that you were within range and caught her thought."

"It was heavily screened. But I am the Mother of the Host."

"Exactly who *is* she, that she should have had knowledge of this plot?"

"Alas—a most promising young healer. She was reserved from the customary bidding by Dionket himself. She should have been sent to the King's couch long ago. But for reasons that are not yet clear to me—you will want to investigate this—she was secreted in the catacombs of Redact House by the connivance of Mayvar and the Lord Healer. With your Awful Father in such low spirits over recent melancholy events, I bethought me of this girl as a potential source of comfort. She had stunned the entire company at the bidding banquet with her empathy. I—I confess that I saw in her reminders of my own self as a young maiden, lulling my dolls to sleep and dreaming of the babies I would some day bear . . . But enough of that. As it is my duty to assure the consolation of our King, I charged your brother Culluket to discover what had become of Minivel. A royal command superseded even Dionket's authority over the girl and she was duly produced. Culluket is much too forthright to deal with the mental preparations that Minivel required—your Awful Father being in the delicate condition he is, we could not risk her putting him down—and so I undertook the coercion and redaction of the young woman myself. I worked with her all yesterday afternoon, and she went to the Thagdal last night as eagerly as a nymph. He never knew that she despised him. And of course your Father never heard Minivel's deep avowal of revenge, since he was distracted by his own passion. I had her sing for him and vouchsafe the most maternal forms of solace in addition to the usual. She was a great success."

"And all unwitting," Nodonn now suggested, "she may become the key to our victory as well."

The door to the suite opened. The King's Interrogator, handsome and stern in a hooded cape of dark burgundy, pushed Sukey in ahead of him and motioned for the escort of garnet-armored guardsmen to remain outside. Culluket saluted Nontusvel and his brother.

"Awful Mother! Brother Battlemaster! I've questioned the woman Gwen-Minivel and laid bare all that she knows."

Sukey stood with a resolute face. Her eyes and nose were reddened from weeping and her hair hung in strings. She still wore the diaphanous love-gift robes the Queen's attendants had dressed her in the night before.

Nontusvel and Nodonn studied the intelligence that Culluket's mind displayed to them.

"Child, child," mourned the Queen. "Not only the treason—but a human lover as well! A lowly gray—Stein Oleson, man-at-arms to Aiken Drum. And you have conceived his child!"

"Stein is my husband," Sukey said.

The Interrogator, so like and so unlike his gentle mother, pushed back his hood. "The penalty for that action alone would be death, Gwen-Minivel. Death for you, for your unborn child, and for the father of the misbegotten. You have abased your silver torc and forfeited all claim to Tanu kinship. You are no longer Gwen-Minivel but merely Sue-Gwen Davies, an outlaw human. You and any persons who are accessories to this treason or to the larger infamies you have revealed to me will answer to our justice—no matter how high their station."

Sukey's swollen lips smiled. Her thought was clear: We lose our lives. But you will lose your whole world, even though you continue to live!

"Send her away," said Nodonn. "We must discuss this."

As Culluket turned Sukey over to the guards, the Queen said, "Let us go into the atrium where there is more air. I don't feel at all well."

The Second Redactor took his mother's arm, and the three of them went into a little enclosed courtyard that was a bower of autumn roses. The Queen and Culluket sat on the marble coping of the central fountain. Nodonn paced the flags, his armor's facets throwing prismatic refractions into the garden shadows.

"What have you done with the man?" Nontusvel asked.

"There was a row, of course." Culluket's tone was dry. "Stein and Aiken Drum were at the Coercer College, breakfasting with Gomnol, if you please! Naturally the young mountebank and the Lord Coercer claimed to know nothing of Stein's relation with Sukey—which was the ostensible reason given for my taking him into custody. Stein became quite violent, even in spite of his torc. Gomnol had no choice but to subdue him and turn him over to us, however.

The truth of our accusation about the woman leaked from Stein's mind as from a sieve. He'll be imprisoned until the Grand Combat and set up in one of the gladiator events. The girl goes into the Great Retort, of course."

"And Aiken Drum?"

Culluket's laugh held admiration in spite of himself. "Now there's a cool one! You need no redaction to know that there must have been collusion between master and man in both treasons. But Drum insisted upon playing the innocent. He demanded that Gomnol and I inspect his mind together, right there on the spot. Without the proper softening process our examination had to be rough and ready —but the little wretch was a match for us. We couldn't discover a particle of treachery hidden anywhere in his mind. No knowledge of Stein and Minivel, no knowledge of any plot against the torc factory or the time-gate."

The Battlemaster stopped his pacing and sat down beside his brother on the edge of the fountain. He stirred the water with one finger. Little simmers of steam arose. "You and Gomnol did the interrogation . . . together."

The Queen looked from Nodonn to Culluket. "You can't mean—"

But Culluket gave a slow nod. "It could very well be. Gomnol is capable of it! I suspected nothing . . . Rumors of the King's impotence have been circulating among all members of the High Table, and we know our precious Lord Coercer cares for nothing if not the main chance. He has undoubtedly realized that his earlier appraisal of Aiken Drum as a metapsychic nova was mistaken. Furthermore, the disallowing of his genetic scheme featuring Elizabeth and the Thagdal has made necessary a slight revision in his dynastic scenario."

"Oh, the ingrate!" cried the Queen. "Gomnol allied with Aiken Drum! This is what comes of admitting Lowlives to our High Table! We must do something about him at once! Imidol must issue the challenge to Gomnol at this year's manifestation of powers."

"He'd lose," Culluket said flatly.

"What then?" the Queen implored. "Gomnol will throw in his lot with the Lowlife rebels! Isn't it obvious?"

Culluket looked puzzled. "But Gomnol wouldn't destroy his own torc factory, his power base. It's counter to the man's entire psychology. Somehow, Aiken Drum has managed to keep this part of the plot from him."

"Then let's tell Gomnol!" cried Nontusvel. "Turn him against that horrid little golden beast!"

"Peace, dearest Mother." Nodonn's sun-bright countenance relaxed the agitated Queen with its warmth. "There are so many things afoot—so many intrigues and plots and counterplots—that they collide with one another and entwine in a tangle that seems to defy unknotting. The northern insurgents with their iron, perhaps with the Spear; the monstrous Felice, murderer of our sister Epone, who now wears stolen gold; the rebel general Guderian and her saboteur cohorts; Aiken Drum, whose loyalties lie Tana-knows-where; the King's schemes; the anthropologist and his survey; and the Lord Coercer—who would manipulate us all! A formidable snarl."

"But not," Culluket insinuated, "beyond your power to unravel, Brother Battlemaster?"

"I," said Nodonn, "have a Sword."

The Queen drew in a sharp breath. "You *can't!*"

"They are humans. They have outlawed themselves. Aiken Drum poses a peculiar problem because of his great popularity with our citizens. We'll need strong proof of his treason, but he can be dealt with. And so can Gomnol—much more easily, I believe. This entire mess can be turned to our advantage."

"Are you so confident of your own ability?" Culluket asked. "The iron alone is a mortal threat to our survival here. If you should miscalculate, the entire High Kingdom could be thrown into chaos."

Ever serene, the Battlemaster said, "We of the Host have agreed that it is necessary to return to the simpler way. To the old customs that we followed for nearly a thousand years. The superficial glamour of humanity's bastard culture has blinded too many of our people—even the Thagdal himself—and brought us to the brink of ruin. But Tana has been compassionate. It is not too late to turn back. The very conspiracies of these Lowlives show them up clearly as the danger we could only suspect before. Not even the most obtuse of our people will be able to ignore the human peril when I have done with my counteraction . . . And there is also *this.*"

He held up a pale-green plaque. Culluket exclaimed, "The survey! Congratulations, Brother! May I inspect it?"

Ignoring the request, Nodonn said, "The human anthropologist has been unwise enough to deliver an honest evaluation. His survey points to the inevitable ascendency of humans and hybrids in the Many-Colored Land, should we Tanu continue to exploit humans genetically and permit them to occupy positions of power. The King has studied the survey but he still waffles over the implications. He and the other moral weaklings at the High Table may think that the status quo can be maintained simply by destroying all copies of the survey and the computer file of data, and doing away with Bryan Grenfell and Ogmol. But thanks to my darling Rosmar, we have not only a copy of the book—but also the anthropologist himself safely tucked away. Dearest Mother, it is my intention to force the anthropologist to reveal the truth about his own human race at the culmination of the Grand Combat. I will produce him just prior to the Heroic Encounters so that the conspirators of the peace faction have no time to prepare opposition. When the peril is made clear, the combined wrath of our entire Tanu battle-company will fall upon those who are traitors to our ancient ideals. Upon Gomnol! Upon Aiken Drum! And upon any of our other kinsmen who have become so depraved as to consider humanity essential to our survival here."

The Queen raised a hand to her lips. "But then the Thagdal—"

Nodonn was relentless. "Queen and Mother, if he persists in his folly, his time has come. I will be merciful. The choice, at the end, will be his own."

Culluket hastened to say, "You, as Mother of the Host, are wholly exempt from his fate."

Nontusvel had her mental screens up. Her eyes refused to meet those of her sons. "Sometimes . . . our ways are very hard. I thought there might be another way."

Nodonn swept on. "As for the sabotage plot in Sue-Gwen Davies' mind, there are ways to turn that affair to our advantage if we work quickly. We have no details of the proposed assault on the torc factory. Obviously, the northerners did not take Aiken Drum and his loutish crony entirely into their confidence. But we do know the date —the twenty-second, two days from now—and we can presume that the attack will take place at night when activity around the Coercer Headquarters is minimal. The second part of the Lowlife plot, the attempt to send a message through the time-gate, must certainly take place at dawn on the twenty-second."

Culluket exclaimed, "Gomnol would certainly try to stop the factory attack if he knew about it. We can beat him to the punch and take the credit ourselves!"

The Battlemaster threw back his glorious head and laughed. "Redactive Brother, what a simpleton you are! But never mind. The planning of campaigns is my duty. You'll see how well I've fulfilled it soon enough. Now then . . . you must summon all of the top fighters of the Host, who have by now arrived in Muriah. This very noon our Mother will hold a sacred reunion in order to impart a special blessing on her warrior children before the games. When we are together and secluded, I will explain the strategy that will deliver *all* of our enemies into our hands."

"The murderer of our dearest Epone," the Interrogator put in, "*she* is reserved to me."

Nodonn nodded agreement. "Extract all useful information from this Felice and then it shall be as you request. But this female monster must be able to fight in the gladiatorial games when you're through with her. It is part of my overall strategy. The others will go into the Great Retort. These Lowlives must all suffer the most public destruction, as an example to the others. I will brook only one exception. I have other plans for Guderian."

"Both she and Felice wear the gold," cautioned Culluket.

"Felice's will be removed by her own iron," said the Battlemaster. "She will wear gray as she spills her blood on the White Silver Plain. Guderian's torc will not matter, as you will shortly discover."

Nontusvel's tears had dried. She rose from the fountain's edge and said brightly, "If we're going to have a great crowd for luncheon, I must consult with the cooks at once. You will excuse me." They kissed her hands and she rushed away, trailing fragmented thoughts of hostessly menu planning.

Culluket turned a level eye to the Battlemaster. "There is still one human whose position remains to be clarified. I must insist that you be straightforward in a matter of such high seriousness."

The image of Mercy seemed to hover between the brothers.

Nodonn's glowing face was unreadable and his mind as well. "The others of the Host were too polite to question my choice of consort—or too prudent. But since you dare to be frank, I'll tell you what I have discovered about her. From my first meeting with Rosmar, I was struck by the incredible affinity, the sweet consonance of thought between us that was so different from the relationships I had known with other human women—even with women of our own race. And so after I took her to wife, I had Greg-Donnet prepare a genetic assay of my remarkable bride."

"And?"

"Mercy-Rosmar's plasm is almost identical to our own. She has more of our genes than she has of human. Tana alone knows how to account for it—but then I am no scientist."

Culluket, who was, looked profoundly shaken. His screens hid a storm of intellectualizing but could not efface the tinge of suspicion pervading it.

The insouciance of the Battlemaster melted into something black. For one terrible instant the startled Culluket was wrapped in a second skin all lined with needles, and the point of each one was the source of an electric charge that inflamed the pain receptors of his epidermis almost to the point of overload. He would have fallen, would have lost consciousness except for the grip of Nodonn's great mind.

As swiftly as it had come, the agony was wiped away, replaced by a sensation of utter well-being.

And Nodonn's thought: Cogitate as you will Redactive Brother. But never again doubt my judgment or hint that Mercy-Rosmar is anything but loyal.

Master of every obscenity!

"Now you're behaving like a simpleton again," chided the voice of Apollo. "Just remember who it is who will be king. And never make the mistake of thinking you can teach *me* anything about the inflicting of pain."

13

TOGETHER WITH many other sightseers from Muriah, Katlinel the Darkeyed went down on chalikoback in the evening cool to wander over the White Silver Plain and satisfy her perennial curiosity about the everyday activities of the ancient Foe, encamped now in harmless splendor all about the northeastern end of the battleground.

She rode over the wide bridge spanning the canal. The bed of the watercourse was paved with limestone blocks, and it ran three meters deep with star-spangled fresh water. The flow came from that huge spring, the Well of the Sea, whose waters had been the rationale for the siting of the field of combat from the earliest coming of the Tanu to Aven. Here and there the Little People dipped buckets or filled skins. Farther downstream, some Firvulag women were washing clothes; and still farther along, where the canal waters shallowed as they curved east and met the Great Lagoon, were the quaint bathing tents of the modest folk.

Katlinel let her chaliko have its head. It ambled down the long central avenue of the tent-city where bonfires burned atop cairns of heaped rocks. The large earth-colored pavilions of the Firvulag nobility were here, awnings and flies fringed in gold and silver, and embroidered designs ornamenting walls and roof panels. Every Great One's tent was fronted by a tall pole from which floated the richly jeweled standard of its occupant, all decorated with hair plumes and gold-plated skulls of vanquished foemen. Every standard was topped by the effigy of a different monstrous head, which represented the favorite illusionary aspect of the Firvulag warrior.

The Little People were everywhere. Some wore their handsomely chased obsidian armor; but most were more casually attired in trousers and jerkins or gem-studded robes with borders of fur (which must have been very uncomfortable in the sultry dusk). Pointed caps were the most common headgear among men and women alike. The grander ladies had veils floating from theirs, or decorated padded brims, or ornamental horns, or long lappets that hung before or behind their ears. It was customary for the lofty Tanu to refer to their shadow-kinfolk as "little." But most of those that Katlinel passed were at least equal to humans in stature; and now and again she caught a glimpse of some doughty champion who far surpassed any Tanu in height and bulk. It was being said in the capital that more Firvulag than ever before had come south for this year's Grand Combat, cheered by their triumph at Finiah. The army was rumored to include certain proud fighters who had disdained to contend of late because of the contamination of the games by human participants. Medor had come out of hiding, and the hideous Nukalavee who fought under the guise of a flayed centaur with all the raw muscles and sinews and blood vessels exposed to strike horror into his opponents; and even old Pallol One-Eye the Firvulag Battlemaster had returned, breaking his twenty-year sulk.

There were supposed to be nearly 50,000 of the Little People encamped on the Plain already—nearly two-thirds of the entire Firvulag population. About half of this number were fighters, and they outnumbered the Tanu knights and their human auxiliaries by about three to one. Eventually, almost the entire chivalry of the

Many-Colored Land would be arrayed against this concentration of the Foe.

Firvulag hawkers importuned Katlinel as she rode among the campfires and the jolly groups of feasters and dancers. She was offered jewelry and precious trinkets on every hand, since this was the craft that the Firvulag excelled in above all others; there were also vendors of sweets and salted nuts and hard cider and strange fortified wines. But she resisted their pleas. Only when she reached the end of the long avenue and circled around among the squat black tents of the humbler folk did she succumb at last to temptation in the shape of a goblinesque little maiden with thick blonde braids and a pert scarlet hennin, who offered flagons of carved myrtlewood filled with a marvelous perfume distilled from forest flowers.

"Thank you, Lady." The diminutive seller bobbed a curtsy as she accepted payment. "It's said among us that the Dame's Hesperis breathes forth a scent that even the most reluctant swain finds impossible to resist."

Katlinel laughed. "I'll remember to wear it with caution."

"Well, I've heard," was the saucy retort, "that some of your Tanu gentlemen need all the help they can get."

"We'll see about that at the games," Katlinel said, and rode on, smiling.

Another chaliko fell in beside her own as she passed through an area crowded with dining and drinking tents. When a drunken ogre came carousing out and seized the reins of her mount, the rider on the other beast closed in even before she could spin a defensive illusion. One mental bolt sent the Firvulag oaf staggering into the arms of his jeering mates, who dragged him away with a breezy apology to Katlinel for the imposition.

"I am in your debt, Exalted Lord," she said, bowing her head to her rescuer.

He was a handsome figure, tall and broad-shouldered, wearing a close-fitting coif beneath a visored cap adorned with a small golden coronet. The coif hid his hair and throat and fell over his shoulders in a very short cape, all scalloped and jeweled at the edges. His hose and doublet were deep violet.

"It is my pleasure, Exalted Lady. I'm afraid that some of my countrymen take their celebrating too seriously, too far in advance."

She studied him with frank surprise as they rode on together. "You amaze me, Lord. With your neck covered, I mistook you for one of my own people."

"And which are they?" inquired the other, the faintest taunt in his fine voice.

Katlinel flushed and gripped her reins, ready to spur the chaliko away from the upstart. But the man reached out a hand and the animal stood still.

"Forgive my impertinence, Lady. It was unforgivable. But it is obvious that your beauty derives from human as well as Tanu blood. And I perceive from your silver and green gown that you are—as I—of the illusion-spinners, and one of rare power. If you will forgo your just annoyance at my crude banter and think instead of the small service lately done for you, perhaps we may yet ride on for a few moments and speak together. I have a great curiosity about your people."

"And a clever tongue as well, Firvulag Lord! . . . Very well, you may ride with me for a short time. I am Katlinel, surnamed the Darkeyed, and I sit at the High Table in the very lowest chair, being the least among the Tanu Great Ones."

"Surely not for long!" He doffed the crowned cap; the purple coif covered his skull. "I am known as the ruler of Meadow Mountain. My domain lies far to the north, on the fringes of the Firvulag realm. Never before this have I attended the Grand Combat. My people are so occupied with the daily problems of survival that they have scant heart for religious games."

"A heretical notion, to be sure. But one that I can sympathize with."

"There are those among you who are not ardent members of the battle-company?"

"Many," she admitted, "especially among the hybrids such as myself. But the force of tradition remains strong."

"Ah. Tradition. But of late the old ways seem shaken. Humanity, once so docile and useful, rises up in revolt against your High King."

"In alliance with you Firvulag!"

"The Tanu were the first to use humans. Shouldn't we as well? We Firvulag are, it's true, more hidebound than you. Why—most of my people will not even mount an animal such as this, preferring to march on their own sturdy legs."

"But you have no such scruples?"

"I've been forced to be a realist, Lady. Tell me—is it true that human scientists are honored and fostered among the Tanu? That you've used their specialized knowledge to enhance your own technoeconomy?"

"I belong to the High Faculty of the Creator Guild. Most science, excepting that of healing and psychobiology, falls within our province. We have many human scientists at work in our College, educating our young people as well as engaged in practical application of their knowledge. Agriculturalists, earth scientists, engineers of every sort, even specialists in the social sciences—all have placed their talents in the service of the Many-Colored Land."

"And geneticists?" the Lord of Meadow Mountain inquired softly.

"Most certainly."

He said, "If only we were not Foes. If only we were free to cooperate, to have a free interchange of ideas and resources. I know that we Firvulag would have much to offer you. And you . . . could do so much for us."

"But that is not the *way*," she said.

"Not yet. Not so long as the stern old battle-company rules your High Kingdom."

"I must leave now," Katlinel said.

"Will you come again and talk? There is still more than a week before the Combat begins and we officially become Foes once more."

She held out one hand and he took it and saluted her in the classic manner. His lips were cold. A flash of metapsychic insight told Katlinel that they were also illusory. But the mind that opened to her in momentary hope—that was not cold at all.

"I'll come again tomorrow night," she said. "Shall I ask for you among your friends?"

"Few here would call me that." His smile was both rueful and cautionary. "Ride here and I will find you. It would be better if none of your people knew that you condescended to have converse with Sugoll, Lord of Meadow Mountain—which humans of Elder Earth call the Feldberg."

"We of the High Table do as we please," said Katlinel. She spurred the chaliko up the trail leading from the salt plain to Aven.

14

GOMNOL PANNED the infrared spot slowly over the blackness of the Catalan Gulf. "Still nothing. And the Flying Hunt will be moving their search into this area in another hour if they stick to their grid. Are you certain the saboteurs planned to land tonight?"

"Goddammit, yes," growled Aiken Drum. He squatted in an embrasure between a pair of battlements, peering through an ordinary lens-ocular. He and the Lord Coercer were on the highest turret of Guild Headquarters. "Arrive tonight, farspeak me to whatever rendezvous seemed safest, confer about the best way to crash this place, then mount the assault during the wee hours Monday morning after a day's rest and recon. Don't dump on me if your spies were too incompetent to locate 'em."

"I believe your friends are here already," Gomnol said. "They could have come in obliquely along the coast with the traffic from Tarasiah and Calamosk and Geroniah and the rest of the Spanish cities. Suppose they sailed southwest into the Catalan backwaters after shooting the Glissade, then simply doubled back along the Aven shore? If they're down on the coast now, we'll never spot them —and neither will Nodonn and the Host, airborne or not. There are half a hundred little creeks and inlets along this northern side of the peninsula, and all full of caves where they could hole up out of far-sense range." He shut off the power of his big viewer. "You'll just have to wait for their hail, even if it does increase the chance that the Host might find them first. What a pity your saboteur friends didn't trust you to fly out and meet them as soon as they reached the Basin."

"Aw, shut up," said Aiken. "I'm trying my seekersense on Felice's pattern. She might not be too good at screening yet."

"And then again, she might! We'll have to be very cautious with *that* one . . . And that great booby, Stein! If our block in his mind doesn't hold—if Culluket recognizes it and gets other redactors of the

Host to join in a multiphase probe—Stein is going to open up! I can't risk the Host knowing my involvement in this affair and neither can you. We're going to have to put Stein out of the way."

"Gumball, will you stop griping my ass?" Aiken's button eyes held a vicious glitter. "Stein's mental block will hold. You just try killing him or Sukey and the whole thing's off between us. You grab?"

"Only too well. But I must point out the risk we're running. If the Host obtains firm proof of our treason, we will be declared outlaw humans. No rules of Truce or other precepts of the battle-religion will protect us. I know how powerful you've become—that's why I agreed to follow your leadership in this affair. But the massed minds of the Host are capable of annihilating both of us if they act in full concert under Nodonn. I've had forty years of experience with the Tanu and you've been here three months! If you won't listen to my advice, you'll end up with your head on a pike—for all your high metafaculties!"

The trickster came down from the battlement, a conciliatory smile making his teeth shine in the dark. "Gumball—baby! I told you we'd be buddies. I know I need you. Hellfire, man, even if you weren't Lord Coercer and the craftiest intriguer in the whole kingdom—*you're the boy who knows the torcs.* Who the hell wants to be king without subjects? You gotta keep those collars rolling out, sweetie! Jeez, I almost blew my cortex when old Elizabeth gave me the marvelous news about these turkeys coming south to sabotage your place. And they want to close the time-gate! Not only cut off the supply of warm bods, but their futuristic goodies, too! No more real Scotch for you and me. Sweet houghmagandy!"

Gomnol laughed. "There's scant chance of either happening now. You and I and the Tanu may have our differences, but the valuation of the gate and the factory is hardly one of them. Not even Nodonn would dare go against the King and public opinion by treating these sabotage threats lightly."

"But he might try to muscle in on our act," Aiken warned. "Just like he did with the Delbaeth Quest. He'll try to make it look like *he's* the one who sniffs out the plots and snuffs 'em, and we can't let him grab face from us. We've gotta catch these human saboteurs red-handed doing their thing so we can show what loyal citizens we are."

"It would be more prudent to take the factory saboteurs as soon as we discover their hideout. But your idea does have PR advantages. I've arranged for neutral observers—Lord Bormol of Roniah and the

Lord of Swords—to witness our brilliant defense. Both of them belong to the Coercer Guild and they'll be able to vouch for my zeal in case that scheming hothead, Imidol, attempts to say later that I was in league with the invaders."

"I wish I could be here to help." Aiken spoke with every evidence of sincerity. "But you can't fly, and one of us has to handle the timegate operation personally. We can't just warn the castellan and hope for the best. This Madame Guderian isn't any dummy, the way she orchestrated Finiah. She'll have something sneaky planned. Probably wild diversions while she creeps up on the gate invisible. But with *me* waiting to pop her illusion—have no fear!" He added quietly, "Just be sure you do as well with Felice, Gumball."

The Lord Coercer was replacing the protective pod over the infrared scanner. "I'll have my best human golds ready for her. Iron weapons won't do the saboteurs a bit of good against *them*." In a nonchalant manner, he asked, "What do you suppose became of the Spear and the aircraft after Finiah?"

Aiken lifted his golden shoulders. "Haven't the faintest! Sure as shit the rebels would've kept on using both of 'em in other attacks if they were still operational. I thought Velteyn claimed to've shot the plane down."

"He said he penetrated the craft with his ball lightning," Gomnol corrected. "But no one saw the flyer crash and no wreckage was ever discovered. We certainly must find out what happened. If the weapon and the ship are still usable, we could be in very serious trouble, my boy."

"Aaah," Aiken scoffed. "If they still had a zapper and an aircraft, would they come down south by riverboat and try this lamebrain attack on your fortress?" Aiken was reasonable. And his mind was artistically screened. "You got nothing to worry about. We'll worm the whole thing outa Felice and her ragtag commandos and you can have your reception committee and observation team all primed and ready . . . And save a few prisoners for questioning—okay? Even if the bird and the zapper they used on Finiah are a terminal fewk-out, it would be awfully nice to know where they came from. There might be others!"

The strange bedfellows eyed one another for a long minute. Neither one could detect the presence of any suspiciously screened chicane in the other. They were both experts.

"Well—guess I'll do a little eyeball scan," Aiken said at last. "I'll get down to the shore and be ready when Felice and her gang give a shout." He flipped a hand at the Lord Coercer in farewell.

A longtailed moth, lime-green with windowpane eyespots, went fluttering from the high tower, down the northern cliffs, and over the dunes and badlands to the shore of the Catalan Lagoon.

* * *

O Aiken.

Hey! That you sweets? Longtimenothink! Thought you long gone.

How *could* you Stein/Sukey trapped Cullukettorturer?

Elizababe misread me not! Blame me not having done damnedest under friggertytough chew! Sukey leaked to Queen re Stein so Cull pounced. Options for me: [1] Let Cull take Stein; [2] fight & get us *both* taken. Yes? Yes! Threw good mindblock Stein won't betray others/me. He/Sukey secure for now Cull thinks he knows all. Before Combat I spring pair detorc ship off to safe lovenest + unborn Steinling happilyeverafter.

And Gomnol?

Elizacraftybeth you know.

AikenDrum + Gomnol = KingYou + GrandVizierHe.

Why not?

Permit probe implementation?

You can't probe longdistance and I'm too busy now to come. What matter no trust little ConnYankeeMerlin anymore?

Not allied Mordred.

Who he? And why you care anyhoo GrandDropoutMaster?

Aiken don't betray ourfriends! Beware not only for theirsake for yours O trickster-selftricked unto the end dear Aiken don't.

Relax Elizababeballooner. When I king all well but interfere not thwart not ambitions gods/superfolk lest juggernaut squish you grab?

O you Aiken do what you must but woe to you because of what you must do.

You oracles all alike anal pain. Keep aloof overflying like before whynot? You got balloon now so take off get lost! But let me alone nothing stops me now nothing not you not Brede not Archangel-Nodonn not old GroupGreen gangomine not even chocolatekryptonite by friggertydamn!

• • •

Elizabeth?

. . .

You gone?

. . .

(Laughter.)

* * *

The longtailed moth followed the call to a deep cavern on an inlet of the northern coast of Aven. The saboteurs, like the Firvulag, knew that the simplest way to escape detection by Tanu searchers was to hide underground. Felice guided Aiken to them by means of a gossamer mind-thread, tuned nicely to his intimate mode, which no other being could possibly farsense. And when the gold-clad little figure appeared with a silent snap on the other side of their shielded campfire, Felice was standing there in the looted blue-glass armor that Old Man Kawai had adapted to her small stature, the Spear gripped in one gauntleted hand—and murder in her eye.

"You tipped 'em off!" Her coercive power closed like a bear-trap.

"Me? *Me?*" He squirmed in her mind's clutches. She was stronger than he had expected. A lot stronger. He could break free—but was it wise to let them know how his powers had matured? And *now* what the hell had she done? A big muffer of a boulder plugging the cavern exit! Where had it come from, so silently, so soon? Goddammit, was she a creator, too—or had that been just a deft bit of the old PK?

"Felice, baby, you are making one helluva booboo. *Yhhh!* Lay off the marbles, kid, for chrissake! I didn't tell 'em! Give me a chance to *explain!*"

She relaxed her holds, both coercive and psychokinetic. A great cage of light-blue flame sprang up to encircle him. (Well, that was that. She could create.) For the first time he paid attention to the others standing behind Felice, disguised as guards and serving women. He only recognized the nun.

"Amerie!" cried the shining youth. "Tell her she's gotta let me explain!"

"Talk fast, Tricky-Pockets," Felice said.

He seemed to bare his innocence to the gold-torced fury. Stein and Sukey—*they* were the ones who had inadvertently blown the gaff—not him! Since the information he gave Felice was basically the truth (and since he was marvelously adept at concealing the seams that joined truth to semitruth and falsehood), the girl's redactive power, weakest of her five metafunctions, could find no fault with his recital. Still glowering, but reluctantly won over in spite of her deeper instincts, she turned off the cage of astral fire and set him free.

Aiken whipped a snowy handkerchief from one of his pockets and wiped his sweating face. "My sweet Lord, you're a brute, Felice! Really learned how to use your collar in a hurry, didn't you?"

She did not answer.

Aiken assumed his most ingratiating air. Addressing himself to the others, he said, "Everything's all set, guys. We've got an inside man —a gold-torc who's lived here for years pretending to be loyal, just waiting for a chance to strike a really valid blow for humanity. He's going to deactivate the lock on a very small service door that hasn't been used in years. They used to shovel their rubbish out of the keep and right over the edge of the cliff, see? There's a little narrow trail giving access to the door but you can walk on it all right. I checked. You'll have to come onto the trail from above, through town. But for the getaway, you can rappel right down the cliff face into the old dump and hightail it into the badlands. A little luck and there'll be such a reeraw going on that you can make it back to these caves before they even know you're gone."

With a magician's flourish, he hauled a large sheet of durofilm out of another pocket.

"Look! I brought you a complete map! City, Guild buildings, interior of the headquarters block showing your route from the service door to the torc-making rooms. See—this is where you are, and here's the old dump, and here's the Coercer HQ at the edge of the cliff and the door. You just come into town in your disguises—you look bonzo, by the way!—and lose yourselves in the greenway bushes just west of the Coercer House wall."

He spread the map on the floor and most of the saboteurs hunched down to study it. But Felice said:

"What about the Spear?"

Aiken was offhanded. "Oh. Right. Is that it you got there? Big sonuvabitch, isn't it?"

"If we could get it working," the girl said, "we could hit the Coercer headquarters from a distance. There'd be no need for a penetration at all."

"I gotcha. Oh, absolutely. I kinda forgot all about that old zapper, what with our having an inside man at the skonk works all ready to let us walk inside."

"Who is it?" asked the biggest of the desperados. He wore the blue cloak and bronze half-armor of a captal of the provincial guard.

Aiken frowned in anxiety. "I can't tell you his name. If any of you got captured, there's no way you could avoid giving him away. And we can't let that happen. This guy is not only loaded with meta-functions, but he's also in a high position. A perfect undercover agent for later on, see? Now lemme give this a good think. Like I say, I'd almost forgotten about this Spear. A real long shot—but if I *could* fix it and warn our inside man to get out of there . . ."

Felice silently handed the great glassy lance to Aiken. Chief Burke brought up the powerpack and its cable, which they had toted from Hidden Springs in a leathern chest. Aiken stroked the blue-lacquered weapon with steady fingers, lifting the cap-lock to inspect the studs, hefting it into his right armpit and pretending to take aim at Felice's big rock plugging the entrance.

"Pam!" he ejaculated. A wavering little spark, the size of a firefly, emerged from the business end of the device and drifted through the air. It collided with the rock and fell into an impotent shower of red-glowing dust.

"So much for refueling the zapper with my mind-power!" He gave them a sprightly wink. "Now let's have a look at the juice box."

He jabbed and thrust at the pack's peculiar sunken fasteners with several of the tools that he carried in his golden suit. "Gonna take more than I've got here to get it open," he said. "Tell you what! I'll change it into a piece of straw and myself into a bird and take it back to my workroom. If I get it open and figure how to recharge it, I'll bring it back here before midnight tomorrow, and warn our coercer pal what's up, and you can blast the place to hell and gone from out in the lagoon. But if I give you a mind-squeak at twenty-four bells telling you it's no go, you carry on with the other plan. How's that sound?"

His eyes flicked eagerly from face to face.

"I think," said Felice, "that we should postpone any decision until you come back here with the Spear. Operational or not. And I think you should go along with us on the torc factory assault."

"I'd like nothing better," he said earnestly. "But I'm supposed to go to this combatant's banquet at the palace. These folks are just sitting down at table around midnight. There's no way I can get out of going. I'm one of the hottest contenders in the light humanweight class!"

"I don't like this," said Felice.

"You still don't trust me." Sorrow clouded the golliwog face. He gestured to the map. "What else do I hafta *do?*"

"You've got it all planned, haven't you?" she said archly. "We just follow your little red lines on the map. Time all picked, route all picked, getaway all set up. What would you say if I told you that we'd make our own penetration at our own time? Not on Monday at all? Just to make sure there's no nasty surprises waiting behind the rubbish door?"

He flung his hands into the air. "It's your gig, babe, not mine. But without the zapper or my inside man opening up for you, you'll need one helluva can opener to break into that fortress. To say nothing of losing your sync with Madame's hit of the time-gate."

Chief Burke said, "Felice, maybe I could go back with him."

"And how'd you let us know if there was any funny business?" She was sarcastic. "Farspeak me through your broken gray torc?"

"Come along yourself, then," Aiken suggested to her.

The others burst into a storm of protest.

At last Felice said, "We'll have to carry on with your suggestion about the Spear. But God save your ass, Aiken Drum, if this is one of your hookem-snivey tricks!"

"Piffle," said the golden man. He picked up the Spear and its heavy pack as though they were toys and cocked his head in the direction of the barricading boulder. "Are you going to be a gentlewoman and open your little door for a lad with his hands full?"

Felice crossed her sapphire-armored arms and gave a tinkling laugh. "Suppose you show us how *you'd* do it, Fancy Pants."

Aiken emitted a martyred sigh. He faced the cave entrance and stuck out his tongue. The mass of mineral suddenly seemed shot through with thousands of small holes that grew and grew until the huge rock was nothing but a lacy webwork. It collapsed in another instant of its own weight, making a sound like smashing glassware.

"Shoddy workmanship around here," observed the jester.

He changed into a crescent-winged nightjar. *Kutuk-kutuk!* The bird gave a mocking call as it slipped out into the night, a straw and a lump of moss caught in its claws.

None of the people inside the cave could see the direction it took: straight north, toward the mainland of Europe.

* * *

Gumball?

Yes Aiken.

They bought the house and lot and the little white fence around it too. Exactly as we planned. They'll futz around for a while when I don't farspeak back tomorrow night. But then they'll decide some monster ate me and go ahead with their plan. What else can they do? Right? You be ready when they come in that back door. Felice is in blue armor and loaded with metafunctions. Be sure your boys have their heaviest screens up. Besides her there are six men dressed as gray guards and two dames got up as servants in those stripy robes. None of them have any mental firepower at all. They'll be easy to stop if you look out for the iron.

And Felice?

Do whatever you have to do and watch your sweet petard.

I understand. You go now to Castle Gateway?

On swift little wings. Plenty of time. You just have yourself a nice day tomorrow and be sure the welcome mat is all shook out and ready at midnight. Bye-bye!

Bon voyage to you Aiken Drum.

* * *

"I knew it! I knew it!" Felice raged.

"It's half past midnight," Uwe said. "We *must* go now. It will take at least three hours to get into the city, even if we do secure mounts at the main dockyard, and more time to make our way along the cliff. We cannot wait any longer to hear from Aiken Drum."

"It's a trap!" the girl insisted.

Amerie urged her, "Try to make mental contact one more time. Try both him and Elizabeth."

Felice's wild brown eyes fixed on some distant vista. She held her fingers to her golden torc. They all waited.

The little athlete seemed to shrink smaller than ever, despite the blaze of glass armor. "Nothing. Neither Aiken nor Elizabeth. Nothing. We can't go. It's a trap. I know it."

Chief Burke stood over her. "That little gold mamzer might have pulled a fast one at that. But there are other ways to explain his silence. He could be in a position where he doesn't dare farspeak us. Perhaps some exotics came and hauled him away to the party before he could get a word off. Isn't that possible?"

"No! I mean—maybe." Her expression was frantic. "Oh, Peo—it all depends on his farspeaking skill! And I don't know enough about this business yet to tell whether he's capable of it or not. I suppose you could be right."

"Then we're going to have to get on with it," said the Native American.

"Can't we wait? Look over Guild HQ in daylight ourselves, the way we planned to back in the beginning? Make our own plan for penetration? . . . My PK and creativity and coerce are coming on *strong*, guys! I think I could fuzz the minds of the guards at that place so we could walk right in the front door. Hell—in this blue rig-out and with you as my loyal escort, I'm just another Guild member to any big guns that happen to saunter by. I can shield the bunch of you easily. And by God, I'll smear that torc factory into marmalade just as soon as I get into range. Not with thunderbolts! Soft and sneaky—with PK that just liquefies the walls! Then we can escape before anyone knows what's happened. But not out that door of Aiken's—we'll go out one of the windows on the northeastern corner of the building, as far away from that service door as we can get. It'll be easy with my PK and Basil's climbing equipment."

Chief Burke hesitated.

Uwe contributed his placid opinion. "If Felice is certain that her metafunctions are equal to the task, there's no reason why we can't follow her modified plan *tonight*. Khalid knows the city. We can take a completely different route from the one laid out by Aiken Drum. The Coercer Guild complex is huge. If they're waiting in ambush at this rear door, they may be careless elsewhere."

Felice gave a crow of joy and kissed the graybeard. "Yes! As long as we don't follow that joker's blueprint, I'm ready to go tonight."

"Do the rest of you agree?" Burke asked. There was a murmur of acquiescence. "Then hoist your little tushies and get your disguises in order. We're off to the main landing stage to steal some horses—I mean, chalikos. If my future ancestors could only see me now."

15

"WAY! Way for the exalted Lady Phyllis-Morigel!" the captal sang out.

The mob of barenecks and grays and well-dressed Firvulag that
crowded the central square of Muriah parted minimally to let the
mounted party pass. Even in the early hours after midnight the
place was a crush of commerce and amusement and carnival display.
The Little Folk were by ancient custom night people; and down
here in the south, where daytime temperatures in the Mediterranean
Basin soared to heights that were barely tolerable to specially
adapted humans, let alone a race that had evolved in cold uplands,
the Firvulag were abroad almost exclusively between sunset and sunrise. Those who wished to cater to them kept a similar schedule.

There were plenty of Tanu and gold-torc humans about as well—
most of them, like the Lady Phyllis-Morigel and her train, having
recently arrived in the capital and seeking lodgings. Some of the
Great Ones stayed in the palace; others were accommodated with
relations; the keenest fighters headed for the pavilions that had been
erected on the turfed racecourse northwest of the city, where they
could practice their martial specialties. But the visitors with no special accommodation arranged in advance usually did what the Lady
Phyllis now did: They demanded, as was their right, the hospitality
of their Guild.

She and her eight attendants rode unhindered into the great
courtyard of the Coercer complex. Hostlers took charge of their
mounts. An urbane silver majordomo, calm in the midst of the
hullabaloo, assigned the lady and her handmaids a suite in one of
the dormitory mansions; the men-at-arms were directed to a barracks.

Felice's coercive power settled without trace over the will of the
majordomo. "We will pay our respects to the High Faculty of the
Guild, such as may be up and about, before retiring. Coming as we
do from doleful Finiah, we have need of fraternal support and sym-

pathy. You will be glad to conduct us into headquarters personally."

"I will be glad," the man repeated mechanically, "to conduct you into headquarters personally."

He led them from the basecourt, through the gardens, and across the plaza that fronted the looming block of the keep. The stronghold had been hung with extra decorative lights and was a veritable blaze of blue and amber. None of the Tanu or gold-torc humans outside the building paid any heed to the new arrivals. Felice's mind was apparently overshadowed by grief. Her raven standard, borne by Chief Burke, had long streamers of silver and black fluttering from its finial, the Tanu symbol of bereavement.

They came to the guards at the main entrance. The majordomo said, "This Exalted Lady will confer with the High Faculty."

The squad leader lifted his great bare sword of blue vitredur in formal salute. "The Exalted Lady will confer with the High Faculty."

"We will follow you," Felice told him.

"You will follow me," said the guardsman.

The majordomo bowed and retreated. Felice and the others walked between ranks of blue-and-gold-armored gray-torcs who stood like empty-eyed dummies on both sides of the foyer. There were no other people in sight. The bronze of the saboteurs' military harness jingled faintly. At each step Felice took, the jeweled sollerets on her feet chimed on the marble floor. She lowered the visor of her crested sapphire helmet. The others, as if hearing her mind's command, loosened iron weapons that had been sheathed in gold-plated wooden scabbards. Folding compound bows appeared from under capes; two of the men passed spares to the "serving women," who now shed their outer robes to reveal half-armor worn underneath.

They mounted a great staircase, with still no sign of Tanu or human Guild members. Felice conjured up the image of Aiken's map, then tried to verify their position with her farsight. But the effort was still beyond her and only Khalid's spatial sense kept them from getting lost in the maze of corridors. Farsensing and seeking, like creativity, were subtle things needing experience; while coercion and PK had burgeoned within the gold-torced athlete like jungle plants, long starved for light and moisture, that suddenly achieve their rampant growth under tropical sun and rain. Felice could control this ushering guardsman with ease, just as she had blanked the minds of the thirty other grays they had passed since penetrating the headquarters building. But now—

A bronze door opened. A Tanu woman in a gown of navy blue came into the corridor and halted at the sight of the procession, giving a telepathic greeting.

Allhail CoerciveSister from Ninelva and let me assist your seeking—

"Peo!" Felice cried. "I can only hold her for a second!"

The big Native American stepped forward, his face impassive under the bronze rim of his plumed kettle-helmet. He drew an iron shortsword, pulled the woman toward him with one arm as if embracing her, and sent the point of the weapon up behind her rib cage and into her heart.

The guard who had been leading them stood quietly, a blue-and-gold robot awaiting orders.

"Did she get off a warning?" Burke asked.

"No," said Felice. "Back inside that door with her, and then out of here. We've still got a way to go."

They began to trot down the corridor, turning to right and left and passing through ornamental gates and doorways until none but Khalid retained any orientation. The lighting grew dimmer. There were occasional heedless squads of guards, whom they ignored—and finally a truly massive pair of doors more than ten meters high, embossed with the heraldic male face and flanked by six grays in full blue-glass armor.

"This has to be it," Felice murmured. To their oblivious escort, she sent a coercive command: You will unbar the entrance to this torc factory.

I am unable to do this. No gray can do this.

"Shit!" hissed the little woman. "Stand back and we'll hope for the best!"

The six guards at the doorway pivoted right and left and marched away like jeweled mechanical dolls, followed by the gray who had led them in. Felice stood before the huge bronze valves with helmeted head thrown back and both fists clenched at her sides. The polished yellow metal along the juncture went greenish, blue, blotched purple—and then began to glow as the power of her psychokinetic faculty sent the molecules of metal to vibrating, going from solid to molten within thirty slow seconds.

The nonmetas watched it transfixed, their iron weapons ready. Heat from the melting bronze and its pungent smell beat at them, making them draw back from the small figure that now raised glittering blue arms and bade the ruined portal swing wide.

Behind the door was darkness. Felice stepped forward, ignoring the pool of still-liquid metal that smoked on the floor.

A burst of azure fire seemed to explode in the vast black beyond the open door. And then another appeared, strontium-red, and another of violet—blazing images in human form almost twice the height of small Felice. There were flashes of green light and rosy-gold and malevolent scarlet, all hovering in the dark. Crowds of them. Fifty or sixty or more, all massed in midair with swords and shields raised but visors open so that the saboteurs could see the contemptuous triumph in the exotic eyes of Nontusvel's Host.

"I am Imidol," thundered the voice of the blue leader. "Your death."

Felice sent a three-meter ball of flame rolling at him. "Iron!" she shrieked. "Iron! I'll bring down the roof!"

Four explosions rocked the corridor. The jewel-armored Tanu came flying out of the huge inner chamber like avenging angels. The invaders loosed their arrows. There were agonized shouts, falling meteors, lightning bolts, the deep rumble of falling masonry, a smell of ozone, dust, ordure, broiling meat.

Amerie, backed against the opposite wall of the corridor and blinded by fumes and metallic reek, shot her arrows wildly at tall glowing figures. Pulses of emotional energy smashed at her unshielded mind. There was a metapsychic conflict going on as well as a physical one, but she, lucky normal, could only perceive its overtones. When her quiver was empty she clutched her short-shafted javelin in both hands, consigned her soul to Jesus, and got ready to die.

A crash resounded as a wall came down—fortunately falling in toward the torc factory and not into the corridor. The meta-powered jewel-lamps along the walls had all gone out and the only light now came from the glowing armor of the Tanu, the bursts of astral flame, and occasional puddles of molten slag. The place was thick with smoke. Amerie fell to her knees and sought air along the floor. Things lay there—shattered blocks of limestone, metal lamp-fittings, pieces of jeweled and bronze armor, and softer dark masses that glistened and oozed.

Amerie crept slowly through smoky hell. Uwe Guldenzopf's bearded face shone momentarily in a lurid blaze. His head lay close to the wall. There was no body.

Sobbing, still carrying her iron-tipped spear, she followed the wall. There were more detonations behind her and a noise like an avalanche. A female voice uttered awful whooping shrieks like a warning siren. A great glowing rose-colored form went soaring over her head toward the center of the tumult—then another that shone green and white. The mental bombardment increased. She flattened herself on the floor, beyond praying. One of her feet was completely numb. The corridor was filled with a brain-blasting throb that made her teeth and even her eyes respond in a harmonic of sympathetic pain. The fumes and fire diminished, as suddenly the whole scene retreated to a distance. She floated above her body—poor thing—and saw that one leather boot was burned black, still smoking, and the sooty bronze of her cuirass backpiece had a deep indentation above the area of her kidneys. Her right arm was raw from elbow to wrist and there was a glimmer of white bone.

"What are you waiting for, angel?" she asked testily.

But she did not die. Taking up residence in the battered thing lying on the floor once again, she let her eyes open. She saw a short human figure in shining blue armor standing over her.

"Well, I'm glad to see *you!*" she shouted, joyous in relief. "Did we win after all?"

One jeweled gauntlet raised the blue visor. A man with a large nose and humorous eyes looked down at her, smiling with small, perfect teeth. She had never seen him before.

"You did not win," said Gomnol.

Amerie felt her damaged body rise from the floor, sustained by the Lord Coercer's psychokinetic power. He walked back into the inferno with her drifting after him like some grotesque balloon-doll. The smoke was pushed away before him and little flames extinguished themselves as he passed. A radiance streamed from Gomnol's face, illuminating the ruins. There were giant motionless forms clad in dulled glass lying here and there, and smaller shapes. She saw Vanda-Jo, mouth still wide in her last silent scream; Gert and Hansi, mated in death as in life, were crushed beneath a stone lintel. Khalid Khan sat against a wall looking like a parody of a pietà, a Tanu warrior spitted by an iron spear cradled in his dead arms. "Salaam aleikoum, bhai," she whispered, and Khalid was lost in the dark.

"Only superficial damage to the factory itself," Gomnol remarked in a pleased tone. "It was stupid of me not to have foreseen this contingency. It's going to be a great bore having to express gratitude to the Host for having saved my bacon, especially since you people seem to have killed a number of them. Ah, well. No real harm done."

A sunburst of rainbow light now shone in the murk ahead. Amerie heard a deafening voice intone: "Welcome, Lord Coercer! Better late than never."

Gomnol came into the area where the bronze doors had been. The last rags of smoke and vapor dissipated. Dozens of brilliantly gleaming knights were standing about in negligent attitudes, leaning upon broadswords or glass lances. Chief Burke and Basil, burned and bloody, wrapped from ankle to neck in glass chain, hunched on their knees at the feet of a ruby-armored demigod. And Felice was there, flat on the floor, helmet off, eyes shut, face and neck colorless except for the soft gleaming of the golden torc and the shine of her hair.

Gomnol sent Amerie floating toward the other prisoners and lowered her softly. To the blue titan who had addressed him, he said, "Our thanks to you, Brother Imidol, to Lord Culluket, and to all the members of your Host. A timely intervention, indeed. I see that the torc factory suffered no serious harm."

"It is quite safe."

"Splendid!" A small golden container at Gomnol's waist popped open and a cigar emerged. The Lord Coercer bit off the end, ignited the tobacco with psychoenergy, and blew a fragrant plume toward the ruined ceiling with a fine air of savoir-vivre.

"My own sources of information had made me aware of a possible sabotage attempt tonight," he said. "Unfortunately, we were misled into believing that the invaders would try to penetrate from the rear of the keep. My forces were in ambush there. Lord Bormol and the Lord of Swords had kindly volunteered to watch with us. They should be here at any moment."

Gomnol swept the massed force of the Host with a confident glance. "If you permit, I'll relieve you of the tedium of the mopping-up operation. Redactors are on their way to succor our fallen brethren. Those who are not too badly injured will surely be out of the Skin in time for the Combat."

Imidol's glaring face was as carved from rock crystal. "We have lost fifteen of our sacred number to the iron. They rest in Tana's peace, beyond the help of the Skin."

Gomnol frowned, studying the tip of his cigar. "Terrible! Monstrous!" He gestured at Felice. "But I see you have avenged yourselves on the Lowlife woman."

"She is not dead," said ruby-clad Culluket. "I have her in mental bondage. Our revenge will be taken in due time."

"Aye," said all the others. "Revenge against *all* traitors."

Gomnol stood stark still. Smoke from the cigar curled playfully in the air currents entering through the breached ceiling.

"This woman showed a formidable psychoenergy," said Imidol.

"Much greater than any of us could have anticipated," Culluket added. "She killed three of our company by her mind's power alone."

"It was only with the greatest difficulty that we all combined and subdued her," came the concerted voices of the rose-gold twins, Kuhal and Fian.

"But not," Imidol concluded, "before she had perpetrated one *final* crime—you understand that this is what we shall say."

The Host blazed brighter and brighter. A certain insinuation of the Second Coercer took unmistakable form within the massed minds.

"Stop!" Gomnol cried. The mightiness of his metapsychic power roared out to prevent them, to fend them off while shielding his soul from the combined stroke of forty-seven exotic minds focused through the hatred and jealousy of Imidol, son of Nontusvel and the Thagdal, who would surely be named Lord Coercer by acclamation once the human usurper was dead.

"You cannot . . ." came the agonized gasp of Eusebio Gomez-Nolan, "you cannot . . . combine against a brother. Tana forbids it!"

No brother you but a HUMAN and a traitor and a conniver with the monster Aiken Drum we know it we are sure so die . . . die . . .

"No proof! No . . . proof!" Gomnol's body twisted, the spine bowed backward in tetany. He fell in his armor as heavily as if he had been turned to stone.

Imidol cried out, "We of the Host have our proof! Proof for the others may come later. For now you will seem to die a hero—last victim of the monster Felice—until it suits us to reveal the full fabric of your treachery! Die, Manipulator. Die."

A last sound came from Gomnol's mouth. The contorted limbs relaxed. The face within the bizarre sapphire globe of his helmet went gray, then white. A skull with perfect teeth grinned at the Host of Nontusvel. The cigar on the floor beside it consumed itself in fragrant patience.

* * *

Culluket the Interrogator placed gray torcs around the necks of Amerie, Chief Burke, and Basil. And then the mountain climber, who of the three badly wounded prisoners retained the most strength, was forced to take an iron blade and sever Felice's golden torc.

"No gray for her?" Imidol inquired.

"Later," the Interrogator said. "It taints the pleasure if I make things too easy for myself."

16

HELPING HIMSELF to early bugs, the nightjar whipped around the predawn sky. Behind the foothills of the Jura the sky was already pink. Mobs of herbivores down on the plateau were stirring. There was activity in Castle Gateway, too—but, maddeningly, no trace of any invisible human skulkers anywhere.

The nightjar made a futile low pass. It was a bloody nuisance that he hadn't been able to locate Claude and Madame yet. They *had* to be hiding underground. No doubt with Madame's illusion-spinning creativity reinforcing the natural psychic shield of the dense granite and hard-baked soil. But they'd have to come out to make the sortie against the time-gate. And when they did, he'd nab 'em.

As yet, none of the castle personnel knew that Aiken had arrived. He'd flown right up the valley of the Rhône, stashed the Spear in the upper branches of a big old plane tree down on the bottoms, and winged it on up here to do the search. Who noticed whether or not a nightjar flew around in the daytime? He'd hoped to spot their hideout, turn back into himself, and lead a castle search party right to the spot (tah-*dah!*).

But the damned old love-birds had foiled him. Ah, well.

It was really kind of cute, when you thought about it. Weird, but cute. (I mean—of course they couldn't. Could they? A hundred and thirty-three?) It was kind of a shame they couldn't have been content to Darby-and-Joan it off in the Hercynian Forest somewhere with the munchkins instead of messing around in the games of the big boys.

But there it was. No helping 'em now. But he'd zap quick and merciful so at least they'd be spared getting dragged down to the Grand Combat and distilled alive in that glass thing the Tanu fancied for traitors. Gomnol had tried to convince Aiken that the ceremonial death of the old folks was strategically necessary. (He *would* think so.) But to hell with him! Gumball's sadism would have to be content with the two old heads on pikes.

Aha! Activity again. The main gate of the castle was opening. Plenty of soldiers coming out, in addition to the white-garbed portal keepers. Just about dawn, too.

He banked, hunched his wings to stall, and plummeted down to keep an eye on things.

Above him, gray on gray-pink and outlined in mallow on the sunward side, was a strange cumulus cloud. Its bottom sagged in udderlike formations. One of the bags elongated like a vaporous Tanu breast as turbulence within the cloud increased. The bag stretched lower, became a dangling sleeve, then a miniature tornado with vortex winds spinning at several hundred kilometers an hour. It twisted and groped through the air, humming loudly. But morning winds were keening over the plateau and the people on the ground did not notice the new sound. They gathered formally about an area of bare rock.

The nightjar did not observe the little tornado either—not until it vacuumed him up, spun him off with a great tangential toss, and landed him in a nearly dry waterhole some three kilometers away . . . The stunned trickster regained consciousness a few minutes later and sat cursing the solicitous little hipparions that came to nuzzle his muddy face.

And then his mind flinched from a far, far obliteration of a familiar psychic pattern; and he knew about Gomnol. By the time he pulled himself together and flew back to the time-gate, it was too late there as well.

* * *

"Chéri, the time has come," she said.

He stretched, yawned, smoothed his silver hair back, then reached out and caught her by the wrists.

"Fou," she whispered, when she was able.

"We both are. We make a pair—like antique bookends."

She laughed softly, but that brought on the coughing which she had been at such pains to suppress. And there was blood. He said, "How long has this gone on? Angélique—why didn't you tell me?"

"I have taken Amerie's medicines. What else was there to do? You would have been made anxious for nothing. Say no more about it! It is time to go. And soon it will not matter."

"Goddammit, we'll get away!" he insisted, voice all raspy.

She kept back as he removed the top course of granite rocks from the wall, and enough from the center of the barricade so that the two of them would be able to squeeze out. An undermined acacia tree sagged down like a curtain in front of the opening. Beyond was the deep dry watercourse where she had first found shelter in the Pliocene Exile some four years earlier.

It had been Claude's idea to hide in this place, not even a kilometer away from the time-gate area. Under cover of her illusion of invisibility, they had come six days earlier during the hours that the moon was down and burrowed into the arroyo wall, enlarging the hole that had already been formed by the roots of the scraggly tree. They had walled themselves in with boulders from the streambed. From time to time during the nights, when her metapsychic senses told them that it was safe, they would venture out. The hole had been enlarged into a chamber nearly head-high, three meters long and two deep. It had suited them.

As they crept from the place for the last time, Claude heard her half-joking little murmur of farewell: "Adieu, petite grotte d'amour."

He said, "Two old spiders in their hole, you mean. But you didn't devour me, ma vieille! Still—it's just as well our time was short."

"It sufficed," said she, mind all asmile. "But now I think we have both reached the point of plus qu'il n'en faut . . . more than enough."

She handed him the amber with the message she had signed, then covered them both with her mental cloak. They scrambled up the steep wall. The surface of the savanna was fully four meters higher than the streambed. No one from the castle could have been able to farsense their hiding place, not unless there was a powerful metapsychic deliberately searching for them and alert for her illusion. They had only a short distance to walk and moments to wait before they fulfilled the duty they had set for themselves. And then, back to the hiding place, where they would hope for the best, should the alarm be raised . . .

Last night—or rather early on this morning—they had tried to find out what had happened to the saboteurs. Madame had sent her mind's ear straining over the long kilometers that separated them from the Balearic Peninsula . . . But the distant mumble refused to fine-tune. She could not hear and dared not call. And so the two of them had simply prayed for their friends, made love again, and slept. She muffled her coughing in the blankets. Her mental alarm woke them at the preselected time.

As evanescent as morning wind, they approached the crowd of people near the time-portal. In the east, the sky was now greenish yellow and the day would be hot. (But their cave had been cool, and they had had plenty of water and food and the soft decamole couches, and so the brief days had passed without effort. He had told her about Gen and she had told him about Théo, and then they had explored one another as only the wise old ones can, the lucky ones who are still strong and alive to danger—for the adrenals hold the great secret of old lovers, but only for those who are brave.)

They were almost at the gate. It was nearly time.

. . . And the world around them abruptly turned black.

Both of them cried out. The sound did not propagate. They seemed to stand yet on solid ground, but all around was darkness . . . until there came a pinprick of light that swelled to a sun, to a glowing face, to the face of Apollo.

"I am Nodonn."

Well, it's finished, Claude told himself. And now she'll die with the guilt.

A voice was speaking aloud. They knew that no one heard it but themselves. "I know who you are and what you would do. I have decided there must be an end to you and your meddling."

Angélique's thought was resigned: You Tanu have won this time. You may kill us, but others will come to shut this devil's gate.

"They will not," said Nodonn, "because I have chosen you." The flaming mask was enormous, its mind-light numbing. "My people have never understood the great harm you did to us in opening this way across the aeons. They would brook no interference with it. Not even I dared to close the time-gate by force. But now there is another way. You will do my will and at the same time achieve those goals you have set for yourselves. The goals you have both sought ever since coming to this Exile. I presume you understand."

Claude replied: We understand, all right.

"My people will believe that you two alone are responsible for the closure. The supposed calamity will be more acceptable to them when they learn that the insurgent leader and the man who bombarded Finiah have been removed from the Many-Colored Land . . . But you know that I cannot coerce you into this final deed. The torced guardians at the gate would detect my intervention. And so you will have to act freely—and visibly."

She said: Yes. It will be the ultimate proof to those at the other end of the gate.

Claude said: And I'm glad I blasted your damned slave-city! Maybe you think closing this time-gate will make you Tanu safe from any more human uprisings. You're in for a disappointment! Things are never going to be the same here again.

The sun-bright face darkened. Nodonn's voice rolled in their minds. "Go back where you came from, accursed!"

Claude said: You fool. We came from here.

And then their human ears heard birdsong again. The true solar disk was breaking over the rim of the highland beyond the Rhône. Not a stone's throw away, a shimmering block hung in the air just above the square of stones where the portal guardians and soldiers waited.

Their illusion of invisibility still intact, the two old people began to run over the dry sod. Four human time-travelers materialized within the tau-field and were assisted to alight.

Angélique stumbled. Claude seized her hand, shoving aside soldiers and bewildered timefarers.

"Jump for it before it recycles!"

One of the armed guards gave a shout and rushed forward, waving his bronze sword. Fully visible, the old man and woman stood side by side in midair, hands linked. The temporal field reversed itself and they disappeared.

In the sky above, a nightjar shrilled its furious *kutuk-kutuk-kutuk* and flew away.

* * *

Only one of the auberge clients whose trip had been so unexpectedly aborted was not suffering hysterics. Still holding his plankton net and sack of specimen bottles, he answered Counselor Mishima's questions warily.

"They were just standing there, I tell you. We only saw them for a split second when those mirrors in the machine's walls cut off. And then they were skeletons! And then dust . . . I really must demand an explanation, Counselor. The brochure states most emphatically that there is no hazard in the journey through time—"

One of the other counselors, kneeling in front of the gazebo, broke in. "Alan, come and look at this."

Mishima said, "Please go upstairs and wait with the others, Dr. Billings. I'll be with you in just a moment."

When the man had gone the two counselors bent over the pile of ashy powder. There was a peculiar gold ornament half-buried in it, a kind of barbarian necklet. When Mishima lifted it, glittering flakes —all that remained of the internal components—sifted from small openings and mingled with the dust.

"And here . . . oh, God." The other counselor had discovered the two flat pieces of amber. The writing was clearly visible within. "We —we'd better rush these things up to the director, Alan."

Mishima sighed. "Yes. And tell that Billings chap and the others that they needn't wait after all."

The twin rings carved from jet were not discovered until later, when the gazebo's dust was reverently swept up to be stored—until the investigatory panel's work should be finished—in a durofilm sack in the auberge director's safe.

* * *

Six million years away, in the room without doors, Elizabeth and Brede wept. Foreknowledge, as Elizabeth had suspected all along, had only made it worse.

* * *

THE END OF PART TWO

PART III

The Grand Combat

1

By the time of the Galactic Milieu the mountain was worn away to a remnant. It rose from the Mediterranean as the island of Menorca, easternmost of the archipelago that had been called the Hesperides. Monte del Toro, not 400 meters above the sea, marked its greatest eminence on eroded Elder Earth. Most of its ancient labyrinth of caves had by then been opened to the sun by wearing elements or, in the case of the deeper caverns, drowned by the encroaching sea.

But six million years in the past, the mountain had another aspect. When exotic newcomers to the Balearic Peninsula first saw its shadowed mass with the twin crags flanking a summit meadow (where Bryan and Mercy would lie), they named it the Mount of Lugonn and Sharn—after the Tanu and Firvulag champions who had fought their ritual battle at the Ship's Grave. Later, the mountain was simply called the Mount of Heroes. By a rare express command of Brede, it was made the property of the Guild of Redactors. Their college of healing and mind-exploration was built on the southeastern slope overlooking Muriah and the White Silver Plain. After the Times of Unrest and the banishment of Minanonn, the very caves within the mountain were annexed—at first to serve as secure crypts for the interment of the Great Ones, and latterly for far less sacred purposes.

* * *

Felice had vowed to herself that she would never cry aloud.

Her mind's voice might rage and the Interrogator laugh; but somehow, through all the days, she remained steadfast and never uttered a sound through the jaws wedged open. She had willed this one thing: paralysis of her vocal cords; and they of all her betraying flesh had obeyed.

Culluket had gone slowly, learning her, utilizing both redaction and coercive power, now strumming like an artist, now thumping with overwhelming crude malice. And if the sensory overload sent her into fugue, he coaxed her back with tweaks at the core of the brainstem to restore full-alert wakefulness when it was time for the next refinement to be demonstrated.

Mental humiliation of her, he had discovered to his surprise, was not nearly so effective as the purely physical assaults upon her feminine dignity. But she was still a child, of course. A perverted child. She had yielded up the required information rather quickly (the Spear of Lugonn in the possession of Aiken Drum, the Ship's Grave and its trove of flying machines, the schemes for producing iron weapons, the fortified villages abuilding in the north); and the data were sent to Nodonn so that action could be taken following the Grand Combat.

That had satisfied the others of the Host, leaving Culluket free to satisfy himself.

To peel open her mind slowly, like a fruit, so that he could observe and then savor all of the strange humors of the alien murderess. Her secret horrors, the massive psychic wound from the loss of her golden torc (and yet that not as devastating as one might have expected), the monstrous metapsychic faculties for coercion, psychokinesis, creativity, farsensing, now walled up and latent like ravening beasts in squeeze-traps, never to be freed again.

Taste the rage! Watch the agony deepen at the forced sharing.

Flay, open to reveal the unsatisfied needs, the infant deprivation short-circuiting the pleasure and the violence pathways deep within the cerebellum. Delicious possibilities there! Realize them. Replay from multiple vantage points the filth, until even she, wretched Lowlife, understands her own vileness. Inhumanity proven by a nonhuman male, exquisitely skilled.

He worked her, shock following shock, pain piled upon pain, her body's degradation translated into maceration of ego; her hatred and fear of other beings clarified as hatred and fear of her self.

Leave her bereft of everything she has ever valued, waiting for dissolution. (Her body had to be unharmed, of course; but he would fulfill his promise to the Battlemaster if he delivered her able to fight in the Combat as a petit-mal automaton.)

But she would not go mad.

Piqued, he rummaged in the wreckage, trying to discover the explanation. He almost missed it. But there—a minute spark barricaded within a stubborn shell of screening that resisted all his attempts at puncture. Diminished and encapsulated, the being that was Felice continued to abide.

If only he could make her speak, cry out! That was the way, the key. He knew it! One voluntary sound and the last defense would fall.

But she would not. After days had passed and the Combat was almost upon them, he dared go no further for fear of extinguishing life, along with that stubborn remnant of shielded identity.

"Keep it, then," he said, "for what good it will do you."

And after pleasuring himself with her one final time, he clamped the gray torc of slavery around her neck, released her jaws, and had the attendants take her away to a cell in the deepest of the catacombs.

* * *

. . . Steinie?

Lovelove you're awake. "Does it still hurt, Sue?"

He knelt on the damp stone floor next to the niche with its straw-stuffed mattress and took her by the hand. There was just enough light to see her, cast by the single Tanu jewel-lamp set like a sad star in the high ceiling of the cell, surrounded by stalactites.

"There's only a leftover ache now. I'll be all right. Lord Dionket said there was no permanent damage. We'll be able to have others later on."

But not him Sukey not my first unbornson. "It *must* have been my fault. We shouldn't have . . . after we were sure you were pregnant." Stupidstupidselfishprickbabykiller!

"No!" She struggled up, sitting on the edge of the stone bed and taking his face to kiss. "Never think it was your fault. I'm certain it wasn't." (And *will* the certainty into his mind through the silver torc still worn; but hide the reality, O never let him find that out.) "You must stop thinking about it now, love. Get ready for the escape! The Combat starts tomorrow. I'm sure that Aiken has waited until the last minute so that the Tanu won't bother to come after us."

Stein growled deep in his chest. He shook his head, like a bear warding off attacking bees. Alarmed, Sukey perceived the random neural firing within his brain that signaled the onset of a spasm induced by his maladaptation to the gray torc.

"Damn Aiken Drum," Stein groaned. "He said . . . he promised . . . but first you, now me . . . . *Christ*, Sukey, my skull's exploding—"

She held his head to her breast and plunged within his mind, as she had at ever-shorter intervals during their time in Muriah. Once again, she was successful in stopping the threatened conflagration. But if the torc stayed on him much longer, he would not survive.

"There, Steinie. There, love. I've got you. I've fixed it."

Water dripped from the ceiling of their prison cell—regular, musical. The wild beating of Stein's heart slowed and his rough exhalations eased. He lifted his head to meet his wife's eyes.

"You're sure that it wasn't my fault?"

"Believe me. It wasn't. Sometimes these things just happen."

Still kneeling beside her, he sank back to rest on his heels, great helpless hands turned palms up, the image of a shattered giant. But Sukey was not deceived. She could see into his mind.

If he could not blame himself, he would look elsewhere.

*   *   *

Aiken Drum hoisted the heavy Spear of Lugonn easily, menacing the ornate chandelier in Mayvar's audience chamber in the Hall of Farsensors. The glassy lance shone golden, now that the last of the disguising blue lacquer had been cleaned from it. The powerpack was fully charged.

"Take *that* for your yoni, witch!" he chortled, striking a wicked pose.

Mayvar's smile was indulgent. "Tomorrow, my Shining One. Tomorrow it all begins. But there will be five days of it, remember. And you can use the Spear only at the very end, after midnight on the fifth day when the Heroic Encounters take place, and even then only if Nodonn decides to use the Sword. *And* if you survive to meet the Battlemaster at all—"

"If? If?" he squealed in mock fury. "You clapped-out old seeress! Are you going to renege on your own Making? Do I have to prove myself to you again?"

He cast down the photonic weapon with a ringing clang and launched himself, suddenly naked as a fish, at the scarecrow figure lounging on the amethyst throne. There was no one else in the chamber and the seat of power was quite large enough for two.

"Enough . . . enough!" she wheezed, laughing until tears trickled through the furrows of her cheeks. "At least let me live to share the triumph and give you your name!"

He let her go, still feigning vexation at her apparent lack of confidence. Perched on purple velvet cushions with his legs crossed, he stuck two fingers under his golden torc and pulled. The metal stretched like an elastic band, then sagged as limp as half-pulled taffy. He began to fling the gold about, spinning it thinner and thinner, catching loops of it on the toes of each bare foot and weaving cat's cradles with the flexible filament that had been a golden torc.

"So doubt me, Hag! And I'll give back this silly gift of yours and go my own way. Who needs you? I've got my quiverful of powers all honed and ready at last and I'm a match for any of 'em now! Bring on the Firvulag spooks! Bring on Thagdal and Nodonn!"

"If you would be king, you must play by their rules," she said flatly. "If they suspect that you are fully operant without the torc they may yet combine against you. And strong as you have become, my Shining One, the massed minds of the battle-company could kill you, given the incentive."

"The fighters are crazy about me. And the ladies think I'm cute!"

"But the Host spreads rumors. They say you co-conspired with Gomnol and Felice's saboteurs. They say that your inept handling led to the closing of the time-gate. Far more ominous, they say that you would mate with the operant woman Elizabeth and engender a race of fully operant humans here in the Many-Colored Land."

"Me and the Ice Lady? What a detumefying thought!"

His smirk was as jaunty as ever, but the golden skein melted back into a circle, which he replaced about his neck. He began to put his suit of many pockets back on. "But you may have a point at that. A good thing Elizabeth is about ready to pack it in and fly. I can't understand why she's hung around this long. Not unless she really does give a damn about us after all."

"Don't think of her." The crone patted his head. "Don't think of anything but the Combat. Your participation in the preliminaries should present no special hazard. And no one may challenge you in the manifestation of powers if I nominate you Second Farsensor. But once the High Mêlée begins you will need to muster all the bravery and cleverness and metapsychic power at your command. It's not enough for you simply to survive the fighting. You must show yourself an inspired leader and a destroyer of the Foe. Then, as the Combat draws to its climax, contingents from all the guilds may rally to follow *your* banner rather than that of Nodonn! Thus you will be seen as a valid kingly aspirant in the Heroic Encounters at the end."

Aiken said in a wistful little voice, "You *sure* I can't use iron?"

Mayvar cackled. "Oh, you jester . . . on the day when you become King of the Many-Colored Land you may do as you please. But never dream of using the blood-metal in this Combat. It would be said that you were allied to the Lowlives in the north. Why do you think I cautioned secrecy when I gave you the weapon to use against Delbaeth?"

Aiken laced his fingers behind his head and rocked back and forth, contemplating limitless vistas.

"When I'm king we'll change all kinds of rules. With a cohort of gold-torc humans armed with iron, we'll mop up the human rebels and take care of the Firvulag, too. But we won't slaughter 'em—hell, no! Now that the time-gate's closed, I'll have to scrounge up subjects anywhere I can. And look at all of the neat things the gnomies make! Fancy jewelry and chaliko tack and booze that's just stone faraway! Nope—I'll pacify the Little Folks by threatening 'em with the ultimate weapon and we'll have one big happy kingdom under Good King—"

He stopped rocking. His black eyes widened and his mouth dropped in stunned surprise. "Oh, *damn*," he whispered. "Mayvar—can you hear it? It's mostly on the intimate human mode but enough slops over into the gray band for you to pick up if you spread it out and listen sharp. You grab? It's Stein."

"Vengeance," Mayvar said. "He blames you. Incredible!"

The golliwog youth sat stiffly on the edge of the amethyst throne, farsensing for all he was worth. "Still no firm conclusion. But mulling it over, the stupid ox . . . How I promised to keep Sukey safe. But she wasn't kept safe. Ergo, my fault! Can you beat that for idiot logic? Sure as shit, that little broad is unconsciously leaking some part of the truth to him. Women! It'd be enough if she just hinted the miscarriage wasn't spontaneous. Looks to me like there's only one thought moving Stein—blame it on somebody besides himself."

Mayvar said, "You did promise no harm would come to Sukey. The word of a gold-torc nobleman and royal aspirant—"

"What about your precious rules?" he exploded. "Play by the rules, you said! Are you tellin' me now I should have gone against the King *and* Queen just to spare Sukey a little houghmagandy that shouldn't have done her or the kid any harm? If Stein wasn't such a thickheaded—"

Mayvar had cocked her head, still farsensing. "Hear what his mind cries out! This is no joke, Aiken Drum."

His tirade against her forgotten, Aiken focused again. The farspoken maunderings of the half-crazed Viking were mostly being broadcast through his torc on the uniquely human spectrum, and they were so chaotic that even human listeners would have been unlikely to expend the effort needed to decipher them. But if a person were patient and lifted aside the ramblings and mutters and the mixed-up business about Sukey—there was something else.

The saboteurs coming to invade the torc factory, thinking they would receive Aiken's help with the Spear. Aiken's cosy arrangement with Gomnol.

"Oh, Christ," breathed the trickster. "His mind-block's going. And with Gomnol dead, my puny redact isn't going to be able to nail the lid back down tight enough."

"You must act at once. If Stein's thoughts are brought to the attention of the Host, they will use him to prove you reprobate and unworthy of aspiring to the kingship. They will serve you as they did Gomnol."

"God . . . I'll have to get both Stein and Sukey out of here tonight—not wait till after I'm king, like I planned."

"It is late for that course of action." She showed him what the safest course would be, at the same time trembling at her test of him.

"I couldn't," he told her. "Not Stein and Sukey!"

"Alive, they will always be a threat to your sovereignty."

"No! There's gotta be another way!"

"You feel an obligation to them? Your honor? Your half-jesting promise? Your pride?"

"Not them! Anybody else I'll zap to charcoal, but not them." Not the crazy dumb lovers see how they suffer because of one another shrunk/enlarged by the giving but what would it be like? Poor doomed damned saps wondered at but denied by the safe avoider as I avoid/deny you dying womanbodymind.

He repeated, "Not them."

Mayvar rose from the throne and swayed there hooded, looking like the calyx of some huge, unopened violet flower. He knew but could not see her fresh tears. "Blessed be my Making. I knew that you were not as Gomnol . . . and there is another way."

He bounded up and grabbed her by the arms. "What?"

"Remain here and make ready for tomorrow. Trust me. I will see that your friends are sent out of Muriah tonight."

2

ON THIS COMBAT EVE, every true member of the ancient battle-company had thoughts only for the coming clash of Foes, the joint celebration of life and death that they believed was their reason for continuing existence in the Many-Colored Land. But there were a few who had rejected the ancient traditions, and these came together—even one who had not set foot in the capital city for five hundred years—to consider whether or not this year's Grand Combat might be the great turning point foreseen by Brede.

To their exasperation, the Shipspouse herself would not attend the meeting, would not confirm or deny the possibility. "The Combat itself will manifest the Goddess's Will," she had told Dionket, "and then you will know what you must do." But the Lord Healer had not been satisfied with that. What did a mystic know of power struggles? Her vision was so disconcertingly *long*.

And so he had summoned the leaders among the antibattle faction, even the pair long banished, to a secret chamber deep within the Mount of Heroes; and when Katlinel dared to bring in the two outsiders, the extraordinariness of the times excused it and even lent it a mad kind of suitability.

DIONKET LORD HEALER: Greetings to you all, fellow traitors and peacelovers, and especially to our Psychokinetic Brother Minanonn Heretic, and our Coercive Brother Leyr, so long absent from our cabals, and our distinguished Foeman—

SUGOLL: Ally.

DIONKET: —now so fortuitously allied, the Lord Sugoll, ruler of Meadow Mountain, and greatest of those called Howlers . . . Sisters and Brothers, we are indeed poised on the brink. Say, Mayvar.

MAYVAR KINGMAKER: Aiken Drum is ready. The human youth is fully operant, possessed of all faculties save redaction in a truly remarkable degree. I believe no single Tanu or Firvulag champion will withstand him. Failing catastrophe or a mass attack by the entire battle-company—which cannot happen unless he is attainted unworthy according to our ancient code—he will become king five days hence after defeating both the Thagdal and Nodonn at the culmination of the Grand Combat.

MINANONN THE HERETIC: A human . . . barely more than a child. A trickster, if rumor does not lie! *This* is your pivotal figure?

MAYVAR: I have tested him in all the ways. He is flawed—and who among us is not?—but he will be worthy.

ALBERONN MINDEATER: Kid's got good stuff. Nerve. Heart.

BUNONE WARTEACHER: Jisum! Both kinds.

MAYVAR: He can be cruel, but he is capable of love all unrealizing. I have been true to my Making.

LEYR THE BANISHED: But—a little human mountebank?

KATLINEL THE DARKEYED: You loved a human once yourself, Father. And our races are merged, for better or for worse.

MAYVAR: Aiken Drum will engender operants. Not so many as Elizabeth might with her fuller penetrance, but enough.

GREG-DONNET GENETICS MASTER: Have no fear, kinfolk! Aiken's genetic assay is *colossal!* I mean—compare him to Nodonn, for instance. The Battlemaster is gorgeous, but we all know how few pureblood offspring he's sired. And his hybrids haven't a High Table candidate or even a first-class power in the lot.

BLEYN BATTLE-CHAMPION: Who wants to be the one to remind Nodonn of his deficiencies?

(Rueful laughter.)

LEYR: Well, you've seen this boy fight and I haven't. But it's hard to swallow the notion that *any* human could stand up to Nodonn, much less this stripling with a silly name.

MAYVAR: He will receive another name, according to our custom, after he survives the High Mêlée.

MINANONN: Look here. Granted this Aiken Drum licks Nodonn in the Encounter—and I'm not nearly so sanguine as you seem to be on that point, Kingmaker—both the post of Lord Psychokinetic and the governorship of Goriah will fall vacant when the boy assumes the throne.

DIONKET: Exactly. And now that Sebi-Gomnol is dead, the Coercer Guild must also seek a new leader.

LEYR: Almighty Tana! Is *that* why you got Minnie and me back here?

KATLINEL: Father—surely you can best Imidol in the manifestation of powers. His coercive will is much weaker than Gomnol's was.

LEYR: Ye-es, but don't underestimate the enemy, Katy-girl. Imidol won't settle for a simple manifestation the way someone like Aluteyn would. He'll want a battle-trial—minds *and* weapons—during the Mêlée.

DIONKET: This is true. And you are much older than Imidol, Coercive Brother, and there is considerable risk. But we know your mind. If you were victorious and reascended to the High Table you would play a moderating role . . . no matter who became High King.

LEYR: Dammit—Minnie's the peaceloving heretic, not me!

ALBERONN: But you'd never favor the extermination of humanity—nor of us hybrids—as does the Host of Nontusvel.

LEYR: Of course not—!

KATLINEL: And much as you love Combat between equals, Father, you have scant heart for the senseless slaughter of the Hunt, or the perversion of the Low Mêlée that has come about since the advent of torced human fighters, or the unsporting tactics used against the Foe in the High Mêlée itself.

LEYR: Bad business, those gray shock troops and the whole matter of mounting our fighters on chalikos. Small wonder the Foe sulks and makes Lowlife alliances.

DIONKET: The Host must not be allowed to dominate the High Table! We appeal to you, Leyr. And to you also, Minanonn.

MAYVAR: We stand at a crossroads, Brothers and Sisters. We may choose our turning or have it forced upon us.

LEYR: Very well. Perhaps I'm getting soft-headed in my old age . . . but I'll challenge that young brawler Imidol.

MAYVAR: And you, Minanonn?

MINANONN: You see me allied to your cause in the event of Nodonn's defeat, contending against Kuhal Earthshaker for the leadership of the psychokinetics.

MAYVAR: You have the power. You were Battlemaster once.

MINANONN: Five hundred years gone, before my enlightenment. And you know me little, Kingmaker, if you think that I would sacrifice my principles now to become a killer once more.

DIONKET: For an end to killing!

MINANONN: Not even for that.

MAYVAR: If the Guild presidency might be decided in a peaceful manifestation of powers and not in battle-trial?

MINANONN: That will never happen under the Thagdal's regime.

MAYVAR: But if our faction forces a change of the rules under a new king?

MINANONN: Then I would willingly aspire. However, until the dawn of that unlikely new day, I must take leave of you, Sisters and Brothers. I fly back to my place of banishment in the wilderness. Farewell.

(He goes.)

BUNONE: Until we meet again, dear Brother Heretic! When our faction controls the Many-Colored Land and I forgo my war-teaching for fancy embroidery!

ALBERONN: That you may, and pink and blue to boot, Lady, if you undertake further Quests with Aiken Drum.

BUNONE: Shame on you, Creative Brother, for not considering the feelings of the Kingmaker.

MAYVAR: I have no illusions about the sexual faithfulness of my human protégé. I see him as he is.

DIONKET: Tana help us if you do not.

LEYR: Yes—how about that, Kingmaker? What happens if this trickster of yours plays his own game once we've put him on the throne?

BLEYN: We can all move into Minannon's cave in the Catalan Wilderness.

MAYVAR: He *is* worthy! I am certain of it! Under him, we will be able to inaugurate a new era. The only questionable factor was the influence of Gomnol—and he is dead. With the time-gate closed, we will push gradually for the emancipation of the grays, an end to involuntary human concubinage, abolition of the Hunt, and peace between Tanu and Firvulag at last. What was impossible under the Thagdal or Nodonn is not only feasible but certain if Aiken Drum is King of the Many-Colored Land.

SUGOLL: Let us speak of others who also share this land.

GREG-DONNET: Oh, listen! This is marvelous—and so *logical*, from a eugenic standpoint! Positively elegant! I couldn't contain my enthusiasm when Katy came to me. Of course, she and Sugoll will be only a token of what might follow as the old racial prejudices are broken down. But later—the results will be very similar to the injection of Aiken's genes insofar as ultimate improvement of the metapsychic phenotype—

LEYR: What the *hell* is this little capon blithering about?

KATLINEL: Sugoll and I, Father. The merging of all three gene pools.

LEYR: Katy?! Do you mean to tell me that you and this—this Firvu-lag—

KATLINEL: Howler.

SUGOLL: My body is, of course, an illusion. Like all of my subjects, I am a mutant. Katy accepts me as I am. But let there be no mask-ing between us, either, father-in-law elect. Look.

LEYR: (!) Compassionate Tana.

GREG-DONNET: Their children will be beautiful. Their minds, at any rate! And I'm off with them to the North Country this very night to look into the teratogenic thing and see if it might not respond to a little fiddling. Anyhow—monster is as monster does.

LEYR: Katy . . . oh, Katy.

DIONKET (embracing her): Blessings, Creative Daughter. And upon you, Lord of the Howlers. You take with you the flower of our High Table. Be with her a bridge.

SUGOLL: Threefold, we may hope. Farewell.

(He goes, with Katlinel and Greg-Donnet.)

BUNONE: Cheer up, Leyr. At least they'll be out of this mess. You can work off your steam on Imidol. I rather like that Sugoll fellow myself. A lot of style for a Firvulag . . .

MARY-DEDRA: Then we only wait? Wait for Aiken Drum to con-quer?

ALBERONN: Some of us must take the active role in his cohort during the High Mêlée. There are numerous volunteers, admirers of his prowess, especially among the hybrids. But Aiken Drum will re-quire captains following his banner as well. Bleyn and I have offered ourselves.

BUNONE: And I.

LEYR: Oh, hell. Why not? I'll throw in with him, now that the world's turned upside down . . . But there's one tradition they haven't dared to meddle with: warrior's privilege! How about it, fighters? A little practical preparation for the Grand Combat, hey?

ALBERONN + BLEYN + BUNONE: Warrior's privilege! No noncomba-tants allowed! Roll out the barrels!

(They go.)

DIONKET: The rest of us will have other work.

CREYN: And may I remind you, Lord Healer, that some of the work awaits to be accomplished yet this night.

MAYVAR: You have secured it, Mary-Dedra?

DEDRA: It is here, Lady Kingmaker, in this golden box.

MAYVAR: As a human, Dedra may touch it without peril. Open and show us, child.

DIONKET + CREYN: Ah.

DEDRA: It was where Elizabeth farsensed it, hidden beneath a granite sett in an obscure corner of the Coercer House basecourt. Lord Gomnol must have put it there himself long ago against—some contingency. No one saw me remove it.

CREYN: And it is certain, Lord Healer, that this tool of the blood-metal may safely remove torcs from humans?

DIONKET: I have it from Elizabeth, who learned it from Madame Guderian herself. Both silvers and grays have been liberated by means of iron in the north. As to the safety of the operation . . . that depends upon the individual's reaction to the withdrawal. We will give the tool to Sukey and hope that her redactive powers are sufficient. When the fugitives are safely away and she is certain that she need not coerce Stein for his own good, she will cut his torc, removing him from Tanu influence and mind-hearing permanently.

MAYVAR: But we will give *her* another option, poor little one. It is the wish of our future king.

DIONKET: I see. Gold, instead of the silver she now wears. She would retain her metapsychic powers and still be free, while her mate remains a bareneck. And she must make the choice . . . This putative Crown Prince of ours is a fiend!

MAYVAR: It is late. Long past midnight. We must act.

CREYN: I will fetch them. They will trust me—even Stein.

DIONKET: Culluket is away, engaged in a premature warrior celebration with the Host. It will be safe. And Elizabeth is already waiting on the mountaintop.

DEDRA: *Elizabeth?*

MAYVAR: We have had to change the plan for the liberation of Stein and his wife. A boat could be too easily intercepted. And Elizabeth's hot-air balloon carries three.

* * *

The hellad drawing the calèche let out a whicker of surprise when it came to the dark summit and saw the huge thing moored there, swaying in a gentle west wind.

"Creyn?" Elizabeth was standing next to the gondola. Her red jumpsuit, like the scarlet balloon, was black in the light of the waxing moon.

"Make Stein walk, Elizabeth. I'll help Sukey."

"I'm all right," Sukey insisted, climbing down from the carriage. "I just thought it would be safer if Steinie were out . . ."

"I have him," Elizabeth said. "The balloon is ready. Thank God you're a small person, Sukey. This will be crowded, but we'll be all right if we keep Stein sedated while we're in the air."

"Elizabeth—" Creyn's voice broke.

"Upsy daisy, Stein. Now you, Sukey. No—don't touch that cable. It opens the maneuvering vent, dumps hot air that we need to rise."

The tall exotic was still standing by the carriage. The hellad drooped in the traces. "Elizabeth!"

"Yes, Creyn?" She came toward him, thinking he wished to say goodbye.

"Brede . . . charged me to explain that . . . *this* was not foreseen by her. Nor planned by the rest of us. Believe me! The cell next to Stein and Sukey . . . I could not help but perceive how little sanity was left to her, for all her uninjured body, and how the Combat would surely snuff it out whether or not she survived physically. And remembering that she had been your friend . . . I consulted Brede. She said that the choice must be your own."

He lifted a blanket. Curled up on the floor of the carriage, frail and vulnerable as a sleeping child, lay Felice.

He said, "You could force-feed the balloon piloting data to Sukey . . . a few minutes' work for a Grand Master. The hazard for them would be very small—"

Brede!!!

I hear Elizabeth.

You did this!

It is as Creyn avers. I did not foresee it, did not plan it. It is the work of the Goddess. Of God.

No. No! Oh—*damn* you! All of you!

* * *

The balloon rose, wafting unseen as the westerly breeze took it over the lights of Muriah. As it gained altitude above the Great Lagoon it met a wind-shear. The semidirigible envelope shuddered, caught momentarily in opposing currents. Continuing ascent injected it fully into the other airstream.

It changed direction away from Corsica-Sardinia and sailed southwest, toward the Isthmus of Gibraltar.

3

THEY WAITED for dawn.

Tanu and Firvulag and torced humanity gathered in splendid array on the Plain, which was pearl-colored now because of the traditional Mist of Duat that the creators of both battle-companies had conjured as a sky-canopy. A low droning sound, part growl and part minor chord, swelled on the still air. The commonalty of the Firvulag, standing on the sidelines all mingled with the Tanu and human noncombatants, were voicing their ancient overture to the Combat.

Firvulag warriors in obsidian armor all decked with gold and jewels stood in a vast mob some 20,000 strong, dwarfs and giants and middle-sized stalwarts all mixed together, some bearing the ghastly effigy standards, some clutching naked weapons. Their great battle-captains were massed nearest to the east-facing stage where the royalty of both races had assembled. On the opposite side of the marble platform waited the Tanu army. Disdainful of the informality of their shadow-brethren, they were ranged in elegant ranks according to their guilds: the violet and gold farsensors, the blue coercers, the ruby and silver combatant redactors, creators armored in beryl tints, and glowing rose-gold psychokinetics. Up in the front rank of the Farsensor Battalion, an impudent little human posed among towering jeweled champions. His armor of gold-lustre glass was adorned with amethysts and canary diamonds, and his cloak glittered uniquely black with a violet edge. He bore high his banner with its strange device.

The light in the east brightened behind thick mist. The chain of silence rang.

Eadone Sciencemaster came forward from the group of Most Exalted Personages and raised some small instrument to her eyes. Thagdal and Yeochee stood immediately behind the Dean of Guilds, the Tanu monarch attired in blue-white diamond armor, the Firvulag wearing sharply faceted black.

"The First Day begins," Eadone declared, bowing to the Kings and stepping aside.

Thagdal gestured. Nodonn Battlemaster came to salute the two sovereigns, trailed by gigantic Sharn-Mes the Young Champion—who as representative of the losers in last year's Combat had only a subsidiary role to play in this opening ceremony. Nodonn carried a glass weapon similar to the big two-handed swords used by both exotic races; but this Sword had a great flaring basket-hilt and a thin cable leading from its pommel to a box worn at the Battlemaster's waist.

Glowing like an aurora, Nodonn formally offered the Sword to Thagdal. The King declined it with equal solemnity, saying, "Be thou our deputy. Open the sky to this Grand Combat."

Nodonn turned, facing east and the veiled sun. He lifted the photon weapon. A brilliant emerald beam stabbed the low-hanging cloud deck, piercing the gray and allowing a widening shaft of solar radiance to spotlight its summoner, the two Kings and the Firvulag general standing behind him, and the rest of the Most Exalted Personages on the platform. Warriors and noncombatants together sang the Song, the soaring Tanu chorus counterpointed by the deeper, more sonorous voices of the Firvulag. The break in the clouds expanded, just as it always had for long thousands of years on the foggy planet Duat, where the ancient rivals had been accustomed to use both mental force and laser beams to insure a sunny sky for their annual ritual war.

The Song ended. The vault of the Pliocene heavens glowed blue above the White Silver Plain. Fighters and spectators gave a mighty cheer, and the First Day of the Grand Combat began.

* * *

Felice awoke to stillness. Physical. Mental. Emotional.

She was half-sitting on the bottom of some cramped container, crushed up against the sleeping form of a disheveled young gold-torc woman she had never seen before. Standing like some herculean statue almost on top of her, but looking out and away, with mind a singing blank, was a man both gigantic and familiar.

But he was not the hated Beloved not him.

Human-hairy legs rising to a grubby green tunic. A waist cinched by an amber-studded belt. Great hunched shoulders. Hands resting on the padded top rail of the box. Motionless homely blond head.

Above, the blazing gridiron within the mouth of a vibrant scarlet gut. A blue sky.

What? Some new amusement of the tormentor? But *his* mind was no longer with her. He was gone and she remained. The strength had been given to her and she remained.

The gridiron thing was of a peculiar complex design, glowing with such heat that the air for meters around it was all ashimmer. It was mounted at the tip of a decamole frame that was attached to the decamole container that imprisoned the three of them. There were silvery cables depending from a wide ring around the red maw's opening, and these were also attached to their open-topped cell. Beside her, projecting from the wall of the box, was a fat shelf. She raised herself painfully and saw a digital instrument cluster:

ALT—2104.3; TER CL—2596.1; VAR— $+$ .19; ENV—77[green]; AMB AT—17.5; PO FX—37:39N, 00:33E; GD SP—66.2; HDG—231; F RES—2299.64HR; ZT—07:34:15.

She and Stein and the woman were in Elizabeth's balloon.

Free.

Felice pulled herself upright and stood beside the rigid man. There was absolutely no sensation of movement through the air, no wind. The heat generator above their heads was silent; but if she strained her ears she could hear minute cracklings as hot air swirled within the semidirigible envelope, and a tiny zip when a high venting panel gaped momentarily and then closed.

Free. And her mind . . .

Fingertips touched the cold gray circlet around her neck. She smiled. Unfastening the knob-catch, she removed the dead torc, held it over the rail of the gondola, let it fall into the deep basin of the Empty Sea.

Now grow, small cherished thing.

So fragile, so deceivingly meager, the kernel of her identity within the brain-vault opened. Psychoenergies gushed forth in giddy torrents. The strictures, the wounds, the debris from the torturer's work that seemed to presage madness (so Creyn the redactor had believed) were swept away. A fantastic new edifice that was the unwitting legacy of the Beloved reared in glory. It expanded, it filled, it recovered and restored and reorganized as it grew. In seconds only, the mental seedling burgeoned into a mature and executive psychoorganism. She was whole. She was operant. And he had done it! She was coercive, psychokinetic, creative, farsensing—all thanks to him. Willing destruction, he had engendered life. Crushing her to near-nothingness, he had forced her into Union (and poor Amerie had been right about that much, at least).

She abode in midair and delight. Gratitude warmed her. She loved him more than ever and thought about how to show her thankfulness. Reach out? No, not yet. But later, yes. So the Beloved and all his kin would know what she had done, just before they died.

The method . . .

She looked over distances. There could be no return to Muriah, the White Silver Plain, and the Combat. She could deal with many of them in direct confrontation, but never with them all. And it would have to be all.

Under the soaring balloon the Southern Lagoon narrowed toward the Long Fjord that lay south of Cartagena during the early Pliocene. Milky waters, dull-gleaming in early sunlight, had swallowed her gray torc. The alkali flats were punctuated by eroded volcanic necks from which jagged walls of old lava radiated. Where the short Spanish rivers dropped from the Betic Cordillera, the shores were stained with black and brown and vermilion alluvial fans. Receding on her right hand lay Aven. The Dragon Range of its midsection was still visible back in the haze. Somewhere on the other side of the peninsular neck would be the large city of Afaliah and the rich plantations of its dependencies.

Were human minions even now tending herds or overseeing ramas who mined ores in those mountains? Would they recognize the drifting speck of the balloon for what it was? Probably not—but her illusion-spinning power rendered the big red envelope invisible, just in case. Firvulag? There would be wild ones in the Betic high-lands who had scorned to attend the Combat. But they could be no threat at such a distance, and their powers of farspeech were so weak that they would surely be incapable of spreadnig any alarm. Tanu? None. They were at the Grand Combat. All of them. All gathered together on the salty plain deep in the Empty Sea . . .

Yes, of course.

That was how. And so fitting, like a reverse birth, with the amni-otic flow initiating. It would not be easy, even for her as she was now. But—yes! Stein had been a crust driller. He would know the great earth faults, the zones of instability.

She smiled up at him. The bright-blue Viking eyes stared unseeing ahead. Every five seconds they slowly blinked. The unconscious mind of him below Elizabeth's expert restraints cycled easily, at peace. Felice could now admire the Grand Master's handiwork that had shunted to harmlessness all but the sustenance circuits of the gray torc. There remained certain grave dysfunctions within Stein's brain, but they were capable of being healed.

And the little woman? His wife, of course. Gently, Felice went probing among the secret places of Sukey's sleeping mind. After a time she found the well-concealed thing that would motivate Stein to help her engineer the murder of the Tanu race.

The estuary below narrowed rapidly. The fjord, deep and blue, snaked through a region of ancient vulcanism that linked Europe with Africa. Eroded cindercones, ash beds, and areas of dark rubble made a kind of sill across this part of the Mediterranean Basin. West of the fjord-pierced barrier, below the region that would be called the Costa del Sol by inhabitants of Elder Earth, was a sizable lowland; there lay the islet-studded Great Brackish Marsh, with its areas of open water where Bryan and Mercy had once anchored their yacht. Farther to the west the waters shoaled into playas and then blazing alkali deserts. The active volcano of Alborán poked up amidst barren wilderness, smoking in a desultory fashion. Beyond was a deep evaporite basin; and then the abrupt southerly curve of the Betic Range, which joined the two continents at the narrow and precipitous Gibraltar Isthmus.

A thin forest grew along the fjord. It looked like a lonely and pleasant place to stop.

Scanning Sukey's mind once again, Felice perceived the simple maneuvers needed to land the balloon. Heat reduction and cutoff, vent action, her own override of the vagrant low-level wind currents that threatened to send the balloon into an undesirable area. There! Into a sheltered nook below one of the old volcanic cones. A spring greened level and ashy soil. The bottom of the gondola touched down, lifted, came securely to rest. Holding the envelope in position with her PK, she tugged the deflation cable. The apex gaped and residual hot air vomited from bellying scarlet fabric. A normal human would have seized a line and jumped out to deck the still-stiffened envelope so that it could be secured or completely deflated; but the masterclass psychokinesis of Felice simply lowered the thing by mind-power. The touch of a stud began evacuation of the structural members of the envelope. Within a few minutes the decamole bag of the red balloon stretched tidily at one side of the gondola, flat and expired.

"Wake up, everybody!" Felice cried brightly. "Breakfast time!"

* * *

Bryan had been imprisoned in a comfortable suite in the highest level of Redactor Guild headquarters. The sleeping chamber was windowless, extending into the flank of the mountain; but the sitting room had a balcony that overlooked the southern section of Muriah and the orchards, olive groves, and suburban villas that extended from the city outskirts to the land's-end promontory where Brede's small residence stood. Beyond that curved the White Silver Plain. He could not see the Combat, of course. The ritual battlefield lay nearly three kilometers away and below the peninsular rim. But as the sun climbed there were occasional heliographic flashes from that direction; and now and then, when the wind shifted, he thought he heard distant sounds of thunder and music.

If truth were told, Dr. Bryan Grenfell was deeply disappointed at missing the Grand Combat, even though the handsomely sinister Culluket had explained that he was going to play a very special rôle later in the celebration and so had to remain offstage, as it were, until his time had come. But almost every anthropologist delights in ritual spectacle, and Bryan, whose specialty ordinarily kept him busy studying statistics and other less colorful manifestations of culture, was at heart a sucker for a good show. He had looked forward to this stylized brawl between the exotic races . . . but here he sat in glum coventry on the balcony, imbibing pale Glendessarry with the sun still on the wrong side of the yardarm, while almost every other human or exotic inhabitant of Muriah was out cheering the preliminary sporting events that were taking place down on the sparkling salt.

She came through the locked door, found him, and laughed. "Mercy!"

"Ah, your face, my darling love! That dear, astonished face!"

She ran to him, trailing cerise and gold gossamer, and reached up to kiss him. Her wired and jeweled headdress was so elaborate that he felt he was caught with her inside some fantastic bird cage where dangling ornaments tinkled and chimed. With her auburn hair concealed beneath a golden hood, she looked unfamiliar, alien: Lady of Goriah, wife to the godlike Battlemaster, aspirant President of Creators—all these, easily. But where was his lady passing by?

"Silly juggins," she said. There was a snap and she stood transformed, wearing the simple long dress of the portrait he had carried next to his heart.

"And is this better?" she inquired. "Now do you know me?"

He let his arms gather her in, and it was as always (again), the soaring into light and the inevitable fall into darkness, from which he returned a little later each time.

They sat together on a shaded divan on the balcony when he had recovered, and he explained to her about the picture he had used in searching for her, and the strange reactions of the people he had shown it to. They laughed over that.

"I tried to imagine your life in the Pliocene when the computer first gave me your portrait, back in the auberge," he said. "You and your dog and the sheep and the strawberry plants and all. I visualized you in some idyllic pastorale . . . and I'm afraid there were even times when I was Daphnis and you were Chloë, God save the mark."

Once more she laughed, and then kissed him.

"But it wasn't at all like that," he said. "Was it?"

"You really want to know." The sea-eyes were opalescent this day, still slightly misted from the ecstasy. When he nodded she told him how it had been—how the Tanu examiner at Castle Gateway had been astonished, then terrified at the result of her mental assay, throwing the entire establishment into a swivet. How she had been granted the unprecedented honor of being flown to Muriah, where the members of the High Table had themselves confirmed her enormous creative potential.

"And it was decided," she said, "that after I had been filled with the Thagdal's grace, I would go to Lord Nodonn. He came to fetch me, having in his mind to make me just another of his human ladies. But when we met—"

A smile of wintry satisfaction touched Bryan's lips. "Enchantress."

"No . . . but he could see within my brain the differences. There was love, too. But Nodonn would not have made me his true wife because of that alone."

"Of course not," Bryan said dryly, and once again she laughed.

"He and I are not as romantic as you, dear Bryan!"

Not as human, something hiding inside him twitted.

She said, "By the time we reached his domain of Goriah we were pledged to each other. He took me as consort in a faerie wedding that seemed the fulfillment of every wonderful dream I'd ever had.

Ah, Bryan! If you could have seen it! All of them dressed in rose and gold, and the flowers and the singing and the joy . . ."

He held her tight against his breast, looking over her head to the horizon where the mirror flashes were. He knew he was dying of her, and that it didn't matter. The elfin lover was as nothing, her metapsychic powers were nothing, not even her imminent ascension to the High Table of exotic nobility mattered. With one small portion of her heart she loved him, and she had promised that he could stay until the end.

She shattered his reflection with a droll commonplace. "Dierdre had pups! Four of them. They're all over the palace, the little devils, snow-white and full of the dickens. Fortunately, we Tanu love dogs."

He had to burst out laughing, restored to the still improbable here and now of a bright sunny morning, October 31, six million years before the time of their birth.

"Shall I show you the games?" she asked. And then in quick explanation, "Ah, no, love—I can't take you to the White Silver Plain as yet. But I can project images of what's happening for us to watch together. It'll be just like a glorified Tri-D, but with all the sensations. I needn't return to the others until tomorrow, when they have the manifestation of powers."

"And you go up against Aluteyn?"

"Yes, my dear. But I'll win over him, never fear. The poor man is old, more than three thousand, and tired. His time has come. He's as much as admitted to Nodonn that he'll welcome the life-offering."

"And will the Thagdal as well?" Bryan asked her. "Aiken and Nodonn are bound to meet in this Combat. No matter which one wins, the King himself must be challenged by the victor. I can't believe that Nodonn would continue to defer to Thagdal after a victory over Aiken Drum."

Mercy's bright gaze turned aside. "Nor would he. If my Lord wins—and he must win!—he will become king and restore the old ways. Matters have . . . progressed too far for him to consider any other course."

For only a moment, the scientist in him prevailed. "Mercy, the old ways can't be restored. The human advent, the adulteration of the exotic culture by our technology, the hybridization of the races—it can't be reversed! Nodonn must see that."

"Hush, Bryan. No more of such portentous talk!" She waved her hand and the distant tournament sprang to life in the thin air beyond the parapet. "Look! We'll watch the games together and between times you'll love me again and again from the excitement! But don't fear that your civilized sensibilities will be too affronted, for no people meet death in the First Day Events. All the wonderful violence is only for the sake of sport."

"So I'm civilized, am I?" Laughing they fell back again onto the cushions. All around spun the preliminary contests of the Combat— the Tanu knightly jousts and chariot races and chaliko races; the ramshackle Firvulag hurling competition and the Little People's gnomish version of highland games; the Contest of Animals in which Tanu and Firvulag and gold-torc humans matched purely natural skills against fierce Pliocene beasts (and could Bryan believe his dimming eyes when he saw who was to be the opponent of the giant ape?); and then the Fray of Warrior-Maids, wherein Tanu and human gold-torc women contended against one another in the lists with horrific illusions and genuine weapons, stopping only short of ritual decapitation so that the losers could be restored by the Skin in time for the real hostilities on the day after tomorrow.

Bryan and Mercy watched the spectacle all afternoon and on into the night, for no one seemed to sleep during Grand Combat time when the days lasted from dawn to dawn. And she was right about the excitement inflaming them, and when she rose to go he was so sated that he could not be roused.

"Oh, you've truly found that which you searched for," she told him, kissing his forehead. "So you won't begrudge me my share of the bargain, will you? Wait until they come for you, dear love. And after it's over, we'll meet one final time."

Her magnificent court costume restored, she went out through the locked door just as she had entered.

4

As THE LAST of the chariot races ended, there were deafening cheers from the Tanu stands and flower garlands draped around the necks of the three blue-dyed chalikos; and a trophy, of course, and the royal accolade from the King himself. Only the bookies reacted to the victory with understandable ennui—not that the race was fixed, but what kind of odds could you give against the Queen? They always let her win the last one.

"Congratulations, Nonnie," Thagdal said, kissing her as she alighted from the gilded wicker vehicle. "You showed 'em again, old girl."

But he didn't want to watch the Tanu youngsters in their point-to-point, or the humans and hybrids boat-racing while Fian Skybreaker whistled a breeze and the noble ladies shuddered delightedly at the occasional dump into the perilous chop. They debated for a moment whether to view the Firvulag caber-tossing or the sword dance —for there was always the chance that a careless contestant would split a gut or get a foot chopped off. But even these diverting possibilities had little appeal to the King.

"I'd rather just go into the pavilion and take it easy for a while," he confessed. "I'm in a rotten mood, Nonnie."

She led him away. Once they were secluded within the white silk, she wove metapsychic screens and blotted out the carnival hurly-burly. They served themselves lunch, for none of the little ramas were allowed on the White Silver Plain lest their sensitive minds be damaged by the emotional tempests of the Combat; and the gray-torc servants and barenecks, by long tradition, were free at this time to watch the games and indulge their gambling lust.

The King did not eat much. His apprehension was so patent that Nontusvel finally made him lie down on the royal camp bed so she could administer the sovereign remedy. And in the self-revelatory murmurings that followed, he told her all the bad news. About the defection of Katlinel and the Genetics Master, which had come to his attention just before the Opening of the Sky. About the message from Redact House, disclosing the escape of Aiken Drum's minion, Stein, together with the latter's ingrate paramour and Felice . . . and even Elizabeth.

"There's real trouble brewing, Nonnie. These are bad times and the worst is yet to come. Aiken Drum denies any knowledge of the escapes—and would you believe it? Both Culluket and Imidol confirm that the little bastard's telling the truth! But if Aiken didn't free the prisoners, who did? And where's Elizabeth? She's not working with the healers any more. Has she gone off with Felice? Or is she hiding, getting ready to connive with Aiken Drum in the Combat?"

"Oh, Thaggy—surely not! Elizabeth is nonaggressive. Riganone determined that when the woman first arrived here in Muriah."

But the King, not listening, only raged on. "And that damn Katy! Look what we did for the half-human chit, raising her to the High Table and all! And she goes and confirms everything Nodonn's been saying about untrustworthy hybrids. Tana knows why she took Greggy with her, but there's been hanky-panky in the computer room."

Nontusevel said anxiously, "You don't suppose Greggy managed to get his own copy of Bryan's survey?"

Thagdal chewed his ornately braided mustache. "If he did, he'd be in a pretty position to play both ends against the middle. The human middle! And you know who's perched right there on the divider grinning at the lot of us . . ."

"Greg-Donnet is too dear and simple to fall in with any of Aiken Drum's intrigues—even if the boy were able to muster a following."

"Hah! I've had my doubts about the simplicity of Crazy Greggy for some time now. And Aiken is popular with our petty nobility, make no mistake. Did you see where he's going to fight the ape?"

The Queen looked shocked, then began to giggle. "The gigantopithecus? Oh, Thaggy! The clever little devil. I mustn't miss it!"

"Nobody wants to miss it," the King said gloomily. "That little joker has the crowd in the palm of his hand before he even gets into the blood events. They *like* the runty bastard, I tell you! And when he really starts to put on a show with his damned masterclass metafunctions in the battles, they'll respect him as well as lionize him. He'll romp through the High Mêlée giving a good account of himself and attract enough opportunists under his banner to support him in his bid for a Heroic Encounter with Nodonn."

"A few urban dilettantes and hybrids!"

Thagdal shook his head. "He's got at least three High Table champions lined up already. And contingents from Roniah and Calamosk and Geroniah and Var-Mesk have declared for him, too. Mayvar's made sure all the provincial lords know about Aiken Drum's golden balls."

"They'll never choose that clown over Nodonn!"

"Face it, Nonnie. Our son the Battlemaster has metafunctions to burn and more panache than me and my Awful Father and my Unspeakable Grandsire all rolled up in one. But eugenically speaking, he just doesn't cut the mustard. And that's all those hinterlanders think about: strong genes, more kids, population growth to keep us ahead of the Firvulag horde. No . . . we've got to be realistic. If Aiken survives the High, he'll go after Nodonn in the Encounters. And if he should win, the whole damn company'll accept the kid as Battlemaster by acclamation. Then *my* ass'll be on the line."

"Nodonn will defeat Aiken Drum," the Queen declared. "He's your designated heir. If necessary, he can invoke ancient privilege and use the Sword!"

But then Thagdal had to admit to her that Aiken had the Spear.

For a long time after that they sat together hand in hand, each contemplating the end apart from the other, and finally, with some measure of serenity, admitting that it might be more bearable if shared.

* * *

The balloon riders decided to camp on the fjord, at least until the next day. Felice assured Sukey that it would be impossible for any hostile observer to penetrate her illusionary defenses. She further invited Sukey to enter her mind and discover something of the wonders newly wrought there. All that Sukey knew of the ring-hockey player had come second-hand from Stein. (This poor little child with the big brown eyes and tattered chemise—*this* was the ballbreaking bull dyke Stein knew back at the auberge?) Any misgivings Sukey might have entertained were dispelled by the aura of goodwill and kindly power shining from Felice's mind.

Resting for a day [thought Sukey] would give them time to assess one another, get cleaned up, and make rational decisions about where to go from here. Most especially, it would provide the opportunity for that delicate operation, the removal of Stein's torc.

The double-lever steel cutters were in one of the gondola lockers.

"I'll be able then to complete most of his mind-healing myself, even with his torc off." Shyness made Sukey hesitate before explaining to Felice. "There are certain mental lesions that Elizabeth couldn't mend, you see. Very old injuries made worse by the torc. But their cure is not so much a matter of redactive skill as one of . . . love."

Felice gave a light laugh. "Stein's a fortunate fellow! If you like, I'll work the cutter so you'll be free to concentrate on his mind. If there's a need, I can coerce him into quiet as well."

Sukey nodded. The two of them bent over Stein, who lay with eyes wide open on the wiry turf. At the severing, the giant cried out. But the caregiving mind was there with her soul-mortar and balm, guiding his psychoenergies into the channels prepared by Elizabeth. There would be no serious postaddictive trauma for Stein. The anomalous brain-circuitry of the torc and all trace of its insult melted away before Sukey's healing. More whole than he had ever been, Stein Oleson lived.

"He'll do for now," Sukey said. "I'll wake him."

Stein's eyes saw her. For a long time they saw nothing else.

Felice left them together and went to study the fjord landscape, the porous blocks of lava and masses of unconsolidated ash and scoria supporting meager vegetation. It was not until hours later—long after Felice had washed their clothes, and Sukey had collapsed in a brief reactionary episode, and Stein had taken his turn as comforter—that Felice began to speak in a matter-of-fact way about her plan for genocide.

They were sitting around a little fire in the shades of evening. The huntress had shown casual power by zapping a lagomorphic creature resembling a short-eared jackrabbit. They had grilled it for supper, and with the sweet biocake from the balloon rations they had had tangy wild grapes. Stein and Sukey, enjoying digestion and sweet peace, sat cradled in each other's arms not really hearing what Felice said to them.

". . . and the torc factory was essentially unharmed by our attack, so the third phase of Madame Guderian's great scheme remains unfulfilled. Humanity can still be enslaved by the torcs. It doesn't matter that the time-gate's closed. Don't you see? All the Tanu have to do is rescind their ban on human-human reproduction, and in time the pool of potential slaves will be bigger than ever. And don't think that only torced humans cooperate with the exotics! You should have seen the bareneck human finks blubbering to go home after we blasted Finiah. Those stupid pathetickers *preferred* life under the Tanu!"

Stein said to Sukey, "We could go to Bordeaux. Where Richard and me figured the wine-loving exiles would live. There could be free people there, like Madame Guderian's bunch. Only not making war with iron weapons. Just living easy. Sorta Robin-Hooding it. I could build us a nice cabin—"

Felice interrupted. "You haven't been listening to me."

"Sure I have, Felice. You could stay with us. Both Sukey and me owe you. So do all the human beings in Exile. What you and the others did—"

"We weren't able to finish the job, Steinie. As long as that torc factory is intact, no bareneck human is safe from slavery. The Tanu will be Hunting for us as long as they're top dogs in Exile. And remember that human traitors wearing torcs aren't poisoned by iron. They're no more vulnerable to it than ordinary bareneck folks are. All the Flying Hunt has to do is spot concealed human settlements from the air, then send in parties of torced humans to do the dirty work."

"Aw, hell. There's gotta be someplace wild enough to be safe. Not all *that* many of the Tanu can fly. The big guns like Nodonn'll be up north where Guderian stirred up the hornet's nest—not in Bordeaux. That's a good spot. Richard and me were worried about ordinary human outlaws in the Pliocene. You grab? We wanted to pick a secure site for our base of operations. So we noodled with one of the geology boffins at the auberge and came up with Bordeaux. It has big tidal swamps with islands of good high land. Richard figured the place'd be perfect."

"Do you know where Richard is now?" Felice's smile was dreamy. "I do. I can farsense him easily with my new power. He's in a broken-down exotic flyer in a parking orbit forty-nine thousand kloms out, going around and around the world with the dead body of his lady. He looks at the environmental readout every now and then and laughs. And it is pretty funny, when you think of his costume and all. Because the oxygen is nearly all used up."

Sukey, shocked to wakefulness, broke from Stein's clasp. "Oh, *no!*

Felice, how can you—how can you sneer at him in such a heartless way? Richard was your friend!"

For the first time, Sukey dared to assay a strong redactive probe into the girl. The mental lancet shattered on impervious smoothness. Sukey uttered a soft cry of pain.

"Don't do that, dear. I'd rather keep my thoughts private until I choose to reveal them. I believe that's a simple courtesy among the metas of the Milieu. Richard is unimportant." And so are you, Redactorwife, so take care! "But Stein *is* important . . . to a certain plan of action that I have in mind. I know how to bring about the real solution to all our worries."

Stein and Sukey stared at her.

Felice said, "I want to wipe out all of these Tanu bastards once and for all—while they're gathered in one place for the Grand Combat. And as a bonus, we'll get quite a few of the Firvulag, too. I never did trust those little friggers and neither did Madame Guderian."

Stein said, "If you expect me to go along on another invasion of Muriah, don't hold your breath, sister!"

"Oh, no, Steinie. Nothing like that." Her fingers caressed the hollow of her throat. "I had a golden torc. It made me operant, with wonderful powers. And then I was caught and the Tanu took my torc away and tried to punish me. But their tortures backfired, Steinie. I'm a strange sort of person, you know. The suffering made me fully operant. Without a torc. I'm as good as the metapsychic world shakers of the Galactic Milieu. My PK and creativity are stronger than the powers of any of the Tanu Great Ones."

"No shit," he drawled. "So buck for Queen of the World at the Combat!"

Once again, the dreamy smile. "I have a better idea. That's why I need your help . . . I want to pop the cork at Gibraltar and let the Atlantic into the Med Basin. Drown the exotics like rats in a barrel. I'll do the heavy blasting, and you'll show me where to put the shots so the walls come tumbling down."

The Viking gave an involuntary shout of exultation. "And Pharaoh's army got drownded? Sweet Christ!"

"*Stein!*" wailed Sukey.

"I thought it might appeal to you," Felice said smugly.

"No!" Sukey cried.

He took her in his arms again. "Don't be silly, babe. What d'you take me for? There's human beings in Muriah! Elizabeth and

Raimo. And Amerie and those two guys that got caught with her. And even the Fancy Pants Kid! He needs a swift boot, all right—but not drowning."

Felice said, "Aiken Drum is almost certain to beat Nodonn in the Grand Combat and become king. Do you think *he'll* close down the torc factory? Or free the slaves and deprive himself of all those trusty human subjects? Don't make me laugh!"

"Dammit—the others!"

"Amerie and Peo and Basil were terribly wounded. They're as good as dead. The only way they could survive would be if the Tanu put them into Skin. And why should the exotics do that? They plan to roast them alive in the life-offering in four days' time."

"Raimo . . . Bryan," Stein protested.

Felice laughed. "They're goners, too. Let's say they loved and lived. As for Elizabeth . . . she could save herself if she wanted to."

Stein's brows lowered in truculence. "You gotta give *her* fair warning. She helped Sukey shrink me. She gave us her balloon."

The little athlete waved one hand in dismissal. "All right. A farspoken warning once the thing is in train and she can't do anything to stop me."

"Stein, you can't!" Sukey cried. "Felice is—inhuman!"

"Oh, yes," the girl agreed. She stirred the fire with a long stick. The tepee structure of burning pine branches collapsed in an eruption of orange sparks. "But so are the Tanu and Firvulag inhuman! If I let in the sea, the Tanu will be virtually wiped out and the Firvulag reduced to a manageable small population. Free human beings will still have to fight against the torc wearers that remain in the mainland cities. But with the exotic masters and the torc factory gone, at least we'll have a chance. *You'll* have a chance."

Not looking at his wife, Stein said, "Sukey—she's right."

"Steinie, what about all the humans in Muriah who'll be drowned?"

He scowled. "All of 'em that I had anything to do with were Tanu-loyal to the toenails."

"But Felice is talking about the murder of nearly a hundred thousand living persons! You can't help her, Stein! Not if . . . I mean anything to you. Felice is insane! Culluket had her for a week. That's enough to—" She broke off, biting her lip.

Felice was unruffled. "He tortured you, too, Sukey. And you didn't go mad. Did she tell you about that, Stein? About the interrogation ordered by the Queen? Don't you want to get back at the people who tortured Sukey?"

"Stein knows all about what Culluket did," Sukey cried. Sudden fear blazed up. But Stein didn't know about—

"And don't you want revenge on Thagdal, Steinie?"

Puzzled, he said, "On the King? But why? He was always a pretty good old buffer. A real sport on the Delbaeth Quest."

"Felice, don't!" Sukey pleaded. "Don't!"

"Sukey didn't tell you what happened *before* her interrogation, though—did she, Stein. She didn't want you to do something foolish and get yourself killed by the Tanu . . . or by anybody else. Ask Sukey how the Queen found out about the sabotage party."

"Don't listen to her, Stein! She's lying!"

"Am I lying, Sukey? I can see the whole thing, right there in your memory bank. Too bad Stein's torc is off, or I could relay it right to him. You've tried to wall off that memory. But I can read it. Do you know that you've been letting it leak? Something in your sneaky little subconscious let just the smallest bit of the memory seep out for Stein to catch! You wanted him to catch it. And he did, too. Just a suspicion. A need to . . . blame."

"Please," Sukey whispered. "Don't do this to him."

"Blame?" the Viking's forehead wrinkled. "How could I blame Sukey for betraying the invasion? I never should've told her anything about it. Even Aik warned me not to. I blame myself—blame him, too, for putting—"

"Ass!" Felice hissed. "Not blame for *that*. For the baby."

Sukey hid her face on Stein's chest. His arms dropped away from her body. He seemed to see something deep in the dying campfire. Resin in a burning brand popped. Sukey's sobs were quiet, hopeless.

"King Thagdal," Stein said at last. "In spite of what Aiken and Mayvar and Dionket promised. He had Sukey."

"When she was already pregnant with your child. And some women—they have to be careful in the first weeks. Before the little embryo is latched on tight. So now you know who to blame."

Big arms came up, enfolding the shuddering form. Stein did not look at Felice nor at his wife. He watched the flames. "We'll have to do a recon from the air. Surface, too, maybe. Can you make the balloon go any direction you want?"

"Of course."

"Tomorrow, then." He repeated: "Tomorrow. Early."

* * *

Elizabeth returned to the room without doors.

There was nowhere else to go unless she was willing to wait passively in Muriah until the Host finally deciphered her personal snuff-sequence and finished her off. Since the escape of the balloon, they had had a dozen top-line farsensors locked onto her, so there was no possibility of her slipping away from Aven by ordinary means. And the Shipspouse had declared, with every evidence of sincere regret, that she was incompetent to teleport her to safety. It was a pity, Brede had lamented, that Elizabeth herself did not possess more PK! For a very short time, Elizabeth had believed the exotic woman's protestations.

But then the sly Two-Faced One had given herself away. Her great racial vision—her foresight—if only Elizabeth would help her to make the last clarification! There was a role to be played by one of them, or both . . . and if they studied in Unity, they would surely discover the truth.

Elizabeth would have fled Brede's room—and Dionket had offered her sanctuary in his conspirators' hideout up in the Mount of Heroes. But she knew that even the natural shielding of the rock was insufficient to shut out the hostile ones. Nodonn now coordinated more than two hundred of them with growing sophistication. If any of them happened to discover that one pattern of assault, and launched it while she was asleep, she would never awaken.

Only in the room without doors was she safe from them. As for Brede . . . there was a way to be rid of her importunities as well. Away, false Unity. Away, seductive two-in-one with your cheating prolepsis that led only to another *using*. Elizabeth would accept no comfort if the price was responsibility. Not in a situation so hopelessly barbaric, so alien to her human metapsychic nature. True human beings would always be defeated in this Exile that was controlled by exotic races. And Elizabeth was too weary and heartsick to condemn herself to a wait of six million years.

The mind-voice of Brede kept calling: We need you! All three races do! Only look and see how it might be. Look and take comfort.

I will not look. *I will not be used.* You tricked me once to attain full operancy, to become adept. And not for the sake of your people, as you said, but to gain access to *me*. To be able to reach me with your temptation, O well-named Two-Face. But I will not be your savior, exotic. Such a role cannot be coerced. You have no comfort for me. My comfort is six million years distant and this Pliocene theosphere is inhuman and untempered by incarnation. So let me alone. Let me alone . . .

Cocooned in the old fire, Elizabeth drifted away. Brede's calls became fainter and fainter, finally dwindling into silence.

5

"THE STRAIT was only about twenty-five kloms across in our time," Stein told Felice. "And that was after six million years of scouring by ocean currents. You won't be able to blast a gap anything like that wide, you know."

The two of them leaned over the rail of the gondola. The red balloon, held motionless by the girl's PK, was poised 300 meters above the crest of the Gibraltar Isthmus. The heights were rounded by erosion. Cedar trees grew in the western downslope valleys. There were dunes and rippling grassy hillocks on the Atlantic side of the landbridge, but on the Mediterranean flank the isthmus was barren, falling off in an awesome escarpment with sharp buttresses and a tumble of great shattered blocks at the foot, below which were smoother sediments dipping to the Alborán Basin.

Felice said, "The terrain-clearance readout and altimeter put that Gib crest at only two-sixty-eight. If you're right about the isthmus being riddled with caves like a Swiss cheese, I should be able to rupture it. Looks to me like it's overdue to crumble from natural causes. And that eastern dropoff goes way below sea level."

"We could see Gibraltar from my satellite," Sukey said. She smiled into the blue, cloudless sky. "The place where Europe kisses Africa, we called it! We were very sentimental about Earth."

Felice ignored her. "Where would be the best place for my first zap, Steinie? Don't worry about the shockwave hitting the balloon. I'll spin a big bubble-shield around us. How about if I blast that little headland sticking out?"

"Hold it, dummy!" he exclaimed. "You want a real tidal wave? Or just a slow-creeping thing like a friggerty filling bathtub that gives 'em plenty of time to make a getaway?"

"Did you see my satellite up in the night sky when you worked in Lisboa, Steinie?" Sukey asked. "Up above the world so high?"

"Hydraulic pressure!" Stein said, smacking left fist into right palm. "That's what we need, kid! A good head of water. A great big surge that comes crashing through the estuary of the Southern Lagoon to the White Silver Plain and floods the battlefield fast!"

"My thoughts exactly," Felice said. "I'll torch the isthmus in a lot of different places. The gap's bound to widen and let a zillion tons of water in. For crissake, the whole Atlantic's pushing!"

Sukey said, "Most of us on ON-15 spent a lot of time looking at Earth. Especially the people who'd never been there. Fourth-generation satelliters like me. Odd that we'd want to do that, wasn't it? We had everything we could possibly want in our beautiful satellite."

"Little Miss Smartass! Even if you hit the fault lines, touched off a major subsidence, you'd never get an opening here more than five-six kloms wide to start with. Okay! The sea squirts through and you got the most hellaceous waterfall in history. But Muriah is almost a thousand kloms away from here! And you saw that big bugger of a dry basin between here and Alborán."

"You mean—it would swallow the surge?"

Sukey said, "Our lovely hollow satellite. Wherever you stood on the inside surface of the cylinder, the central axis was up. It spun to simulate gravity. Sometimes the strangeness of it drove Earthsider visitors crazy! But we were used to it. The human brain is an adaptable organism. For almost everything."

"That damn basin would kill our head of water deader 'n Saturday night in Peoria! So don't go zapping this isthmus yet, baby. First we gotta go back and seal up the fjord. Get the picture?"

"Build up *another* head of water?"

"Checko. With the fjord shut, that old volcanic line between the Costa del Sol and Africa forms a natural dam. A kind of threshold maybe two hundred and fifty kloms north to south—but not very wide, not very high. The marsh is west of it, taking the outflow from that Spanish river. The fjord is—what?—a hundred meters deep? So if we plug it, we got a long, long dam! And not made of tough rock like Gibraltar, either. Just unconsolidated ash and cinders and lava hunks."

"It would be much safer inside Hollow Earth than at Bordeaux, Steinie," Sukey said. "It's still not too late for us to find the way."

"I think I understand," Felice said, nodding. "When we get a good head of water behind this soft dam, *then* I rip the thing open."

"If you got the gigawatts, kid."

"Wait and see, big boy! You're sure the dam will hold until I'm ready to blow it?"

"Looked like it. And if you're as good as you say you are, you could always shore it up if it started to crack too soon."

"Kaleidoscopic! Let's highball it to the fjord and I'll show you how good I am!" Felice began to manipulate the heat generator. The balloon mounted rapidly into the air.

"They might not want to let Felice into Hollow Earth, Steinie." Sukey's face was anxious. "Violence isn't allowed in the peaceful realm of Agharta. Only kindness. But what'll become of her if we don't take her with us? Poor Felice . . . all alone with the dead ones!"

Stein took his wife's shoulders and gently pressed her down. "You rest awhile, Sue. Take a nap, maybe. Don't worry about Felice or Hollow Earth. I'll take care of everything from now on."

Sukey's mouth trembled. "I'm sorry you can't go, Felice. Steinie's changed now. He's gentle and good. He'll fit in. But not you . . . Let's go to Agharta *now*, Stein. I don't want to wait any longer."

"Soon," he assured her. "Try to sleep." He made her as comfortable as he could on the floor of the gondola.

Felice's creative metafunction conjured two air masses of dissimilar pressure. A wind began to blow from the Atlantic, carrying the balloon directly toward the fjord. Felice's eyes shone. "If I pedal real fast, Steinie, we can be there and back before lunch. You're *sure* this ploy will do the job?"

"When that clinker dam lets go, you'll have one vicious grannybanger of a tidal wave chargin' down that narrow Southern Lagoon. Make old Noah eat his heart out."

Sukey buried her head in her arms. One gleam of hope shone through her nightmare. Elizabeth! With this new golden torc, it might be possible to—

Silly fool! (Sukey's sanity tottered.) Don't you think I've been expecting you to try something like that? (You can't get me—I'm running!) I've got you screened so thick you couldn't even spit without my say-so! (But you'll never catch me where I'm going.) Warn them, would you? You little hypocrite! Deep down inside your stupid virtue you want this just as much as we do! (No, no, no.) Yes, yes, yes!

Escape . . .

Sukey tried to drag Stein along with her. But his torc was gone. She could no longer pull him like a child. She could only beg, plead with nonmeta rationality, and hope that he would change his mind and follow her as she retreated.

Deep down there, the way to Agharta still had to be open.

* * *

It was something to keep him busy, and it did not require moving about on his rudely splinted broken legs, and so Basil spent most of his waking hours scraping away at the solid rock wall of their prison cell with a vitredur spoon.

By the seventh day, he had made an indentation approximately fifteen centimeters long, four high, and one deep. Chief Burke, in one of his last fully lucid moments, had told him, "Keep working! When you break through, we'll be able to post a letter: 'Help. I am a prisoner in a dungeon in Middle Earth.'"

But that about marked the end of the brave jests and stiff-upper-lipping, for Burke became delirious and addressed Basil from then on as "Counsel for the Defense," shouting tirades that apparently reprised his wittier pronunciamentos from the bench. Amerie was less noisy in her ravings, only leaning toward the more bloodthirsty psalms when the agony from her suppurating burns was most intense. By the tenth day of their imprisonment, the nun and the big Native American were helpless and incapable of speech. It was left to Basil, with only one of his fractures compounded, and that not even gangrenous yet, to remove their single daily meal from the turntable door-wicket, exchange the full slop bucket for an empty one, and tend to his dying friends as well as he could in pitch-darkness.

When these melancholy chores were done, he would return to his patient scraping at the letter slot.

Sometimes he dozed when the pain permitted it, and dreamed. He became an undergraduate again and punted on the Isis; squabbled with other dons over esoteric fripperies; even climbed mountains (but always with the summits out of reach—alas for the Pliocene Everest!).

He might have dreamed the bizarre woman as well.

She was gowned in metallic red and black all adorned with flame-shapes and beadwork, and wore the butterfly-shaped padded headdress of the middle fifteenth century. She was not a human being, not a Tanu either, and she seemed to have two faces—one comely and one grotesque. He tried to warn her tactfully about the slop bucket as she came shimmering through the stone wall, but like many an apparition, she only smiled and looked enigmatic.

"Do tell me how I can be of service to you, then," Basil said, resting on his elbows in the muck.

"It's ironic—but I really do need your help," said the woman. "Yours and that of your friends."

"Oh, hard lines," Basil said. "You see, they're more or less dying. And I think my left leg's finally going off. Getting rather noisome where the fibula ends protrude from the flesh."

The woman glowed. She had a kind of haversack, all bejeweled like the rest of her, and she took from it a considerable quantity of very thin transparent membrane, resembling plass. With no ceremony, she knelt down on the floor amidst the garbage and stinking puddles and smears of excrement and began wrapping the unconscious Amerie in this stuff; and when the nun was packaged like a choice cut in a butcher case, she enswathed Chief Burke.

"They're not quite dead, you know," Basil protested. "They'll smother."

"The Skin does not bring death, but life," the bizarre woman said. "You are needed alive. Sleep now and have no fear. Your gray torcs will be gone when you awake."

And before he could open his mouth in further demur, she had *him* entangled in the membrane, and then the dream of her faded away along with Peo and Amerie and the dungeon and all the rest of it.

* * *

Up until the time that Felice blew up the fjord, Stein had lived his whole Pliocene experience as some misbegotten culture-drama.

It had been wilder and scarier and more vivid than the immersive pageants he had been thrown out of way back in the Milieu of his young manhood; but when you came right down to it, life in Exile was just as stone friggerty unreal. The bloodletting in Castle Gateway, the fever-dream sequence culminating in the deep-redact by Elizabeth and Sukey, the auction banquet and the fight with the animal in the arena and the slaying of the dancing predator and the Delbaeth Quest . . . unreal! Any day now, any minute even, his participation in the show was going to come to an end and he would turn in his Viking costume and go out the exit and back into the real world of the twenty-second century.

Even at this moment, with his mind convalescent and suspicious, some evaluating segment of the cortex refused to accept the balloon journey as anything but an extension of the dream. Down below lay a pretty fjord entrance of colored lava cliffs. A big cindercone at stage right. Fakey-looking evergreens like overgrown bonsai clinging to the heights. Small wooded islets with flowering shrubs and mangrove thickets dotted here and there on mirror-smooth water. A big flock of pink flamingos over in the shallows, scoffing up lunch.

Unreal! He could see the posters:

SAVOR YOUR ANCIENT FAERIE HERITAGE
IN FANTASTIC PLIOCENELAND!

But all of a sudden, while he still floated in reverie, Felice leaned from the gondola and pointed a finger.

Their balloon was enclosed in the metapsychic shielding. But the flash, the concussion beating around them, the clouds of dark dust and fountaining earth and rock—they were not make-believe. He had known this kind of destruction before. He had caused it. The blasting of the fjord and the small volcanic cone next to it shocked him more profoundly than anything else he had lived through since passing the time-gate. He saw with vision new-born the roiling dust and steam, the ruined marshland, the bodies of the birds. His ears, preternaturally acute, heard Sukey's sobs and the mad giggling of Felice.

Real.

One of his hands reached out to the balloon controls and increased the output of the heat generator. They began to rise and shortly it was possible to survey the results of Felice's strike. What had been the entrance to the channel was now piled deep in rubble. Stein's earth driller's eye estimated that the landslide from the demolished cindercone bulked at no less than half a million cubic meters.

Felice grinned at him. "Now do you believe, Steinie?"

"Yeah." He turned from the gondola rail. His guts were tied in the old familiar knot. He tasted bile as he knelt to comfort poor cowering Sukey. "I believe, all right."

"We'll fly slowly over to the eastern end of the fjord, then. I'll whomp up quieter slides to block the rest of the passage—but I couldn't resist trying one little zap over here. My first shot! Did I blast rock like a pro?"

"One—little—zap?" Stein muttered.

"Well, actually I was afraid to really let loose this close to Muriah. I mean—only six hundred kloms away! They might have seismographs or something. It wouldn't do to let them know that something unnatural was going on. But a single small zap can pass for an earthquake. Right?"

"Sure, Felice. Sure."

Sukey clung to him, shivering. Ghostly drumrolls, relics of the monstrous explosion, still flailed and echoed among the ashy hills. Real. It was real. Sukey was. And Felice was.

After a time, the little blonde athlete extinguished the protective bubble and let the ambient atmosphere in again. She hung partly out of the car, laughing as she triggered rockfalls. Dust floated up on the thermals and settled all over the decamole surfaces. That was what made Stein's eyes water, what set his teeth on edge.

"Oh! Sorry about the mess, guys." The bright goddess banished the sifting grit in a flourish of psychokinetic power. "All finished here! Now we'll hurry back to Gibraltar and get down to serious business."

"You see, Steinie?" Sukey whispered to him. "*Now* do you see?" But he said nothing, only held her very tight.

Westward again flew the red balloon, impelled by Felice's wind. Over Alborán and its train of extinct subsidiary cones; beyond the deep dry basin; up the slope that rose to the Gibraltar rampart; across the crest and out over the sea, to stop suspended above the Atlantic, where white scallopings of surf fringed the great beach that stretched unbroken from the margin of the Guadalquivir Gulf in Spain south to Tangier.

"Now come up and stand beside me, Stein," Felice ordered him "We're far enough out over the ocean to be safe from the fallout. Show me where to begin . . . Come *on*, Steinie!"

"Yeah, yeah." Sukey was gripping the front of his tunic with extraordinary strength. He unfastened her fingers.

"No," she begged. "No, Stein, no."

"Stay down," he told her, kissing the white knuckles of her hands. "Don't look."

Felice took hold of the load cables and clambered aloft. She stood barefooted on the rim of the gondola, facing the shore. "Show me! Show me right now!"

He pointed. "Where that deep straight-line ravine comes down north of the little point. Can you—can you see under the ground at all? Through the rocks, like Aiken could?"

She gave him a startled look over her shoulder. "I never thought of it! But if he could . . . *oh!* It's like—funny great piles of lights and shadows! Huge sandwichy chunks leaning every which way. Other darker stuff, some blobby, some too opaque to see through at all. How marvelous!"

His jaw tightened. He was as far away from her as he could get in the small gondola, the instrumentation shelf jabbing into his rump. He did not dare to look at Sukey.

Felice burbled on. "Those are rock formations that I see, aren't they? Under that straight ravine is a great big surface that slants away underground toward the south. A kind of meeting place between two gigantic slabs of rock that are—bent."

"It's one of the faults at the continental-plate boundary. You start by hitting the strata above the slanting interface of the slip. Bust the whole thing up. You'll need a string of strong shots. Start deep under the water if you can, then come ashore underneath, still blasting, and continue right into the hillside."

"I get it. Ready? There—!"

Stein closed his eyes. He was under the sea again himself, riding his drill-rig in armor, in control of emerald fury. When he blasted, great blocks of planetary crust moved or were melted. Muted thunder spent itself harmlessly against the sigma-fields that sheltered him. He torched his way through the lithosphere, the screen of the rig's geodisplay showing the Earth's structure in three dimensions—

"They're cracking, Steinie! Way down there! But not the rocks on top. What's wrong? There are only tremors on top. The isthmus is still solid!"

"Dumb broad. You think this is gonna be easy? Keep hitting it north of the slip. Farther inland!"

"All right—you don't have to get nasty!"

The ground quivered. There were a few minor landslides. A peculiar change came over the pattern of Atlantic waves reflecting from the small pointed promontory.

He said, "That's enough. Now get this damn balloon over onto the east side of the isthmus."

The gondola lurched but Felice clung easily to the web of cables. The balloon seemed to be dragged through the sky by a genie force.

It crossed the Gibraltar crest a kilometer high and came to a halt in emptiness above the dry Alborán Basin.

"Now look under the rocks again," Stein said. "As deep as you can. Tell me what you see."

"Um . . . the shadows make this big bend. A huge U-shape lying between Spain and Africa. The bottom of the U points to the Atlantic. But the cracks are all different here. There are smaller ones branching out of the U's curve. And way, way down is this hot thing—"

"Stay the hell out of that! You're starting to blast at the surface now. But below sea level, on this eastern slope. About where the yellow rocklayer is. You grab? Tunnel in. Push the junk out of the way. Hit the caves. Then blow the roof out. Never mind about making the cut wide or straight. Just dig deep and head in the general direction of that other slanting fault you were working on."

She nodded, turned her back to him. There was a fearful blaze of light and unending noise. The balloon's gondola swayed gently as the girl shifted position; but the other two passengers felt none of the shock waves, tasted none of the dust. They floated unscathed while Felice smote the earth and debris boiled up. The easterly wind carried streamers out over the Atlantic. The girl sent bolt after bolt of psychoenergy into the landbridge which was, at sea level, perhaps twenty kilometers wide at the narrowest part. She hacked out a long crevice, never more than fifty meters across except where some great cavern's roof was undermined, creating a sinkhole. Clogging masses of rock exploded into dust for the winds to scatter.

She struck. She struck! Five kilometers in. And ten. Carve and rend! Make a sluiceway for the cleansing waters. Fifteen kilometers in. Blast. Blast! Slower now, through the heart of the rotten isthmus. On to where the Atlantic waits. Strike. Strike. Wearily now, but continue. Find the energy somewhere. In some other space, some other time? Who cares where the power comes from. Only focus. Hit! Hit again. Again. And now so close. And now . . . now . . . yes. Through.

Through?

Laugh. See, Felicia Tonans, ignorant child-flinger of mindbolts! See what you've done, boobing it!

You've let the cut become shallower and shallower as you drove westward, weakening. And now the breakthrough, when it comes, is a ridiculous anticlimax. The penetration is a scant meter below natural sea level. The Atlantic enters diffidently, trickling along the rough hot floor of your incompetent chasm. It has been long millions of years since the waters flowed in this direction, toward the Empty Sea. The way is strange . . .

"Felice! For God's sake! You gotta do better than that—it's just piddling through! Plane out that friggin' gradient!"

She drooped, still clutching the balloon cables. The protective bubble attenuated. Around them, heat rose. With it came a smell of rock dust and molten minerals.

"Tired. So tired, Steinie."

"Get on with it! The rock underneath is busted to hell along the main fault. Keep going! Hit the sucker, I tellya! The rock'll rupture from water pressure if you just get the cut deep enough. Can't you *see* that with your damn X-ray vision?"

She didn't reply, didn't even cuss him out, only swayed a little with her eyes shut and her little bare dirty feet trying to grasp the gondola's padded rail.

He screamed at her. "*Do* it, you almighty bitch! You can't just stop. You said you could do it! God—you said you could do it!" The car rocked with the vehemence of his rage, his fear, his shame. Oh, shame.

Felice was nodding slowly. Somewhere, the strength she needed might be found.

Call for it, seek it. Search it out among these infantile, asynergic sparks of life-force that are Earth's Pliocene Mind. The two-in-one (now oddly separate) refuse you, as you knew they would. And the many-in-All so much farther out, who had also helped before on the River Rhône, now withhold and try to show you other ways. But you have chosen and it must be, and there is one other source of the energy, so bright, so early-rising, who will not turn away. Here then is a better Unity for you, here is power to brim your height and depth and breadth at least until the end. So you accept. The energy comes. You harness it with your creative metafunction; mold, compress, convert. And then you hurl it down . . .

With no metapsychic shield in place, the balloon caught the full force of the shockwave and was thrown far up and away. Stein gave a great shriek and so did another. Bodies inside the gondola flopped as helplessly as dolls, crushed against decamole surfaces, against bruising human flesh and bone.

Deafened, Stein and Sukey struggled together in the tossing basket. Neither could help the other. The tough envelope billowed, struck the hot grid of the generator but rebounded unscorched, whirled in a vortex. Spiraling upward, the balloon broke free at last from the storm-cell of ionized turbulence. What had been a distorted, kiting scarlet blob smoothed and reexpanded. It sailed in the high thin air, slowly descending to its altitude of equilibrium.

Stein dared to rise, to look out.

Below, the waterfall of the western ocean flowed.

All of the smoke and dust was streaming over the Atlantic, making it easy for him to see what they had done. The gap in the isthmus widened even as he watched. Brown and yellow rocks on either side appeared to melt like sugar in the torrent's press. To the east, the cataract outflow poured into the Empty Sea across a front nearly ten kilometers wide. A blanket of mist, grayish tan from suspended dust that muddied the droplets, hid the Alborán Basin floor.

He heard Sukey's voice. She climbed to her feet and stood beside him. "Where—?" she asked.

He said, "She *might* have been able to fly. Like Aiken could. Try with your golden torc."

She pressed the warm collar, looking down at the streaks of wrath streaming westward from the sundered isthmus. Unless the surface winds shifted, no one at Muriah would see the smoke.

"There's nothing, Stein. Nothing."

The balloon continued its descent. Seeming not to have heard her, he consulted the instruments. "Three-five-two-eight meters, heading oh-two-three. Another airflow up here. Pretty close to the direction we want to go." He manipulated the heat generator.

"Steinie, I've *got* to tell Elizabeth!"

"All right. Just her. Nobody else."

The balloon attained equilibrium. The ground-speed display told of their progress, but it seemed to the man and woman that they hung motionless in the clean blue sky.

"She doesn't answer me, Stein. I don't know what's wrong! My farspeech isn't very strong, but Elizabeth should be able to receive it on the human mode"

He gave a sudden start, grabbed her by the upper arms. "Don't you try calling the others!"

She squirmed. "Stop it, Steinie! I didn't. Nobody else can—" She gaped at him. He was opening one of the lockers, taking something out. "Oh, no," she whispered.

"I love you. But you can't stop it. Even without Felice to break the dam, the flood's going to happen. The whole nightmare wiped out. Elizabeth . . . if she's still there, she'll save herself. You don't have to worry about her. You don't have to worry about any of them anymore."

Cold metal touched her neck. Her vision of him, of the anguish-scarred and merciless Viking face, blurred with her tears.

"Don't be afraid," he said. "It's better this way."

With great care, he slid one blade of the steel cutters behind her golden torc. He began to close the handles. The double levers worked.

Brede! her mind cried. *Brede!*

The shorn torc fell away, hurting. But even with its loss the reply came:

Be at peace Little Daughter it will happen as foreseen.

6

THE SECOND DAY of the Grand Combat initiated the first of the battles to the death: the Low Mêlée, also known as the Contest of Humans. In the time before the opening of the time-gate, these preliminary fights had served to showcase the talents of novice Tanu warriors of special expertise; but now only gray-torcs took part in them. Hundreds of male gladiators and a small number of gray women contended in elimination bouts that featured every conceivable form of martial art. One section of the ritual battlefield was partitioned into smaller courts so that the spectators could savor the blood sports at close range. The bookmakers had their finest hour; but a groan went up from human and Tanu fans (especially the Finiah refugees) when it was announced that two of the top-ranked gray contenders had been scratched. Neither Stein nor the infamous Felice appeared in the lists and no explanation was given for their absence.

The fighting continued from dawn until noon, accompanied by much festivity and culminating in a bloody free-for-all symbolic of the original character of the event. Victorious grays who were without injury retired to prepare themselves for the High Mêlée on the morrow, where they would join the silvers and golds and veteran gray warriors in the ritual war pitting Tanu against Firvulag. Battered gladiators who had acquitted themselves well in the tournament were escorted by redactors to the medical pavilions, where they joined the recuperating warrior-maids in the Skin wards. The handful of badly wounded losers who still lived and the cravens were sequestered in a handsome glass structure resembling a box-seat section canopied in silver and black cloth, which stood at the far southern end of the battlefield on top of stout scaffolding. Its walls were transparent and unbreakable.

In theory, the remaining time of the Second Day was devoted to choosing Combat leaders by means of the manifestation of powers—after which the Foes separated for a final War Feast and invocation to the Goddess prior to the start of hostilities at sunrise. In practice, the great captains had all been selected hundreds (or even thousands) of years ago and now merely stepped forward to dare any upstart to usurp their privilege. If a challenge was forthcoming, both parties might manifest their metapsychic powers on the spot and be judged by the battle-company of their race. The reigning champions also had the option of dueling contenders with both weapons and metafunctions at any time during the High Mêlée.

As overall losers in the previous year's Combat, the Firvulag presented their captains first. The regal platform was expanded into a much larger Dais of Challenge with the two Kings and noncombatant nobility enthroned well back out of range of any stray thrusts. Rivals were supposed to confine their psychoenergetic coups to one another—but accidents had been known to happen; and so a squad of shield conjurers from the PK Guild took up positions around the perimeter of the stage to protect the crowd with an invisible wall. The Tanu Marshal of Sport then introduced the Firvulag Great Ones, who simply stood forth and then retired to applause from the triracial assembly when no challenges came from the ranks.

The presentation of the Firvulag leadership was swift, almost perfunctory. Medor, Ayfa, Galbor Redcap, Skathe, Nukalavee the Skinless, Tetrol Bonecrusher, Bles Four-Fang, Betularn of the White Hand, and finally Sharn-Mes all accepted plaudits and stood down unchallenged. Lastly, in a major but fully expected break with the tradition of recent unhappy years, the Firvulag Battlemaster was proclaimed by King Yeochee. Not Sharn the Younger, who had undertaken the thankless job during the past twenty Combats—but Pallol One-Eye himself.

The irascible old First Comer, gigantic in his full suit of obsidian mail and monstrous crested helm, ascended the Dais of Challenge to tumultuous acclaim. There were many—Tanu and Firvulag as well as human—who had never seen his power manifested. Others, now that he had returned to the Combat after his long absence, jested that his faculties must surely have atrophied from disuse. No one dared challenge him; but as a technical neophyte he was obliged to demonstrate his primary metafaculty before the assembled field.

Pallol stood with legs wide apart and spike-studded arms flung out. He leaned back so that he appeared to be gazing directly at the high sun. His visor remained shut but the hushed onlookers knew, nevertheless, that it hid not one eye—but two. The right was a normal orb having an iris colored deep red. The left was of a color unfathomable, usually shuttered behind a patch but now beyond doubt naked and dreadful.

Clouds summoned by the awesome creative power of the old ogre materialized in the sky. They were thick and dark and low-hanging, with unnatural ruddy lightning blinking in their depths. The black-armored monster did not move. Of its own volition, his helmet visor slowly opened.

Twin purple discharges scorched down from the clouds into Pallol's gauntleted palms, begetting a shattering clap of thunder. From the gaping helm a coherent scarlet beam blasted skyward, carving a tunnel through the cloud in the manner of a cannonball punching through a snowbank. The sun illumined Pallol's Eye. His visor closed. The sky brightened to blue.

"Slitsal, Pallol!" cried the chivalry of the Firvulag. "Slitsal, Pallol Battlemaster! *Slitsal!*"

King Yeochee arose from his throne and roared out, "We confirm Pallol One-Eye as Battlemaster, to defend our racial honor in this Grand Combat!"

Thus ended the Firvulag manifestation of power, and the Tanu prepared to take their turn upon the Dais of Challenge. At this point in the proceedings in years past, many of the Little People among the spectators had tended to drift away discourteously, being by that time of the day ferociously hungry as well as sweltering in their armor or heavy clothing under the Mediterranean sun. But on this occasion the Firvulag held their places. The grapevine had promised a widespread shakeup in the Tanu hierarchy and none of the Little People wanted to miss the fun.

Things began tamely enough as the lowest-ranked among the

Tanu Great Ones ascended to acclaim. Bleyn the psychokinetic hybrid was unchallenged, and after him came Alberonn Mindeater, another mixed-blood who had earned his place at the High Table through creative mastery in battle. And then there stood forth Lady Bunone Warteacher in her silver-green armor and hawksbeak helm, and Tagan Lord of Swords—these two being most directly responsible for the training of the gray-torc warriors and cheered most loudly by the humans and hybrids in the crowd.

After the fighting specialists came the Guild Presidents. These could, by ancient custom, delegate a Combat deputy if they were not inclined to take to the battlefield in person. Any challenge, however, would have to be answered by the principal in a manifestation of power.

The Marshal of Sport announced: "The President of the Guild of Redactors, Dionket Lord Healer!"

Unarmed and empty-handed, the gaunt figure in simple scarlet-and-white robes ascended the dais.

"Is there a challenge?"

There was not. Dionket gestured and a tall warrior wearing ruby armor came and stood beside him. "I delegate Lord Culluket the King's Interrogator as Second Redactor, to defend our Guild's honor in the Grand Combat." The two retired to cheers from Tanu and humankind. The Firvulag hummed mockingly.

"The President of the Guild of Psychokinetics, Nodonn Lord of Goriah!"

The rosy-gold one came forward, not to claim leadership as Lord Psychokinetic, but to await challenge. There was none, of course, and so he delegated his brother Kuhal Earthshaker as Second, since he himself would undertake the role of Battlemaster. As the two stepped down the Tanu cheers were louder, the human distinctly subdued, and the Firvulag humming more vicious.

"The President of the Guild of Coercers, Sebi-Gomnol Lord Coercer!"

The crowd noise chopped off.

King Thagdal rose from his throne, diamond armor ablaze. "Our dear son Sebi-Gomnol having been gathered unto Tana's peace, we declare the Presidency of the Guild of Coercers vacant and call for aspirants to stand forth in this manifestation of power."

Imidol the sapphire titan mounted the dais to howls of Tanu acclamation. Then came another tall form, his blue armor and helmeted head cloaked and hooded in dull-bronzen brocade. The Marshal of Sport cleared his throat.

"Awful King and Father! Noble battle-company of the Tanu! Here before you aspirant stand Lord Imidol—"

Cheers and jeers.

"—and Leyr the Banished, predecessor to Sebi-Gomnol in the Presidency of the Guild of Coercers."

Gasps and hoots came from Tanu and Firvulag alike as the bronze fabric fell away. The deposed Lord Coercer stood decorous beside his louring young rival.

For a long moment Thagdal was silent. He had known what was in the wind, of course. And thousands of years ago on far Duat, another unseated and exiled Great One had dared to attempt a comeback, so there was precedent. He addressed the two: "Will you manifest here and now or will you duel?"

And Imidol responded, as was his right as a member of the High Table, "We will duel unto the death in the High Mêlée at such moment as the Goddess may choose."

Tanu spectators applauded stiffly while the Little Folk whooped and screeched at the evident discomfiture of the Foe. The blue-armored coercers stepped down.

"The President of the Guild of Creators, Aluteyn Craftsmaster!"

The stout old Tanu in the jeweled caftan came forward as the Marshal called for any challenge. Gulls flew overhead, uttering creaky cries in the ensuing silence. A light eastern breeze blew Aluteyn's silver-vermeil hair and long mustaches back from his stony face. He glared over the heads of the vast crowd and seemed to contemplate the pale lagoon that lapped the White Silver Plain in shallow harmlessness.

"I challenge," said Mercy.

The crowd opened for her. She came up to stand facing Aluteyn, wearing for form's sake a delicately wrought suit of parade armor, silver-lustre glass all embossed and enameled with green ornamentation and inlaid with emeralds. Mercy's head was bare except for a narrow emerald diadem, and her glorious red hair floated free.

"Awful Father! Lord Creator! Noble battle-company!" cried the Marshal. "Here before you challenging stands Lady Mercy-Rosmar of Goriah, wife to Nodonn Battlemaster."

"Will you manifest," Thagdal inquired, "or will you duel?"

"I will manifest," declared Aluteyn Craftsmaster. "Let the Kral be borne forth."

The ceremonial cauldron, which Creator Guild personnel had kept covered at one side of the dais, was placed between Mercy and Aluteyn. The Firvulag throng was now almost out of control, straining close to the platform on their side of the field and making an uproar of derisive twitters, growls, and a deep bourdon drone of humming that now reached a crescendo of maddening whole-tone intervals.

The chain of silence was shaken again and again. Finally Mercy was able to speak.

"I, Mercy-Rosmar, call upon Aluteyn Craftsmaster to devastate if he can the creation I will manifest here before you."

She and the old man confronted each other across the huge kettle, arms extended. An emanation like a wispy rainbow began to stream from Mercy's mailed fingers. In response, a flood of blackness flowed out of the Craftsmaster's hands, enveloping not only the small colored whirlwind but Mercy and the entire cauldron as well. The Tanu spectators gave a triumphant shout. Torced humans and Firvulag groaned and hissed.

The black tide swelled into an inky amoeboid blob. Beneath it, the side of the platform nearest the Firvulag commenced to fizzle and flame as though the white stone were being attacked by some ectoplasmic acid. The Little People shrank back as the PK shielders made a gesture.

Aluteyn laughed.

But something was glowing within the dark mass like a rare green star emerging from a coalsack nebula. The blackness thinned. Mercy reappeared, poised in vapor above the dissolving dais, and the cauldron was there with her. She glowed more brightly. Her rainbow vortex spun into the depths of the Kral and started something to sparkling and tinkling down there. The black tide went splashing back to menace its creator.

Aluteyn cried out. A great thing like a hammer of night came smashing down on Mercy and the Kral. But this creation of the Craftsmaster, like the other, frittered away to impotence. Mercy's rainbow tornado now rose from the cauldron and grew until it was more than four times the height of the Lord Creator. It began to show thickening clots of multicolored light. Aluteyn caught it in a huge black net and pounded it with psychoenergies, trying to force it back into the kettle or turn it upon the woman. But it eluded him. It expanded and solidified high above the heads of the throng . . .

And manna rained on Tanu and Firvulag and humans alike. The

air was filled with a soft hailstorm of rainbow bubbles, countless thousands of them, which when seized and broken open released sweetmeats, cold fruits, rich little cakes, and a whole cornucopia of other delicious edibles that were greeted with jubilant enthusiasm by the famished spectators of all three races.

"Slonshal, Rosmar! Slonshal, Rosmar Lady Creator! *Slonshal!*"

She stood with lowered eyes, having fully restored the dais, with one silver hand resting on the brim of the empty cauldron. The mob was still yelling and grabbing, for never before at the Grand Combat had any creator produced fully tangible organic matter that endured instead of quickly fading away. (Mercy's astral hors d'oeuvres were far from illusory; the stomachs of the throng testified to it!) And so her talent was hailed not only for its novelty but also for its practical value.

"I delegate," she said at last in a small clear voice, "Lord Velteyn of Finiah as Second Creator, to defend our Guild's honor in the Grand Combat."

The Tanu contingent made such a bedlam hailing the bereaved former ruler—now presented with a perfect means of restoring his damaged prestige—that few heard the second part of Mercy's speech:

"And I call upon Aluteyn, late President of the Creator Guild, to choose between exile from this noble company or life-offering to our compassionate Goddess."

"I choose the offering," said proud Aluteyn. Virtually unnoticed, he walked without escort to the Great Retort and joined the other condemned ones who waited inside.

Mayvar Kingmaker stood forth unchallenged as leader of the Far-sensor Guild. None were surprised when she designated Aiken Drum to lead the Guild's fighters, rather than the Host's nominee, the female warrior Riganone. Finally Thagdal the High King came forward, proclaiming Nodonn to be Tanu Battlemaster, and the manifestations ended.

With one last thundering cheer, the crowd dispersed to the two tent-cities that now stood on either side of the Well of the Sea. There they would spend the rest of the day and most of the night in feasting, drinking, and amusement, until dawn would begin the Third Day of the Grand Combat and the opening skirmish of the ritual war.

* * *

Some eight hundred kilometers to the west of the White Silver Plain, scorpions and spiders and alkali ants that lived on the slopes above the Alborán Basin were drowning by the millions. Small flying predators such as wasps and brown-flies survived longer, keeping ahead of the creeping saltwater until night coolness loaded their wing membranes with condensation and forced them down.

7

It LACKED a few minutes until sunrise. The armies confronted one another, poised and ready.

The overwhelming numbers of Firvulag were on foot as always, dancing and leaping in undisciplined mobs around the battle-captains of their choice like great black-armored insects. The effigy standards with festoons of gilded skulls bounced up and down, daring the Foe to seize them—for in this manner, as well as in the taking of heads, was the Grand Combat victory judged. The Little People were armed with dark glittering swords, spiked clubs, chain-flails, and halberds with odd-shaped blades. They carried no bows and arrows or other projectile weapons, these, as well as the war-steeds, being contrary to their traditions of battle. Many of them had spears; but they were accustomed to fling these at the Foe rather than thrust, and so the weapons usually caused little damage to the heavily armored Tanu riders and mounts.

A few Firvulag could not resist shape-shifting in anticipation of the Mêlée. A ghastly winged serpent shot up amidst the cohort commanded by Karbree the Worm. In another part of the field, a stinking explosion heralded the temporary appearance of a cyclopean horror that splattered the salt with foul ichor, prompting obscene protests from its indignant comrades-in-arms. Out near the lagoonside flank, a formless mass of yellowy-green protoplasm went rolling and bumping along, hooting like an insane calliope.

The Tanu force faced this trollish rabble with dignity and splendor. In the front ranks, armored in bronze and glass and bearing colorful pennons, were the troops of gray-torc cavalry and the human charioteers; all were armed with bows, spears, and blades, and responsive to the mental commands of their hybrid and gold-torc human officers. Behind them the five great battalions of the metapsychic guilds sat their steeds, both warriors and chalikos aglow with near-fluorescent brilliance. The coercers and psychokinetics were most numerous, the creators somewhat fewer in number, and the farsensors and combatant redactors constituted the smallest units, since most of their membership undertook support roles during this part of the Grand Combat.

Contingents from the various Tanu cities gathered around local champions bearing banners that must not fall into the hands of the Foe. Certain knights of high repute had their own adherents, Tanu and human; and besides the golds and silvers there were among them numerous glass-armored grays who had proven themselves in the Low Mêlée. Later, when the battle heated up, the regional groups and even the guild segregation would be abandoned as fighters gathered to follow the banner and mental commands of the heroes who acquitted themselves most valiantly—and also showed the most powerful defensive shielding ability. The royalty and field generals of Tanu and Firvulag stood well apart at this early stage, ready to observe and evaluate strategy and commend noteworthy feats.

The sky above the Great Lagoon was golden. As the upper limb of the sun appeared, there was a vivid green flash that persisted for a full twenty seconds before dissolving into white dazzle.

"Omen! Omen!" Screeching like banshees, the Firvulag horde leaped forward. Their mailed feet raised a din that caused the salt to tremble.

The Tanu waited in arrogant rainbow array, banners high and chalikos held firmly in check.

The sunlight strengthened. Nodonn Battlemaster rose into the air mounted on his armored charger, blazing to rival the solar disk. His mind and storm-loud voice sounded the ancient Tanu war cry:

"Na bardito!"

Glass trumpets held by the fighting women blared. Seven thousand gem-studded shields rang like bells as they were struck with the flat of vitredur swords. The uncouth bellowing of the Firvulag was overwhelmed as the tall exotics and their human allies repeated the cry.

"Na bardito! Na bardito taynel o pogekône! *Forward, fighters of the Many-Colored Land!*"

The armies swept together, beginning the three-day encounter of massed minds and weapons. The clash of their meeting could be heard far away on the Mount of Heroes by those who had ears to hear.

* * *

"This year it will be different!" Sharn-Mes had vowed to Pallol. The Firvulag Battlemaster, clothed in his illusionary guise of a monstrous black otter having six legs, flaming fangs and claws, and a coruscant opal the size of a dinnerplate lidding his Eye, professed scepticism. But then, he had not been there at Finiah!

The young general and the old, surrounded by aides and cronies, watched from behind a formidable screen as the early skirmishes took place. But after the first hour, even Pallol had to admit that the Little People were handling themselves with singular éclat. There was a marvelous and fresh sense of valor among them. Finiah had lifted their spirits—and even more, it had opened them to new ideas.

Sharn, wearing the shape of a three-meter albino scorpion, all waxy translucent, with glowing organs in his body cavities, pointed out an impending engagement with his farsense.

"They're coming close to us, Battlemaster. But no more tactical retreats now! Just you watch our lads when the Lowlife cavalry charges!"

A troop of gray-torcs came galloping hell for leather, ready to cut and trample a tight phalanx of some sixty Firvulag, who appeared to be making their customary stubborn and futile stand. But on this occasion, just before the mounts' pounding claws slashed down on the mound of overlapping black shields, the foot-soldiery scattered and went dodging among the tall animals, slashing at unarmored bellies with pole-knives, or swinging axes at the vulnerable leg tendons of the chalikos.

"I'll be damned!" interjected Pallol.

The gray-torc charge disintegrated. Hamstrung and mortally wounded steeds threw their riders and then staggered, screaming and tripping over their own gushing bowels, until they died. There were still the unhorsed humans to contend with; but in hand-to-hand combat the superior numbers of the Little People gave them the advantage, even though the grays were often physically stronger and compelled to fight to the death by their banner-carrying officers. Visions of battling goblins and other ghoulies and ghosties came and went in the midst of the struggle. The aether throbbed with hideous mental projections. The gold-torc human officer in coercer blue managed to zap out and hack to death half a dozen of the Firvulag before disappearing beneath a pile of stalwarts, but it was plain to see where the advantage lay now.

"That belly-sticking maneuver's not bad," Pallol had to admit.

"The humans used it at Finiah," Sharn said. "It was an innovation of some Lowlife metalcrafter who acted as an ad hoc leader. He said later that the tactic was traditional among members of his ancestral ethnic group. The hamstringing was suggested by a Lowlife holy woman, of all people. She had seen it used by the terrible Morigel in her murder of Epone."

"Morigel? *The Raven*—? Oh, you mean that human monster, Felice." Pallol shook his fierce carnivore head. "Té be thanked *that* one's out of the picture! Rumor has it she escaped the clutches of Handsome Cull and flew away in a big ball of scalding-hot blood. Damn superstitious claptrap! But wherever she's gone, I hope she stays there."

The Firvulag had finished butchering the last of the cavalry troop, and now raised thirty severed heads, still in crested bronze helmets, at the ends of their lances. One head wearing a blue-glass burgonet with draggled golden plumes was impaled on the pike of its own standard. The visor of the helmet was open and the dead eyes seemed to look down on the bloodied azure banner with mild astonishment.

The phalanx of Little People came rushing up to the knot of leaders. "Manifest, Battlemaster!" howled the dwarfs, dancing around Pallol and Sharn. "Manifest—like in the good old days!"

"You fellows . . . I'm prouder'n hell of you!" croaked the demon otter, swallowing a lump in his throat. "You bet I'll manifest for you!"

He lifted the opal lid from his Eye and zapped the waving heads to white bone. The skulls flew up and spun like a swarm of meteors just over the cheering warriors' speartops, then swooped down to land in a pyramidal pile on the sidelines, surmounted by the disgraced blazon. Every one of the skulls was now plated with gleaming gold, ready to be picked up by the trophy makers.

"Slitsal, Pallol!" yelped the phalanx. Brandishing their freshly cleaned weapons, they went dashing off to seek a new engagement with the Foe.

* * *

In a tangled heap lay two Firvulag bodies and one human being only pretending to be dead, the latter praying that he would be able to hold out until sundown, when it might still be possible for him to desert.

With great caution, Raimo Hakkinen groped again in the region of his high-rising rump. Once more there was only the dull *ching* of a glass-plated gauntlet striking the skirt of articulated tassets that armored his derrière. Damn! Forget again. He had no hip pocket. He had no flask of good old Hudson's Bay Demerara. No water, even. Nothing to drink at all unless you fancied blood. From the ventilating slot in the visor of his pink-glass sallet came a faint sob. It went unheard in the battle tumult all around him . . .

They'd had to coerce him into it, of course.

Those giggling Tanu she-fiends had dragged him away from the War Banquet and stripped his poor emaciated husk of a body right in the middle of the armorer's showroom while they selected a suitable PK harness for him. A gray squire had snickered while dressing him in the undergarments: first a cotton singlet and briefs, then the beautifully engineered suit of padding, tough woven-gauze fabric enclosing pea-sized plass bubbles, fully protective, airy, and weighing only a few grams. The six exotic women themselves had strapped on all the sliding plates of gold-chased pink glass, telling him how brave he was going to be and how gloriously he would prove himself on the White Silver Plain. Armored to the neck, he had to kneel before them while they mockingly dubbed him "Lord Raimo" with a big sword of rosy vitredur. Then he was forced to pleasure all of them in the only way left to him, and after that humiliation was over they clapped on the magnificent crested helmet that rather resembled a visored sou'wester, sheathed his sword in a scabbard hanging at his side, and hustled him outside to the skittish armored charger all ready to bear him off to battle. The chaliko had its coat dyed a violent fuchsia with acid-yellow mane and fetlock featherings, a parody of the Psychokinetic Guild's heraldic rose and gold. When the women teleported him into the saddle he barely had time to grab the reins before the great brute reared, nearly flinging him ass over teakettle backward.

Somehow he stayed aboard and was rewarded with six separate zonks on his silver torc's joy-buzzer.

They all trotted over to the Plain together from the Tanu encampment, joining the vast parade of bejeweled fighters and well-wishers streaming along the torch-lit and bannered avenue in the gray false dawn. The six ladies waxed symphonic on his happy-circuits to work him up to a fine pitch of euphoria; and when they reached the staging area of the battlefield they switched abruptly to the hypothalamic trigger, charging him with adrenalin and insane hostility toward the Firvulag Foe that lurked less than a kilometer away in the murk. He joined the Muriah-town ranks of his fellow silver PKers, hyped to the eyeballs with battle ardor.

Then the army waited in place for another whole hour. And with the passing of time and the withdrawal of the women to the distant sidelines his frenzy weakened and what remained of sanity began to assert itself. He discovered that the Tanu witches had forgotten to turn control of their man-toy over to Kuhal or Fian or some other officer of the PK battalion. He was unfettered! No one was coercing him any more!

When the charge sounded at last and he was off and running, waving his sword with the amok multitude and yelling with both voices, he was cold sober and scared out of his mama-reamin' mind.

At first, his chaliko saved him. It was a well-trained destrier, for all its evil temper, and it knew how to lash out with its claws whenever members of the Firvulag infantry came running at them. Raimo charged in a middle Tanu echelon, between the elite grays and the splendid ranks of provincial champions. By the time he was in the thick of the fighting there was enough dust and shape-shifting and preliminary slaughter going on to keep his erstwhile comrades occupied with matters other than *him*.

It was time to think about escape.

He wheeled about, slashing at the air and hiding behind his shield when illusionary monsters loomed up in the uncertain sunrise glare. Waves of Firvulag-generated terror swirled around him and blended with his own home-grown funk. He rode through a nightmarish hullabaloo where the combatants of both armies flashed into and out of view like images on a fritzed holo-projector. Only one aspect of the war was relentlessly real—the headless bodies, mostly human and Firvulag, and the dying animals staining the salt with sticky crimson and hot excrement.

Once he raised the visor of his helmet and vomited with discretion so as not to spook his mount. For the most part, the tall beast stepped carefully among the corpses while he tried to guide it in the direction of the ascending sun, which looked like a cut-out white disk heavily curtained in dusty haze. In that direction lay the eastern arm of the lagoon. If he reached the shore, it might be possible to swipe one of the Firvulag boats; and if his broken-down PK had a few watts left, he just might make it to Kersic.

Luck. Just a little luck. Didn't he deserve some after these months of living hell? Just keep up the good work, Horsie, and kick! Kick the crap outa those little turdlings when they come at us!

The chaliko fought well. And the Firvulag, he discovered, only threw their lances and never made use of arrows or darts, so he was fairly secure behind his shield in the high saddle until—

Something like a gigantic purple spider came scuttling out of the misty dazzle and got behind him. One of its appendages thrust up under the armored tailpiece of the chaliko's crupper. The animal let out an earsplitting scream and fell heavily forward, impaled by some kind of long-shafted pole-arm. Raimo was pitched from the saddle and hit the ground with a sound like a demolished xylophone. He saw the spider waver and dissolve, and then, cavorting around and around him and chortling in a falsetto squeal was a Firvulag in gore-smeared half-armor—the spitting image of Grumpy the Dwarf in Disney's 2-D cinema classic.

"Now I gotcha! Now I gotcha!" the manikin shrilled, waving a black glassy blade with a terrible notched edge.

"Help!" Raimo cried. He tried vainly to rise. His chaliko thrashed in death agonies, its great claws almost on top of him. *Helphelphelp-help* . . .

Sweet houghmagandy, Chopper! That you?

Aik! Aik, for the love o' Christ!

A beam resembling that from a sodium-vapor searchlight stabbed from the clouds of dust. It flicked harmlessly over the collapsed pink knight, but when it detected Grumpy it steadied and intensified. The Firvulag warrior's limbs flew out in spasm and his obsidian sword arced away. Orange-yellow light licked up and down the exotic body, melting the cuirass and leaving a path of smoking wound. The Firvulag uttered piercing shrieks. A voice out of thin air said, "That's a good fix," and the astral beam swiveled to shine into the transfixed dwarf's open mouth. There was a small, exceedingly nasty explosion.

"Open your eyes, Chopper. Your shining knight has come to the rescue."

Still prone, Raimo tilted up his visor. A huge black chaliko all armored in gold looked down at him, its benign eyes peering from the openings of a gilded chamfron. It had a monocerine faceted spike of amethyst mounted on its forehead. Sitting the magnificent beast was a diminutive human glowing as from a self-contained power source. He carried no weapon, no shield. But he held high a purple banner whose golden-hand blazon gave the finger to the Exile world. A black-and-violet cape rippled unstained about Aiken Drum's gold-lustre armor. He grinned as he PK-hoisted Raimo to his feet.

"There you go, Chopper. Good as new and ready to raise hell! See you later!"

"Wait—" the former woodsman pleaded. But the Shining One was gone. The battle noise intensified and so did the clouds of smoke and dust. It sounded as though some desperate engagement were coming right at him.

He stumbled about until he recovered his sword and buckler. Avoiding the thrashing chaliko and the fearful mess that had been Grumpy, he started off in the direction opposite from the worst of the psychocreative detonations, away from the clang of glass and bronze weapons, the bellowing of thousands of human and inhuman voices that filled his ears and mind. Within a few minutes he was completely disoriented. There was no clue to show him the way to the shore, no sure route to escape.

"What am I gonna do?" he whimpered.

Survive until sunset, something reminded him, and there would be a recess of three hours while the field was cleared of the wounded and the dead. If he could manage to hide until then—

He tripped over the two decapitated Firvulag and stopped his aimless flight. There was no natural cover on the Plain—so why not? Still shrouded in thick dust clouds, he flung himself down and burrowed among their dark-dripping limbs. Then he withdrew his consciousness into that inadequate little closet of refuge Aiken had taught him to use when the women drove him to the brink of madness. Unless someone beamed a thought right at him, he was safe. Almost all sensation, almost all pain ceased. Raimo Hakkinen waited.

The sun climbed high, heating the White Silver Plain and generating rising air currents that lifted the pall of dust. The warriors of both sides renewed hostilities. Great deeds of heroism were accomplished by Tanu and Firvulag alike, but the gray-torc levies were being decimated by the new tactics of the Little People, which placed the Tanu in a potentially dangerous position.

Raimo lay unmoving, even though some skirmishes took place only a few meters away from him. He suffered cramps and heat and thirst. Flies descended to feast on the blood and lay their eggs in dead flesh, and some of them crept into his helmet. Rousing from his stupor for a moment, he used the shreds of his psychokinetic power to squash them against the insides of the sallet. From time to time he groped deliriously for booze. The fuchsia and yellow feathers of his helmet crest shaded him slightly, but he still broiled in his shell of pink glass until late afternoon when the sun declined at long last and silhouetted the spine of Aven against blood-red light before it disappeared.

A single horn sounded a silvery note that reverberated in his mind.

The noises of battle faded. A wind of luxuriant coolness came rushing over the salt. The armies withdrew.

Soon, Raimo told himself. Soon—when it was a bit darker.

He was wide-awake now but still lying motionless. Unfortunately, he had concealed himself in a spot precariously close to the huge Tanu encampment. Redactors and farsensors on missions of mercy were spreading out onto the quiet Plain, guiding bearers to the wounded Tanu and human knights. And there were others as well, leaders mounted on fresh chalikos assessing the results of the first daylight action. If any of *them* detected him—!

He tried to suppress all thought projection, shrinking back into his little skull-closet. I am a dead thing let me be I am dead pass me by ignore me go away go away . . .

"Oh, you are, are you?"

The voice was in his mind and ear. He refused to open his eyes.

Laughter. "Come on now, Psychokinetic Brother. You don't look as badly wounded as all that!"

The Firvulag bodies, those precious sheltering bodies, shifted. He began to slip down onto the salt; but someone held his head, compelling him to look out through the opened visor of his sallet.

Two Tanu women—one in purple, one in redactor's red and silver. Behind them, a pair of stolid male barenecks with a litter. The stiffened Firvulag corpses lay like discarded headless mannequins beside him.

"He is not wounded at all, Sister," said the farsensor. Her deep-eyed face was grim and shadowed beneath the hood of her cloak.

"It's true," the redactor confirmed. "His mind also is untouched by the Foe. He is a malingerer. A craven!"

In a panic, Raimo scrambled to his feet. The cramped muscles of his legs refused to hold him up. He fell—and then the full force of Tanu coercion flowed from both women to his torc and held him in thrall. He stood perfectly still, a statue encased in jeweled pink plates crusted with other people's blood.

"You know the penalty for cowardice, Lowlife," said the farsensor.

He had to reply, "Yes, Exalted Lady."

"Go to the place then. Go where you belong!"

He turned from them and began to trudge across the battlefield, to where the Great Retort of glass stood waiting on its high scaffold.

* * *

Seven hundred kilometers to the west, the body of a young plesiosaur lay stranded on the rocks of the Alborán Volcano.

It had been hunting tunny-fish in the Atlantic, oblivious to any danger. And the tunnies themselves were chasing flying squid, and the squid in their turn had pursued a shoal of silver sardines that had been browsing upon the microscopic organisms of pelagic plankton. The unexpected current had seized them all, large creatures and small, and sucked them into the Gibraltar rift.

For a hellish quarter of an hour they had been buffeted and churned and then they were flung over the incredible waterfall. The young plesiosaur's graceful neck snapped as it impacted into the foaming pother of the new Mediterranean Sea. It died instantly. The tunnies, torn and battered against submerged rocks, succumbed not long afterward, as did the squid. Because of their small size, most of the sardines managed to traverse the falls shocked but physically unharmed. When their brains regained a measure of equanimity they attempted to go about life as usual, but the turbulent water filling the Alborán Basin was so full of silt that their tiny gills were clogged and every one of them suffocated. Of all the creatures that had been pulled through the newborn Straits of Gibraltar, only the hardy plankton survived.

The body of the plesiosaur had floated eastward until it came ashore on a slope of the Alborán Volcano that had once stood 600 meters above the floor of the adjacent dry basin. Gulls and carrion crows feasted on the carcass before the rising flood reclaimed it and set it adrift again in the misty dark.

8

IN THE RECESS BEFORE DAWN, Nodonn flew over the battlefield with Imidol and Kuhal and Culluket, studying the dismal results of the first round of the High Mêlée. The nearly full moon was setting and the stars shone dim. In keeping with their mood, the four brothers had dulled their own metapsychic illumination and rode the sky like wraiths.

Firvulag medics, firefly lanterns bobbing, were busy among the masses of dark bodies. Over in their camp was a great circle of bonfires signaling a warriors' collation in progress. The Little People were singing a loud polyphonic chant, punctuated by throbbing drums.

"I don't recall hearing that one," Imidol remarked.

"One of their fight songs," Kuhal said sourly. "The kind they sang when they used to win every other Combat back in the days when you were still clinging to Mother's skirts and learning to coerce black beetles. The song's a victory lay, actually. Let's hope it's premature."

"That they should dare to voice it at all—!" Culluket's face blazed momentarily crimson.

"We're not even behind in the banner tally," Imidol protested. "It was a shame about Velteyn, but Celadeyr of Afaliah can take over his Creator Battalion."

"What's left of it," Kuhal snarled.

The Battlemaster had offered no observation. Now he led them lower, to a large area where the scarlet-and-violet glow of Tanu agents of succor had concentrated. He said, "Velteyn was an impetuous fool to underestimate Pallol. He of all our battle-captains should have known the new mood of the Foe. And do not minimize the disaster, Youngest Brother! The ranks of the creators have been reduced by fully one-quarter of their number—and Celadeyr is not one of the Host."

Culluket was a shade too neutral. "Well, it was your idea to have Mercy designate Vel as Second Creator. I warned you about his impaired judgmental outlook."

"And now," the truculent Kuhal appended, "our late brother of Finiah overlooks the Firvulag revels! Doubtless from empty, gold-socketed eyes."

"We have two more rounds," Imidol said, radiating confidence. "This fiasco with the gray-torc cavalry was a fluke. We'll bounce back."

"The Skin pavilions are overflowing," Culluket warned.

"I've been considering that," said Nodonn. "The most seriously wounded Tanu and human golds will have to be transferred to the healing rooms up in Redact House so that the field medics can devote their skills to patching up the battleworthy. We will undertake a second innovation as well. Culluket—you will farspeak the Lord Healer and instruct him to begin admitting the best of the fighting grays to the Skin. The wounded incompetents of our own race must resign themselves to sitting out the rest of the Combat in Muriah. We'll have no time for aging has-beens and bunglers in *this* war."

"Tana's teeth, Brother!" Kuhal exclaimed. "Thaggy will supernova if you go against tradition like that!"

Nodonn was adamant. "Our customs can stand a little bending. We have more to worry about than the injured pride of traditionalists—or even the Kingly honor. I admit now that I made a serious mistake putting Velteyn in a position of command. I was moved by sentiment, and you saw how popular his designation was at the time."

"Celadeyr is a good leader, even if he isn't of the Host," Kuhal said. "But we've lost a sure High Table candidate in Velteyn, and we'll have to look sharp from now on . . . And I'm talking to *you*, Youngest Brother!"

Imidol blustered, "I'll take care of Leyr when the time's ripe! You just watch your own psychokinetic ass, Brother!"

The eastern sky was deep violet. Venus hung over the gunmetal smoothness of the lagoon.

"This day," Nodonn told the three, "we must all take great care. The battalions will be fragmenting as the pressure of battle builds and the Firvulag Great Ones emerge to do personal combat. With so many grays and creators gone, we are even further outnumbered— but we still have the advantage in total mindpower. When you take to the field yourselves, be more prudent than our luckless brother,

Velteyn. He erred in trying to gather outguild fighters to his personal banner too early by means of spectacular but foolhardy tactics. He gambled and lost. But let me remind you that there is another gambler fighting amongst our ranks . . . and he is playing a masterclass game for the highest possible stakes."

The four brothers talked over technicalities for some time after that, letting their steeds drift in the dawning. Down below, the Plain was being cleared rapidly. Firvulag dead were loaded into special coracles on the lagoon strand, to be immolated on the water during the return journey of the Little People to the mainland of Europe. The headless Tanu and human bodies were shrouded and stacked beneath the glass box of the Great Retort, where they would fuel the distillation of the imprisoned in the ultimate Combat offering of life and death.

* * *

For a hundred years, the eggs of the brine shrimp and the spores of minute algae had waited for rain.

Safe beneath the cracked saline crust of the playa, they had husbanded their tiny portions of life-force, resisting heat and drought and chemical action until yet another extraordinary once-in-a-century rainstorm should drench the Pliocene Betic Cordillera, swell the Proto-Andarax River, and fill the Great Brackish Marsh to overflowing.

Then for a few short weeks the thousands of square kilometers of dry lakebeds that lay between the normal western boundaries of the marsh and the gentle Alborán Rise would burst into teeming life. The brine shrimp and the algae and a few other hardy aquatic forms would thrive until the waters drained and evaporated away, leaving fresh eggs and spores entombed in the sediment to await the next Hundred-Year Storm.

No rain fell. The Pliocene sky of early November was clear and the bed of the Andarax carried only a thin trickle from the Spanish heights into the basin of the Mediterranean.

Nevertheless, the playa filled. The water spread and deepened in a manner unprecedented.

Brine shrimp hatched by the billions, ate algae, and hastened to lay the softer-shelled eggs that they produced in a well-watered environment. The water was muddier than usual and it harbored alien competitors, oceanic plankton that vied with the shrimp for the drifting greenery and even tried to prey upon the little crustaceans themselves. But the creatures of the playa had no true awareness of that, nor of the fact that they would never have to endure the long drought-sleep again.

* * *

"Trust me!" said Aiken Drum, amid the fire, smoke, mind-bellowing, and carnage.

"If this doesn't work," Bunone Warteacher told him, "there's a good chance that Nukalavee will nail you."

Aiken jabbed his saucy banner skyward. "Fear not! Just keep your fewkin' illusions intact and see that none of the gang here tries any heroic chivalrous bullshit to louse up the ambush. You hear me talkin', Tagan baby?"

The Lord of Swords said dryly, "We are so menaced by the Foe that I will bow to any expedient giving promise of reprieve. Even to you, Aiken Drum."

"Attaboy, Coercive Brother! Look sharp, then. I'm off!"

The golden figure on the magnificent charger vanished in a puff of purple smoke.

Lord Daral of Bardelask said, "Have confidence, Lord of Swords. Aiken has led us with brave ingenuity all this day. We have more than twoscore of the Firvulag battle standards through following his banner—as well as the head of their hero, Bles Four-Fang!"

"Lying in ambush isn't our *way*," grumbled Tagan.

"It's a way to win," Bunone shot back. "You old soldiers give me a pain in the—heads up!"

Out of the dusty imbroglio surrounding the six depleted Tanu companies emerged a new sound—an infuriated roar from more than a thousand throats, carrying over it a whistling squeal that reminded the human fighters of a kind of Brobdingnagian electronic feedback. In an instant, all of the five hundred or so mounted knights disappeared, transformed into piles of miscellaneous corpses lying on both sides of a fairly clear corridor perhaps thirty meters in width and nearly ten times as long.

"The illusion is firm," Celadeyr told them. "And now—en garde!"

Into the cleared area came galloping a hipparion, one of the donkey-sized three-toed horses of the Pliocene Epoch. It was bridled and plumed and caparisoned with purple and gold garniture. Standing upon its back, waving a small-sized version of his digitus impudicus banner and laughing like a maniac, was Aiken Drum. He was wearing his golden suit of many pockets.

Charging hot on his trail was a legion of monsters, Firvulag stalwarts clad in their most fearsome illusions, led by a towering apparition resembling a centaur from which the skin had been flayed. Its raw muscles and sinews and red and blue blood vessels glistened and throbbed; the eyeballs started from its skull in frenzied rage; a lipless mouth with broken tusks gaped as it voiced its appalling scream. Nukalavee the Skinless, one of the premier Firvulag champions, pursued the small figure on horseback, flinging lightning balls that hit some invisible metapsychic barrier around the fleeing jester and exploded into harmlessness.

"Nyaa-nyaa!" cried Aiken Drum.

The hipparion galloped flat out. The youth bent to peer backwards through his legs and stick his tongue out at Nukalavee, clinging to the reins with one hand and flourishing his midget banner with the other. Then he dropped the flap of his golden suit.

Nukalavee's feedback howl soared to a hundred and ten decibels. The trampling Firvulag mob came to be entirely encompassed by the twin lines of corpses.

Bunone and Alberonn and Bleyn gave a simultaneous mental command:

Now.

* * *

"Wake up, Bryan. Can you hear me? Wake up now."

The dream of darkness began to fade, that cavern swallowing him with sweet and awful finality. He opened his eyes and there were Fred and Mario, the silver-torc redactors who had been his warders. And there was Creyn, now setting aside a small golden censer from which lingering acrid fumes swirled.

"I'm quite all right," Bryan said. (But soon to return to be engulfed.)

The deepset exotic eyes with their flat-blue pupils were very close to him. "Tana be thanked, Bryan. We had feared for you."

Good old Creyn was concerned. But why? She had promised to come for him.

"You have been asleep for three days, Bryan."

"It doesn't matter, really."

"No," the Tanu healer replied in gentle agreement. "I suppose it doesn't. But you must rise and prepare yourself now. Mario and Frederic will help you dress appropriately. It's time for you to leave Redact House. In an hour, after the sun sets, we will have the sec-

ond Recess Before Night. There is to be a gathering of the entire
Tanu battle-company in extraordinary conclave. You are summoned
to the White Silver Plain."

Bryan managed a slight smile. "Another command performance
before Their Awful Majesties? I should think they'd have . . . more
diverting entertainment these days than the likes of me."

"You are summoned by Nodonn," Creyn said. He extended one
bony hand all covered with rings and lightly touched the fingers of
the still recumbent anthropologist. "You have no torc and so I cannot reach you in the fullness of fellowship, nor heal you even if it
were allowed, or possible. You are unaware of what you have done,
and in Tana's mercy you may never know. So go, Bryan. Receive
your last gift. Goodbye."

Bryan's wondering gaze followed the exotic man to the door of the
suite. And then Creyn was gone and Fred and Mario were helping
him into the sumptuous bathroom.

* * *

"They weren't listening to me!" Bewildered, Thagdal sank back
into his throne.

The banqueting pavilion was a turmoil of conflicting thoughts
and shouts. Nobody was sitting formally at table any more; they
were jumping up on top of them to deliver impromptu harangues; or
gathered around this champion or that, consuming heroic quantities
of liquor as they debated and quarreled about the remarkable events
of the day, the Tanu comeback in the face of lengthening odds and
what—or who—had been responsible for it.

"I thought it was a lovely speech, dear," Nontusvel assured him.
"Setting differences aside and all working together. What could be
more logical?"

The King only gave a hollow laugh and drank from his gilded-
skull goblet. Morosely, he stared into the inset carbuncle eyes.

"Remember this good old boy? Maglarn Wrinkle-Meat. Ugliest
mother's son of the whole Firvulag tribe, and a fighting fool. I
finally zapped him through the gizzard after we'd walloped each
other for three mortal hours in the Heroic Encounters. Now *that*
was Combat! None of this hole-in-a-corner sneaking around and
dirty tricks. But now—! The Foe fights dirty, and so do we. And
unless some miracle supervenes, the dirtiest trickster of the lot will
end up King of the Many-Colored Land."

"Here's Nodonn," Nontusvel said softly. "He has . . . brought someone with him."

The King looked up and uttered a mild blasphemy. "I might have known who had that anthropologist stashed away! My boys combed the whole city and half of Aven and couldn't find hide nor hair of him."

Nontusvel regarded her husband with sorrow. "But they found poor Ogmol, didn't they?"

The royal beard sparked ominously. "You're an innocent, Nonnie. I was trying to save us all."

The arrival of the Battlemaster inspired cheers from the thousands of feasters, and a single impudent *nyaa*. Nodonn made his duty to his parents with accustomed serenity and then took Bryan around to a prominent position in front of the High Table. The human scientist appeared dazed; an odd smile touched his lips and from time to time one of his hands strayed to his open collar, from which came a telltale golden gleam.

"Noble battle-company!" intoned the storm-loud voice. The chain of silence was not needed. "We have suffered defeats in this Grand Combat . . . and victories!"

Plaudits and groans and not a few drunken curses.

"The first round of the High Mêlée saw us faced with disaster when our gray-torc cavalry and charioteers faltered in the face of novel tactics from the Foe. The misfortune was compounded when the commanders of the gray levies, half-bloods and gold-torcs, as we know, failed to rally their troops according to the tenets of our ancient battle-religion."

Catcalls and shouting of indignant denials, mingled with taunting epithets and a scattering of "Shame!"

The Battlemaster held up one mailed fist. "Let those deny it who will! The ranks of humankind were shattered. And as a consequence we suffered grave setbacks. The blame, however, lies not with humanity, fellow warriors of the Tanu, but with ourselves!"

The hubbub, which had been swelling in intensity, suddenly fell away to silence.

"We have come to depend overmuch upon humanity in our Grand Combat. We have become lax and decadent as we adopted first their domesticated animals as battle-mounts, and then their very selves. Yes . . . we adopted humanity. They fight our battles, they grow our food, they operate our mines and factories, they administer our commerce, they infiltrate our sacred guilds, they mingle their very blood and genes with our own! But that is not all. We are faced with the ultimate humiliation—and once again, we have brought it upon ourselves. For a human now aspires to our High Kingship!"

In all the vast tent there was no sound. And then came the mighty bellow of Celadeyr, Lord of Afaliah: "And is this to our shame, Battlemaster? When Aiken Drum goes himself to meet the Foe, unarmed and unafraid, while certain Exalted Personages rest secure behind impregnable screens, dithering about antiquated tactics that no longer dismay the Firvulag—much less defeat them?"

A thunderclap of mental and vocal shouting greeted this sally. Celadeyr added, "The Foe has consorted with humans. This is how Finiah fell. This is how their pikemen learned to devastate our cavalry. Shall we then return to the ancient ways you champion and all lose our heads—rejoicing that at least our honor is intact? Or shall we follow this golden youth, the chosen of Mayvar, and know victory?"

This time the outcry made the very walls and ceiling of the pavilion billow and the cups and plates dance on the tables. The face of Apollo was apparently unmoved; but Nodonn was now glowing so furiously that those closest to the High Table fell back, shielding their eyes from the rose-gold glare.

"I only wish to show you," the Battlemaster said, and now his voice was very soft in the reborn silence, "what the price of such a victory must be. You will see and hear what future lies ahead of us from the lips and mind of this human scientist, who enjoyed the highest reputation in his own Galactic Miileu. His survey of our relationship with humanity and the attendant stresses was commissioned by the Thagdal himself in the hope of confuting my own long-stated opposition to human assimilation. This scientist carried out his analysis freely, without prejudice. Many of you were interviewed by him or by his associate, our late Creative Brother Ogmol."

Now Nodonn held high the book-plaque that had been Bryan's love-gift to Mercy.

"Here is a copy of the survey he recently completed. He will explain it to you himself. He wore no golden torc while he worked— and he wears one tonight only so that you may examine his mind yourselves and see the truth of his statements. Because I compel him through the torc, he will carry out the survey's extrapolations in full, including the impact of humanity's use of the iron. Listen to what this man, Bryan Grenfell, says. It will not take long. And then return to the White Silver Plain for our night affray and *think* as you contend against the Firvulag! When dawn brings the final day of our Grand Combat, you may then choose which banner to follow until the end—that of your Battlemaster, or that of our true Foe."

* * *

The marshgrass flats and the lotus beds of the Great Brackish Marsh were gone now, and mangrove jungles where the ibises and egrets and pelicans once nested were completely submerged. Only the highest islets still poked above the rising waters; here crazed animals fought one another in the dwindling space until they were drowned or pushed off to swim for their lives. The luckier of the refugees found sanctuary on the great dam of volcanic rubble; but it was necessary for them to keep climbing higher and higher up the clinkery slope as the water continued to rise. Once the summit had been attained, many of the animals were too weary and traumatized to go farther (and down the eastern flank of the dam it was all desert, anyway); and so they crouched there beneath the moon that lacked one day to fullness—the tusked water deer and the otters and the pygmy hippos and the aquatic hyraxes and the long-bodied felids and the rats and the turtles and the snakes and amphibians and a myriad other displaced creatures—not one showing aggression toward another, instincts of predators and prey alike dulled by the devastation of their world.

The water rose higher. The weight of it thrust against the natural dam; water seeped into every crevice and percolated through the coarser strata of ash. Some found its way among the debris clogging the Long Fjord. When this reached the head of the narrow Southern Lagoon estuary, a thousand little jets of water squirted from the rubble-face.

The water in the erstwhile Great Brackish Marsh was now more than eighty meters deep where once the flamingos had waded. For the first time in more than two million years it was possible for a fish to swim from the cliffs of southern Spain to the Morocco shore.

9

HE WAS SUMMONED again from the warm dark.

Why oh why couldn't they simply leave him in peace? Leave him to savor the last of her alone? He had done the sun-god's bidding, explaining to the barbarians why the shutting of the time-gate was good, why the Tanu should wean themselves from their overdependence upon human technology.

Ingenious, the way that the Battlemaster had twisted the statistics to his own ends; but of course he had to spare Mercy and the loyal hybrids. Pogroms were so wasteful and Apollo ever a prudent husband-man.

But Bryan had justified it all, speaking through his golden torc. Poor Oggy had been so right about it being a boon to communication. (And so it was, provided you had angelic backing when it came to sloughing over the dicey bits without getting caught.) When the little lecture was finished, the mood of the crowd was turning away from Aiken Drum. Bryan wasn't surprised. Barbarians were a hot-headed and fickle lot, and this tribe was almost as mercurial as the Irish.

Nodonn had taken him then to the place where Mercy waited. And she had shown him what he had been missing by not accepting the golden torc before. Even knowing that it was the end, that he would not survive the cave this time, he had gone freely to her, into the bright flight and the long fall.

Free but never free of you with your wild wild eyes, Mercy. And will I love you till I die.

"Come out of it, son. Help a little. I'm not the best redactor in the realm, but there's a few tricks left in the old man's bag. Come on, Bryan. You remember me."

I die I did but die I see her passing by I die . . .

"He's not gonna stop free-wheeling until you zorch him in the stem, Craftsmaster."

"You shut up, you damned male trollop. I pulled *your* marbles together, didn't I? . . . Come on, Bryan. Open your eyes, son."

A great round irascible face, hair and trailing mustaches of silvery gold, all backlighted by a yellow morning sky with strange streaky red clouds. He closed his eyes, willing the memory of her and her warm dark to return.

But it would not, not yet. In an unsteady voice, Bryan said, "Hullo, Lord Aluteyn."

"That's good!" An arm slipped around him, lifting. A glass of water, not very cold, was held to his mouth.

"I'd rather be left alone," Bryan whispered. Oh, let me go down, down! But where was that sea unreflecting of stars?

"No you don't, son. Not yet."

He peered out of the mind-cave resentfully. A crowd of people, looking very seedy, crouched all around him. Gold and silver and gray torcs and now all of them able to *feel* at his mind in the most disconcerting way. "Do stop that, all of you," he told them peevishly. "It's not decent when—when I'm—"

"You're not quite ready to shuffle off, son. I've patched you up a little, as well as I could. Just tell us what happened at that conclave last night. What's Aiken Drum up to? There's something very odd going on. Since I'm deposed, I've had a block put on my metafaculties to restrict my range to the immediate vicinity. But I don't need my powers to feel the ground tremors and the changes in the local earth currents, and see those anomalous clouds. Has your young friend Aiken Drum been doing any fancy mucking-about with Aven's geology?"

Now Bryan's eyes were fully open. He began to laugh, then trailed off in feeble coughing. The glass of water met his lips. "I should think . . . Aiken Drum had quite enough on his plate already . . . without conjuring up earthquakes." He sank back against the Craftsmaster's arm. A singular pang shot through him. *What if he wasn't going to die?*

A contemptuous voice. Raimo? Yes, it was Raimo Hakkinen, that poor devil.

"He's no help! Maybe we can get some fresh dope when the next batch of losers is tossed in here at sunset. Though what difference it makes to *us*—"

"I thought I was beyond caring," the Craftsmaster said. "But I do care! I'm one of the First Comers, and I care! If there is a genuine danger, then I must give warning. My honor demands it!"

The Raimo Hakkinen voice was muttering something scornful. Other voices, other thoughts, came sloshing in disorderly waves against Bryan's brain. A few persistent interlopers picked through the ruins like bored ghouls.

"A really big earthquake might crack this thing so we could escape!" the Raimo voice said. Exclamations. Protests. And the probing. How many of them were there mauling him?

"Mercy," he groaned aloud.

Something like an arm of silver-and-green light swept all of the prying minds away from him and showed him how to put up the screen. He did. But when he turned to descend again he could not find the cave. His mind and voice howled, anguished, *"Mercy!"*

Run search cry hunt the dark with the golden torc's horrible light driving it back whenever he spotted it afar off. She would not wait. She was gone. And he might not die.

"Mercy," he whispered again, and woke to the compassionate gaze of the old Craftsmaster. After a long time, he asked, "Where is this place? What is it?"

"It's called," Aluteyn said, "the Great Retort."

* * *

Brede Shipspouse led the three humans along the deserted corridor deep within the secret wing of Redact House. They were free of their gray torcs, dressed in fresh clothing, and at a loss to know who she was or what she wanted of them.

"My identity is unimportant," said the masked exotic, stopping in front of a closed door. "The only one who matters lies within, lost now in a reverie of self but soon perhaps to awaken."

Brede's brown eyes fixed on Basil. "You are a man of action and ingenuity. In a few brief hours your talents will be called on. When the time comes, you will know what to do. All of the things you will need—including maps and many sophisticated devices confiscated from time-travelers—will be found stored in lockers inside this room."

The headdress of the Shipspouse tilted far back as she addressed Chief Burke, and her eyes crinkled with humor at the big Native American's expression of suspicion. "You will organize and lead the survivors. It will be difficult, for there will be the Skin patients to care for, and even the able-bodied will be reluctant to follow a bareneck human. But you will lead them, nonetheless."

Brede's hand now rested on the latch of the door. She said to Amerie, "Your task will be the most difficult of all, for you will have to help her during the terrible time of adjustment. But you were her friend—and you are the only one of the original group left for Elizabeth to turn to. You will understand her, even though you are not a metapsychic. She does not need a fellow initiate now. She needs a friend . . . and a confessor."

The door opened. Within was a large dimly lit room, three of its walls carved from the living rock. The wall at the far end had a long horizontal slot, glassed over, that revealed a late afternoon panorama of Muriah and the saltflats to the south. There were storage lockers lining the side walls and in the center of the room, a low cot with a figure in red denim lying on it.

"Remain here until tomorrow morning. Do not leave this place before dawn, no matter what should happen. You will not see me again, because I must go down to be with my people in the hour that I have foreseen. When Elizabeth wakes, tell her this: *Now you are free to make a true choice.* Guard her well, for she will soon be the most important person in the world."

Brede faded from their sight, enigmatic to the last. The three of them exchanged glances and shrugs, and then Amerie went to examine Elizabeth while the men opened the lockers.

* * *

With the Fifth Day now winding down to the final hours of the High Mêlée, both armies were inflamed and hopeful of victory, even though the Firvulag knew very well that the odds were lengthening against them.

King Yeochee spent most of the afternoon in the darkened Tent of the Seers, where talented crones used farsensing powers to project choice bits of action for the noncombatant Little People to view. The duel between old Leyr and Imidol of the Host had been particularly gripping . . . and poignant, too, for Yeochee remembered well what a firebreather the old Lord Coercer had been before his banishment by Gomnol. Even though Leyr was one of the Foe, that had been a hard way for him to go—sliced up slowly like a salami and then forced, by the superior metafaculty of the young coercer, to open his gorget and cut his own throat. Ah, well. Youth would have its day.

He left the seers and rambled on to the field hospital where the wounded were being treated preparatory to disembarking for home.

Boats had already begun to leave Aven, and many more would sail before the Combat had its official finale at dawn. The post-Combat Truce, like that prior to the games, was only one month in length—and overland travel with the wounded was a slow business, especially since they could not utilize river boats on their homeward journey.

Yeochee wandered up and down the rows of battered and bloody gnomes. A word of cheer from the Old Man always seemed to bolster the warriors' spirits, and they needed all the help they could get. There was no magical healing Skin in the field hospital of the Little People. All they had were their rough and ready surgical skills, fortitude, and the superior resistance of a tough race that had matured in a natural environment fraught with hazard. Nearly half of the original Firvulag complement was now hors de combat. But the Foe, King Yeochee reminded the smirking casualties, had lost almost the entire 2000 of their gray elite corps and most of the 1500 silvers—as well as a respectable number of the rash and punier-powered among the Tanu and human golds.

"We still have a chance!" the little King asserted. "We're not licked yet. This might just be the year that the Sword of Sharn comes home!"

The broken warriors croaked and gargled and whistled. Yeochee hopped on top of an empty bandage crate, knocking his crown askew again.

"So we haven't got as many high-point banners as they do! So we've only got four skulls in the 'Most Exalted' class! Damme if two of 'em don't belong to the Host—and one of those a High Tabler! Velteyn and Riganone are worth ten extra points right there, and that offsets our loss of poor old Four-Fang and Nukalavee. We've still got the Heroic Encounters to come, and one good upset there could wipe out all the Foe's advantage in the Petty Nobility tally. If they do beat us, it'll be by a squeaker. But they won't beat us! We're going to fight, and we're going to win!"

The tent rang with ragged cheers. One game soul even managed to turn on his sparkling centipede apparition for a moment.

Wiping away a furtive tear, Yeochee stood proudly and let his regal aspect come slowly upon him. His dusty fur-trimmed robe turned to obsidian parade armor, blazing with a thousand gems. His tall crown (sitting foursquare) sprouted its ram's horns and beak of enameled gold, and brushed the roof of the great hospital tent as he attained his full stature, dark and terrible, eyes glowing like green beacons.

"This is the end of my term in office, warriors. And I confess that I never dared hope to see the old days of glory restored before my retirement. But those days are at hand! Even if we fall a little short this time . . . *just wait till NEXT year!*"

"Let's hear it for Yeochee!" somebody yelled. And the maimed and mangled hauled themselves up and hailed the Sovereign Lord of the Heights and Depths, the Monarch of the Infernal Infinite, the Undoubted Ruler of the Known World.

Illusionary aspects flashed and flared and the tent seemed crowded with a thousand monsters. But then as quickly as they had appeared they were extinguished, and the little man in the dusty robe with the tilted crown was saying, "Té lift your fighting hearts, lasses and lads," and all the brave demons turned again to bloodstained and weary gnomes.

Yeochee slipped outside into the evening calm of the Last Recess. He would still have to get something to eat and say his prayers and then get into harness to join Pallol and the generals overseeing the last of the Mêlée. In the four hours before midnight, the free-for-all battle would have its wild climax. Some of the Firvulag shitfires were sure to be bucking for the empty champion slots—and Yeochee wanted to be there on the spot with the commendation if any of them came through. No proxy accolading for him!

The sky looked rather strange. Wispy cloud-tails coming out of the west still showed purplish against indigo. It was too early for the rains, though. The King shook his head. The big full moon was sullen orange in leftover dust and smoke blown out over the lagoon. Bearers with the newly wounded and the decapitated dead were wending their way from the battlefield, across the Well-of-the-Sea Canal, and past the great pile of skulls encircled by exultant bonfires. The heap of gilded trophies had never been larger. And how fine those captured banners would look hanging among the old soot-stained blazons draping the stalactites at High Vrazel! Perhaps they wouldn't win back the lost Sword of Sharn. But they would at least have acquitted themselves with honor.

"And that's the important thing!" Yeochee whispered fiercely.

Out on the salt, the glowworm processions carried in their burdens.

10

At MIDNIGHT on the White Silver Plain, when the silver moon rode high behind thin clouds that rippled like watered silk, the two armies lowered their weapons and finally disengaged. Bareneck hostlers led all the war-chalikos away. Swift psychokinetics cleared a great circle of bodies and debris. All around its perimeter the rank and file of Tanu and Firvulag gathered indiscriminately in the fellowship of utter physical exhaustion.

The Kings came forth with their entourage of noncombatants, Thagdal bearing the trophy Sword. And after them swarmed the commonalty from the camps who wished to view the Heroic Encounters with their own eyes. At the last, in an action so unprecedented that it defied comment, Brede came.

No one needed to have the tallies posted; each mind knew what the Mêlée score was—the Tanu holding to their precarious noble body-count lead, which could be overtaken if there were any significant upsets during the Encounters. The great champions of the sibling peoples would now fight individually; they were nearly equal in metapsychic as well as physical prowess. None of the Firvulag heroes were of the gnomish build; they were all massive and some of them were giants. The Tanu (with one exception) were also outstanding physical specimens, their somewhat lighter musculature outweighed by the wider range of their mental powers. So well matched were the Great Ones of the two battle-companies that the winners of the Encounters were almost always adjudged on points. It had been many years since any hero had been slain in the Combat's final scoring event.

Referees from both races took their positions. Heralds sounded a fanfare of glass and silver and the Firvulag drums began to beat. Out of the black-armored multitude came Pallol One-Eye, bearing his terrible effigy battle standard, which he implanted in the salt. The nine Great Ones of the Little People emerged from the throngs of their adherents to declare fealty to their Battlemaster: Sharn-Mes, the veteran Medor, Gablor Redcap, the female heroes Ayfa and Skathe, Tetrol Bonecrusher, Betularn White-Hand, and—newly accoladed in place of the defunct Bles and Nukalavee—Fafnor Ice-Jaws and Karbree the Worm.

While the cheers for the Firvulag champions still resounded, Nodonn came forward to plant his sun-faced blazon. Those who gathered beneath it were Imidol, Culluket the Interrogator, Kuhal Earthshaker, and Celadeyr of Afaliah, field-promoted to the High Table and now Second Creator, who had chosen to follow Nodonn after all. But then, with the crowd's murmur building to a new crescendo, Aiken Drum strolled out and planted *his* banner, and to him adhered Tagan Lord of Swords, Bunone Warteacher, Alberonn Mindeater, and Bleyn.

The assembly erupted. This partisan division among the Tanu heroes signified that Nodonn's position as Battlemaster and heir apparent was challenged by the little gold-clad human. Tanu and Firvulag viewed such a split in leadership differently; among the Little People, there would have been a popular election to settle matters, just as in their choosing of kings; but the Tanu resolved their intramural conflict on the field of honor. The Heroic Encounters between Tanu and Firvulag might not be broken for partisan jousts, and so the total performance of each aspirant's attachés would decide whether Nodonn or Aiken Drum ultimately met Pallol. The ensuing Encounter of Battlemasters would bring to a close the scoring; and following would be the awarding of the victory trophy by Thagdal—who would either yield up the Sword to King Yeochee or keep it himself.

This officially marked the end of Grand Combat hostilities. But not the end of the fighting—for the two rivals for the field leadership of the Tanu would then have their duel, the winner earning the option of declaring fealty to the reigning monarch or challenging him on the spot.

The prospect of provoking the downfall of Tanu royalty gave a nice added incentive to the already victory-hungry Firvulag heroes and they began stamping their mailed feet on the salt in a gesture of defiance that was immediately taken up by all of the Little People among the spectators. The ground shook. The Tanu knights blazed in furious retaliatory display. The aether and air vibrated with insults and it seemed that a riot might break out.

Then from the crowded area where Thagdal and Yeochee stood,

there stepped a woman dressed all in black and red with her face hidden. The chain of silence was held unmoving between her out-stretched hands. The mob fell back and the mind-storm calmed.

The Marshal cried out: "Let the Encounters begin!"

Now there was frantic whispering and a cudgeling of wits among the spectators, trying to compute the odds for this decisive event. Poor Karbree was bumped from the field because of the Aiken Drum-Nodonn combination, leaving eight subsidiary heroes on ei-ther side. As each Firvulag contestant stepped forward in order of reverse seniority, Thagdal—as present custodian of the victor's Sword—was entitled to name a Tanu opponent. It was a time of suspenseful calculation. Would the King succumb to the temptation to shave points in favor of Nodonn's boys? Would he risk the loss of the Sword in order to beat out the little human? Past matches be-tween Nodonn and Pallol had been very close, pointwise. Was it possible that the small golden manikin had stronger metafaculties than the glorious Apollo? (Physically, there was no comparison.) And yet—the upstart must have something going for him or he wouldn't be in a position to challenge at all! Not since the Times of Unrest had there been such a wild windup to the Grand Combat; and a heretic aspiring to the Tanu throne was nothing compared to the prospect of a *human* King of the Many-Colored Land . . .

Thagdal raised rainbow-glinting arms.

"For Fafnor Ice-Jaws—Culluket the Interrogator!" (It figured; the novice Firvulag versus a High Tabler notorious for his mind-tricks and dubious courage.) "For Betularn White-Hand—Celadeyr of Afa-liah!" (Two codgers, but the edge clearly belonged to mean old Celo.) "For Tetrol Bonecrusher—Alberonn Mindeater!" (Nod to the Firvulag. Was Thaggy getting sly in this match?) "For Galbor Red-cap—Tagan Lord of Swords!" (Nope, guess not. Tagan had beaten this boy before.) "For Skathe—Bunone Warteacher!" (A tossup. Nothing harder to handicap than battling broads.) "For Ayfa—Bleyn!" (Now there was a real mismatch! Sharn's wife would take that hybrid apart like fried chicken. This one could finish Aiken Drum.) "For Medor—Kuhal Earthshaker!" (Now the big guns. Pretty close, but this Tanu threw a helluva PK punch.) "And for Sharn-Mes—Imidol Lord Coercer!" (Anybody's fight, Imidol being so young. But coercers were a nasty lot and this boy was overdue.)

"You will come forth," Thagdal said, "contend throughout the allotted time, and then withdraw promptly before the next contestants. And may the Goddess of Battles look upon you, judge your valor, and make her choice!"

* * *

"Listen to me, Coercive Brother!" the Craftsmaster pleaded. "The ground tremors! The electromagnetic changes in the crust! Can't you feel them yourself?"

The cheery-faced human gold in the blue armor shrugged. "With the fans making such a brouhaha over at the Encounters, I should bloody well hope the Earth would shake! It's two losses and two wins for Aiken Drum's folks now, and the lads of Nodonn have a win, a loss, and a tie between Kuhal and Medor. So you see we're down to the wire in this last tilt with Imidol versus Sharn-Mes—not only in the Battlemaster sweepstakes but very likely in the whole friggerty Combat to boot! And I'll thank you to stop impeding me in me duties so I can get back to the action!"

Gray soldiers herded into the great glass enclosure the last of a draggled column of men and women, cleared from the dungeons and lockups of Muriah and brought to the White Silver Plain to make their last offering. These were not fallen nobility or craven fighters, but the saddest dregs of the realm—the traitors, the criminals beyond rehabilitation, the rebellious barenecks too feeble to provide sport in the Hunt, women worn out by childbearing, and above all the mind-burned, who shuffled along through the impetus of their gray or silver or gold necklets to stand in neat lines along the show-window front of the Great Retort and stare out at the moonlit battleground with empty eyes.

"Read me!" shouted Aluteyn to the commander of the guard. "Check my mind! There's something funny going on, I tell you! Just give me permission to farsense the King—or Lady Eadone Sciencemaster."

"None of your guff now," warned the human coercer. "Just ease off, old fellah-me-lad. Cash in your chips like a man." He sent a mental order to the soldiers, turned his back, and hurried outside to where his mount waited.

"I told you it wouldn't do any good," Raimo said gloomily. "But nice try, Al."

Aluteyn's teeth ground together as he looked out of the thick, clear front of the Retort. "Damn them! Damn them! This Mediterranean Basin is unstable! Over to the east, between Kersic and that long archipelago that you future people call Italy, there's a zone of crustal instability I've had my eye on for a couple of hundred years. What if it has a major disturbance? There could be a seiche in the lagoon!"

"What's a saysh?" asked mystified Raimo.

"A tidal wave. A little one," said one of the craven gold knights, chuckling. "Wouldn't that be a kick in the nuts for all the brave gladiators on yon battlefield? Och, we know how the Tanu love to get their little trotters wet!"

"The lagoon's too shallow to slosh up much," somebody opined.

"It might make things too wet to light the fire under the Retort!" another shouted.

"Not bloody likely. You ever *see* one o' these here conflagray-shuns, cockie? Ask old Al Tub-o-Guts Craftyfuckinmaster here! He usta be the one to touch off the corpse pile every year. Goddam psychoenergy from the whole goddam Guild o' Creators'll broil us in the goddam box even if it pours goddam pups and pussycats!"

"I must give warning!" Aluteyn cried. "It's my duty! If I could only communicate—"

"Send 'em a stargram C.O.D.," a harsh voice suggested.

A woman said, "We could act out your message in charades when they come to light the bodies!" Her giggle was hysterical and infectious. Laughter spread.

"Testify like those muffers Shadrach, Meshach, and Abednego! Too bad we got no Nomex angel in here like them old-time Israeli cats had!"

The rabble of the doomed cackled and taunted and wept.

Meanwhile, Aluteyn Craftsmaster, former Lord Creator, used what was left of his metapsychic power to etch a warning message on the inside of the Retort's smooth front pane. It probably wouldn't do any good, but he had to try something.

* * *

"You *lost!*"

"It was a lousy Firvulag trick he pulled on me, Battlemaster," protested Imidol hotly. "I really had Sharn-Mes worried, him and his damn scorpion suit, and if I'd just had three more seconds—"

"You lost, and your bungling and inexperience may have cost us the Grand Combat!"

The sapphire titan removed his helmet and dumped a bucket of cold water over his still-smoldering hair. "You know you can beat Aiken Drum in the one-on-one."

"Fool!" The Battlemaster raged to incandescence. "Have you forgotten the Firvulag? They now lead us in the point-scoring!"

In the minds of the eight Tanu champions and Nodonn hung the telltale scorecard:

CULLUKET	(LOST)	vs.	FAFNOR
CELADEYR	(WON)	vs.	BETULARN
ALBERONN	(WON)	vs.	TETROL
TAGAN	(WON)	vs.	GALBOR
BUNONE	(LOST)	vs.	SKATHE
BLEYN	(LOST)	vs.	AYFA
KUHAL	(TIED)	vs.	MEDOR
IMIDOL	(LOST)	vs.	SHARN-MES

The Battlemaster gestured to the four allies of Aiken Drum who stood around the defeated coercer hero. "And thanks to our turncoat brothers and sister here, we must send a puny trickster into the Encounter against Pallol One-Eye!"

There was a puff of purple smoke. "I thought I heard my name taken in vain," chirped Aiken Drum. "Don't tell me, Brother Sun-Face, that you have doubts about me being able to put a lid on the Big Eyeball?"

Nodonn said, "He is five times more mighty than his blood-cousin, Delbaeth, who led us such a merry chase on the Quest. And he does not strike and run away, as the Shape of Fire did. He stands! Do you think that your mind will be able to shield you indefinitely from that Eye? Are you confident that your psychocreative power is a match for his? Or will you expend yourself in defense, human youth, using all of your strength to fend off his energies while he demolishes you with a single blow of his armored fist?"

"How would you like *me* to kill *him?*"

The eight champions and the Battlemaster broke into bitter laughter.

Aiken frowned. "No. Seriously. I could kill him. Just like I did Delbaeth. I'd have to do it in a human way, and you and the rest of the High Table have to all agree that I can do it my way without getting zapped by the lot of you for breaking some holy fewkin' rule."

Nodonn's face within the fantastic rosy-gold helmet was bright with contempt. "You may not use the Spear on Pallol, Lowlife. Only against me."

Aiken flipped one finger toward the Battlemaster. "That's not what I meant. And don't be impatient, Sun-Face. Your turn's coming!" He glared at the champions in turn. "Well? Am I going to pull your baked patoots out of the fire and win this damn shindy for you —or not? My trick's no more dirty than the ones the Firvulag and their human pals pulled on you guys at Finiah." And Aiken's mind showed them what he proposed to do. "Yes or no, dammit? Give the rest of the Table a holler or I'm gonna just take off like a skyrocket and leave you here with your thumbs in place."

"Go and be damned!" Imidol yelled. "The Battlemaster will meet Pallol if you default. And he'll win!"

"Are you sure?" inquired the jester softly. "Will he win by enough points to clinch the ball game? Nodonn can't decapitate Pallol. But I can. And you know what that'll do to our score. We win, walkin' away!"

"I will confer with the High Table," said Nodonn.

Fifteen seconds later he said, "You will fight Pallol One-Eye in your human way, without prejudice."

* * *

The moon was descending now, having done its work. It still shed light on the Mediterranean Basin, but its tidal effects, so long inconsequential on the shallow water, were just beginning to make themselves felt in the area west of Aven where the dark waters lapped a crumbling lava crest.

11

AIKEN DRUM advanced on Pallol One-Eye.

The giant did not bother to shape-shift. He waited, an ebon monolith planted in the middle of the white-salt circle, and chuckled. The sound reminded some of the hushed spectators of a metal dustbin caroming down a long flight of stairs.

Fools! What fools the Tanu were, sending this puny creature

against *him!* They had forgotten, that was it. His long absence from the field had dimmed their memories, just as their fatal contact with Lowlife humankind had softened their wits. This insect, this gaudy midge in his golden glass and jaunty purple-feathered crest, was not even worth toying with. He would die in a single thunderclap thrust, incinerated by the incomparable blast of psychoenergy from Pallol's Eye! . . .

Aiken Drum had come to a standstill. He had no lance, no amethyst sword, no weapon at all that Pallol could discern save a small golden ball and a dangling leather strap wide in the middle and thinning toward the ends.

Holding up one admonishing forefinger in the universal gesture that begged a moment's wait, Aiken transferred the strap to his teeth and concentrated on trying to manipulate the ball in some way between his mailed fingers. Still laughing, Pallol removed his awesome helmet, tucked it under his right arm, and with the other hand raised the patch over his Eye.

ZAP went the scarlet beam. It struck an invisible metapsychic barrier, a three-meter dome covering Aiken, and disintegrated into a web of lightnings.

Aiken scowled, continuing his struggle with the ball. Was he trying to unscrew its halves? Press some button or lever countersunk in it?

ZAP!! This time, one portion of the psychokinetic screen glowed an ominous blue. The ogre bellowed in glee. "Now we'll see how well you hide, you insolent little pismire!"

A salvo of coherent radiation beams sprayed at Aiken's mental shield. Globs of energy like great static discharges hit the screen from all angles, making it glow blue, green, sickly yellow. The crowd of spectators emerged from their fascinated trance and began to shout. Tanu clanged their shields and tooted horns. Firvulag whooped and smote their tomtoms until the drumheads split. The great white-salt circle of the fighting-ground was walled by a mass of shining colored bodies and leaping nightmare shapes.

At long last the two halves of Aiken Drum's golden ball fell apart. He grinned up at Pallol in a friendly fashion, paying no attention to the ferocious bombardment of the metapsychic screen. The barrier was fading from vermilion to dull lake red, the signal of imminent collapse.

"There we go, Goliath baby! All set now!"

Aiken placed a small silvery object in the wide section of the leathern strap and swung the sling around and around his head. Something flew through a hole in the screen, flickered among the light beams, and struck Pallol smack in his normal right eye.

The Firvulag Battlemaster roared. Both gauntleted hands clutched at his face. The awful left Eye closed and from the right one spurted blood that was black in the pallid moonlight. The ogre's howl diminished in strength, and slowly, as a monumental structure folds and crumples when the charges of demolition engineers undermine its supporting members, the monstrous armored form bent, sagged, and crashed to the salt.

Mayvar Kingmaker came out of the crowd with Aiken's own purple-glass sword and presented it to him. He cut off the head of Pallol with a single swipe and held it up. The once-potent Eye was shuttered. In the other socket something silvery glittered in a mass of bloody tissue. Delicately, Aiken plucked the fatal missile out. He zapped it with his creative faculty so that the late Lord Gomnol's cigar cutter was as shiny and clean as ever and the long vision of the farsensors in the crowd could read what was stamped on the metal:

SOLINGEN—INOX STEEL

"Here's to the new era," said Aiken Drum. "Long live Me."

* * *

Six hundred kilometers to the southwest of Muriah, the long natural dam that stretched between Spain and Africa was finally starting to give way—not in one spot but in a hundred, all along its waterlogged and crumbling length. Stressed unbearably by the weight of the ever-deepening water, great slices of the ash and scoria barrier went sliding forward down the eastern slope. As the impounded sea gushed over, the breaks grew and merged with one another until it seemed that the entire unstable dike would be shoved into the estuary of the Southern Lagoon by the pent-up pressure.

Saltwater crashed among dark lava buttes in the desolate country east of the vanished Long Fjord. It flooded across moonlit flats, found new drainage channels among gypsum dunes and spindly towers of striped evaporite. The ground trembled and the air was filled with a stupendous roar as nearly 200 kilometers of dike-length subsided within fifteen minutes.

The volume of rushing water was too vast for the narrow estuary of the Southern Lagoon to accommodate and the flood rose higher and higher in the phenomenon called hydraulic damming. Ahead of the catastrophic surge flew a hurricane blast of air. The pale waters of the long lagoon seemed to recede in horror before the onrushing dark wall, then surrender, rise to meet it, and merge at its nearly vertical face. The wave was 230 meters high.

Freed of their last restraint, the waters of the Western Ocean raced toward the White Silver Plain.

* * *

The throng of Tanu and humankind sang the Song while all of the knights held high their glowing jeweled swords. Beneath the waving white banner with its golden face stood Thagdal and Nontusvel, and behind them, seeming to generate her own shadow in spite of the multihued dazzle, was Brede. The Tanu Great Ones were also there; but of the Foe, only King Yeochee and the noncombatant Firvulag nobility stood waiting for the latest and most disappointing in a long-unbroken string of similar humiliations. The Firvulag champions, and many Little People among the spectators as well, had withdrawn—too overcome by sorrow even to stay for the rare spectacle that was soon to follow.

Aiken Drum plucked Pallol's standard from the ground. With a psychocreative flourish he removed the demon-otter effigy that had been mounted amid the dyed scalp locks and dangling chains of skulls. Displaying the head of the fallen Battlemaster to the crowd one final time, Aiken made a magician's pass. Pallol's head was transformed into a golden death mask; in the socket of the left eye was a star ruby the size of a grapefruit. When the head was impaled upon its own battle standard, Aiken Drum raised it high and approached King Thagdal.

Before he could speak, a gaunt figure in purple robes came from the ranks of Great Ones and stood beside him.

The Marshal of Sport, already flustered by the outrageousness of the whole affair, seemed to choke on his stately announcement.

"Awful King—and Father! The referees and—and judges of the Tanu and Firvulag races have—conferred and made their last accounting. And—uh—the victory belongs to the noble and valorous Tanu battle-company of the Many-Colored Land!" After a pause for cheering, he resumed. "Here before you, craving your royal accolade as Premier Champion of this Grand Combat, stands Lord Aiken Drum—"

"No," said Mayvar quietly.

There was a breathless hush.

"No longer Aiken Drum," she said, "for now I bestow upon him at last his Tanu name—that taken by every human admitted to our battle-company and fellowship. I have kept Aiken Drum's true name hidden in my heart for so long because I wished to let him show you himself that he is worthy of it. I, Mayvar Kingmaker, have never had doubts of him. And on this field of battle he has proved that he is truly one beloved of the Goddess . . . Therefore, with confidence and love I call him! He is the Shining One! He is the Young Lugonn."

The crowd, stunned first by incredulity, began an uproarious clamor of voices and minds, horns and beaten shields. There were those who rejoiced and those who shouted enraged exception; but the tumult was so vast that no one could say where the hearts of the majority lay—with the young Battlemaster or with the old.

Thagdal stepped forward, his face stiff as that emblazoned on his royal banner. He accepted the Firvulag standard from the hands of the little golden man and passed it immediately to Bunone War-teacher. Eadone, Dean of Guilds, now came to the fore bearing something upon a long velvet pillow. The crowd noise ceased. This was the moment they had been waiting for. Would Aiken Drum—Lugonn—pick up the holy Sword of Sharn and pass it in fealty to the Thagdal, as Nodonn always had done? Or would he—

The shining small figure lifted the huge thing, leaving the tethered powerpack on the pillow that Eadone still held. Taking the hilt in both hands, he pointed the Sword blade-down and drove it into the salt at the feet of the King, then turned his back on Thagdal.

There was a slow letting-out of breath. The throng seemed stupefied, as did all of the royalty, both Tanu and Firvulag, gathered beneath the emblems of the two Kings.

Into this void stepped the dark personage who had guided both races for a thousand years. Her garments of scarlet and black repeated the colors of the sky, for it was nearly dawn. Her face, clearly visible, was wet with tears.

"Let it be, then," her mind and voice spoke together, "as I have foreseen. Let the two heroes contend with Sword and Spear on the White Silver Plain in the last Combat."

Mayvar led out the four Tanu champions who had declared for the Shining One in the Heroic Encounters. They carried with them the Spear. Bleyn fastened the jeweled baldric holding the powerpack around the little human's shoulder and hip. Nodonn materialized out of thin air and stood next to the Sword. He pulled it from the ground and held it high while Kuhal, Imidol, Culluket, and Celadeyr girded him in the harness.

The throng drew far back. Impelled by some psychokinetic force, the heroic pair separated, gliding a few centimeters above the salt, which now had assumed a dull-red luminescence in the overcast dawn. Visible haloes of defensive mental energy englobed the tall rosy-gold apparition and the diminutive form of the trickster. Both stood ready.

"Begin," said the Shipspouse.

There were twin bursts of emerald fire and simultaneous concussions that forced all of the torced spectators to shield their senses for an instant. When the audience recovered, the thunder still reverberated over the Plain. Both contestants stood firm, psychic barriers and glowing armor intact.

Again came the green explosions and the monstrous clap of sound —but this time the echoes did not dwindle. The deep rumbling became louder and the ground shook under the heroes' feet. A wind rose out of nowhere, adding its howl to the deeper note. The red-and-black sky suddenly was obliterated all along the western horizon.

Thagdal the King saw the wave and cried the first mental warning. Summoning every erg of his metapsychic power, he erected a wall. "To me! To me, all of you!"

They joined him—Firvulag and Tanu and torced human—in a massed mind-thrust never before attempted in Exile. Nodonn lent his psychokinetic strength, and Lugonn, and all of the Little People strove with their creativity to shore up the King's mental bastion that held back the onrushing sea, to prevent it from breaking over them all. But the dark water mounted higher, higher, and the weight of it pressing their defending minds was unimaginable millions of tons . . .

The wave broke.

"I am still King," Thagdal told Nontusvel. The sea crashed upon them. Drowning, he was content, and he sent the last of his dwindling force in a touch of comfort to the Queen, for he had not let go of her hand.

* * *

The primary wave-front rushed on into the sunrise, losing height rapidly as it spread into the expanse of the Great Lagoon. A secondary surge washed the shoulder of the Aven Peninsula, flooding inland for several kilometers before draining away down the cliffs. The waters caught those still remaining in the city by surprise, and most of them perished, including all but a handful of the ramapithecine slaves.

Amerie would have rushed out of the room high on the Mount of Heroes, except that Chief Burke seized her and held her tight, and she fought him and screamed until she was exhausted and could weep no longer. And then Basil came and crouched there with them under the terrible window. Both Amerie and the rugged old lawyer understood when the former don whispered his ancient prayer.

"Elevaverunt flumina fluctus suos, a vocibus aquarum multarum. Mirabilis elationes maris. Mirabilis in altis Dominus."

Together, they waited for Elizabeth.

12

THE MIND-CRIES as they passed!

They reached Elizabeth even within the cocoon of fire. The first scattered leavetakings at the start of the Mêlée came like tentative drops introducing a storm; and then whole gusts of them went flying by in increasing numbers—crying out, afraid and disappointed and raging and eager. There were lulls. And then the death gales rising again, rushing past her refuge. All those disembodied minds hurrying beyond space and time to the many-in-All that she had shut out, and a very few spinning their own fiery cocoons to drift apart from the stream, denying, going their own lost way.

But she was not free to follow the river of Mind. She was anchored yet to Earth. When the final disjunctive cataclysm happened, she felt the shock even within the hiding place, and had to let her mind's eye observe. Too amazed to grieve, she watched and heard the torrent passing.

Many of them were persons she knew. And at the end of the great storm-surge of mortality there came one that was all too familiar. Brede's mind swept by her with a final appealing touch. And then Elizabeth saw an alien thing, vast and bright and loving, come to meet its mate, an escort into irresistible light . . .

Elizabeth awoke.

The face leaning over her belonged to Sister Amerie, and it had the drawn, haunted expression that comes after there are no tears left.

"I know," said Elizabeth.

The nun extended her hand, touched Elizabeth's tightly clenched fingers. "There was—an exotic woman. She knew this would happen. She healed us. Brought us here to you. And there was a message: 'Tell Elizabeth that now she is free to make a true choice.' I hope you understand."

Elizabeth sat up. After a moment she was able to rise from the cot and walk to the window in the natural bunker where Basil and Chief Burke stood, now unable to take their eyes from the scene below the mountain.

Morning had broken fully and the heavily clouded sky gave a gray and pitiful light. The White Silver Plain and both tent-cities and the entire expanse of carved and sparkling sediments that had once rimmed Muriah from its cliffs to the lagoon shores had vanished. In its place was a sea. It was the color of dull jade and its white-capped waves ran eastward toward the far horizon. Driven by the strong wind, breakers crashed over the small curving point of land at the peninsula's end where Brede's house had been. Muriah was now beyond reach of the waves; however, smashed houses and trees and pools of draining water showed where the earlier surge had devastated most of the capital city.

Now you are free to make a true choice.

Outside the door of their room was noise. Her mind perceived the anguished jumble of thoughts. It was hard—well-nigh impossible, given the unbearable emotional load of them—to distinguish Tanu from human, or these from the Firvulag who were apparently gathered among them. There were no masters and slaves, no friends or Foes; there were only survivors.

"I think we should go out now," Chief Burke said.

Elizabeth nodded. The four of them turned away from the window and walked to the door. Burke lifted the latch.

Now you are free to make a true choice.

There stood Dionket and Creyn and others wearing the garb of redactors. Behind them milled numbers of the survivors. Elizabeth gently fended their minds, met the eyes of the two healers.

"Give me just a few minutes." She gestured to the red balloon jumpsuit she still wore. "I'd like to find some other clothes."

* * *

Torn from its base, the huge glass box that was the Great Retort wallowed in the flood, the bodies inside of it tumbling and piling with each violent oscillation. Eventually the Retort settled on a fairly even keel. Half of its bulk was below the waterline and the conscious ones among the prisoners felt they were adrift in some bizarre parody of a glass-bottomed boat. The black and silver awning that had roofed it was all tattered and it snapped as the gale took hold of the ornamental superstructure. The benches and tables, the commodes and food dishes and water jars were all flung together with the bodies of the condemned.

Raimo Hakkinen spat out saltwater, salt blood, and a tooth. He lay up against the front wall, close to the door. Water was leaking in through crevices around the jamb.

"Come on," he croaked, stripping off his undershirt and ripping strips from it with his teeth.

Only one person from the pile of casualties nearest him responded, a woman dressed in a suit of armor-padding. They bit and tore apart her short gambeson; the collapsed plass bubbles made excellent caulking.

"That ought to hold her," Raimo said, offering a gap-toothed smile.

"She floats!" The woman stared in a dazed fashion at the brownish water, swirling with unimaginable debris, that surrounded them outside the four transparent walls. "Just like some crazy aquarium—except—those things on the outside aren't fish—" She turned away and was violently sick. Raimo backed off on hands and knees.

"Maybe I can find a water jar that didn't break."

He went creeping among the bodies and the mess. Quite a few people were alive, but there were plenty of deaders, too. He located a container of water snuggled amid three corpses. And wasn't that one over there—

He turned the body over. "Bryan? You all right?" The lips smiled. "Bryan?"

"He cannot hear you," said the voice of Aluteyn Craftsmaster. "Your friend has passed into Tana's peace."

Raimo shrank back, holding the water bottle. "Uh—too bad. We came down to Muriah on the same boat together. And if the rumors I heard about him and Lady Rosmar were true, maybe the two of us—well, sorta suffered the same way."

Aluteyn gently unfastened Bryan's golden torc. "Not quite the same way, Raimo. But neither of you has to suffer any more." He put the torc around Raimo's neck, removing the silver one he had been wearing. "I think Bryan would have wanted you to have this. Your brain is mending, thanks to my little patch job, and we may find more skilled redactors among our fellow survivors. Or—later."

"You think we'll make it? You think this damn glass box'll float long enough to take us to shore?"

"Those who programmed restraints on my metafunctions are doing so no more. I can generate a moderate PK wind, even keep out the sea by reinforcing the walls of the Retort, now that I have recovered my full consciousness." He gestured to the sprawled bodies. "If you will help me to sort out the ones who still live—"

"Let me go get the dame who was helping me to caulk the door." Raimo grinned and tottered off. The floor of the Retort lurched in the fierce currents, setting the bodies to rolling.

The Craftsmaster gave one last look at the smiling face of the dead anthropologist. Then, groaning with pain and resignation, he began to work again.

* * *

She was a strong swimmer and a woman of courage. Using her fatigued creativity, she could still fashion twin bubbles from a portion of her court dress and position them behind her arms so they would help to buoy her up. And when the sun came out at last to shine on the swirling muddy waters and she began to faint from weariness and shock, Mercy called out:

"My Lord! Where are you, Nodonn?"

No answering thought came. It was hard, almost impossible, to muster the control needed for long-range farspeaking. She was so deadly tired! But finally she gathered the strength and called again. "Nodonn! Nodonn!"

O come daemon lover, angel of light, come. How can you be dead and I not?

She floated in the midst of the flood. Faint thoughts, faraway and garbled, made a vertiginous twitter in her brain. None of them were his thoughts.

"Nodonn," she kept whispering. And once, "Bryan."

Her head flung back, hair trailing like tendrils of dark seaweed, Mercy drifted in the sea. Finally the sun went down and it was cold. Her legs and lower body numbed. She suffered from thirst, but she was so weakened from shock that she could separate the sweet water molecules from the salt with only the greatest effort. Creativity, of all the metafunctions, is most vulnerable to trauma and sorrow.

"Then I will die along with his world," she decided, "for it's all gone now, all the brightness and the wonder and the song."

A small yellow light.

It bobbed, flickered, grew. She decided to wait, since the radiant entity gave evidence of having farseen her, even though it stayed coyly beyond her own mental sight. After an hour or so the glowing thing drew close by. She saw it was the Kral—that great golden cauldron sacred to the Creator Guild—and she cried out.

"Creative Brother! Do you know if Nodonn lives?"

"Is that gratitude?" asked Aiken Drum.

He leaned over the rim of the kettle, extended an arm all covered in golden pockets, and painfully lifted her up. She was deposited in a heap on the curved metal beside him and he grinned down at her.

"Sorry to be so crude on the teleport, Merce lovie, but I'm feeling a little wonky myself yet. Lie still and I'll see if I can conjure you dry."

"You," she said. "*You* live."

"The baddest penny of them all. When I saw that we didn't stand a chance with our King Canute act, I figured every man for himself and spun myself a little air capsule. Popped up and only had enough strength left to float. This tub was a mighty welcome sight, I can tell you. I'd just about had it when it came sailing by, chirky as you please."

Slowly he dried her, cleansed her of salt and filth, clumsily restored her torn clothing. By the time he finished she was nearly asleep.

"The gown," she murmured, "is supposed to be rose-colored—not gold and black."

"I like gold and black better."

She tried to rouse herself. Her whisper retained a trace of the old coquetry. "Now then . . . what's in that naughty mind of yours, Lord Lugonn Aiken Drum?"

"Go to sleep, little Lady of Goriah, little creative Mercy-Rosmar. There's plenty of time to talk about that tomorrow."

* * *

Winter rains swept over the Bordeaux marshes. The great river was silty, and the fish were shy, but there were still plenty of wildfowl and the small antlerless deer with the tusks, and in higher parts of the large island where the oaks and chestnuts grew, succulent mushrooms. Sukey craved them now and had nagged Stein until he agreed to go for a basketful. And then she was sorry when it began to rain so hard, and saw to it that there was a fine hot stew waiting for him and a good fire in the cabin hearth.

He returned when it was nearly dark. Besides the mushrooms, there was a haunch from a half-grown wild porker. He said, "The rest is cached up a tree. I can fetch it tomorrow. Cook this pig meat well, remember."

"I will, Stein. I wouldn't take a chance. You know that." She caught up one of the wet, calloused hands and kissed it. "Thank you for the mushrooms."

"I'm all soaked," he admonished her. "Wait." He stripped off the squelchy buckskin jacket and pants and the rawhide moccasins and warmed himself at the fire while she leaned against him, watching the flames and smiling secretly. In the summer it would be born, and there would be plenty of time to search for other humans then, in the days of lasting calm weather when the great balloon would sail very slowly and land with scarcely a jolt. Next August or September, they would leave. And in the meantime, this wasn't so bad. They were all alone, completely safe, with plenty of food and a snug cabin and each other.

"Eat now," she told him. "I'll take care of your things and see to this meat."

Just before they were ready to go to bed the rain stopped. Stein lifted the door flap and stepped outside, and when she heard him returning she came to stand beside him in the peaceful, dripping dark. The stars were out.

"I love it here," she said. "I love you. Oh, Stein."

He encircled her with one great arm, saying nothing, only looking up into the sky. Why should they leave this place? They had often talked of it, but why was it necessary to seek out other humans? Who knew what they would be like? Besides, there were wild Firvulag in the mainland wilderness. He knew, for he had seen their will-o'-the-wisp dancing lights once when he had gone exploring in the dinghy.

The two of them had been very lucky in avoiding contact with exotics on their way to this haven. It would be madness to run the risk all over again, doubly mad to take a newborn infant on a journey in the balloon. A balloon was too unpredictable. It flew its own way, not yours. If an unexpected strong wind took them, they might be carried hundreds of kilometers before being able to descend safely. They could be carried southeast, all across France, over the Mediterranean . . .

Never. He would never return there to look on what he had done. He would never do it.

"Oh, look!" Sukey cried. "A shooting star! Or—is it? It's moving too slowly. Too late, it's gone behind a cloud! And I forgot to make a wish."

He took her hand and led her back inside their little home. "Don't worry. I made the wish for you," he said.

* * *

The lights on the orbiting flyer's display were all dead now, and the exotic alarms no longer sounded a warning. Without power, without oxygen, the craft faithfully maintained its parking orbit, going around and around the world at an altitude of something less than 50,000 kilometers.

During most of its orbit, the dull-black surface of the flyer made it virtually invisible against the backdrop of space. But now and then sunlight would strike the flight deck's front port, brightening Richard's face and causing a brief beam to reflect back to Earth.

Around and around the little broken bird went, endlessly circling.

* * *

In the Hall of the Mountain King at High Vrazel, the decimated council of the Firvulag met to discuss new business: the election of a new Sovereign Lord of the Heights and Depths, Monarch of the Infernal Infinite, Father of All Firvulag, and Undoubted Ruler of All the Known World.

"We're going to be in trouble this time," Sharn-Mes warned them.

"How so?" queried Ayfa.

He told her and the others the bad news. "The Howlers are demanding the franchise."

* * *

The great black raven spiraled downward to the place where its fellows were feeding. All along the North African shore, the scavenger birds were prospering as never before. The bounty had persisted for nearly four months now and still showed no sign of scarcity.

Pruuk! grated the newcomer. It ruffled its feathers malignantly when another bird was slow to move aside on the carcass of a porpoise. *Pruuuuuuuk!* it repeated, lifting its shoulders and opening its wings. It was a huge bird, half again as large as the others, and its eye sparkled with a mad gleam.

Uneasily, the rest of the flock moved back from the meal, leaving the great stranger to dine in solitude.

* * *

"They're coming! They're coming!" Calistro the goat-boy shouted as he dashed up the length of Hidden Springs Canyon, his charges forgotten. "Sister Amerie and the Chief and a *lot* of others!"

People swarmed from the cottages and huts, calling out to one another in excitement. A long train of riders was wending its way into the village outskirts.

Old Man Kawai heard the commotion and stuck his head from the door of Madame Guderian's rose-covered house beneath the pines. He sucked air through his teeth.

"She comes!"

A small cat came running from the box under the table, nearly tripping him when he spun about to snatch up a paring knife. "I must cut flowers and hurry to greet her!" He pointed a stern finger at the cat. "And you—see that your kittens are groomed so that you do not disgrace both of us!"

The gauze-screened door slammed. Muttering to himself, the old man chopped off an armful of the heavy June rose clusters, then rushed down the path scattering pink and scarlet petals behind him.

* * *

THE END OF PART THREE

Epilogue

REMEMBERING THE INCIDENT of his childhood, the young male ramapithecine came again to the Lake of Giant Birds.

There was a trail that some larger creatures had made more than a year ago, now kept open by other animals, for it had been a dry summer and the crater lake a boon to the thirsty. The ramapithecus was not in search of water, however.

Slowly he crept out into the open area along the crater rim. There was the bird! When he crouched under it, he wondered why it seemed smaller. And the hole in its belly was gone, along with the climbing-up thing. But this was *his* bird. He knew. The memory burned within him. His mother screaming her anger . . . snatching, flinging away a precious joy that gleamed the color of the sun.

He searched. Into a bush. That bush, that gorse bush. He extended a brown-haired arm into the spiny thicket. Careful. Scratch at the dusty soil. Dig, probe.

His hand touched something smooth and hard. He drew it out with great care. It was as he remembered. The knobs snapped open, the halves turned, and this time it fitted around his neck snugly enough so that it could not be slipped off over his head. It would not be taken away from him again.

He got up and started down the path to the forest where his mate, more timid, was waiting for him. The sunshine was brighter, the smell of the maquis more pungent, the trilling of birds and insects more distinct. All of the things around him were transformed. It excited and pleasured and scared him a little, all at the same time.

I'm coming! Yes, I am!

He leaped in his joy and the lesser creatures on the trail hastened to get out of his way.

* * *

THE END OF *THE GOLDEN TORC*

Volume III of the Saga of Pliocene Exile, entitled THE NONBORN KING, *tells of a realignment of power structures during a turbulent period in the Many-Colored Land, wherein human and exotic antagonists receive their first intimations of a new-old menace from the western morning.*

APPENDIXES

Apologia Pro Geologia Sua

Map of Northwestern Europe
During the Pliocene Epoch

Map of Western Mediterranean Region
During the Pliocene Epoch

Map of Eastern Aven (Balearic Peninsula)
During the Pliocene Epoch

Apologia Pro Geologia Sua

THE ANCIENT LANDSCAPE depicted in this saga represents Europe during the so-called Mio-Pliocene Regression, when the Mediterranean was at its lowest ebb prior to the opening of the Straits of Gibraltar. The timing of the latter event has not been firmly established, but it may have taken place about 5.5 million years before the present, and I have rounded off this figure to 6 million years. During the Miocene Epoch, the Mediterranean Basin received Atlantic waters via two channels that opened and closed a number of times—the Betic Channel in southern Spain and the Rif Channel, which extended across northern Morocco, Algeria, and Tunisia. The rupture at Gibraltar took place after the Rif and Betic channels had closed. With the opening of the Gibraltar Gate, the filling of the Mediterranean might have been a fairly rapid thing; perhaps only a hundred years after the cataclysm, influx from the Atlantic would have filled the basin of the Empty Sea completely, drowning the ancient Valley of the Rhône almost as far north as Lyon, and undoubtedly initiating tectonic adjustments that not only altered the Mediterranean floor into its present topography of abysses and shallows but also caused profound modification of the geology of the Italian peninsula, Sicily, and other unstable regions.*

* The only other events remotely comparable to the flooding of the Mediterranean were the "Great Missoula Floods," which took place during the Pleistocene Ice Age in western North America. Melt waters from the Cordilleran Glacier of the Rocky Mountains flowed toward the west until they met a lobe of the Okanogan Glacier, which blocked Clark Fork Valley near the present Lake Pend Oreille in northern Idaho. This formed Glacial Lake Missoula, one of the largest freshwater bodies ever to collect in the western part of the continent. More than a thousand feet deep in some places, it inundated the valleys of western Montana until the natural dam of ice and rubble broke. Some

The map of the Empty Sea that I have drawn is entirely speculative, especially in its treatment of the Southern Lagoon Estuary, the Great Brackish Marsh, and regions now known as the Alborán Sea and the Algerian Basin. There are, however, volcanic remnants that make my rubble dam at least remotely plausible; *viz.* at Cabo de Gata; at Cap de Trois Fourches, Morocco; and of course at Isla de Alborán itself.

I have postulated that Pontian flora and fauna were contemporaneous with the Mediterranean flood. The climate, geography, vegetation, and animal life of Pontian times are essentially as set forth in the novel—but geologists and paleobiologists will be quick to detect a few fudgings that I hope can be forgiven in the spirit of good fun. Ramapithecus, that enigmatic and fascinating hominid of many aliases, is placed as late as the Pontian by virtue of a jaw described in 1972 by G. H. R. von Koenigswald, to which he gave the name *Graecopithecus freybergi.*

The structure called the Ries (or Rieskessel) is the subject of some controversy—one school of thought accepting it as an astrobleme, while another holds it to be the result of a cryptovolcanic explosion that brought to the surface "meteoritelike" materials. Arguments for the latter viewpoint are summarized in G. H. J. McCall, *Meteorites and Their Origins* (New York: Wiley, 1973). The more dramatic impact hypothesis is elegantly supported in E. Preuss, "Das Ries und die Meteoriten-Theorie" (Stuttgart: *Fortschritte der Mineralogie,* 1964, 41:271–312). McCall seems not to have considered the Preuss material in his later survey. In my novel, trajectory, velocity, and mass data are from Preuss. Both K/Ar and fission-track testing of the Moldavite tektites (usually considered of identical age with the Ries) yield—alas!—an approximate age of 14.7 ± 0.7 million years.

---

500 cubic miles of water drained from the lake through the Grand Coulee within a period of about two weeks, scouring the Washington landscape known as the Channeled Scablands and draining into the Pacific through the Columbia Gorge. Hydraulic damming in the gorge piled the flood waters some 400 feet above sea level in the region adjacent to Portland, Oregon. The flooding was apparently repeated a number of times. In comparing the Missoula Floods to the filling of the Mediterranean, one should recall that the Mediterranean Basin now holds about one million cubic miles of water; but in early Pliocene times, the basin is presumed to have been much shallower.

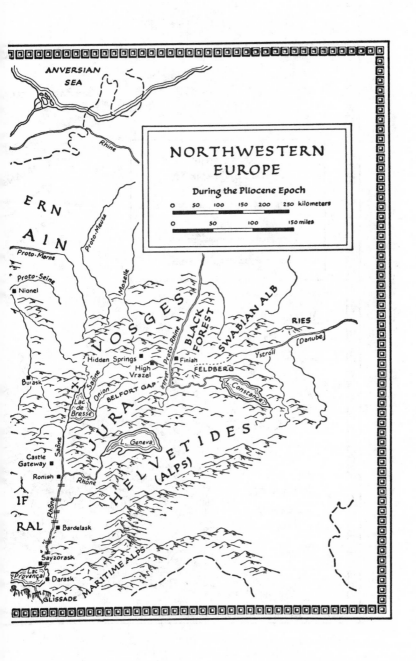

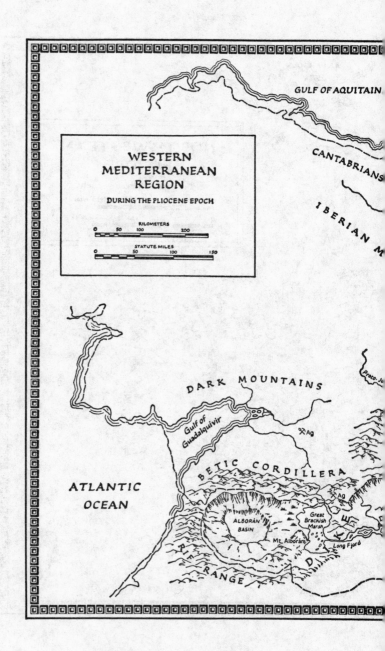

WESTERN
MEDITERRANEAN
REGION

DURING THE PLIOCENE EPOCH

KILOMETERS
0   50   100   200

STATUTE MILES
0   50   100   150

GULF OF AQUITAIN

CANTABRIANS

IBERIAN M

DARK MOUNTAINS

Gulf of
Guadalquivir

Ag

BETIC CORDILLERA

Ag

ALBORÁN
BASIN

Great
Brackish
Marsh

ATLANTIC
OCEAN

Mt. Alborán

Long Fjord

RANGE

Proto-Ju

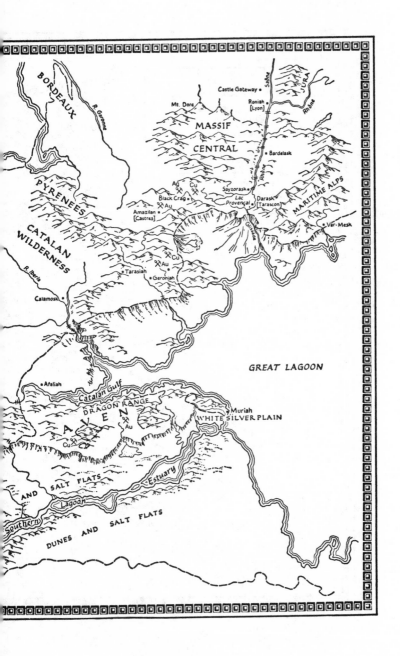

EASTERN AVEN
[BALEARIC PENINSULA]

DURING THE
PLIOCENE EPOCH

KILOMETERS

0 5 10   20   30   40   50

STATUTE MILES

0   5   10   20   30

DRAGON RANGE

GROVES

AND

PLANTATIONS

FOREST PRESERVES

DUNES
AND FLATS

Southern   Lagoo

CATALAN GULF

MURIAH
AND
ENVIRONS

Plain of Sport

Coercers

Square

Main Dock

MOUNT OF
HEROES

Palace

Psychokinetics

Redactors

Creators

Arena

Farsensors

Well

Tanu Camp

Firvulag Camp

Brede's House

Dais

Lists

Battlefield

Retort

Area
of inset

WHITE
SILVER
PLAIN

GREAT LAGOON

Estuary

SOUTHERN
SALT FLATS